The Princess Brides

by
Jane Porter

THE SULTAN'S BOUGHT BRIDE

THE GREEK'S ROYAL MISTRESS

THE ITALIAN'S VIRGIN PRINCESS

Harlequin Mills & Boon Limited,
Eton House, 18-24 Paradise Road, Richmond, Surrey TW9 1SR

THE PRINCESS BRIDES
© by Harlequin Enterprises II B.V./S.à.r.l 2008

The Sultan's Bought Bride, The Greek's Royal Mistress and *The Italian's Virgin Princess* were first published in Great Britain by Harlequin Mills & Boon Limited in separate, single volumes.

The Sultan's Bought Bride © Jane Porter 2004
The Greek's Royal Mistress © Jane Porter 2004
The Italian's Virgin Princess © Jane Porter 2004

ISBN: 978 0 263 86132 7

05-0908

Printed and bound in Spain
by Litografía Rosés S.A., Barcelona

THE SULTAN'S BOUGHT BRIDE

by

Jane Porter

100 Reasons to Celebrate

We invite you to join us in celebrating
Mills & Boon's centenary. Gerald Mills and
Charles Boon founded Mills & Boon Limited
in 1908 and opened offices in London's Covent
Garden. Since then, Mills & Boon has become
a hallmark for romantic fiction, recognised
around the world.

We're proud of our 100 years of publishing
excellence, which wouldn't have been achieved
without the loyalty and enthusiasm of our
authors and readers.

Thank you!

Each month throughout the year there will
be something new and exciting to mark the
centenary, so watch for your favourite authors,
captivating new stories, special limited
edition collections…and more!

Jane Porter grew up on a diet of Mills & Boon® romances, reading late at night under the covers so her mother wouldn't see! She wrote her first book at age eight, and spent many of her school and college years living abroad, immersing herself in other cultures and continuing to read voraciously. Now Jane has settled down in rugged Seattle, Washington, with her gorgeous husband and two sons. Jane loves to hear from her readers. You can write to her at PO Box 524, Bellevue, WA 98009, USA. Or visit her website at www.janeporter.com.

Don't miss Jane Porter's classic
The Sheikh's Virgin
available in October in the M&B™ collection
The Desert Sheikh's Marriage.

For CJ Carmichael.
Thank you for everything, Carla. I am so very
lucky to call you my very good friend.
Jane.

PROLOGUE

"YOU'RE not going to go." Princess Nicolette tossed the heavy parchment paper into the garbage can. "You just pick up the phone and tell the sultan—or sheikh—or whatever he is that you're not doing this disgustingly barbaric arranged marriage thing again. For heaven's sake, Chantal, you're a woman—not a human sacrifice!"

Chantal's mouth curved, but the tight smile didn't touch her gray eyes, or her tense expression. "He's wealthy, Nic. There's a chance he might be able to buy Lilly's freedom, and if this is the way—"

"It's not the way! Absolutely not the way. You barely survived one hellish marriage. How could you even consider another?"

"Because our country needs it. Our people need it." Chantal's slim shoulders lifted, fell, as did her voice. "My daughter needs it."

Chantal's resignation killed Nic. Her sister had lost her spirit, her backbone, her courage. The last couple of years had virtually annihilated the elegant princess, the eldest of the Ducasse royal grandchildren.

"*You* have needs, too," Nic shot back. "And you need to be treated kindly, lovingly, with respect. Another marriage of convenience—to another playboy—will only crush you." Nic's emotions ran high. If Chantal couldn't fight anymore, then Nic would have to do it for her. "And I know you want to help Lilly, but your daughter needs to come home to Melio, Chantal. She doesn't need another foreign country, another foreign culture, or another foreign nanny saying *no princess, you can't princess, don't smile princess, we don't approve of laughter, princess!*"

Chantal winced. "You're not helping, Nic."

Nic dropped to her knees, and wrapped her arms around

5

Chantal's legs, holding her sister close. "So let me help. Let me do something for a change!"

Chantal's fine dark brown eyebrow arched and she lifted one of Nicolette's long blond curls. "You'll marry the sultan?" Chantal gently mocked. "Come on, Nic. You'd never agree to a marriage of convenience. And you're not even close to being ready to settle down. You're still sowing all your wild oats."

Nicolette pressed her cheek to Chantal's knees. "I'm not sowing wild oats. I'm just dating—"

Her sister laughed and tugged on the long blond curl. "You don't date, love. You hunt and destroy."

"You make me sound like the Terminator! I don't destroy men. I just haven't found Mr. Right yet."

"And how are you going to find the right man when you sleep with all the wrong ones?"

"I don't sleep with everybody."

"But you do like sex."

Nic eyed her sister thoughtfully. "Uh-oh, big sis doesn't approve."

"Big sis worries about AIDS. Venereal disease. Herpes. Pregnancy."

But that wasn't really what Chantal worried about, was it? Chantal wasn't thinking about Nicolette contracting a disease. She was worrying about her sister's reputation. "Is this where you make the Good Girls Don't speech?"

"Well, Mother's not here."

"Which probably makes you glad because Mother wasn't a Good Girl, either!"

Chantal stiffened. "Don't speak of Mother that way, and more importantly, you know we all need to make good marriages. This has been the plan for five years." Because their kingdom, consisting of two small islands in the Mediterranean Sea, Mejia and Melio, would be split at year's end. Mejia would revert to French rule, Melio to Spanish rule if the royal Ducasse family couldn't pay their taxes and trade agreements.

Chantal had been the one to suggest marriages of convenience. If the three princesses all made good marriages they could save Melio and Mejia, infusing the economy with new money, new alliances, new *power*. So Chantal had been the first to marry to Prince Armand Thibaudet of La Croix and it'd been a nightmare from the start.

So, no, Nic hadn't been overly anxious to marry, but that wasn't to say she wouldn't do her part. "You don't think I can marry well anymore, do you?"

If Chantal had heard the hurt in Nic's voice she gave no indication. "I don't know anything about your reputation, but I do know we all have a responsibility to take care of Melio. Succession depends on us. Melio's security, and stability, must come through us. We *are* the next generation."

"I've never shirked my duties. While you've been gone I've taken over your charities along with mine."

"Charities are all very well and nice, but it's money we need. *Millions* of dollars. And you have had two proposals, Nic."

"Years ago."

"Exactly! And nothing since. Because all the European royals know you've been voted by the press as the Ducasse princess least likely to settle down."

The criticism rang in Nicolette's ears. It still rankled Nic that Chantal continued to perceive duty…responsibility…as the best of personal virtues. "You're saying your sultan, King Nuri, would never propose to someone like me?"

"Well, he didn't, did he?"

Nic stared at Chantal for a long moment, realizing that even if duty-bound Chantal wanted to go to Baraka to meet the Sultan, Nic wouldn't let her. Chantal had been through too much in the past few years. No one but Nic knew about Chantal's private hell. Even Joelle, their youngest sister, knew little about the abuse Chantal suffered at the hands of her late husband.

"There's no reason for any of us to marry the sultan," Nic said after a moment. "We can get him to help us without giving up our freedom, and yes, I do value my freedom." Her gaze locked with Chantal's. "We'll get Lilly free. We'll bring her home."

Chantal shook her head. "Her grandparents will never let her go."

"They will if pressured properly." Nic's gaze held her sister's. "They will if King Nuri insists. You did say he was immensely powerful."

"And wealthy," Chantal whispered.

"So I'll go to King Nuri and ask for his help. He won't say no to his future bride, will he?"

"Nic—"

"I'll go, pretend to be you, get him to fall in love with me—"

"*Nic.*"

"He's a man, Chantal. I know how to manage men."

"It's not going to work. You'll never be able to pass yourself off as me. You're blond, I'm dark—"

"I'll dye my hair. As a brunette I could pass for you." Nic suddenly laughed, empowered. "I'll sneak in, sneak out. He won't even know what's happened."

"Oh, Nic, this is a disaster waiting to happen!"

"Not if I'm smart," she answered smugly. "Trust me. I can do this. I'll put together a plan, and you know me, Chantal. When I want something, I always win."

CHAPTER ONE

KING MALIK ROMAN NURI, sultan of Baraka, stood on the ancient harbor wall constructed nearly seven hundred years ago, in the shade of a sixteenth century Portuguese fortress and watched the royal Ducasse yacht sail into his harbor, ship's purple and gold banners flying high.

His princess was here.

His thick lashes lowered as he heard his band strike up a song of welcome, and he wondered at her thoughts, the thoughts of the beautiful Ducasse princess who'd left her home for his. Her world was Western, his was Eastern. She must feel some fear. He felt fear for her. She was coming to a world far different from her own. Her life would never be the same.

Did she even know it yet?

Standing on the gleaming wooden deck of the *Royal Star*, the Ducasse yacht named after Nic's late mother, Nicolette adjusted the long dark head covering she'd donned, and listened to the ship's flags snap in the hot afternoon wind, even as her own body crackled with tension.

She was determined. Focused. She knew what she had to do.

Her plan would work. There was no reason it shouldn't.

She'd arrive in Baraka, pretend to be Chantal, proceed with the wedding, and then once Chantal and Lilly were safe in America, the wedding would be called off.

Simple. Doable.

With her narrowed gaze on the horizon, the formidable stone walls of Atiq, Baraka's capital city, took shape. The fortified rampart facing the sea appeared to be centuries old, buffeted by storm and sea, and countless marauding neighbors. Nic could easily imagine those ruthless neighbors—The Greeks. The Romans. The Turks. The Portuguese. The French.

Everybody wanted to own something. If not a woman, then a piece of land. She could just picture the sailors, the soldiers,

9

the adventurers grabbing up chunks of soil and sand. Anything for power.

Nic stifled the wave of irritation. She had to be careful, needed to keep tight rein on her temper. She had to be charming, not angry. Sweet-tempered, not feisty. It was vital King Malik Nuri believe she was really Chantal.

Pulling the head scarf closer to her face, concealing her mouth and nose, she drew a deep breath and chased away all thoughts of conquerors and kings. Instead she studied the looming port with the dots of green palm trees shadowing the glaring white walls of the inner city.

For a moment, Nic's curiosity upstaged her emotions. Was this where she'd stay during the next couple of weeks? Did the sultan live in the harbor city of Atiq? Or was his palace else-where…perhaps tucked inland, protected by the massive dunes of the Sahara?

And as her gaze focused on the distant horizon, music wafted over the water. She spotted the enormous crowd gathered on the rampart walls. Hundreds and hundreds of people waited for her. *So much for sneaking in and out.*

Beneath Nic's long robe, something she'd cheerfully put on as it aided her disguise, her toes curled inside her sleek leather pumps, the shoes matching her hidden lavender silk suit per-fectly, the suit vintage designer—something from her mother's collection, and she shook her head at Chantal's choices all over again.

Why on earth would someone like King Malik Roman Nuri choose Chantal for his bride? And why on earth would Chantal even consider saying yes to yet another unfaithful husband?

Nic had spent all last week on the Internet, poring over media archives. She'd done her research and she knew King Malik Roman Nuri for what he was. A handsome, but irredeemable playboy.

From the few grainy photos she'd been able to pull up, he was certainly attractive. He had hard, masculine features, a thick head of hair, and apparently a stunning libido.

The gossip magazines claimed the sultan, Malik Nuri, was The Casanova of Arabia. According to several sources close to the sultan, King Nuri had mastered seduction, turned lovemaking into an art, and kept numerous mistresses—all in splendid style.

Fine. He was a world-class lover. He spoiled his mistresses. After Chantal's experience with one manipulative and unfaithful husband, she certainly didn't need another who'd never keep his vows of fidelity, much less loyalty.

Nic grit her teeth. Chantal deserved a prince of a man, not a sultan unable to keep his royal trousers on!

The band's bright notes jarred her, even as they filled the air. Two weeks, three weeks, she told herself, fighting her temper, not a day more. They'd leave for the United States as soon as it could be arranged. She'd propose a wedding in her mother's home town, something very small and private, yet meaningful, and once they were in Baton Rouge, Nic would call the wedding off.

If she handled this right—flattering the sultan, giving him the kind of attention she knew how to give a man—the whole charade would be nothing but a feminine escapade. The engagement would be short. Sweet. *Painless.*

"Your Highness?" The ship's captain had appeared at her side. "We have arrived."

Nic turned to the captain, a man she'd known nearly half her life. He'd aged in the past decade, but then hadn't they all? And he didn't know what she knew: this would be his last voyage as captain of the *Royal Star*. The *Royal Star* was being put up for auction on the ship's return to Melio. "Excellent."

"We've just about moored, Your Highness. Are you ready to disembark?"

"Yes." And then she swallowed around the fierce lump in her throat as she looked up into Captain Anderson's weathered face, the creases at his eyes deep from years of squinting against the sun. "And may I thank you for your years of loyal service, Captain? You've been truly magnificent."

"It's been my pleasure, Your Highness." He bowed. "We'll see you on your return home."

With the stringed instruments plucking, drums and tambourines beating, Nic stepped onto the gangway and halfway across, colorful confetti streamed down. It wasn't paper confetti, the bits of orange and red and pink were flower petals and the sweet scented petals drifted onto her covered head and shoulders.

It was like entering a dream world—the music, the colors, the hint of spice in the air. Nic had the strongest sensation that this new world would soon dazzle her with its exotic secrets.

By the time she reached the end of the gangway, time had slowed. Faces blurred. People were cheering and clapping but none of it sounded real. The language was different, the faces weren't familiar, there was nothing here that resembled the life she'd known.

Her gaze searched the crowd, trying to find a landmark…a personal touchstone. She found none. Instead the heat beat at her, hot and humid and oppressive, and the noise rang in her ears, too loud, too insistent, and for a half second everything swam before her eyes, a blur of orange and crimson, sharp, discordant sound, and she blinked once, trying to clear her head, trying to find herself again.

Nic gripped the gangway railing and tried not to dwell on the fact that she, Tough Girl, was suffering from a case of nerves. Focus, she lectured herself. Find a face in the crowd. Get your legs under you. Pull yourself together.

And she did.

She found a remarkable face in the crowd. It belonged to a man of course, she'd always had a soft spot for the opposite sex, and this man certainly caught her interest, quickened her pulse.

Arresting, was the first word that came to mind. Darkly arresting. She liked his strong hard face with the dark sunglasses, the thick black hair which framed his wide brow. She even liked the way he wore his sophisticated dark suit, with his crisp white shirt open at the collar.

He looked cool, calm, different from the others.

Her gaze clung to him, grateful for the normalcy. No robes, no camel, no chanting from him.

Good.

His sunglasses shaded his eyes and added to his mystique. She tried to imagine what his eyes would be like. Dark? Sable brown? Golden, perhaps?

It really didn't matter, not with that thick, slightly wavy hair, and a face that made her think of lips…kisses. His jaw was as broad as his brow, his nose rather long but his lips curved faintly. They were *very* nice lips.

Then he pulled off his sunglasses and she inhaled a little,

intrigued by his expression. It was arrogant. Proud. Challenging.
He looked like a man who enjoyed a good fight. Interesting. She
enjoyed a good fight, too.

Nothing turned her on as much as a man wrestling with her,
rolling her beneath him, pinning her hands to the bed.

Mmm, it'd been too long. Too bad they weren't in Melio.
What she wouldn't give for a night alone with him. She'd like
to test his pride as well as taste his intensity. He'd be great fun
on board the *Royal Star*, or for a night playing in nearby Monte
Carlo, but there was no way anything was going to happen here.
She was Chantal, she reminded herself, ending the brief fantasy,
and she was in Baraka to discuss a wedding.

Conscious of a thousand pair of eyes resting on her, cymbals
still clanging in her ears, Nic wished the sultan would step forward and get the introductions over.

For a moment no one moved, then a small, very stout robed
man with dark mustache and beard moved toward her.

"Princess Chantal Marie Ducasse?"

The man barely reached her shoulder. Nic was tall, taller than
either of her sisters, but this man would have been short standing
next to even them. "Yes."

He bowed. "May I present to you, His Royal Highness, King
Malik Roman Nuri, sultan of Baraka, prince of Atiq."

The crowd shifted expectantly and their tension sent arrows
of dread straight through her middle. For a half second she regretted agreeing to this, wishing she'd stayed comfortable and
ignorant at home.

Then she straightened her shoulders and the front row of the
crowd opened, allowing a tall man in a dark suit to pass through.
Him.

No, she silently cried, not *him*. Anyone but him. But he was
moving toward her, slowly, languidly, and her legs went weak.

This was not a good thing.

She swallowed, tried to see past his sunglasses which were
again hiding his gaze, but instead looked at his mouth. The
mouth that had made her think of lips, and kissing and...sex.

Her mouth dried. She suppressed a wave of horror. She'd seen
the Sultan's picture on the Internet and she wracked her brain,
trying to put together the grainy photos with this man but it

didn't fit. She'd imagined a shorter man, heavier set, easily managed and rather spoiled...

This man didn't look easily managed at all.

"His Royal Highness," the short man intoned with a deep bow.

Her heart thudded, turned over, and her legs felt quivery. "Your Highness?" she murmured, hearing the doubt in her own voice.

The sultan closed the distance between them and studied her for a long silent moment. Nicolette was the first to look away, glancing down to the ground to hide her confusion.

But the Sultan wouldn't let her escape. He tilted her chin up with his fingers, again gazed down into her face, and then apparently satisfied, he kissed her on each cheek.

"*S-salamu alikum,*" he said soberly, his voice so deep she had to strain to hear him.

"Peace on you," the short man translated with another bow. "His Highness welcomes you to his beloved Baraka. Land of a thousand dreams."

Land of a thousand dreams. Interesting. And rather provocative, too.

"Thank you," she murmured, her cheeks still hot from the brush of his lips, and her brain racing to assimilate everything she was learning—such as the fact that the sultan didn't speak English. "Would you please tell His Highness that I am flattered by the warm welcome his people have given me?"

The translator passed the message on before turning back to Nicolette. "His Highness thinks it would be good to get you out of the sun. His car is waiting just there," and he pointed to a dark limousine behind them, surrounded by uniformed guards.

The translator sat on one long seat in the limousine while Nicolette and the silent sultan sat on the other.

She and King Nuri didn't speak during the brief drive, and although he barely looked at her, Nic had never felt so uncomfortably aware of anyone before.

She was conscious of the way he sat, feet planted, knees parted, thigh muscles honed. She felt the way he breathed— slow, deep breaths as if he owned the very air. His fragrance was light and yet the faint hint of spice made her want more.

He shifted abruptly, his arm extending on the back of the

black leather upholstery seat, his hand precariously near her shoulder. Nic shimmered with sudden heat, her skin prickling all over. She felt each fine hair on her nape rise, and her nipples tighten.

Bizarre. Impossible. She hadn't responded to a man this strong since…since…

She shook her head, not wanting to go there. It was bad enough trying to cope with her dazed senses without throwing memories of Daniel into the mix.

"Your luggage will follow," the translator volunteered after a few tense minutes. "But if there is anything you require before your luggage arrives, you need only ask."

Nic nodded jerkily, grateful for the protective head scarf, knowing her cheeks were as hot as the rest of her. "Thank you."

They reached the outer gates of the palace, and Nic discovered the sultan's palace was actually a modernized fort, although to Nic's mind, the huge and richly embellished main gate seemed more suitable for decoration than defense.

Once inside the ornate gate, a miniature city appeared, gardens, courtyards, white stone buildings each elegant and unique, nearly all fronted by endless white marble columns.

Guards in white trousers, white shirts, black boots and white robes bowed as King Nuri led Nicolette and the translator across the central courtyard to the central building. The building they entered was larger than the others and the facade grander, but the large carved doors failed to hint at the grandeur inside.

The great doors were gilded, and in the interior the ceiling soared, at least two stories in height, every surface covered in gold, mosaic murals, and bronze detailing. Gold, treasure, and impossible beauty.

Awed, Nicolette followed King Nuri into an elegant salon, rich crimson carpets covered the marble floor. The King gestured to one of the low couches in the middle of the room.

Nicolette gratefully sank down on the edge of one couch, the cushion covered in stunning ruby silk, cocooned by the luxury and elegance.

"Refreshments?" the translator offered as a serving girl entered with a silver tray.

The smell of dark rich fragrant coffee made Nic's mouth water. She'd never needed fortifying as much as she did now. "Please."

Still standing, King Nuri gazed at Nicolette with unnerving focus. Then he broke the silence, and when he spoke, his voice was so deep and smooth that his words sounded like honeyed candy.

The translator explained the sultan's words. "His Highness trusts your journey was safe."

She nodded, forcing a calm smile. "Yes, thank you."

"No problems on your journey?" The sultan added.

Nic listened to the sultan's voice in her head, lingering over his syllables. He had the most unusual voice. Deep. Husky. Again her pulse lurched, her heart finding it hard to settle into a steady rhythm. "The trip was uneventful," she answered, knowing she'd better find her footing fast. If she couldn't control her response to him, how could she possibly control *him?*

"Hamadullah," King Nuri answered, the corner of his mouth curved in a small private smile.

She forced her attention away from the Sultan's lovely mouth. Remember his stream of mistresses, she told herself. Remember his reputation. "What does *hamadullah* mean?"

"It means, 'Thanks be to God'."

Nic mulled over the King's response.

King Nuri spoke again, and the translator hastened to explain. "It is customary here to express gratitude to God for our blessings."

Nic shot King Nuri a quick glance. His lips curved fractionally. Hollows appeared beneath his strong cheekbones. "And my arrival is a blessing?"

"Without a doubt." The translator answered, speaking for the sultan.

She shot King Nuri yet another wary glance. She'd thought she was prepared for this trip, thought her plan was bullet proof, but now that she was here, and he was here, and they were together…this wasn't at all how she'd imagined it. She'd pictured him rakish. Handsome but a little thick in the jowls, a little paunchy at the waist. She'd told herself he'd flirt outrageously, come on too strong, and probably wear flashy clothes, but that wasn't the man facing her now.

The sultan took a seat close to her on one of the low couches.

When he reached for his coffee, his long arm nearly brushed her knee and she shivered inwardly, tensing all over again.

Had she hoped he'd touch her?

Had she feared he'd touch her?

The sultan was speaking Arabic again, and Nic glanced from King Nuri to the translator and back. The King's profile was beautiful. He was beautiful. Definitively male.

"His Highness expresses his satisfaction that you are here. He says that he and his people have waited a very long time for this day."

Nic's fingers tightened around her small espresso cup, trying to keep her calm. The King was practically reclining, and his eyes, a cool silvery green-gray, rested on her as if he found her absolutely fascinating.

Thank God Chantal wasn't here. King Nuri would have seduced her, married her, and abandoned her in no time. If he was a man who lived off his conquests, then Chantal, so broken by marriage and life, wouldn't be enough of a conquest.

"I look forward to getting to know His Highness," Nic said in her most careful diction. "And to discussing my ideas for the wedding."

"*Your* ideas?" The interpreter asked.

Nic couldn't hide her impatience. "Yes. Of course. It's my wedding. I have ideas about *my* wedding."

No one spoke for a moment, and King Nuri's dark head tipped, his black lashes dropped as he studied her. His cool gaze examined her face, taking in each feature, the curve of bone, the very shape and texture of her lips.

The translator expressed her thoughts to King Nuri.

Then the sultan spoke, and the translator turned to her. "The king understands that you have just arrived, and everything feels quite new and alien, but he also asks you to trust him with the wedding details so they will comply with his beliefs and our customs."

"Please tell His Highness that I'd like to trust him with the wedding details, but a wedding is quite a personal event, and I insist I be part of planning it."

"The king thanks you for your concerns, and assures you that you need not worry, or be troubled. As the wedding details are set, there is nothing for you to do in the next two weeks but relax and familiarize yourself with our life here in Baraka.''

Nothing to do in the next two weeks but relax? Nic puzzled over the king's answer. ''What's happening in two weeks?''

The translator bowed his head. ''The wedding, Your Highness.''

The wedding already planned. The ceremony here. In two weeks. It couldn't be. Surely this was a language problem, an issue with the translation. ''I'm afraid we're losing something here. Are you telling me that the wedding date—and all the detail—has already been set?''

''Yes.''

Nicolette touched the tip of her tongue to her upper lip. She'd been in Baraka, King Malik Nuri's North African kingdom, less than two hours and already things were wildly out of control. What had happened to *her* plan? What about the quiet, private ceremony she'd dreamed up in America? ''How can it be *set?*''

The robed translator bowed his head politely. ''His Highness has chosen a date blessed by the religious and cultural calendar.''

Nicolette glanced past the stout translator to King Nuri reclining on the sofa. This was going to be far more difficult than she'd anticipated. King Nuri was the kind of man she'd assiduously avoided—smart, suave, sophisticated—and far too much in control. ''But the king hasn't consulted my calendar,'' she said firmly, turning toward the sultan, meeting his gaze directly to convey her displeasure. ''He can't set a wedding date without my input.''

The translator nodded again, his expression grave, and still unfailingly polite. ''It is customary for the king to consult with his spiritual advisors.''

''The king is very religious then?''

The translator paused, appeared momentarily at a loss for words before recovering. ''The king is the king. The ruler of Baraka—''

What nonsense was this? ''And I am Princess Chantal, of the royal Ducasse family.'' Her temper was getting the best of her. She hated double-speak, especially hated royal double-speak. This is one reason she'd always dated commoners. *Playboys,* her sister's voice echoed in her head. ''Perhaps you'd care to remind your king that nothing is set until I say it's set.''

The translator hesitated. He didn't want to translate this.

Nicolette's jaw hardened. "Tell him. *Please.*"

"Your Highness—" the translator protested.

She shifted impatiently, set her cup on the low wood table. "Perhaps it was a mistake coming to Baraka. I'd assumed King Malik Nuri was educated. Civilized—"

"Western?" the king concluded, languidly rising from his sofa to again dominate the royal chamber.

Nic's jaw dropped even as her stomach flipped.

So he spoke English. But of course he spoke English. She'd discovered on the Internet that he'd gone to Oxford for heaven's sake. Yet he'd allowed all introductions, all awkward conversation, to be made via the translator. He'd had their first meeting conducted like an interview.

"Why did we have a translator?" she demanded, head tilting, scarf sliding back, revealing her long dark hair.

He didn't look a bit apologetic. "I thought it might make you more comfortable."

Wrong. It was to make him more comfortable. A passive display of power. Nic scraped her teeth together. Think like Chantal, she reminded herself. Be Chantal.

But Chantal's become a doormat.

And yet it's Chantal he wants, not you.

The sultan was waiting for her to speak. Her eyes flashed fire even as she struggled to retain her flimsy smile, nodding her head the way she'd seen Chantal nod graciously so many times on official state business. "How considerate," she said from between clenched teeth, rising as well. "I really ought to…thank you."

King Nuri's lips curved faintly. "My pleasure." He lifted his hand in a small imperial gesture and the translator discreetly exited the room.

They were both standing, far too close for Nic's comfort, and the sultan studied her fierce expression for a long moment before knotting his hands behind his back and slowly circling her.

It was an examination. A study before a purchase.

Like a camel at an open-air market, she thought uneasily, as he circled a second time, his hawklike gaze missing nothing.

"Do I meet your approval, King Nuri?" She choked, her

sarcasm lost as her voice broke. This was not going to be a two-week vacation. She was scared. Not for Chantal, but for herself. King Nuri had a plan, and as the wild beating of her heart reminded her, his plan was swiftly annihilating her own.

CHAPTER TWO

THE king continued his examination, coming round full circle a second time before stopping in front of her, just inches away.

Nic held her breath, fighting for poise, trying not to blink or flinch but keep all responses hidden even though he did something crazy to her senses. Her head swam and her pulse quickened and right now she found herself fascinated by a dozen little things like the line of his jaw, the shadow of his beard, the deep hollow at his throat—

"You're taller than I expected," he said, breaking the taut silence.

She'd inherited her father's height, as well as his blond hair, and her height had been a problem for a lot of men, "So are you."

His eyes narrowed thoughtfully. "Your coloring is a little off, too." He shrugged. "But then I suppose people always look different on television."

"You *are* disappointed."

One of his flat black eyebrows lifted. "Did I say that?"

Nic's temper flared yet again, and she didn't understand it. Normally men didn't trouble her. Men didn't upset her. She was usually so adept at handling them. She understood the way they thought, the things they wanted, how best to soothe their fragile, ruffled egos. But the sultan didn't appear fragile, or egotistical, and so far, she hadn't a clue how to deal with him.

Malik calmly met Nicolette's furious blue gaze.

The princess had cheekbones and an attitude, he thought, smiling faintly. He didn't know why it made him smile. The attitude he'd expected—she was one of the beautiful Ducasse sisters after all—but the cheekbones intrigued him. In the princess the cheekbones were sculptural, architectural. Something one wanted to touch, trace, caress.

She'd only just arrived and yet he wanted to take her face in

21

his hands and stroke the sensuous curve of cheekbone that stretched from her hairline to just above her full mouth.

But then, she didn't just have cheekbones. She had lips, too. Lovely, full lips and wide winged eyebrows that reminded him of two birds flying free.

Where was the restrained regal face of Chantal? This wasn't the face of a gentle princess. The face before him had an edge of sensuality, and fierceness. He had no doubt that this woman could be strong, very strong, and he'd be a fool to let her long soft curls and soft full lips tell him otherwise. He knew from his own mother that the most delicate beauties could hide a tiger's heart.

"Did you bring no one with you?" he asked, breaking the tension. "No secretary or valet? No one to handle your social calendar?"

Nic shrugged. "I didn't think it necessary, Your Highness. I have cleared my calendar, made myself completely available to you."

"How thoughtful."

"I try," she said demurely, bowing her head, missing Malik's speculative expression.

She was up to something, he thought, looking at her bent head, her dark brown hair shiny, silky. Her hair was long and she wore it pulled in a low, loose ponytail. The style flattered her high cheekbones but somehow did little to soften her strong jaw. She had a firm jaw and chin for a woman. She was a woman accustomed to getting her way.

"But of course you need help," he said after a moment, knowing why she'd traveled alone, and understanding it had little to do with the Ducasse family's strained finances. It wasn't that she couldn't afford help. He guessed she wanted to be incognito. She didn't want any familiar staff assisting her.

The princess, he thought, was playing a game.

"Since you weren't able to bring anyone from home, I'm happy to provide staff for you," he offered sympathetically. "I have a few people in mind, and all have undergone rigorous training as well as a thorough screening for security."

The deepness, the richness of his voice still sent little shock waves through her. Nic felt the tremors on the inside, wondered how any man's voice could be so husky. "I don't really need a staff, Your Highness."

He brushed aside her protest. "You have a very busy schedule, Princess. You have many functions, and many activities planned. It is vital you have help organizing your calendar, as well as your wardrobe."

She blushed. She'd never been serious about fashion, and the few smart pieces she had were gifts from various French and Italian designers. "I brought very little in the way of wardrobe." Her polished smile hid her inner turmoil. He was not going to be easy to negotiate with. "I thought this was just a preliminary visit. Get acquainted, set the date—"

He thrust his hands into his trouser pockets, looking alarmingly Western. "But of course the date is set. We discussed this—"

"No, Your Highness, we never discussed this. You might have suggested a short engagement, but no date was ever set." She loved that she could be firm. No one had ever been able to bully her. "I would have remembered."

He gestured casually, and shrugged. "Regardless, I think two weeks is sufficient time, considering the fact that we both are anxious to move forward with our lives. One of the first staff members you'll meet is your wedding planner—"

"Two week engagement?" she interrupted, torn between laughter and indignation. Two week engagement for a princess? "It is impossible to prepare for a wedding in fourteen days."

"It's two weeks from Saturday which makes it eighteen days."

The issue wasn't fourteen days or eighteen days. The issue was not getting married…or at least, not getting married *his* way. If he wanted a wedding, she'd give him a wedding, she just wasn't about to be a bride, trapped in Baraka. "I have thoughts on the wedding, Your Highness. I've made some preliminary arrangements of my own."

"You have?"

"Yes. As my mother was American, I thought we'd fly to the States for the actual wedding." She saw his incredulous expression and hurried on. "I'd hoped to marry in my mother's parish church, just outside Baton Rouge, Louisiana."

His jaw tightened. "I've never even been to Louisiana. Have you?"

"No, which is why I want to go. I'd like my mother's family to be able to attend—"

"They can attend the wedding here."

"They're—" she swallowed hard, "—poor, Your Highness. Most have never been outside their county, much less on an airplane to a foreign country."

"So we'll send my jet. Problem solved." The Sultan walked to a bureau hugging a far wall, retrieved something from the top drawer and returned to her side. "Your schedule," he continued, handing her an appointment calendar. "As you can see, you'll be quite busy helping plan and prepare for the wedding here. Some things you'll do on your own. Many things we'll do together—"

"King Nuri," she interrupted, fingers burning from the brief touch of their hands, "forgive me for being obtuse, but I don't understand why we can't at least discuss my ideas for the wedding."

He lifted his head, met her gaze, his cool silver gaze still. "But of course we can discuss your ideas," he said after a moment. "I think its essential to incorporate as many of your family traditions into our ceremony here. This is exactly what I wish you to tell your wedding planner. You'll be meeting with her later today—"

"Today?"

"Tonight." He shrugged. "But to ensure you're not over-whelmed, your assistant, Alea, and the wedding planner will discuss your agenda, make sure you're comfortable with your various duties, as well as answer any question you might have with your schedule. I think you'll find both women most help-ful."

She suppressed a wave of panic. A wedding planner. A per-sonal assistant. How many handlers did she need? "I'm quite capable of handling the preparations myself."

"I realize you have a great deal of experience at planning receptions and the sort, but you're to be my wife, Queen of Baraka. It wouldn't do to have you inundated with fatiguing details. I've brought in the most competent professionals avail-able. I know you'll like your staff—"

"But I don't need a staff!"

"You do." He smiled almost benevolently. "It'll help you manage the stress."

"I don't feel any stress."

He smiled even more benevolently. "You will."

Actually, she had lied. She was feeling unbelievable stress at the moment. If she couldn't get out of Baraka...if she couldn't get her sister and Lilly to the States...if the wedding went forward without an escape route...

To hide her worry, Nic opened the bound leather calendar and skimmed the pages, noting the various names and dates written in. Meet personal assistant, first Arabic lesson, first fitting for wedding gown, selection of wedding ring, second Arabic lesson, first engagement party, culture lesson, third Arabic lesson, city tour with King Nuri, fourth Arabic lesson. And on and on all the way until the wedding.

Eighteen days of activities. Eighteen endless days of pretending to be somebody she wasn't. Eighteen days of acting as if she were about to become King Nuri's queen. "I have something scheduled every day."

"Exactly."

It boggled her mind. He'd thought it all out. He was *training* her for the wedding. Language lessons, beauty lessons, public appearances, private activities with her betrothed. It was a whirlwind of activity to ensure a smooth wedding and transition into married life. "King Nuri—"

"Malik," he gently corrected.

"Malik," she amended, wondering where to even start with her concerns. "Is this all necessary?"

"You're to be Queen."

"Yes, but some of this can happen after the wedding. The language lessons...the cooking classes..."

"It is better to take care of as much as possible now, before the wedding." His tone allowed for no argument. "I expect you'll be carrying my child soon after the wedding, and I understand some women do not feel up to much activity in their first trimester. My desire is to simplify your life so that after the wedding you are free to concentrate on the family."

This was definitely not part of the plan.

The plan was to rescue Lilly via America—*not* get stuck here in Baraka with a wedding ring on her finger and a sultan's baby in her womb. "You want to try for children immediately?" Nic prayed she didn't sound as horrified as she felt. Nic loved kids— other people's kids. She wasn't the nesting sort. Felt no intense maternal urges. Had never been one to want to hold the babies when friends came by the palace with their latest.

"But surely you want more children?"

More, that's right. He saw her as a mother already. She had one daughter, what was oh, five or six or seven more?

"Yes, of course, but we're still strangers...."

"We won't be in a few weeks time." He gestured to the calendar she held limply in her hand. "If you'll check your schedule you'll see we spend a significant amount of time to-gether every day. Some days we'll be dining alone. Some days we'll be entertained. Other days we'll be shopping for necessities like a marriage bed."

Marriage bed. A fate worse than death.

Nic felt the blood drain from her face. She didn't want a marriage bed. She wasn't going to share any bed with Malik Roman Nuri, especially no bed that had "husband and wife" hung over it.

Making love was one thing. Getting married for the rest of your life was another. Unfortunately, King Nuri had them on a fast track to the ceremony, and right now, he was providing no loopholes.

Wasn't this just what Grandfather Remi had predicted? He'd said for years that one day Nic was going to meet the man who was more than her match.

"Not all men are going to roll over and play dead just because you snap your fingers," Grandfather had said. "There are men who can be shaped, directed, and then there are men who do the shaping."

Malik watched her face, seeing the wariness in the princess' blue eyes. He'd never seen a less eager bride in his life. But then, he understood some of her apprehensions. When he real-ized he'd have to marry, he'd had plenty of his own.

He was marrying out of necessity. The issue of succession had become more pressing since the assassination attempt last year. His younger brother, Kalen, wasn't about to leave London, having renounced all ties to Baraka and his royal family. Malik had sisters with young sons, as well as numerous male cousins, but none had remained in Baraka, all choosing Western culture over their own.

That left the issue of succession to him. He needed heirs. Boy or girl, it didn't matter. He could rewrite law, change the rules. The key was having a direct descendant. And he'd chosen the Princess Ducasse to bear him that descendant. "I don't want you to worry," he added soothingly. "I shall be a loyal, monogamous husband dedicated to fulfilling my responsibility as husband and mate."

Nic's head spun, the words husband and mate swimming through her tortured brain. *Mate...mate...mate.* "Most royals have separate bed chambers," she said at length, fingers knotting around the calendar. "Is that not the custom here?"

"My parents always shared their bed."

"Ah."

"Yours did not?" he swiftly rebutted.

She was losing focus. King Nuri was too smart, too fast, too sharp. He was taking their discussion places she really didn't want to go. "My parents had a love marriage." Her parents' marriage had been scandalous. Surely he would have heard of it even here.

Her parents had married against the wishes of her father's parents and it'd been shocking at the time, the golden boy, Prince Julien marrying the trashy American pop star. Everyone said the marriage wouldn't last the year. It lasted ten, and they were still together, still happy together when they died in the car accident on the coastal road near St. Tropez.

Nic glanced at the calendar in her hand, the edge of the small appointment book pressed to her palm. "Apparently I meet my staff in an hour and a half."

"After you freshen up. Tea and sandwiches will be served to you in your room. You'll even have time for a short nap."

Suddenly her temper snapped and she turned the little leather book around, flashing the pages. "Really? Are you certain? I don't see it in my calendar."

King Nuri didn't even glance down at the book. He simply stood there, considering her. After a moment he said, "If you do not want this marriage, Princess Chantal, say so."

The quiet authority in his voice echoed in the elegant salon.

Ashamed that she'd so completely blown her cool, Nic slowly

closed the leather book, drawing it against her chest. "I'm sorry."

He waited until she looked up from the intricate pattern of the crimson carpet at their feet. "I do not hold a gun to your head, Princess. This isn't obligatory. If you are dissatisfied with me as a groom, speak now. This is the time to break off the plans, not one week before the ceremony, not one day before the ceremony. The wedding is a fortnight away. We have not yet publicly celebrated. If you have reservations, tell me. I will not judge you, and I promise I will not be angry or cruel."

His words streamed in and out her ears, but the only thing she heard was the phrase, *if you have reservations*...

She *only* had reservations. Nothing about this was right. Nothing they were discussing was going to come to pass. She was a hypocrite. She was standing here, lying to him, intentionally deceiving him.

But how could she tell him the truth? If she told him who she really was, and why she was in Baraka, the engagement would be off, his assistance would end, and all efforts to free Lilly and Chantal would be for naught. No, she couldn't tell him. Couldn't stop what she'd started until they were in America, Chantal and Lilly secreted away and Nic was boarding the first plane home.

"Well?" he quietly prompted, clearly at the end of his patience.

He'd never forgive her for dumping him at the last minute. He'd never ever forgive her family for humiliating him...

Nic closed her eyes, forced herself to block out everything but little Lilly's delicate face. Lilly, like a butterfly, so small, so fragile, so painfully vulnerable.

Just thinking of Lilly trapped in La Croix made Nic's temper flare. How could people...society...be so unjust? Girls should be raised without fear and intimidation. Girls should be protected.

She opened her eyes, met Malik's dark gaze. "My only reservation is that I am to be married so far from those I love." *Lie, lie, lie.* She wanted to be married in America only because the country was vast, Louisiana was clannish, and her mother's network of old friends and distant relatives would definitely provide cover for Chantal and Lilly once they went into hiding. "I would feel much more comfortable if you'd be willing to consider my…thoughts…my request.''

He stared at her for a long, heated moment, before inclining his head. ''If it means so much to you, yes. I shall consider your thoughts, and think more on your request.''

Nicolette felt a dizzying wave of relief. She could do this, she told herself, encouraged. She'd pull this off yet. ''Thank you, Your Highness.''

''But of course. I want you happy. Our wedding is special. The day of the wedding will be a national holiday in Baraka. The ceremony shall be televised, so all our people can celebrate with us.''

No pressure there. ''Excellent.'' Some of her relief faded. Standing up the sultan in front of hundreds of thousands of his people was not her idea of a good time. ''What a fabulous idea.''

''Thank you.'' His silver gaze glinted. ''Now let me show you to your suite. I'm sure you could use some time alone.''

In her room, Nicolette fished out her own pocket organizer from the bottom of her suitcase and flipped quickly through her scribbled notes. Hotels, rental cars, bank numbers, phone numbers, maps of downtown Baton Rouge and vicinity. She'd already wired money to the Bank of Louisiana's Baton Rouge branch, bought a used car, had it gassed and prepped with maps and an emergency road kit, and spoken to the priest at her mother's childhood church. Everything was set. Everything would work. It was simply a matter of getting them there.

It seemed as though no time at all had passed before a knock on her door forced Nic to zip her notes back into the inner compartment of her suitcase. She ran her fingers through her hair and opening her door, discovered a cluster of women in the hall. Nicolette's new staff had arrived.

For two hours the women chatted, introducing themselves, explaining how each would assist the princess. They all spoke excellent English.

The wedding planner was young and very efficient but there was little opportunity to discuss the wedding in detail. Nicolette's assistant, Alea, was beautiful with dark hair and kind eyes and there were numerous other maids as well who fussed over the princess. Nicolette's head spun with all the names and various duties. She'd never had this much help in her life.

At nine fifteen, Nic's bedroom door opened again, and an attractive young woman, elegantly dressed in a vivid emerald-green gown with elaborate gold embroidery at the seams, entered Nic's room.

The other women sitting with Nic immediately rose and bowed. "Welcome, my lady," they all chorused, several falling into deep curtsies.

The young woman—close to Nicolette's own age—approached Nic with a cool smile. "I'm sorry I'm late." She stopped before Nic, and she took a moment to scrutinize Nicolette from head to toe. "I am Lady Fatima, cousin to the sultan, a member of the royal family. I've been asked by my cousin to help you adjust to our customs."

Fatima's words were polite but Nic heard the aloof note in Lady Fatima's voice. Lady Fatima did not intend for them to be friends. But Lady Fatima didn't need to feel threatened. Nic had no intention of permanently staying. The sooner she and the Sultan headed to America, the sooner the charade could end.

The women finally left close to midnight, and Nic fell into bed exhausted.

There were too many people getting involved, she thought, curling on her side, too many people spelled trouble.

But you're already in trouble, a little voice mocked her, and she bunched her hand in her silk coverlet, knowing that if she wasn't very careful, she could soon be trapped in Atiq forever, married to the sultan, mother to his sons. And Grandfather Remi would have the last laugh of all.

Nic, married.

Nic, Queen of Baraka. Royal Babymaker.

Nic didn't usually wake up in a bad mood, but her dreams had been so intense, so upsetting, that by the time she headed into her mammoth adjoining bathroom with the enormous white and sunken tiled tub, dread filled every muscle and pore.

She needed to talk to Chantal. She needed advice quickly. There'd never been a back up plan, and that was a mistake. Nic realized now that they should have discussed emergency measures, like other destination alternatives to America, and how to extricate Nic from the engagement without creating an international scandal.

Not waiting for the bath to completely fill, Nic sat in the tepid water, soaped up with the scented bath gel and quickly rinsed off before dressing. She usually thought fast on her feet but right now she had no ideas, no answers, no possible escape routes.

The *Royal Star* had returned to Melio. She'd traveled without a great deal of cash. Even if she wanted to run, how on earth would she get out of here?

Well, if you really had to run, you could always tell him the truth, the little voice chanted as Nic combed her long dark hair, pulling it back into a smooth coil at her nape.

But if you tell him the truth, Lilly remains in La Croix.

Not if he develops feelings for you…

It's horrible to use a man like that.

Yet lots of men have developed feelings for you, and you've never worried overly much about hurting them before…

A knock sounded on her door. Relieved to escape the conflict of her conscience, Nic took the bobby pin from her mouth and tucked it into the coil of hair at her nape. "Come in."

Malik entered her room. "Am I interrupting anything?"

She pulled another pin open with her teeth and plucked it into the coiled mass. "I'm just doing my hair."

He entered her room, closed her door behind him. "You do have beautiful hair."

The sincerity of the unexpected compliment made her flush. "Thank you."

"I've always loved hair that color. I was admiring the shade yesterday."

Nic didn't know what to say. It was a bottle-brown, something Nic had washed in herself. "I'm flattered, Your Highness."

"It's odd," he continued, "but I've never been attracted to blondes."

Nic's hand shook, and the coiled hair, not properly anchored, slipped loose, delicate pins tumbling free. "You don't like blondes?" Men *loved* blondes.

"Not particularly."

"Why not?"

"I don't want to be stereotypical, but…"

"But what?"

"Well, in my experience, I've found most blondes to be…shallow. Self-absorbed. Less intellectual."

Nic blinked to chase away the veil of red before her eyes. *In his experience.* What kind of blondes had he met? "My sister, Nicolette, she's a natural blonde, and she's extremely intelligent."

"Really?" He frowned skeptically.

"Yes," Nic answered firmly, outraged that he could hold such a ridiculous prejudice against women based on hair color. "Nic holds advanced degrees in mathematics and science."

"Speaking of your sister," he said, changing topics. "That's why I've come. As we're not married yet, I wouldn't normally visit your room uninvited, but since your sister called, I thought it might be urgent."

"Which sister?"

"I could have sworn she said Chantal."

"Impossible." Chantal must have made a mistake and said her own name.

"Exactly." His gaze met hers and held. "Chantal's here."

"Maybe it was Joelle. Sounds a bit like Chantal."

"Maybe."

"Or Nic," she added, seeing a spark of a smile in his eyes, and the cool mocking smile put her teeth on edge. What was he thinking? What did he know?

"Didn't sound like Nicolette," he answered, reaching into his pocket, pulling out the phone. "This sister sounded sophisticated. Refined. And from what I've heard, that's not your sister Nic."

She tensed at his criticism. He didn't even know Nicolette and yet he sounded as if he were the font of all wisdom. But he was holding the phone out to her, asking her if she wanted to take it. "Do you want to call?" he was asking. "I have the number saved."

So who would have called, Nic wondered? Her grandparents didn't even know she was here—so obviously they hadn't phoned. Joelle knew Nic was gone, but believed she'd headed off for a visit with Chantal in La Croix, leaving only Chantal to phone, but that wasn't a call Nic wanted to make in front of King Nuri. "I can phone later."

His expression didn't change. His arm remained extended,

offering the slim phone. He was dressed casually today, khakis, crisp white shirt, the sleeves rolled up a couple times on his forearms. "It could be urgent. Just hit Redial."

Nic tried not to glare at him as she took the phone, moving past him to stand at the window overlooking a pretty interior courtyard. Pressing the redial button, Nic heard the phone ring and almost immediately was connected with Chantal.

"Thank goodness it's you," Chantal said, wasting no time on preliminary greetings. "I've been worried sick."

"No reason to worry. Everything's fine." *Lie again.*

"So how is it going?"

Nic knew she couldn't tell Chantal the truth. Chantal was the typical first born, big sister. A worrier, overly responsible, Chantal was also a guilt-ridden perfectionist. The last thing she needed was one more reason to blame herself. "I'm fine. Honestly."

Chantal hesitated. "How…how is he?"

Nic tried to close her eyes and blot out King Nuri's presence, but he wasn't easy to dismiss, and even with her back turned, Nicolette felt his proximity. The man radiated energy. "Okay."

"Is he giving you any trouble?"

"No." Nic glanced over her shoulder, caught Malik's eyes. He'd been watching her with interest. As well as amusement. "How is Lilly?"

Chantal let out a small breath. "We're making plans. I've been in contact with mother's high school friend, Andrea. She's agreed to help us once we reach Baton Rouge."

"Good."

There was a moment of silence on the line. "I appreciate what you're doing," Chantal said quietly. "I'm not sure it's the right thing—I still think it's awfully risky for you—"

"No regrets," Nic interrupted. "No second thoughts, either. This is for Lilly. I love her dearly. You know that."

"I do."

"Okay." Nic's heart felt tight. There was so much at stake. Just hearing her sister's voice made Nic realize all over again how much depended on her. "We'll talk soon."

The call ended, Nic returned the phone to King Nuri. "Thank you. You're right. The call was important."

"I heard you mention your daughter. I trust she's fine?"

Nic saw Lilly's wide blue eyes, already too troubled. Four-year-old children weren't supposed to worry so much. "Yes."

"When is she going to join you?"

"Soon." Nic mustered a tight smile. "I hope."

He nodded, hesitated. "I don't see you again until later this evening, and I imagine you've looked over today's agenda. Did you have any questions?"

His question suddenly reminded her of why she'd woken in such a lousy mood. He might exude raw sensuality, but he was nothing short of a dictator. "I'm not a child, Your Highness."

"I didn't think you were."

She felt her temper swell, her anger was fueled by completely contradictory emotions. She'd never been so attracted to anyone before, and yet he was entirely unsuitable for a relationship. "So why have you—without consulting me, or asking for any input—put me back into school? According to my schedule, I have classes from morning until afternoon, starting with a two-hour Arabic lesson in fifteen minutes."

"I've done only what is necessary—"

"Forgive me, Your Highness," she interrupted sharply, "but these are decisions I should be making for myself. Perhaps here men decide for the women, but in my country women have a say about what happens in their lives."

CHAPTER THREE

HIS cool silver gaze rested on her face, his eyes touching her lips, her nose, her cheeks, her eyes. "A man naturally wants what is best for his woman."

She felt a shiver race down her spine. His woman. But she wasn't his woman. She had no intention of ever becoming his woman. "A woman finds it difficult to respect a man that doesn't allow her to use her brain."

"This isn't a political exercise, Princess Thibaudet. I'm simply asking you to study our language and culture—"

"All day long."

His jaw tightened. "It's not as if you're actually in school. You'll be studying with my cousin Fatima, who is not only a member of the royal family, and close to your age, but a true Barakan scholar. I expect that the two of you will become great, close friends."

Great, close friends? Nic flashed back to last night, and Fatima's cool welcome. The Sultan was dreaming. "Yes, I've met Lady Fatima, and Your Highness, my frustration isn't with the teacher, but the lessons themselves. I'm concerned that less than twenty-four hours after arriving I've already lost—" she broke off, biting back the word *control*.

She wasn't upset because she was going to learn a new language. She was upset because she was quickly losing control...of the wedding, her environment, her independence itself. Nic had spent her entire life fighting to keep the upper hand and yet less than twenty-four hours after arriving she felt as if she'd become a possession instead of a woman.

Nic struggled to find a more diplomatic way to say what she was feeling. "I'm asking you, Your Highness, to give me more input into organizing my schedule. I'd find the lessons and activities less objectionable if I had a choice."

35

"But what would you do differently? Everything I've chosen for you is good for you."

He didn't get it. Because he was a man, and a powerful man, he didn't understand what it was like to be told where to go, when to go, how to get there. "But that's precisely my point, Your Highness. Women want to choose for themselves!"

He sighed, glanced at his watch, and shook his head. "As interesting as this is, I've people waiting in my office, and I'm afraid I've spent all the time on this discussion that I intend to spend. I regret that you're unhappy with my choices, but I expect you'll enjoy the lessons once begun."

And that was it. He was done. He turned away, headed for the door and Nic watched his departing back in astonishment. He was serious. He was really done.

The fact that he'd walk out on her blew her mind. Her temper surged yet again. "I'm not going to the lessons," she called out. "I'll look my schedule over and see if I can't adapt the activities to better suit my needs."

Ah, that caught his attention. She suppressed a smile of satisfaction as he stopped at the door, and slowly turned around. His silver gaze grew flinty, his expression implacable. "The lessons are set."

"Nothing in life is set." She lifted her chin, temper blazing, emotions high. "And I won't be dictated to. If you wish a marriage with a modern princess, than you'd better expect a modern partnership. I didn't travel this far to become a royal doormat."

His dark head cocked, his jaw rigid. "A doormat?" he repeated softly. "I find the description highly offensive. I have nothing but the utmost respect for women, and the women in my life are cherished and protected. And if you learning our language is so objectionable—"

"It's not the language, Your Highness!" She was walking toward him, frustration and irritation coiled so tightly inside her she couldn't keep still. "I've never minded learning your language, but I shouldn't have to be immediately immersed in language coursework first thing on arrival. Your country is bilingual. Everyone in Baraka speaks French. And my country is also bilingual. We speak Spanish and French."

He folded his arms across his chest. "But French is part of our colonial past while Arabic is the future."

She stopped in front of the sultan, arms folded just like him, mimicking his pose. "So why marry a European princess, Your Highness? There must be plenty of Arabic princesses if that is indeed, *your* future."

He didn't answer her question but leaned toward her, brow furrowed, and she instinctively held her breath as his lips grazed her ear. "It's not too late to put you on a plane and send you home."

She gritted her teeth, eyes narrowing. How typical. Met with conflict, he'd rather send her home than compromise. "Maybe you should. You're not ready for the reality of marriage, Your Highness."

Suddenly his hand was against the back of her neck, his fingers curled against her warm sensitive skin. She shivered. He felt the shiver and his fingers tightened perceptibly. "You can not blame me entirely, Princess. You've changed. A month ago you were most eager for this union. Two weeks ago you expressed nothing but eagerness, willingness."

He'd drawn her close, so close that she was nearly held against his chest. She could feel his body's warmth, his leashed energy, his innate strength. There was no escaping him this time. Not until he chose to let her go. "What has caused this change of heart, Chantal? You're nothing but difficult today."

"I'm not difficult. I'm merely honest." He was manhandling her, dominating her, and his arrogance infuriated her. There was no reason to trap her like this against him, render her helpless with his body...his will. "Yet it appears I'm not allowed to have an opinion."

His fingers stroked the side of her neck, his thumb drawing small circles which she found maddening. She liked his touch. She hated his dominant strength. It was as if her body loved the pleasure, but her mind detested his control.

"Of course you're allowed to have an opinion," he answered calmly. "But your opinions so far express only displeasure and discontent—"

"You can't say that based on the ninety minutes we've spent together!"

He forced her head back, ensuring that she saw his full displeasure. His jaw flexed. His silver gaze shone brittle. He was barely hanging onto his temper. "Do you ever stop and think before you speak, Princess?"

"And do you bully everyone into doing what you want, King Nuri? I understand you're the sultan, but surely, others—your family, your subjects—are allowed a modicum of free speech?"

"You've tasted more than free speech," he retorted, pressing a finger against her lips. "In fact, I've heard all I want to hear from you."

"Well, I won't be quiet!" she talked despite the finger shushing her, talked to push him away, talked to keep from falling apart. The tension between them was overwhelming and Nicolette had never been so afraid. He excited her. He terrified her. She could only imagine how wild, how explosive their love-making would be.

"You won't?"

She swallowed convulsively, feeling prickly with heat, her nerves screaming in anticipation. The tension crackling between them was unlike anything she'd ever known before. But then, she'd never challenged a man as powerful as Malik Nuri before. "No." She drew a quick, shallow breath, trying somehow to regain her footing again. She could hear Chantal in her head, hearing Chantal's disapproval. Chantal would never, ever challenge a man like this. Chantal believed in tact, diplomacy, quiet strength.

Nic's strength wasn't even close to being quiet.

But she wasn't here as Nicolette, rebel middle daughter. She was here as Chantal, and King Nuri had expected agreeable Chantal.

His head lowered, his lips brushed her cheek. "I can not have a disobedient wife."

His deep cultured voice penetrated through her, electrified the most inner part of her. Her belly clenched in a knot of pleasure and fear. She craved, physically craved, his voice, his strength, his power. She wanted him to touch her. She wanted his hands all over her.

You're mad, she choked inwardly. You've lost your mind if you want to take King Nuri on this way.

But she did. She wanted to provoke him. Test him. See how far he'd let her go. She wondered where he'd draw the line and what he'd do to make her toe the line.

Power. Control. Submission. Domination. She was strong. Very strong. So strong that she'd never met a man who could match her strength—until today. "A husband shouldn't require obedience. He should desire a spirit of cooperation, and mutual respect."

His lips hovered above her cheek. "But a woman can't respect a man if he lets her walk all over him."

"I don't believe you've allowed me to walk anywhere near you, Your Highness."

He tipped her chin up and his silver gaze burned into her eyes, seeing the fire and rebellion she couldn't possibly hide. "You refuse to capitulate."

His touch was making her head spin. "But why should I have to capitulate? If you're serious about wanting a wife with an education and a sense of self-worth, then you'd welcome my thoughts."

"I do welcome them. I just don't expect my bride to challenge every request I make."

"I'm not your bride yet, and you're not making requests. You're making demands. There's a difference. We both know it." She jerked her head back, put her hands to his chest and gave a firm push. There was no way she'd let him knuckle her under.

His gaze swept down, from her warm cheeks, to her lips and even lower to the full swell of her breasts. "And if I ask you to attend language classes?"

The weight of his gaze on her breasts made them ache. It was as if he was touching her, caressing her, and her nipples peaked, hardening. "I'd consider your request." Her voice had dropped, grown husky. He had to know what he was doing to her, had to know the sensations he was stirring within her.

His gaze slowly lifted again, traveling up her neck, over her full, soft mouth, past her flushed cheeks to her eyes. "Not everything between us needs to be a fight."

His inflection was nearly as husky as her own. She felt warmth creep through her, a seductive wash of awareness...and desire. "I'm not fighting now."

The corner of his mouth lifted in the briefest smile. "No. But I expect this is but a momentary reprieve."

Oh, that smile of his. It was dangerous. Mysterious. It was as if he knew all sorts of things about her that she didn't even know. "You don't like to fight?"

He coughed, cleared his throat. "No." His silver gaze warmed, the gray-green depths turning rich, molten. "There are too many other things I'd rather do with women, particularly if she happens to be *my* woman."

There. His woman again. More possession. And she didn't want to be a possession.

"Now let's see how well this works," he continued softly, a husky note of compulsion in his voice. "Princess Chantal, I'm asking you to please consider attending the language and culture classes that begin in—" he glanced at his watch "—fifteen minutes. It's important to me that you familiarize yourself with our culture. Can you manage to squeeze the lessons into your busy schedule?"

He really wasn't giving her a choice, though, and she knew it. He was asking her, but he was fully expecting her to say yes. Damn him. Malik Roman Nuri was really hard to manage. "I'll check my calendar," she answered crisply. "But if my morning is open, I'll do my best to make the first lesson."

His eyes gleamed. His smile was mocking. He reached for her again, his fingers curling through her long hair. "You, Princess, have had too many Western men."

His words, his touch, his knowing smile made her tremble inwardly. The power continued to shift. The boundaries seemed practically invisible. He touched her as if she was already his. And her body was responding to him as if it were the most natural thing in the world. "I said I'd try."

He released her leisurely, drawing his fingers from her thick hair even more slowly. "You will. We both know you will. You're in Baraka now, *laeela*. My will, Princess, will soon be your command." Taking her hand in his, he kissed her knuckles. "Enjoy your time with Fatima. I'll look forward to getting a full report on your lessons tonight."

Nic watched him leave, feeling a bubble of hysteria form in her chest. How was she going to convince him to go to America? How was she going to convince him to do anything? He wanted her to submit—not the other way around!

You're in so much trouble, she told herself, feeling like a ship with a hole in the stern. She was going to sink. The only question was how much time did she have left before she went down?

Nicolette met Fatima in an airy salon, where the wood shutters at the tall arched windows were folded back, allowing the bright sun to bounce off the pale apricot walls and drench the marble floor with its dramatic black and ivory diamond pattern.

The language lesson seemed to last forever, but then a serving girl carried in almond pastries and mint tea.

Fatima poured the tea, glancing at Nicolette as she did so. "You know we have a saying here, Princess Thibaudet. *There's no escaping death and marriage.*" Fatima smiled grimly, handed Nicolette her tea cup. "It's true, you know. A girl's place is in the home. Tending to the family."

Nic shrugged, sensing the other woman's hostility thinking of the life Chantal had lived so far in La Croix, knowing that they were supposedly discussing Chantal's future, not hers. "I don't have a problem with that, Lady Fatima. I have a daughter. I'm comfortable being home. I've lived this way for years."

Fatima blew delicately on her hot tea. "Your daughter will marry a man chosen for her, too, then?"

Nic startled, picturing her young niece being forced to marry against her will. Never. "There's no reason for Lilly to do that."

"Yet…if you are to marry the Sultan," Fatima's smile was hard, and it made her dark eyes gleam like polished onyx, "your other children will have to follow our traditions. Surely it would be better for Lilly to do the same."

Nicolette couldn't answer. She felt cold on the inside. Scared, too. "Your cousin has never spoken of this to me."

"Not yet, no. But he will. After I have introduced our culture to you." Fatima sipped from her cup. "That is my job, you realize. To introduce you to our ways."

Nic stared into her small cup, her emotions growing hot, replacing the ice around her heart. Had Chantal considered this? Thank God Chantal was not here. Thank God she would not have to listen to this. Be tortured like this. Chantal and Lilly had been through too much already.

Gracefully Fatima set her cup on the low table, lifted the plate of pastries out to Nicolette. "Please."

It'd be impossible for Nic to eat now. She'd choke on the pastry. Her throat was dry as dust.

Fatima inclined her head. "Back to our discussion about your daughter. Do you really think it is fair to her to make her an outcast? To treat her differently than you'll treat your children with the sultan? Please try to think of it from her perspective, of what would benefit her most. How do you think she will feel being different? And how shall your choices impact her later? Because, Princess, no Barakan man will ever marry her, and if she can't marry here then you are choosing to send her far away."

Nic's tongue pressed to the roof of her mouth. She felt horribly close to choking. "She's *four,* Lady Fatima. Just four years old. A little girl still. I think these decisions don't need to be made for a number of years."

"Time passes quickly."

Not quickly enough, Nic silently retorted, furious, hanging on to her temper—barely. Fatima's company was becoming intolerable. "And you," Nic said, turning the focus onto the twenty-five-year old. "What are your cousin's plans for you? Is there a husband on the horizon, or are you going to remain here, devoting your life to him and me?"

Fatima's eyes narrowed. "I haven't heard who he has selected for me, but I am interested, of course. Why? Have you heard something?"

"No."

For the first time since they sat down together this morning, Fatima expressed uncertainty. "But if you do hear something, you'll tell me?"

"Of course, Lady Fatima. We should help each other, not hurt each other, don't you think?"

Returning to her room, Nic glanced at her calendar, unable to believe that every morning would be spent in virtual hell with Fatima, unnerved by the fact that she was making every decision—including decisions about meals and coffee—based on a calendar. *Malik Nuri's calendar!* It was an insult to her intelligence. A test of her control.

Insult or not, Nic knew that according to the calendar, she had just enough time to freshen up and change before dinner. According to her appointment book, she and King Nuri would be dining alone together, and Alea had clothes already waiting, a pale pink trouser set with a long slim silk overcoat.

Nicolette wasn't in the mood for pink, but she didn't have the energy to protest, especially not when she had more pressing matters on her mind.

Managing her emotions—and reactions—around the sultan was an issue. Lady Fatima was already posing a problem. And Nicolette was no closer to convincing the sultan that the wedding should be moved to Baton Rouge than when she arrived yesterday afternoon.

So think of tonight as an opportunity, she told herself, as she was escorted to King Nuri's quarters. This isn't a chance to fail, but a chance to succeed.

They ate Western style, sitting at a small table in one of the elegant courtyards. Torches illuminated the tiled walls, reflecting off the ancient mosaics decorating every surface. During the meal, Nic struggled to think of a natural way to bring up her concerns about the wedding—and Lady Fatima—but no opportunity presented itself. But the wedding first.

"I attended the lessons today," she said, cringing a little at her inept opening. There had to be a better way to approach the topic than this. "Lady Fatima is certainly…knowledgeable."

"She is, isn't she?"

Nic forced herself on. "She expressed thoughts that troubled me."

"Indeed?"

He wasn't being very helpful here. "Despite her education, she sounds quite conservative, at least in terms of women's roles in your society."

His shoulders shifted and the candle light flickered over his face, his features even, controlled. "Fatima has always been most comfortable as a woman. She embraces the unique differences between men and women."

Was he purposely taunting her? "Sounds perfect for you. I'm surprised you never considered marrying her."

His gaze clashed with hers. "Did I say that?"

"Did you propose?"

"No. I respect her immensely, but she's like a sister to me."

Finally some insights into his world. Ever since arriving in Atiq, Nicolette had floundered, struggling to get her feet on the ground. Just who was Malik Nuri? What did he want? What did he really believe? "Have you ever proposed to anyone?"

"I've waited a long time to marry." His expression revealed nothing, and his tone was deceptively mild. "I've waited a long time for you."

"Not me—"

"Yes, you, Princess."

She wasn't sure what to say next. Maybe she should just be glad he'd presented her with an opportunity to address her wedding concerns. "Have you had a chance to think about my request? It really does mean a great deal to me...marrying in my mother's parish." She tried to keep her tone casual, although beneath the table her fingers were knotting her linen napkin. There were so many undercurrents between them—personal, physical, sexual.

"Your mother, the American."

"I know you want to be married here, in Atiq, but perhaps we could find a compromise. Instead of just one ceremony, we could have two. We go to Baton Rouge for my church ceremony, and then return here for a traditional Barakan ceremony."

"Two ceremonies?"

"It's not unheard of, Your Highness—"

"Malik. Please. We're discussing our wedding."

The way he said *our wedding* made her blush and she nodded awkwardly, immediately aware of the size of him, the strength of him, as well as the sense that despite the differences between them, they'd be eventually matched in bed. "Dual ceremonies are being done more and more these days," she said, voice almost breaking. "It's one way of addressing the various aspects of culture."

He hesitated, lips pursing. "Perhaps. I've never thought of drawing this out, but that's not to say we couldn't make it happen."

Yes. Nic felt herself exhale in a deep rush. But her relief was tinged by something else...an emotion far more personal, one that had nothing to do with Chantal and Lilly and only to do with her attraction.

"We'd marry here first, then," he added, as if thinking aloud. "You're already here. The plans have been made. After the palace ceremony, we could fly to Louisiana, invite your friends and family to join us there."

His words popped whatever brief fantasy she held. She was

being ridiculous, the daydream she had been having of a lazy afternoon in bed was even more ridiculous. He was a sultan. She was a princess. She wasn't even the princess he wanted. "Your Highness—" she saw his frown, and quickly substituted his name "—Malik. I appreciate you considering my suggestion, and I'm grateful you're willing to travel to the States, but if we should do all that, I'd really like to walk down the aisle first...be a bride in white."

"A bride in white," he echoed thoughtfully.

And then remembering she was supposed to be Chantal she forced a tight smile. "I know I've done it before, but it's still...traditional."

"And you're the traditional sister, right?" He leaned away from the table and the candles, having burned low, turned the table into a shade of rose-gold. "You mentioned this morning that the Ducasses are half French?"

It was a quick switch. He was very good, she thought, rinsing off her fingers in her water bowl, wiping her hands dry. He controlled the conversation. He controlled her physical reactions. He controlled her emotions. This was certainly a first for her.

"French and Spanish," Nic answered after a moment's pause, gathering her wits about her, knowing she needed them more than ever. He let nothing slide. He remembered every word she said. "Although throughout history many Ducasse kings took English brides."

"Royal brides?"

"Only royal brides."

"So you were raised speaking...?"

"French for father, English for Mother, and our nanny was from Seville, so we spoke Spanish with her."

"Any other languages?"

Her heart was no longer racing. She felt calmer again, dignified. "I read Latin, of course, know some Greek, a fair amount of Italian and can get by with my German."

"A linguist."

She shrugged. "I'm a mathematician. They say language and math use the same parts of the brain."

"Interesting." His fingers tapped the table, his expression almost brooding. "I didn't realize both you and Nicolette studied mathematics at university. I knew she had—you'd mentioned that this morning—but didn't know you had as well.''

Nic gave herself a hard mental kick. You're Chantal, act like Chantal! But it was proving harder to do than Nic ever expected. Having never wanted to be anyone but herself. ''It's all the same gene pool,'' she said lightly. The table had been covered by an elegant purple cloth shot with gold threads so the entire table seemed to glimmer and shine in the soft candlelight.

''Speaking of the parental gene pool, I met your father once,'' Malik said, again changing the topic, keeping her firmly off balance. Candlelight flickered across his face, playing up the length of his imperial nose, the uncompromising line of his jaw. ''Years ago, when I was still in my teens, I heard him address a group of leaders at a European economic summit. He was brilliant.''

''He loved Melio.'' Nic pictured her country's beautiful old port, the narrow tree-lined streets, the pretty farms tucked between rocky hills. ''He wanted the best for Melio, and was willing to make whatever sacrifices were necessary—''

''Except for giving up your mother,'' the sultan interrupted thoughtfully. ''Your mother wasn't ever negotiable, was she?''

Her mother, the American pop sensation...a star who'd risen from the poorest roots imaginable. Her mother had grown up hungry. Hungry for food, warmth, love, shelter. Hungry for recognition.

Only Nic's grandparents hadn't seen it that way. They'd thought her mother was hungry for power and they'd done everything in *their* power to break up Julien and Star's marriage. They'd wanted so much more for their Prince Julien. ''He would have given up the crown if he had to,'' she answered flatly.

''Your grandparents nearly disinherited him.''

She shook her head, finding it all so ludicrous. ''My grandparents underestimated my mother.'' Nic had never visited her mother's birthplace in Louisiana, but she knew it was considered rural. Rough. Poverty stricken, crime ridden. Definitely not roots to be proud of. ''Mother may have been born poor, but she wasn't afraid of challenges.'' No one worked harder than her mother. She had little formal schooling, having dropped out of high school before earning her diploma, but she'd dreamed big and that counted for something.

Malik's gaze rested on Nic's flushed face. "You got along well with her?"

"Very." Nic had adored her mother. In some ways they were one and the same. Fearless. Absolutely fearless. "I'm glad she wasn't your typical princess. I'm glad she was poor, blue collar, American. She took nothing for granted. She taught us to take nothing for granted."

A maid appeared with a tray and a steaming pot of coffee and two small cups. As the maid poured the coffee Nic wondered how on earth had they gotten onto this topic in the first place. It was not her favorite topic. Nic was too much like her mother to understand those who'd criticized Star.

Malik waited for the maid to leave again. "Would you say you're the same kind of mother to Lilly? What is your relationship with your daughter like?"

And suddenly Nicolette felt wrenched all over again, remembering how everything they were saying, everything they were doing was a lie. She was supposed to be playing Chantal, instead she kept speaking from the heart, answering his questions honestly, openly.

Think like Chantal…think like Chantal. And Nic could see Chantal in her mind's eye and knew that yes, Chantal was a fantastic mother. Chantal was the ultimate mother. "I think I'm more protective than my mother," Nic said after a moment. "And Lilly, I think, is more trusting than most children, and considerably more vulnerable."

Malik sipped from his small cup. "Perhaps it's losing her father so young in life."

Nic couldn't help her jaw hardening. Armand…Armand… how she hated Prince Armand Thibaudet. "Perhaps," Nic agreed quietly, but her voice came out cold, flat. "Or perhaps it's that she's very bright for her age, quite intuitive, and she senses that things are not…as they should be."

Malik stared at her, considering her, his expression curious, almost speculative. After a minute ticked by, he shifted in his chair, leaning back to make himself more comfortable, and yet the intensity of his gaze made her burn from the inside out. "From what I understand, your first marriage wasn't a love match."

Her stomach was in knots. She could hardly concentrate. "Far from it."

"Yet you came to Baraka…?"

Because I didn't have a choice, she wanted to tell him. You were pressuring Chantal, and Chantal's had enough pressure. "I want Lilly happy," she said at last, feeling the weight of the world rest on her shoulders. Somehow, in less than forty-eight hours, he'd tied her in knots. She wasn't Nic. She wasn't Chantal. She didn't know who she was anymore. The only thing she did know was that the chemistry between her and King Nuri was wild…stunning…she'd never had this kind of response to anyone and there was no way—absolutely no way—she could let the attraction get out of hand.

CHAPTER FOUR

LATER that evening, after returning to her room, she lay in bed, staring at the wood shutters where just the faintest edge of light could be made out around the edges. She couldn't sleep.

Couldn't turn her brain off.

She was beginning to worry, really worry. First her dinner conversation with King Nuri played in her head, and then as soon as that conversation ended, she heard her last conversation with Chantal begin, the conversation they had just hours before Nic had boarded the *Royal Star* yacht.

"It's just a meet and greet, right?" Nicolette had asked, drumming her fingers on her locked steamer trunk. *"You wouldn't actually marry him. It's just a chance to say hi—bye—and know what you're not getting involved with?"*

Chantal's eyebrows lifted. "Be careful, Nic. This isn't one of your fun-loving Greeks. This is King Nuri—"

"A man—"

"A King."

Nic shrugged. "So he's a royal, but so are we—and just because a man says jump, it doesn't mean we have to."

So she didn't have to jump, but the wedding was less than two weeks away and she had no idea how she was going to make this work.

What if she couldn't get out of Baraka? What if she wasn't able to break off the engagement in time?

There was no way she'd go through with this marriage.

Not even to rescue Lilly?

The little voice in Nic's head made her sigh, close her eyes. She knew she'd marry Bluebeard if it'd save Lilly. But oh, let there be another way...

There had to be another way...

Once again Nic woke up in a bad mood. She hated lies.

49

Detested hypocrisy. And yet here she was, about to begin another day pretending to be someone she was not.

Alea had breakfast waiting outside in Nic's private courtyard, and after wrapping herself in one of the long silk robes from her wardrobe, Nic wandered outside, pulling her hair into a ponytail high on the top of her head.

She caught a glimpse of herself in the koi pond outside. Brown hair. Long messy ponytail. Dark circles under the eyes.

Princess heading to disaster.

Alea sat with Nic while she had her breakfast. "It's going to be a busy day," Alea said, studying Nic's calendar. "Language lesson. Culture lesson. Then a wedding gown fitting—"

"No."

Alea looked up from the appointment book. "Did you want lunch before the fitting?"

"No. No, I don't want to go to the wedding gown fitting—"

"It's only scheduled for an hour."

Nic covered her face with her hands, rubbed her forehead, hating the headache that never seemed to go away. "I just wish...I mean...why can't the fitting wait?" Nic shook her head. No use complaining. Alea hadn't made the schedule and Alea couldn't change her schedule.

But Alea frowned, feeling responsible. "Do you want me to send a message to His Highness? Would you like to speak with him?"

Nic's gaze rested on the courtyard's lacy latticework, and her view through the open bedroom door to her suite of rooms. The ceiling in her bedchamber was high, and painted gold and blue, the floor covered in graceful tile mosaics—all lovely, all intended to seduce the senses, subdue the will—but Nic didn't want to be seduced and subdued. She wasn't here to be charmed. And she wasn't about to be wooed.

"These rooms," Nic said, "they're incredibly beautiful. Are all bedrooms in the palace like this?"

"Oh, no, Princess. There are just a few of these special rooms. They are reserved for the sultan's favorites." Alea smoothed a page in the open appointment book.

The sultan's favorites? As in plural. Very nice. Nic's eyebrows lifted satirically and she glanced around once more seeing the palatial use of space, large outdoor sunken pool, koi pool, and colorful mosaics with fresh eyes. "This was part of the harem."

"For the sultan's chosen."

Ah, well, that was much better, wasn't it? Nic thought pushing away from the table, thinking it fitting that she moved from one excruciating test to another. Breakfast in the harem followed by Arabic lesson with the cousin. How could life get any better?

Nic survived the arduous lesson, and then happily the study turned to geography. Today Fatima pulled out a map of Baraka and its neighboring countries and Nicolette loved learning about the various geographical points of interest—the mountain ranges, the river, the great deserts.

Abruptly Fatima folded the map. "What do you know about our weddings?"

"Very little," Nic answered, wondering why Fatima had taken the map away. She'd been enjoying the lesson immensely and they still had plenty of time left. At least fifteen minutes.

"You should know about our weddings," Fatima continued tersely. "They are very important in our culture, and they are very expensive." Fatima's lips curled but she didn't seem to be smiling. "Wedding celebrations generally last a week. The wedding itself takes place over several days. Yours will probably be at least three days. Each day of the wedding week you'll receive more gold and jewelry from Malik. And then finally on the wedding day, you'll be carried in on a great table, covered in jewels and all the gifts Malik has given you."

Nicolette was appalled, disgusted that she'd be paraded about on a table like a roasted pig at Christmas.

"You are very lucky," Fatima added forcefully. "You are grateful for your good fortune, aren't you?"

A murmur of voices sounded from the doorway and Nic glanced over her shoulder to see the servants bowing. King Nuri had entered the room and Nic couldn't be more relieved.

"Good morning," Fatima greeted, rising.

"How is the lesson coming?" he asked, approaching them, wearing dark casual slacks and a long-sleeve shirt the color of burnished copper. The shirt flattered his complexion, enhancing his features and the inky black of his hair.

"Good," Fatima said stiffly. "We're done."

"Fine. Then allow me to steal my princess." He bent his

head, kissed Nicolette on each cheek, and waved off Fatima, indicating she was free to go and turned to Nicolette. "You're certain the lesson went smoothly?"

She glanced up into his face. His expression was guarded. She wondered if he'd heard something when he first entered the room. "It went smoothly. Your cousin is quite knowledgeable."

"She is," he agreed. "And at times a little formal." He hesitated a moment. "I thought I heard her speak of our wedding customs."

So he had heard something. "She was describing the ceremony. I must admit, it seemed a little...otherworldly to me."

"Which part?"

She felt heat rise to her cheeks and tried to shrug casually. "The part where the bride is draped in gold and jewels and carried in, reclining on a table."

He laughed, the sound deep and husky, and far too sexy. "It's not exactly the same thing as walking down an aisle in virginal white, is it?"

It amused him, this little play acting of hers. The princess was determined to stick with the role, even though it didn't suit her at all.

He'd known she was Nicolette from the moment she arrived, and yet he'd gone along with her charade, curious to see how far she'd let this go. He'd heard she was tough—spirited—independent, and her fire intrigued him. As well as challenged him. She might be a player, but so was he. He'd play her game. And he'd beat her at her own game.

Watching her face now, he secretly hoped she would give him a good run for his money. Women had always fallen at his feet, swept away by his power and money. Women had always been...too easy. But Nic wasn't easy. And he liked that.

The fact that she'd come to his country and try to play him...now that was daring. She was a born risk-taker. Good for her. Too many people played it safe throughout life.

"Should we go try on that wedding gown now?" he asked, feeling almost guilty for enjoying himself so much. And yet it'd been a long time since he'd felt so enthusiastic, or optimistic, about anything.

He saw how the word "wedding gown" made Nicolette's jaw clench. It was all he could do to keep his expression blank.

"You're going to accompany me to the fitting?"

"Why not?" he answered with a shrug.

The tip of her pink tongue appeared, briefly touched the edge of her teeth. "Is it customary?" But she didn't give him chance to answer as she immediately continued. "Because somehow I can't imagine it's allowed here. According to your cousin Fatima, the men and women are still so segregated. Once girls hit puberty, women begin to lead separate lives…" Her voice drifted off. She tried again. "Perhaps I've misunderstood her, or perhaps I've misunderstood you."

"No. You didn't misunderstand."

She waited for him to elaborate but he didn't. She swallowed. "But aren't you…I'd think you'd be…as sultan…" Her confusion showed in her eyes. "More traditional."

It was rather refreshing to see her struggle. Very little gave Princess Nicolette pause. She'd arrived here thinking she had the upper hand. She'd do this, and do that, and it would be just as she planned.

But nothing in life went just as one planned. And the game was on.

"Alas," he sighed, "I am not the most traditional sultan. I've traveled a great deal, lived abroad. I hope you are not disappointed."

He felt her gaze as they walked through the palace, down one mysterious corridor and then another. She was thinking, and she was struggling to come up with some definitive conclusions but so far she hadn't.

She couldn't.

She didn't really know him.

He smiled on the inside. He liked her. He'd liked her for a long time, not that he knew her well, either. But he appreciated what he saw, admired her attitude. He knew she was the Ducasse princess who didn't want to marry. He'd heard all about her escapades, the problems she'd created in Melio, the headaches she'd given her beloved grandparents. He'd heard, too, how she didn't worry about what others thought—she loved her family—but she wasn't going to give up herself just to please them, either.

Like her, he'd dated extensively. He'd never worried about marriage, had known he'd have to marry one day, after all, he was the eldest son of the powerful Sultan Baraka, and he'd assumed that his bride would be loving, loyal, dutiful, and he'd imagined a quiet woman from his own country. But after the attempt on his life, his priorities changed.

He needed more than a quiet, obedient bride. He needed a woman who could face the challenges of life with courage, intelligence and humor.

They'd reached the end of the hall, and Malik opened the door to a very modern salon. The salon was outfitted with low couches covered in bright orange and violet velvet fabrics, the pale yellow walls were sheeted in long mirrors, and in the middle of the room was a small curtained platform for wardrobe fittings.

An elegant woman entered the room, and she bowed to King Nuri, and then turned to Nicolette. "Your Highness," she said, smiling. "It is an honor to meet you, and an even greater honor to dress you for your wedding. You must be quite excited."

Excited was the last word Nic would have used to describe her emotions at the moment. Dread, disgust, terror, anxiety, fear...those were the emotions she felt right now as she stepped up onto the platform.

"Do you have any thoughts on the type of gown you'd like to wear?" The designer asked, summoning two assistants who helped begin with the measurements.

Nic felt King Nuri's watchful presence, and she glanced up at the curtains hanging from the ceiling. She knew the curtains could be closed, offering greater privacy, but no one moved to shut them. "No. I don't really spend time thinking about these things."

"You'd never had any ideas about the gown? The color, the style, the fabric."

Nic shook her head. Once, four or five years ago, she and her sisters had spent the night before Chantal's wedding to Prince Armand planning their futures and Nic and Joelle had sketched their wedding dresses and described the kind of wedding they'd each have. Nic had said she'd do a Sleeping Beauty wedding, all pink and coral and green, because she'd have to be Sleeping Beauty to get married—go to sleep, wake up with a kiss and get dragged to the altar fast before she knew what was happening.

Joelle and Chantal had laughed, of course, but now the idea of being dragged to the altar fast appeared incredibly real.

With the measurements taken, the designer summoned for fabric samples, and the assistants carried out bolt after bolt, displaying them first before the sultan and then draping them across Nicolette's shoulder.

The fabrics were all costly—rich delicately woven silks with even more delicate threads of gold. The colors were exquisite, sheer pastel hues ranging from grass-green to young lemon, the pink of dawn to the coral plucked from the sea.

"This is just the beginning," the designer said. "Later many dedicated hands will embroider fantastic patterns, but first we must find the right silk for you."

Malik had been watching everything closely from his position on one pumpkin-hued sofa. He suddenly spoke to the designer in Arabic.

The designer listened attentively, bowed and turning to Nic, she smiled. "You are very fortunate, Your Highness, the sultan wishes you to have a gown made from each."

Nic wished everyone would stop telling her how fortunate she was. She did not feel fortunate. She felt trapped. And a gown of each color would only trap her more.

Turning, she glanced at King Nuri where he reclined on the plush sofa. His rust-colored shirt had fallen open at the collar, exposing the higher plane of his chest. He was all hard, honed muscle.

She tried not to imagine how lovely all that hard, honed muscle would be naked. She was already far too aware of him, far too attracted to him. The last thing she needed was proof of his sensuality…sexuality…virility. "I appreciate your generosity, Your Highness, but I do not need so many expensive gowns."

"It gives me pleasure to dress you," he answered lazily, a spark of possession in his eyes.

Nic swallowed, thinking she didn't like the possessive light in his eyes, or the expense, and waste, of gowns she'd never wear. She wouldn't be here long enough to wear even one of them. "I understand you are a generous man—"

"Proud, too."

The pitch of his voice made her stomach flip. He looked so relaxed, and yet she felt distinctly uneasy. Was she imagining the note of warning in his voice?

Shaken, Nic looked down, saw the latest bolt of fabric wrap

her breast and hips, the silk a wispy blue like the blue of the sky after a hard cleansing rain. She liked the blue. It made her feel almost calm.

"And one of the blue silk, too," he said, breaking the silence. "That is my favorite so far."

The fitting ended soon after, concluding in silence. The designer bowed deeply to the sultan, thanking him profusely, and then excused herself leaving Nic and King Nuri alone.

Nic heard the great wooden door softly close behind the seamstress. She remained where she was on the dais, feeling strangely alone, and unusually foolish.

"Which will be my wedding gown?" she asked, stepping off the platform and adjusting the band collar on her simple white linen overcoat and long slim skirt.

The sultan cocked his head. "Does it matter?"

No. It didn't matter. She'd only been making conversation, trying to fill the awkward silence. It wasn't as if she'd ever wear the gown anyway. "You're angry with me."

"No. Not at all." He extended a hand to her. "Come. Sit here with me so we might speak more comfortably."

She moved to sit on a sofa across from his but he shook his head. "Here." He placed a hand on the pumpkin silk sofa where he reclined.

Gingerly she sat next to him. "Comfortable?" he asked.

She ignored the mockery underlying the question. "Yes." Maybe he wasn't angry, but there was something on his mind.

He adjusted one of the gorgeous gold tapestry pillows, placing it behind her back. "Better?"

"I wasn't uncomfortable."

"Yes, but one could always feel more peace...more pleasure." He folded his arms behind his head, studied her face, her expression outwardly serene. "Did you enjoy the fitting?"

"I think I mentioned before that I'm not particularly fashion conscious."

"But the newspapers and magazines are always proclaiming your strong sense of fashion. Aren't you the clear favorite in the design world?"

Chantal was, of course. Every designer loved to dress the very slender, and inherently elegant, Chantal Thibaudet, the beautiful widowed princess of La Croix. Chantal had been beloved as the eldest Ducasse daughter, but once married and widowed, the public embraced her even more.

Nic's emotions ran riot. Chantal didn't obsess about fashion. She'd always been stylish, even sophisticated. The family used to joke that even as a baby Chantal would tug on her bonnet until it had a jaunty angle.

But Nic found the public's love affair with beautiful, fashionable princesses burdensome. She'd rather spend a day figuring math problems than go clothes-shopping. "One of the drawbacks of being in the public eye, is the constant pressure to maintain one's image. I've often felt there is too much value placed on appearances, Your Highness. I personally dislike having to worry about clothes and fashion when there is so much happening in the world that is of real importance."

"You always surprise me." The sultan smiled, and it was a genuine smile, one that reached his eyes and made the grooves along his mouth deepen. The warmth of the smile was almost unbearably appealing.

Nic's mouth dried. He looked so comfortable in himself, so physical and sexual at the same time. "That's good?"

"Yes." His smile faded but the warmth remained in his eyes. He exuded intelligence, as well as compassion. He wore his mantle of authority well. "Do you know why I selected you, Princess?"

It was hard to concentrate with him looking at her like that. She wanted to focus and yet she felt so many emotions that she had no business feeling. "I know you wanted better Mediterranean port access."

"But there are numerous Mediterranean ports, and numerous single European princesses interested in marriage." He hesitated, speaking each word with care. "I chose you, because I respect you. I believe you are like me. You understand the responsibilities of being a princess of the royal Ducasse family, and your loyalty, along with your sense of duty, make you an ideal mate."

Nic couldn't breathe. She felt the air settle in her chest. He had it all wrong. She lacked Chantal's sense of duty. Her loyalty was to her own family. That's why she was here. Not for Melio, but for Chantal and Lilly. "You don't worry I'd run away...fail to fulfill my obligations here?"

"You didn't in La Croix."

No, Chantal hadn't run away. Not in La Croix, not in Melio, not ever. But that's because good Chantal, first born Chantal, had been a pleaser since birth. All she'd ever wanted was to do the ''right'' thing, and yet the thing that had driven Nic crazy was the thought, how did Chantal even know what was *right?*

Nic had never known what was *right*. She'd had to search for meaning, ask questions, test, push at each and every limitation. In her world, there'd been no ''right,'' there had only been truth, and truth wasn't something one accepted blindly.

Truth required testing. Truth required proof.

''Marriages that are not love matches can work. They do work.'' His voice was deep, his tone thoughtful. ''My parents had an arranged marriage which lasted fifty-some years.''

''They are the lucky ones.''

''Your grandparents' marriage was arranged. They are still together today, and you can not tell me they do not care deeply for each other.''

Grandfather Remi cherished Grandmama Astrid. They were a true couple. They'd been together so long now, functioned so well together, it was as if they couldn't exist without the other. Ever since Grandmama had had her stroke, Grandfather's health had declined. Until Grandmama's stroke, Grandfather had been robust. Vigorous. Not anymore.

''They do love each other,'' Nic said, finding her voice. ''They're wonderful people, too.''

She swallowed, reminding herself that she couldn't answer just as Nicolette. She had to be Chantal. She had to think like Chantal. ''Which is why I accepted Prince Armand's proposal,'' she added huskily. ''If my grandparents thought Armand and I would be a good match, then…''

She shrugged, but she didn't feel indifferent. Armand was the lowest sort of a man, the kind that would abuse a woman verbally, physically, a man who didn't feel strong unless he completely dominated—subjugated—the woman who loved him, depended on him.

''You implied last night that Lilly wasn't happy,'' Malik said. ''Tell me about her life in La Croix.''

Nic hesitated, uncertain yet again how much she could, or should say. ''It's not a positive place to raise a child.''

"Yet her grandparents are there, and from what I've heard, her father's family apparently dotes on her."

"Her father's family is obsessively controlling."

"Obsessively?"

"Complete control freaks," Nic retorted, unable to hide her bitterness.

His eyebrows flattened. "An awfully American expression," he said thoughtfully. "Not one I would have ever thought you'd use. Your sister, Nicolette, now she'd say something like that…"

Could he be anymore condescending? Suddenly Nic was fighting mad. She'd love a good fight, would welcome an opportunity to spar. It was so unfair that women were trapped in bad marriages, unable to take action because mothers with young children couldn't afford to work, pay for food and shelter along with childcare. The economics alone kept women down. "Yes, she would, and she does," Nic answered hotly. "Unfortunately I've picked up some of Nic's expressions. We've just spent a week together in Melio."

"Ah." Malik's eyes narrowed slightly at the corners. "That explains it." He paused. "Because I've wondered. You haven't seemed quite yourself since you arrived. I'd always heard you, Chantal, described as gentle, controlled, emotionally contained."

"And I'm not?"

His mouth pursed. "No."

"But…but why? I think I'm exactly the same."

He shook his head. "Even your mannerisms are different. You move your body more. Your gestures are sharper, less… refined."

Ouch. Chantal the Persian cat, Nic the tiger, Joelle the lovable tabby.

"Perhaps the years at La Croix changed you." His gaze met hers, held. "Made you stronger. Fiercer. Angrier."

"Angrier?"

"You are angry."

No use even debating that one. She was angry. Deeply angry that Chantal would suffer such horrible treatment by the Thibaudets, angry that Chantal and Lilly were trapped, angry that there was no one who could help rescue them, angry that the world didn't seem to care very much when women were hurt, when women were verbally, emotionally, mentally abused.

Abuse should never be tolerated. Ever. Ever.

Children shouldn't be hurt. Women shouldn't be squashed, smashed, pushed around. Just because women were smaller boned than men, lighter in weight, softer skinned didn't mean that it was okay to make them stepping stones or punching bags.

Someone had to do something.

Someone had to care enough to say, enough is enough. I've had enough. No more.

"You're right. I am upset," Nic said after a long moment. "Very upset." She bit her bottom lip, felt the softness of the skin in her mouth and regretted that she hadn't been there for Chantal when Armand had bullied her, intimidated her. Nic was heartsick that she hadn't known Chantal's misery until too late, until the emotional scars were hidden but not at all forgotten.

She drew a slow breath to calm herself, trying to buy herself time. "I think it's easy for people to ignore those in need. I think it's easy for people to close their door, shutter their window, pretend that it's enough to take care of yourself, enough to have a full stomach and comfortable bed."

Malik's gaze grew intense. "What happened in La Croix?"

She pictured Chantal's gaunt frame, sad eyes, the abuse Nic only recently knew Chantal had suffered. "What didn't happen?"

CHAPTER FIVE

"I TAKE it your husband wasn't exactly…a good husband?" Malik's deep voice echoed concern.

Nic pressed her nails into her palm. Surely it was okay to tell the sultan this. After all, if she wanted him to help rescue Lilly, she needed his sympathy, and the only way he'd sympathize with Lilly's plight was if he knew the truth. But the truth was hard to say, painful and shameful, and Nic knew Chantal would be furious with her for speaking it aloud.

Like many abused women, part of Chantal believed that somehow she had brought the pain on herself, that she must have done something wrong along the way, that Armand's cruelty wouldn't have happened if Chantal had been a better wife, woman, mother.

Malik's long tanned fingers tapped the rim of his glass. "Did he hit you?"

Nic held her breath. The air felt hot and sharp inside her lungs. She could hear Chantal in her head, no no no, could see her sister's beautiful eyes pleading, don't say a thing, don't tell him what horrible things I went through. He'll think less of me, he'll think I'm bad, that I'm somehow…dirty.

Nic's eyes filled with tears. Damn Armand to hell. He had no right laying a hand on Chantal. No right putting his fist to her face. "Yes."

Malik's eyes searched Nic's. "Did he ever touch your daughter?"

"He was rough." Nic swallowed. She didn't like talking about her sister's marriage, didn't like airing such horrid secrets. It was shameful, she thought, understanding for the first time why Chantal couldn't talk about the abuse, why Chantal only wanted to move on. Forget.

"Were Armand's parents aware of the problem?"

61

Her shoulders shifted. "They couldn't have been oblivious. Armand lost his temper in front of them frequently."

"But they did nothing?"

"No. But his mother did come to me once. She'd intimated that early in her marriage Armand's father had behaved the same, but that it was our duty to forgive them, that they are good men. They just don't manage their anger well."

"She wanted you to put up with it since she had to."

Nic nodded. She'd told Chantal the very same thing. "They say abuse often perpetuates itself." She felt a gnawing restlessness. She needed to get up, move, escape this dreadful dark emotion filling her. Chantal had been through enough. Chantal would be saved. Chantal would have a chance at freedom. Independence. There was no reason for Chantal to ever have to agree to a loveless, arranged marriage again.

"I want Lilly out." Nic swallowed, forced herself to focus. "I want her away from La Croix." She drew a slow breath. "You're the only one who could possibly get her out."

"Her grandparents won't let her leave the country?"

Nic's gaze was direct. "They can be persuaded."

Malik said nothing.

Nic felt the lump in her throat grow but it only made her more determined. Lilly would get out. Chantal would be free. "There are all kinds of persuasion," she added, glancing at her hands, then up into his face. "I believe her grandparents might accept…compensation…if you will."

"Buy them off?"

"It could be possible."

"Those are desperate measures."

Nic smiled but her eyes felt hard, her skin felt cold. "And I am a desperate woman."

He stood, held out an arm. "Come, let's walk. It's feeling a little close in here."

Nic rose, slipped her trembling hands into the pockets of her slim linen overcoat, wondering if she'd alienated Malik with her honesty. Then so be it, she immediately answered. If he couldn't handle truth, if he couldn't deal with reality, then he wasn't the right one for her. Correction, the right one to help Chantal.

Because she was here for Chantal. This wasn't about her…this wasn't for her… Or was it?

Nic sucked in a breath, wondering what was happening. She was feeling a kinship with King Nuri, a new sense of belonging. But Baraka wasn't home, and wouldn't be home. Her life was in sunny Melio on the other side of the Mediterranean with its scent of cypress and oranges, shades of olive-green and dark green, the rocky cliffs and the sun drenched pastures.

Malik's arm rested lightly around her as they walked from the palace to one of the exterior courtyards, massive even by European standards, and the warmth of his body against hers flooded her with hot sensation.

She wanted so much more than just an arm on her waist. She longed to feel him all the way against her, wanted the pressure of his chest, his hips, his legs. She drew a deep breath, exhaled even more slowly. The desire to be part of him was growing stronger day by day. This was a dangerous place, she thought, and somehow the splash of fountains and the sun glinting off cobalt-blue tiles while the scent of jasmine hung in the air only added to the ache inside her.

She glanced up into his face, her gaze taking in his hard, regal features, his dark hair combed back from his broad brow. He looked pensive. Preoccupied.

"Did I shock you?" she asked, wishing she didn't care one way or the other what he thought, but she did care, she cared very much. The fact was she liked King Malik Roman Nuri more than she'd liked any man in oh—years.

He was hard, sexy, sensual. Male. She knew by the way he touched things, he understood fingers, skin, pressure, sensation. She knew by the way he moved that he was aware of himself, aware of others. Even now with his arm lightly around her waist she felt his strength and energy ripple through her, hot, sensitive, alive.

"No."

"You've gone quiet."

His palm pressed against the dip in her spine, warm, strong. Nicolette had never felt so safe. She'd never felt in danger before, but this was different. Malik Roman Nuri was a man who cared about women. Protected women. He was a man who'd always do what was right for the women in his family.

"You've given me much to think on." The pressure of his

hand eased. "I realize that you come here with unique needs of your own."

Was that a polite way of saying she had an agenda? She wasn't going to deny it. Arranged marriages were about strengthening one's position, forming an alliance, creating stability.

"We both want something," she answered frankly. "The question is, what do you *really* want from me? You already know what I want from you."

"Do I?" He shot her a curious glance. "I know you want freedom for Lilly, and stability and security for your country, but what about you? You don't strike me as a woman who has no dreams for herself."

The splash of the fountain soothed Nic's nerves. She listened to the gurgling water and it sounded cool, refreshing. She felt more at peace than she had in days. "It would be enough for me to know that my family is happy, healthy, and safe." And Nic realized that it was true. Maybe she didn't have her mother's talent and desire for fame, but she had her mother's courage. She wasn't afraid to risk all to ensure that those around her would be protected.

Nic knew she was tough. She'd always been strong. She didn't need approval. She wanted to stand on her own two feet. "And equality," she said after a moment. "Equality for women. Everywhere."

Then remembering where she was, standing in what had to be one of the most luxurious courtyards in the world, Nic realized she was speaking not just to Malik, but to a sultan, a king of a country that had once been part of the powerful Ottoman Empire, in a country where men outnumbered women in higher education ten to one.

Perhaps she'd said too much, been too honest. Nic glanced up at Malik again, tensing inwardly, waiting for his reprimand.

Instead he nodded, his expression sober. "I agree."

Another night of restless sleep. Another morning where Nicolette did not want to get up. The more Nic liked Malik, the more difficult her charade became.

But Alea wasn't about to let Nicolette spend the day in bed.

"Princess," Alea said, tugging on the covers Nicolette held over her head. "You must get up. You're going to be late."

"It's just a language lesson."

"But Lady Fatima will be waiting."

Let her wait.

"And I've Italian espresso," Alea encouraged in her cheerful singsong. "You love Italian espresso."

True, Nic loved her coffee. She could drink coffee all day. "What else do I have on my schedule?" Nic asked, her voice muffled from beneath the covers.

Alea hesitated. Nicolette knew what that meant, too. It meant that Nic had another exhausting day, lessons, appointments, luncheons—all accompanied by Fatima.

"You have the state dinner tonight, and the King will be taking you, of course." Alea was trying her best to be encouraging. "And the first of your new gowns are ready. You'll be able to wear the dress tonight when King Nuri introduces you to his aides and advisors."

Nicolette slowly lowered the covers. As much as she wanted to stay in bed and avoid the lessons and day's appointments, she knew she couldn't. She also wanted to see Malik later. Seeing him had somehow become the highlight of her day.

Several hours later, after the language lesson ended, Fatima took Nicolette on a tour of the palace, pointing out unusual details like pre-Roman bronzes unearthed at various sites in Baraka, a beautiful bronze of a young boy dating back to the start of the imperial era, gold coins that had been minted during the Almohad dynasty when Baraka was part of the territory that included Morocco, Libya, Tunisia, Algeria and part of Spain.

For a little while Nicolette forgot the tension existing between her and Fatima. Nic enjoyed the tour, finding the description of ancient treasures and artifacts riveting. She'd always loved history, was passionate about early civilizations and had once fancied herself becoming an explorer.

But in the end, after university ended, she'd never used her degrees—mathematics, history or otherwise. Instead she'd become a professional princess. For whatever that was worth.

At one point during the tour, Fatima opened a set of pale gold wood shutters, and the sun poured in. Looking out, Nicolette saw the cloudless blue sky, the far away peaks of the Atlas

mountains and the not so distant date and palm trees. For a
moment Nicolette felt swept back in time, sucked back one hundred, three hundred, a thousand years. Here, nothing would
change quickly. Here, certain elements were constant—the burnished sun, the torrid desert, the tribal conflicts, the unwavering
faith of the people.

King Malik Roman Nuri was part of these elements. He might
have French ancestry, a Western education, but he was as steady
and deep as the sky over the Sahara.

Maybe Chantal would like it here. Maybe Chantal would be
drawn to Malik just as she, Nic, was drawn to the sultan.

Maybe she'd made a mistake telling Chantal not to come, that
it'd be disastrous to accept the King's marriage proposal, because truthfully, there was great beauty here. Even the ordinary
felt exotic, luxurious, mysterious. Time moved more slowly. No
one was hurried, no one moved too quickly, spoke too quickly,
no one seemed too busy to converse or smile—well, except for
Fatima, that is.

Standing at the window, Nic tried to imagine Chantal and
Lilly in Atiq, and somehow the exotic beauty overshadowed the
two of them.

In her heart of hearts, Nic knew that Chantal would disappear
here. Chantal would say all the proper things and agree and try
to be pleasing, proper, the wife of a king, but trying hard to
please another would just diminish Chantal further.

Chantal needed a life away from nobility. Service. Duty.
Chantal needed to learn how to be selfish.

Nic's thoughts haunted her as they finished the tour of the
palace rooms. They'd virtually viewed the entire elaborate
sprawl of villas, suites and chambers. There were buildings for
everything, rooms reserved for the royal family and then the
formal rooms for entertaining and even the old wings were spacious, coolly elegant, steeped with a gracious mystique.

Heading back to Nic's suite in the palace, they crossed paths
with Malik walking with two of his advisors.

Malik greeted her formally, using the polite Arabic greeting,
kissed her on each cheek and then briefly introduced his aides.

Nicolette responded politely, murmuring words of greeting,
although she couldn't remember exactly what she'd said surprised by the flood of warmth coursing through her.

She didn't know why the fleeting touch of his mouth to her skin should make her lose track of her thoughts, and yet suddenly she wasn't sure what she was doing here, or why they were all together. Uneasily she glanced up into Malik's face, and his expression was the same as it'd been when he'd briefly kissed her—cordial, considerate, attentive.

And something more.

Possession?

Nic gave herself a quick mental shake. Not possession. He didn't own her. She didn't belong here. She wasn't going to stay. Yet thinking of leaving, and leaving him, made her ache more than a little. He was tapping some emotion she usually kept buried deep inside, and this emotion had nothing to do with sex, and everything to do with life. And possibly love.

He was speaking to her now, asking a question. "How has your day been?"

"Good. Thank you." Nic struggled to find adequate words. "I'm overwhelmed by the history here, as well as the beauty. The palace is truly exquisite."

He smiled at her, creases fanning from his eyes. "I'm glad you're enjoying yourself."

She liked the way he smiled at her. It was a small smile, barely discernible, but she recognized it and knew it was for her.

Possession.

The word whispered through her head, nudging her, worrying her, reminding her of what was at stake.

But even as the warning voice whispered in her head, something peculiar was happening in her heart. She didn't feel like Chantal, the betrothed. She felt like Nicolette, the betrothed. She actually felt possessive of Malik.

But that couldn't be. She wasn't here for a relationship. She couldn't form any bonds, no attachments whatsoever. If she wanted to fall in love, let her fall in love with the country, the history, the culture.

She forced a light note into her voice. "I hope I'll have a chance to see more of the palace at a later date. It's truly wonderful. Everything has been designed with perfection in mind."

"Perhaps I'll have time later this week to complete the tour," Malik answered, shadows forming beneath his strong cheekbones. "The palace is a thousand years old. Countless artisans have devoted their lives to embellishing the palace's natural beauty." He then nodded at the others, indicating that Fatima and his advisors were to continue on.

Malik waited until the others had disappeared before continuing. Some of his formality eased. "You could be comfortable here then?"

"How could I not be? You've thought of every comfort imaginable."

His eyes warmed, the silver glints brightening. "And I have quite an imagination."

Nic knew he wasn't just speaking of creature comforts now, and again she felt as if she'd stumbled into another world, one existing just for King Nuri and her. Their conversations had become increasingly private, their references more personal, their innuendos more blatant.

"I'm sure you have a good imagination," Nic agreed with mock seriousness. "Most men think they've a good imagination."

"You doubt my imagination?"

"I'm certain you are imaginative…for a man—"

"Double standards?"

"Of course."

He shook his head. "You're forcing me to respond to your challenge."

She tried to keep a straight face. "I'm not challenging you, Your Highness, I'm simply stating a fact."

"A fact?"

"Yes. Most men think they know what women want, and women need—"

"Oh dear, another problematic declaration." He folded his arms across his chest. "I had no idea you were so chauvinistic."

"I'm not."

"Indeed, you are." He held up a hand, his gesture imperial. "But unlike you, I do not endlessly engage in debate. Words accomplish nothing. I, personally, prefer action."

Her breath felt trapped inside her lungs. She could barely nod. "Yes."

"Good." And moving forward, he clasped her face in his hands and tilted her face up to his.

The way his fingers splayed across her jawbone, the slow

caress of his thumb beneath her lower lip, the shrewd expression in his eyes sent a shiver through her. Expectation. Desire. *He was going to kiss her.*

Then his head descended and he did kiss her—slowly, curiously, as if he'd wondered for quite a long time what this kiss would feel like, as if the kiss was crucial to some little part of the universe.

Her mouth softened beneath the pressure of his, her lips parting ever so slightly at the tingling pressure. Malik smelled of cedar and cardamom, sweet, spicy. His lips were cool and firm and she felt helplessly fascinated by the slow sensual questing of his lips against hers. He wasn't directing, commanding, demanding. He was simply touching her, letting her experience…him.

And it was unbelievable. He—like the kiss—was warm, sensual, fragrant, her body responded by softening, sending sharp sparkly darts through her belly, to her breasts, and between her thighs. She hadn't felt longing like this in ages. She actually clenched her knees, surprised by the waves of tension and sensation, pleasure and expectation.

Malik trailed one hand down her cheek, his fingers cupping her ear, skimming her cheek and she opened her mouth in a silent gasp. He was doing everything right, *too* right.

Heart hammering, she broke away, took a quick, unsteady step backwards. "Not bad." Her voice came out breathless, high. "For a start."

His expression mocked her. Heat glowed in his eyes, along with a measure of confidence. "You want more."

"That's not what I said—"

"But you want more."

Arrogant man, she thought, and yet he had a right to be. His kiss had melted her bones, turned her into a shivering bundle of need. "I wouldn't be adverse to—" and she drew a quick breath to steady the pounding of her heart "—challenging my assumptions."

"We shall see what we can do." He smiled. "But unfortunately we have business first. You're aware of tonight's reception? It's a political affair."

She nodded, head still spinning a little. "I'll be meeting your cabinet members, and their wives."

"I want them to like you, Princess."

Her eyes locked with his. "Is it important that they do?"

"No." And he dropped his head, kissed her on the corner of her mouth and whispered, "I just want them to like you as much as I do."

Back in her own suite of rooms, Nicolette trembled as she sat in the deep steaming bath, emotions still running high, tension rippling through. Malik's parting words, spoken in his sexy, husky voice, had shaken her nearly as much as the kiss.

He liked her. Not because she was a European princess. Not because she represented a powerful alliance. He liked her because he liked *her*.

And that alone made her happy. She'd no intention of becoming anyone's wife, but she was quite curious about King Nuri—in and out of bed.

Nic could hear Alea in the next room, humming as she laid out Nic's clothes for the state reception. Would Malik kiss her again later? Would they even be alone later?

Nicolette thought she could endure just about anything at the dinner if it meant she'd have ten minutes alone with Malik.

No, ten minutes wouldn't do.

An hour. A solid hour of uninterrupted time alone.

It'd been months and months since she felt anything remotely this strong. Years since she'd had a really satisfying love affair. Years ago, she'd had a fantastic lover, and he'd ruined her for all others. A man that couldn't use his hands, his mouth, his sense of touch wasn't a man at all. It wasn't enough to be physically endowed. A man had to know how to please a woman, although most men thought if they just kept thrusting long enough they'd reached the goal. Problem was, most women needed a hell of a lot more than that. But try telling that to a man.

Even playboys, rich gorgeous, sexy playboys didn't know what turned on a woman most of the time. Fortunately, Malik didn't seem to fall into that category. His brief kiss, his tantalizing caress, conveyed a world of knowledge and experience she was anxious to try.

Alea's footsteps sounded on the marble floor as she made her way through the bedchamber to the walk-in closet across from the bath. Nic could hear her sorting through hanging clothes in the closet.

"Yellow or green?" The young assistant called to Nicolette. "Two dresses arrived earlier this afternoon."

Nic swiped at the steaming water, the jasmine scented bath oil forming smaller pools on the surface. "They're not for the wedding?"

"Oh, no, Princess. You will have special gown for wedding. These are just for you to look beautiful."

"Which do you like better?" Nic asked, content to have the decision made. Some things she fought for. Some things she delegated. Fashion she delegated.

"The green, I think. The color will look striking with your lovely dark hair."

Her dark hair. Nic suddenly sat up, touched the top of her head where her hair had been pinned up on extra large Velcro rollers. Brunette. She was a brunette. It still seemed strange to think she'd gone dark.

Would she ever become blonde Nic Ducasse again?

Four hours later, the long dinner had ended, and instead of providing entertainment, King Nuri had encouraged his guests to mingle—a decidedly Western approach—but one he hoped would give Nicolette a chance to meet more of his cabinet members. But looking at her now, cornered by a dozen robed ladies—including his cousin Fatima—Malik realized he'd made a tactical error.

Nic wasn't getting a chance to meet anyone. The women were keeping her firmly sequestered in the corner. Men on one side of the room, ladies on the other. Malik could imagine the topics the women would be discussing, too. Conversation would be limited to domestic events—marriage, childbirth, health of the elders. There'd be talk about servants, discussion about the cost of food, complaints that the weather was unusually hot and yet it was too early for everyone to trek to summer homes.

Nic made a gesture, and slight bow, indicating she was about to leave the others when Fatima touched Nic's arm in a silent reprimand.

Malik stopped listening to the conversation around him and watched his cousin speak to Nicolette.

Fatima tended to be overly harsh with Nicolette.

Malik knew Fatima didn't understand why he'd chosen a woman like Nicolette, or why he'd go so far from their culture for the woman who would be his mate, his wife, who would bear his children. Baraka's heirs.

But he knew what she did not—he needed someone like her. Nic would teach their sons and daughters to set goals, to dream big, to fight for what one believed.

It was what all children should be taught, he thought, watching Fatima's face tighten with irritation. She was angry with Nicolette for being different than Barakan women, and yet Fatima had been given opportunities to travel, to live abroad, to find a more Western husband. But Fatima didn't want to leave Atiq. She was waiting, she said, for the right man.

His lashes lowered as he watched Nic turn away, focus on an object beyond her shoulder and he realized that Nicolette was struggling to conceal her anger. What had Fatima said now?

Suddenly Nic turned her head and looked at him. Her blue gaze met his. The corner of her mouth pulled and her expression turned wry.

Save me, her expression seemed to say. And yet she wasn't complaining. She was half amused, half resigned. The not-so-storybook-life of a modern princess.

It was obvious she'd been through this before, many, many times. The princess at a state dinner. The princess, guest of honor at a charity ball, princess, keynote speaker at a fund-raiser.

She might be the family rebel—she might have covered up her gorgeous blond hair with a horrible brown hair dye—but she never shirked her duties.

She might think she wasn't a proper princess, but she understood family and loyalty, she understood what it was to protect and honor.

She'd make a perfect queen. Little did she know that by taking Chantal's place, Nic had given Malik everything he ever wanted in a bride.

Malik made his way across the room and the ladies surrounding Nicolette bowed and parted, leaving him alone with his betrothed.

"Enjoying yourself?" he asked, seeing that Fatima alone stayed at Nic's side.

Nicolette shot him an exasperated glance. "It's a fine party." Her lips pursed. "If you're eighty."

So she was bored. "Too slow for your tastes?"

"Your Highness, no one is doing anything."

"And what would you like to do?"

"Real conversation wouldn't hurt, or maybe turn on some music and let people dance."

He shook his head regretfully. "We can't dance in mixed company." Then he smiled. "But you and your ladies could dance if we men excused ourselves."

"Dance with women?"

He liked the way her cheeks darkened. Nic didn't blush very often and the pink was most becoming, especially tonight in her lime green gown, the color deliciously cool on her lightly tanned skin, making her look as if she were a mouth watering sorbet. "Of course. Dancing with women can be quite exciting."

The silver charm bracelet on her wrist tinkled as she gestured displeasure. "Your Highness, I don't dance with other women."

"It's not a slow dance with women. It's a fast dance. Energetic." He was trying hard not to laugh at her hand hovering before her mouth, her blue eyes wide and indignant. "The dance gets your heart pumping, your body moving."

"Aerobics?"

"Think of it as an Arabic version of Jazzercise." He saw her incredulous expression. "I know what Jazzercise is. One of my sisters lives in San Francisco. She loves her aerobic classes—"

Nicolette started to laugh. She tried to stifle the sound by covering her mouth but it didn't work. The more she tried to stop laughing, the harder she laughed. Tears filled her eyes. She wheezed behind her hand. "That's priceless."

Fatima looked on in horror but Malik found Nic's laughter sexy...refreshing. Nic had laughed with her whole face. Her laughter was contagious and it healed something in him that had been damaged from the attempt on his life a year ago.

He needed to laugh. He needed to feel hope. Nicolette gave him hope, and wasn't hope a wonderful thing?

He leaned toward her, preventing his cousin from hearing his words. "We could always leave," he murmured. "I'm sure we could find some diversions back at the palace."

CHAPTER SIX

HEAT flared in Nic's eyes. Her soft lush lips parted and his own body instantly hardened. He knew exactly what she was thinking. He was thinking the very same thing.

When he kissed her earlier, he hoped to contain his attraction, curtail some of his less inhibited thoughts, but the kiss did nothing to quiet his imagination. He'd thought of nothing but her since then. Wanted nothing but her beneath him, against him, above him.

When would he be able to take her to his bed? Make love to her properly?

Not while they were here, that was for certain.

First they had to get through their goodbyes, and it took a good ten minutes, but they were finally finished and escaping to the car when Fatima appeared and asked for a return ride home.

Nic groaned inwardly. She'd been thrilled at the idea of a long private drive home. Now the long drive would be anything but relaxing, or private.

The three settled into the back of Malik's waiting limousine, Fatima and Nicolette on one side, the sultan on the other.

"Glad to be gone, Princess?" Malik asked, as the limousine pulled away from the state building.

"I was tired tonight," Nicolette admitted with a small sigh. She'd felt off balance tonight, not quite herself. It was the newness of everything, she tried to tell herself, the different food, the different language and customs. But deep down she knew her headache was due to adrenaline. Her body felt hot, sensitive, her pulse quick like an engine revved.

He'd started something with that kiss. Now she just wanted him to finish it.

In the dim light of the interior Malik smiled briefly, acknowledging her honesty. "Do you find it difficult being the only foreigner in the room?"

Nic plucked at her green silk sleeve, letting the weight of the cool silver beads fall against the back of her hand. "I'm accustomed to being the only foreigner at state events. But I have to admit, tonight I did feel...different."

"*You* are different," Fatima interrupted. "You don't dress like women in Baraka, you prefer not to robe and veil yourself—"

"I've never asked her to, either," Malik quietly reproved his cousin. "Princess Ducasse is entitled to be herself here."

"Then how can she be a proper queen if she isn't a role model?" Fatima flashed.

"Enough," he answered, curtly. "This is not your concern."

Fatima dropped her head, but Nicolette saw the anger flare in Fatima's eyes. Nic struggled to think of something to say. What could she say? She and Fatima had had a rocky relationship from the very first meeting.

The limousine wound through the quiet city streets, turning from one wide palm-lined boulevard onto another. Minutes passed in silence. The air conditioner blew, a quiet hum of artificially chilled air. Nic adjusted her delicate wrap, covering her shoulders more thoroughly.

"Is the air too cool?" Malik asked.

"It's fine, thank you," Nic answered, touched by his concern. "It feels good after the warmth of the party."

"I was warm, too," he said, and then paused, his attention focused on her. Nic felt his interest, his gaze resting on her face, or what he could see in the flashing light and shadows. "Our older buildings were designed with high ceilings to draw the warm air up, but the newer government buildings lack adequate ventilation."

Nic smiled deprecatingly. "I think all government buildings are identical. Perhaps they share the same architect?"

"Or same sensibilities," he agreed.

Fatima sighed heavily and stirred, and Nic fell silent, self-conscious all over again.

Malik ignored his cousin. "Tell me, Chantal," and his deep voice was like velvet against her senses—his timbre, rich, sensual, impossibly male. "When you're queen, what is the first thing you'll do?"

* * *

Nicolette wished Fatima were not here, hanging on to every word. "Do you mean as in programs?" she asked, thinking about all the causes near and dear to her family's heart back in Melio.

"Programs, issues, activities. I'm just curious to know what you'd care about as queen. How you'd spend your time and energy here."

Nic had her causes, too, and since discovering the extent of Chantal's misery in La Croix, Nicolette had taken it upon herself to set up women's centers on each of the islands in Melio where women could ask questions, request help, even seek refuge.

She'd do the same thing here, too. She'd want to do something for women. It'd stunned her that Chantal had been physically abused, but now that Nicolette's eyes were opened, she was determined to reach as many women as she could. If Chantal had suffered in such silence, God only knows the number of women in need. The number of women not helped.

"I'd like to help women," Nicolette answered evenly, knowing that Malik was now aware of Chantal's wretched life in La Croix. "I have the name, the visibility, and the connections—all I lack is the means."

"Which you won't lack as Queen of Baraka."

Nic thought of the women living in Baraka who might be in desperate need of a helping hand. If she as Queen couldn't make a change for the better, then who could?

But you won't be queen, she reminded herself. This is just a game...

But it didn't feel like a game anymore. Not at all.

She slowly peeled off her long pale green evening gloves. Everything about her life here felt real. Her emotions, her hopes, her worries.

"How would you begin?" Malik persisted, apparently genuinely interested in wanting to hear more.

"Education." Nic lay the satin gloves on top of her small beaded purse. Chantal would never support this issue though. Chantal couldn't fight for herself, much less anyone else. "I'd want to improve education for girls—"

"Our education here is excellent," Fatima interrupted. "Girls are treated very well in Baraka. The majority attend school."

"Yes, you did, Fatima," Nicolette answered gently. "You

hold a college degree, and your parents supported your educational pursuit, but that's not the norm for poorer families, is it?'' Nic didn't wait for Fatima to answer. ''If I were queen, I'd like to see all children in school until seventeen, and I'd want to encourage girls to continue to college and vocational programs so that every girl has a choice in life, opportunity—''

Fatima snapped her fingers. ''They *have* a choice. They can choose marriage, they aren't married against their will. Parents and matchmakers consult daughters here. We are not barbaric like some countries. And a wife and mother is always loved.''

As if saying yes or no to an arranged spouse was freedom of choice!

Nic said nothing for a long moment then shook her head. ''There are many ways of being loved. Women should at least have the option to choose how they are loved, and that includes choosing career or home. Women shouldn't be home because they have no other choice, but because it's the place they choose to be. The path they seek.''

''And you, Princess Chantal,'' Malik interjected kindly, diffusing some of the tension, ''are you doing what you want to be? Have you found your path?''

Nicolette met his gaze in the shadows of the car. Ah, tricky question. Had she found her path?

No.

Had she ever tried to find her path before?

No.

Why?

''I think I'm still searching,'' she said after a moment, feeling foolish, aware of Fatima's seething animosity.

''So what are you searching for?'' His question was maddeningly simple.

Nic flashed back to the palace in Melio, her elderly grandparents, her sisters gathered in her bedroom, all of them sprawled on her bed talking about the future, what needed to be done for the future of their country. ''Me,'' she whispered.

Fatima snorted in disgust. ''Typical Western answer,'' she muttered, turning her head away, staring pointedly out the car window.

Heat burned through Nic, a blush flooding her face. Me, she

silently mocked herself. Me, had been such a self-absorbed answer. A childish concept.

Searching for oneself.

Trying to find oneself.

"We're all called to search for the truth," Malik said, and
she looked up to find that his expression had gentled, and there
was compassion in his cool silver gaze. "Without self-
knowledge, we are nothing. If we do not know ourselves, we
can not love ourselves, or anyone else for that matter."

Nic's eyes suddenly watered. She bent her head, focused on
the pair of pale green gloves draped across her small evening
purse, telling herself that no matter what, she couldn't, wouldn't,
cry in front of Fatima. "Thank you."

Arriving back at the palace, Malik didn't have to walk
Nicolette back to her rooms, but he insisted, and she was glad.
Well, sort of glad. Her heart felt very heavy at the moment and
things she thought she could do, things she thought she could
ignore, weren't quite so cut and dry anymore.

She was deceiving a man she greatly admired.

The quiet of the palace, and the spots of moonlight shimmering on the marble floor wrapped around Nicolette, making her
feel truly lonely for the first time since she arrived.

"Do you ever wonder if perhaps you have the wrong sister?"
she asked softly, her voice barely audible.

Malik glanced down at her, his expression one of concern.
"Do you think I have the wrong sister?"

"I just wonder if perhaps I'm not really the one you want…"

His brow furrowed. "In terms of outlook? Attitude?"

Her shoulders lifted, fell, the silk of her gown sliding across
her skin. "I don't know. Maybe I'm confused why you picked
me. Why not one of the others?"

They'd reached her suite of rooms and stood outside her door.
"I suppose I could have proposed to Joelle instead," he said,
rubbing his jaw.

"Joelle?" Why Joelle? She's barely an adult. "She's too
young for you."

"Perhaps you're too old for me."

Nic felt her cheeks burn. "You're at least ten years older than
me, King Nuri."

"But let's be honest, Chantal, shall we? I'm excited about

marriage and the possibility of having a family. You, forgive me, seem so blasé about it all. I would rather have a young bride eager to experience marriage and motherhood than a wife that dreads matrimony.''

''Yet there are three Ducasse princesses. You haven't mentioned Nicolette.''

He waved a hand, brushing aside the suggestion. ''She was never an option.''

''Why not?''

Another impatient gesture. ''She's not suitable—''

''*Why not?*''

He gave her a sharp look. ''If this is upsetting you, we ought not continue the discussion.''

''It is upsetting me, and we should continue the conversation because I want to understand. Nicolette's much beloved by her people—''

''Yes, but to be Queen Nuri, queen of Baraka, one must be more than great, one must be above reproach.''

Apparently Chantal hadn't been exaggerating when she'd said that Nic's reputation was destroying her chances of a good marriage. ''Yet you've never even met her. How can you be so critical?''

He didn't look the least bit apologetic. ''It's common knowledge that she prefers playboys and libertines.''

Playboys? ''*Libertines?*''

''She's not a virgin.''

Nic flushed hotly. ''Neither am I.''

''But you were when you married.''

Nic squeezed the gloves into a ball in her hand. And Joelle was still innocent. Damn him. What was wrong with a woman experimenting a little? Figuring out what she wanted…needed? Why could a man do what he wanted but a woman had to worry about reputation? ''You're not a virgin.''

His lips curved but he wasn't smiling. ''It's a man's duty to know how to pleasure his wife.''

''And a woman has no need to know how to pleasure a man?''

''Her husband will teach her.''

''That's absurd!''

''Why?''

She thought of poor Chantal, married off as a twenty-two year old virgin to a man who didn't give a fig for her happiness, or comfort, and who most certainly didn't bother to educate her in the art of love. Nic was certain that Chantal had never had an orgasm in her life—and if she'd had—it was probably alone.

"My late husband taught me nothing."

"Then he failed in his duty."

"Just as I am quite certain that many men then 'fail in their duty.' Most men still have no concept where the clitoris is let alone how to touch it!"

His stunned silence said more than words ever could. Nic realized she'd said far, far too much and she gripped her gloves so tightly she felt frozen in place.

Why was she so intent on changing his opinion about "Nicolette"? What did it matter if he disapproved of her? Let him think what he wanted to think. It was foolish and irresponsible to let her ego get the better of her. She had to protect Chantal. She had to play Chantal until she'd gotten word that Lilly was safe.

"I said too much," she said, swallowing hard, realizing she was swallowing her pride.

But he said nothing.

She'd have to apologize again. "I was wrong, Malik. I'm sorry. I shouldn't have been so…detailed."

"I didn't realize you'd had so much experience."

"I'm a woman. I have friends. Sisters—"

"Nicolette."

He'd said her name so disapprovingly that it made her stomach free fall. "You really don't like her."

"I don't know her."

Nic nodded painfully, her face still scalding hot, more from anger than shame.

After he'd left, Nic let herself into her suite of rooms, and with her insides still churning with resentment, she changed into her pajamas, and then wandered outside. Trying to calm herself, she walked the length of her private courtyard with the deep still pool and the fountain with the beautiful marble statue.

It was late out, but the night was still hot, and the sultry night air hung on her, making her want to turn around and retreat to the cool dark suite. But she couldn't go inside. She felt even more trapped inside. Scared, too.

Malik occupied her thoughts lately—endlessly. She wanted to pretend it was mere curiosity, cultural fascination, even sexual infatuation, but deep down she knew her interest was so much more than that.

He was an ideal ruler for a country like Baraka where the culture dated back thousands of years and people had been forced to reinvent themselves following earthquakes, fires, tragedies.

And God knows she didn't want to shame him, not in front of his people. Not in front of the world. And certainly not in private, either.

How on earth was she going to extricate herself from this? It would be one thing if he liked Princess Nicolette. It would ease some of her guilt and misery. But he didn't like Nicolette. He'd been most clear from the beginning that he would not, could not make Nicolette Ducasse his queen.

So maybe there lay the solution to her problem.

If she didn't want to embarrass him by breaking the engagement, she'd force him into taking action. She'd continue the masquerade as long as necessary, and then, once Lilly was safe, Nic would she reveal the shocking truth—that she was really that blonde, shallow, wanton princess he so despised.

He'd never marry her then.

Nic crossed her arms over her chest and tipped her head back to take in the dark purplish sky and bit her lip to keep from crying.

She couldn't cry. For heaven's sake! She wasn't here to find true love. She was here to get a job done.

It's a job, she reminded herself, crawling into bed. She was helping those who needed her most.

Early the next morning Fatima was admitted to Malik's office and seeing him still on the phone, she took a seat on a low chair in the corner and waited patiently for him to finish his conversation.

When he finally hung up, he looked up at her. He was wearing a pair of dark framed reading glasses. "Do you know why I wanted to see you?"

Fatima's tranquil expression betrayed nothing. "You will tell me, I am sure."

He studied his cousin a long moment. Fatima had taken an almost immediate dislike to Nicolette and he still hadn't figured out if it was jealousy, insecurity or something deeper. "I've felt your hostility to our guest."

Fatima didn't even blink. "She's not going to marry you, cousin."

"Not if you continue to intimidate her."

Fatima lifted her right hand, a gentle dismissal. "I am being truthful with her, and with you. I do not trust her, Malik. She's playing you."

One of his black eyebrows arched slightly. He barely glanced her way. "That's an awfully Western expression coming from you."

"I've been to the West, I've lived in the West, I understand Western culture as well as you do." Fatima shook her head soberly. "Malik. Listen to me." She stared at him pointedly, one of those dagger sharp stares that is next to impossible to ignore.

He met her gaze, her dark eyes unsmiling. "Listen to me, cousin," she added flatly, no urgency in her voice, just conviction. "She's. Not. Going. To. Marry. You."

Malik pulled off his reading glasses and dropped them on his desk, rubbing his eyes as he did so. "Why not?"

"She's too independent. She's not interested in our country, or culture, and quite honestly, I don't think she's all that interested in you."

Malik frowned, partially agreeing with her, partially disagreeing knowing that Fatima had always been bright, but she didn't know about chemistry, or attraction. She had no concept about physical desire, and when it came to physical desire, the princess was very attracted to him. Nic might not want to marry him, but she definitely was interested in being intimate with him.

"I'm not worried," he said rising from his chair and moving toward Fatima. "She needs me," he said, standing over his cousin. "Her country needs what I can offer."

Fatima shook her head. "But what if she gets just enough from you that she doesn't need the rest? What if she needs less than you think she does?"

Good point. Fatima had always been smart. She'd excelled in school. She could have done anything with her life, but she'd chosen to remain here, at the palace. What would she do with her life, he'd often wondered. A member of the royal family, she was worth a fortune and with her father dead, her mother living in New York, she belonged beneath his protection. Who would ever be good enough for her?

"I'll have to be careful then, won't I?" he answered evenly, and then he smiled at her. She was beautiful. Dark eyes, high cheekbones, firm chin, slightly pointed with masses of long silky black hair. Fatima looked like their grandmother but she had her father's cunning mind. "Now you better go. The princess will be waiting for her language lesson."

Nicolette was waiting in the salon for Fatima, but she wasn't thinking about her lesson. She was thinking that she had the strangest secret. It was her birthday today, her real birthday, but she couldn't celebrate because no one knew who she really was.

It was rather odd thinking she'd reached twenty-seven. Suddenly it seemed like such an old age. Chantal had already been married several years when she turned twenty-seven. So far Nicolette had done...what?

Nothing.

Fatima arrived and the lesson proceeded without incident, and then as the serving girl arrived, bringing the now expected tray of tea and sweet biscuits, the serving girl curtsied to Nicolette. "Princess, His Highness would like you to join him for a late breakfast," the girl said. "I'm to show you the way."

Fatima's face tightened but she didn't protest, and Nicolette followed the serving girl through the corridors and out to one of the gorgeous inner courtyards reserved for the sultan's personal use.

Malik was already at the wrought-iron table that had been set for two. Bright flowers filled a dark green glass vase and Nic decided she'd make this her birthday party. He didn't even need to know it was her birthday. It was enough that she could be with him now, start her day with his company. Already his company meant so much...

"Good morning," Malik greeted, leaning forward to kiss her on each cheek. "I've been thinking of you."

She shivered as his lips grazed her cheek. He smelled lovely.

She wished she could capture his face between her hands and kiss him properly. No more fleeting kisses on the cheeks, but a long, deep kiss, one that would make her melt again. "Have you?"

He leaned forward on the table, his black hair almost glossy in the bright light. "I've also felt very guilty."

"Why?"

"I've been unkind with regards to your sister. I know how I feel about my brother and sisters and wouldn't tolerate anyone speaking harshly about them, and yet I have been incredibly intolerant of Nicolette's idiosyncrasies. Forgive me."

Nic looked away, embarrassed as well as uncomfortable. "She's not really so—eccentric." She'd intended to reply matter of factly, but to her shame, her voice broke. Even when he apologized he made it sound as if Nic was this peculiar woman with cannibalistic tendencies. "Maybe she's not Barakan, but she's good. And kind. And she doesn't say cruel things about people." Nic drew a wobbly breath, shaken. "She doesn't judge people, either. And she wouldn't be here right now, judging you, or judging your cousin Fatima who can't say a nice thing about anyone."

Finished she sat there, words spent, emotion spent, all illusions about a party dashed. It wasn't a fun birthday morning. It was another horrible day living a lie. "Would you excuse me, please?" she whispered.

"No."

His refusal surprised her. She pushed away from the table. He might be king in Baraka, but she was royalty in Europe. "I'd like to return to my lessons with Fatima."

"Even though she's judgmental?"

"I'd rather her be judgmental than *you*."

"Why?"

Tears burned in her eyes and she looked at him so overwhelmed by emotions she hadn't expected to feel that she didn't even think she could find her voice.

"Why?" he demanded yet again.

The rest of Nic's control snapped. "Because I like you. I don't want you to be mean. Or petty. I don't want you to be cruel just because Nicolette isn't your idea of the perfect woman. No one's perfect, King Nuri, and even those of us who aren't perfect, are still pretty worthy of love, and loyalty.''

''I was apologizing—''

''Not really. Not enough.'' Her lip quivered. She felt so wretched she couldn't even bear it. ''It's her birthday today, and I don't think she deserves this—''

''I know it's her birthday!'' He nearly shouted, his voice echoing. ''That's why you're here with me this morning. I wanted to celebrate with you.''

She fought to regain control and her chest rose and fell with each deep shuddering breath. ''How did you know it's her birthday? You don't even like her.''

He stood, leaned across the table, cupping the back of her head, and kissed her. ''Because I like you,'' he said, kissing her again. ''I like you so much I've tried to learn everything I can about your family.''

The tears shimmered in her eyes, making it very hard to see, but if she blinked, the tears would fall. ''How old is she then?''

''Twenty-seven.'' He reached up with the tip of her finger and caught the tears clinging to her lower lashes. ''And I know you're worried about her because she's getting old and she's still not married—''

Nic batted away with his hand. ''She's not that old.''

''But she should be married, shouldn't she?''

And to show her he was teasing, he kissed her yet again, a light kiss, but something happened when his lips touched hers this time. The restraint was gone. The pure intentions disappeared. Instead emotion sizzled and the slow, tender kiss blazed into pure, raw, unadulterated desire.

Nic had felt desire, but this desire took her breath away, turned her belly inside out, made her ache with need.

She reached for him, fingers twining in his shirt, and his lips ruthlessly parted hers, his tongue stabbing at the softness of her mouth, tasting, teasing, making her aware that he'd been gentle with her so far, but he could also be fiercely hungry, and demanding.

Nic clung to him, welcoming the intensity, finding release in the violence of emotion. All her life she'd craved passion, and to find it here—and now—with Malik stunned her.

He lifted his head, stroked her cheek. "Forgive me. Please?"

"Of course." And she managed a tremulous smile, something of a feat considering the intense desire still coiling inside her. It hurt to kiss. It hurt even more to end the kiss. She'd never felt so unfulfilled. "And Nic forgives you, too."

"Then we can still have breakfast to celebrate her special day?"

She grinned ruefully. "Yes."

"And can we start over, pretend nothing's happened?"

Her laugh was soft, husky. "Are you that good of an actor?"

"Depends. Are you that good of an actress?"

Nic thought of the past week at the palace. "No." She laughed yet again, making fun of herself. "I'm a terrible actress. I've never been picked to play a lead in any of our school theatre productions."

He held her chair for her, and slid her chair into the table once she was seated. "Not even though you were a very famous princess?"

She made a face. "I'd like to say there was a bias against princesses, but that isn't the case. My sister, Joelle, is a fantastic actress. She also inherited Mom's voice. Joelle's voice is like an angel's. You have to hear her sing one day—" Nic broke off, blushed. "Listen to me. You've turned me into a chatterbox."

He gestured for coffee and a steward instantly appeared, filling their cups. "You're far from a chatterbox, Chantal. I have to work to make you talk."

Nic reached out to touch the floral arrangement, her fingertip brushing across one crimson rose petal. The damask roses in the floral arrangement made the air smell spicy and sweet. "Men like quiet women."

Malik spluttered on his coffee. "I can't believe you say these things."

"At least it makes you smile."

"I'm just glad you're smiling again."

CHAPTER SEVEN

THEIR eyes met and held. Nic saw the sincerity in his lovely silver gaze, and felt little ripples of pleasure hum through her. They were making small talk and yet below the surface the most intense attraction simmered, and the awareness that they both felt so much, fueled the desire.

"So what is on your calendar today?" he asked, sitting back as a serving girl set a plate of fresh sliced, peeled fruits before him—mangos, papayas, kiwi, pomegranate. The colors were vivid, wet, glistening. Like jewels drenched by the rain.

Nic's mouth watered. She was hungry. But not just for food. She wanted his mouth again, wanted his tongue and the spicy taste of his skin.

"It's busy," she answered, knowing perfectly well that her schedule was packed with appointments, including another fitting followed by two hours in the kitchen with the master chef learning about Baraka's cuisine before being given her first instruction in how to prepare the sultan's favorite dishes.

"Perhaps we've kept you too busy. The strain is showing."

She made a wry face. "Apologies, Your Highness."

He smiled. "Do you need a holiday?"

"No books? No activities? No homework? What would I do?" She feigned shock.

"I suppose you'd have to enjoy my company. If such a thing is possible." He speared a circle of kiwi and put it in his mouth, chewing slowly, letting the ripe sweet fruit dissolve even more slowly.

She watched his firm, mobile mouth take the succulent fruit, watched his jaw move once, twice, saw the long strong column of his throat swallow and she exhaled in a tight, thin stream of air. A day alone with Malik wasn't her idea of relaxing. She couldn't relax around him. She'd begun to crave contact with him too badly. "I know you've many state appointments—"

"Too many," he agreed solemnly.

"It wouldn't be fair for me to add to your pressures—"

"But, *laeela*, you must come first. You're to be my queen. My wife. My lover."

Heat surged to Nic's cheeks. *His lover*. And she loved the sound of that word, even as the image conjured up all the press clippings she'd read, the stories of his many mistresses scattered around the world.

She felt his gaze caress her now, sweeping her cheeks, down the column of her throat to rest at her breasts. She was wearing a turquoise silk pantsuit, the collarless jacket conservative by Western standards, and yet his desire made her feel naked. Exposed.

"Yes, well, of course there are the duties," she said hurriedly, "but right now, if you have greater pressing concerns—"

"Greater concerns? Princess, I'd be amiss not to be concerned with you. I can see you are a little lonely today." The smile faded from his eyes. "I can see you are a little sad. I think you need some company. I think you could use me."

Use him. Oh, indeed. She could use him but that wasn't part of the plan.

The plan wasn't to make love.

The plan wasn't to fall in love.

The plan wasn't to get trapped in this country so far away from her own.

"We can always meet later—for dinner." She pressed her knees together, tucking one foot behind the other ankle. She couldn't let herself want more from him. She couldn't continue to let herself get emotionally invested. "You can tell me what you've done…"

Her voice faded as Malik leaned forward and ran the pad of his thumb over her lips, silencing her. "You need an adventure today. Something new, something fun. Leave it to me."

"Malik."

"Yes, *laeela?*"

Her eyes burned and she closed her eyes as his hand slid along her jaw, and down, along the side of her neck to rest at her collarbone. His fingers were so sure and steady against her warm bare skin that Nic found the lovely sensation almost too excruciating to enjoy.

"Why don't you ever look me in the eye?" he asked softly, the pad of his thumb stroking the hollow of her throat. "When we talk like this, you always look away."

"You're touching me," she whispered, and he was right, she couldn't meet his gaze. He'd stirred intense emotions in her, and even hotter desire, and the combination of the two tried her conscience.

Her heart ached almost constantly and her body felt restless, a ceaseless restlessness that came from wanting.

But the wanting was reckless, dangerous, and even Nic, who embraced danger knew what was at stake here.

Chantal and Lilly.

"My touch shouldn't frighten you," Malik said. "You're not a virgin, not without experience."

She swallowed, her skin flaming with heat, her belly heavy, empty. "It's not lack of experience that makes me wary, and it's not your touch I fear." She looked up into his perceptive pewter gaze. "What I fear is…you."

"You fear me?" He sounded incredulous. "But why? I'd protect you with my life."

Nicolette's heart twisted. The pain startled her. She hadn't felt such strong emotion in years. "Maybe that's what I'm afraid of." Jaw pressed tight, she gazed intently at his hard features, the long aquiline nose, the broad jaw, the stubborn set of his chin. "You place too much trust in me. You haven't known me long enough to offer your life in exchange of mine."

His palm suddenly cupped her cheek. "But you're my betrothed."

"We haven't exchanged any words, had a formal declaration."

"You are here."

Tears thickened her voice, tears she wasn't going to cry. "But appearances can be deceptive."

His expression turned thoughtful as he sat back in his chair. "Are you thinking of leaving?"

"No."

"But you still have doubts?"

She hated talking like this. Now that she'd met him, gotten to know him she didn't want to be the one to disappoint him. "I was born with doubts. Of the three of us, I was the princess most likely to—'' She broke off, realizing she was about to make another Nicolette pronouncement, and he was suspicious of those Nicolette pronouncements.

"To?" he prompted softly.

"You don't want to know."

"I do."

She shrugged helplessly, as if to say, I warned you. "Most likely to initiate world war."

He coughed.

She flexed her fingers, tension coiling throughout her body. "I know. I'm sorry."

"What can we do? How can I help?" He sounded so tranquil, so comfortably conversational. "Is there something that I could do? Something I could tell you?"

She closed her eyes, felt the late morning sun warm the top of her head, wrap her shoulders in heat. She didn't know what she was doing anymore. Didn't know how she'd lost control of the situation. She wasn't supposed to get involved here. She was to have been a guest…just a guest… Instead she'd started to feel things, genuine things, for Malik Nuri.

Nic swallowed, opened her eyes. Malik should have been troubled but he looked calm, as if all his concern was for her instead of himself. "I don't want to—'' her mouth had gone dry and she reached for her glass of juice, took a sip, wetting her lips "—humiliate you."

"I'm glad. I hate being humiliated." But the corner of his lips lifted, and he sounded downright cavalier.

She didn't know how he could joke at a time like this, yet she smiled at his humor, her emotions strung up like the rope of flags on the *Royal Star*.

"But you're not going to humiliate me," he continued confidently. "I know you. You're like me. You understand duty, and responsibility. You love your country, your people, and your family. You'll do what's best for them."

He was speaking matter of factly and she found herself hanging on each word, as if she couldn't wait to hear what he'd say next. "If you give me your word now," he added, "I know the ceremony will take place. You wouldn't cancel at the last minute, now when it'd be so awkward for both our families. Never mind national pride."

National pride. Nic couldn't speak, couldn't make a sound, and life seemed to crystallize around her—the sun shining through her glass, filling the guava juice with shimmering light, the heady scent of the damask roses, the forlorn cry of a seagull above, a reminder that the Atlantic sea wasn't so very far away.

"You're free," he added even more gently. "You're free to go home now. I'd never keep you here against your will."

He didn't even know who she was, she thought, and if she did marry him, pretending to be Chantal, what would happen later when he found out later she wasn't Chantal? Would he say fine, one Ducasse is the same as another, or would he want Chantal—the good one—the obedient one, and divorce her on grounds of fraud? Deception?

But if Nic confessed the truth now, what would happen to Chantal and Lilly? What if they were close to getting home to Melio? What if Nicolette ruined it for them now?

She couldn't imagine that all this…subterfuge…should be for naught.

"I'm not going anywhere." Her voice sounded rough. "I'm staying right here." Nic looked up at him and prayed he wouldn't see the tears in her eyes. "I'm on holiday today, re-member? And you've promised me to show me something new…something fun."

"I remember."

After the meal, Nicolette quickly changed shoes, applied some sunscreen to her face and returned to the front hall. Her heart felt heavy when she saw Fatima waiting.

Fatima looked at her. "This wasn't my idea," she said stiffly.

Nic could barely nod, ridiculously disappointed. Just then the car and driver pulled to the door and Malik arrived. Like Fatima, he'd changed into a *jellaba,* and like his cousin, his long robe was made of expensive fabric with ornate needlework lining the seams.

"Do I need to change?" Nic asked, touching the neckline of her turquoise jacket.

"I have a *jellaba* you can wear if you'd like," Malik an-swered, lightly circling her with his arm. "But I see no need for you to change. You'll find that many of our young people favor jeans and T-shirts. Between our French colonial past, and the flood of tourists in winter, you'll find that our city center is quite Western.''

''Is that where we're going?'' she asked, settling into the back seat.

He suddenly spoke in Arabic to his cousin, and Fatima, who'd just sat down next to Nic, reluctantly moved, relocating herself to the opposite seat. Malik took the vacated space next to Nic.

''Is this proper?'' Nic whispered to Malik as the king stretched an arm across the back of the seat, his fingertips brushing her shoulder.

''It's my car,'' he answered, looking down at her.

''Yes, but your cousin—''

''Knows you're to be my wife.'' He reached for her hand, kissed the back of it. ''Now relax. I want you to enjoy yourself. You're not allowed to worry.''

''Not about anything?''

''About nothing. Not even Lilly. I've everything under control.''

Something in his tone made the fine hair lift at the nape of her neck but she didn't dare ask. He'd said not to worry, and for one hour, she could try to do that much, couldn't she?

With a small convoy of police escorts, the limousine wound through numerous avenues, the streets growing narrower with each turn until they'd reached the market square.

Merchants and peddlers had filled the square with colorful bazaars, their booths offering every kind of ware imaginable. Baskets mounded with fruits and nuts. Copper pots. Bolts of fabric. Leather goods.

Nic sat forward on her seat, anxious to see everything. Malik's fingers trailed down her spine until his hand settled in the small of her back. ''You're eager to explore.''

She couldn't contain her curiosity. She loved getting out, doing things. It'd been hard being so cooped up in the palace during the past week. ''I am.''

The driver parked and the security circled the limousine. Malik climbed out, extended a hand to Nicolette and then Fatima.

As Nicolette stood, she realized that nearly all of the women bustling around the market were wearing the long colorful *jellaba*. ''Do you still have the...coverall?'' she asked, indicating his jellaba. "I think Fatima and I would draw less attention if we looked the same."

Fatima aided Nicolette in settling the long navy *jellaba* over Nic's head, covering her pantsuit.

"Would you care to have a look around?" Malik asked Nic once she was finished dressing.

"Yes," Nic answered, ready to see as much of the medina as she could. She'd wanted to visit the city hub ever since she arrived.

"Fatima will walk with you," he said. "I'd like to go with you, but I think it's less complicated for security if I wait here."

She understood, especially as the market was very crowded and it'd be difficult for a group—much less the sultan and his escorts—to pass through the congested square.

As she and Fatima set off, the sun shone high above, and a hot wind kicked up dust, tugged at the crisp canvas awnings, blowing the palm trees dense green fronds. Nic was nearly overwhelmed by such exotic beauty—the blue and white striped stalls, the massive clay pots of pink and green olives, baskets piled high with dried dates and apricots, the pervasive spice of peppers, and all the while the hot wind brushing and whipping the fronds so the very air seemed to whisper.

Exquisite, she thought, taking it all in, savoring all that was new and mysterious.

"*Balek!*" a man shouted, lumbering past with a cart full of goods.

Balek. Nic smiled. Watch yourself. She'd understood the Arabic word.

Contented, Nic followed Fatima around the parameter of the bustling square, the old buildings fronted by hundreds of souks, each one selling something different, just as each merchant sized the shopper up, setting new and different prices.

Now and then she stopped to examine intriguing merchandise and gradually Nic forgot Fatima's hostility, losing herself in the pleasure of being somewhere altogether new.

As she moved slowly from one seller to another, the sun beat down on her head, the rays penetrating her dark *jellaba*. Time to turn back, she thought. But looking up, hoping to catch Fatima's eye, Nic realized she'd lost Malik's cousin somewhere along the way. Surprised, but not distressed, Nic actually felt...relief. She'd been in many foreign countries, traveled a great deal. It didn't cross her mind to feel fear. Instead, for one brief moment, she felt free. No Fatima, no sultan, no marriage, no worries.

And with that thought in mind, she wished she had money on her and she'd find a café somewhere and buy an iced coffee and just sit in the shade and watch everyone. Atiq was amazing and Nic loved the medina, responding to the history of the inner city with the cobbled streets, whitewashed buildings and dazzling sunlight.

A hand touched her arm and Nic turned. An older woman stood before her, the woman's gray hair partially covered with a long scarf. "Lost?" The elderly woman asked.

Nic smiled. "A little."

The woman stared up at Nic for a minute, her dark eyes puzzled. "You are a very beautiful lady," she said in her halting English.

"Thank you. *Merci,*" Nic answered, switching to French hoping it'd be easier for the older woman. "That's lovely of you to say."

The woman smiled gratefully. "You're not American?" she asked in French.

"No."

The older woman's mouth pursed as she studied Nic's face. "French?"

"Half." Quarter, actually. Julien, her father had been half-French, half-Spanish.

Suddenly the old woman wagged her finger. Her frown faded as she smiled, deep lines creasing her skin. "I know who you look like." She beamed wider. "The American singer. Star."

Star. Mom. And Nic could see her mother, long dark hair, flashing eyes, a wicked sense of humor.

"You know who I'm talking about?" The woman clasped Nic's arm. "Superstar. Married a Spanish prince."

But Mom didn't marry a Spanish prince. He was a Melian prince. Her eyes felt gritty and she blinked, blaming the hot wind. "Thank you."

She patted the older woman's hand where it rested on her arm, the elderly woman's fingers thin, the skin delicate. "I'm very flattered, and you are very kind."

The woman beamed wider, spaces showing between her bottom teeth and reached up to pat Nic's cheek. *"Allah ihennik."* *God make you safe.*

Nic's heart squeezed. A lump filled her throat. "And you," she murmured as the elderly woman shuffled away. She watched the elderly woman fade into the crowd.

It'd been years since anyone said she looked like her mother. With her blonde hair, the family always said she was like Julien, but Nic remembered when she was little, her mother used to sit Nic on her lap and comb her long hair and point to their reflections in the mirror. "You have Mommy's eyes," her mother would say, drawing the boar bristle brush through Nic's curls. "And you have Mommy's mouth and chin."

"And Mommy's nonsense," her father called to them from the bedroom where he'd inevitably be sitting in a chair, or lying in bed, with a stack of state documents. Her father was always reading, preparing, studying up on economies, politics, world events. No one cared more about the future than Prince Julien Ducasse.

It was odd, Nic thought, setting off, threading her way through the crowd, but when her parents died everyone talked about what a tragedy it was, what a loss of beautiful young glamorous people. And beauty was all very nice and fine, but beauty wasn't their strength. Their strength had been their intelligence, their spirit, their drive. Both her father and her mother were real people, not glossy paper dolls, or coat hangers for expensive couture.

What a gift that elderly woman had given her today, what a lovely birthday gift. To be told she looked like her mother. To have a stranger stop her and say I see Star in you…

Nic closed her eyes, pressed her hands to her heart, held all the emotion and welling of love inside.

Now it was time to get back to Malik before he started worrying, and rounding a corner lined with narrow stalls, Nicolette glanced around, sensing she hadn't gone in the right direction. Where had she made a wrong turn? Nothing looked familiar, but then, the maze of merchants and crowded souks was enough to disorient anyone.

Standing at the corner, hands on hips, Nic became aware that she was drawing attention. Women avoided her but men were curious. It was obvious she was a foreigner, and even though she was wearing a traditional coverall, she stood out as different.

Where was she? Where was the central market?

What would Malik say when he found out she'd lost Fatima and was wandering somewhere inside the endless medina?

Nic moved toward a woman to ask for directions but the woman drew her scarf closer to her face and hurried on.

Nic wrinkled her nose. That was not the response she wanted. Glancing left, and then right, the streets much narrower than they had been earlier. What she needed to do was backtrack…

Nic set off again, returning the way she'd come, but the street didn't lead to the market. Instead the street ended in a narrow alley, and alley led to yet another alley.

This was definitely not the right direction.

Nic chewed the inside of her lip. The sun had dropped, but the heat was still intense, and there were fewer people out now.

Nic batted a fly buzzing her face and sighed. She couldn't panic. She hadn't been gone that long. Twenty minutes. Thirty at the most.

She rubbed the back of her arm across her eyes, catching the dampness on her brow. Think. Which way did you come? Where was the sun? In Baraka the markets—like the mosques—are built facing East. All she had to do was orient herself to the East and she'd find her way across.

Malik was waiting at the side of the car when Fatima arrived alone. "Is the princess here?" Fatima asked, bending down to peer into the darkened car windows.

He felt as if his heart stopped, his muscles turned to stone. "She's supposed to be with you."

Fatima looked at him, wide-eyed, innocent. "I thought we were together. We were just browsing through the market—"

"You lost her."

"No."

"*You* lost her."

His normally quiet voice boomed. Fatima shook her head. "I didn't. I thought she was with me. I was sure she was following me."

He snapped his fingers, and his driver appeared. "The princess is missing." He spoke quickly, urgently. "Summon the

security officers, let them know we must find her. In the meantime, I'm going to call the palace, request additional guard.''

The chauffeur bowed, hurried away. Fatima watched Malik
call the palace on his phone, tears in her eyes. "I didn't mean
to lose her, cousin. I wouldn't do that."

He silenced her with a lift of his hand. "I don't want to hear
it. You've had a problem with the princess since she arrived."
He turned his back on her, spoke to the captain of his military
guard, requesting assistance, giving the captain his location at
the market square.

Tears continued to well in Fatima's eyes. "Forgive me,
cousin."

But he couldn't look at her. "I trusted you," he said, his deep
voice curt, his tone bitter. "And you have shamed me."

Fatima climbed into the back of the limousine and buried her
face in her hands. Malik paced before the car, waiting for the
driver to return. Malik intended to set off and look for Nicolette
himself, but suddenly she was there, a flushed princess, hot,
tired, but obviously grateful to have found her way back.
"You're still here." Nic smiled in relief. "Thank goodness."

"I'd never leave you."

"I know, but I—"

"I'd never leave you." His gaze swept her, a quick inspection
to ensure she was truly in one piece. "Are you okay?"

"I'm fine. Just embarrassed. I don't know how I managed to
lose Fatima." Nic paused, glanced around. "Is she back yet?"

Malik's expression darkened. "She's in the car."

"Good. I was afraid she was out looking for me, and I didn't
want to put her in any danger." Nic shook her head, incredulous.
"It's hot."

"It is," he agreed, spotting the driver returning through the
square with the security officers. "Let me take care of this," he
said, indicating the officers approaching, "and then we'll head
back to the palace."

Back at the palace, Nic returned to her suite and discovered
Alea waiting with open arms. "Are you alright, Princess?" Alea
cried, touching Nic's arm as if she were an apparition.

Alea's concern was almost comical. "I'm fine." Nic grimaced. "I was lost. The city was hot. But I found my way back
and everything's okay."

"Well, we're going to take good care of you," Alea assured Nicolette. "First, a shower to cool you off, wash away the dust, then a good soak in the hot tub, after that, a massage, help relax every muscle—"

"That's not necessary, Alea. A shower is all I need."

But the young woman wasn't listening. She was already off, heading into Nicolette's luxurious bathroom, opening doors, turning on the shower. "Come, Princess," Alea called above the steamy shower spray. "Let's get you started."

An hour and a half later, Nicolette winced as the experienced masseuse dug her elbows into the knots in Nicolette's back. The massage wasn't Swedish style, Nic thought, wincing again, but after an hour of steady kneading, rubbing, twisting, Nic was beginning to feel boneless.

But gradually the deep tissue massage gave way to a softer touch, longer strokes that soothed instead of hurt. Relaxed beyond belief, Nic drifted in and out of sleep, happy to just lie there and be mindless.

No worries now, she thought sleepily. It'd be impossible to worry.

The masseuse finished by working Nic's hands, feet, lightly kneading, working each little joint.

Stepping from the table the masseuse held up Nic's warm silk robe. "Your Highness."

Nic dragged herself off the massage table, her limbs so heavy, she wanted to slide into bed. Instead she forced her arms into the robe's quilted sleeves and belted the tie around her waist. "Thank you."

"My pleasure." The masseuse opened the door, gestured to Nic's pink marble bathroom. "The steam room, Your Highness?"

"No thank you, not again. I think I'll just shower."

"As you wish." The masseuse bowed, and excused herself and Alea appeared.

"How do you feel, Princess?"

"Lovely." Nic covered her mouth, hiding her yawn. "I can't even keep my eyes open."

"You won't have to. Rinse off the oil and then I'll finish you off with a nice scented lotion to keep your skin soft. Afterward, you can put your robe back on and you'll find refreshments waiting for you in your sitting room.''

Nicolette spent forever in the shower, letting the hot water rain down on her head. She couldn't remember when she last felt so languid. She was relaxed, almost too relaxed, she didn't feel the slightest urgency...about anything. She shampooed her hair, once, twice, and then finished with the delicious fruit scented conditioner that made Nic's mouth water.

After finally stepping from the shower and toweling dry, Nic allowed Alea to slather her in lotion. She couldn't protest the indulgence even if she wanted to. She simply didn't have the energy. The heat from the market place, and then the two hours of pampering, had taken all speech away. Nic might as well have been a rag doll.

With her hair lightly blowed dry, Nic slipped on a clean robe, this one a gorgeous coral silk embroidered with gold and green threads, and headed for the sitting room where hot mint tea and sweets waited.

But that wasn't all that waited.

Malik Nuri waited as well.

Nic froze in the doorway, one hand going to her chest, checking the drape and coverage of her thin silk robe. ''Your Highness.''

''I thought I'd join you for tea.''

She'd never felt self-conscious around any man before and yet Malik did something to her, made her feel absolutely naked. And truthfully, right now she was rather naked. Her silk robe didn't conceal much.

''It is your palace,'' she said, tension curling in the pit of her stomach.

His eyebrow lifted. ''That's not the same thing as a 'yes, I'm glad to see you', is it?''

Nic licked her bottom lip, conscious she wore absolutely nothing beneath the robe, not a chemise or even a thong. Just skin. Warm, still slightly damp skin from her hot shower and application of body lotion.

And he knew it, she thought, with a curiously expectant shiver.

''Of course I'd enjoy your company,'' she said, surprised yet again by her flutter of nerves. She shouldn't have this kind of response—at the very least, she shouldn't act on this response.

"Any company?" he teased. "Not my company?"

Her gaze took in the way he reclined on the sofa cushions, his own robe open at the chest, his long muscular legs covering the length of the settee.

He was gorgeous. And he knew it. "You know I enjoy your company," she answered softly.

"And my touch."

She had to bite the inside of her cheek to keep from laughing. "Did it ever cross your mind that you're still single because you're arrogant and conceited?"

He smiled. "I'm not conceited."

"But arrogant?"

"*Laeela*, I wouldn't be a proper sultan if I didn't have a certain amount of confidence."

CHAPTER EIGHT

HIS smile was slow, wicked, and rising from the couch Malik walked to a console panel on one of the walls. He touched a few buttons, and music sounded, spilling from hidden speakers. It wasn't Eastern music, but a popular rock and roll ballad. "You did say the other night you wanted to dance."

She couldn't tear her gaze from the small smile playing at his lips. He was tall, dark, handsome in a bone-melting kind of way. "I didn't think you danced with women."

"Not in public."

She couldn't speak, adrenaline coursing through her veins and he moved toward her, his energy leashed, his powerful body graceful, languid. "But then," he added in that deep sexy voice of his, "there's lots of things I can't do in public that I love to do in private."

He stood before her, arms loose at his sides, his chest bare. "Come here."

Her mouth had grown dry and Nic shook her head in a desperate plea for sanity. "You have no dinner engagements tonight?"

"None."

She touched the tip of her tongue to her lips, trying to moisten them. "No appointments?"

"Completely free." His smile was in his eyes. His arms were strong, relaxed. He had all night. He could afford to wait. "I thought you'd like this song."

The group was one of her favorite bands. She'd met the band members on their last European tour, too. "I do."

"So come here."

She didn't know why she couldn't go to him, but her legs wouldn't move, her feet felt rooted to the floor, and dread hummed through her, reminding her that she was not who or what she seemed. ''You come to me,'' she whispered, praying he wouldn't, praying he'd turn and walk away.

He laughed. He was so confident he could find her insolence amusing. Malik closed the distance between them, pulled her against him, shaping her body to his, silver gaze glinting with laughter. ''Like this, princess?''

She shuddered at the press of his thighs, his body hard, his torso firm. Nic's eyes closed as Malik bent his head, pulled back her robe and kissed her bare shoulder.

He must have felt her shudder as he kissed the same sensitive spot again and this time as the shiver raced through her, he cupped the side of her breast, feeling her nipple harden in his hand.

Her legs went weak and she hid her face against his chest as the music wound around them, warm, seductive, intimate. Nic found herself drawn closer against Malik's chest, his smooth hard bicep pressed to her shoulder. She liked his arms around her. She liked the way he slid his hands down her ribcage, as if counting each rib, shaping each rib, until he reached her hip bones. He knew how to make a woman feel like a woman, and when he rested his hands in the small of her spine, she thought she could stay that way forever, savoring his warm, his spicy fragrance, how easy he was with her. No strangeness, no awkwardness. No formality. No royal games.

Just Malik and Nic.

She felt a twinge of guilt. Make that Malik and Chantal. But she didn't want to be Chantal anymore. She wanted to be herself with him. She wanted him to want *Nic*.

Impulsively she reached up and touched his prominent cheekbone, tracing the sweeping length of bone and the shape of his chin. Everything in his face was strong, everything in his eyes was mysterious. Yet she knew he'd answer any question she put to him. He'd talk openly, candidly, about any subject she chose.

What would it be like to love you? She silently wondered, letting her hand return to his shoulder, feeling emotion grow and swell inside her chest, her heart strangely tender. For a second her eyes burned, little pricks of pain everywhere.

She'd love to spend hours with him. She'd love to take it all so slow. No rush, no hurry, no goal. Just time together.

She'd never been one of those glassy-eyed optimistics. She

didn't believe in excess of hope, didn't believe in romantic dreams that couldn't be fulfilled. Dreaming for her was a precursor to action. If she desired it, she did it. It wasn't a challenge but a fact. If there was something she wanted out of life, she went for it.

"Thinking about Lilly?" Malik asked, interrupting her thoughts, his fingers playing her spine, sending rivulets of feeling in every direction.

Nic shook her head, feeling guilty. He must think she was a terrible mother. She sighed heavily. She was in this so deep, wasn't she?

What was she doing here? What was happening between them? They were on a collision course with disaster.

Nic felt as if she were beginning to suffocate and she stepped back, putting space between them so she could try to think. "Can we sit down?"

"Certainly." He took a seat, and she knew he expected her to join him, but she hesitated. If she sat next to him in her little flimsy robe she might as well give up the battle now. If he touched her again, peeled the robe from her shoulders, kissed that sensitive spot on her neck, or her collarbone, she'd hold his lips to her skin and ask him to just keep on going...

"Maybe I should go put some clothes on first."

"Why?"

"You know why."

He cocked his head, studying her. "I can't believe you're so afraid to make love with me."

Talk about honesty. Nicolette flushed. "If you were a terrible kisser we wouldn't have a problem."

He rubbed his brow, ruffling his crisp black hair. "I could try to kiss badly. If that's what would make you happy."

She groaned, exasperated. "It wouldn't."

"You're very difficult to please, Princess."

"Yes. I know." Nic felt like she was losing her mind. "Even more so than usual."

"What's wrong?"

She pressed her hands to her head, trying to quiet all the guilty recriminations, the little voices that wouldn't let her rest. "I think I'm developing a split-personality."

Malik had to work very hard at keeping a straight face. "Really?"

"Yes."

"Tell me about them."

Nic paced in front of him. "There's the virtuous Chantal," she said, shooting him a swift glance, "and then there's the impulsive Chantal, the one that really likes you."

"So what is the problem?"

She stopped pacing. "If I don't even know who the real me is, how will you?"

"I can tell." He gestured to her. "Come here."

He was making her nerves dance, and she moved toward him, drawn to him despite her better judgment.

Malik reached up to clasp her hand, his fingers locking with hers, and smoothly, firmly, he drew her down onto his lap, and she gasped at the naked touch of skin. Her thighs rested against his, and even though they were wearing their robes, the silk fabric didn't contain him. He was aroused and his body pressed against her, teasing her tender flesh, making her even more sensitive.

His hands curved around her hips, his fingers firm on her hipbones and he tilted her hips forward, and back, shifting her pelvis between his large strong hands.

"You belong to me." He placed a kiss on her mouth. "Married or unmarried, queen or friend, you can call us what you want, but you," and he shifted her again, pulling her forward so his erection rubbed inside her thighs, at the apex of her thighs, "you were made for me, and I for you."

Her mouth had gone dry. She couldn't think of a single thing to say. Of course she wasn't his, and there was no way she belonged to him, but it'd been years since she felt this raw physical craving for anyone.

"Do you do this with all your wives?" she asked breathlessly.

"Harems are passé," he answered, his hand rising to cup her breast through the silk fabric, his thumb strumming her nipple, playing the taut peak as if he had all the time in the world. And indeed, he did. He was planning on keeping her, making her his wife legally, and in Baraka wives were permanent.

Oh, if he kept touching her like that, she'd do just about anything. She linked her hands around his shoulders, needing to hang tight and as he strummed her nipple his other hand played on her hip.

Nic couldn't stand the tension within her. She dragged herself closer to him. "I want you." Her voice sounded faint, breathless, and indeed, she was seeing stars, her vision dark and silvery all at the same time.

"I know," he said, and he kept playing her body, playing the nerves and she was shivering against him, dancing a helpless dance.

She felt heat rush through her in a torrential wave. He'd turned her so on, turned her into an inferno. She felt her skin prickle and burn across her cheekbones, along her brow and even her lips felt hot, full, aching.

"No, Malik, you don't know how much I want you. You just think you do..." She bent her head, pressed her face to his neck, breathed in his spicy cologne and the warm scent that was him, and he smelled delicious, smelled like everything she wanted in life.

Keep me, a tiny voice whispered inside her. Keep me forever and never let me go. It'd been since Daniel, she thought, reaching for Malik again, sliding her hands up through his hair, tightening her fingers against his scalp, feeling the crisp cool strands of Malik's hair bunch in her fist.

"I think I know what you need," he whispered against her mouth, pulling her closer so that their two bodies felt almost as one.

And as close as they were, it still wasn't enough. Nic needed to be possessed by, filled by him. There'd been years of dates and several lovers since Daniel but no one made her feel like this anymore, no one made her want like this. This was as hot and intense as she'd ever known. "Can we make love? Is it illegal to be intimate before the wedding?"

"It's not illegal." His lips brushed the corner of her mouth. "If it were, I'd change the law." He lifted her long heavy hair from her neck, stroked her sensitive nape.

She shuddered against him. He held her in his thrall. He was powerful but he never used force. He didn't need to speak harshly, or use strong language. He didn't need threats or boasts. He wore his confidence like his silken robe. Comfortably.

Naturally. He'd do anything for his people. He'd protect them at all costs. He'd protect her, too.

Malik lay her down on the settee, and stretched out over her, his weight braced on his elbows. "You're trapped," he said, studying her lying beneath him. "My prisoner."

"So what are you going to do to me?"

His gaze settled on her mouth. "Make you talk."

"Talk?"

"I want to know what you think about when you go so quiet on me." He traced her lips with the tip of his finger, lightly following the bow shaped curve of the upper lip and the swollen lower lip. "I want to know what you don't talk about."

She felt her lips quiver from his caress. "Why do we always have to talk?"

"Because I want to make sure you know what you're doing. I want to make sure I know what you're thinking. Better to face the facts than run away from them."

He was caressing her ear, lightly running his fingertip along the curve of her outer ear and then gently along the sensitive lobe.

She couldn't think when he was doing that, couldn't concentrate on anything but the way he made her body blister and burn. "All right. Ask me a question."

"What does no one know about you?"

What did no one know about her?

She tried to blot out the delicious sensations he was stirring within her, by staring up at the elegant domed ceiling, all gold and cobalt-blue tiles, and the breeze outside the open window rustled the thick date leaves. What did no one know about her? What had she kept hidden from everyone for all these years?

Daniel, of course.

She'd fallen for him so hard.

He'd worked at the palace. A mechanical engineer. Daniel built and restored race cars and she'd wanted it to work between them, had wanted to be with him as much as she could, but their relationship was doomed from the start. Perhaps her father could get away with marrying her mother, but there was no way she could run off with Daniel Thierry. No way she could live with him. No way she could love him. But that didn't stop her from wanting him with a desperation that nearly drove her mad.

She might have run off with him too, if it hadn't been for Chantal's wedding to Prince Armand. Somehow Nic couldn't run away with Daniel when Chantal was marrying a man she didn't love in hopes of protecting Melio's future.

Chantal had been such a beautiful bride—not radiant the way magazines liked to say—but poised, ethereal in her loveliness. With her warm brown hair and gray eyes she looked like a Dresden figurine. Perfect. Flawless. Petite. Her full skirts and long veil with the high diamond tiara captured the fairy tale elements of the royal wedding and her picture was on the front of nearly two hundred magazines the week after the wedding.

Chantal was happy, Nic assured herself, not blissful, but happy enough.

Yet the fact that Chantal had the strength and conviction to go through with an arranged marriage undermined Nic's insistence on doing only what she pleased.

Truth was, she couldn't run away with her beautiful Daniel.

Truth was, there couldn't be a future with Daniel.

He might kiss her senseless, and he might make her laugh, and she might feel most comfortable with him, but he wasn't even remotely what Melio needed.

A month after Chantal's lavish wedding Nicolette ended it with Daniel.

It was the hardest thing she'd ever done as an adult. In fact, she changed her mind once, getting back together with him for a stolen night, but later, the next day, she forced herself to call him and make a complete break.

He was out shopping when he answered his phone. She could hear the voices of other shoppers, could hear him periodically place things in his basket, could hear the mundane sounds of normal life all around him and it cut her, realizing in that moment it was really all over. She'd never be part of his real world again. She'd never do the ordinary things with him that she'd wanted to do. No trips to the movies, no snuggling under the covers late on Sunday morning, no going out on the spur of the moment for sushi or Chinese.

Don't take my calls, she'd said. Don't let me change my mind.

In the store, in the middle of his shopping, Daniel went quiet. He'd said absolutely nothing.

She'd felt the tears rise, felt the distance growing by the second. No one had made her feel so good about herself, and losing him—leaving him, was breaking her heart.

She had to talk quickly to get the rest of the words out, and they came in a rush. "If you see my number, don't pick up," she said, holding the tears back. "If I show up at the garage, don't talk to me. Don't let me change my mind."

"If that's what you want," he finally said.

Is that what she wanted? No. Is that what Melio needed? Yes. She held the phone tighter, closed her eyes, and tried to be responsible. Think about Grandmama and Grandfather, she told herself. Think about Joelle. Think about all the people who have worked and sacrificed to get us to this point.

"It's what's right," she said, emotion strangled inside of her, strangling her. If only he'd give her a good reason to throw respectability and responsibility away.

But he didn't. He'd been a citizen of Melio his whole life. Yes, he'd gone to school in Rome, studied beneath the great DeLaurent family, but when he'd come into his own, he'd returned to his island kingdom and like everyone else, he understood the burden on the Ducasses, knew that one day the princesses would inherit.

He'd known from the beginning their relationship could go nowhere. But he'd taken a chance. Gone with his heart. And she had to admire that. The odds hadn't been good, but Daniel had let the love carry him as far it would, and when it ended, he'd been a man.

He'd let her go without a word of complaint.

Staring up at the gold and blue domed ceiling, Nicolette blinked back tears. Giving up Daniel had put her emotions into a deep, cold storage and for the first time in a long time she could admit what her decision had cost her.

True love. A chance at lasting happiness.

She felt Malik's gaze. He'd been patiently waiting for her answer. "I've no secrets," she said at last. "My life is public knowledge."

He leaned forward, took her chin in his hand, turning her head to stare into her eyes. "Yet you cry."

She tensed. "I'm not crying."

"I see tears. And sadness. You lost something and it's never been returned."

My heart, she agreed silently, even as she masked her surprise that he'd read her so accurately, that he'd nailed the emotion and need. "My parents died when I was ten."

"This isn't about your parents—"

He was interrupted by a rapid knock on the door. The outer door opened and Alea's young voice could be heard calling for admittance. "Your Highness, forgive the interruption, but you're needed immediately."

Malik sat up, closed his robe. "What's happened?"

"Lady Fatima, Your Highness. They've called an ambulance for her. She's terribly ill."

Nic waited for Malik to return. He did not. Instead he had servants bring Nicolette a dinner tray to her room.

Later a grim-faced Alea appeared to help Nicolette prepare for bed. Alea didn't volunteer any information about Fatima, and out of politeness, Nic didn't ask.

But once Alea left, carrying away the remnants of dinner, Nicolette paced her room. She was concerned about Fatima despite how the other woman had treated her. And after what had been interrupted between herself and Malik she felt like she was going crazy. She wanted to make love, not fall in love. She wanted passion, not emotion. She wanted to be with Malik now, not committing to the future.

Why was this so hard? She'd been with other men before, had made love but hadn't worried about falling in love. Why couldn't she do that here? Why couldn't she stay breezy, light, keep it all superficial?

Because Malik wasn't superficial, that's why.

Nic slumped on the foot of her bed, pressed her fists to her eyes. She could see him even now, handsome, proud, intelligent, kind...

God, he was kind. He had such warmth and dignity and she couldn't bear to hurt him. Disappoint him.

But she was. No matter what she did now, it'd disappoint. No matter what choice, it'd be wrong.

He wanted Chantal. She was Nic. He wanted forever. She only believed in the moment.

She didn't even believe in marriage for heaven's sake!

Letting her hands fall to her sides, Nic inhaled slowly, trying to calm the wild beasts stampeding inside her. Breathe, she told herself, just breathe.

But it was a struggle to even breathe. It was such a struggle being here, pretending to be someone she wasn't. She'd stopped trying to pretend that she was handling the situation well.

What she needed to do was reduce it to the most elemental form, and in this case, it was physical attraction. Sexual attraction.

She wanted to make love with Malik. Maybe making love is just an escape, another form of running away, but at least making love, she'd feel something besides this…panic.

Making love she'd feel like herself again.

She hated pretending to be Chantal. She missed her natural hair color, missed her own strengths, and missed her own dreams.

If she could just become Nic again. If she could just find her sense of humor, and sense of adventure, again.

If she could just stop worrying about Melio, her grandparents, Chantal and Lilly, and the kind of future Joelle faced as well.

Her brow creased as she stared across her room to the door with the delicate arch. It was a lot to worry about.

But if she could just escape the worries for a while…

If she could just be with Malik, feel his arms around her, put her cheek on his chest…

If she could just close her eyes and think about nothing but sharing the moment with him. Just be close to him. Warm skin, his body, his heart beating beneath her ear…

And maybe his hands taking hers, pinning her arms down against the bed, his mouth on hers, his body moving over…

Maybe his body in hers…

Maybe…

Nic bit her knuckle, feeling as if she were dangerously close to losing control. She—who'd needed so few people in her life—had never felt as if she needed anyone or anything like one long intense night in Malik's bed. He was a king. He had to know what she was feeling. He carried so many responsibilities on his shoulders. Surely he could give her some advice.

Or at least, be able to help her forget.

Just to be a person. A woman. Just to be Nicolette and loved for herself, wanted for herself…

Nic fell asleep waiting for some word from Malik and early the next morning, woke with an even heavier heart than before.

She had to go. That's all there was to it. Time to go home, wash out this awful brown hair color, answer her mail, check her email, start dating again…

She swallowed hard, hating the lump that filled her throat. She'd miss Malik. She liked looking at him, liked listening to him, just liked him period.

Nic showered, dressed, wondered where breakfast was. Leaving her room she noticed a small congregation of servants in the hall. The gathering of servants troubled her. She hung back in the shadows watching the servants speak. She knew enough of palace life to know that the small groups of guards and servants meeting, murmuring, parting, only to assemble again further down the hall was not normal palace protocol.

Something was definitely wrong, and from the hushed tones of the guards and servants the problem had to be serious.

Had Fatima been sick before, and Nic didn't know?

Guilt assailed Nicolette. What if Fatima had been recovering from something…in remission from cancer or leukemia?

Nicolette returned to her room, quietly shut the door, worrying about Fatima without really knowing what Fatima was facing.

Alea arrived a little later with coffee and a message from the sultan. Nicolette opened the folded sheet of paper. He'd written a note, letting her know that due to Fatima's poor health, the morning's language lesson had been cancelled.

CHAPTER NINE

MALIK sat in a chair next to Fatima's bed, his hands folded together, his expression grim. His thoughts raced, confusion and anger. "I don't understand."

Fatima's dark head turned away. "I can't talk about it."

"You have to," he shot back, his deep voice curt, tense. How could she do this? What on earth had she been thinking?

Fatima wouldn't answer. She continued staring at the wall and Malik felt a welling of helpless rage. He rose from the chair, towered over the bed. "They wanted to keep you overnight at the hospital. Maybe I was wrong to bring you home. Maybe I should take you back—"

"No." She rolled over, looked up at him, tears in her eyes. "I won't do it again."

She looked so small, so defenseless and his anger melted. He loved Fatima like a sister. They'd grown up together. He trusted her. "But why would you try something like that in the first place? What if help hadn't come in time?" He shook his head, exhausted, worn out from the night spent at the side of her bed. "Is your life really so unbearable?"

She covered her face with her hands, unable to bear his censure. "Forgive me."

"Help me understand."

She cried harder. Malik felt sick at heart. "I've sent for your mother," he said after a long moment. "She and your sister are coming from New York."

"No, Malik!" She scrubbed her face dry, struggled to sit up, grimacing at a wave of nausea. They'd pumped her stomach at the hospital and she was obviously still sore. "Mother will be furious. She'll be so upset."

"And I'm not?" he demanded, not knowing whether to shake her or put his arms around her. "Fatima, you could have died."

112

She shuddered. "It was a mistake. I knew it was a mistake the moment I did it. That's why I called for help."

"But why?" He couldn't let it drop. He couldn't let it go. You didn't swallow a bottle of pills without good reason. What had pushed her over the edge? "Fatima, you must be honest with me. I insist."

She looked at him, then past him, her dark gaze going vacant. "You were supposed to marry me."

He froze, air bottled in his lungs. *What?*

Staring down into Fatima's averted face, he could see her agony. Her face was still pale, her mouth pinched, her eyes glassy, and he felt her tremor of fear and anger, hurt and confusion. Her agony was real. "Explain this to me," he said more gently, trying for a calm he didn't feel.

She wouldn't meet his gaze. "Father said you were to be my husband. He said I was to wait for you."

His heart fell.

For a long moment he felt horribly destructive—look what he'd done to Fatima? And then reason set in. He hadn't done anything to her but treat her as a member of his own family.

And now he wracked his brain, trying to think of a time when marriage with Fatima might have been discussed, but he could remember no such conversation. It was common practice in Baraka for cousins to marry, for family to intermarry. Cousins were considered favorable marriage partners as it consolidated a family's power.

Fatima filled the silence with her slow, painful words. "It'd been widely assumed that we would marry—"

"By whom?"

"My family. Your family."

"I've never heard this before."

She shrugged wearily. "My father said your father had agreed. It would keep the wealth in the family, simplify inheritance." Her body slumped, no energy left. "Ever since I was small, I'd been raised to think that you…and I…" Her voice drifted away, she bit her lip, trying to hold back the tears.

You and I rang in his head. You and I… "So you took an overdose of sleeping pills?"

She shrugged yet again, her slender spine bent beneath the weight of it all. "I didn't understand why you'd decided to go elsewhere for your bride when you have me here single, waiting.''

And suddenly he understood. Not just her pain, but also her shame.

In the West, Fatima was still considered young; she was just in her mid-twenties, but in Baraka that was old for women who remained unmarried. Men didn't believe a woman couldn't remain pure—untouched—for that many years and a bride's purity was as important as her dowry. Indeed, a great part of the wedding celebration was the confirmation of the bride's virginity.

Malik sat down in the chair next to her bed, reached for her hands, held them between his own. She felt so cold, her skin chilled. ''I didn't realize—'' He broke off, heartsick. Or did he?

He'd known she'd always hoped to make a royal marriage. But he hadn't realized she'd always hoped to marry him…or had he?

He clasped her cold hands in his, trying to warm her. His thoughts were broken, disjointed. He'd confronted her this morning wanting to make sure she understood the shame she'd brought on the family by her actions, and yet now he saw the shame she'd been enduring for years.

People would have been wondering, whispering, why a wealthy royal like Fatima Nuri was still single. They would have wondered why her cousin went outside Baraka for a wife…they would have gossiped about Fatima's reputation, and her shame. Shame. *Hshuma,* he thought wearily. *Hshuma* was such a heavy burden for everyone.

She bowed her head, stared at her hands. ''Forgive me.''

''I do.'' He felt her tremble and his heart smote him. He'd unwittingly hurt her. No wonder Fatima had been so angry, so resentful of Nicolette. Fatima had feel rejected. Supplanted.

Fatima couldn't bring herself to meet his eyes. ''What have you told my family?''

Nothing yet, thank God. ''Just that you were very ill, and they needed to come quickly.''

''Ah.'' Fatima gently disengaged her hands, putting distance between them. ''When do they arrive?''

''Later today.''

''Will you tell Mother about what I…did?''

He'd been asking himself the same thing. What did one do

in this circumstance? "No," he decided quickly, and knew it was the right decision. There was absolutely no reason to bring more shame to her, or on the family. "But you have to know this behavior—what you did—isn't acceptable. The choice you made, that's not a valid option. You are loved by all. Your life is of great value—"

"Please," she pleaded, fresh tears welling. "Please don't. I won't do it again, I won't try anything like that again. I just felt so ashamed, so horrible about what happened at the market yesterday. I'd never mean to hurt the princess and yet—" She broke off, shook her head, tears spilling. "Maybe I did lose her on purpose. I don't know anymore—"

He hugged her. That any member of his family should hurt so hurt him. "The princess returned safe. Do not worry, or blame yourself anymore. You must get rest. You need to take care of yourself."

She nodded slowly, fatigue etched in the tightness at her eyes and mouth. "Maybe I'll go with Mother to New York for awhile. Maybe a change of pace…"

"I'll arrange it for you." Malik kissed her forehead, and stood. "You've nothing to worry about, Fatima. Just get some rest. Everything will work out."

"Malik." Her voice stopped him at the door. He turned around to face her. Fatima's eyes looked huge in her pale face. "I…can I ask a favor, please?"

He nodded.

"Would you consider taking the princess to Zefd for a few days…just while Mother is here? It'd be easier to pack and leave for NY without worrying about Mother saying something to Princess Chantal. I know Mother will be disappointed that I didn't—" She broke off, frowned, drew a deep breath. "You see, Mother had also hoped you and I…and she doesn't know about your engagement to Princess Chantal."

He nodded. "I understand. I'd planned on taking the princess there next week, we'll just go a few days early. You're comfortable explaining my absence to your mother?"

Fatima smiled weakly. "Yes. And thank you, cousin."

Malik stopped by Nicolette's room personally to tell her they were going to visit another home of his for a few days. Nicolette saw the shadows in his eyes, felt his strain. "How is Fatima?"

He shook his head.

His silence put knots in her stomach. "If she's ill, we shouldn't go—"

"She'll be herself soon. I don't want you to worry. You have enough on your mind."

"But—"

"No." This time he was adamant, his tone forceful. "I do not want to discuss this further. Have Alea pack. Tell her you are going to Zefd."

Several hours later Nicolette and Malik left noisy, congested Atiq behind, traveling in a luxuriously outfitted four wheel drive vehicle, the interior seats leather, the windows tinted, the middle console between two of the passenger seats built to house a mini refrigerator, a stereo, and a DVD player.

Malik sat silent the first half hour of the trip, staring blindly out the window. Nicolette knew he wasn't angry with her. Rather he was wrestling internally, in a battle with himself.

Finally she wouldn't let him sit in silence any longer. He'd had over an hour to beat himself up. Now he'd have to talk to her.

"I've never seen a four-wheel drive vehicle like this," she said, her voice breaking the heavy silence.

"It's custom," he answered, his expression even more brooding. "Built for the desert. To handle the dunes if necessary."

"It's quite plush. You could live in here."

"If necessary."

He wasn't making this easy, but Nicolette doggedly inspected the entertainment system, remembering the hidden speakers and stereo system in her room at the palace. "Lots of interesting gadgets."

"A king should be entitled to a few play things."

She cocked her head, hearing the anger and self-loathing in his voice. What had happened last night? What had happened with his cousin? "Please tell me about Fatima."

"There's nothing to say."

Pain deepened his voice and Nic's heart ached. "I've been worried," she said softly. "And I know you care about her very much."

Malik continued to stare out the windows. The hills were giving way to steep red tinted mountains. "She's going to go to

New York for a while, spend time with her family there. She agrees with me that she needs a change—''

"And until then, we're leaving her alone?"

"She won't be alone. Her mother and sister are arriving from America this afternoon."

Nic assessed the situation, understanding suddenly that she was being sent away deliberately before Fatima's mother arrived. "You didn't want me to meet your aunt."

"Fatima wanted to avoid any potential problems."

"Meeting your aunt would have created problems?"

He turned his head, met her gaze. "My aunt wished me to marry my cousin, and Fatima, wisely wanted to save you, and herself, from further embarrassment."

So that explained Fatima's hostility. Nic exhaled slowly, thinking of the past week, all the time the two had been forced to spend together. Fatima must have felt hurt, and humiliated. "I didn't know."

He made a rough sound, impatient, angry. "I didn't, either."

Her lips parted in surprise but Malik's pained expression stilled the words on her lips, leaving them unspoken. He looked staggered even now. Nicolette had never seen him so quiet, so closed. It was as if he'd gone inward and shut all his emotions down.

Something horrible must have happened last night... "I'm sorry, Malik. I really am."

"I am, too."

Nicolette suddenly wondered if perhaps she'd done something far worse by coming here than just masquerading as Chantal. Had she perhaps destroyed people's futures...their lives? "Was there a reason you couldn't marry?"

His powerful shoulders shifted. "I didn't choose her," he said flatly, turning to look at Nicolette with a piercing gaze. He stared at her hard, staring at her as if he could see all the way through her. "I chose you."

Nicolette felt a wave of panic. Fatima loved Malik, she'd hoped to share her life with him, and all the while Nicolette was playing a part, biding her time before she could escape back to Melio.

How would Nic's disappearance affect Malik...Fatima...the Nuri family?

She swayed on her seat, feeling dizzy, sick, scared of what she'd started. Her breezy words spoken to Chantal returned to haunt her, I'll sneak in, sneak out, and be gone before the sultan even notices…

Wrong.

"She's going to be okay," Malik said, sensing Nicolette's panic, seeking to reassure her. "Don't blame yourself. I chose you. You didn't create this…problem."

Nicolette heard the emotion in Malik's voice, felt his worry, his personal struggle. He blamed himself.

He cared about Fatima. He loved his family. He'd spent his life trying to protect those he cared about. And in that instant, Nic realized that all those European gossip magazines had gotten King Malik Roman Nuri wrong. He wasn't a Casanova. It'd be impossible for him to take women to bed just to discard them later.

Malik cared about women. He didn't take advantage of them.

She felt tears start to her eyes. "No wonder you enjoy your gadgets." She covered his hand with hers. "You should be entitled to a few fun toys. It's not easy being King."

He lifted her hand to his mouth, kissed the back of her fingers. He was trying hard to lighten his mood. "You will enjoy Zefd. It will be good for us to spend a few days in the mountains."

But Nic didn't want him to put on a happy face for her sake. She searched his eyes. "Are you going to be okay?"

Leaning forward, he brushed his mouth across her cheek, and then once more on her lips. "I'm glad you're with me, *laeela.*"

"I'm glad I'm here, too."

They spent two hours traveling in and out of the rugged red and pink mountains, climbing slowly, steadily to the peak of one mountain, to descend on the other side, and then start climbing all over again.

Late afternoon they reached an open valley, the barren ground dotted here and there with oases of green. "Artificial lakes," Malik said, "for commercial orchards of date trees."

On this side of the mountains the landscape looked brighter, clearer, and more unusual. It was the quality of light, Nic thought, the way the golden rays hit the rose and gold sand, reflecting off the pink and red granite cliffs.

Everything here seemed to come from the earth, to be made

of the earth, and would eventually return to the earth. The driver approached a red sandstone fortress, the stark walls high, the parapet clearly etched against the brilliant blue sky. The fortress towered over the rest of the city and yet was still dwarfed by the snow-capped mountains behind.

"So where are we?" Nic's inquisitive gaze took in the magnificent mountains dusted in white and the weathered apricot and terracotta buildings before them.

"This is Zefd. One of the oldest cities in Baraka. My father's family came from here."

As Malik's vehicle entered the walls of the city, people unexpectedly poured out, robed men and women and dozens of eager children. "Did they know you were coming?"

Malik's expression was ironic. "Someone must have alerted them."

The driver parked, but before he opened the door for them, palace guards appeared, forming a protective barrier between the sultan's car and the crowd.

Malik climbed from the car and assisted Nicolette. On seeing the king, the people cheered, and Malik lifted a hand in acknowledgment.

Malik was surprised when Nicolette moved forward, toward the crowd, greeting his people. She spoke only a few Arabic words, but the sincere phrases coupled with her warm smiles appeared to charm everyone.

Standing at her side, Malik watched Nicolette work the crowd, and while "work" sounded cold, it was exactly what she was doing. She knew her job, he thought, seeing how gracefully she handled the press of people, the hands extended, the small children lifted for her to kiss. She knew how long to chat, how long to listen, and then how to gently break free to continue making her way along the edge of the crowd.

He'd known she was strong, intelligent, but he hadn't expected this natural warmth and ease with his people. She was a true princess—regal, royal—and yet she identified with the common man. She would be good for his people.

And very good for him.

But he still hadn't made much headway when it came to knowing her, openly speaking with her. She'd learned to hide herself quite well. She projected so much warmth and charm that one didn't realize how neatly she sidestepped the personal until later.

Princess Nicolette did not wear her heart on her sleeve. Instead she kept her heart buried very deep. But it was her heart he wanted, and right now he wasn't even sure he had that. She was attracted to him, and responded to him, but the fact that she continued to hide her true identity had begun to trouble him. What if she didn't intend to go through with the wedding? What if she still intended to leave him at the altar, the jilted royal bridegroom?

The thought left him cold. His jaw gritted and he felt ice lodge in his chest, close to his heart. He wanted her. He needed her. He had no intention of losing her now.

His temper and emotions firmly in control, Malik moved forward, claimed Nicolette, drawing her with him into his desert home.

"We call this house the Citadel," he said, showing Nicolette around his Zefd desert home. "It was built as a fortress, and although the royal family has lived here off and on for the past two hundred years, it still serves as an important military outpost, one of our stronger defensive positions."

"Does Baraka worry about its neighbors?"

"The neighbors aren't the threat. Our troubles historically have come from within." He opened a door, leading to a large walled garden dominated by an ancient argan tree. The tree's upper limbs were enormous and gnarled, like spiny green dragons fighting.

They took a seat in the shade and were immediately served with glasses of ice cold, very sweet mint tea.

Malik's expression became contemplative and he drummed his fingers on the table. When he spoke next, he chose his words with care. "We have a complex society in Baraka, our culture that of Berber, Boudin, Arab, African. Throw in some French colonialism and you have intense conflicts."

She considered him. "How intense?"

"We've had more than our share of political turmoil in this century. Unfortunately, the last fifty years have been especially...explosive."

She reached for her glass, sipped the icy beverage gratefully. "The tensions have boiled over?"

"Violently."

"It seems I do need to learn Baraka's history," Nic said, setting her glass down.

He hesitated, staring off, his gaze on the red mountains beyond, the manicured palm trees lining the exterior citadel wall. "Baraka was in the midst of a violent civil war when I was born. This war lasted fifteen years. Everyone took sides. Many fought on behalf of the royal family, others fought for the insurgents. You see, we'd been under French rule for so long that people were fighting simply because they were angry, and scared, and no one knew what was best. I was still just a small child when my grandfather was assassinated, but I've never forgotten that day."

His brow furrowed as he remembered those dark violent years. "My grandfather's assassination ended the war." He turned and looked at her, his expression curiously blank. "Because you see, my grandfather was universally loved. He wasn't supposed to be killed. This wasn't a fight against him, or the family, but a fight about culture...custom...a fight to be recognized. The country virtually shut down the day of Grandfather's funeral. All the people took to the streets. I've never forgotten the sound of weeping, thousands of people weeping, and it taught me that nothing is more important than life. Than family."

"I'm surprised you haven't married before then."

"It didn't feel urgent."

"And it is now?"

His mouth opened as if to speak but instead he closed it, shook his head.

Truthfully, he'd never worried about marrying, having children, he'd been certain it was a matter of timing and sooner or later he'd meet the right woman...but it hadn't happened, and here he was, in his late thirties, and without a wife, an heir, or a family of his own.

And with one assassination attempt against him already.

Malik drank his tea, let the cool liquid pour down his throat and ice his raw emotions. It'd been a difficult twenty-four hour period. He was feeling the strain of Fatima's desperate measures, Nicolette's masquerade, and his own need for closure. He just wished he knew if she'd come through, meet him on her own terms. He wanted her on her terms, he wanted her heart, her laughter, her commitment. But he couldn't push her…yet.

He turned his head, looked at Nic whose features were grave, a deep furrow between her eyebrows from thinking hard, listening so intently.

"The years of war changed the way I looked at society," he continued. "It impacted the way I view our culture and the idea of stability. I learned early that we must embrace change, that without change we die."

"I would have thought you'd be afraid of change. After all, change triggered your grandfather's death—as well as that decade and half of turmoil. One would think you'd associate change with danger."

He shrugged. "But chaos and turmoil surround us, whether or not we choose to recognize it. Just because we don't see turmoil, or because we're not immediately impacted, doesn't negate its existence. Chaos can happen at any time."

"So your philosophy is…?"

Talking with Nic was good for him. "Change is good. Change is necessary. It doesn't mean that one can't revere the past and respect tradition, but tradition is pointless unless one can use tradition to teach, to use as a benchmark, to show one where and how to aim."

She leaned back in the chaise. "You like being King."

"I love being King."

CHAPTER TEN

NIC couldn't look away from his remarkable face with the light silver eyes. He was so quiet, so controlled. She'd had no idea he'd been through so much. Another man might have been angry, bitter, cruel, but Malik had accepted the tragedies with grace.

Baraka, she whispered to herself. *Baraka,* Fatima had once told her, meant Grace and peace. Malik had that peace, didn't he?

"There are dangers, of course," he said after a reflective silence, "but we all face danger at different points in our life. The secret is to be aware of the danger, to know how one is vulnerable, and then embrace truth, and life, and move on."

He rose, took her hand in his, and tugged her to her feet. "You still look hot, *laeela.* Let me take you to your room. You'll be pleased to know you have your own private swimming pool."

It was good news and Nic took a long, leisurely swim before dinner. The bottom and sides of the pool had been painted a sapphire blue and as Nic floated on her back, she stared up at the high pink stone towers surrounding her, one tower covered in purple bougainvillea, while climbing roses draped another tower wall, the petals the palest shade of pink. With jasmine and sweet orange blossoms scenting the air, and the setting sun painting the ancient walls a dusty red, Nicolette closed her eyes and felt…bliss. *Baraka,* she whispered to herself. Grace and peace.

Nicolette was to meet Malik in one of the walled courtyards for dinner. The Citadel staff had planned a special welcome supper for the princess, and the outdoor party delighted Nic, especially as it was a very exclusive party with just two guests— them.

A big bonfire had been built in the courtyard and a tent had been strung up to provide the sultan with additional privacy.

123

Malik had Nic sit beside him, cross-legged on a red woven rug, and together they dined on roasted lamb, artichokes, saffron rice, and endless nuts and sweets before sitting back to enjoy the evening's entertainment: a juggler—who juggled fire, talented singers, and traditional dancers.

The evening was unlike anything Nic had experienced in Atiq and was by far her favorite. She loved eating outside, relished the heat and glow of the fire, and embraced the sensuous beauty of the place. ''If I was from Baraka, this is where I'd want to live,'' she said, resting her head on her knee, watching the flames crackle and dance. ''This just feels right. I can't explain it, but it feels like…home.''

Malik looked at her and a small muscle pulled in his jaw. ''You say extraordinary things when I least expect it.''

She turned her head from the fire, smiled at him. She felt pleasantly relaxed, a little bit sleepy. ''What did I say?''

He gave his head a slight shake, drew an imaginary circle on the red blanket. ''This is my home, my spiritual home. Whenever I have doubts, I come here.''

''Doubts about what?''

His lips curved. ''My ability to lead.'' His smile turned self-mocking. ''As well as my struggle to find the balance between what I need, and what my people need.''

Glancing at him, she saw that his brow had creased, and shadows haunted his eyes. He had such a noble face it hurt her to see him struggle. Nicolette felt her chest tighten. The depth of her emotion staggered her.

She wasn't supposed to care this much. She wasn't supposed to admire him. She wasn't supposed to want him.

She shouldn't have come to Zefd, shouldn't have loved the red mountains, the pinkish walls of the citadel, the gnarled trees that seemed to spring from the middle of the boulders. She shouldn't love the way the wind rustled the fronds on the date trees. Shouldn't like sitting on a carpet by a fire eating rice with her fingers and feeling peace, real peace, for the first time in years…

This *couldn't* happen. She couldn't fall in love with Malik or his desert or his kingdom. She wouldn't let herself want the conversations with him, the quiet with him, the life with him…

He was too soulful, too powerful. He'd turn her life upside

down. He'd expect her to give up everything she treasured, including her freedom and her beloved family at home.

Tears burned the back of her eyes. She felt as if she couldn't breathe properly. "I'm exhausted," she said, crossing her arms over her chest, overwhelmed by all that she felt sitting here in the dark with him. What she needed was time alone, quiet to figure out her way home. Melio felt light years away. How would she get back?

More importantly, how would she ever forget? If she left Malik, she'd leave her heart in Baraka with him.

"I'll walk you in," he said, rising.

"No need." Nic said hastily, trying to ignore the panic building inside of her. Whatever pretense she'd been able to manage had fallen behind like Atiq's white washed stonewalls. "You have dozens of valets and butlers and maids to escort me to bed."

"I know. I pay their salaries." He smiled sardonically. "But I am the sultan, and you, *laeela,* are my princess."

He walked her through the semidark corridors, candles lit in high wall sconces, the soft flickering yellow light reminding Nicolette of a medieval castle and yet the blue paint, and the gold and black mosaics were exotic instead of frightening.

He opened the door of her room, checked inside, made sure all was in order. "Is there anything you need?"

"No."

He said good night then, and left her. Nicolette shut the door, leaned against the door, wishing with all her might that Malik would have stayed. She needed to be with him. Needed to be close to him. Even if they never made love, she just wanted one night in his arms.

She slowly started to undress and a knock sounded on her door. Opening the door, Nic discovered Malik. A lump filled her throat. She was so glad to see him and it'd only been a couple minutes since he left. "Get lost?"

His crooked grin tugged on her heart. "I forgot something," he said.

"What?"

He wrapped his hands around her arms and pulled her against him. She felt the hard length of his body touch every soft curve of hers. Dropping his head, he kissed her. Malik's lips felt wonderfully cool against her heated skin and she closed her eyes.

"This," he murmured against her lips.

"You returned for a kiss?"

"What is more important than love?" With the tip of his finger he outlined her brow bone and then her small, straight nose.

She shivered at the touch, and yet questioned his words. Love. But he didn't mean *love*. Not in the Western sense, the way she knew love. He meant love as one that is familiar, important, betrothed.

After all, everyone had arranged marriages in Baraka. No one married here for love. There was a way of doing things, the bridegroom paid a *sedaq,* bride price, to the family of the bride, and the bride presented the groom a dowry, and in her case it was the ports and harbors of Melio.

"I don't know," she answered, belly tightening, nerves jumping as he continued to touch her, his hand exploring the column of her throat, the sensitive spot at the top of her spine, and now her long hair which she'd just loosened.

"You have lovely hair," he said, fingers sliding through the long strands.

"Thank you." The words stuck in her mouth.

"I'm so glad you're not a blonde. I think brunettes are much more striking," he added, holding a tendril up to the light, letting the dark brown and rich auburn highlights glimmer against his skin. He turned the long strand over. "You haven't ever wanted to be fair, have you?"

Her mouth dried. "I don't think I'd look bad as a blonde, and it's just a hair color. The face would be the same. The eyes. The nose—"

"The lips," he interrupted, covering her mouth with his in a kiss that stole her breath, turned her inside out. *This* was a kiss. This was so hot. This was so hungry and male.

Her insides felt tight. Her belly felt tense. She was achy everywhere, wanting something he was promising with his kiss but so far not delivering.

She wanted him.

All of him.

"Could you stay the night?" she whispered against his mouth, one of his hands against her breast, inflaming her nerves, her skin, her imagination.

"We were interrupted last night."

"We were," she agreed, and then remembered what had interrupted them. She felt a pang of conscience, saw Malik's expression darken. He, too, remembered. "I *am* sorry. For her, for you—"

"I appreciate your sensitivity, but in this case, you have nothing to apologize for. I've always known I could marry from within the family. The option never appealed to me." He lifted her chin, kissed her mouth, felt her lips tremble beneath his. "It will be good for her to go to America for awhile. Fatima has many family members in New York and Washington, D.C., and her immediate family knows many families. She will find the right man. I am sure of it."

Nic felt a stab of sympathy for his cousin. If Fatima truly loved Malik, she would not find him easy to forget. "I hope so," she whispered.

He circled his hands around her long hair. "We were discussing the night."

Her hands hovered at the buttons on his shirt. "Yes."

"Do I spend the night?"

"Yes." And then as she unbuttoned the first button, and the second button, she remembered one huge but crucial detail. She wasn't a natural brunette. He'd notice as soon as he saw her naked. The hair on the rest of her body was blond. *Natural* blond.

Nic's fingers were motionless now. "But if you're worried about impropriety, perhaps we just spend the night together... without making love."

"Or maybe you're worried that you can't spend a night with me without wanting to make love."

She laughed softly, embarrassed, amused. He was very funny for a sultan. Very sexy, too. "You have extraordinary confidence."

"I should. I'm very good."

This was getting quite interesting. This was the stuff she'd been dying to know. "Good, how?"

He laughed, too. "How do you think?"

"I'm supposed to be a virgin," she answered primly, ignoring the shimmering heat in her cheeks, the languid warmth throughout her body. She loved the verbal foreplay with him as much as actually touching. She loved letting the desire start with the eyes, the lips, letting words tease. She loved making love, but better than making love, was the idea that making love could be so damn fun.

"I believe Western culture has had all the virgin births it can support. You have a daughter. I'm quite sure you'll never have that virginity restored."

"So we can definitely do some things tonight, just not...everything." She'd returned to unbuttoning his shirt again. She almost had it all the way unbuttoned now, and with each button she felt her desire ratchet up another notch. "What would please you?"

His shirt fell open. He looked down at her, heat in his gaze. "You."

Nic sank down on the edge of her bed. Malik towered above her. She tried to keep from staring at the magnificent proportions of his upper body. He'd looked great in a robe last night, but in slacks and a shirt he looked...oh...unreal. "And what about me pleases you, Your Highness?"

He studied her, considered her. "Your mouth."

"My mouth."

"Your hands."

She gripped a pillow. "My hands."

"Your mind."

She wanted to throw the pillow out of the way and beg him to take her and to hell with the consequences. No one had ever liked her mind before. "You like it better than my body?" She knew she had a decent body.

"I adore your mind."

She couldn't suppress her smile. "Why?"

"It's sharp. It's smart. It's funny." His head cocked. "You're funny. I'm having a fantastic time watching you, wondering what you're going to do next. You're very daring."

What did he mean by that? What did he know? "You mean...marrying you? A stranger?"

He laughed softly, and the sound just melted Nic. She felt so hot, she pressed her knees together, pushed the pillow to her thighs.

"You'll never admit the truth, will you?"

"What truth?"

He wasn't going to answer that one. "Never mind. It's not important. I'll leave you to your sleep." Malik bent down, kissed her gently on the mouth, a long slow kiss that made Nic's head spin and tummy flip as if it'd taken flight. *"Tasbah ala khir."* *Good night. Wake up happy.*

"You're not going to stay?" Disappointment washed through her in waves.

"No." He sounded regretful and he kissed her again, parting her lips ever so slowly, flicking the inside of her lip with his tongue. "You wouldn't be able to keep your hands off me. And I wouldn't be able to keep my mouth off you. And I love to kiss, *laeela*. Everywhere."

Malik returned to the fire outside. Hours passed, and he couldn't make himself go to bed.

His guards wanted to stay up with him—security had been stepped up a year ago—and he knew it was for his own good, but tonight he needed space.

He reminded his guards that he was within the locked walls of the Citadel, his own fortress, a fortress that hadn't been conquered in five hundred years. "If I'm not safe here," he said to his men, "then where?"

They laughed because they were supposed to, and they retired. Finally alone, Malik's thoughts raced. He found himself thinking of not just one thing, but many, and his thoughts weren't linear.

He thought of Nicolette, his siren, and knew he'd met his match.

He thought of Fatima and her sorrow and shame, and he wished he'd known what she was expecting, wished he'd tried to find her a good match before. But she'd never wanted to marry. She'd told him many times that she'd rather stay single, than marry a stranger and leave the palace.

He thought of his younger brother, Kalen, now living in London, having studied at Oxford—just like he did—but unlike Malik, chose to sever his ties with Baraka, become a true citizen of the United Kingdom. Malik had never understood it but he'd accepted it.

But with Kalen choosing to become a U.K. citizen, he'd forfeited all rights to succession. Kalen had been second in line for the throne but now...

Malik had been furious with Kalen on moral grounds—they were Arabs, their home was North Africa—but it wasn't until the attempt on Malik's life a year ago that he understood Kalen's fears.

Kalen didn't want to get caught in politics. He wasn't a politician. He was a businessman. He thrived in the high-powered world of banking, loved the urban rush, felt like he'd found a true home in London. Malik couldn't stay angry with his brother. Every one deserved a chance to lead a happy life, a life of meaning and value. If Kalen found that meaning in London, who was he to criticize his brother?

Malik contemplated the glowing orange red fire, and knew he'd lived a good life. It'd been a very full and interesting life. He'd been blessed. And in the past several years he'd been so busy living—doing—that he'd spent very little time in contemplation.

If it weren't for the assassination attempt a year ago, he wouldn't be as contemplative as he was now.

The threat on his life last winter had forced him to become cognizant of all that he'd been given, of the blessings heaped on his head—wealth, prestige, education, power, respect. In reality, he'd been denied little. Looking back he saw that he'd lived large, loved readily and regretted nothing.

Not true, he thought, stopping himself. He did have one regret. He was sorry he'd waited so long to take a wife, start a family. He wanted a child. Needed a child. He needed an heir in case the unthinkable happened. And quite frankly, the unthinkable happened somewhere in the world every day.

A log shifted in the fire, rolling, and red-hot sparks shot up, into the still black night. Malik's eyes narrowed as he watched the sparks burn brightly then fade just as swiftly.

Life was like that, wasn't it? One was here, present, accounted for, and in those hours one had youth and life, one believed in forever.

One wanted to believe there'd be forever.

And then something happens and it changes all the naive assumptions, forces one to confront the very things human beings shy away from. Mortality.

He couldn't deny his mortality any longer. He, King Malik Roman Nuri, had a price on his head. There'd been one assassination attempt already. Malik knew there'd be another. It was simply a matter of time.

Malik crouched by the fire and stared into the shimmering red heat, letting the acrid bite of smoke waft around him, stinging his eyes, filling his nose. He could taste the smoke, feel the smoke and it reminded him of his younger days.

He'd been to battle. He'd returned from battle. He'd led his country for the past fifteen years and Baraka had benefited from his leadership, but he knew history. He'd studied history. Each man was but one part of the whole, and time was a continuum and would continue long past one man's years.

Malik knew he wasn't going to live forever, and he could accept that as long as he provided for his people. And in this case providing for them meant providing leadership. He needed a child desperately. And while the mantle of leadership would fall to his child, Malik also vowed to love his child with all his heart, and all his strength.

A rustle of fabric caught his attention and Malik turned to see Nicolette coming toward him. She was wearing one of the traditional robes, and the head covering had slipped back, exposing her chestnut hair.

"Did you ever go to bed?" she asked him, joining him at the fire.

"No," he answered, straightening.

She studied his profile for a long moment in the firelight. "Thinking of Fatima?"

He made a hoarse sound. "I'm thinking of everything."

He tipped his head back, gazed up into the sky. It was hours till dawn and the heavens were huge, endless, a dark purple punctuated by countless stars. Here in the middle of the mountains he was more nature than man. Here he was part of the wind, the sun, the sand, the air itself. He wasn't king, wasn't royal, was just a common man.

Sighing, Malik ran a hand through his hair. "I miss this life," he said at length. "I don't get away from the city often enough."

She said nothing, and he felt her watchful gaze.

"I used to spend many of my holidays here," he added, filling the silence, knowing she wanted him to speak, that she'd joined him to hear what was on his mind. ''The mountains here, the red sand, it's always been special.''

He turned to look at her. Her blue eyes were a clear lucid blue even now, in the middle of the night, and he thought she looked real, no longer guarded. So often she hid her emotions behind a mask, and perhaps they, royals, always did. The world was always watching so one had to be careful. But it was good to see her calm, rather contemplative, too.

''My brother and cousins also enjoyed the trips across the mountains,'' he added. ''They liked the nights like this, when we camped out, the night spent huddled around the fire, but they've all left Baraka now. But I could never call any other place home.''

''You shouldn't have to. This is your country. You were born here, raised here—''

''And you were born and raised in Melio but you're forced to leave.''

Nic stood still, finding his words both painful and surprisingly honest. ''I've known for awhile,'' she answered after a long moment. ''Once we realized the situation, we all knew we'd have to leave.''

''And that doesn't break your heart?''

Her eyes closed and Nic felt his deep voice seep through her, into her heart, into her veins, touching her everywhere. And that doesn't break your heart?

How could a man of his power, his position know?

How could a thirty-seven-year-old sultan understand the difficulty of the decision, of the rocky heights and depths of emotion? ''One does what one must,'' she murmured, voice failing her and tenderness suffusing every bone and nerve.

''One could always rebel.''

She shot him a swift glance. His gaze was steady, penetrating, and she felt no one had ever looked at her, or listened to her, with Malik's focus. He truly heard her. He paid attention to not just the words she said, but the meanings beneath, to all the unspoken breaths and nuances that made conversation potent. ''I'm no saint. I have rebelled,'' she hesitated. ''Many, many times.''

His dark gaze traveled her face. ''Yet you're here now.''

Nic felt heat warm her face every place his eyes rested. He

was no ordinary man. He possessed extraordinary strength. There was nothing weak or passive about him. "I want what's best for my family."

He suddenly reached out, touched her temple with the pad of her thumb. "And not for you?"

She shivered as his thumb caressed the arch of her brow. "I need very little."

His thumb stroked along her hairline to the curve of her jaw. "You might be surprised."

Her face suddenly felt so naked, so bare—as if he'd peeled away some false self, leaving her real self exposed. She wanted him to touch her again, wanted his thumb to find her mouth, wanted his hands to frame her face, wanted him to surround her with his strength.

Bone to bone. Skin to skin.

Heart to heart.

Nic bit her lower lip, drawing the soft skin hard between her teeth.

She pulled away, turning from him. He needed a wife. He thought he'd found his queen. And yet in a matter of days she intended to leave him.

He caught her shoulders, wouldn't let her retreat. "I see the sadness in your eyes again, and last night we were interrupted, but I don't think we will be again."

"There's no sadness."

But his fingers were firm on her shoulders. "No sadness? Why, *laeela,* you have the Sahara in your eyes—endless, speechless, lonely."

"I'm not lonely." How could he read her so well? There were times it felt like he was part of her...another half of her...how could anyone—much less a man—understand her so well?

"You have been alone too long." Lowering his head, he kissed her forehead, very very gently. "I think it is the fate of being such a beautiful princess. There is no one as beautiful as you—"

"Malik."

He cupped her cheek with his hand. "Life in a high stone tower."

"No. It's not like that. I haven't lived like that. I'm not—" She broke off, swallowing hard.

"Not what?"

How to tell him that she wasn't who he believed her to be? That all his assumptions were wrong because she wasn't the good, virtuous Chantal but Nic, the one who did what she wanted to do, the one who'd taken Chantal's place to keep Malik's necessary marriage from taking place.

Everything he needed, she'd prevented.

Everything he wanted, she'd keep him from having.

This was wrong. She was wrong. Nic clasped Malik's hand, pressing his palm more tightly to her cheek. She met his gaze and in his eyes she saw kindness. Such compassion. It was almost as if he knew she harbored secrets that could hurt him, and yet he'd already forgiven her.

But it couldn't be.

He didn't know...he couldn't...*could he?*

He released her, stepped away, returning to the fire where he prodded a burning log with a stick. The log rolled over, wood popping, sparks shooting high. "So, are you going to tell me?"

There was so much to tell him. But she'd been playing the charade too long. Nic couldn't figure a way out.

"Just say it," he said coolly.

"Can we sit down?" Nic's legs had begun to shake with fear and fatigue. She knew she had to start opening up a little. She'd suffocate if she didn't.

He took a seat on the dark crimson carpet with the gold and black threads. Nic sat down near him and was relieved he didn't pull away. "I'm worried."

He waited.

Her heart pounded. She felt almost dizzy. "I'm worried about the future." The words tumbled from her lips. "I'm worried about Melio. I'm worried about my grandparents, worried about Lilly—"

"And us. You're worried about us."

"I am."

His jaw jutted. He suddenly looked very weary. "I am, too."

"You are?"

He nodded slowly. "I'm also concerned about the future."

She heard the weight of the world in his voice. Please don't let her be the cause of his unhappiness. Please don't let her add to his burdens. "Why?"

"I don't believe in divorce. I don't want to marry to be divorced."

CHAPTER ELEVEN

HE DID doubt her, then.

"I'm not modern enough for us to marry and live apart the way some royals do," he added decisively.

Nic rubbed her fingers against the plush rug. "If we married I wouldn't want to live apart."

"*If* we married," he said, repeating her words, revealing her own noncommittal words. "You haven't made up your mind."

She wanted to protest, but her mind stayed blank and she just looked at him, wondering how on earth someone got from here to there, how chasms were crossed, oceans traveled, mountains climbed. She didn't have the strength anymore. Didn't have the courage right now, either.

The sky looked so big. The stars so high. Nic had never felt so small. Helplessly she reached for him, touching the back of his hand, her fingers sliding over his, covering them. "I want to be with you."

"Just tonight, or forever?"

If she answered honestly, and said just tonight, there'd be no tonight. If she lied and said forever, there'd be tonight but no forever.

There was no way to win this one.

He lifted his hand, pressed his fingers up against hers, and she wrapped her fingers around him. "I'm scared of marriage. It terrifies me."

"Because of Armand?"

Back to the game, the charade, the mask that Nic hated wearing. "I've just…never…wanted to be married." She couldn't be Chantal and herself any longer. She could only be herself. She could only speak for herself. "I just never fantasized about getting married, having babies. That was more Joelle and—" She broke off, swallowed and tried again. "Then I grew up, and saw that the fairy tale belongs in books. Once married, your options are limited.''

''And what are our options again?''

She marveled at his calm. ''Once you marry, you give up your freedom to choose. You don't get to be with anyone else, you have no more partners, no more different paths—''

''But how many paths do you really have, *laeela?* As a Ducasse princess, your options are limited.''

Maybe that's why she was frustrated. She didn't have the choice others had, couldn't just do what she pleased. Duty and obligation had hung over her head since birth.

''Besides,'' he continued, ''I don't feel limited. When I was younger I enjoyed being a bachelor, but I'm midway through my thirties now. I know what I want.''

''But it's not me you want. Not really.''

''But I do. Really.''

''Because of Melio, and the Mediterranean ports.''

''Initially.''

Her heart pounded, and yet she felt a disconnect from her body. ''What about me do you want?''

''Everything.''

''Because I'm a princess—''

''Because you're smart, spirited, independent, interesting.''

Nic didn't know how to reply to that. What was she supposed to think...feel? ''But you wouldn't marry me if I weren't a Ducasse.''

''And you wouldn't marry me if I weren't a Nuri.''

She was getting nowhere. ''I don't see how our marriage would work. We're both so strong and opinionated—''

''You think a marriage between a strong person and a weak person would be better? You think we're both better off with a spineless partner, one with frozen emotions?''

She searched his eyes. Did he mean it? Could he really accept her—hothead, stubborn streak, and all?

She moved to withdraw her hand and yet he wouldn't let her fingers go. ''What are you afraid of—and it's not sex. I know that much.''

Nic glanced down at their hands, fingers linked. It was good like this, comforting touching like this, but the warmth and comfort of joined hands could quickly become a ball and chain. "Marriage traps a woman."

"No."

"You're a man, you don't know."

"I'm a man. And I'd never trap a woman."

Her nails dug into her palms. "It's not even a choice men make. It just happens. Marriage...motherhood...children. It changes a woman. Your priorities change...they must change."

The heat in his eyes burned her. He stared at her so intensely it made her almost dizzy. "Is that such a bad thing?"

"It is if you value your freedom."

"And your freedom is so valuable?"

Nic was finding it harder and harder to breathe. The air felt heavy, close, pressing in on them. He didn't understand, he hadn't seen what she'd seen—her mother's career ended, her incredible voice and talent hidden from the world, her energy devoted to supporting her father's efforts, and then Chantal, locked away in a chateau in La Croix, trapped. Ignored. Lied to. "It is to me."

She looked away, remembering the delicate gold birdcage she'd seen earlier in the day with the pretty orange and yellow birds inside. Her heart had gone out to the tiny songbirds. It'd kill her to become what Chantal had become. She'd rather die than be trampled by a person she'd trusted...

"You'd clip my wings," she whispered, feeling tears start to thicken her throat. "I'd hate it." She swallowed the threat of tears. "And I'd hate you for it."

He brought her hand to his mouth, kissed her curled fingers. "Hate is such a strong word."

She looked at him, her chest tightened, heart knotted. "Hate is such a strong feeling."

He released her hand and leaned back, letting the fire warm him. "You know hate, then?"

Her nerves were frayed. She'd said things she'd never intended to say. "I did love someone once," she said after a long moment's silence. "And it couldn't work. Denying the love was so hard. It did something to me. Broke something in me."

"Your heart," he supplied softly.

Nic shrugged uneasily. She didn't believe much in romance and Valentines, and no one had ever said life would be simple, but she'd never expected it to get so challenging so quickly, either. "Getting over Daniel took me years. Forgetting a love doesn't happen all at once. I had to work at it, over and over. There were days I didn't think I'd make it without picking up the phone and calling him."

"Did you pick up the phone?"

"No. But I wanted to." She closed her eyes. *Badly.*

"What happened?"

"By the second year I'd learned to ride the pain out. And date like mad. I must have been out every night of the week." She had to make him understand, had to get him to see. "I'm not innocent anymore. I've lived enough to know the way the world works, how relationships evolve. Sooner or later you'd want me to be something, someone, other than I am."

"Maybe you did have a bad first marriage, but your parents— they were happy. Everyone knows they were extremely close."

Nic flexed her fingers. "Mom shouldn't have given up her career. It shouldn't have happened."

"It would have been difficult for her to tour, be with your father, and have a family."

"*Exactly.*" She shook her head. "And you might not think it now, or know it now, but eventually I wouldn't be what you wanted. I wouldn't be what you needed. You'd try to change me. It happens all the time. People fall in love with one thing, but eventually its not enough—" She broke off.

Malik studied her for a long moment before getting to his feet, and tugged her up, too. "We need a change of scenery. Come."

The Citadel's Moorish doorways were horseshoe shaped, dramatic arches carved of wood and stone, ornate lattice work and elegant filigree. Each of the arches in the fortress was unique and when Malik led her through a doorway into a bedroom, Nicolette froze.

Candles flickered on the low round table by the bed, in the sconces on the wall, in the niches tucked around the opulent bedroom.

"Where are we?" she asked, watching Malik deliberately close the thick dark wood doors, locking the latch.

"My bedroom."

He pressed her against the wall, his hands framing her face

then sliding through her hair, his fingers threading between the long silky strands. "I want you." His voice sounded rough with desire. "And you can trust me, *laeela*. I won't let you down."

Nic swallowed, holding the tears back. He was talking about Armand. He was referring to the horrible life Chantal had led in La Croix but he didn't understand that she wasn't that woman. Compared to Chantal, Nic had had it easy. Her life was uncomplicated.

But she couldn't hold back the rush of emotion. She loved the feel of his chest against hers, loved the strength of his ribs and hips. He was hard—nearly as hard as the wall—and she loved being caught like this, loved being covered like this, her body hidden from all, reserved for just him.

She lifted her lips, wanting to feel him take her mouth.

Wanting to feel him take her—finally.

She was such a strong person, so determined, and yet despite all her strength and drive, she yearned to feel a connection with another. And she felt that bond with him.

He kissed her, covering her mouth with his, and with his hands braced on either side of her head she felt his body brush hers, a slow, lazy contact that left her craving more. She pressed up against his long torso, bringing her hips to meet his, sighing with pleasure when she felt the hard ridge in his trousers.

Malik lifted his head, lips curving wryly. "Do all men feel this way about you?" he asked, even as his hand trailed down one loose tendril of hair, across her shoulder, over her collarbone, to the peak of her breast.

"Like how?"

"Like they can't live without you." His palm covered her right breast, her sensitive nipple hidden in the palm of his hand. "As if life wouldn't be worth anything if you weren't there."

Nic swallowed, trying to think when her body was melting, sending conflicting signals to her brain. Desire, hunger…so hard to stay focused on the practical and the plan. "I don't think that's the common response men have to me, no."

"What about the one you loved all those years ago? What was his name?"

He was kneading her breast, fingers playing the soft tissue. She forced her fuzzy brain to clear. "Daniel?"

"Yes."

She tried not to gasp as he leaned into her, his knee parting her thighs and she felt his hard thigh press against the apex of her legs, heightening sensation not just there, but everywhere.

She might as well have been naked. His skin was so warm against hers, she felt her temperature rise, hotter and hotter and as his hand caressed the length of her, shaping from her breast to her waist, hip, and back again she thought she'd go up in flames any moment.

Nic shivered as his hand returned to her breast, his fingers burning through her thin *jellaba*, her breast aching in his hand, the nipple hard and sensitive. Pressed as she was to the wall, his hips held her still so each caress of his fingers made her dance against him, shuddering with pleasure.

She could feel his heat and strength throughout her body. She'd become a dancing girl, trembling against him, arching helplessly, needing more than just his hands on her breasts, wanting his hands on naked skin—her belly, her hips, between her legs. She wrapped her arms around his shoulders, drew him closer. "Blow out the candles," she begged in his ear. "Blow out the candles and let's just be together."

He stripped her in the dark, leisurely removing each item, not that they were difficult to take off. She was wearing only her thin cotton nightgown covered by the modest *jellaba*. But in the dark, with Malik's hands slowly wandering over her, Nic felt as if she wore gold and silk threads, gossamer fabrics of great beauty.

She didn't speak. He didn't speak, and his touch was that of a man who had infinite time. His whole pleasure seemed centered on exploring her, hands lightly caressing the curves of her body. His lips followed his hands, his mouth brushing across her heated skin savoring her softness, her warmth, her texture.

When he knelt at her feet, she took a step backwards. "Not that," she protested. "Not yet."

He kissed the inside of her thigh. "I'm not doing that. Not yet."

She felt his smile against her thigh and it made her smile. She knew him so well already, could picture his silent amusement, the tolerant gleam in his eye. His confidence knew no end.

With him kneeling at her feet, his hands traced the line of her leg, from the curve of her buttock, to the indentation where cheek met thigh, and down the back of her thighs to her knees. His fingertips drew invisible patterns at the back of her knees and then inside her kneecaps, light deft strokes that made her feel so hollow on the inside, and then his hands were teasing down her shins, circling her ankles, finding her sensitive insteps and between her toes.

By the time he'd reached her toes she felt as if she were humming with energy. She felt deliciously awake, her senses alert. Eager.

Standing, Malik stripped off his clothes and reaching for Nicolette, pulled her into his arms, letting their warm naked bodies just touch, and Nic drew a small breath, responding to the brush of his body against hers, aware of things she might not have felt if the lights had been on. She felt the smooth hard plane of his chest, the way his hip bone pressed against her skin, the silky hair at the juncture of his legs. He was so firm, and strong, and she loved the way she fit against him, loved how his arms wrapped around her.

When he lifted her into his arms and headed for the bed, Nic pressed her face to his neck and inhaled the spicy scent of the fragrance sill lingering on his warm skin. His biceps pressed against her soft breast, his hand clasped her naked bottom, and desire shot through her, sharp, intense, demanding.

He placed her in the middle of his enormous bed, but Nic didn't lie passively beneath him. She encircled his shoulders, drew him down to her, felt the rigid length of him nudge her thighs even as she offered him her mouth. His jaw scraped across her skin, the new growth of his beard making her own skin feel raw, and with the cool silk coverlet beneath her heated skin, she felt incredibly wanton.

In the dark, with her sight denied, all the other senses became highly tuned. She could smell the smoke of the fire in his hair, taste the mint of tea on his breath, feel the firm satin texture of his skin, and the dense, thick muscle.

He didn't even need to ask her to do anything. As his hard body touched hers, she opened her legs for him, wanting to be with him, thinking nothing had ever been more natural in her life.

He filled her slowly, entering her with remarkable control, ensuring she had plenty of time to adjust to his size. Nic hadn't realized he was so well endowed until the sense of fullness was almost overwhelming.

Her breath caught in her throat, and she wrapped her fingers around his upper arms trying to make this easier. Malik kissed her slowly. His tongued traced her lips, teasing the swollen lower lip, and as her body relaxed, he clasped her bottom, lifting her hips, allowing her to better accommodate him.

He moved slowly, his muscles sleek beneath her hands. He sank into her, deep, steady strokes, each thrust of his narrow hips powerful yet controlled. She loved the feel of him, relished his languid grace, the warmth of his skin, the satiny texture of his lower back and buttocks.

He already seemed to understand her body intimately, touching her with deft skill, taking his time in building the tension. She was grateful he didn't race to a conclusion, grateful that he, too, seemed to find their joining ultimately satisfying, and yet the friction of their bodies settled into a rhythm satisfying and yet not, because the pleasure demanded more. Each thrust into her made her need another. She met his driving hips, lifting up to meet him, push against him and the tension built.

"Slow," she whispered, fingers kneading his shoulders. "Slow. I don't want this to—"

She broke off, closed her eyes, trying to stop the first tremor, not wanting to reach orgasm yet, not wanting anything about this amazing night to end, but her muscles were wound too tight, the nerves stretched, and his deep thrusting pushed her ever closer to the brink of no return.

Nic kissed Malik with near desperation. She wished she could tell him how right this felt, how as crazy as it sounded, everything about them made sense to her. She'd never felt so right with anyone before. But it was impossible to speak. Words were impossible. He was claiming her, his body demanding her. He buried himself in her, harder, faster, a silent possession which sent Nicolette over the edge, shattering, one intense contraction after another.

Malik came even as she did, and she felt his hard body surge and shudder in her arms, his jaw clenched as he struggled to contain his passion. Tears came to her eyes as she held him tightly, wrapping her arms more closely around his shoulders, listening to the fierce pounding of his heart beneath her ear. His body still throbbed inside hers, making her own body pulse in small aftershocks of pleasure. It was such simple lovemaking, she thought, kissing his chest, right above his heart, and yet it was the most satisfying experience she'd ever known.

Malik shifted, turning them both so she lay cradled against his chest. They lay like that for long minutes, utterly quiet.

Malik's royal bedchamber was dark and yet in the dark Nicolette saw colors she'd never seen before. Making love with him had been everything she'd ever wanted, and more. She'd never felt this close to anyone, nor so loved. When he was in her, part of her, she truly felt as if they were one.

With her cheek resting on his chest, she let the steady beat of his heart sink into every bone and muscle, and the peace stayed with her. The minutes stretched. She exhaled slowly, inhaled, exhaled again, and she thought just maybe everything was going to work out.

Nic felt like talking, really talking. Usually after sex she just wanted to get up, shower and put her clothes on. It wasn't that sex had ever been bad, but afterward, she hadn't felt comfortable with the intimacy part. But that was different now. She wanted to know everything he thought. Wanted to feel what he felt.

"Was that okay?" she whispered tentatively.

She felt a rumble in his chest. "Yes," he answered. "Was it okay for you?"

She sighed and smiled in the dark. "I thought it was amazing. I've never felt anything like that before."

"I'm glad it gave you pleasure." He stretched a little. Their bodies were still damp and her long hair fell in a tangled heap across his chest.

Nic pushed up on one elbow, looked down at Malik and even though it was dark she wanted to face him, feel his breath, be close to him. "It wasn't just pleasure, it was…more. You gave me…" She didn't even know how to explain it, but what they did, what they were together was perfect. Nothing had ever felt more right in her life.

"Yes?"

But she couldn't find the words. Instead she bent her head, found his mouth, kissed him tenderly, and as her lips teased his, she touched his cheek, feeling the sharp bristles of his beard along his jawbone.

"You're beautiful," she whispered wonderingly, letting her hand slide down his jaw, to his chest, her nails dragging lightly across his nipple and the unyielding muscle.

"I'm not."

"You are."

"My nose is too big," he complained, palming the fullness of her breasts, playing her nipples until they pebbled in his hands.

She felt her womb clench, flooding her body with warmth. "It's not," she whispered, trying to ignore the electric current running through her, the dampness between her legs, the fierce desire building all over again.

"My mouth's too wide," he added, cupping her bottom in his hands and pulling her back on top of him.

She shuddered at the rigid feel of him. He'd recovered already and his erection pressed between her thighs, the thick tip already sliding against her warm slick flesh. "The best lips I've ever kissed," she murmured hoarsely.

"And the last lips you'll kiss," he answered, wrapping his hands around her thighs, and parting her wide.

Even in the dark Nic gasped. Gripping his shoulders, her thighs spread wide in his hands, she could do nothing to stop him from enjoying her his way.

He was so naturally sensual, so comfortable with bodies and the physical, that as he rubbed her naked, sensitized flesh against his rigid shaft she felt as if there was a whole world of love-making she knew nothing about. His touch demanded trust. His skill was far beyond anything she'd ever known before.

Again he let his erection slide across her wetness, and she closed her eyes, seeing bright sparks, the pleasure and sensation so intense. She could feel the straining tip, the warm silken head running along her cleft, and she squirmed, trying to take him, wanting to take him. Once, twice, his swollen shaft slid across her opening, teasing her where she was so moist and pliant.

But he wouldn't enter her. His lips brushed her bare shoulder. His fingers kneaded her thighs, parting her wider and wider until she thought she'd break.

"What are you doing to me?" she demanded, panting.

"I was just remembering a conversation," he said, one hand leaving her thigh to reach between their bodies. He found the damp heat of her. Slowly he slid one finger into her core, which felt as if it had come alive, pulsing around his finger. Yet the slow thrust of his finger gave no relief. The slow, tantalizing touch only crazed her senses.

"Do you remember our conversation about men, women and sex?" he continued, turning his finger slightly, stirring every possible nerve ending.

Nic bucked against his hand. She needed more. God, she needed more. "No."

"You were saying that in your experience—"

"I can't talk," she interrupted hoarsely, as he slid his finger out of her warm body, and she felt utterly lost, completely bereft. "I can't even think."

He lifted her up by the rib cage, holding her torso above him, and his lips found her navel, and he licked his way from her belly button to her sternum, completely avoiding her breasts. "I'll help you then. You were telling me, I believe," he said, letting the air cool her damp hot skin, "that most men have no idea how to touch a woman."

Nic squeezed her eyes shut. Oh dear God, not this, not now. Not that conversation.

He arched her backward, bending her back at the waist and as he did so, his hard shaft thrust against her exposed flesh, the delicate bud so ripe it hurt.

"You were saying men had no idea what women wanted—"

"Malik!"

He stroked the rigid length of him against her tender flesh over and over. "Now help me, Princess," he said stunningly conversational. "Just where is this clitoris?"

My God. He was going to melt her brain. She was losing it. She burned and throbbed everywhere. Her skin felt hot and she felt desperate. "I eat my words," she choked. *"Please."*

And then the tip of his finger found her, right at the sweet spot between her legs. "Am I getting close?"

"Stop talking," she gasped, breathing shallowly in great gulps of air. His touch was exquisite. That delicious play of his finger.

He stopped touching her. "I'm afraid I don't know what to do—"

She leaned over him, covered his mouth in a desperate kiss.

"You do know, you're doing it, please Malik, please, you're making me mad."

He kissed her back, drawing the tip of her tongue into his mouth, and sucking on the tip, tight hard rhythmic sucks that had her swinging her hips.

And then catching her hips, he plunged into her, hard, deep, burying himself in her tight sheath and she cried out, and he pulled her against him, so that her nipples rubbed against the crisp hair of his chest and his hard abdomen pressed to her naked belly and the heat was intense, the heat inside her an inferno. She was so hot, so wet she was melting inside. She gave up, gave her body to him, gave the rest of her resistance, too.

He'd captured her whole—heart, mind, body and soul—and the orgasm was spectacular, but nothing like the release of control.

She'd found love. She'd found the other half of her soul.

Nic didn't remember falling asleep after they'd made love the second time. She didn't remember anything but the joy and comfort of being in Malik's arms. But when she woke, dawn was breaking, a pale blue skin beyond the shuttered window.

She stirred sleepily and Malik kissed the top of her head.

"You're mine now," he said, his deep voice gruff. "You're only mine."

"Mmmm," she agreed, snuggling closer. "I know."

He stroked her hip beneath the light silk coverlet. "No more maybe about the wedding."

"No." And then it was like a massive stone fortress breaking. Nic saw light, way down at the end of the tunnel. There was no reason not to marry Malik. She should just do it. It was the right thing for everyone—Melio, the country's economy, her family. "I'm glad we're getting married in six days." She curled against him, "It's just six days, isn't it?"

"Five now."

"Sounds good." She lifted her face, brushed her mouth across his chin and sighed when he found her lips, kissed her deeply. "It'll be nice to get it over with."

"You're sure?"

"Yes." And wrapped in his arms, Nic pictured the ceremony they'd have in Atiq. She'd wear one of the new gowns made for her, and Malik would look gorgeous no matter what he wore and the whole picture felt right.

Except for one little but crucial detail. Lilly.

"I want Lilly here," Nic said, clasping Malik's arm, needing to feel his strength. "She has to be here."

"She will be."

"Her grandparents, the Thibaudets, might not let her—"

"They will." He kissed the top of her head. "Don't worry, *laeela*. I'll take care of everything."

CHAPTER TWELVE

NIC stretched, rolling onto her side with a deeply contented sigh of pleasure. Now that was brilliant sex. Just one night and Malik had spoiled her forever.

Opening her eyes she discovered Malik standing, arms crossed, watching her from the front of the bed.

She sat up, combed her long hair back, the covers at her waist. "You're dressed."

"I've been in my office working the past couple hours but I returned to have breakfast in bed."

His expression made her breath catch in her throat. "Are we talking orange juice and scrambled eggs?" But her body was already responding, her bare breasts tingling, the nipples peaking.

His gaze rested on her full breasts. "Sure."

She felt heat rise through her, a blush that pinked her skin from head to toe. "I mean, on a *plate*."

His deep laugh echoed, the sexy husky sound coiling in her tummy, making her feel hotter, emptier. She could almost feel his hands on her, his hard body slowly filling her, all silky heat and strength until she was dissolving around him. Pleasure. Endless pleasure, endless sensation.

"If you insist," he mocked, moving to ring for the breakfast tray. It arrived minutes later and Malik took the tray from the male steward, carrying the tray to the bed where Nic waited.

Malik lounged on the bed next to her, his powerful body at ease and cradling her coffee, Nic felt as if the night had been one long, sexual dream. The lovemaking had reached a level of eroticism Nic had never experienced before, and yet it had felt completely natural, too.

"How do you feel?" he asked, popping a miniature almond and apricot pastry into his mouth.

The muscles deep inside her clenched. He was more man than

ten men together. Again heat swept through her, burning her. "Fine. Thank you."

He lay on his side, his elbow propping his weight. "Have you changed your mind about the wedding?"

"No. Have you?"

He laughed once. "I knew I shouldn't have gotten intimate with you. Now you'll have forever confused love and sex."

Nic nearly rolled her eyes. "I've never confused love and sex before."

"Yes, but was the sex that good before?"

Blushing all over again, Nic gave him a reproving look. "No one's ever made me beg before."

"I withheld nothing."

Her blush deepened. No, he had not. He gave her everything—and more.

"I want you." His voice suddenly dropped, throbbing with raw naked need. "I want you like you won't believe. What I feel for you—what I want to do with you—" He shook his head, warningly. "This is dangerous, *laeela.*"

She couldn't breathe. She wanted him in her, now, filling her. She felt fierce, demanding, her body all melting need, a need that could only be answered by him. "You might be right about that."

His hungry gaze held hers. "I had an idea."

"Yes?"

"I think we should get married in Melio."

It was the last thing she'd expected him to say. "Marry...in Melio?"

"You could have your family with you—"

"I thought we were going to have just a traditional wedding here. You know, televise the ceremony, big national holiday."

"We'll just broadcast the ceremony from there."

Panic raced through her. "It'd be too much of a strain on my family. My grandparents aren't well—"

"Which is why we'd go there. There'd be no traveling for your family. The cathedral is just down the street from the palace."

She leaned forward, planted a desperate kiss on his lips, trying to distract him. "We can see them later...after our honeymoon.

Really, Malik, let's not complicate things. It'd be too much fuss. Royal weddings are such big deals in Europe.''

He wasn't to be distracted. "Perhaps we ought to think about your grandparents' needs. I know how it feels to worry about one's family. I know what a comfort it is when you know that your family is looked after, and I know it'd greatly reassure your grandfather to know that while ours is an arranged marriage, it isn't cold, or unbearable.''

Did he even know what he was doing? "There would be so many preparations.''

"Taken care of.''

Her mouth dry, she reached for her juice glass off the tray and sipped slowly, trying to give her mind a chance to clear. "What do you mean...taken care of?''

"As I said to your grandfather earlier—''

"What?''

He wrapped his hand around hers, securing the glass in her fingers. "You better drink. You look pale.''

But she couldn't drink. She couldn't think.

He urged the glass to her lips, tilted it against her mouth. "You need some sugar. Drink up. I don't want you fainting on me now, not when we've so much to do before we fly out.''

Nic nearly bit through the glass. She forced herself to swallow one mouthful before she pushed the glass away. "I don't understand any of this.''

"You're a widow, not a divorcee. You're entitled to a lavish second wedding, and so this morning, after waking I've been on the phone. I called your grandfather first, and then had my office staff begin shifting all wedding arrangements from Atiq to Porto Terza.''

He'd called Grandfather...

Nic blinked. "What did you say to him?''

"That you were here, and you'd agreed to marry me—''

"Who did you tell him I was?''

Malik looked at her as if she'd lost her mind. "Who do you think?''

She reached for her juice, slurped it down, and wiping off her mouth she looked up at him. "You told him I was Chantal.''

"Yes.''

"And Grandpapa said...?''

"That no, you couldn't be Chantal because Chantal was in La Croix. He'd just spoken to her a few minutes earlier."

Nic's eyes searched his. "Malik?"

"Yes, *laeela?*"

"What are you thinking right now?"

"That I have an imposter princess."

Pretty accurate description. She set her glass down very carefully. Thank goodness he wasn't getting angry. She didn't think she could have handled that on top of all this. "I am a Ducasse princess."

"But not Chantal."

"No." He smiled at her, rather pleasantly actually, considering the circumstances.

Her stomach felt funny. She'd drunk the juice too fast, maybe. "I'm…"

"Nicolette."

She nodded awkwardly. "How'd you guess?"

His black eyebrows lifted. "Are you serious?"

"I just thought…"

"We've spent the night together. It's been pretty intimate, but that's not how I knew." He hesitated and her heart lurched sickeningly. "I've always known," he admitted. "From the moment you arrived."

"What?"

"I've spoken with the real Chantal on the phone before. You're smart, Nic, and you're beautiful, but you're nothing like your older sister."

She lay back on the bed, dragged the covers to her shoulders, and stared at the ceiling. "That's why you called grandfather."

"He knew you were here all along."

"Just like you did." She squeezed her eyes shut. This was just getting worse and worse. "Why didn't you confront me? Why didn't you make me confess the truth?"

His laughter drifted over. "I was…amused. I found your charade entertaining."

He didn't just say that. He couldn't have just meant that. She'd been in emotional turmoil and he'd been having fun? "So what happens now?"

"We go to Melio and get married."

"You still want to get married?"

He made a rough sound, impatient, disbelieving. *"Yes."*

"What else did he say, my grandfather?"

"That you had it coming." Malik's laughter was soft, goading. "He said to remind you that he'd once said—"

"I'd meet my match." She opened her eyes again, feeling as if she were riding a roller coaster. What was happening? How had everything turned so fast? Her head was spinning. "Maybe we could just stay here and skip the big wedding."

"Skip the wedding?"

"I'll be your mistress."

The covers came flying off her and Malik loomed over her, his expression incredulous. Malik, for all his sensuality, was quite old-fashioned. "You didn't just say that."

She felt a quiver shoot through her. "Our children could still be your heirs."

"Make a princess a mistress?" he drawled derisively. "I don't think so."

She'd always been such a truthful person. All her life she'd pushed at the limits, refused to accept the boundaries, but at least she'd always been honest. "You wanted Chantal."

"But I've made love to Nic."

She shook on the inside, and she realized she hadn't just been lying to him. She'd been lying to herself. She loved him. She'd fallen in love with him.

"Malik." She hadn't realized she'd even spoken his name aloud until he reached for her, lowering the weight of his body, his hips and chest covering the naked length of her. She shuddered at the pleasure of his body on hers and closed her eyes, overwhelmed by everything. She'd fallen for him. So hard.

But how?

Opening her eyes she looked into his silver gaze, the cool depth lit by a small silent smile, she knew how.

He was amazing. Gorgeous and physical, sexual and sensual, he was smart. And patient. Tolerant.

"You don't have to marry me just because we made love," she said, her voice hoarse.

He kissed the side of her neck. "You're still running away."

"No."

"You can't run."

"I can." But her voice wobbled.

Looking down at her, his eyes warmed to hot liquid silver. "You can't," he chided gently. "I won't let you go."

But she knew those were just words. He was teasing her, playing with her. Enjoying her.

And God, he did enjoy her, didn't he? She felt it in every nerve and fiber of her body. She felt his humor and pleasure, felt his interest, felt his concern. He would always do what was best for her. He might say he'd never let her go, but if she wanted out, wanted to leave, he'd never keep her with him against her will.

"I never planned on getting married." It felt as if the words were wrung from her. "I never planned on staying in Baraka."

His smile faded and he shifted his weight, moving off of her. "I know."

They spent the rest of the day apart, even had their meals alone, but late that evening Malik came to her bed and his kiss was hard, possessive, territorial. Malik stretched her out beneath him and she felt the volatility of their emotions in the intensity of their lovemaking. He wanted her, and he wanted her to know that there was no way in hell he was letting her go.

Two days later they returned to Atiq, but they weren't staying for more than a few hours. Malik was giving her time to pack and then they'd be off, heading to Melio where her family was waiting.

In her room, Nic asked Alea for help. "I need a really good hair stylist," Nic said, telling Alea exactly what she intended to do. Alea looked horrified but Nic felt calm. Malik knew who she was. It was time to become a blonde again. Nic was more than ready to rinse all signs of Chantal away.

Nic wore a robe and head covering on the way to the airport. She wasn't ready to shock all of Malik's household staff. Let Alea pass the word while Nic was in Melio.

They boarded on schedule, and Malik's royal jet took off from Atiq's airport at two in the afternoon. The flight from Atiq to Porto Terza in Melio would take about three and a half hours but three and a half hours sounded like forever to Nic right now.

They'd only been in the air a few minutes when Malik leaned

forward and tugged the head covering off. "Can I see what my fiancée looks like?"

She silently endured Malik's inspection. His intense examination reminded her of her first day in Baraka, when he'd circled her twice, studying her from head to toe. "Do I pass?"

"Is that your natural color?"

"You don't like it."

"You're very blond."

She turned her head, stared out the window biting her lip. But she couldn't keep her temper in check. "You don't have to marry me."

"You could already be pregnant."

What kind of answer was that? "Well, don't do me any favors!"

He surprised her by laughing. "I won't." His laughter faded and still studying her, he asked, "Does Daniel still work in the palace garage?"

"Yes, why?" Nic blinked in surprise. "And how did you remember his name?"

"I'm very good with names." He gave her a long, level look. "Do you still love him?" Malik's silver gaze was no longer cool. He seethed with emotion.

"No. I don't love him. I'm marrying you."

"Do you love me?"

She pointedly held his burning gaze. "Do you love me?"

He said nothing. He just looked at her as if he knew her, and understood her. He looked so kindly and intently that she felt hot sparks shoot through her belly, into her veins.

He wanted her. He loved her. Maybe he hadn't said *I, Malik Roman Nuri, love you,* but the words, it was there in his body, in his eyes, in his heart.

He might not even use the word love in the Western sense, but the emotion she saw in his eyes was the emotion she wanted to feel when the man she loved looked at her.

She felt a surge of raw emotion so strong it hurt.

Malik unbuckled his seat belt. "Let's get something to drink from the bar. I think we both need to relax."

Three hours later the jet circled once over Porto Terza before making its final descent.

Safely buckled back in her seat, Nic's breath caught in her

throat as she gazed at Porto Terza from the air. In the late afternoon sunlight, the ocean gleamed purple and turquoise, the surface of the water sparkling in sheets of silver white, and Porto Terza's historic buildings shone a rich creamy beige against cliffs of dark green. *Melio.*

Nic suddenly reached for Malik's hand. "I'm nervous."

He grimaced. "You're not alone, princess. I am, too."

The plane's wheels touched the tarmac and settled into a smooth taxi down the length of the private runway. They'd arrived at the Ducasse family's airport, a small terminal reserved for the royal family and visiting dignitaries, and Nic's insides were turning over again. She couldn't pretend it was excitement or happiness. It was dread. And fear. She'd come home to Melio to marry—a sultan, no less.

A chauffeured Mercedes sedan waited at the airport for them. Within minutes they were entering the palace gates and sweeping up the grand driveway, shaded by palm trees planted over a hundred years ago.

The palace was a graceful stone building with a Palladian entrance, a domed center court, and elegant wings flanking either side. Massive marble lions guarded the front door and Nic shot Malik a nervous smile as they climbed the front steps. "This is home," she said, nodding at the navy uniformed staff members who'd quickly assembled in the hall to greet them.

Malik took a moment to gaze around the grand entrance. The Porto Terza palace was smaller than many European palaces, and yet the charm lay in its style and scale. Although the central staircase was quite grand, and all the floors and columns were two shades of marble—pink and gold—the palace interior was sunny and warm like the late afternoon sunshine outside.

Footsteps sounded above, and Joelle appeared at the top of the stairs. "Nicolette!" She dashed down the stairs and threw her arms around her sister, whispering in her ear. "You've got everybody in an uproar. What have you done?"

"I don't know," Nic answered weakly.

Joelle drew back, studied Nic's face. "You're really getting married?"

Nic didn't know whether to laugh or cry. She turned, gestured to Malik. "Joelle, the groom's right here."

There were endless introductions for the rest of the evening.

A private predinner reception with Nic's grandparents, King
Remi and Queen Astrid, and then a massive sit down dinner
with nearly all of the King's advisors. Nic had no chance to be
alone with Malik. Her grandfather kept Malik firmly at his side.

Nic went to sit with Queen Astrid once dishes were cleared
and everyone was free to informally socialize. "Are you angry
with me, Grandmama?" she asked nervously.

Her grandmother's stroke last year had made it difficult for
her to speak, but she managed a small smile. "No," Queen
Astrid mouthed. "Grandpapa and I know you."

The next morning Nic woke and her first thought was that
there'd been no word from Chantal. The wedding was in two
days.

Where was she? Why weren't she and Lilly here? They were
supposed to be here. Her grandfather said Chantal had planned
on leaving with Lilly yesterday to help Nic with last minute
wedding details. But Chantal hadn't arrived and Nic went in
search of answers.

Grandfather was worse than no help. He was the bearer of
bad news. "They're not going to make it," he said, motioning
for Nic to move from the doorway and sit in his private office.
"I didn't want to upset you yesterday, not when it was King
Nuri's first day here, but apparently the Thibaudets don't think
it's wise for Lilly to travel so far for such a short period of
time."

Nic felt the old anger return. It was all she could do to keep
her voice quiet. "Then let her come for a couple of weeks! Lilly
hasn't been home to Porto Terza in nearly two years. It was all
she could do to keep her voice quiet. *Two* years, Grandpapa.
Don't you want to see her?"

"Of course I do."

"Then call King Phillipe, tell him you and Grandmama insist
that Lilly come—"

"The child's not well, Nicolette."

Tears started to form in Nic's eyes. "If she's not well it's
because La Croix is bad for her! All I ever hear is how fragile
Lilly is, how small and delicate for her age. Maybe she needs
someone to get her out of there."

"You're being overly dramatic."

Nic stared at him, not understanding how he could ignore the facts. He hadn't seen his granddaughter in fourteen months. He and Grandmama had gone to La Croix to visit Chantal and Lilly a couple months before Lilly's third birthday. Well Lilly was four now. And her grandparents who were just an hour and a half away by plane had had no visit since then.

Was he afraid of the truth? Did it make him feel helpless, powerless, or was he just too tired to face the reality anymore? "The Thibaudets have taken over her life. Chantal has little say in Lilly's upbringing. They've pushed Chantal out—"

"This isn't right. I don't like this." He stood up, leaned on a corner of his desk. "You mustn't speak of Phillipe and Catherine this way. I've known the Thibaudets my whole life. Queen Catherine and your grandmother were close, childhood friends."

Nic swallowed the lump lodged in her throat. "That doesn't mean—" She broke off as her grandfather headed to the window, walking slowly, virtually turning his back on her. He'd aged a decade in the past year. She couldn't stand it.

"I'm going to bring her home, Grandpapa. You don't have to like it. You don't have to agree. You just can't stop me."

CHAPTER THIRTEEN

NIC found Malik in a palace salon with a large group of security experts—Porto Terza's chief of police, the captain from the palace guard, plain-clothes detectives, secret service agents from a half dozen foreign countries.

Apparently all of Europe was showing up. Kings, queens, prince, princesses, duke and duchesses. There were political leaders from every superpower, industry leaders from the business sector, fashion scions, celebrities with connections, even the American president's wife had just flown in and was staying at the Porto Palace Hotel, Melio's revered five star hotel property.

Joelle had said that with the ceremony taking place at the palace, and the reception in the Porto Palace Hotel's grand ballroom, the sultan was taking no chance with security and she'd been right. Malik was taking no chances.

She listened as Malik conversed with the blond American secret service agent, the American's strong Texas twang giving away his place of birth. It boggled Nic's mind—a Cathedral wedding with Cardinal Juneau presiding followed by a reception for five hundred at the Palace Hotel...

It was enough to make her want to grab her *jellaba* and run for the desert. Instead Nic stepped from the shadows, caught Malik's eye and indicated she needed to speak with him.

He joined her in the hall a few minutes later. "What's happened?" he asked, immediately seeing the stress in her face.

Nic explained quickly. She left nothing out. Due to some archaic La Croix law, Chantal couldn't take Princess Lilly, heir to the throne, out of the country without the King and Queen's permission, and The Thibaudets weren't going to let Lilly come.

She also explained her grandfather's position on it, and how he—who had the power to challenge the Thibaudets—refused to do so. After she'd told him everything she felt the weight

159

return, the heaviness of her heart that had been there for so long now.

She didn't want to hurt or humiliate Malik, but she also knew herself. She couldn't forget what had taken her to Baraka in the first place.

"I went to Baraka to free Lilly." Her heart felt so bruised she could barely look at him. "The only reason I pretended to be Chantal was to find a way to get Lilly out of La Croix. I can't marry you if she isn't here. I made her a *promise*."

He said nothing, his expression calm, unruffled as always.

"I'm asking you to help bring her home for the wedding." Her eyes were gritty and her throat felt raw. "I don't want to say I won't marry you. I don't want to humiliate you. But she has to be here. That was my goal, Malik, that was my objective all along."

"And I assured you that she would be."

"But that was before—"

"Nothing's changed. I gave you my word."

But the morning of the wedding arrived and Nic woke, heart sick. Chantal wasn't here. Lilly wasn't here. Malik was completely uncommunicative. Whenever she asked about Chantal and Lilly, he simply said, "I'm doing everything I can possibly do."

But what exactly did that entail? What had he done? What hadn't he done? And if he was working so hard on getting them here, why weren't they?

It made Nic crazy. She wanted to jump on a plane with the palace guard, fly into La Croix and scoop up Lilly and Chantal and bring them home.

A knock sounded on Nic's bedroom door and Joelle's dark head appeared around the corner. "I've got coffee."

"Then you can come in."

Joelle carried two cups of steaming café au lait to the bed. "You're not up yet?"

"Don't start," Nic groaned, pushing herself into a sitting position. "You sound just like Alea."

Joelle grinned. "I know." She handed Nic her coffee before taking a seat on the foot of the bed. "You've told me all about her. She sounds great."

Nic was going to say something sarcastic but inexplicably her eyes filled with tears.

Joelle's smile disappeared. ''Chantal would be here if she could,'' she said softly, knowing exactly what Nic was thinking. ''But you can't let Chantal's absence ruin your day. This is your wedding day—''

''No. It's not.'' Nic set her coffee down on the night stand. ''I'm not getting married.''

''Nic.''

''I can't.''

''Nic, he's great. It may have been an arranged marriage, but he's…gorgeous, and sexy and—'' her hand gestured as she struggled for words ''—perfect for you.''

''It doesn't matter.'' She slid from the bed, reached for her old white woven robe. It was a super soft cotton robe she'd had forever and simply loved. ''And don't look at me like that. Malik knows.''

''Does he?''

Nic nodded and swallowed, but on the inside, she wasn't so sure. Malik had to know she was serious. She wasn't going to get married without Lilly in Melio. That had been the deal. That was the arrangement from the beginning.

''There are five hundred important people here.'' Joelle rose up on her knees. ''Grandpapa and Grandmama would be shamed—''

''If Grandpapa can ignore Chantal's misery, then he can learn to ignore his own.''

The phone rang, providing momentary distraction. Nic answered the phone, said a quiet yes, and hung up. Things were going to get ugly, Nic thought, taking a deep breath.

''The wedding dress is on its way up.''

There was a quiet rap on the door. When Nic opened the door her heart fell. It was the designer from Baraka. She'd personally flown the gown in. A gown that Nic knew she wasn't going to wear today after all.

''S-salamu alikum.'' Peace on you, the designer said, offering the traditional greeting with a deep bow and a smile.

The woman carried the garment bag to Nicolette's bed and laid it flat. ''I think you'll like the gown,'' she said. ''The sultan has been most anxious that you approve.''

Nic could feel her stomach start to rise. It was like the Danube flooding. She should have talked to Malik this morning, told him she'd meant what she said, asked him to put a stop to the ceremony before it was too late.

But the designer was intent on the task at hand, and she unzipped the garment bag, and drew out a sleek white satin gown with the narrowest shoulder straps imaginable. The gown was cut almost straight across the collarbones, with a very sexy hour glass shape, then flared behind the knees in a long silk train. The train made the dress. The train was hopelessly romantic, a sleek white satin edged with a wide curling ruffle that curved in on itself like icing on a cake.

"Nic," Joelle whispered. "It's like the dress you drew…no sleeves, skinny straps, form fitting curves and not much else."

"No beads, no pearls, no lace, nothing sparkly," Nic recited numbly.

The designer was waiting anxiously for a response. "You're unhappy?"

"No." But Joelle was right, this was the dress she'd sketched on the last night the Ducasse sisters were together, the night before Chantal married Prince Armand. Joelle had been just a teenager, fifteen or sixteen. Chantal had been the mature one at twenty-four. They'd talked about their futures and Chantal had goaded them into drawing their future wedding gowns.

How long ago it seemed. How different things were now compared to then.

"I have to talk to Malik," she choked, queasy, dizzy, unable to let this continue another moment longer. "I have to make a phone call."

Joelle waited, chewing her thumb as Nic dialed Malik's room, but there was no answer. Yet Nic let it ring and ring and ring until the palace switchboard cut in, telling Nic what she already knew—Malik wasn't in his room.

Nic hung up. Stared at the phone, thinking. "Maybe he's already checked into the suite we're using tonight."

"No, he's not." Joelle snapped her fingers. "I completely forgot. He's at the airport meeting the King and Queen of Sweden. They were arriving with members of Spain's royal family and King Nuri thought it'd be nice to welcome them in person."

"Four hours before the wedding?" Panicked, Nic hung the phone up. She had to reach him before this went any further. She couldn't possibly walk down the aisle like this. "Couldn't somebody else do that?"

"Grandpapa was going to go, but King Nuri thought it would be too much for him considering everything that's happening today."

Sensitive of Malik, Nic thought, emotions swinging wildly yet again.

"Your Highness," the designer said, drawing Nicolette's attention, "and this is to hold your veil."

Nic turned around and gaped as the designer presented her with the most magnificent diamond tiara Nic had ever seen.

The tiara was tall, with small fragile arches, and elegant curves and ripples so that the tiara itself seemed to undulate like the desert sands of the Sahara. Within each arch hung a perfect pink tear drop diamond—nine in all—with eight smaller teardrops nestled in the sea of white diamonds below. The arching headband was covered in what looked like a swirling ribbon of miniature pink and white diamonds.

"Incredible," Nic breathed, utterly captivated by the gorgeous pink and white wonder, but with trembling hands she passed the tiara back. "Can't keep it. Far too expensive, obviously an heirloom—"

"It was his mother's. His cousin, Lady Fatima, hand-carried it here today."

"Lady Fatima's here?"

"Indeed. She flew in with her family for the wedding, and brought the crown for you. She'd been keeping it for the sultan's future bride since the sultan's mother died."

Nic turned away, covered her mouth, tried to keep it together. Fatima, who'd waited years for Malik, was here today to lend support.

The designer added with a smile. "Lady Fatima said to remind you that the sultan's beloved must be draped in gold and precious jewels and carried on a table, but that you somehow have managed to miss out on the table."

Nic suddenly laughed, even as tears filled her eyes. Fatima was here. Malik's family was here. How could she not show up? How could she not tell him in advance…just leave him there, in front of five hundred, standing at the altar?

Nic tried to call him over and over during the next three hours but he couldn't be reached, and no one seemed to know anything. Finally it was time to dress and go, or do nothing at all. The moment had come to make a decision.

Joelle stood in Nicolette's room, wearing her pale pink maid of honor gown. She'd been pacing in the hallway until she couldn't bear it anymore and now she was on the verge of tears. "You have to get ready, Nic, or we'll be late. The ceremony begins in thirty minutes."

"I can't—"

"You can! You must." Joelle's eyes welled with tears. "Nic, I don't know what this is about. I don't know if you two had a fight, or you've just got cold feet, but he's been here for you, every step of the way. He cares about you, and I know you love him. It's obvious. It's all over your face."

"I do love him." There was no doubt in her mind about that. "But we weren't ever supposed to be married, we weren't ever supposed to be together. He wanted a different Ducasse—"

"No." Joelle grabbed Nic's wedding dress and shook it in front of her sister. "Maybe he did, maybe he wanted Chantal, but he fell in love with you, so get your dress on and put your tiara on your stubborn blond head and let's go. Because Nic, I know you. You'll never forgive yourself if you hurt him. You love him, and you can't bear to disappoint those that love you, too."

Nic felt an icy shiver rush through her, and goose bumps prickled her skin. That was exactly why she was so upset. Nic had promised Chantal she'd free Lilly. She'd given Chantal her word and it was killing her to let Chantal down. A promise was a promise.

But you also promised Malik. So it must mean it's better to disappoint Malik than Chantal.

"Oh my God." Nic's voice came out broken. "What have I done? What am I doing?" Her chest felt like it was burning up, all ice and heat, all uncontrollable fire. "I do love him. I do and I don't want him standing there, facing everyone, waiting for me."

She blinked and tears fell. "Help me, Joelle. I can't be late."

The distance between the palace and cathedral was less than a mile but it felt like forever to Nic. She was crushed that Chantal and Lilly hadn't come, but she also knew that Malik Nuri was the heart and soul of her future and there was no way she'd stand him up today.

In the back of the chauffeured limousine Joelle squeezed Nic's hand. "Are you okay?"

Nic nodded even though her heart felt like it might explode. Then the car rounded the corner and the Cathedral came into view. Thank God. They'd reached the church with five minutes to spare.

The Cathedral had been built in the Baroque tradition, a lovely domed ceiling painted with a glorious blue and gold vision of heaven complete with angels and all the saints frolicking in eternal joy.

King Remi was waiting for them in the back of the Cathedral. And Nic, who'd been battling for calm, nearly lost her composure when she spotted her grandfather resplendent in his coronation suit, the one he wore for only the most official state business with the purple ribbon and medals of honor.

"Grandpapa," she whispered, leaning forward to kiss him. She smelled the brisk aftershave he'd worn his whole life, a scent old-fashioned and yet elegant, just like him.

His dark eyes filmed with tears. "Tell me you're happy, darling."

She ground her teeth together, knowing she'd walk on fire if she thought it'd give her grandparents peace. They'd been through so much and she knew they were tired. Tired and Worried.

"I'm so happy," she whispered, heart aching, throat sealing closed. Unable to bear so much emotion, Nic impulsively hugged him again, wanting to cling to her childhood for just one more minute. Grandfather Remi to her, King Ducasse to everyone else. "And I'm sorry I spoke sharply to you the other day. I forget you're eighty-five and I'm twenty-seven sometimes."

"You were right." Nic felt her grandfather take a deep shuddering breath. "Your father would never forgive me if I let any of his girls marry, or live, unhappily."

"But I love Malik."

"You should." He drew back, and one of the chapel's dark doors squeaked. A little girl peeked out around the door in a pink silk dress embroidered with great rose-hued flowers.

"Aunt Nicolette?" The soft brown curls, the uncertain smile, the high soft voice of a very young child.

Lilly. "Baby," Nic cried, running toward her niece and swinging her up into her arms. "My little Lilly baby, you're here!"

Lilly's uncertain smile turned positively elfin, the shyness turning into laughter. "I'm not a baby, Aunt Nicolette. I'm four years old. I speak French and Italian and I know how to ski, too."

"You better stop crying," a feminine voice whispered in Nic's ear, even as an arm wrapped around her waist. "You don't want to walk down the aisle with a shiny face."

Chantal. Chantal and Lilly here. Nic couldn't believe it. "What…how…?"

"Grandpapa." Chantal hugged Nic again. "He came for us this morning. He told Phillipe and Catherine they were welcome at the wedding, and he'd like them here, but even if they didn't come, he wanted Lilly and I there." Chantal shrugged. "So here we are."

"Grandpapa did that?"

Chantal nodded. "Well, Malik flew him there, of course. But you already knew that, didn't you?"

No, she didn't, Nic thought, fighting to keep the tears from spilling, but she should have known. Malik was a man of his word.

There was a moment when the organ's triumphant notes filled the glorious fairytale cathedral and the sunlight streamed through the stained-glass windows, and Nic stood at the back of the church, holding her dearest grandfather's arm, seeing her sisters and little Lilly at the front of the church on the left side, and Malik standing on the right, and it was like the moment when she stepped off the yacht in Atiq. Time blurred, lives changed, Nic's senses swam as the past and future came together in a glorious glow of rose, cream and gold.

Nic could smell her flowers—a stunning bouquet of mango calla lilies, conga roses, the most elusive pastel pink tipped cymbidium orchids, and she remembered the way the flower petals had rained down on her head as she stepped off the gangway.

The sun was shining today, just as it had that day, and as the light poured through the high stained-glass window, patterning the guests and floor in bits of blue and gold it was like the domed ceiling of the palace in Baraka. The exotic beauty laden with mystery and promise.

And finally, she could see Malik, her sultan in a long black morning coat, his thick black hair combed back from his handsome face. And when he turned and looked at her from the front of the church it was like the very first moment their eyes met on the harbor wall in Atiq—magic. Just one look and her life would never be the same.

Nic didn't remember walking down the long aisle where each pew was marked with a spray of orchids and rose buds. She didn't remember the prayers, the words spoken, the periodic burst of music, or the cathedral choir. The ceremony was a blur, it was all a strange and haunting beauty, a dream world, she thought, and she didn't wake until Malik lifted her veil and kissed her on her lips.

''Hello, Blondie,'' he whispered, and he smiled at her, a gorgeous, wicked, sexy smile that melted her all over again. She, who'd never imagined herself marrying, had found true love by pretending to be someone else. Impossible. Incredible. It was an ending plucked straight from a child's storybook.

The reception at the Porto Palace Hotel defied description. Entering the grand ballroom was yet another step into a dream. The sixty three round tables were skirted in luminous pink and purple silk covered by square toppers each hand beaded so the crystals glittered and shone in the candlelight. The pink silk cushions on the chairs were tied with the palest green ribbon, and the flower centerpieces spilled over in a riot of fragrance and color.

Candles shone everywhere—on tables, on pedestals, in gold sconces on the wall—and the cake in the corner was nearly eight feet tall, each one of the nine delectable layers painted different shades of pink and apricot and gold.

She and Malik were inseparable. They ate. They danced. They kissed. They visited with guests. They cut the cake. They danced some more, and this time when dancing, Nicolette knew that she had to be alone with Malik, now. Right now.

"Let's go," she said, linking her fingers with his. "We've been here long enough. Surely we can sneak out?"

He reached up and gently touched her earlobe. "Sneak out?"

Just like that, the words she'd spoken to Chantal four weeks ago, came rushing back. *I'll sneak in, sneak out. He won't even know what's happened.*

It didn't exactly work out that way, did it?

But she and Malik did manage to leave the reception at midnight, exiting quietly through a side door, slipping into one of the royal family's chauffeured cars. At the palace they practically ran up the stairs, and Nicolette was laughing so much by the time she reached the top of the second landing, that she had to lean against one tall marble column, struggling to catch her breath.

Malik reached out with his arms and trapped her against the column. "It's been forever since I've kissed you."

"We kissed yesterday."

"That wasn't a kiss." His lips brushed her cheek, his nose touched her ear and she shivered as his breath caressed her skin. "I want a kiss where I can taste you…everywhere."

The husky note in his voice sent a shot of adrenaline through her. "I think we need a room for that," she answered, grabbing his tie and giving it a tug, pulling him toward their bedroom suite.

Inside their room Malik took control. Despite his own impatience, he wouldn't let them race. He took his time unhooking her snug gown, and with each hook his mouth touched her neck, her back and sometimes he kissed her, and sometimes he licked her and sometimes he bit her, and the wait for the touch became harder to endure.

Her breathing slowed and her belly felt hot and tight with wanting. "It's okay to accelerate things a little," she urged, as his hands became more deliberate, and the wait between bites and licks even longer. She could feel the cool air against her heated skin, feel her breasts swell, aching, her nipples extended begging to be touched and yet he was content kissing a vertebrae in the middle of her back.

But he didn't hurry. His fingers trailed across her skin, making her body burn. She felt feverish by the time her dress spilled open and he pulled her backwards against him, his arms moving around her waist, clasping her, holding her to him. She felt the rigid length of him against the white silk of her panties.

The quiver of her body against his, sent a shudder through him and Nic gulped air as his hands encircled her waist and slowly moved up, shaping her, letting the fullness of her breasts fill his palms and then finding her nipples through the silk of her corset. She whimpered as he pinched the distended nipple. Sensation exploded through her. Hunger, craving, every physical desire.

She was already dissolving against him when his hand slid down her tummy, to the edge of her silk panty, and then lower, finding the heat and moisture between her thighs. She leaned against him, legs disgustingly weak, and the teasing torment of his fingers sinking slowly, deliciously into her creamy heat made her clasp the back of his thighs and hold on to him for dear life. "It's not fair," she choked, struggling to get sound through her throat. "You're still dressed."

"We've time."

"Not that much," she answered breaking away to look up at him through heavy lashes. "I've a wedding and thank you gift to give to you."

Dark color touched his cheekbones. "I don't want gifts."

"But you'll want this." She fought to get control, astonished at the way she responded to him. She felt utterly wild, completely without inhibition. "I want you to undress for me."

He stared at her a long moment and she felt his gaze rest on the full curves of her breast. Her finely boned corset pushed everything up, just barely obscuring the nipples. She could tell he liked her in the corset. He liked her wearing just thigh high stockings and high heels and looking like something from a pinup magazine.

No wonder. He liked hot sex, too. "Your shirt," she commanded.

He watched her face as he started to undress. The shirt came off and she drank him in. His dark hair gleamed, his upper body beautifully bare, the muscles sinewy, arms chiseled like stone.

"Now your belt," she directed coolly. "Then your socks, and trousers."

Silently he unbuckled his belt, slowly drawing it from the loops in his slacks. Her heart began to thud harder, faster as he tossed his belt onto the down-filled chaise. With a lift of his eyebrow, he unzipped his black trousers, letting the material fall open, exposing his taut, flat abdomen with the fine trail of dark hair that disappeared into the low waistband of his silk boxers.

Her mouth went dry. Very dry. Her heart did the craziest somersault. He was hers. Hers. As in forever.

As he stepped from his trousers, she told him to sit down on the bed.

He gave her a sardonic look, but he obeyed, taking a seat on the edge of the mattress, the muscles in his thighs hard, smooth, like the small knots of muscle in his abdomen.

She moved toward him, and putting a hand on each of his knees, she parted his legs to make room for her. Kneeling between his legs, she felt primal, powerful, *female*.

Nic caressed his thighs, felt the muscles bunch beneath her hands.

He reached for her, slid a hand through her long loose hair, turning the blonde strands over, savoring the glossy corn silk color. "You don't have to do anything for me."

"I know. You've made that abundantly clear from the beginning." She caressed the length of his quadriceps again, feeling the warm smooth plane of muscle, and as her light touch slid inward, along the taut muscle of his thigh, she heard him groan. Caressing his thigh again, she explored the width of his chiseled muscle, the shape, the length, the way one muscle wrapped another.

She felt him shudder, saw his erection press against the silk of his boxers, the fabric barely containing him.

Good. He was getting a taste of his own medicine.

Nic caressed him again, this time stroking his belly, his buttocks, the skin beneath his scrotum—anything but his rigid shaft. And when she knew he was reaching the edge of his control, Nic tugged his boxers down and wrapped her hand around the length of him.

"What was that about a kiss isn't a kiss if you can't taste everything…?" she murmured, lowering her head until her long hair fell forward, brushing his naked lap. She heard him swallow yet another groan. Nic brushed her lips across the smooth warm tip of him, and followed the soft kiss with a lick, and she was just about to kiss him again when he slid his fingers through her hair.

"So you've forgiven me then, *laeela?*" His voice came out hoarse. "No hard feelings about getting you here?"

Her hands stroked him, loved him. "Hard feelings about what?"

"Going to Chantal, asking for her help."

Her hands stilled. "I don't understand."

"You love me?"

"Yes."

He titled her chin, looked into her eyes. "I love you. You made me complete today. I feel whole again."

He was saying the right words but there was an undercurrent here that was wrong, and Nic was tired enough, worn down from the wedding and all the stress and nerves that she couldn't put two and two together to make four.

What had Chantal done?

What had Malik done?

Why would Nic need to forgive anyone?

Malik adjusted his boxers, covering himself, and pulled her onto his lap. "Chantal introduced us," he said calmly. "I asked her, too."

"No. You'd proposed to her. You sent her the formal of-fer—" Nic broke off, a flutter of fear winging through her. She tried to stand. Malik wouldn't let her go.

"Stay here," he said, holding her securely. "We have to talk."

But she'd gone cold, icy cold everywhere. Her arms and legs felt like polished marble. "That letter you sent her," she was struggling to get the words out. Her lips were stiff. Numb. But she managed to stagger to her feet. "You never intended to marry her?"

"No. The letter was essentially my bait."

Bait? She was beginning to understand how it'd worked. It'd been a con. The letter had been a *con.* Nic took a step away, not knowing where to go, what to think. Chantal hadn't truly set her up, had she? Chantal and Malik couldn't have set this whole charade up, could they? "You never wanted my sister."

"You're the one—and the only one—I've ever wanted."

CHAPTER FOURTEEN

STANDING there in her strapless silk corset and her insubstantial thigh high white hose, Nic saw how ridiculous she looked. How ridiculous she must have looked for the past three weeks.

He'd known she was Nicolette from the moment the yacht docked at his harbor wall. He'd known the only Ducasse coming to Atiq would be Nicolette. There had never been any other Ducasse princess...just a plan to force Nicolette to the altar and fill the Ducasse coffers.

The icy cold in her face gave way to a burning heat. She was blushing now, embarrassed. Ashamed. Here she'd been feeling so noble. She'd felt so good about her decisions...her compromises. Her *sacrifices*. She was giving up her own best interests for the sake of Lilly and Chantal's happiness.

But now she saw it was just a big joke. She'd been set up. *Set up*. How could Chantal do this? Chantal wasn't a trickster. Chantal wasn't cunning and manipulative. How could she sell her own sister out?

"You're angry," Malik said, lying on his bed, the sheet low on his hip, watching her fume and pace.

"Damn straight." Nic stared at him through new eyes. He was a schemer. A player. A playboy.

Oh God, she'd married just what she'd sworn she'd always avoid.

"She did it to help you," he said, arms folded behind his head now.

Shut up, she wanted to tell him. "Marriage doesn't help me."

"It helps your country." Because Melio gets money, a serious investor and developer, as well as a strong arm to keep bullying neighbors at bay. "She said you'd all agreed to marriages that would improve your country's situation, and position," he continued remorselessly.

Nic couldn't listen to this. They'd both tricked her. They'd both known she hadn't ever wanted to marry but they'd ignored what she wanted, what she'd believed, and forced their own wishes on her. "Did she come to you, or you go to her?"

He smiled, as if finding her question touching. "Trying to figure out who's the villain?"

"You're both the villain," she retorted grimly, "but yes, I'd like to know who initiated this...sham of a marriage."

His expression grew dark. "It's not a sham. It's a real marriage. Legal. Consummated. Permanent."

"You haven't answered my question."

He shrugged, as if the answer was obvious. "I went to her. After I went to your grandfather."

Her lips parted. "You went to Grandfather? In the very beginning?"

"Of course. He is the King. No one else could give me permission to marry you, and all it would take is his permission."

Ridiculous! "What about *my* permission? What about my free will?" It stunned her to think that Grandpapa could be in on this, too. It was as if the entire kingdom wanted Nicolette settled, married, belly fat with baby.

He patted the bed. "You came to Baraka of your own free will."

"Because I thought I could go! I thought a couple weeks as a brunette, a few state dinners, and then voila, off to Baton Rouge, see Chantal and Lilly safe, and then I'd be back to Melio, back to blonde, back to life as I prefer it."

"You're shivering. There's no reason to let yourself get so worked up." He sat up, pushed the covers aside. "Come back to bed, *laeela.*"

She couldn't even look at him. All those comments he'd made about her sister "Nicolette," those remarks about her beautiful brown hair, the digs against blondes. He'd been having a grand time, hadn't he? He'd really enjoyed himself, and he'd planned it all. Every little bit of it. "I can't."

"You can." His voice dropped. "You will."

"You can't boss me around. I never let you before, and I'm certainly not about to start now." She was shivering, she realized, seeing how goose bumps covered her arms. She needed to get dressed. "I can't believe what a fool I was. Such a romantic idiot."

"Nothing's changed."

"Nothing?" she sputtered, turning to face him, eyes wide with shock. How could he say nothing had changed? Their whole relationship was...a lie! "I don't even know you, Malik Nuri. I thought...I thought..."

"You thought what? That I was a fool, that I was just another man you'd lead around like a little spoiled poodle?"

"I've never treated a man like that!"

"You've treated every man like that. You use your beauty against men. You dazzle them, you win them, you dump them. I wanted you, and I was willing to take some risks to woo you. You can't be angry because I beat you at your own game."

Damning words, she thought, fighting tears. But he was right, of course. She was furious with him—and herself—for precisely that reason. She'd thought she could pull the charade off—and she'd expected to escape from her charade relatively unscathed. Instead she was married. Instead she'd be spending the rest of her life in Baraka.

"You were so dishonest." She sputtered the words, riding an endless roller coaster of emotion. She was married, *married,* and it was all a...trick. He'd set her up and then tricked her...coerced her...into marrying him, knowing perfectly well her fear of commitment. He'd found a way to get her to the altar and more.

"You weren't honest, either," he answered calmly, completely unruffled by her furious outburst, "and I never blamed you. I knew you. Understood you. You're competitive. You like to win."

"This isn't about winning."

"*Laeela,* it's only about winning."

She couldn't even see straight. "Yes, but two wrongs don't make a right!"

"I'd planned to tell you the truth."

"When?" she demanded, marching toward the bed. "Because I don't remember you coming clean, either."

"No, I didn't confess. I figured I'd tell you, when you told me. But you didn't. So I didn't." He smiled like a cat with a big bowl of cream. "Nic, darling, you wanted me. You have me. Forever."

He really didn't need to add that last part, she thought bitterly, wanting to grab a pillow and cover his smiling face. "But I didn't *want* to be married."

"But if you're going to be married, aren't you glad you married me?"

"So not the point, Your Royal Highness."

"Some points become pointless." His massive shoulders shrugged carelessly. He'd become the ultimate male, all contented authority. "We are married, and we're going to enjoy our life together. We certainly enjoy each other."

"Not anymore," she flashed, turning away, unable to stomach this a moment longer. This whole time, all these weeks...the night she'd spent in his arms...

"What was my bride price?" she whispered, her gaze on the sparkling lights of the port. It was quiet now, but if she hadn't married Malik, it could have been jammed with cruise ships and passengers, the very thing the Ducasse family had been desperate to avoid.

He didn't leave the bed. "High."

She swallowed hard. "How high?"

"Twenty-five."

"Twenty-five...?"

"Million."

"Dollars?" she choked, turning around, staring at him incredulously. "Tell me that's not dollars."

"It's not dollars. It's pounds. My bank in London handled the transaction."

Nic slowly sat down on the window sill. The glass felt cool against her nearly bare back. The wire in the silk bustier pressed against her underarms. "That's it?" she jested, feeling absolutely flattened. She'd been an extremely expensive wife. Not to mention extremely reluctant.

"Another twenty-five million when our first child turns fifteen."

She couldn't take this in. She couldn't believe anyone would spend that kind of money...even if one wanted a royal wife. "Why fifteen?" she asked, giving up on even keeping the facts straight.

"At fifteen, our son or daughter could legally assume the throne, without need of a guardian. That's important. Guardians often attempt to seize control. So fifteen is important."

She felt her eyes burn. Carefully she drew a breath, refusing to let even one tear form. "Are you planning on going somewhere in fifteen years?"

"No."

"I see." But she didn't see. She didn't understand anything right now. Standing, Nic glanced around for a robe, something to wrap around her now that she'd grown cold. Instead she picked up her discarded wedding gown. Stepping into the slim skirt, she fought to keep her tears from falling. What a terrible end of a beautiful day.

"Errands?" he asked quietly, his tone losing all playfulness.

She swallowed the tears. She didn't care if he was watching her, looking at her with that combination of worry and understanding. He could pretend he understood her. He could pretend he cared.

She hiccupped, stuck her arms through the thin straps and held the back of her dress together with one hand. "I think I'd prefer sleeping alone tonight."

"There's no reason to do this—"

"There is," she interrupted fiercely. But she ruined her defiance by letting her lower lip quiver. "I'm hurt. And angry. I'm going to go to my old room. I need to be alone."

"Why?"

"I have to think."

Malik slowly rose, wearing nothing but his boxer shorts. "You'll just get angrier."

"Probably."

"But if it's what you want…?"

"It is."

He didn't approach her, didn't kiss her. Instead he headed for the bathroom. "Good night."

The worst wedding night in history, Nicolette told herself for the hundredth time, fighting tears all night long. She couldn't sleep and she couldn't rest and yet she was too tired to get up and actually do anything, either.

But morning did arrive and Nic dragged herself into the shower, and then put on a least-likely-to-be-a-princess outfit—ratty jeans and a super soft pink cotton T-shirt. The pink reminded her of her gorgeous floral bouquet from yesterday, and her eyes stung.

This was all her fault.

Well, Chantal and Malik's, too.

Chantal entered Nic's room while Nicolette was sliding her feet into a pair of leather loafers.

"One of the housemaids said you'd slept here last night," Chantal said, glancing at Nic's bed, the sheets tossed on only one side of the bed. "You slept alone?"

"Glad the housemaids are keeping everyone informed," Nic answered, standing. She was *not* in the mood to talk. Her heart hurt. She felt…used.

Chantal sat down in the armchair near the window, gracefully crossing her legs. "I'm sorry, Nic."

Nic looked away, fighting the angry words that came to her lips. She didn't want to fight with Chantal, not when Chantal was still so ecstatic about getting Lilly free from Armand's family in La Croix. It was the first time Lilly had been away from La Croix in nearly two years. And now that she was home here in the palace, Lilly would be safe.

"You should have told me." Nic's voice came out husky.

"It was a bit underhanded—"

"A bit?"

Chantal blushed. "But I knew you'd like him, Nic. I know your type. I just wanted you two to meet. I thought you'd hit it off, and you did. And I knew you wouldn't marry him unless you wanted to."

Nic exhaled in a rush. "We agreed you'd never play matchmaker with me."

"But stop for a minute and think about the big picture," Chantal said, moving toward the door. "You haven't just saved one country, you've saved two. Melio needed King Nuri's money, but King Nuri needed you."

King Nuri did not need her, Nic fumed, leaving her bedroom, heading outside. King Nuri wanted a royal marriage, and heirs—don't forget the heirs—but he didn't need *her*. In this instance, any fertile princess would surely do.

She set off for the water, cutting through the extensive palace grounds, zig zagging through the rose garden, the perennial garden, the formal maze, the little rock garden with the imported alpine flowers that one royal from Salzburg had planted in hopes of bringing a little bit of Austria to her new home.

But Nic didn't pay attention to any of the glorious flowers or the pale morning sunlight glinting off the water. She was thinking of Malik and his trickery, thinking of Chantal who had trapped her into marriage—two people she respected, two people she trusted.

She couldn't believe it.

Couldn't understand it.

Why not just introduce her and Malik at a party, say, "Nicolette, this is King Nuri, sultan of Baraka, and I thought you two would hit it off together..."

Nic kicked a pebble, watched it bounce, and on reaching it, kicked it a second time, this kick sending it flying so high and far that it disappeared over the stone wall into the port itself.

"Nice kick," a male voice drawled.

Nic turned around and spotted a man in jeans and a thin cashmere turtleneck sweater leaning against the wall behind them. She sized him up, saw that he was young and fit, and from the way the sweater clung to his biceps, obviously quite muscular. "I used to play football," she said irritably.

"I bet you were good."

"Very good." She was so mad, so mad at people—and men—that she had no desire to be nice to anyone. "Enjoy the sunshine," she said, eager to move on.

But his voice stopped her. "It must feel pretty wonderful bringing a man back to life."

What was that? Nic turned, looked at the stranger, a scathing retort on her lips when she realized that this man spoke like Malik, same kind of rich, cultured tone, same husky pitched voice except his accent was more English, more uppercrust, less...desert.

He was dark like Malik, too, but his eyes were golden— amber—and his expression was harder, more cynical. He might be wearing jeans but he was already an old soul. Jaded.

He drew on his cigarette, held the air in, turned the cigarette to look at the burning tip and then exhaling, dropped the cigarette and crushed it out. "I take it he didn't tell you about the— attempt?"

"Who?"

His eyebrows lifted, satirical. "King Malik Roman Nuri."

And she suddenly put it all together. "You're a cousin or…"

"The younger brother."

Kalen, she silently said, understanding. "You came for the wedding."

He laughed. "I was the best man."

"I didn't—"

"See me. I know. You only had eyes for my brother." He looked at her for a long moment. "Congratulations on the wedding. I guess that makes us family."

She nodded, crossed her arms over her chest, still angry, still hurt. "What did you mean by the 'attempt'?"

"The assassination attempt." His golden gaze met hers. "Last year."

It seemed there were many important things Malik hadn't told her. Nic put a hand to her stomach, feeling sick. Somebody had tried to hurt Malik.

Her Malik?

"He hushed it up," Kalen continued calmly, as if his news were inconsequential. "Baraka's secret service agents arrested the shooter and Malik acted as if nothing had happened. But something had. Obviously. He wasn't the same afterward."

Kalen's jaw grew tight, and for the first time Nicolette saw how Kalen's cavalier attitude hid his deep family ties. "There was a time I almost thought I'd have to return to Atiq. Put on the old *jellaba* again," he continued lightly, but his golden gaze was hard and angry. "He'll never tell you, but the attempt killed something in him, stole his spirit. And then he realized that he had to provide for his country. It was his duty."

Duty, she silently echoed, hearing Malik's voice in her head and one of their many, endless conversations about duty and choice, responsibility…

She took several steps away, leaned on the low stone wall overlooking the water. "He wasn't going to tell me."

"Probably not," Kalen answered calmly. "He's a king."

Nic felt the roughness of the wall bite into her knuckles. He was a King. He was also a man. A very great man. Her chest squeezed. Malik should have told her so many damn things. She pushed off the wall, furious all over again. "I better go back."

Kalen's dark head inclined. "He'll be worried about you."

Nic felt a rush of pain, and just like that Kalen had diffused her anger. How had Kalen managed to find the chink in her armor so quickly? She loved Malik. She'd never want Malik to worry—especially not about her. She never wanted to add to his burden, create more stress in his life. She wanted to help him. Protect him.

Love him.

She shook her head, struggling to smile but couldn't. Her heart had never felt so bruised. Less than three weeks ago she'd met Malik for the first time. Now she couldn't imagine her life without him. "Will we see you again before you return to London?"

"I doubt it." His smile gentled. *"Allah ihennik."*

"May God's peace go with you, too, Prince Kalen."

Nic started off, back up the stone path leading to the palace gardens.

"Queen Nuri—" Kalen called out.

She stopped, glanced over her shoulder and saw that Kalen still leaned against the low stone wall.

"I don't know what he told you, but he loves blondes." Kalen's teeth flashed white. "He'd never marry a brunette."

Nic waved farewell, bit back a smile. The Nuris were impossible. How could she have married into this family? How could she possibly have agreed to marry *anyone* after only three weeks?

Climbing the palace staircase, she headed for the elegant guest suite which had been given to them as a bridal suite. The door was unlocked and Nic walked in, through the grand entry, the elegant sitting room and into the bedroom where Malik was still in bed.

Enjoying breakfast in bed.

Nic dropped into a chair opposite the bed. "Bastard."

He looked up from the newspaper he was reading in bed. He was wearing a scholarly pair of glasses and a tray with freshly baked croissants, juice and coffee sat next to him in bed. "Good morning, wife."

"You're right. I don't like losing. I thought…"

"You could win," he concluded, pulling his reading glasses off. "But you did win. You got me. And you know I love you."

"And you know I was terrified of marriage." She balled her

hands. "So far, my early impressions of marriage aren't positive, either."

He smiled sympathetically which was the wrong thing to do. "It's not funny, Malik. You don't just manipulate women into marriage."

"Let alone extremely popular, eligible princesses."

"Let alone," she agreed hotly.

"I wanted you."

"But life doesn't work like that."

"It does. If you find your soul mate."

She crossed her legs, shook her head, thinking he was so unbelievably confident. "But you'd be honest with your *soul mate*," she answered, her voice growing husky. "You'd tell her the truth—"

"Just like you told me the truth?" He set his paper aside. "Come on, Nic, this isn't about honesty. It's about power. Control. You're angry because you were outsmarted."

"You didn't outsmart me."

"I did. You're just a sore loser." He pushed the covers away and climbed from the bed. "I detest sore losers."

He was naked. Beautifully naked.

"You're cheating," she whispered, "you can't walk around naked when we're fighting."

He ignored her, pulling her to her feet, closing the distance between them. She sighed as his hands slid around her waist, moving to the small of her back and then lower, to clasp her backside. "You're still cheating," she gasped, as his hands continued a very slow, thorough caress across her bottom.

"I've never met anyone so obsessed with winning." He kissed the side of her neck, then lifted her long hair and kissed the pale skin at her nape. "But all's fair in love and war. And you have to know, *laeela*, I'd do anything to keep you from running."

"But why, Malik? And why me?"

His hands stilled on her hips. He stared down at her, his expression unusually fierce. "I've become a realist. I'm driven by practicality. And although I knew you weren't interested in marriage, I admired your independence. You didn't see marriage as a means of getting things. You wanted a relationship where you were an equal—"

"Yes, and yet what did you do? You trapped me into marriage, you live in a country where women aren't equal—"

"And I know if anything happens to me you will stand by our children no matter what," he interrupted. "I can imagine no other woman as the mother of my children. I chose you, not based on beauty or title, but out of respect."

Nic's eyes burned, so hot and scalding she had to look away. "Surely there were better suited women in Baraka."

"I needed a wife who wouldn't be intimidated by power or politics. You're not just a princess that understands duty, you've studied math and science, you've traveled extensively. And best of all, you embraced my country and our customs."

She hated the lump filling her throat. She struggled to swallow, lifting her chin as she did so. "There was an assassination attempt last year."

He looked at her strangely. "No one knows."

"Your family knows."

His eyes narrowed. He considered her for a long moment. "Kalen had no right."

Damn these arrogant men! It didn't matter if they were a sultan or a king, they were all the same. All they ever thought about was their reputation. "He loves you." She glared at him. "Although why, I don't know."

He reached out to her, clasped her face between his hands. "I've waited years to marry. I didn't think I'd ever find anyone right for me—but you are right for me, and I know in my soul, where my hope and my ancestors live, that you are the only one for me."

She pushed against his chest, feeling the smooth hard muscle beneath her fists. His skin was warm and fragrant. His nearness was doing crazy things to her senses. "Do you have any idea how much I love you? Do you have any idea how much your life means to me?" She heard the catch in her voice, felt the heartbreak on the inside. Knowing his family history, knowing how his grandfather had died must add to his fear.

"I don't want anyone to hurt you," she whispered, knowing the burden he carried, understanding even better the great love and compassion he felt for his people. "I don't want anyone to take you from me."

"I don't want anyone to take me from you, either, but if the unthinkable should happen, *laeela,* I know you will be a tiger in the palace. You will fight like hell for our children. You will do whatever is necessary to protect them—''

''But nothing is going to happen to you.'' She wrapped her arms around his waist, burying her face against his chest. ''I'm not going to let anything happen to you. For better or worse, you are my other half and if you're going to give me children then you have an obligation to stick around and help raise them. Understand?''

''Is that an order?''

''It's the first edict from Nicolette Nuri, Queen of Baraka.''

He laughed softly, and lifting her chin, he studied her as the morning sunshine illuminated her face. ''Yes, my beloved Nicolette.'' He dipped his head, kissed her deeply, thoroughly. On lifting his head, he gave her a little wicked smile. ''And now, Queen Nuri, your husband, the King, and Sultan of Baraka requests that your clothes come off. The King wants you naked and kneeling in his bed.''

''Naked and *kneeling?*'' She balked indignantly. ''Well you can tell your King—'' she broke off, and despite blushing wildly, her curiosity got the better of her. ''Why does he want me kneeling?''

Malik was trying desperately hard not to laugh. ''There are still a couple choice positions for the royal newlyweds to try, including the King's personal favorite, Catch the Tiger.''

Nic didn't know whether to be amused or mortified. ''I certainly hope it's nothing to do with the tiger's tail.''

''Most definitely not. The King wouldn't want to harm your tail. You have a beautiful tail.'' And kissing her again he reached for the hem of her pink T-shirt and tugged it over her head. ''And never forget, you have free will. You can stop me anytime.''

Stop him? Nic thought, hearing the zipper on her jeans go, and swoosh as the faded denim came down over her hips. *Not a snowball's chance in hell.*

EPILOGUE

THE fire glowed on the soft red sandstone walls. The Citadel had always been so beautiful and mysterious at night, and Nicolette watched four-year-old Zaid's face, the boy's big green eyes impossibly wide as Malik threw another log on the fire and hot orange sparks shot up into the dark sky.

Malik was telling tales now, stories of the boys' brave Barakan ancestors, of the battles once won and lost here in the dramatic mountains. Sitting on the red wool carpet, Nic felt little Aden press his face against her middle, his heart pounding like mad through his two-year-old chest, and she shot Malik an exasperated glance. Her husband was nearly as bad as the children. He loved bringing the children to Zefd, loved these nights when they sat out by the fire and they pretended to be nomads and Bedouin instead of a powerful king and his sons.

"You're scaring them," she whispered to Malik over the little boys' heads.

"It's a campfire. We're telling campfire stories."

"They're still just little boys."

His brow furrowed and he shot a protective glance at Zaid and then Aden who peeped up at his father from beneath his mother's arm. "Should I stop?" he asked the children.

"No, no," cried Zaid, and of course little Aden chimed in, trying to copy his brother, wanting to be brave like Zaid.

Nic groaned to herself. Malik knew better than to ask the children, but then, men were men and they never changed. Yet she didn't really want him to change, either. She loved him so much, and she loved to see Malik like this—so relaxed, so happy here in Zefd. When they were here at the Citadel, together like this, Malik's cares seemed to melt away and right now, Malik looked nearly as young and carefree as the boys.

He needed the break, she thought, heart softening. They

should have made this trip months ago. But at least they were here now, and Malik was making up for lost time with his boys.

Nicolette knew she'd done many good things in her life, but nothing was better than making the children. The children had made her and Malik's lives complete.

Nic ran her hand across Aden's small head. His black hair was still silky, the long loose curls nearly reaching his shoulders. Someday the curls would be cut. The baby would grow up.

Please don't let time pass too quickly, she said in a silent prayer. Let time slow. Let us stay together for as long as we can.

Malik caught her gaze. He felt the wash of her intense devotion. "You love your boys."

Her chest suffused with bittersweet warmth. "I do. All of them."

A log rolled over, shooting up another stream of sparks, and Nic thought back to the past five years, and she knew she'd change nothing about them, and nothing about their marriage. Malik was perfect for her: the right combination of strength, integrity and sensuality. He kept her on her toes. He never let life get boring. And best of all, he'd taught her that sometimes one has to lose, to win.

THE GREEK'S ROYAL MISTRESS

by

Jane Porter

CHAPTER ONE

THE jet, part of La Croix's royal fleet, groaned and shuddered and Princess Chantal Thibaudet glanced up, her tea sloshing in her cup.

It'd been a relatively smooth flight until now. They'd been in the air for nearly three hours—almost halfway home to La Croix enroute from her week stay in New York—and although the princess's secretary and ladies-in-waiting were happily visiting in the back, Chantal was desperate to get home to her daughter again.

Yet she managed not to fidget, her expression remaining calmly neutral, too ingrained by years of public service to ever give away what she was truly feeling.

Chantal's lips curved slightly, fighting a self-deprecating smile. It still amused her—the vagaries of life. People didn't want to know the reality behind the palace doors. They wanted the beautiful hair and smile, the tiara, the stylish clothes. They wanted the fairy tale, not the truth.

The truth. Ah, the truth. Now that was something else altogether...

Chantal's smile faded and for a moment the bleakness of her future stunned her, the walls, the rules, the silence...it wasn't the life she thought she'd have. She'd always been so good, so earnest about everything, she'd been sure life would turn out differently.

Abruptly the plane dropped, a sharp somersaulting lurch that had Chantal's retinue giggling and glancing nervously around, checking other's reactions. Chantal herself skimmed the clusters of passengers. Her own skittish assistants, a couple members of the media, several men interspersed, executives, friends of the Thibaudets, airline personnel.

She hated rough flights. They were inherent in flying, and she'd grown up on airplanes, but now that she was a mother, Chantal dreaded takeoffs and landings and the rough patches of

5

air in between. Yet outwardly she feigned calm and took a sip from her cup.

No sooner had she lifted the cup to her lips than sound exploded from the back of the jet. The aircraft shook, a shiver like teeth chattering, metal scraping metal. The jet dropped yet again, a steeper descent, and suddenly the teacup saucer seemed miles away.

She didn't like this.

Uncrossing her legs, Chantal planted her feet firmly on the floor, doing her best to look relaxed. Unconcerned.

They weren't going to crash. It was just turbulence. Nothing serious. Planes hit pockets of turbulence all the time.

A flight attendant in the red and cream uniform of La Croix Royal airlines came hurrying toward her. "Let me take your cup," she said, swooping the cup and saucer from the princess. "We don't want to get you burned."

The plane was jolting now, great shudders like a silver belly dancer in the sky, and passengers were murmuring in the back even as Chantal's hairdresser began to cry.

Glancing up, Chantal's gaze met one of the male passengers. He was sitting not far, just across the narrow aisle in a matching leather chair, and his dark gaze continued to hold hers, his expression calm, compelling. He wasn't English, or French. He was too hard-looking, beautiful but hard, face all severe lines and planes—an uncompromising line of brow, nose, mouth, chin.

"It's bumpy," she said, raising her voice a little, compelled to make a connection. She didn't want to be afraid, hoped she didn't look afraid.

"Yes."

Chantal had the feeling that he resisted company—people. "Do you fly a lot?" she asked, trying to keep from thinking about the terrifying shimmying of the plane.

"Yes." His dark gaze was nearly as hard as the line of his cheekbone and jaw. "And you?"

"Quite a bit." She swallowed. But she'd never been afraid like this before. Her fear was intense. "I've never—" She broke off as the plane sank abruptly, and someone behind her screamed.

The hair rose on Chantal's nape and gripping the arms of her chair she concentrated on breathing. Be calm. Be calm. Be calm.

Heart racing, eyes burning, she turned and looked at the man across the aisle. She couldn't disintegrate. She had to remain focused.

Talk to him.

Make contact with him.

She drew a shallow breath, her head spinning. "You have an accent."

His black eyebrows dropped. "So do you."

Maybe he was Latin. Italian? Sicilian? The burning in her eyes turned to tears. She felt ashamed of her loss of control. "I'm from Melio," she said, naming her independent country off the coast of France and Spain.

"I'm from Greece," he said, suddenly rising. He crossed the narrow aisle, took the empty chair next to her.

Ah, Greek, she thought, even more unnerved by his close proximity. "I'm Princess Chantal Marie—"

"I know who you are."

Of course he did. How silly. She struggled to sound normal. Natural. "What's your name?"

"Demetrius Mantheakis."

Her lower lip quivered. Her throat felt swollen, a lump lodged right in the middle. "That's quite a mouthful."

His gaze held hers, eyes so intense they dazzled her. "Yes."

The jet groaned loudly and did a strange ripple as if it'd become serpentine. Flexible. Mobile.

Chantal's lips parted. She gasped in air. She turned to Mr. Mantheakis. "This isn't turbulence anymore, is it?"

"No."

She hadn't thought so, and she nodded, exhaling slowly, trying to ignore her fear, which had become a huge, tangible thing. The fear was cold and heavy, like that of breaking a sweat in the middle of a bad dream and wanting to wake, needing to wake, and yet being unable.

Demetrius leaned toward her, his broad shoulder bumping hers. "How's your seat belt?" he asked, but he didn't wait for her to answer. He reached over and checked the tension on her seat belt personally.

His actions said more than words ever could, and her fear grew, spreading within her. "You don't have to do this."

"Do what?" He stared at her, his dark gaze narrowed and focused on her face.

She thought his voice was like gravel, hard, sharp, and she found herself thinking his Greek accent wasn't like the Greeks she'd ever known. His tone was harder. His inflection harsher. "Entertain me. Distract me. Whatever it is you're doing."

"I call it company."

She tried to smile but couldn't. She felt wild on the inside, her heart pounding, her pulse racing. They were flying over the Atlantic Ocean, heading back to Europe. There was nothing below them but water. Even if they needed to land, they couldn't.

She turned to the window. The shuddering of the plane, the inky clouds, the sense that destruction was just a heartbeat away heightened her senses, time stretched endlessly so that the future was impossible—far, far out of reach.

Lilly.

She felt the acid at the back of her eyes. She pressed her knees tight to keep from letting tears form. Princesses don't cry. Princesses don't show emotion in public. Princesses must be above reproach.

But her daughter's face swam before her eyes, the sweet pale face, the fair hair, the little lips shaped like a Valentine.

She covered her face with her hands, rubbed her eyes, drying the tears before they could fall. She couldn't lose control. The captain hadn't made any announcement. The flight attendants were buckled into their jump seats but they looked quiet, focused, professional.

The jet shuddered and banked steeply left. Chantal sat forward as the plane continued to verve left. She glanced to her window again.

"I can't see anything," she said, the jet appearing to settle back into a more normal flight pattern. The world beyond her window was dark, thick with heavy cloud, and the plane sailed through the dense blackness shuddering every now and then as if to remind passengers that the danger wasn't over.

"It's dark out," he answered calmly, leaning back in his seat, his body relaxed, no tension anywhere in his big, powerful frame.

She wished she could take comfort in the fact that he was at ease, but his confidence shook her even more. "Can the pilots see?"

"They fly by equipment."

But what if their equipment was wrong, she wanted to ask? Instead she thought back on life, the choices made, the opportunities passed up. "Moments like these are great for self-analysis," she said with a brittle laugh. "Nothing like facing one's self."

"Regrets?" he asked.

Her eyes felt like they were on fire. "Dozens."

"Name one."

She shook her head, her hands gripping her armrests tightly. "There's too many. I can't think of just one, but all of them, all that life experience, all those hopes and dreams..."

"Life's never what you think it's going to be, is it?"

Her eyes sought his. He looked so big, so imposing and yet he projected strength. Calm. "No."

"What's turned out different for you?"

She gave her head a slight shake. She couldn't talk about this. She couldn't talk about anything.

Suddenly she flashed back to her weekend in New York.

She'd been the guest of honor of New York's annual Fashion Week, and the event chairs had booked her into the royal suite at the Le Meridien in New York, a sleek, glossy hotel with a strong French influence. She supposed they thought she'd be most comfortable with the French accent, but she hadn't come to New York to find France, or Melio, or even La Croix. She'd come to New York to find a bit of her past, at least her mother's past, but it hadn't worked out like that.

How could she ever find her mother, or even herself, in a posh hotel with sleek marble lobbies and even sleeker chrome and cherry wood restaurants and lounges?

But the hotel had been an interesting juxtaposition: all the white and black marble flanked by chrome and wood. The lounge was like that of a cruise ship with its enormous circles of light—portholes—and the small tables scattered tightly together reminded her of the tables on the deck, surrounding the pool. Life at the Le Meridien New York was crowded and upscale, chic and noisy, and maybe this was New York after all. Maybe the throb and hum of street noise mingled with clank of cutlery and surge of voices over the sweet bluesy voice of the singer—maybe this was exactly New York and maybe this was why Chantal knew she'd always be a stranger here.

This wasn't her island, her husband's kingdom, or her elegant and refined way of life.

But maybe that was New York's allure. She remembered her view from her royal suite, the view over the dark brooding cityscape with its Gothic-like points and steeples, soaring building, bright lights, water towers perched precariously on top of slim and squat towers alike. New York was about change, and choice, power and sacrifice, and as the city had pulsed around her and past her, she knew she didn't have that kind of strength. Or courage.

"Life's a puzzle," she said softly, still thinking of her week in the city, and all that she'd seen and heard. Places like New York and London reminded her that there were so many different people in the world, and so many ways of doing things.

"It can be. Or it can be quite straight forward."

It'd once been quite straightforward for Chantal, too. But not anymore. Not since her marriage, Lilly's birth, Armand's death. Nothing was clear. Or simple. And thinking of the lack of simplicity reminded her of her waiter just that morning in the hotel's restaurant. She'd had her own table—her personal secretaries and valets seated at one nearby—and her waiter defied description. Literally.

"There was a waiter at the hotel's restaurant," she said slowly, picturing the tall waiter, who had to be at least six-foot-one or -two, and had long hair, a soft voice, sloping shoulders, soft waist, full hips, and yet, he was a man. At least he'd been born a man. "The waiter didn't fit his body. I don't know if he'd been taking something to become more feminine, or maybe he was simply willing it, but..."

"But what?"

"I admired him." Chantal looked up, into Mr. Mantheakis's eyes, and she felt her insides wrench. "I admired him for refusing to spend his life as someone, or something, he didn't want to be...for being unable or unwilling to spend the rest of his life in a body that didn't fit, or playing a role that didn't suit."

"Seems the waiter took drastic measures."

"I think he was brave," she whispered, breaking the gaze, turning to glance out her window at the darkness surrounding the plane.

In the restaurant this morning she'd been first puzzled, then confused, and finally sympathetic. And her deep sympathy made her feel an ounce of the pain he must have felt to have changed his world so.

She knew what it was like to start out as one thing and to battle it constantly. To struggle through the days, to deny the natural impulses again and again, to order oneself to do it because...because.

"Coffee?" the waiter had asked her this morning, with a voice that was pitched soft like a woman's and yet still distinctly male.

The waiter's voice had buried deep in her heart where she tried not to let emotion go. She'd felt such empathy for him that she tried to smile, and yet her eyes filled with tears. This poor man must have endured years of pain. "Please," she'd said, forcing herself to speak, and looking up, she'd met the waiter's eyes, and smiled, really smiled, even as she thought that no one got through life without tremendous pain.

"But you're brave." Demetrius Mantheakis's voice brought her attention back to him. "You've done incredible things in your life."

She shook her head, the memories of the morning still burning inside her heart. "No. Not like that. I've never really fought for anything." And suddenly her voice broke and Chantal closed her eyes, wishing she could disappear. She didn't want to feel this much. Didn't want to think this much.

"If you could do it over, what would you fight for?" he persisted.

Chantal stirred uncomfortably in her seat. She wanted off the plane. She wanted away from this man who asked hard questions and wanted real answers. It'd been a long day, but she didn't know how not to answer him. There was something forced in him, something about him that compelled her to speak. "Happiness," she said at last.

"Happiness?"

Her shoulders lifted, fell. She couldn't believe she was telling him this...sharing this. "I never thought it'd be so elusive. I always thought we'd all have an equal shot at it."

"And you didn't?"

She never talked to people like this, and yet now that she'd started opening up, she couldn't seem to stop. It was as if he'd unleashed a storm inside of her. "I don't know what went wrong. I tried so hard to do the right thing, and I always thought, if you just try hard enough, just be good enough, honest enough, kind enough, compassionate enough...if you work hard enough and give enough you'll discover that elusive happiness that others seem to have. You'll find happiness and—" She broke off took a breath, the aching emptiness inside her like a live thing, humming.

Deep grooves formed at his mouth. "And what?"

"Peace." *Peace.* She didn't close her eyes but on the inside she felt so weary and empty that she would have if he hadn't been watching her so closely. But he doesn't know you, she reminded herself, he knows your name, but that's it. He'll never really know you. And even if you survive this crazy flight— something that looked decidedly remote at the moment—they'd never see each other again. Was there really that much harm in opening up? Being honest? Speaking from the heart?

Her entire life had been dictated by duty, country, economy. As the oldest of King Remi Ducasse's three grandchildren, she was destined to be the future queen and monarch of Melio. She'd known since her teenage years that it was her duty to marry well, provide heirs, secure financial stability and guarantee independence from their powerful neighbors Spain, France and Italy.

To speak from the heart. To live according to the heart. These were not choices she'd been allowed to make. Her heart had long ago been overruled by her head and her innate loyalty and desire to do right had long ago eclipsed impulse and sentimentalism. There was that which was right, and there was that which needed to be done, and she knew when she married one day she'd marry a suitable match, a match arranged by her grandfather and his advisors. She'd bring prosperity back to their tiny kingdom, and stability.

That was her job. It was the job she'd do.

And it was the job she'd done. Tragically the moment she married Armand, Chantal knew she'd made the worst mistake of her life and having Lilly only made it worse.

But just thinking of her young daughter made her smile on the inside. Lilly was everything. Absolutely the greatest, purest joy life could bestow. A gift. A reward. A lifeline.

Suddenly the plane groaned again, metal scraping, the body of the jet rippling now as if in agony.

Chantal clenched her hands in her lap as the lurching plane shivered and shrugged as if struggling to molt its gleaming silver skin.

What was going to happen to Lilly?

She knew her brother-in-law, King Malik Nuri, the sultan of Baraka had been working on freeing Lilly, trying to find a way to escape the archaic La Croix laws, but so far nothing had worked, which meant, if the plane went down, or broke apart, or did whatever it was that planes do, then Lilly would be trapped forever with the Thibaudets in La Croix. Chantal couldn't bear the thought. The Thibaudets, Armand's parents, were cold and hard and they would control every choice, every thought, every breath Lilly took.

Her head spun. Her stomach heaved. She was going to be sick.

From nowhere a hand pressed to the back of her head, forcing her down, urging her face to her knees. ''Breathe.''

Demetrius Mantheakis's touch was firm and yet his voice was calm.

With his hand against the back of her head, and her nose bumping her knee, she felt utterly bewildered by the turn of events. Earlier today she'd been in New York, wrapping up her trip and missing Lilly dreadfully, and now she was getting ready to say goodbye...

Eyes squeezed closed she fought for control. You have to be okay, you have to be able to let go. No one lives forever...no one gets forever...

"Breathe," the voice above her commanded again.

"I can't." Her voice broke and the tears fell onto her knees. "I can't—"

"You can. You must. Come on, Chantal, be tough."

His hard voice was like a slap, right, left. After a moment she felt calmer. She was breathing again. More deeply. More regularly.

"I'm fine now," she said, and she pushed up, against the weight of his hand.

Little by little he let go of the back of her head.

Sitting upright, she tried to meet his gaze but couldn't. Demetrius Mantheakis scared her almost as much as the shuddering plane.

Demetrius watched the princess knowing that they were in trouble, knowing that he was calm because there wasn't a great deal either of them could do now. They were either going to make it, or they weren't going to make it. Either way he'd be with Princess Thibaudet. If they survived he'd be there. If they died, he'd be there. He could afford to be calm. Certain decisions were already made for them. It was a matter of waiting.

"I'm fine now," she said again, and this time her voice was deeper, calmer.

He studied the way she sat in her chair, her hands clenching the armrests. "There's nothing wrong with being afraid." He saw her head jerk up, her blue gaze meeting his. Emotion darkened her eyes, etched fine lines around her soft mouth.

"Are you afraid?" she whispered.

"To some degree, yes."

Chantal looked away, her fingers pressed to the cool metal armrests. She wasn't a little afraid. She was very afraid, and for the first time in years she only wanted the truth. Just the truth.

Save the promises and the pretense and all the flowery phrases people were always trying to give her. "Are we going to make it?"

"We're going to give it our best shot."

Demetrius's steady voice made her want to scream. He was so fixed, so contained while she felt absolutely sick with fear. If it weren't for Lilly then she could go, she could say goodbye, she could accept that she'd had her turn, lived her life, but there was Lilly and Lilly needed her.

God, give me sixteen years, Chantal prayed, *I want sixteen years. Sixteen more years for birthdays and hugs and conversations late into the night about anything and everything Lilly could possibly want to discuss.*

I won't ask her to live for me. I won't ask her to be anything for me. I won't ask her to become anyone but Lilly. I just want to be there for her. I want to open doors for her, and then tuck her in late at night, knowing she is home, knowing she is safe.

Chantal flexed her fingers, dug her nails into her palms. "If I don't make it home—"

"You'll make it home."

She wanted to believe him, she really did. "But if I don't, promise me you'll tell my daughter—"

"Chantal."

His hard voice, fixed, like a slab of rough hewn marble, dragged her gaze up, all the way up from his chest to his open collar to his chin and jaw and mouth. Once her eyes met his, she felt cold and hot, a tangle of live nerves. "You don't call me, Your Highness."

"But you're not my highness. You're Chantal Thibaudet—"

"I hate that name." She grew even colder, ice crystals all over her heart. "I am not Thibaudet. That was my husband's name."

"And he died."

She swallowed convulsively. "And he died."

"And you're not going to die."

"No."

His lips curved into the faintest glimmer of a smile. It was like a black wolf. Teeth bared. "That's the first positive answer I've heard from you."

"And that's the first smile I've seen from you."

"I don't like smiling."

She laughed. For a moment, as incredible as it was, she forgot the shuddering plane, the dips and lunges in space, the wretched nausea pervading every limb. "You don't like smiling?"

"Fools smile."

Chantal choked on her muffled laugh. "You must be joking."

His head cocked, his dark eyes met hers and the feral intensity in his eyes made her shiver inwardly, a shiver that had nothing to do with the plane and fear, and everything to do with awareness.

Like Armand, he possessed tremendous confidence. But she knew what happened with men like Armand. They decimated those around them, tearing into them, bite by bite until nothing remained. No spirit. No self-esteem. No sense of self.

Her laughter died in her mouth, strangled in her throat. Hard men, strong men weren't the kind of men she wanted to know.

The jet suddenly plunged down, a steep free for all, and somewhere behind Chantal a woman screamed, a long terrified cry that seemed to go on and on as the jet hurtled toward the ocean below.

Demetrius's hand reached out, covered hers, held her fists tightly in his. "I'm here."

She gripped his hand with all her might. "We're going down."

"We're going somewhere fast."

There was an edge to his voice now, a hardness that spoke volumes. He felt the urgency, and the peril. He was meeting her where she was. Two human beings...mortals...no distinction between anyone now.

"Thank you," she choked, her mouth all sand, her heart beating so hard her eardrums sounded as if they'd explode. "Thank you for doing this. Being with me."

"My pleasure."

Yellow masks dropped.

Chantal stared at the bright yellow cup swinging in front of her, and then she remembered all those flight briefings, all those routine instructions. She reached for the mask, pulled it over her head, settling it on her nose. The mask fit.

She turned, looked at Demetrius. His mask was in place. His eyes creased.

Her mouth trembled. Tears filled her eyes. "I want to go home."

"To your daughter."

She nodded, hands gripping the arms of her chair so tightly she thought the bones would snap.

"Tell me about her," he said, his voice coming from very far away. "How old is she? What's her favorite color?"

Chantal blinked, dragged in air, felt tears well. The jet was in a downward spiral and he was trying to keep her from falling apart. Trying to keep her mind occupied. "Four." The pressure in her ears, the pressure in her head was intolerable. She blinked, head spinning, ears feeling as if they were going to burst. "Green." Blinking dizzily, Chantal dragged in another excruciating breath. "Her favorite color is green."

The plane was tumbling, spinning, and her seat belt strained, pulling tight across her lap, barely holding her into her seat. With a thud she felt Demetrius's arm strain against her chest, battling to pin her back into her seat. "What's she like?" he demanded.

Chantal couldn't focus. The pressure in her head made her want to scream like the others in the back who were crying out for God and help and deliverance. *Shy.* She closed her eyes. *Lilly's shy.*

Her blood was pooling in her head, in her ears and she knew she couldn't withstand much more pressure.

Lilly.

She pictured Lilly, kept her daughter's face before her, held love for Lilly in her heart. And as the world spun past, Chantal realized for the first time that love couldn't be contained. Love isn't trapped or shaped inside the body but is alive throughout the universe.

Love is inherent in every living organism, every cell, every creature and man.

Lilly would be fine.

Lilly would have Aunt Nic and Aunt Joelle, she'd have Grandfather and Grandmamma and there would always be the people in Melio who'd love her, embrace her, accept her.

She'd be fine.

A voice sounded on the jet's speaker. The captain announced that they were going to attempt to land. ''Brace yourself.''

Brace yourself. For the worst. For the best. For the rest of your life.

Demetrius's arm was now forcing her head down again, shaping her into a ball. ''Hold on.''

I love you, Lilly.

''Hold on,'' Demetrius ground out yet again, his hand in a death-grip against the back of her head.

I'm holding.

CHAPTER TWO

FOR a moment nothing happened. They were still flying-floating-hanging suspended and then in the next moment they bore straight down, down, down, gravity and turbulent air rushing at them in a frenzied battle that left her gasping for breath.

Then the ground came up at them, grabbing for them as if two giant arms were reaching up into the sky. The jet slammed against the earth. Bounced. Slammed down again. Bounced up higher, metal exploding, popping, screeching until Chantal was sure they'd be consumed by the heat and metallic noise, the smell of burning rubber and gas.

A plume of black smoke filled the cabin and as smoke poured into the cabin, the jet skidded sideways, a runaway plane sliding into the night.

The jet's momentum carried them along, and inside the battered plane they were being thrashed about, thrown to the right and left, narrow seat belts barely restraining.

Something bright flared, color, light, heat. Fire.

The plane was on fire.

But the jet was still moving, still sliding, still racing along like a giant's plaything, until the body snapped apart, nose gone, tail falling away, the belly sawing open.

Dazed, Chantal saw the night sky overhead. Blinking, she tried to focus on what must be stars even as something warm and wet dripped on her from above. She drew a shallow breath, finding it hard to breathe. Everything was so hot, the air so thick and steamy. Smoke and petrol burned her nose and she gagged a little. Had to get this mask off. Had to get out of here.

A hand groped at her waist, reaching for her seat belt. Stupidly she tried to rise but her legs wouldn't hold her. It was like coming off one of those carnival rides, the spinning teacup one that threw equilibrium to the wind.

Again Chantal tried to rise, but her chest hurt, her legs trem-

19

bled. Her body refused to cooperate even as her mind screamed. Have to get off. Have to get out.

Her face was wet, sticky. Must be raining. Or was that acrid burning smell petrol?

"Take my hand," a voice commanded. Demetrius's voice, she dimly registered. But she couldn't seem to find him, or his hand, and she turned weakly in her seat, stared back behind her, realized that the others were gone, that the tail of the jet was somewhere behind.

"Chantal."

He said her name so harshly that her head jerked back. He was standing and she stared at him in shock. His face looked blurry. Only his dark eyes made sense. They were fierce, black.

He pulled her to her feet and Chantal tried to move but her legs were soft, pillowy, the strangest weakest sensation. "I smell fire," she said, her voice eerily calm.

"The tail section is burning."

"Where is it?"

"Behind us."

She nodded, accepting this, and with her hand in his she tried to follow him across the pale taupe carpet with the bold gold and black border. Funny how the carpet looked the same.

But then the carpeted aisle ended abruptly, falling off away, and a huge scrap of silver sheet metal jutted up, twisting into the sky like a postmodernist garden sculpture. "Careful."

Again his voice was hard, ruthless and she nodded. There were no words left, no thought in her mind. She would have followed him anywhere at that moment.

He jumped down first, then lifted her from the carpet into his arms.

"I can walk," she protested as he carried her away from the tangled wreckage.

"You're bleeding."

Her head fell back, she stared into his face. His jaw was set, his expression ferocious. "I'm not bleeding."

He didn't answer. He just kept walking, carrying her as if she were nothing, moving swiftly to an unseen point in the distance.

From nowhere a siren sounded in the warm heavy darkness, the mournful siren piercing the humid night.

Thank God. Help's arrived. Gratefully Chantal closed her eyes.

With the princess slumped against his chest, Demetrius carried her from the burning plane to the clearing up ahead. He intentionally was taking her away from the other survivors who were gathering away from the wreckage. He was glad she'd passed out. He wasn't in the mood to talk, or try to explain what had happened.

He'd failed. Plain and simple.

He'd been hired to protect her. And he hadn't protected her. Regardless of the circumstances, he took full responsibility for the crash. The crash should have never happened.

He'd swapped flight crews, substituting the cockpit flight crew for his own. He'd changed flight attendants, too, unwilling to take the chance that the danger would come from one of those that were paid to serve the princess. He'd done his best to screen all those traveling with Chantal, and he'd felt reasonably confident that those flying with her were loyal.

In the end, the problem had been the jet itself. He'd had it inspected. Obviously the inspection hadn't been thorough enough.

You'd think after ten years he would have learned something. He got into this line of work by default. There'd been a breech in family security and he'd paid the ultimate price. The tragedy had turned him into a vigilante, and later a security expert. He was too ruthless, too cold to be a good bodyguard, which was only one of the reasons why he didn't take personal assignments, but after King Nuri of Baraka, Princess Chantal's new brother-in-law, had explained the situation to him, Demetrius couldn't say no. His company routinely provided high profile, celebrity security detail, but Princess Chantal Thibaudet's situation was different.

Widowed at twenty-seven, she was a stunning member of the royal family with a four-year-old daughter and someone wanted her gone. Dead.

The maliciousness of the intent, as well as the fact that a young child would be left orphaned, made his blood freeze. The widowed princess was far too visible, and far too vulnerable.

After studying the files, Demetrius knew he couldn't refuse the job. King Malik Nuri and the elder Ducasse royals didn't know how to handle this sort of threat. But Demetrius did. When it came to offering the dirtiest form of protection and intimidation, Demetrius was on a level of his own.

He didn't mess around.

He usually didn't make mistakes.

He'd made one today and he'd never forget it. The princess and her family could damn well believe he wasn't going to make another mistake, not when it came to her safety, nor her daughter's future.

The ground grew soft beneath his feet and the voices and cries of the passengers faded with the distance. They'd found land in the middle of the Atlantic—God only knew how the flight crew had managed to do that—he owed them hugely. They'd be compensated.

He heard a dull roar, the endless, monotonous sound of water against sand. Apparently the jet had landed within a couple hundred feet of the ocean. If they'd overshot the runway even a little bit, they would have broken apart in the water. Another miracle.

Demetrius crouched down, set Chantal in the still warm sand. He checked her vitals as best as he could and she seemed fine. It was the bump on her head that worried him. Part of the upholstered wall in front of them had come flying back at them.

He wished he had a flashlight. He wanted to check her eyes, see if they were as dilated as he feared.

She stirred, lunged forward. *"Lilly?"*

The terror in her voice cut him. "She's fine, Chantal." He wrapped an arm around her to keep her still. "Lie back, relax."

"Where is she?"

"Home."

Her expression cleared and she drew a slow breath. "She wasn't on the plane."

"No."

Her eyes closed. "Thank God." She drew another breath and

her eyes opened. She looked at him in the dark. He could see the whites of her eyes, the glimpse of white teeth as she bit her lip, organizing her thoughts, controlling her emotions. "We made it."

"We did."

She swallowed. "And the others?"

"I know there were survivors. I saw quite a few passengers gathering outside the wreckage."

She struggled to free herself. "We should go. We need to be there. I should be there." Her voice sounded hollow. Numb. She was in shock, probably had no idea what she was even saying. "I need to go help. People are hurt—"

"Can't."

"I must."

"It's not safe."

"Why?"

He stared at her for a long moment, before shaking his head, expression grim. "Too volatile."

She frowned, bemused. "The plane, you mean?"

"Among other things," he said, gently releasing her and watching her settle back on the soft sand.

The sand felt surprisingly warm beneath her and pressing her knuckles into the fine grains, Chantal's brow creased. Were they really still alive?

It seemed impossible. Improbable.

Eyes narrowing, heart pounding, she struggled to focus on Demetrius's face and process his words. It had sounded as if he were speaking in a megaphone—loud but not clear—and she struggled to understand why her hearing was off, why he sounded so far away when he was standing so close.

Gingerly she reached up to touch her forehead where it throbbed. It hurt to lift her arm, and her fingertips came away crusty when she touched her temple. She probed a little more and felt something gummy, still warm and sticky. Blood.

She must have hit something pretty hard then. Odd. She didn't remember hitting anything, but in the moments when the plane had been on a collision course with the earth, everything seemed to fly at her—a leather purse, a high heel, a paperback novel. It was as if they were in outer space: astronauts operating in zero gravity.

"Did you ever lose consciousness?" she asked tiredly, wiping her hand on her short suit skirt. Somewhere along the way she'd lost the matching woven pink and mossy-green jacket.

"No."

She nodded. She felt so strange. Almost otherworldly. How could they have survived what they did? "And you're not hurt?"

"No."

Again she nodded; thinking that time had changed, evolved, become almost 3-D. She could see them on the jet, could feel the terror still, could taste the smoke and blood and fear, and yet here they were, on some remote island off where? In the middle of the Atlantic? "Where are we?"

His thickly built shoulders shifted. "Off the coast of Africa, I believe."

"It's impossible. There was no land..."

"Our excellent flight crew found some."

Chantal gave her head another bemused shake. She felt as if she'd been through the spin cycle on a washing machine but they were *safe*. Alive. "Where's the plane?"

"Over there." He gestured inland, back to the thickly forested land behind them. "Everyone's just on the other side of the trees."

"We're that close to the water?"

"We very nearly parked offshore."

She didn't know why, but his expression, his dry tone, even the words he used, made her smile faintly. "We're lucky to be here."

"Very."

Nodding numbly, she stared off into the distance, seeing the endless line of dark water, feeling the heavy humidity in the air, the glance up into the sky, which revealed a half-hidden moon.

She couldn't absorb it all.

The danger was still so recent, so real, she couldn't quite believe they'd come through relatively unscathed. And then her heart tightened. What about the others? She had to know about her attendants, her staff. Most of the young women that worked for her weren't married yet, but they were still someone's daughter, sister, girlfriend. She had to check on them. Had to know the facts.

She struggled to rise, the effort making her body throb. She hurt. All over. "I need to get back to the plane."

"No."

Teetering to her feet, she ignored him, just as she ignored the pain pulsating hot and sharp around her lower ribs. "I'll never forgive myself if they're hurt and I sat here doing nothing."

He rose and settled his hands on her shoulders. Firmly. Heavily. He held her immobile. "I can't let you go back."

"You don't understand—"

"I do." And then suddenly he pressed a finger to her lips, silencing her. "Shh. Someone's coming."

His gaze was fixed on the grove of trees behind them and he touched his side, just beneath his arm. She knew the gesture. Her secret service detail had done the same thing numerous time before. He was checking for a weapon. A firearm.

He carried a firearm?

Demetrius was moving in front of her, shielding her. "Who's there?" he called.

A male voice replied in Greek.

Demetrius relaxed slightly, but not much. She felt the power in his body, his broad back tight, muscles hard, ready. He spoke to the other man rapidly, his voice deep, short, no-nonsense.

He was a man accustomed to being obeyed.

Chantal glanced up at him, took in the back of his head, the width of his shoulders and wondered who he really was and what exactly he was doing on her plane.

The man by the trees faded back into the darkness and Demetrius drew her down onto the sand. He sat close to her. "You can rest easy now," he said roughly. "That was the pilot. There are some injuries, no casualties."

She felt an almost dizzying wave of relief. "You're certain?"

"Everyone's been accounted for, and while some of the injuries aren't pretty, none appear life threatening."

"Thank God."

He nodded. "They've radioed for help. We're going to stay here until help arrives. It's safer."

She wanted to ask, how was it safer? But she didn't have the strength, or energy. She was tired. Sore. She thought she'd do just about anything for a couple of aspirin. Maybe it was better to sit, and rest. She felt as if she could sleep for months. Years. "Okay."

"Okay."

And some of the weight rolled off her shoulders. Her head felt a little lighter. The worries less agonizing. There was nothing she needed to do. Nowhere she needed to go. She could just sit here and be.

How strange. How wonderful.

Time passed. Slowly. Chantal felt drowsy and yet she struggled to keep her eyes open. As the hour passed, a warm wind picked up, banking heavy clouds overhead and sweeping the sand into whirling dervishes.

"Follow me," Demetrius said, taking her hand and pulling her to her feet.

She winced as he tugged on her arm. Her ribs were really sore.

He found a spot on the beach he liked. The position faced the water, was backed by a high hard dune, and provided an unobstructed view of the forest and the clearing. If anyone approached, he'd see.

Gathering some fallen branches from the forest, a few palm fronds, several fragrant eucalyptus branches, he built a miniature lean-to into the sand dune. It didn't take him long to put the shelter together, but by the time he was done, dark storm clouds had virtually obscured the white moon.

"It's going to rain," she said, frowning up at the now nearly black sky.

He nodded, and watched her gingerly creep backward into the lean-to, her lips pinched, her face a study in concentration. She was hurting.

He'd felt her tense as he drew her to her feet a few minutes ago, and he'd thought perhaps she was simply stiffening up. Maybe she was. But it could be more serious, too.

He didn't want to confront her, or risk offending her unless he absolutely had to, but he'd been hired for a job and he'd do his job. He took a seat next to her in the little shelter, the warm sand against his back. "Why don't you take your shoes off, Princess? You might as well get comfortable."

She glanced at her high heels. They were the palest pink suede banded by a darker pink leather trim. Biting her lip, she bent down to slip one shoe off and then the other. As she tugged each heel off, her lips pinched again, a needle of pain between her brows.

"Where does it hurt?" His deep voice sounded harsh even to his own ears.

"I'm fine."

"That's not what I asked."

Her fine dark eyebrows furrowed with displeasure. "Pardon me?"

She sounded positively imperial and frigid, shifting into the glamorous and untouchable Thibaudet Princess. "You're hurt," he said bluntly.

"No."

"You wince every time you move."

"A little bruising, Mr. Mantheakis."

She was trying hard to put him in his place, but she didn't know that he didn't believe in a caste system. He'd come too far to subscribe to class, status or social pecking order. In his world, people were people. Period. "It's worse than that."

"It's not." She averted her face, tilted her small straight nose higher, and yet he saw her hands burrow deep in the sand.

She might want to project cool indifference, but she was suddenly afraid. Afraid of him. She wanted to leave, to return to the others.

Terrifying her would solve nothing. He sought to gentle his voice. "I need to check for injuries."

"Absolutely not."

"It won't hurt."

She drew a deep breath, her nostrils flaring. The wind rustled through their small shelter, tugging at the princess's hair, catching one long tendril and blowing it across her cheek.

She caught the curl, and forced it back behind her ear. "I want to return to the plane."

"You know we're not going to do that."

Chantal attempted to rise but Demetrius's arm wrapped around her, pulling her back against him.

She inhaled sharply as she felt the heat of his body through his shirt, the hard planes of his chest against her back. "Let me go."

"I'm not going to hurt you."

His deep voice sent shivers through her and she felt a sob form inside her chest. He was so much stronger than she was. He was completely overwhelming her...dominating her. "You've no right to touch me."

"You're making this harder than it has to be."

She closed her eyes, turned her face away, her cheek grazing his chest. She felt the smooth thick muscle of his shoulder, felt the warmth of his skin and the even thud of his heart.

He was strong. Very strong. It crossed her mind that nothing invaded these walls of his arms. He was a power unto himself. Law.

Like the ancient Greek warriors and conquerors, the Greeks that founded civilization, changing the world forever.

"Please let me go," she whispered, a new fear welling.

"After I make sure there are no other injuries."

"There are none. Trust me."

"Can't take your word for it, Princess. Sorry."

Her breath was coming more rapidly, and opening her eyes she looked up at him, into the hard edges of his face. His cheekbone was high, almost too high, giving his face a harsh angle, and his chin, blunt cut, did nothing to ease the arrogant lines.

Pulse quickening, she knew he wasn't someone she wanted to negotiate with. "I haven't broken anything."

"I have to check you anyway—"

"No." He was mad, out of his mind. "No, no, no, and no." There was no way she'd let his hands go anywhere on her body. "I'd know if I'd hurt something—"

"You didn't know you were bleeding."

"I thought it was rain."

"Exactly." He shifted, placed her on the ground and he crouched in front of her.

She avoided looking at his chest and her gaze settled on the taut muscles of his thighs, his trousers snug around his quadriceps.

"If you'd unbutton your blouse, Princess."

She nearly choked on her tongue. *"Mr. Mantheakis."*

He didn't reply. He was waiting. And he was patient. Very patient. Patience alone gave him tremendous strength.

Chantal felt a stirring of genuine panic, sensing she'd lost power, considerable power. "I'm not about to take my clothes off. I'm wearing very little as it is."

"I'm only asking you to unbutton your blouse. It's not as if you're naked under your blouse. You're wearing a bra."

Naked. Bra. Blouse. This was *her* body they were discussing, her clothes, her privacy. "Yes, but—"

"Do I need to unbutton your blouse for you?"

"Don't you dare. You've no right, no—" She broke off, startling when his hands reached for her, fingers brushing the full curve of her breast. *"Stop!"*

"I'm not in the mood to argue."

"Back off."

"Be quiet."

Chantal's jaw dropped. My God, another Armand. These insufferable arrogant boorish males were everywhere. She slapped at his hand. "I might be a silly thirty-year-old princess, but I'm not a complete fool. You don't have to take my blouse off to check for broken bones. You can inspect for damage through my blouse just as well."

"I'm looking for deep contusions."

"Thank you very much, but I have my own doctor in La Croix."

"We're going to be here all night, possibly all day tomorrow. We can't afford to wait until you reach La Croix. Now please unbutton your blouse. I promise I won't lose control."

She felt her cheeks heat. "Don't make fun of me."

"I'm perfectly serious."

She didn't know whether to be offended or chagrined. "I'm not accustomed to undressing in public."

"Then you can relax. This is definitely private."

Unconsciously she crossed her arms over her chest, scared, chilled, shivering at what? Being looked at by a man?

Yes. Precisely.

No one had touched her, looked at her since Armand had died, and when he'd been with her, he hadn't been particularly...kind.

Armand had married her to create a political and economic alliance and while the countries had benefited, Chantal had died on the vine.

It was worse than she'd ever imagined. It wasn't the life she thought she'd ever live. She'd been the oldest, the bravest, the surest of herself. She was going to do it all right, make things work for her sisters, her grandparents, for Melio's people. She could do anything, be anything and oh—she'd failed.

She'd been so wrong about everything.

Armand didn't love her. He hadn't even tried to love her. She'd been anything but what he really wanted.

Silly Chantal, silly disillusioned princess living in the tower.

Demetrius's hand settled on the middle of her back, his palm was warm, firm, and it slid up to wrap her shoulder. "Your blouse, Princess. Now."

CHAPTER THREE

THE heat from his hand felt explosive.

Chantal sucked in air, head spinning at the unexpected contact. It'd been so long since anyone touched her. For the past few years there had just been Lilly's arms. Lilly's hugs.

She'd forgotten what a man's hand felt like. Forgotten what even her skin felt like.

His hand lightly gripped her shoulder. Fingers pressed against her upper arm. It wasn't an intimate touch and yet her pulse quickened, blood racing.

Oh God, to be thirty and so lonely...

To be a woman and to not feel anything like a woman.

"Relax." He lightly rubbed her upper arm. "I won't hurt you."

"I know." And she did know. He wasn't the kind of man who'd raise a hand in violence toward a woman. But there was still the other current running through her, the small electric sensation of being touched. Of feeling...real.

His palm slid back up her arm, over her shoulder, covering her collarbone, and then to the upper swell of her breast.

Chantal closed her eyes, held her breath, her body intensely alive. She was both scared and curious.

With her eyes closed, lips parted, she could almost imagine a life she'd never lived. Could see herself someone's wife with a pretty whitewashed house with blue shutters and a view of the sea. She could see the colorful boats tied up at the dock, bobbing happily on the water. She'd hang the laundry outside, sheets and shirts and skirts drying in the sun...

Herbs and cucumbers and tomatoes in the garden. A loaf of crusty bread in the oven. Climbing roses that smelled like musk...

His palm rested on her breast, above her heart. Her pulse raced. Her body flooded with heat. She could feel the hardness of his palm against the softness of her skin.

She couldn't move. Couldn't think. Couldn't speak. All her nerves were tuned to the heat of his hand against her body, the feel of his palm on her breast.

"Unbutton your blouse, Princess."

His voice danced across her senses, the no-nonsense Greek inflection riveting. He expected her to obey. He expected her to do exactly as he said.

And yet...and yet...how could that authority, that firmness, that awareness make her feel like this? Something in her responded to his immovable presence, to the maleness, to the fact that he was so different from her.

It made her aware...made her feel...

"Come on, Princess. Or I will."

She trembled, and reached for the first button on her blouse. She couldn't believe she was actually unbuttoning the pink silk blouse. Where was her mind? Where was her will? What was happening to her? How could she be losing control? And yet she didn't stop. Her fingers kept moving. She unbuttoned the delicate blouse until it hung open and then looked at him, muscles tight, nerves wound to the breaking point.

His eyes held hers. He didn't move. He didn't look down at her chest. Instead he stared into her eyes until she felt dizzy and she shuddered, overwhelmed by the strange sensation that she was falling, and yet she couldn't put her hands out, couldn't break her fall.

His hand moved, infinitely slowly, a warm path across her breast, beneath the edge of her blouse to the heated skin below. She jerked at the touch of his skin on hers. The sensation was sharp, hot, and heat curled in her belly, daggerlike fingers of fire.

He heard her hiss. His eyes narrowed. "Does that hurt?"

Yes. No. She struggled to swallow around the lump blocking her throat. "It's...sensitive."

His heavy black brows flattened. But he said nothing. Peeling her blouse back, his gaze dropped, lashes lowering, and he studied her, his gaze taking in her pale skin already darkening with bruises, mottled shades of yellow, green, blue.

"Lean back if you can," he directed. "I'm worried about your ribs."

Goose bumps danced across her skin, the fine hair lifting on her arms, at her nape. His hand made her skin feel so hot, nerves stretched, her body taut, listening as if trying to comprehend what was happening.

What was happening?

What was happening inside her, around her, to the world at large? Chantal felt caught in something so big and chaotic, the dark sky rippling with restless energy, a rumble of thunder and then a deeper growl that stretched from one end of the sky to another.

Her eyes closed as his palm slid across her breast to her shoulder and back again, now slipping along her ribs, beneath the breast, his fingertips gauging the width and span of bone, but this was no impersonal inspection. She felt heat at each pass of his fingers, each stroke across her skin sent little licks of fire, sparks of heat shimmering deeper and deeper into her, sensation burrowing so strong that her womb came to life, all aching emptiness and tension.

No one had made her feel like this in years.

No hand on her breast, no fingers on her hips, no careful exploration of the indentation at her waist. And now this man, this man's hands, this darkness and hot, stormy night everywhere.

Lightning split the sky, wild white fingers of light beyond the edge of the shelter and Chantal shivered.

"Did that hurt?" His mouth was so close to her ear that his deep voice seemed to come from inside her, and she shivered yet again.

"No." Chantal felt almost feverish with heat. His touch was unreal. He was making her feel so much. She'd been alone so long and suddenly his hands, his strength, his close proximity reminded her of everything she'd missed.

Love. Making love. Sex.

Maybe sex was overrated when you were getting it, but take it away, deny it altogether and the body stopped feeling like a real body. Leave the lips just for speech, the hands for tasks, the body just to do essential chores and the life starts to drain away. Bodies have nerves, bodies have skin, bodies contain a spirit, a heart and endless imagination...

His hand settled on her ankle, slowly inspected his way to her knee, and then skimmed her thigh, first outside and then inside and Chantal gasped. Squeezed her eyes. Tried to get control.

"Other leg," he said matter of factly and yet Chantal couldn't stop her from leaping, her pulse to leaping, her belly in knots, her nerves so tense she jumped when his palm circled her left ankle.

"Don't," she choked, knowing she was losing it, losing perspective, losing whatever it was that kept her contained, the iron wall around her emotions. Suddenly she wasn't the fortress of before. She was an open gate and she was begging the forces in.

"Almost done," he said calmly, continuing his examination, ankle, calf, knee—oh knee, her knee was ticklish, all tender nerves and she flinched.

"Not hurt," she whispered breathlessly, willing him to just hurry, just get on with it. If he would finish with this silly med check of his, then she could get back to being the ice princess who needed nothing, no one, not even love.

But he wasn't hurrying. Not in the slightest.

If anything his inspection slowed, his fingertips still resting in the hollow behind her knee, the lightest touch imaginable and yet it sent arrows of feeling up her thighs, between her thighs, feeling that was nearly as intense as the loneliness she never told anyone about.

She wasn't supposed to need.

She wasn't supposed to want.

She wasn't supposed to feel.

Finally, finally his hand wrapped her thigh, moving up, the outer thigh, the back of her hamstring reaching the sensitive skin where thigh met cheek and she jerked so hard that tears rushed to her eyes.

Chantal drew a ragged breath, and then another, completely undone by everything that had happened in the past few hours. She shouldn't be letting him touch her. She shouldn't be responding when he was touching her.

"You're very bruised. You've cracked some ribs. But I think that's the worst of it." His deep voice hurt her ears. Everything about him was making her twist on the inside, her chest, her heart, her emotions so wound up she didn't know how to escape or where to go.

A crooked fork of lightning split the sky just above their heads, and in the stunning bright flash of light, Demetrius's eyes met hers and they were so dark they sank through her, reaching the restless, anxious place where she needed so much and didn't even know how to live with the reality of her life.

He was a man. He was different from her. Altogether different.

"You said you were Greek," she said, conscious of his hand resting on her thigh, near her knee, she dropped her gaze and went to work on the small buttons on her blouse.

"Yes."

Dammit. Her hands were shaking so bad she couldn't even get one button back through the hole. "You live there now?"

"Yes."

"You're in Athens?"

She felt rather than saw him lean toward her. He reached for her blouse. Began to button the silky fabric himself. "I've my own island near Santorini."

He sounded bored, indifferent, but she didn't believe it for one minute. In her experience, Greeks were the proudest of men, the most male. They were passionate, too, and possessive of their women. One of Chantal's college friends had married a member of the Greek aristocracy and she'd been a pampered, and jealously guarded, wife ever since.

Her gaze lifted, she searched his face. His eyes did something to her. They were so dark. So intense. His entire face was hard...fierce. The only softness was at his mouth. There was just a hint of a curve to his lower lip, a suggestion of sexuality that matched the edgy hum in Chantal's veins.

She thought the exam had been difficult. But the matter of fact touch now, the way he buttoned her blouse was worse. She felt so much, needed so much, and the depth of her need appalled her.

Tears filled her eyes again. She clenched her hands at her sides.

"What's wrong?" he demanded gruffly.

She shook her head, afraid to speak. What in God's name was happening to her? Why was she falling apart now?

Thunder boomed, an ear-shattering clap followed immediately by scorching white fingers of light.

"Come here," he said, his gravel accented voice husky, and he dragged her into his arms.

Within the circle of his arms Chantal felt twin rivers of feeling—fear and need.

Hold me.

Let me go.

Want me.

Don't touch me.

His hands reached up, tangled in her hair, tipped her head back. She felt his gaze, a direct piercing look that penetrated all the way through her. "Princesses aren't allowed to cry," he said roughly, and she struggled to smile.

"I know. Rule number one."

"What's rule number two?" He was holding her before him, his hands in her hair trapping her. She couldn't escape his voice, his eyes, his body.

"Not to do anything publicly that would embarrass the family."

"Is that a warning?"

"No. Just a rule."

"And is this public?"

They were in the middle of nowhere, her staff hidden away, back behind the forest with the plane wreckage. "I don't know anymore."

"There's no one here," he said, and his voice was like silk and sandpaper at the same time, sensual, stirring strokes across her senses. "Just us. The sea. The sky."

"And the storm," she added as thunder boomed yet again.

He picked up one of her clenched hands and studied her small fist. "And your fear."

"And my fear," she echoed, her heart beginning to pound harder, heavier.

"Why are you afraid?"

She struggled to swallow, to moisten her mouth, which had

become so dry. Her skin prickled all over. She did feel fear. Tremendous fear. As well as tremendous excitement. ''I don't do…this.''

''This?'' He considered her, a long level gaze. ''Why not?''

Her heart pounded so hard she couldn't catch her breath. ''It's not allowed.''

Demetrius's jaw tightened. Then his head tipped and his mouth covered hers.

Chantal stiffened. For her, all thought stopped, all reaction stilled. She was frozen in endless time. For a long moment she was nowhere, nothing, unable to respond, and then the ice broke, and her mouth trembled, her lips softening beneath his.

She felt his warm breath and the texture of his lips—his mouth both firm and cool. It'd been so long since she kissed anyone she couldn't even remember how she was supposed to do this and yet she couldn't pull away. She needed his touch, this touch, needed the incredible sensation that shot through her, electrifying her.

He kissed her so slowly that she wasn't even sure if they were kissing or touching and her mouth quivered against his, her nerves tightening, her emotions just there, beneath the surface. Her chest contracted, her eyes burned, her breath became more and more shallow. Had she ever felt a kiss like this before? Had she ever been so afraid before?

Chantal reached up to touch his face, uncertain if she was trying to bring him closer or push him away. He was invading her world, ignoring her boundaries. She couldn't let him do this and yet she didn't know how to stop him. It was as if his kiss was life itself. The thunder rolled and boomed, bone shuddering claps overhead and the heat in the air, the humidity of the impending storm, made her want to peel off everything and press herself against him.

''What do I do?'' she choked against his mouth. ''I don't know what to do…''

''Hush. I do.'' And lifting her in his arms, he settled her in the sand, her back against the soft grains, the white lightning visible beyond their shelter.

She felt his big, hard body come down on hers, felt the length of his torso, arms, legs. His shoulders covered her, her hips cradled his. She felt as if she'd finally come home.

Demetrius braced his weight on his arms, aware of her fragile ribs, and the pain she'd feel if he allowed her body to support his.

It'd been a long time since he'd been with a woman like this. It wasn't that he'd remained celibate since his wife died, but he hadn't felt something with anyone in so long that feeling anything was stunning. And he wasn't just feeling a little emotion. He was almost overrun by emotion.

They'd been so close to death, and so ready to accept whatever came next, that the relief at returning to life was dazzling. Dizzying.

He felt Chantal's breasts rise and fall, felt her body stir beneath his, her hips lifting, seeking, and lowering his head, he covered her lips once more with his.

He kissed her deeply, kissed with a hunger that words could never explain. Unless you'd been where he'd been, unless you'd seen what he'd seen, unless you knew what he knew, words wouldn't explain the need to merge completely with another, to find release and mindlessness, maybe even an hour of peace.

Peace, he thought, lips parting hers, tongue flicking across the soft, swollen inside of her lip, tasting her mouth and the warmth and wetness within. Peace hadn't been his in years.

Nothing had been his in years.

He'd lost his family, his wife, his circle of friends.

He'd lost it all when he realized he couldn't continue in the Mantheakis tradition, when being a member of his family, his clan, was killing him as surely as it'd killed his wife.

Something had to give.

So he'd given up his past, his future, his soul. But now, here, with the princess, he wasn't quite so disconnected. He felt almost alive again, felt hard and heated and warm. Felt her warmth all the way through him, too.

He'd had sex numerous times in the past few years but he'd never made love.

And somehow, he wanted to make love to the princess who seemed nearly as alone as he was.

His chest burned, hot, hotter, and yet gently he settled his hips against her, even as he kept the brunt of his weight on his arms. He felt her softness shape him, accept him, felt the painful ache of his erection press against her skirt, now hiked high on her thighs.

Her fingers grappled at his shirt, pulling the fabric from his chest. He inhaled sharply as her hand found his bare skin, her fingers seeking skin, muscle, tendon and then he took her tongue in his mouth and sucked the tip of it instead.

She was making him burn. She was making him want. She was making him feel like a young man first falling in love. But this wasn't love. It was fear. It was exhilaration. It was gratitude for making it through another day.

Her fingertips brushed his nipple and he stifled a groan. Her touch unsettled him, light, searching and yet edged with desperation as if she too knew it was this one moment, and only this moment, that whatever was happening would never happen again.

If that were the case, he'd hold her, fill her, give her all that he'd withheld from the women who'd entered and disappeared from his life in the years since Katina died.

With her assistance, his shirt came off. His slacks were next. The underclothes disappeared from them both and when he lay her down again they were both completely naked and their skin felt so right that way, one body close to the other.

He felt the princess draw a quick breath as his hand caressed her hip, shaping her curves. She was so slender, delicate, and he urged her closer yet, her shoulder brushing against his, her soft breasts pressed to his chest.

He briefly shifted his weight, settled between her legs and immediately felt his body seek for hers, searching for her warmth, her heat, and he felt the softness of her against him, felt the way her body gave.

This was madness, he knew, this wasn't why he'd agreed to protect her. This wasn't part of any job description he'd ever known, but he couldn't stop. Not now. Not today. Not when the thunder boomed and the lightning crackled and their bodies and skin was the only thing keeping them sane.

Reaching between their bodies he lightly touched Chantal's smooth flat belly, cupped her mound, slipped his hand between her legs to feel if she was ready for him, and she was. Her body was warm, wet, willing. Was this right? he wondered, even as he kissed her more deeply. How could making love be an answer to anything?

And yet her body felt wonderful, and her warmth called to him, drawing something in him that he'd refused to recognize in years.

She wasn't just a body, but a woman, a woman with a life that had been as challenging as his.

And when he entered her, slowly easing into her, pushing as deep as he could go without hurting her, he felt something inside him split, a small tear, and he knew then, that he'd made a huge tactical error. This wasn't a woman he could have. But she wasn't a woman he could forget, either.

The storm was over. It had to be morning, but Chantal didn't want to open her eyes. She didn't want to wake up until Demetrius was gone. But Demetrius wasn't moving. He was lying right next to her, his body curved around hers, his hand resting on her bare hip.

She'd spent the night in his arms. All night in his arms. The lovemaking had been intense, explosive, almost frightening in its carnal volatility. They could have been animals instead of people, two starving human beings.

But she *had* been starving. Starving for years.

Shuddering at the image, Chantal opened her eyes, her heavy lashes fluttering up to face the clear pale blue sky, the morning light the sheerest shade of gold, the air still and warm, the only sound that of the crash of waves on the beach.

Pushing up on her elbow, she winced at the stab of pain and combed her hair back from her face as she tried to stay calm.

This wasn't something she should have done. This wasn't something she could condone. Frantic grapplings in the dark were reserved for teenagers randy with hormones, not a middle-aged woman with a young child.

Swallowing the icy lump in her throat, hating how it matched the even heavier icy rock in her stomach, she slowly rolled out from beneath his hand, biting a groan of anguish at the sharp pain stabbing deep in her ribs, spreading into her chest, radiating through the middle of her back.

My God, she hurt. But she forced herself to her feet, and stepped over the scattered palm fronds. The storm had blown their little shelter to bits, and the high ocean tide had practically swept them out to sea.

Not that the storm, or the tide, had stopped them last night. Nothing had stopped them. Not even dignity, pride, or common sense.

Limping along the beach, Chantal searched for her missing clothing, and tried to pretend she wasn't stark naked.

This had to be someone else's life. This couldn't be her, this couldn't have been her horrible nightmare.

She'd had sex with a stranger.

Not just once, but two, three times.

Cringing, she turned, scanned the sea, saw nothing beyond the beautiful beach, so peaceful now, the sand swept clean by rain and sea, and then glanced back at Demetrius who still slept.

Who the hell was he? She knew nothing about him. Absolutely nothing. He could be a reporter. A friend of her father-in-law's. He could be married. He could be infectious.

Chantal froze, her insides cramping.

She could get pregnant.

They'd had unprotected sex. Three times. She could definitely get pregnant.

Panic rose, a wide wave of panic even stronger than last night's high tide. She pressed her hands to her eyes, blocked out the vision of what they'd done, what they'd been to each other then, and tried to focus on facts. On reality.

She'd never been highly fertile—she and Armand had had a year of unprotected sex before she conceived Lilly—and she shouldn't be in that part of her cycle, anyway.

Besides, lots of people had unprotected sex and they didn't get pregnant. The timing had to be next to impossible. The chances, the odds...

What was done, was done, she sharply reminded herself. Don't get hysterical. Just get your clothes. Get dressed. Get out of here.

She searched for her blouse, her skirt, and spotted them on the beach, wet, bedraggled, soggy with saltwater and sand. The surf must have carried them out and then brought them back again. Sighing, she hurried across the unscarred sand for her things. The clothes were chilly, damp and gritty but Chantal dragged the blouse on anyway and stepped into the short skirt, the pale pink silk fabric now stained a dappled purple gray.

What a waste of a couture suit.

Sick at heart, Chantal turned slowly, away from the ocean with the fingers of white foam to the long sandy expanse behind her and froze. Demetrius was awake, and watching her.

He was half-sitting, propped on one elbow. His expression was closed, guarded. What on earth was he thinking? But no, actually, she didn't want to know what he was thinking right now. She didn't want to have any part of him. What she wanted was to run—get as far away from him as possible but there was nowhere to go—at least not yet.

Slowly, deliberately, she headed toward him, trying to ignore that the cold wet blouse clung to her bare breasts, that her soaked skirt hugged her hips like shrink-wrapped cellophane, and her undergarments were probably floating out at sea.

Yet on reaching his side she saw her crumpled petal-pink lace bra and matching pink panties bunched in his hand.

Chantal's eyes burned. Her stomach hurt. Her pride felt battered. "Please," she said, putting out her hand in an imperial gesture.

Silently he handed her the delicate under wire bra and lace panties.

"Thank you," she gritted, tears of shame scalding her eyes.

"My pleasure." His eyes glowed at her, a warning in the dark depths. "Princess."

CHAPTER FOUR

DEMETRIUS was angry. Ridiculously angry. He had no right to be angry, either.

He knew last night was a one-time only, he knew when he woke this morning that he'd never let his control slip like that again, and yet the knowledge did nothing to ease the hot, livid emotion building inside him.

The fact that he still had any emotion inside him shocked him.

He'd been the vigilante—the terminator—so long he hadn't thought he could care about people, needs, *feelings*. But he was caring about something at the moment, and it was a mistake. Emotions got in the way of him doing his job.

"How are the ribs?" he asked, his voice coming out short, curt. He shouldn't still be sitting here naked. He shouldn't still be fighting desire. He shouldn't even be thinking about stripping the still damp skirt and blouse off her curvy body and putting his mouth against her sun warmed skin and drinking her like a sweet strawberry Italian soda.

His body hardened. It was impossible to forget how she'd felt beneath him. He was ready to take her again, ready to slide his hands across her breasts, her belly, her thighs. Ready to feel her squirm and whimper and cry with pleasure.

"Fine," she answered crisply, balling her undergarments tighter into her hand.

He felt his lips twist in a savage smile. Last night she'd been broken...open...but this morning she'd remembered who she was, who he was, what her title represented. Princess Chantal Marie Thibaudet, born Princess Chantal Marie Ducasse, probably the world's most beautiful, famous princess. No one was more photographed. No one was more regal.

And she was regal now, even with her long dark hair loose over her shoulders. Even with the wet clothes clinging to her slender figure, she managed to tip her straight nose, press her

43

full mouth tight. She'd become so perfectly proper again. She'd become exactly who she was supposed to be and even though it was right, it made his head hurt, his pulse pound, made him want to lose his temper as only he could lose his temper.

And he had one hell of a temper, too.

"Do you mind turning around?" she said icily, gesturing with her finger.

He ground his teeth together. Did she honestly think he hadn't seen everything? That he hadn't memorized every curve of her body, every dip and hollow and soft satin place?

But she was staring at him, pointedly, and with an exasperated sigh he rose.

Chantal's heart stuttered and then nearly broke through her chest as Demetrius slowly got to his feet.

How she could have fallen so willingly into his arms?

He was huge. Muscular. Intimidating. Armand had been an aristocrat, medium height, lithe, slender, with hands like a pianist—long slender fingers, narrow wrists. Demetrius Mantheakis was anything but narrow and slender. He was thickly built, broad through the shoulder, deep in the chest, thighs, butt hard with tight, compact muscle. Dark hair shadowed his chest, formed a fine trail down his flat, carved abdomen to a thatch at his thighs. Male, his body screamed, I am all male.

She wanted to avert her eyes but knew it was too late. They'd been...intimate. Very. Besides, she'd been married before, conceived a child, delivered a child. It wasn't as if she didn't know how men's bodies worked, how men and women came together for pleasure and procreation.

But their joining last night had had nothing to do with procreation, which left just pleasure.

With his back to her, she struggled out of her blouse again, groaning softly at the effort of trying to hook the bra. Each lift of her arm, each twist lanced pain through her, hot and sharp. Blinking back tears, she tried to get the hook to take a second time.

"Enough," Demetrius ground out, turning around. He took the delicate straps of the bra from her and deftly hooked the bra closed. "It's absurd to not let me help you."

"I don't want your help."

"Too bad, isn't it?" He bent down, picked up her blouse from her feet and held it out.

"You shouldn't—" she broke off, bit hard on the inside of her cheek, held the recriminations in. She couldn't blame him. She'd allowed it to happen.

Worse, she'd *wanted* it to happen.

He buttoned the blouse for her, even tucked it into the waistband of her skirt, and heat filled her at the brush of his fingers against her skin. Eyes closed, she felt her stomach clench and remembered the way his body had joined with hers, how his body had taken hers, a deep, relentless assault on her frozen self.

How to stay cold when someone so hot, so hard was taking your breath away? He'd filled her completely, driven every thought from her mind until all she felt, all she wanted, all she needed was him. Each thrust of his hips rocked her world, creating wave after wave of excruciating sensation. She couldn't survive pleasure like that. It'd been so intense, too intense, and yet he wouldn't let her hold back. He just kept driving into her, hard, thick thrusts that sent her shattering.

"Thank you," she said stiffly as he finished his task and took a step away. And she commended herself for sounding so cool when on the inside she felt feverish all over again. She had to forget. She had to put the memory of her shuddering response out of mind. Had to block out how she'd held onto him for ages, her body rippling with aftershock after aftershock, her nails pressed to his shoulders. Had to forget that he'd just about finished her off when he kissed her breast, suckling her aching nipple.

How did some men know exactly what to do? How could Armand, with all his experience, never give her any pleasure? How could lying with Demetrius here on the beach become the most sexual, sensual night of her life?

"What about the panties?" he drawled.

She went hot, cold, and she fought to keep her gaze above his waist. He was so powerfully made, and with his magnificent body completely naked, she discovered he was hard, very hard. She found his arousal this morning shocking and exciting. What did *he* think of last night? Was it good for him, or had it all been about her?

His dark eyes met hers and held.

She felt a shiver race up and down her back. In the morning light he looked even more dominant than he did at night. While the storm had raged, he'd held her safe in his arms and now she knew why. Demetrius wasn't about to be blown away by sea breezes or tropical storms. He wasn't about to be blown away by anything.

"I can help you," he reminded her.

"*Please.*" She meant to sound sarcastic, instead it came out breathless. She was losing control again, and she knew she couldn't. "This was a mistake, Mr. Mantheakis—"

"I think we're past formalities now, Chantal."

The way he said her name sent another hot shiver racing through her, flashes of feeling in her belly. She was burning hot on the inside. "Could you please put some clothes on?"

He smiled. Grimly. "Of course, Princess."

Relations were most definitely strained, Chantal thought, disgusted with herself. He'd been wonderful on the plane, the kind of man she might have actually enjoyed as a friend, but now...now...

Never.

"What exactly do you do?" she asked, digging into the sand with a little stick, trying to ignore the growling of her stomach, the heat around them, the near sweltering conditions. According to her watch, it was close to noon and he still refused to let her return to the plane wreckage—something she found utterly absurd—but at this point, with tender ribs and a stunning headache, she wasn't going to test him.

"I have my own business."

She tried to imagine what kind of business he'd be in. "You're successful?"

"Very."

She nodded and poked the stick deeper into the hole she'd dug, finding water down below the surface sand. "And you have your own island?"

"Yes."

Chantal heard a droning sound overhead, a faraway hum of engine. "Do you hear that?" she asked, tilting her head back, scanning the endlessly blue sky. She didn't wait for Demetrius to answer. She struggled to her feet, pressing her right arm to her side to keep the tender ribs and surrounding muscles as still as possible.

Suddenly a plane swooped low overhead from behind the tall trees of the rainforest. Chantal let out a shout of relief. "They found us!"

The plane circled the island. It descended even lower, making a final approach. "We should go. It's landing," she said, checking the buttons on her blouse, then the hem of her salt-stained skirt.

Demetrius didn't move. "That's not our plane."

"It's a rescue plane." She was hot and hungry and ready for a shower and clean clothes. And if he wasn't going to head back, fine, but she wasn't about to waste another minute here. "Fine. Stay here. I don't care."

He reached out, circled her ankle, held her still. "It's not our plane," he repeated.

She very nearly kicked his hand, his fingers so warm, too warm against her bare skin. "Let go."

"Once you sit down."

This wasn't even about power. It was survival, pure and simple. Demetrius Mantheakis was too much for her. She couldn't handle him, couldn't even handle herself around him. "I don't want to sit down. I want to go join my staff. I want to board the plane—"

"We're waiting for a different plane, Princess."

She could feel his fingers wrap around each of the small bones in her ankle, feel his warm firm palm along the back of her anklebone and she shivered. His fingers tightened.

"I don't think you understand me, Demetrius. I don't want to wait for another plane. I want this one."

"I'm sorry."

She yanked on her ankle, got nowhere at all. "*Stop.* Just stop this game right now. I want to go."

"You can't."

She felt a shaft of cold, her skin prickling with heightened nerves. "You're beginning to frighten me."

"I've no desire to frighten you. It's my job to protect you." He released her, fluidly stood. "Your safety is my number one concern."

She stared at him for the longest moment, eyes searching the hard planes of his face, the dark stubble on his square jaw. "Why? What do you mean?"

"You've no idea who I am, do you?"

She hated the confusion filling her, and her lips pressed, her heart beating double fast. "No." There was much more she wanted to say but she'd learned years ago to ask only the most pressing questions, to fight only the most essential battles. But surely, this was one of those battles. "Who are you?"

His eyes creased at the corners. He looked as if he were enjoying a private joke. "Your shadow."

She might have learned to bite her tongue, but Chantal hated sarcasm and cryptic answers. It was so typical of the kind of answers Armand and his people gave her, answers indicating that she didn't need to know certain things, answer indicating that as a woman she ought to be ignored...lied to.

Her nails dug into her palms. She'd had it with the lies, had it with the silence. "My shadow? As in—" her eyes searched his, trying to see past the hard veneer that hid his thoughts and all his emotions "—bodyguard?"

"Exactly."

She frowned, increasingly uncomfortable. Maybe she'd never handpicked her security detail, but she'd always been part of the final selection process and been promptly introduced to new staff. "I didn't hire you."

"No."

She felt a muscle twitch between her eyebrows, a small convulsive tug. "Then...?"

He gave her a long, level look, as if weighing what he could tell her, weighing what he would tell her. It was already clear to her that he wasn't accustomed to confiding in women. But then, she wasn't an ordinary woman, either. "Your brother-in-law, King Nuri, hired me—"

"Malik?"

"—With your grandfather's blessing."

Chantal felt cold despite the simmering heat. She reached up, blotted her forehead with the back of her hand. Her skin was beaded, damp, and yet she felt chilly on the inside. "I'm afraid the heat is getting to me. I don't understand. Nothing you're saying is making sense—"

"You're not listening, then."

She needed a bath. Sand and sea coated her skin. The heat and humidity wasn't helping, either. "Then say it again."

"Your family hired me to protect you."

"Why?"

"You're in danger."

No. She wasn't. How absurd. "Somebody would have said something to me. My sister...my grandfather."

"I've been shadowing you two weeks, Princess."

Her head snapped back. She stared at him appalled. "Two weeks?"

"Everywhere you've been, I've been."

"The fashion shows?"

"The receptions and cocktail parties."

A world shimmered precariously beyond her reach, a whole world rotating on an axis and she could see it, imagine it, but she wasn't part of it. "The breakfast at the hotel?"

"I know exactly the waiter you were talking about. She was my waiter, too."

Chantal noticed that Demetrius had referred to the waiter as she. Demetrius understood the waiter's need to be someone else, too. Somehow the thought settled her, calmed her. She focused her thoughts, forced herself to regroup. "Why do you think I'm in danger?"

But before he could answer there was a loud humming noise and the humming turned into a full roar. The jet that had landed fifteen minutes ago was taking off.

For a long moment she stared at the belly of the white glossy jet, watching the wheels, the tilt of the aircraft's nose.

Then panic hit and she screamed. "No. No. Not without me!"

She chased after the plane, running barefoot along the beach, blindly kicking up saltwater and sand.

But the jet kept rising and the wheels folded, disappeared. Tears filled her eyes as the jet sailed off, away from the island into the endless blue sky.

She dropped to her knees, tears of hurt and rage filling her eyes. She wanted to go home. She needed to go home. She'd never been away from Lilly for more than a week. Seven days. That was her limit. She'd made it clear from the beginning that she'd fulfill her royal duties, but when scheduling her appointments the staff had to accept that no matter the occasion, no matter the reason, she'd never leave her daughter for longer than a week.

She should have been home last night. Which made today day eight.

"My jet will be landing shortly."

She hadn't heard Demetrius approach and she shook her head, hating him, hating him for keeping her away from her daughter. "I wanted to be on that plane. I wanted to go home. Now. Today." She reached up and wiped away her tears, feeling overwrought. "You have no idea how much I miss Lilly."

Demetrius stared down on Chantal's dark hair, the long strands blowing in the gentle breeze. The first clouds were appearing on the horizon. True to the tropics, the wind would pick up, rain clouds would gather, there'd be another spectacular storm later.

She was wrong about one thing, he thought, watching the breeze lift and blow her hair. He understood how much she missed her daughter. He'd lost his wife and child. And he'd never stopped longing to see them, touch them, hold them just once more.

He'd made endless bargains with God, promised his heart, his home, his soul if Katina and their daughter could be spared.

God, he learned, didn't bargain.

"I miss her," Chantal repeated softly, tipping her head back to watch the jet—now just a speck in the sky—disappear from sight.

"And she'll miss you, but better we keep you safe."

"So when does your plane arrive?" She asked, unable to keep her voice from breaking.

"Soon."

"And your plane will fly me to La Croix?"

He was silent a long moment. "We're not going back to La Croix."

Chantal was glad she was sitting. Her bones felt dangerously weak. "Not going home?"

He took a step toward her and then another, until his body dwarfed hers, his shadow stretching long, a tower of a man. "Not immediately."

"My daughter's in La Croix," Chantal said quietly, firmly, grateful she'd spent years learning the art of camouflage.

"I know. But we're not going there."

"Where are we going then?"

"To the Rock."

"The Rock?"

"My island."

Chantal fought down her anguish. "And Lilly?"

"She'll be safe in La Croix with your family."

Armand's family. Chantal averted her head, faced the ocean, watched the waves, which were beginning to turn dark green beneath the early-afternoon clouds. A storm was moving in. Again. She suppressed a shiver. She didn't want to be here when the next storm hit. Didn't think she could survive being caught in the middle of another storm with Demetrius Mantheakis. He was a storm in and of itself. "My daughter should be with me."

"She will be."

"They won't let her leave the country." She spoke carefully, finding it painful to speak difficult truths out loud. "Part of my...contract...as princess is that I can leave, but Lilly, who shall inherit the throne must stay behind." She felt the lump block and fill her throat, cutting off air, making her head swim. "She's La Croix's only heir."

"Then for now she remains with her father's family."

The Greek's voice sounded flinty, almost indifferent and Chantal bowed her head, hiding her pain. "I need her." She could barely squeeze the words out. It was nearly impossible for her to claim what she needed most. And she needed her daughter. Her daughter had been everything for her so long...her daughter had been her sole reason for living, breathing, her daughter was life itself.

"You'll be with her again." He crouched in front of her, forced her chin up, stared long and hard into her eyes. "Eventually. Once it's safe. For you, and her."

Chantal swallowed around the hot pain filling her, a lance through her heart. "You don't believe she's in danger, do you?"

"No. But you definitely are."

She flinched, but it wasn't his words, which frightened her, it was him. She realized the others were gone. She realized they were alone, truly alone together, and the situation terrified her. Him, her, alone. Him, her... "And once we're on your island...?"

"I'll be able to keep you safe my way."

She hesitated, unbalanced. "*Your* way?"

"My people, my island, my control."

He called this an island? Chantal asked herself, leaning sideways in her seat to see the land loom up below them.

Greek islands were supposed to be beautiful. This was a piece of black rock in the middle of the sea.

Moments later the jet touched down on the shortest runway imaginable, and the moment they deplaned they were traveling in a dark Mercedes convertible with Demetrius at the wheel.

Still wearing her stained silk suit, Chantal pressed her hands to the side of her seat, her nerves absolutely shot.

During the flight, they'd had a hot meal and slept, but Demetrius had spoken very little.

But now, driving, he glanced at her, and finally she registered on his personal radar screen. "We're almost at the house," he said.

She couldn't imagine how anyone could live on such a barren black rock. "A real house?"

"With indoor plumbing." Rare amusement lurked at the corner of his mouth.

But she wasn't amused. The last thing she felt like doing was laughing.

''So when can I call my daughter?''

The amusement faded from his expression. ''You can't.''

He couldn't keep her from phoning her own family. He didn't have that kind of power. ''You forget, Demetrius, you work for me.''

''Actually, Princess, I work for the sultan.''

She chafed at the way he said, *princess,* resenting his authority and the mockery she heard in his voice. ''He's not going to approve of how you're treating me.''

''He knows my methods.''

''I wouldn't be so sure of that,'' she flashed, pressing her fists to her thighs, trying desperately hard to hang on to the last scraps of her royal dignity. Somehow he'd managed to strip her of everything else.

''And so do my people,'' he added, shooting her a warning glance. ''Don't think they'll loan you a phone, a boat, or a plane.''

''*Your* people?''

His head, with the thick jet-black hair, inclined. ''The Rock is my world. Everything on this island is part of that world, and it's the only world I trust. Those that live here, work here, work for me.''

''Are you sure you don't own them?'' she flashed, provoked beyond reason, remembering her years in La Croix. Armand had acted like he owned her and she'd hated it.

But Demetrius wasn't perturbed. He looked at her, shrugged. ''Of course not. They're not objects to possess. But I own their loyalty. They are my people.''

She stared at his profile now, questions racing through her head, making the short drive from airport to house interminable. How did she know she could trust him? How did she know anything he said was true? It was quite possible he was the threat.

Emotion coiled inside her, tighter, tighter until she felt like a child's wood top about to spring loose.

What if, just what if, he really hadn't been hired by Nicolette's sultan? What if he worked for someone else? What if...?

She shot him another suspicious glance, unsettled by the high bridge of his nose, the hard prominent cheekbones. The lines in his face were so dominant, so strong. She'd never known another man with a face that looked as if it'd been gouged from stone.

"If there's something on your mind," he said flatly, his gaze never leaving the narrow twisting mountain road, "say it."

Say it? She silently wondered, thinking of the past. The problem was she'd spent too many years silent, biting her tongue, holding back her protests. She didn't know how to say what she needed to say, didn't know the words...

There'd been years and years of being politely ignored. Years where the attention was focused on the man—the male definition of experience. In La Croix she'd never been a woman, not a real person, much less a royal princess. She'd simply been a companion. It was as if each tour, each visit, each appearance was strictly for Armand's benefit. She was only seen when she was at his side.

His side. *His* pleasure. *His* interest.

Now and then guides and interpreters would engage her in conversation when she was alone, on her own, waiting. But the moment Armand appeared, all friendliness vanished. Silence fell. Energy, attention focused exclusively on Armand.

She'd had no idea how strong her feelings were until she wasn't allowed to express them. Armand's culture was the culture of men. It wasn't merely arrogant—it was oblivious to the feminine. For most La Croix men, a woman was to be seen, not heard, to be beautiful, but pliable, to comply, compromise, acquiesce.

Acquiesce.

She'd spent her life giving herself up, giving herself out, giving, giving, would there ever be time for herself? Room for herself? How was a woman supposed to survive in a world like this?

"I can't answer your fears if you don't tell me what's worrying you—"

"I'm not afraid."

"And I can't help you, if you don't tell me what you need," he continued as if she hadn't spoken.

Help her? How could he possibly help her? He was a man. Anger surged through her and balling her hands into fists, she held the fury in.

Suddenly she pictured herself standing on the top of Demetrius's mountain and screaming up into the sky, screaming at the stars and the sun and the dawn, screaming at the night. *Look at me. See me. I am real, aren't I? I must matter, don't I?*

I matter.

I do.

"We're here," Demetrius said abruptly, parking in front of a tall whitewashed house, stark, simple.

The air caught in her throat. She'd never seen such a severe looking house in her life. How could he live here? The building looked as cold and hard as a hospital.

Or a prison.

Demetrius turned off the engine. "Welcome to your new home."

CHAPTER FIVE

"THIS isn't my home," Chantal said fiercely, still sitting in the Mercedes convertible, her gaze fixed on the large white plaster house, the no-nonsense windows, the intensely blue sky behind the barely visible terra cotta tiled roof. Even the stairs wrapping the side of the house were boxy, rectangular, all straight white lines and angles.

He stopped on the front steps and faced her. "For the next month it is."

Month? Was he out of his mind? She struggled to scramble from the convertible, her right side tightening with red-hot pain as she pushed open the car door. Her ribs had been on fire ever since they boarded the plane but the physical pain was nothing compared to the loss of Lilly. "You don't actually mean a *month.*"

His dark narrowed glance swept over her face with its furrowed brow and compressed lips. He shook his head once, a short, impatient shake of his head. "You're in no condition to fight with me. You can hardly stand up straight."

Was that a challenge? Ignoring the intense throbbing between her ribs, Chantal forced her shoulders back. "I'm fine."

He gestured dismissively, indicating her paleness, the pinched muscles at her mouth. "I'll let the doctor be the judge of that. He's on his way."

Inside the house, Demetrius climbed the stairs to his second floor bedroom suite, checking messages on his cell phone's voice mail at the same time.

Most calls weren't urgent, but the message from palace security in Melio was. He called the chief of security as he walked to his bedroom window that overlooked the front driveway. The princess was still leaning against the hood of his car. She looked furious. Frustrated.

He didn't exactly blame her. He was damn frustrated, too. Sex

56

had been a mistake. He should have never lost control. But blame would do nothing now. The mistake had been made, and he'd learned long ago that once history was written, you couldn't go back and rewrite it.

Those first couple years after he made the break with his family—*The* Family—he expected a bullet in his back any day. You didn't leave the family. He'd been the first in decades. But his anger had been so huge, his loss so severe, that somehow the different warring sides respected his pain, accepted their part in the tragedy, and they let him go.

Of course there had been attempts to bring him back 'home', attempts to influence him—persuade—money, psychological intimidation, physical threats, but Demetrius was far too angry, emotions far too numb, to fear death. So he got life. And he had his revenge and he carved out his freedom for himself, one job at a time.

The vigilante had become the professional, the expert on solving crime, predicting crime, protecting from crime.

Now his security firm was considered one of the best in the world, if not the best, and he'd made a fortune off people's fear, built an empire on the notion that what happened to Katina should never happen to anyone else.

"Demetrius? Still there?" Avel Dragonouis, the Greek security expert Demetrius had sent to Melio to work with the palace detectives came on the line. "Sorry to keep you waiting."

"What's happened?"

"There was a camera in her room at the palace here," Avel said bluntly. "We found it patched into a wall. It's not particularly hi-tech, can't be police or government equipment, either. This is your typical consumer video camera."

Demetrius felt his gut tighten. "Where was the camera?"

"Positioned over her bed."

A Peeping Tom pervert, too. "Has anyone checked her rooms in La Croix?"

"So far the king and queen have refused to cooperate in our investigation—"

"We just want her room checked," Demetrius interrupted bitterly, exasperated by Princess Chantal's inflexible, in-laws.

"They feel it's an invasion of privacy."

"Better to lose the princess, right?" Demetrius sighed, rubbed his forehead. "Fine. Keep me posted."

Hanging up, Demetrius glanced out the window again, saw Chantal nervously rub her hands against the car's glossy paint.

Her head was bent. Her face concealed. And yet he felt her vulnerability keenly. Her royal family, the Ducasses, were worried sick about her, and yet in La Croix, the Thibaudets couldn't be bothered.

The Thibaudets needed investigating.

Before stepping into the shower, Demetrius made one more call, this time to his Athens office. It was time a serious inquiry was launched into Phillipe and Catherine Thibaudets' lives. Demetrius wanted to know everything about them. He also wanted to know everything possible about Armand, their late son, their only child, the prince Chantal had married.

No detail was too small, Demetrius told his Athens assistant. No detail irrelevant.

In the shower Demetrius reflected on everything he knew about Chantal. Her American mother. The idyllic childhood in Melio. The loss of her parents at fourteen. Her protective relationship with her sisters. Her difficult marriage. Her young daughter. Her pride.

And it was her pride that jeopardized her most.

The princess didn't know when to ask for help. The Princess didn't know how to ask for help.

He was right to bring her to the Rock. The Rock was the ultimate refuge, the island was off-limits to everyone. No one arrived by boat, plane, or helicopter without his permission. The few families living and working here had been with him for years, most were people he'd saved in one way or another, and for those rescued from the sure hand of death, life on the Rock was secure and sweet.

People here knew exactly who he was, and exactly what he did, and they were grateful he didn't pull any punches.

Dressing in khaki-colored linen slacks and a black knit short-sleeve shirt he ran his fingers through his short dark hair and returned down the stairs to discover the princess had entered the house and was wandering through the lower floor.

Chantal passed through virtually empty rooms, the interior of the house as Spartan as the outside. As she moved from one room to the next, the whitewashed walls remained empty, the furniture low and sparse, no decoration anywhere. No pictures, no books, no television, nothing for entertainment or pleasure.

And suddenly he was there, appearing so silently in the doorway, that she felt a shudder deep inside her. He terrified her. Not because he'd ever hurt her, but because he'd made her feel so much on Sao Tome, the island the plane had landed on. He'd made her want so much again.

Briefly her gaze met his before she looked away, heat creeping through her face, burning her. "Your house is empty," she said, nerves strung tight, body humming with a restless energy she couldn't explain.

"I have what I need."

Even without looking at him, she felt the way he studied her, assessed her. He was an expert in observation. "So what do you do here?" she asked, trying to fill the peculiar quiet. "How do you pass the time?"

"I work."

"You have an office here then?"

"Downstairs."

He hadn't moved from the doorway. He was so big he filled the opening in the white plastered walls and the light pouring through the open window lit his face, clear defining light accenting the broad jaw and brow.

"You've been a bodyguard for a while now?" she asked, picking through the dozens of questions and doubts filling her brain.

"Awhile."

He wasn't giving her much to work with, was he? "You don't look like a bodyguard."

"Do they come in a standard package?"

"I've had bodyguards before."

"Were they any good?"

She shrugged. "I'm still here, aren't I?"

He said nothing and his silence set loose a fresh flurry of

worries and doubts inside of her. She didn't know how to deal with him. Didn't know how to distance herself, either. He was inconsequential, she told herself. He didn't matter. He had no impact on her life.

But that wasn't true.

He'd rocked her world with his body, and then rocked it again when he'd told her she was in his protection.

Protection. The word was supposed to evoke safety. Comfort. Peace. But she felt anything but safe, comfortable or peaceful right now. ''Is this where you bring all your clients?'' She blurted, panic growing. How could she spend a month here? How could she spend a month with *him?*

''You're the first.''

''And the lack of neighbors?''

''I like my privacy.''

''Do you even have phones?''

''Yes, but I have a security code on them. No one can use them without me dialing the code first.''

Chantal felt precariously close to tears. She needed a bath, a change of clothes, a good nap. But most of all, she needed to find a touchstone, something familiar, something from home to reassure her. Settle her. ''Can I at least call Lilly?''

''No. You're too emotional.''

Because I'm scared! She ground her teeth together, fighting her anger, the waves of indignation. ''What about making a call to my sister, Nicollette? Or to my grandfather?''

He shook his head. ''There's no point. They know what they need to know—the plane crashed, there were frightening moments, but you're now safe with me.''

Safe with him? Chantal nearly choked on the tears she was holding inside. Nothing about Demetrius was safe—much less her own person. She'd stripped for him, opened her body for him, nearly opened her heart for him. How could this...*he*...be considered safe?

''I realize you've been hired to protect me,'' she said tersely, speaking flatly, precisely, empowered by the oldest survival skill of all time: self-preservation. She'd never make it here, not alone with him. ''But I won't be kept isolated from my home and my family this way. Perhaps you enjoy your isolation here on the Rock, but I need my family. I need to be with them. And I need to go home—''

"Even if it kills you?" He interrupted, folding his arms, causing the shirt to gape.

"An exaggeration," she said, trying to avoid looking at his bronze throat and the dense muscle of his chest. She remembered what it felt like to lie against that chest, to have his warm, powerful body arched above hers, hips tight, legs tangled. He made love the way some made war—accepting nothing less than complete and total surrender.

And she'd loved it. Perhaps that's what humiliated her most. She hadn't merely accepted him, she'd wanted him desperately. She'd been completely wanton, craving everything he gave her and more.

He'd been so big inside her, so hard, so hot, and even after he'd come, she hadn't wanted him to withdraw from her. She'd loved the feel of him too much, loved the way their bodies had fit together. There'd been no thought, no control on her part.

She'd dug her nails into his back trying to hold him tighter, trying to merge even closer.

Insatiable, she thought now, ashamed all over again. She couldn't get enough, and he knew it.

Heat flooded her body, mindless heat, her legs trembling a little, her muscles inside her belly clenching.

"When was the last time the Thibaudets visited the palace in Melio?" he asked abruptly.

She eyed him warily. "Six months or so. They flew to Melio for Nicolette's wedding to King Nuri."

"Did anyone else from La Croix come?"

Her shoulders twisted. "Plenty. Both the king and queen have brothers and sisters as well as cousins. Why?"

"Someone close to you, someone with access to you wants you...gone."

Gone? Gone as in *dead?* She blanched but held her ground, those years of training coming in handy as she struggled to mask the depth of her shock.

"There've been two attempts that we know of," he continued

—

in the same hard, uncompromising voice, his Greek accent more pronounced then it had been last night. "The first attempt was foiled purely by chance. The second was nearly fatal."

"I don't..." She swallowed, feeling sick on the inside, nausea and ice somersaulting in her veins. "I don't know anything about an attempt, and certainly nothing about one being nearly fatal."

"You were sick after your sister's wedding." His deep voice forced her to meet his gaze again.

"I had the flu."

"You were hospitalized."

"For a day."

"Two days."

"Dehydration."

"Blood work was done." He moved toward her, touched the base of her neck, his fingertip brushing the hollow of her throat.

She jerked at the touch, her pulse leaping wildly. His touch was hot and sharp, both delicious and disconcerting.

"You were being poisoned," he continued ruthlessly.

"No."

"Your doctor in La Croix alerted the king and queen—"

His words and touch made her head spin, and Chantal glanced right, left, unable to take in what he was saying. It couldn't be true. There was no reason for him to lie to her...and yet, what did she know of him? Who was he? A man. And she knew perfectly well that men had agendas of their own. "I never heard anything about it," she said hoarsely.

"Of course not." The corner of his mouth lifted but he looked harsh, angry, as though he were barely hanging onto his temper. "The good doctor was forbidden to speak of it to you. He was told that you'd done it to yourself, that you'd turned increasingly self-destructive since your husband's death and this was just another attention seeking behavior."

"What?"

Even more slowly Demetrius ran a finger up the side of her throat. "A cry for help," he concluded, and she shivered even as tendrils of heat curled in her belly, re-igniting the fire, turning her into a mass of trembling nerves.

Just like last night his touch scorched her and the need had returned, resurrecting the memory of pleasure. The pleasure had been stunning. Nothing had ever compared to the earthy, sensuality in her life. No one had ever touched her as if she was both beautiful and real, and it felt incredible to love her body, her skin, her mind.

Her mind...

Her mind had always been her greatest strength. Her reason. Her discipline. Her tremendous drive. And yet he was telling her now that the king and queen didn't think she was mentally sound. Worse, they'd actually told her physician that she'd apparently poisoned herself to get attention.

How repulsive. As if she'd ever hurt herself when she had so much to live for! "That's ridiculous," she choked, stepping away, senses spinning, nerves stretched taut. She had to put distance between them before her body betrayed her again. Her mind was strong. It was her body that was weak. "I might have issues with my in-laws, but I've no desire to leave this life."

"And I've no desire to see you leave this life, either."

"Who poisoned me, then?"

"If we knew, I wouldn't have you in protective custody."

Protective custody. What a horrible phrase. She turned, glanced back at him. "Any ideas? Possible leads?"

"The Melio palace security is taking the lead in the investigation. Of course my staff is working with them, but our primary job is to keep you safe, not solve the crime." He hesitated. "But at the moment we have two different theories. The first, that you've been targeted for political reasons. The second, it's purely personal."

"Personal? How?"

"You've got an obsessed fan."

Chantal slowly sat down on one of the plain sofas covered in rich blue fabric and struggled to take it all in. She'd been poisoned. *Poisoned.* That meant someone had been close enough to get to her food, her drink...that same someone could go to the kitchen or the dining room without arousing suspicion.

"It's crazy," she finally concluded, her head reeling, fatigue growing. So much had happened in the past forty-eight hours. And now this news.

"What about Lilly?" she asked quietly, fear welling for her daughter. "Is there any suggestion that she, too, might be targeted?"

"No. Nothing. Her grandparents have her well protected." Demetrius crossed the floor, stood before her, looking down at her bent head. "It's you we're worried about. And we haven't ruled out that the threat might coming from the Thibaudets—"

"No."

"We can't rule it out, Princess. Both attempts on your life happened either at the châteaux, or nearby."

"No." Chantal stood, faced Demetrius, squaring off with him. "I haven't had a warm relationship with Armand's parents, but I know them, and I can't believe they'd ever be part of something so...reprehensible. They might be callous, but they're not malicious."

He said nothing. He simply stared at her, silently contradicting her and she flushed.

He'd be a ruthless adversary.

He'd never accept defeat.

"Queen Thibaudet practically grew up with my grandmother. They were childhood friends. The Thibaudets are essentially good people." Her voice came out husky, pathetically vulnerable.

"Good people that want custody of Lilly," he retorted flatly, without apology. "And they're tired of battling with you—"

"They don't battle with me. They've tied my hands completely!"

"Nonetheless, you worry them. You're a...thorn...in their side." His eyes narrowed, his wide jaw bristled by two day's growth of beard. "Haven't they told you as much?"

She closed her eyes. They had. But how did he know? She opened her eyes, looked briefly up, into his eyes, and then down at his chest. Far easier to keep her gaze there on the black shirt than his dark eyes which hinted at anger, and more. "How could you possibly have heard?"

"Every palace has ears."

A knock sounded on the door and a young maid appeared in the doorway. She bobbed her head and spoke to Demetrius in

Greek. Demetrius answered her and then turned to Chantal. "The doctor's here," he said. "He's waiting upstairs."

Demetrius stood at the far end of the bedroom, his back turned to give Chantal some privacy, while the doctor from Athens conducted a polite, professional examination. She'd been upset that Demetrius had insisted on remaining during the exam but she had to admit that he'd been as detached as humanly possible. The only time he'd glanced toward the bed was when the doctor had asked Chantal to sit up and she'd cried out at the stab of pain.

Chantal's cry had hardened Demetrius's jaw and he spoke quietly, harshly to the doctor, and the doctor immediately apologized to Chantal for causing her pain.

One of her eyebrows arched ever so slightly as she shot Demetrius an assessing glance. He was definitely in charge. Definitely the boss.

A few minutes later the doctor concluded the exam. He'd brought some painkillers with him and suggested the pills for pain relief, especially at night if the princess had difficulty sleeping. "Otherwise, I recommend rest," he said, closing his bag and drawing his suit jacket back on. "Her Highness needs to let the bruised muscles mend. Nothing too physical."

Demetrius walked the doctor out and then returned a few minutes later with the young Greek housemaid.

"This is Yolie," Demetrius said by way of introduction, "and she'll be assisting you while you're here."

Chantal felt as if her life had been completely taken over. First the doctor. Now the young Greek maid. "I don't need help."

"You can't sit up without whimpering like a baby, Princess—"

"Why do you call me that?" she interrupted, finding him overbearing. Arrogant. Controlling. Just the way he said princess put her teeth on edge. He never used Your Highness, or Your Royal Highness, the proper title of respect, much less addressed her with deference.

"What would you prefer? Your first name?"

Her bedroom seemed to have shrunk since he'd returned. She could almost see the white plaster walls move, the ceiling dropped. He dominated his space so completely. She refused to let him dominate her. "Your Highness, will do."

His upper lip curled. "Trying to put me in my place, Princess?"

She flushed, mortified that he'd not just recognized her intention, but called her on it, and she held her breath, battling her rage. She didn't want to be here. She wanted Lilly. She wanted peace. And if she couldn't have that, then she'd at least like to be alone. "I'd like some privacy, please. You may go."

"May I?"

"Yes. And you may take your housemaid with you. I'd prefer to be on my own."

"That's nice. Unfortunately I'm not leaving you alone, not when you're still so bruised. You'll need help drawing the bath and dressing. So drop the pride, and admit you need help—"

"I don't."

"You do. It's your choice. Yolie or me."

She drew in a swift breath. "You?"

His dark head inclined. "I'm more than happy to bathe and dress you."

His mocking tone made her see red. "As if I'd give you that opportunity!"

A warning light flared in his dark eyes. "You did yesterday."

"That's low."

Lines etched on either side of his firm mouth. "But true." He turned, walked to the door. But at the door he hesitated. "Just so you know, Yolie doesn't speak anything but Greek. If there's any confusion, feel free to send for me."

Right. He knew she'd never call for him. "Thank you."

He ignored her sarcasm. "Tonight I'll have dinner sent to your room so you can get some rest. But in the morning feel free to explore the house, and take advantage of the pool and gardens. The island is completely secure. You're welcome to relax or explore."

"I'll need some toiletries. Clothes."

"You'll find that the walk-in closet is lined with everything you could possibly wish for. Shorts, skirts, gowns, tracksuits, swimsuits from all the big designers."

"In my size?"

"Everything's your size. You're the fashion world's darling, and when the big designers heard you needed something to wear, the clothes poured in."

"In a day?"

He laughed. Grimly. "Don't underestimate yourself, Chantal. The clothes arrived within an hour. You're everybody's favorite princess."

CHAPTER SIX

FOR nearly a week after arriving on the island, Demetrius gave her the space she craved, as well as endless hours of time alone.

They didn't take meals together. They didn't sit down together for drinks or conversation. If they met, it was only in passing, and even then Chantal felt tense, awkward.

She wasn't just uncomfortable about what had happened between them. She was ashamed. The only comfort she found was the knowledge that what happened wasn't going to happen again. And the distance between then and now had helped her understand that the explosive chemistry between them had been a result of fear, fatigue, adrenaline. It wasn't normal, or natural, and the same situation wouldn't arise here on the Rock.

But still, she regretted her loss of control. She'd let someone in too close. She'd let Demetrius see—know—far too much of her life and it was dangerous. Dropping her boundaries for even a moment was dangerous.

A week after arriving on the Rock, Chantal left her bedroom and was heading downstairs when Demetrius appeared in the hall, dressed in faded black sweatpants and an old black T-shirt.

"I'd heard you were going for a walk," he said, standing at the bottom stair, waiting for her.

She froze half way down the staircase. They hadn't spoken in a couple of days and his sudden appearance—his very male appearance—unsettled her. He looked far too physical in the faded cotton sweats and T-shirt, the soft fabric clinging to the rugged planes of his chest, his biceps bare, his sweatpants sitting low on his hips, the sturdy cotton outlining the lean line of his thighs.

She knew what he looked like without the clothes, knew the golden skin underneath, knew the curve and knot of muscle. He'd feel warm. He'd feel hard. He'd feel too good.

It'd been a week since their night on Sao Tome and yet suddenly it felt like yesterday. "Yes," she answered, her breath strangled, and she smoothed her short green skirt flat against her thighs, wishing now it was a longer length. It'd looked crisp and fresh this morning in her closet but somehow Demetrius always made her feel exposed.

The nervous kneading of her hands drew his attention and he glanced at her thighs, noting the shortness of her dark green skirt and the length of bare, tan leg revealed.

"So you're feeling better?"

"Yes."

"Ribs not as sore?"

"Haven't had pain in a day or so."

He nodded, pleased. "Good. We'll get started then. You might want to change."

Her eyes narrowed and she eyed him warily. "Change for what?"

"Self-defense classes. It's essential. You have to know how to protect yourself." Demetrius gestured at her slim olive skirt. "So if you're going to change—"

"I'm not," she answered firmly, defiantly. She wasn't going to slip back into a submissive role. He was not in charge. He was not in control. "I'm quite comfortable as I am. Besides, this shouldn't take long."

He shrugged. "Fine. You're the princess."

He led her downstairs, to the bottom floor of the villa. She'd only been to the lower level once, and that was on her second day here. It was Demetrius's floor. She knew his office suite was downstairs, along with a spare bedroom, but she hadn't known about the gym.

The work out room was huge and surprisingly airy. The room accommodated all forms of exercise, from a wall of racked weights and benches to a state of the art treadmill and high tech exercise bike. In one corner a red punching bag hung from the ceiling, while bright blue mats covered nearly half the large hardwood floor.

"Come," he said, kicking off his running shoes at the door. "Join me on the mat."

Chantal removed her leather sandals and cautiously walked to where Demetrius waited for her on the bright blue rubber mat facing the mirror.

"First thing," he said, moving to stand behind her. "Is that you must be aware of your surroundings at all times. You must be conscious of where you are, and what's happening around you."

She nodded, skin tingling, acutely aware of him behind her, sensitive to everything about him. His size. His strength. The hard angle of his jaw.

"You have security detail. Bodyguards. Police escorts," he continued, stepping closer so that his breath brushed across the back of her neck, below her high ponytail. His breath was so warm on her skin and she balled her hands, willing herself not to shiver.

But when his arms encircled her, his hands resting on her hips she jerked violently.

"It's not enough to rely on others to protect you," he continued, his voice in her ear, his hands holding her hips securely. He'd always known how to hold her. Firmly. Calmly. With all the confidence in the world.

"Someone could get distracted," he was saying, even as her pulse raced, her head spinning with sensation.

He was relentless, she thought, his voice assaulting her, his body so warm behind hers.

"There could be another threat requiring immediate attention, your security might need to clear an obstacle, tackle an intruder, jump to protect Lilly. And in those moments you could be left completely exposed." His breath was caressing her neck, her skin, her body growing hotter by the second, her body betraying her yet again.

She burned at the feel of his hands, shuddered when his body came into contact with hers. She caught a glimpse of them in the mirror, Demetrius so large, towering over her, his big arms around her, his legs planted wide.

He was gorgeous and terrifying.

She could see his dark head tip as he spoke to her, saw the intensity in his expression, as well as the urgency.

Her mouth dried. She stared at them, the reflection of the two of them. She looked so small next to him, and it looked natural, too, as if they'd been carved from the same piece of stone, he on the outside, her on the inside, nestled against his chest.

"You need to know what you're going to do before it happens," he said, sliding his hands up her rib cage, wrapping his arms around her chest. "You need to know how you'll handle an attack, know the best way to break a hold. Like this," he said, his arms locked around her chest, his hands practically molding her breasts.

She tingled at the warmth of his hands against her breasts. It was like she had a million nerve endings, and they were all screaming, especially when he shifted and his hips brushed hers, his thighs nudging the back of hers.

"Feel this?" he asked.

She met his eyes in the mirror, mutely nodded. How could she not feel it? She was burning up. Her bare legs no match for the heat emanating from him.

"By the time someone has you trapped like this, it's over."

It was already over, she thought dizzily, heart racing, body trembling from head to toe. She might get off the island, return to royal life, but she'd never get over him.

He tightened his arms a fraction. "I've got your arms pinned to your side. My stance is too wide for you to kick backward, or connect with a knee."

For a moment they stood there, locked together, and again she met his gaze in the mirror and saw something so fierce, so intense in his expression that she wondered how she could have possibly thought that she could manage to control this...that she'd be able to indulge in a physical relationship with Demetrius and not be destroyed.

He wasn't going to let her go, she realized, panic rising. Not now. Not ever. He must have felt her panic because his arms abruptly fell away, and she was free.

Free, but not free. Safe, but not safe. She'd jumped from the fire into the frying pan. Chantal drew a quick breath, glanced at Demetrius.

His dark eyes rested on her. "I'm going to grab for you again," he said calmly. "When I make a grab for you this time, put your arms up, like this.'' He pulled his arms close to his chest, elbows in. ''Then as I bring my arms around, use your arms to break free. Push up and out.''

She did as he said, but she couldn't break free at all.

''Try it again.''

''I can't.''

''You can. Be aggressive, Chantal. You have to power up, shoot your arms out, think explosive.''

Explosive. That's exactly what she was thinking, but not the way he meant. Each time he touched her she shivered. Every time he spoke, his voice burrowed deep inside her, a honeyed heat that she found impossible to resist. She knew how it was in his arms, in his bed. She knew how his body moved against her...in her...she knew too well what he felt like, and how desperately she wanted to feel that passion and pleasure again and again.

I'm lost, she thought, dizzily. *I've never been in so much trouble in all my life.*

They practiced the move until he was satisfied—barely—and then it was another position, him wrapping his arms around her, lifting her bodily off the ground. ''Kick out, aim for my kneecap,'' he said.

His chest was so hard against her back, his arms like steel bands.

''I don't want to hurt you,'' she panted.

''I'll take that chance.''

She felt like she was flailing in his arms, uncoordinated, gawky, weak. Her legs swung, trying to connect with him but unable to find a knee. ''This is ridiculous,'' she said, flushing, her breath coming hard. She didn't want to be fighting him. She didn't want to be in this horrid tug of war in the first place; and it was a war. This was passion versus reason.

She knew her desire for him was illogical. It was pure animal instinct, carnal and physical, and so unlike her real self she knew it'd never last.

''You're not trying,'' he charged.

''I am!''

He put her down, swung her around to face him, his hands resting on her shoulders. "This isn't a game, Princess."

She reached up, knocked his hands off her shoulders. "Don't you think I know that?" She shot back, humiliated. She couldn't understand what was happening inside of her, couldn't understand this crazy love-hate swamping her. "I'm trying. But this isn't natural for me. This isn't like anything I've ever done before."

"Yet another disservice at the hands of your family." His tone was harsh, cutting. "They did nothing to prepare you for reality, did they?"

"You know nothing about my life."

His eyes sparked. "I know all about powerful families, families where duty comes first; families where loyalty and obligation is everything."

"My grandparents did everything they could, and I'm very grateful to them—"

"For selling you off to their wealthy neighbor?"

"It was what was best—"

"For your family. For your country," he interrupted yet again, his voice grating across her nerves, his jaw tight. "Tell me, was saving everyone else worth it?"

"Yes." Her chin lifted. Her eyes met his, clashed, challenging him to contradict her again. "Yes. And I'd do it all over again if asked."

"You're kidding yourself."

And if she was? It was no business of his. He was her bodyguard, dammit. Not her partner. And most certainly not her husband. "Why do you even care?"

"Why don't you care more?"

She shook her head, momentarily speechless. "You have more opinions than any man I've ever met."

He was breathing hard now. "I might have a lot of opinions, but I back up my talk with action."

Her hands balled at her sides. "Unfortunately for you, Demetrius, there doesn't seem to be anyone you can beat up right now."

"Maybe it's you that needs a good swat on your pert little behind."

"Oh!" She seethed with indignation. "I think I need some different company." Marching to the door, she jammed her right foot into one sandal and then the left. "I'm going for a walk," she said in a strangled voice. "And don't follow me. If this is really your island, your *Rock,* then I ought to be perfectly safe getting some fresh air!"

Chantal swiftly climbed the stairs back to the main level, exited the villa through the front door, and crossed the driveway, walking down the long winding driveway. Her eyes were filling with wretched tears and she silently cursed herself, cursed Demetrius, cursed the fact that she—who never used to cry— had become one massive tear duct.

She hated him.

Absolutely positively hated him.

No one else had ever gotten under her skin this way. No one else had ever made her feel so helpless...so confused...so completely off balance. It only took a couple words from him, one long searing glance, and she fell apart, dissolving into a tearful, jagged mass of emotion.

The fact that he had such power over her scared her. Made her furious. Made her want to scream.

Chantal stumbled on a rock and righting herself, laughed at her stupidity. Of course Demetrius was right. Of course it horrified her that she'd married only to lose herself, married only to be destroyed. But it wasn't supposed to have happened that way. It was supposed to be a real marriage. A good marriage. A good life.

She shook her head, hating these thoughts, unable to remember the past, unable to look too far into the future. She never used to dwell on her life this way. She never thought about herself at all. But something had happened the night the plane veered off course, shuddering, shimmying. It was as if the plane on breaking apart had broken something loose inside of her.

The plane was wrecked.

Her world was shattered.

And who was going to fix her? The plane could be replaced,

but what about her? What about this *wanting?* How in God's name would she ever stop feeling now that she'd started?

Demetrius swore beneath his breath, standing on the terrace on the main level watching his princess strut down the driveway, her slender legs bare to mid thigh, her skin the color of sun kissed wheat, her long dark hair swept up in a ponytail high at the back of her head.

He'd never met a more sassy thing. He swore bitterly again. She was making him crazy. She was making him burn.

She was nothing like Katina, either. Katina was blonde, dark olive skin, shy. *Sweet.*

Chantal might long to be reserved, and she played the ice queen well, but she wasn't sweet.

No, she wasn't sweet. She was hot, she was intense, she was smart.

And he wanted her like he'd never wanted anyone. He'd tried to stay away from her. He'd tried to keep his distance, but his self-control was wearing thin.

Very, very thin.

Chantal left the road where it merged onto a smaller path, the grass trampled flat, and followed the dirt path as it began to slope downhill.

She'd had it with men. She didn't want them. Didn't need them. Didn't want anything but to be free. And alone.

She tramped on, arms swinging, temper surging, the warm sun overhead making her thirsty.

If she'd been a real woman, she told herself, she would have told Armand to get lost. If she'd been a real woman, she would have set him straight. She would have left him the first time he raised a hand against her. Instead she tried to reason with him, and then before she knew it, she was pregnant, and the baby changed everything.

Because the baby trapped her in La Croix. Even if she left La Croix, the baby would be Armand's heir.

She should have left him the first time he lost his temper like that, should have packed her bags and headed home and never looked back.

Why did she wait? Why did she hesitate? Love. She'd once loved him enough to imagine a happy life with him. And then when the love was dashed by misery, she still found hope, and hope made her believe that something good could come of her pain. That something good might still happen for her one day. Chantal shook her head slowly, overwhelmed by the endless memories, the mountain of regrets.

The path continued to drop, descend, and rounding the side of the hill Chantal glimpsed the sea again, and then a cluster of houses and whitewashed buildings along a narrow road.

Small red and blue boats were tethered to a low stone wall. Goats grazed in a pasture behind several of the houses. A little tavern with blue painted tables and chairs overlooked the water, hugging rocky land between the road and sea. It was a real Greek village, a charming little town with a shop and tavern and dark-haired children playing football in the street.

She'd been here a week and hadn't even known it existed. Pausing at the edge of the village, Chantal watched the boys. Life in Melio was like this. Little boys teasing girls in the street, little girls sticking out their tongues, little boys growing up into teenagers with crushes on the teenage girls.

One of the boys spotted Chantal and picked up the black and white ball, holding it against his hip. The other boys turned and stared at her.

She felt a funny flutter in the middle of her chest. She was obviously a stranger here, and for a moment she was tempted to turn back around and climb up the hill again, but on the top of the hill was Demetrius and his big whitewashed house that perched above the sea like a predatory bird about to take flight.

No. She wasn't going to go back to the house. She'd walked all the way here. She was going to go on into the village and get some air, and some much needed space.

Space away from Demetrius Mantheakis. Because somehow he'd taken over her life, taken over her thoughts, her heart, her body, too.

She felt the eyes on her as she crossed the dusty road, stepping onto a cobbled sidewalk that must have been part of the island for hundreds of years.

Ducking beneath a canvas awning, she entered the taverna's patio and took a seat at one of the empty tables close to the ocean.

There were four or five older men seated at a table close to the bar. They all stopped talking to look at her, a long measured glance that took in her short linen skirt the color of olives, her fitted white T-shirt, her hair caught up in a high ponytail with wisps now sliding down her neck.

She mustered a smile as she pulled a chair out, but they didn't smile back. Their weathered faces remained perfectly blank. *Fine. Be that way.* Ignoring them she sat down. Leaned on the table. Looked around. Waited. And waited. And waited some more.

Minutes passed, a good five, ten minutes, and yet no one approached her. No one appeared from the kitchen. The young man behind the long bar never made eye contact.

Chantal felt her temper rise. It was hot. Flushed and sticky from the walk, she really craved a cold drink—and some service please. Standing, she crossed the floor, walked to the bar. ''I'd like to see a menu, please.''

The bartender had been washing out coffee cups and reluctantly he turned the water off. ''A menu?''

She hid her impatience. She spoke French, Spanish, English, German and Italian. Surely he understood the word menu. ''I'd like to order something to eat.''

The young Greek bartender had thick wavy black hair that fell across his forehead, long dark lashes, and he stared at her as if she were an alien being, then he looked at the group of older men sitting at the table in the shade. One of the older men said something to the bartender and the bartender shrugged.

Suddenly another voice spoke sharply in Greek and everyone shifted into action. *Demetrius.*

The bartender flushed, the old men at the table, shifted their feet, murmured apologetic words in Greek, and Demetrius moved toward her. ''I'm sorry. You shouldn't have been treated like that.''

He'd drawn her chair out for her and reluctantly she sat back down. If it'd been tense in the taverna before, it was doubly nerve-racking now. "They don't like me?"

He shrugged. "It was a misunderstanding. That's all." But that wasn't all, she thought. The energy in the tavern, at their table, had changed, become charged, electric.

"He wasn't going to serve me," she added, trying to understand the undercurrents.

"No." Demetrius leaned on the table, looked at her, his gaze hard, heated. "They know you're off-limits."

"Off-limits?"

He leaned even closer so they were just inches apart, his dark eyes burning into her, telling her with his eyes what he hadn't yet said with his lips. "They know, *pedhaki mou,* you're mine."

Her heart hammered wildly. He was so close. She could see each dense black eyelash, the tiny bits of copper reflecting in his dark brown eyes. "But I'm not yours." Her voice came out faint.

He simply stared at her, his upper lip barely curving. It was the coolest, most sardonic smile she'd seen in her life; a smile so cool, so sardonic she was forced to look away, hands clasped beneath her chin to keep her wildly beating heart in control.

"You're here," he said softly. "Actions, not words."

Still looking away, Chantal swallowed hard, stared at the line of sand and sea. If she were completely honest she'd admit that the danger waiting for her in La Croix seemed far more manageable than the danger sitting across the table.

Cold drinks arrived. Then a basket of breads and crackers appeared, soon followed by goat cheese, olives, and marinated vegetables.

Life here was like a medieval village. She reached for a hunk of the crusty bread, tore off a piece and dipped it in the fragrant olive oil.

They ate an early lunch, and after they were finished Demetrius leaned back, and watched Chantal. She'd relaxed, he thought, studying her. She'd dropped her guard long enough to enjoy the village, and he could see her take in everything, from the two fishermen down at the water to the group of men at the table next to them.

One of the men nearby laughed, a deep hearty laugh and Chantal looked at Demetrius.

''Zeno,'' he said. ''Our resident Papa.''

Chantal smiled at his explanation, a tiny dimple flashing at the corner of her mouth and his gut tightened.

He wasn't going to let this get out of control again. Not even when she looked at him like that, with a shy glance so full of need and want from beneath her thick dark lashes, her eyes half-smiling up at him, her eyes a warm French blue. She was beautiful—elegant, refined, sophisticated. And yet when he looked into her eyes he saw a world of sadness she prayed no one would see, and most people wouldn't see it, most men wouldn't know what it was, but he recognized the starkness of the pain that made her eyes an even more startling blue.

She'd had her heart crushed, and like the young woman she'd been, she hadn't even seen it coming. Women, he'd learned, were nothing like men. Women looked forward to love and marriage because it was going to be cozy...warm...happy. They were going to be beautiful brides and beloved young wives and then the first of the cherished babies would come along...

Demetrius turned his head away, looked out at the dark blue water and the sailboat sailing across the sparkling waves.

Katina had been like that, too. She'd been so happy to be with him, so happy to be married to him. They didn't have long together, just two and a half years. She was pregnant when she died. Seven and a half months.

His mouth filled with bitterness, the acid of old. There had never been an hour where he could forget. He'd been raised to be a man, and men wanted to protect those more vulnerable. They were driven to protect their women, their children...

Chantal's hand touched his arm. ''Demetrius.''

The red glaze that filmed his eyes faded away. He turned to look at Chantal. She barely came to his shoulder and her thick glossy brown hair gathered in that high ponytail made her look young, far younger than her thirty years.

She was still so innocent, he thought, still so naive. Without thinking he reached out, combed a stray tendril of hair from her dusty rose cheek.

She blushed, her gaze dropping. He couldn't imagine how anyone could raise a hand against her. Couldn't imagine how Armand could do anything but protect her.

Her lashes lifted and she looked back up at him, an uncertain smile curving her lips.

"Have you ever been married?"

"Once." His features looked closed, unreadable.

"Why didn't you ever marry again?"

"Not interested."

"Was your marriage that bad?"

"No. It was that good."

"Oh." She ducked her head again, and she looked so wistful, so much like a kid outside a candy store.

"Would you marry again?" he asked, watching her eyes widen, the sapphire blue so much like the sea.

Her expression immediately shuttered, the veil dropping back over her eyes, hiding thought, emotion, turning her back into the remote ice princess. "No."

"Why not?" he persisted.

Color darkened her cheeks but she looked agonized. "The whole princess thing scares people."

That wasn't it at all, he thought, feeling something inside him wrench. She was lying to him, lying to herself, deliberately twisting the truth.

Her marriage had been horrible. Marriage had scarred her. Scared her.

Aware of a new tension within him, Demetrius leaned forward, rested his weight on the table, moving closer to Chantal, close enough to see all the skin her small T-shirt hadn't covered, the shadow between her breasts and the small golden brown freckle on her collarbone.

He'd never tell her that her vulnerability moved him. That her isolation profoundly touched him.

A princess with her wealth, and her beauty, could have been cold, and yet Chantal was the opposite.

Her softness was everywhere—in her eyes, her lips, in the yearning in her expression. She reminded him of a girl who jumped from childhood to adulthood without a parachute, or the necessary years between.

"I'm not scared," he said quietly, feeling her body hum, watching her face, her emotions barely veiled. "You're a woman, not a machine."

Chantal's mask suddenly dropped and for a split-second she looked at him with outright longing. The loneliness in her eyes cut him. She'd been abandoned too many years ago. Adrift too long.

His body burned. His fingers itched. He wanted to take her face between his hands and kiss her. Kiss her until she melted into him, until those high walls around her fell, kiss her until she warmed, her body and heart as hot as his.

"We've company, boss." The young bartender's voice rang out, breaking the tense silence.

Looking up, Demetrius saw the bartender had binoculars fixed on a point out at sea. "What do you see?" Demetrius demanded, attention abruptly shifted.

"A boat. And it's heading our way."

CHAPTER SEVEN

CHANTAL heard the flurry of Greek, the immediate rise in tension as well as the strange, taut silence that suddenly enveloped them.

Everyone had gone quiet, even the older men. Every head turned to face the sea, all eyes squinting against the sun and the dazzling reflection on the unbelievably turquoise water.

Awareness filled the taverna and Chantal glanced from one man to the next. Something was wrong.

She heard Demetrius speak, Greek words spoken so low and quickly, that she didn't have a hope of understanding, but his tone was unmistakable. He didn't like what he saw.

The pair of young fishermen down at the water also stopped stowing their nets and they, too, faced the water.

What was out there?

Chantal was tempted to rise, but her training was too deeply ingrained. Don't ask too many questions. Don't pry. Don't get involved in business that isn't your own.

But the relaxed atmosphere at the tavern had disappeared. Every man faced the water, waiting.

It was a boat. A small, private sailboat, and it was heading straight to the tiny harbor.

As all eyes stared intently at the cove, a man on board the sailboat dropped anchor and then jumped over the yacht's edge, into the relatively shallow water. He waded toward the low stone retaining wall and the men at the tavern closed ranks around the princess.

Chantal felt the strain, the stress palpable. She could hardly see the beach anymore, but one of the older men from the tavern rose. He was big, burly, the man Demetrius had called Zeno. Zeno headed toward the water, intercepting the young sailor before he could reach the tavern.

"This is a private island." Zeno's deep voice carried. "You're trespassing."

Chantal couldn't hear what the young man was saying, but he was talking, gesturing to his boat, his hands now making shapes in the air, and Zeno didn't look as if he gave a damn. His dark head shook, his arms folded across his chest. "We don't fix boats. Sorry."

The sailor answered and then laughed.

Zeno wasn't laughing.

The sailor tried to brush past Zeno whose arm shot out, grabbed the man by the shoulder and suddenly the sailor was lying flat on his back.

Chantal winced. She saw Demetrius's right hand flex but he didn't move. He wasn't going to leave her side.

"We don't fix boats," Zeno repeated, slowly, loudly, his foot on the sailor's chest. "You need to leave now. Understand?" The man finally understood, whether he wanted to or not. And with Zeno's not so friendly assistance, returned to his boat without further delay.

"That was quite a display of power," she said, completely unnerved. The Rock was like no place she'd ever been before.

Demetrius shrugged. "Everyone works hard here to keep the island safe." With the sailboat disappearing on the horizon, he extended a hand to her. "Come. Let's walk a bit."

But Chantal was still shaken. Demetrius's men had collectively banded together, formed a human shield. She didn't know how Demetrius and his islanders had formed such an intense relationship, but he was right. These were his people. They would protect him, and the island, at all costs.

Demetrius stood next to the table, his brow furrowed as he gazed down at her. "You're not afraid, are you?"

Yes, she wanted to answer him, yes, I am afraid. I've been afraid for years. But whom could she talk to? Whom could she confide in?

"There's nothing to worry about," he continued, his tone softening somewhat. "My people will not let any harm come to you."

She suddenly wished she'd known someone like Demetrius years ago, back when she was still a wife, back when she cringed with fear every time Armand lifted his voice—or his hand. She would have liked to have someone like Demetrius on her side. She would have welcomed his strength. His courage. His counsel.

But there hadn't been anyone like Demetrius then, and she couldn't have him now. She was trapped, and she knew it.

"You're right," she said, forcing a smile to her lips, her face feeling stiff, numb. She couldn't explain the wild swing of emotion, couldn't explain how the physical awareness had turned to something else, how hunger had suddenly given way to a vast emotional need. "Everything's fine."

Rising, Chantal felt self conscious all over again. She couldn't bear being here with him like this. She hated that his company—and even his attempt to comfort her—only reinforced her loneliness. Her wretched inner emptiness. She hated these emotions, hated feeling broken. Once she'd been the strong one in the family. The leader. The big sister. The role model.

She wanted to laugh at the irony. In the end, she was the worst sort of role model. She was a disaster. Spineless. Shattered.

They left the taverna and stepped outside into the bright sunshine. The hard glaze of light momentarily blinded Chantal and she lifted a hand to shield her eyes.

"Need sunglasses?" Demetrius asked.

"No." She actually welcomed the intense light. The sun burned her eyes, imprinting little gold halos against her eyelids, but the brightness, and the heat, chased away some of the clouds within her. She couldn't very well go through life feeling sorry for herself. Yes, her marriage had been painful, but she had a beautiful daughter, a daughter she loved more than life itself.

They walked for a few minutes in silence, and until today Chantal would have never known that the island had another face to it. There was the side she knew well, the black volcanic rock, the arid steep pitch of land emerging from the sea, and then there was this, the softer face, the one that supported a small village with a tiny fleet of fishing boats and the traditional taverna on the beach.

"Tell me more about Lilly," Demetrius said, as they crossed the sand, walked along the low stone wall, the breeze coming in off the water smelling sharp and salty. "What does your daughter like to do?"

"Play games," she answered, putting out her hands to balance her as she climbed up on top of the old wall. They were passing the fishermen and the two young men nodded at Demetrius but otherwise continued working.

"She must have some beautiful dolls."

"She has a couple dolls, but I try to keep the expensive playthings to a minimum."

"Her grandparents spoil her."

She shrugged uneasily, and glanced back over her shoulder at the quaint village. "I don't want her to get used to grand gestures."

"Toys are grand gestures?"

"They're deceptive. Just like fairy tales."

"And you don't read her those, either?"

"Maybe I shouldn't anymore."

He shot her a quizzical glance. "And what would you do instead?"

"Teach her karate. Some of those self-defense moves you were trying to teach me."

He laughed, thank goodness, his dark gaze smiling down at her. "Are you admitting that I might possibly be right about something?"

She bent down, picked up a broken seashell, rubbed the water softened edge against her hand. "You're right about a lot of things. I just don't want it to go to your head. Your ego's mammoth as it is."

"*My* ego?"

"*Massive.*"

He laughed again. It was so unlike him, so unlike the person he'd become. He watched Chantal jump off the wall into the packed sand and head for the water. He followed her, pursuing her to the water's edge.

She was gazing out across the water, and the breeze grabbed the hem of her short skirt, revealing even more of the back of her knees and her slim, bare thighs. His body responded, desire tightening within him, making him feel hard, impatient. He was tired of holding back. Resisting his attraction, resisting her, was wearing him down. But he wasn't the only one wearing down.

Chantal's tension was tangible. Palpable. He could feel her frustration. She wanted off the island. He was keeping her on. She wanted away from him. He wouldn't give her the chance.

But he was doing this for her, he reminded himself, he was doing what he had to do. "My marriage was arranged, too," he said abruptly, not at all sure why he was sharing some private information.

Chantal was intrigued. She faced him, blue eyes wide. "Really?"

"Greek families like mine do it all the time. Arranged marriages bring families closer together. Solidify wealth. Power. I hadn't wanted to marry Katina. She wasn't my first choice—even though she was very pretty—but in the end it worked. Better than anyone expected."

"So your family did a good job."

"With Katina, yes."

Chantal stared at him, incredibly curious. "What did your family do that you didn't like?"

"The list is too long to even start. My family—" He broke off, crossed his arms over his chest, muscles hardening in his arms, biceps curving, triceps thickening. The hair on his arms was dark, semicoarse and his skin was tanned, his wrist was wide and the black and gold watch just emphasized the width and strength of his bones. "My family is well known. Everyone here knows them. They know me. They know who I am, what I've done—"

"What did you do?"

Demetrius turned, his body inches from her. The warm wind lifted his thick black hair and she could smell the musky spice of his skin. She'd never met anyone who smelled like he did and the more she was around him the more she found herself wanting to breathe in the scent that was spicy and strong and somehow, oddly, sexual.

"I wasn't always in the business I am now." His dark eyes were nearly as hard as his jaw. "I come from a very old Greek family with very old ties."

She nodded, indicating the sprawling Greek villa on the cliff behind them. "But you were raised with money?"

"This I earned." His lashes lowered, his expression shuttered. "But yes, there was money. Plenty of money. But we didn't wear our wealth like the nouueau riche. We were a very private family, and in our family, you stayed within the family, worked within the family."

She was trying to read between the lines, and there was a lot being written between the lines. He'd mentioned how private and closed his family was a couple of times. "What did you do for your family?"

The corner of his mouth lifted. "More than you'd want to know."

She met his gaze. "And your family was in which business?"

"All of them."

The hair on her nape rose, a prickling that laced through her middle. "But you don't work for your family anymore?"

"No." His lashes dropped, and as he stared past her shoulder, his jaw wide, a small muscle knotting, popping near his ear. "And what I do now is important. It helps people, doesn't hurt them."

His head turned, his gaze dropping, his dark eyes resting on her face. "I had disturbing news this morning, Chantal."

She went hot, then cold. "Lilly?"

"No."

His answer sent relief surging through her but the rush of adrenaline was almost too much. Her legs felt quivery and weak.

"Let's sit," he said, indicating the low stone wall and she didn't argue, her knees bending, her weight sinking onto the rough wall.

Demetrius sat down next to her. "There's no easy way to say this, Chantal, so let me say it quickly. You know there have been threats against you, including physical threats. Apparently another one was made, and this one resulted in a fatality."

Chantal sat motionless, her arms at her sides. *A fatality?* Demetrius's shocking words reverbrated around her head like a gong against a steel drum.

A fatality? To whom? How? Her heart hammered so hard she thought she'd throw up. With difficulty she forced herself to swallow the awful cold lump that filled her throat, blocking air, slowing thought. "What happened?"

"Someone tampered with your car—" he broke off, jaw flexed, and continued "—the bomb exploded when the ignition was turned. Your young driver, Tanguy, was killed."

Tanguy. Killed? He was just twenty. No more than a boy. "Car bomb?"

"Someone has too much access to you." Demetrius's voice sounded harsh. "Someone knows too much about you."

But she wasn't thinking about herself, or her safety. She was thinking about Tanguy. Remembering how he'd turned twenty only a month ago, remembering how he'd told her about the birthday party his girlfriend had thrown him, remembering how the night of his party he and his friends had stayed up until morning celebrating their friendship and life.

And now he was gone?

"Why was he in my car?" Chantal's eyes filmed with tears. She could barely breathe. "He doesn't drive my car. He drives me in one of the palace sedans."

Demetrius hesitated. His features were hard, his expression shuttered. "He was taking it round to be washed, detailed. He thought you'd be home soon and he wanted to surprise you."

And now he's dead.

Chantal covered her face, pressed the palms of her hands against her eyes.

She felt his hand on her shoulder, his fingers gripping her shoulder blade. "You're going to be safe," he said quietly. "You will be safe here, and we won't return you to La Croix until we know for certain you'll be safe there."

"I'm not worried about me," she answered, dropping her hands. "It's Tanguy. He died because of me."

"You can't think like that. You have to concentrate on safety. Survival. Concentrate on getting through this so you can return to Lilly."

Lilly. Just her name was a touchstone, a reminder of what she needed, what she loved, and Chantal's heart burned. "I miss her."

"I know." He stood. "Let's go back to the villa. We have work to do."

For the next four days Demetrius spent hours training Chantal, teaching her moves, blocks, defensive steps, as well as offensive attacks.

On the fifth day he opened up a locked cabinet, revealing an extensive weapon collection. She immediately recoiled. "I don't like those."

"You're not supposed to," he answered flatly. But that didn't stop him from withdrawing the weapons, showing her how they worked, the damage they inflicted.

He also taught her how to minimize the assault from various weapons, and his relentless explanations, his intensive training, peeled off the protective outer layer and left her feeling deeply exposed.

She'd known nothing about survival, she thought wearily. She'd learned numerous foreign languages, studied art, music, history, fashion, culture. But she didn't know the first thing about protecting herself.

Or Lilly.

And she was missing Lilly, more and more. Chantal's inside churned constantly, her emotions pulled. It'd been over two weeks now since she'd last seen her daughter.

But it wasn't just missing Lilly that was wearing Chantal down. She felt the most ambivalent emotions around Demetrius. All the hours in training had kept them in almost constant contact.

For days now their bodies touched. Their skin brushed. Their thoughts came together.

Yet this was business. He was all business. Professional, cool, detached. And yet his detachment was worse than his passion. After being so intimate, feeling so physically close, she didn't know how to ignore the current of desire running through her. Didn't know if she could ever forget what he'd made her feel.

Or what his touch made her realize she'd sacrificed.

To be the good, dutiful wife, to be the obedient daughter-in-law, she'd denied herself everything she needed. And it was only now, lying flat on her back on the thick spongey mat in his gym, her body warm, damp with perspiration, she realized she'd been living in a sterile metal box for the past years, denied of sound, touch, sensation, love.

Love. She'd never thought she'd find it, never thought she'd dare to hope for more of anything, but somehow isolated here on Demetrius's Rock, she'd begun to dream again. And the dreams frightened her. The dreams teased her, reminding her of who she'd once been, of what she'd once imagined.

"Are you okay?" Demetrius asked, reaching down to extend a hand to her.

"Yes." She was still panting from the exertion of the exercise, and she let him help pull her to her feet.

"Let's call it a day. I've been working you hard. You've earned some time off."

"You're sure?" she answered lightly, trying to hide the crazy conflicting emotion inside of her. She loved being near him. She hated being near him. She wanted more. She couldn't have more.

"Positive. I'm a nice guy. Sometimes." He handed her a towel and her bottled water. "I'll see you at dinner."

"Fine."

But in her bedroom she didn't feel fine. She felt wild. Desperate. Emotional.

She wanted so much right now it terrified her. She wanted so much that her need made her feel primitive. Animal-like.

Where was Chantal Ducasse Thibaudet? Where was the cool, contained woman she'd once been?

In his study, Demetrius stood next to his desk, staring down at the letters he'd just read. The stack of letters was far larger than he'd expected. There were dozens of letters, all written to the princess, all intercepted by the Melio palace security.

The letters were by hand, and they were long, and rambling. The tone of each was downright creepy. Even accustomed to creeps and freaks, Demetrius felt a chill spread through his middle as he reviewed the letters.

Bits and pieces jumped out at him. *You belong to me, Chantal. We belong together. No one loves you like I do.*

He switched letters.

I can't live without you. I have to have you. I have to be with you. I know you feel the same.

Another letter.

Darling, cherie, why don't you answer? Why play these games? You must stop these games now. Come to me immediately. I don't want to be angry with you. My darling, Chantal, you are very wicked to hurt me like this. Don't make me punish you. I don't want to hurt you.

The letters had been sent over a period of three months. The first letters were postmarked roughly two weeks apart, but after awhile they became increasingly frequent until the sender was writing a letter daily.

It didn't help that the letters showed increasing disintegration—moving from hopeful fantasy, to projection of fantasy, to threats of intimidation and violence.

Demetrius reached for the last letter, received by the palace only a few days ago. *Don't think you can escape me, Chantal. Don't think you'll ever escape me. If I can't have you, no one will. Do you understand? If I can't have you, no one will.*

But the man was wrong, Demetrius thought, studying the last letter, the handwriting jagged, erratic, matching the writer's anger and obsession, before restacking the letters and binding them with a rubber band. No one was going to get close enough to Chantal to hurt her. They'd have to go through him first.

She'd bathed, rested, and now Chantal sorted through the clothes in her closet trying to find something appropriate for dinner.

It was her twelfth night on the island, her fifth dinner with Demetrius, her fifth quiet evening where her body would feel hot, cold, painfully alive. Her fifth night where she'd sit there wanting Demetrius to look at her, wanting him to talk to her. Wanting him to want her the way she wanted him.

The dinners together had become a kind of agony. She felt like a teenager again, overcome with hopeless longing. He had no idea, either.

Chantal wondered what he'd think if he knew she sat at the table each night fantasizing about him pulling her into a semidark hallway, pressing her up against the wall, and kissing her as if there was no tomorrow.

Her stomach tensed, her whole body tightening with need. She thought she'd die if she didn't kiss him again soon. She needed something to ease the pressure building inside of her.

Taking a long pale apricot dress from the closet, Chantal held it up to the light, studied the silky apricot folds. She could see herself in this, see Demetrius's hands against her skin, imagine him shaping her against him.

Her skin tingled. Her breasts felt so sensitive. It'd been so long since she felt raw and carnal like this, and the fierceness of her desire made her nerves scream. What was this emotion anyway? Was this love…lust…infatuation?

She put the dress back. Bit her lip. All she knew was that she wanted him. And she wanted him to want her. But she also wanted more than that.

Eyes prickling, stinging, she blinked to keep the tears from falling. She wanted love and sex and no tomorrow. Love and sex and one long endless night.

She wanted a night of no regrets. A night without mistakes. A night to end all nights…

But that's not going to happen, she angrily answered herself, hating how violent she felt on the inside. She was flooded with hormones, overwhelmed by needs that had never been met. She was acting so silly, acting girlish and young, and yet she was thirty. *Thirty.* How could she confuse physical attraction with emotional needs? How could she imagine that sex—even great sex—would be the answer to anything?

Impatient with herself, Chantal dragged a long blue and cream dress from the closet and carried it to her bed. After donning lace panties in the palest shade of blue, she slipped into the long designer gown. The dress was a mix of small silk patterns, the fabric shades of cream and French Provincial blue. The slender silhouette of the gown gave way at the knees to a slight flare, and the silk fabric had been beaded at the bodice, a stunning geometric pattern of blue beading, open at the neckline in a classic keyhole shape.

Nothing about the dress was expected, nothing traditional, and yet the lightness of the fabric, the exquisite beading, the gorgeous neckline made it a work of art.

Calmer, Chantal faced herself in the mirror, and looking at her reflection, her cheeks a dusty rose from the afternoons in the sun, she knew it wasn't just sex she wanted. She wanted sex, and love, and a chance to live a real life, a life where she'd be an ordinary woman with ordinary dreams.

She wanted a life where someone good and strong would love her. She wanted a life where a man would treasure her, adore her, protect her. She wanted a man who'd love her—heart, mind, body and soul.

You're no better than your little sister, Joelle, Chantal silently mocked, picking up her hairbrush, and brushing her long hair until it rippled and gleamed. Her hand pausing midair, she stared at herself, trying to see what it was about her that angered Armand so much, what it was in her face that made photographers shadow her, what it was that Lilly saw when she looked up at her.

Her long dark hair was now shot with streaks of burnished copper, and her skin glowed gold from the time in the sun, but her blue eyes were still quiet. Sad. Too sad. She hated the sadness. She was ready to move on with her life. Ready to go home. Ready to be with Lilly.

Lilly. Her heart squeezed, her breath catching in her throat. God, she missed her. When she thought about Lilly the pain was almost too much.

Indeed, all of it had become too much. Tonight Chantal's heart felt broken.

Downstairs Demetrius stood on the terrace, facing the sea, his back to the house. He'd dressed for dinner, black trousers, crisp white linen shirt, the sleeves casually rolled up on his forearms. He was on his cell phone, and she felt a pang. How lucky to be able to just call up whomever he wanted, when he wanted. He must have heard her footsteps because he turned. Nodded at her. But instead of hanging up, he held the phone to her.

"You've someone who can't go to bed until you wish her good night."

Chantal went hot, cold. She looked up into Demetrius's face, unable to believe what he was telling her.

He smiled reassuringly. "Your daughter's waiting."

CHAPTER EIGHT

JUST when she'd thought she couldn't take anymore, just when the emptiness threatened to overwhelm her, she'd been given this gift.

Her eyes met Demetrius. She struggled to speak, wanted to thank him, but the words wouldn't come.

"She's waiting," he reminded her gently.

Chantal nodded, and shaking, she took the phone from him. "Lilly?" she choked, tears streaming as Lilly's voice echoed across the phone line.

"Mommy!" Lilly cried. "Mommy, Mommy!"

It was almost too much. Chantal ground her teeth together. Lilly was her heart. "How are you, baby?"

"Good. I miss you."

"I miss you so much, too."

For the next ten minutes they chatted about everything. It seemed that Auntie Joelle had gone to La Croix to spend a long weekend with Lilly, and Chantal offered up a silent prayer of thanks to her sister. And in the next breath, Lilly chattered on about all the things she was doing—music lessons, dance lessons, school lessons, language lessons. Lilly had always been kept very busy at the Thibaudets' insistence.

"But when are you coming home?" Lilly demanded at last. "I want you here. I want you home."

"And I want to be home, too," Chantal answered, her heart full to bursting. She drew a breath, steadied her voice. "It won't be long until I'm back."

"Promise?"

"Yes." The tears filled her eyes yet again, but she held them back. "Be good, sweetheart. Listen to your grandparents."

"I do."

"I know. I just—" she broke off, squeezed her eyes closed,

94

pressed a hand to her mouth. She couldn't do this, couldn't say goodbye.

A steady hand touched her back, and she looked up, saw Demetrius, saw encouragement in his warm dark gaze.

She drew a deep breath, calmed herself. "I love you," she said at last, her voice stronger. "And I can't wait to see all the things you've learned and done while I've been gone. Will you try to remember everything and tell me as soon as I'm home?"

"I'll draw you a picture."

Her heart tugged. "Will you?"

"I'll draw lots. I'll make you a picture book so you can see everything."

"I'd love that. I really would."

There was a moment of silence on the line and then Lilly spoke, her own voice suddenly deeper, more serious. "I love you, Mommy."

It was as if Lilly had grown up over night. Chantal bit her lip, pictured Lilly's face, could see the furrow between her light brown eyebrows. "I love you, baby. Sleep tight."

"You, too, Mommy. Bye bye."

Bye bye. Silently Chantal handed the phone back to Demetrius. She couldn't look at him. She had to look away, out toward the water where another stunning sunset played out across the dark blue waves.

"Thank you." Her voice was hoarse, the tears still there, buried in her heart. "That was the nicest gift ever."

He said nothing for a moment, pocketing the phone. His features looked drawn. "It was your sister," he said roughly. "She traveled to La Croix knowing we needed her help to get the call placed."

"She didn't have to do that."

"Of course not. But your sisters adore you. Both of them. I've been speaking with them both all week—"

"You have?"

"And you're their hero," he continued, as if she'd never interrupted. "They'd do anything for you."

"But I'm the big sister," she said, trying to move forward, not wanting to linger on a topic like this when her emotions were already dangerously high. Talking to Lilly had undone her, made her feel so many things.

"Even big sisters need help." He continued to regard her with that intense, piercing gaze. "And your sisters hate that your late husband hurt you."

She stiffened, surprised, flustered. "He's gone. It doesn't matter anymore."

There was a moment of silence. "It doesn't matter that your husband was physically abusive?"

She looked up, around, feeling wildly disorganized. It made her queasy, talking about this, and they still had dinner ahead. "He wasn't a bad person, he just had a problem with his temper, and he always apologized later. He didn't like to lose his temper."

Demetrius let her babble on, his face impassive and yet he hated what she was saying. She didn't even know what she was saying. She wasn't the cause of her husband's anger, just the scapegoat. Yet Armand had successfully destroyed her self-confidence so she couldn't stand up for herself. "You aren't to blame for your husband's weaknesses. Your husband had the problem. Not you."

"But I am still to blame," she said softly. "I wanted us to be a family. I kept thinking if I could figure out what I was doing wrong, we'd be a real family, and that idea of family meant everything to me."

"Why?"

"I don't know. Maybe because I had family taken away from me too young." So of course it crushed her when she realized her new family despised her. It had never crossed her mind the Thibaudets would hate her. Why should they? They'd chosen her.

Demetrius saw her lips twist, a small self-mocking smile that burrowed deep inside of him.

"Family is important," he agreed, feeling the rage claw at him. He, too, would have done anything to protect his family. He'd been prepared to trade his life for Katina's. It'd been the most natural—instinctive—thing to do. "But you sacrificed yourself—"

"I had to."

"You didn't. And if you really believe that, then your family sold you out."

"They did their best." Why did he keep pushing her on this?

"It wasn't good enough." He seethed. His hands clenched at his sides, and even though he turned away from Chantal, he was so aware of her. He felt the shape of her, she barely came to his shoulder, and he felt her size, her softness, the delicacy of her features. "By staying with him, you gave him permission to hurt you—"

"I thought I could help. I thought I could change things."

"Nothing you could have done would have changed him."

"Not even if I'd been better?"

Better? he nearly cried. Better, how? How would you be better? How could you be better? "You must see it had nothing to do with you," he snapped harshly, far more harshly than he'd intended.

Chantal rubbed her bare arms, her nipples peaked beneath the thin silk fabric, obviously chilled. "I'm sorry. I didn't mean to make you angry—"

"You didn't." Guilt suffused him, endless waves of hot emotion. "I'm not angry with you. I'm angry that men hurt women. I'm angry that your husband hurt you."

"We won't talk about it anymore."

"But maybe we should talk about it. Maybe its time to get some of these secrets into the open."

"What good would it do?" She struggled to smile, attempting to be cavalier. "What's the old expression? Let by gone be bygones? Nothing we say will change the—" she broke off as he moved abruptly toward her.

Chantal took another frantic step backward. He was coming after her.

"Maybe it will change the future," he challenged. He looked positively lethal right now, his features harsh, the ridge of his prominent cheekbones jagged beneath taut bronze skin.

"You can't change the future," she protested nervously. "It hasn't even happened yet."

"So what have we been doing? Training. Preparing. Focusing.

Everything we do impacts the future. Every thought, every choice.''

He was stalking her, closing in on her, and she was sure he could see the pulse beating at the bottom of her throat, feel the fear sweeping through her, the fear a crazy combination of panic and passion. Her heart was pounding. Her stomach knotting. How did he make her feel like this? How did he create such hugely contradictory emotions?

The balcony pressed against her back. She lifted her hands, trying to soothe him. This couldn't be normal. This couldn't be the way women responded to men.

"I'm not trying to quarrel. I don't want a fight."

"We're not fighting."

Her legs felt like melting butter. "You're upset."

His dark head inclined. "I'm a little provoked."

A little? Maybe if she'd known more men, had more experience, she'd know how to deal with her emotions, her reactions. But she'd never known anyone like Demetrius Mantheakis, and she couldn't hide, or manage, her response to him.

He didn't stop until he was standing so close that she could see the fine weave in his shirt. Feel the heat emanate from his body. "What's happening?" she whispered, her heart beating so hard she thought it would burst through her chest.

"What do you think?"

Her shoulders lifted. "I don't know. This doesn't feel right. It's...frightening."

"What's so frightening?"

"You. This. All of this." Tension coiled cobralike in her. She'd never felt anything like this, never knew that this kind of energy and tension could exist between two people. The heat alone dazzled her. She felt his strength, his energy, the hard planes of his body and yet he wasn't even touching her. She wanted him.

She wanted his hands. His mouth. His body. She wanted him everywhere.

"Do *I* frighten you?"

His question forced her gaze up, her eyes meeting, locking with his.

His eyes were dark, smoky, filled with a hunger that was so physical, so raw she shivered.

He'd taken her on the beach, held her hips in his hands and driven his body into hers until she couldn't think, couldn't stop, couldn't control her little world another moment longer.

"Yes," she whispered, knowing that even as earth-shattering as the lovemaking had been, it was the aftermath which had really rocked her.

She'd loved being in his arms too much. She'd loved the seduction, the suppression of control, the intensity he stirred within her. He was far too dangerous. Far too real. She couldn't exist in his world. She'd never survive it.

"And your life?" His lips curved but it was not a friendly smile. "Does that ever frighten you?"

She didn't answer. Her mind was racing, still trying to process everything that she was thinking, feeling.

He leaned closer, his jaw hard, tight with anger. He'd shaved between breakfast and dinner and yet his jaw was already dark, and his dark eyes snapped fire. "Does it frighten you that you're like a little mouse in a cage? Absolutely trapped? Completely dominated? That everyone in your world has a say over your life...except you?"

"I'm not a mouse. I'm not trapped." But she was lying through her chattering teeth. The fact that he saw her world, her life, so clearly terrified her. Her little world, the prison that it was, was supposed to be her secret. Just like Armand's abuse was her secret shame. She couldn't discuss these things, couldn't admit such failures out loud.

"Do you have any idea how much danger you're in?" he ruthlessly persisted. "How fragile your world really is?"

She heard his voice, saw his firm lips move, but she'd shifted into panic mode. Her body was stiff, her brain freezing. She was shutting down because she didn't know how to respond.

"When are you going to confront the truth, *pedhaki mou?* You must come to grips with what your life is, and what your life isn't—"

"It's fine. My life is fine."

"It wasn't fine on the plane. On the plane you admitted you

wished you would have done things differently. You said you wished you'd fought for happiness—''

"Leave the plane out of this! That wasn't a normal conversation. That wasn't a normal night. I thought we were going to die. You got me talking and I couldn't shut up."

He smiled.

Chantal swallowed hard, skin prickling, burning. Demetrius didn't smile. Only fools smile. His voice echoed in his head, and something was making her pulse pick up, faster, faster. Too much adrenaline, she thought. Far too much emotion. She lifted a shaky hand, pushed back her hair from her temple. "That night was an anomaly. Nothing about the plane, or—" she drew a swift breath, bracing herself "—what took place on the island fits in to real life."

He cocked his head. "Not even the sex?"

The sex.

It sounded so raw that way, so physical, so heated and fierce. But then, it had been raw. And it had been hot. And she hadn't known that a man could make a woman feel like that. She hadn't known *she* could feel like that.

"Not even the sex," she answered, lifting her chin, trying desperately to prove that she, too, could be a woman of the world, and that incredible sex on a beach was something she was perfectly accustomed to.

"So you're saying that sex isn't part of your real life?"

Flushing, Chantal found herself mentally scrambling for an answer. She hadn't meant it like that, hadn't known he was going to twist her words like that. "I'm widowed."

"Surely, you've had boyfriends since Armand died."

"No."

"Dates?"

"No." She flushed yet again, her skin so hot she wished she could unzip it, cool herself off. "It's not part of my role."

"I didn't realize your role was so rigid."

"It's very...set." She purposely avoided the word rigid. "I married into a powerful monarchy and my daughter is the heir to the throne—''

"She's a little girl. You're the adult. You're entitled to have a life."

"I have a life. I adore my daughter."

"You live only for your daughter?"

"She needs me. She's four."

His dark gaze met hers, held. "What happens when she grows up?"

Frustration welled within her. Chantal didn't want to think about the distant future, couldn't even imagine the distant future. Just getting through today seemed impossible. "I don't want to talk about this anymore."

"First your husband, now your life. Is everything off limits, Princess?"

"Yes!" She shot back, furious, frustrated. He didn't respect normal boundaries, he didn't give her the space and privacy she needed. "It is to you. You were hired to protect me, not torture me, so..."

"So...?"

"Back off." But she didn't just mean verbally, or emotionally. She needed physical space, too. He was overwhelming her in every way possible. "I can't think like this. Can't breathe."

"Then breathe."

She shook her head, stunned. Not even Armand had ever spoken to her so bluntly. Pointedly. But then, Armand didn't talk. He hit. He lashed out and he lashed out when she least expected it, but Demetrius wasn't angry, he was calm. Eerily calm. He exuded control.

"I'll breathe better when you leave me alone." She drew herself as tall as she could manage considering he dwarfed her completely. Six foot one, six foot two, he was taller, broader, and stronger. He'd been built hard, rugged, built to take on the world instead of hiding from it.

"I'm not leaving you." His lashes lowered, his gaze fixed on her mouth. "And I'd never leave you alone."

"Then I'll go."

"Why?"

His voice was but a murmur of husky sound and she jerked

her head up, met his dark gaze, saw the heat in the depths, saw too late that he was as much on fire as she was.

Like the night on the beach.

Something between them burned, hot, incinerary.

Startled, aroused, she stared so long into his eyes that she lost track of time, of place, of everything she was supposed to remember.

God, no one had ever looked at her like that.

"Don't," she whispered, feeling as if she were falling even though she was still on her feet. He was leading her to the edge, she thought dizzily. He was leading her straight to disaster and she was letting it happen.

"I've done nothing." His voice was rough, and yet it brushed her senses, caressed her skin. She felt her breasts grow heavy, nipples tingling, tightening and everything she felt that night on the beach was back, everything she'd wanted was returning in waves.

Waves of longing. Waves of need.

When he looked at her like that she felt young again. When he looked at her like that she wanted to be real again. No china doll on a shelf, no pretty princess posing for the magazines.

She gave up. She leaned toward him, and even as she put herself into his space, she drew a breath. *Foolish, foolish, foolish Chantal.*

She felt his slow kiss all the way through her. It drew the air from her lungs and made her clench her fingers into fists, fighting, resisting a touch so warm, so sensual, resisting a touch that heated her so deep inside she didn't know how she'd ever put the fire out.

Better not to know you could feel this way, she told herself, reaching up to push him away and yet her hand, once pressed against his chest, couldn't let go.

Her fingers clutched at his shirt, her body drawing closer to his, curving against him as if it were the most natural place to be.

He'll ruin everything, a small voice reminded her. He'll take it all away from you. Remember what you've agreed to do. Remember your contract. Loyalty and fidelity to the Thibaudets and only the Thibaudets. She was to honor Armand's memory, uphold his name.

The hot tears seeped from beneath her lashes and she shuddered in his arms, a tremor of complete despair. She couldn't have passion and La Croix, and La Croix was Lilly. Lilly was home.

"You're crying." He lifted his head, stared down at her.

Chantal couldn't look away. His eyes, so dark, so intent, bored all the way through her and she felt as though he were slowly remembering it all, recalling all the words said, all the things done, all the emotion surging through her now. "This is a cruel twist of fate."

Frowning, he wiped away tears from her cheek. "How so?"

She grew hot, cold, and hot all over again, and unable to speak, she leaned against him, feeling his strength, the shape of his chest a curve of smooth dense muscle that invited further exploration. "You're not part of my world. You're not what I can have."

His narrowed gaze took in the wetness of her tears, the softness of her mouth. "What can you have?"

"Nothing." The word was wrenched from her.

"And you accept these limitations?"

Her lips curved in a hard, brittle smile. "I don't have a choice."

"Everyone has a choice."

"Not me." Sanity was returning, little by little, awareness of her, of him, of the restrictions placed on her. She had to stop this madness before she lost reason completely. This wasn't love. It was lust. This wasn't right. It was a product of nerves, of hormones, of imagination.

But Demetrius didn't like her answer, and he wasn't going to accept it, either. He dropped his hands from her face to lightly encircle her waist. His touch was so hot, so electric she felt as if he'd singed her. "And you really believe that?"

She loved the way his hands felt on her, loved the pressure, the touch, the connection between them, and yet when she looked into his eyes she saw a fierceness...a rage...that knocked the wind from her.

His hand rose, stroked her high on her side, over her ribs to cup her breast.

She shivered. *"Demetrius."*

He drew her even closer, and the feel of his palm curving against her full, sensitive breast made her head spin.

This was the way a man should hold a woman. This was the way she'd always wanted to be held. Firmly. Securely. Nothing tentative about it at all.

For a split-second Chantal could imagine a life like this, a life safe in the Greek's arms, his body between her and the world, his shoulders shielding her from the press, his strength holding her up when she didn't think she could smile one more smile, pose for one more photograph. His body taking her body late at night, taking her places no one else could ever take her...

His lips covered hers again, and when his mouth parted hers, she dug her fingers into his shirt again, fabric balled in her palm and she prayed for strength.

Remember your position. Remember your situation. If nothing else, for God's sake, remember Lilly. If you can think of nothing else, think of her.

And focusing, remembering, she pushed away. It took every ounce of strength to walk away from him, but she did. She backed up, one step, two steps, until she found herself half way across the room, staring at him as if he were a mirage, something conjured from her own imagination.

"You're letting them own you, Chantal."

She shook her head, stunned by the emptiness inside her. She felt as if he'd ripped her insides wide-open and let in the warm night air. The emptiness—the massive gaping hole—horrified her. "What have you done to me?"

"It's all you, *pedhaki mou.*"

She swayed, felt the delicate beaded silk fabric of her dress brush the back of her legs. "This isn't me. This isn't who I am."

"And you said sex wasn't part of your real life." He made a rough sound, mocking, impatient. "Maybe it should be. You're a woman that was born to be loved."

Chantal lifted a hand in protest and the glint of her wedding ring caught her eye. She balled her hand, feeling the press of the sapphire against her skin. Her stomach heaved.

What a nightmare. It had all become an endless dreadful dream.

Phillipe and Catherine Thibaudet, Armand's parents, had insisted she continue wearing the ring, just as they'd insisted she continue as it'd been before Armand died. And it had to be that way. It's what she'd agreed to all those years ago. It's the deal she'd made.

God forgive her for signing contracts she didn't understand.

"Don't kiss me again," she said, trying to look taller, stronger than she felt. "Promise me you won't ever kiss—touch me—again."

"Can't."

"Can't?"

"Won't," he corrected. "I don't make promises I won't keep."

CHAPTER NINE

HIS answer took her breath away. She burned all the way through—her heart, chest, body on fire. The noise in her head was so loud it was like a thousand helicopters buzzing.

"You're intentionally making this difficult," she said, her voice coming out hoarse, raw.

"No. I'm just being honest. I could never make that promise, Princess. Not in a thousand years." He caught her by the arm, his hand easily encircling her slender bicep. "But I promise to be true to you. And I'll promise to be with you no matter what, that I shall face every danger with you—"

"Why? I'm nothing but a job to you!"

His features shifted. "But you're a job I like."

The anger and passion in his voice left her reeling, and she shook her head, bewildered. Once more she tried to pull away, and this time he let her go.

She walked away from him, moving across the room to look out the window. The sky outside had grown dark and household staff were silently moving through the terraces lighting fat golden candles, which threw off soft rays of light.

One of the maids stepped into the living room. "Dinner," the maid said, bowing slightly.

Chantal took her seat at the table in the dining room. The long wooden table had been draped with a pure white lace cloth, a half dozen tall white candles softening the stark room with soft yellow light. The dining room boasted a massive plated window with a breathtaking view of the water, which had begun to reflect the moonlight.

But all the moonlight in the world couldn't ease her internal chaos. She felt so exposed sitting there with the lights dimmed, Demetrius's face alternately lit and shadowed by flickering candlelight.

Her dress was delicate, barely there, and yet she felt so hot.

Her skin burned. Her stomach clenched. She couldn't even bring herself to look at Demetrius. How was it possible to want someone so badly?

"You didn't eat much," he said, as the dinner dishes were cleared.

He was right. She couldn't eat much. Even though she felt empty and restless, her hunger had nothing to do with food, and everything to do with touch. Pleasure. Sensation. "Not much of an appetite," she answered, staring at the skewered bite of broiled lamb sitting on her plate.

"I can have the cook prepare something different."

"No. I like lamb."

"Just not this lamb?"

It's not the lamb, she wanted to snap, her fingers tightening, flexing in her lap, her body humming with a nervous, restless energy. She hated the heat in her face, the hunger in her heart, the memory of how it'd been between them. If the sex had been bad, or her body indifferent, she wouldn't be feeling this way. But the night they'd shared on Sao Tome had been stunning and the sex unreal. Everything that had happened between them had been...so not ordinary, and it was that sense of the extraordinary which had swept her up, made her feel, made her imagine that maybe, just maybe, there was more for her, maybe...

"I'm okay. Really." She managed a small tight smile. And it struck her that what she wanted wasn't sex...or a body...it wasn't even a man. She wanted *him*. Demetrius Mantheakis. The hard, tough Greek. But she didn't understand the attraction, didn't know what it was about him that made her pulse race, her imagination fly.

What in God's name was wrong with her? How could she be so pathetic? She'd lived right for years. She'd made the choices she was supposed to make and she'd said yes, Your Highness, no, Your Highness, anything else Your Highness?

"Dessert? Fruit and cheese?" he offered.

She dug her nails into her hands. He was worrying about the fact that she'd sent her plate back to the kitchen virtually untouched while she was going mad with desire. She didn't want food. She wanted *him*.

She wanted him to unzip her dress and slide his bare hands across her back, down to her hips, around her thighs.

She wanted the darkest room, the softest bed, seductive silence.

Instead she touched her neck, wrapped her fingers around her warm skin, feeling far too tense, impossibly sensitive. She touched the very place she wanted his hands, imagined how his lips would feel, not just on her neck, but on her breast, on her tight nipple.

Eyes briefly closing, she could feel the heat rise in her, the yearning so strong she felt as if she was dissolving. "Would you mind if I turned in early?" She asked, struggling to hide the flare of need. She couldn't continue to sit here, across from him, couldn't stand feeling so bare and raw.

His eyes met hers and held. "Yes. I want you to take a look at something first. You can either wait here while I get the information, or you can join me in my office."

"What information?" she asked, shooting him a mistrustful glance. His features were even, his expression perfectly controlled and yet she felt his brooding silence, a stillness in him that reminded her of a hawk perched high above, watchful. Waiting.

"Just come with me. You'll see."

She followed him downstairs to his office suite. It was more elaborate than she'd thought—two interconnecting offices and a separate conference room. He led her to the conference room where papers were spread across the table.

He picked up most of the papers but left a couple on the table. "Have a look at this," he said, pushing several pages toward her.

She glanced down at the papers he'd given her. They were letters. Handwritten. Addressed to her. On one page the handwriting was small, narrow, tightly contained. On the other page the handwriting was bigger, looser, an uncontrollable scrawl. "These letters are to me."

"Yes." He leaned forward, watched her skim one and then the next. "I've kept the worst of the letters from you. But I hoped that you'd recognize the handwriting."

''No.'' She looked up at him. ''I'm sorry. I wish I did.''

Demetrius sighed. ''I didn't think you would, but it was worth the chance.'' He took the letters back from her, glanced down at the page with the wild scrawl. ''The letters were mailed to the palace in Melio, but they're postmarked from La Croix, from the main post office near the Thibaudet châteaux.''

It was a struggle to concentrate when he looked at her so intently. ''So the danger is in La Croix. And it could be someone at the châteaux.''

He nodded. ''We're having the handwriting analyzed, but the detectives working the case are certain it's a man, and someone fairly educated.''

''Hard to believe I could have such an obsessive...fan.'' She felt fear spread through her. ''I've tried to live simply. Quietly.''

''Obviously not quietly enough. Someone's noticed you, and someone wants you.''

Dead, she silently finished, trying to control her pulse, her heart now beating a little faster. And Tanguy had already paid a horrible price for someone's sick obsession. ''Any ideas about this person's lifestyle or occupation?''

''Not at the moment.''

''But there must be some kind of profile—''

''There is. But, unfortunately, these guys don't wear their profiles on their sleeve. The stalker is a predator. They hide their intentions, work hard to appear normal.'' His brows lowered. ''Most think they're normal.''

Demetrius saw her pale. He didn't want to upset her, but he needed her cooperation. They had to apprehend the stalker before the stalker hurt anyone else.

Demetrius's firm had dealt with fan obsession before—many times before. Of all the forms of security work, this was his least favorite. Not because it wasn't vital, but because it was such unpredictable work. The stalker was one of the hardest, most difficult threats to control-because he could be anyone, could blend in anywhere, could hide in a crowd, could slip in, out, silent, secret, unnoticed.

''Why do you do this?'' she asked, her voice shaking a little.

"It's so..." She suddenly shivered. She didn't bother to finish her sentence.

"Sordid," he supplied, his lips twisting. "But that's what I like. What I do—what my firm does—helps people. I'm glad I can help and protect people, because I know what its like to lose sleep when someone you love is in danger. I know its impossible to eat when your insides are sick with fear. I lived that way for three weeks once, and it was the longest three weeks in my life."

His voice was hard, his tone dark. She felt a shiver race through her. "I hope your story has a happy ending."

His features seemed to freeze. His expression turned ruthless. "No."

She felt a chill race through her. Something horrible had happened in his life and the tragedy had made him the man she saw now, the man who refused to let her cower or hide. "How did you survive your loss?"

"Revenge."

She didn't like this conversation, didn't want to imagine how Demetrius had suffered, much less how he might have made another suffer. "Do you...do...that sort of thing today?"

"No. I play by the book now."

"I see."

"You don't approve."

She tried to smile. "I don't like pain."

"No. You'd rather go through life pretending happiness, wearing that lovely royal mask and letting the world think you're beautiful inside and out."

He knew how to hurt her too well. "You are awfully dangerous, aren't you?"

"You're more dangerous. You're dying on the inside and you won't even admit it. I, at least, want to help you."

She stared at him from across the table, air trapped so long inside her lungs that little specks appeared before her eyes. He was right. She hated him for being right. Anger bubbled up in her, resentment that he always seemed to have the answer. "Did it ever cross your mind that I don't want your help? That I've accepted my life—"

"Bullshit."

Her cheeks colored. "Excuse me?"

"Let's not do this, Chantal. We don't have to do this. It was sex. It was nothing more than sex. Let's just keep it at that, okay?" And dropping the letters back on the table, Demetrius headed for the door. "You know your way back to your room, so I'll let you stay and poke around my office if you'd like. But I'm heading upstairs. I need some air. Good night."

He walked out.

She watched him and something in her chest squeezed, vise-like. Tears stung her eyes. It wasn't supposed to be like this.

Inside her room she undressed slowly, removing her dress for her nightgown, and she felt as if she were moving in slow motion.

She'd married Armand because Melio was bankrupt, and she, intellectual that she was, understood that duty came first. That duty would always come first.

But God forgive her, she hated duty. Hated everything about duty. Yet it was too late. She couldn't stop what she'd started. Couldn't escape what she'd agreed to do.

Moving to her bedroom window, Chantal pressed her face to the slick pane, needing the coolness of the glass to soothe her hot skin. She felt wild inside. Tangled. Angry.

And standing at the window, she spotted him below, out on the pool terrace. Her heart pounded. Her thoughts went wild. She wanted to go to him, or send for him. But if she did, what then?

What then indeed?

The loneliness was unbearable, and turning from the window, Chantal leaned against the wall, closed her eyes, her hand sliding inside her robe to cover her chest.

Her skin felt so tender and smooth, warm, warm with the curve of her breast beneath her palm and her even softer silkier nipple against her fingertips. She felt touchable, needing to be touchable, needed to be touched and held and loved.

Her hand slid slowly from her breast, down the middle of her rib cage to her flat abdomen, muscles tensing, nerve endings stirring. She could imagine his hand touching her like this, could imagine the sensation and knew she'd like being with him, knew she'd welcome every touch, every kiss, every caress.

Madness.

Abruptly she drew her hand from her robe and pulled the edges of it together, trying. What are you going to do Chantal? If you make love to him again, you're going to fall in love. You're going to fall so hard you'll never be able to get out in one piece.

She tugged the wood shutters closed, blocking out the mysterious night with the high white moon and the sprinkle of faraway stars.

The silk coverlet on her bed had already been folded back, the cool cotton sheets exposed, and Chantal pulled the top sheet back feeling more alone than she had in years.

A knock sounded on her door before she could climb between the sheets.

She crossed the room, opened the door. Her heart slowed, stopped, the air strangled in her throat. "Demetrius."

He didn't say a word. He just stood there, looking at her, frustration etched deeply in his hard features.

He was still wearing his dark trousers but his shirt hung open, revealing his bare chest. His thick dark hair stood on end as if he'd spent the last ten minutes dragging his fingers through it.

She couldn't tear her gaze from his face. He looked as if he were absolutely tortured. Heart thudding, she opened her door wider and watched his dark eyes grow hotter, the brown depths smoldering, like volcanic rock pulled from fire.

She touched the tip of her tongue to the inside of her bottom lip. Her lip felt fat, heavy, swollen. Her body felt just as heavy. "Do you want to come in?"

"You know what will happen if I do."

Silently she stepped back, drawing the door wider still, and with her breath bottled inside her, she watched him enter her bedroom. He walked slowly around the room, measured steps that matched his close measured gaze. He was looking at everything, taking in every detail, locking it away in his incredible brain.

He sat down on the edge of the bed and looked at her. She felt her legs tremble. "Come to me," he said, and liquid silver raced through her, turning her into endless need.

She went to him and he parted his thighs and pulled her between them. She felt his thighs close, trap her between his legs, his knees on either side of her hips. He was strong. The muscles of his thighs held her firmly, his hands settled on her waist and his fingers burned through her pale peach silk nightgown.

"This is just sex, right?" he demanded harshly.

Her eyes burned and she struggled to smile. "It couldn't be anything else."

A tiny muscle pulled in his jaw, tightening his mouth but he said nothing.

His silence said more than words ever could and she flushed deeply, looked at him, looked away.

He caught her hair in his fist, turned her face back to his. His dark brown eyes held a mixture of pain and anger. "So it is just sex you want."

She didn't understand what he wanted her to say, didn't understand where he hoped this would go. He knew her world. He knew her commitments. He knew what she had to do. "Yes."

The corner of his mouth curved. "Fine." He reached up to cup her breast even before his lips covered hers.

His kiss burned her. His kiss was hard and demanding, his kiss, like the hand on her breast, spoke of ownership. Possession. But he didn't stop there. Clasping her face between his hands, he turned her into a captive and there was no escaping the insistent pressure of his mouth now. His lips were firm, and he explored her mouth with his tongue, tasting her, filling her, heightening sensation until she whimpered for more.

Blindly Chantal reached for him, hands settling on his chest, fingers twining in his shirt as she struggled to meet her need for more contact, more pleasure.

This was raw, she thought wildly, this was fierce and hot and he made her want to strip off her clothes and cool off—or to just drag him over her and have him fill her, really fill her and give her relief.

Funny, but her need for him, physically seemed to come from something deeper, leaping to life from an emotional well inside of her. She'd felt numb for so many years and the numbness was gone, to be replaced by an inferno of desire. For one crazy second she vowed she'd give up everything just to answer the need. Just to satisfy the craving.

He lifted her into his arms, carried her around to the side of the bed, and when he set her on the mattress, he immediately followed, his big body moving over hers, parting her thighs.

Lifting the hem of her nightgown, he impatiently tugged it over her head, and his hands replaced her gown, covering her breasts, touching her hips, molding the softness of her belly.

She felt him caress her hip, the inside of her thigh and then he was touching her there, at the apex of her thighs, his fingertips brushing the dark curls and then between, finding her silken and warm, finding each taut nerve ending.

She gasped softly as he parted her inner lips, and stroked her, once, and again, from the delicate peaked nub down, across the burning tender skin to the tantalizing opening that was craving to be filled by him. The lightness of his touch, the sureness of his touch, made her tense and grasp the coverlet between her hands. She was melting in her need, and as his fingers dipped into her, filling her, she felt herself dissolve, becoming hotter, wetter, her body hungering for him.

"Make love to me," she said, reaching up to encircle his neck with her arms. She drew him down to her. "I've never wanted anyone, or anything, like I want this."

"The sex is that good?" His eyes creased but his voice sounded hard, cynical.

Tears burned the back of her eyes. "You're that good." *I could love you, you know. I could love you forever.*

She closed her eyes as his lips covered hers in another hard, possessive kiss. She felt his body press against hers, felt his hair roughened chest, felt his hard flat abdomen, felt the ridge in his trousers.

Chantal slid a hand down his stomach, fingers groping for the button on his trousers. If she couldn't have forever, she thought, she'd at least have this.

They made love twice—intense, demanding, incredibly erotic sex—and after she climaxed the second time, she curled up in his arms, skin still damp, body still shuddering, and she felt his strong arms wrap around her, holding her securely to him.

She'd never felt so loved in all her life.

But this isn't love, she told herself, this was sex.

Liar.

"You—this—amazes me," she said softly, struggling to find the words even as her palm pressed against his chest, his heart beating beneath her hand. "It's incredible. Being here with you. Like this."

He didn't speak, and she felt his silence all the way through her.

"I won't ever forget it," she added, wanting him to say something. Maybe even to agree. Yes, Chantal, this is wonderful. No, Chantal, I'll never forget you...

But he didn't say a word. He wasn't agreeing. He wasn't conceding. He wasn't going to let her have her way.

"I won't forget you," she added, stomach muscles tightening. "You've...meant...a lot to me."

"It was sex," he corrected almost cruelly. "Remember?"

"Because it has to be." She swallowed, felt pain radiate out through her, replacing the warmth, erasing the pleasure. "This life I have isn't what I want, it's not what I ever dreamed it'd be—"

"So break away."

She gathered the thirty years of hard training into her shaking limbs and rolled away from him, to sit up, her arms encircling her legs. "You don't understand."

"Try me."

"I can't. It's too complicated, too unbelievable to explain."

"Try me," he repeated stubbornly.

The resolve in his voice sent shivers through her. "It's rather dry, actually. Facts and figures, not fun and romance."

He barked a laugh. "I studied economics at university, Princess. I'm sure I can handle the dry details."

"Maybe you will find this interesting then." Her arms tightened around her bent legs, even as she struggled to organize her thoughts, simplify the story into one concise paragraph. "You know that my marriage was an arranged marriage. But most people don't. The magazines never printed anything about it being arranged, and from the lavish wedding no one would guess that the Ducasse-Thibaudet marriage was really about two countries brokering a deal.''

She shot him a glance, and even in the dark saw the grim set of his mouth. Swallowing, she pushed on. ''As you can expect with any important deal, there was lots of paperwork attached, clauses and contracts, plus a wordy pre-nuptial. I never imagined I'd be widowed so young, just as I never imagined my marriage would be so miserable, so I agreed to the terms that seem ludicrous now. But Melio benefited. La Croix provided my country with financial aid. Everyone seemed happy.''

''Except you.''

Her shoulders lifted and fell. ''In any merger or takeover there's bound to be some hurt feelings.''

His jaw tightened and he shook his head once, a short angry shake. ''But this is more than hurt feelings, this is slavery, Princess.''

That was putting it bluntly, she thought, her eyes prickling in the dark. But she managed a brittle smile, a hint of her old bravado. Once she'd been so brave. Once she honestly thought she could do anything.

''Shh,'' she whispered, trying to tease, but her voice broke. ''It's our dirty little secret.''

His arm reached out for her, and he pulled her back down onto the mattress. ''Dirty is the word I'd use.''

He rolled her over, trapping her beneath him. His head descended, his lips covering hers, taking her, and her heart felt as if it would explode.

She loved being with him. She loved being kissed by him. If only this could be real, if only this were part of her world...

He deepened the kiss and she felt herself melt, heart, body, limbs, opening for him, needing him and he knew. He parted her knees, making room for his warm hard body between her thighs.

She shuddered as the rigid length of him pressed against her still damp, sensitized core. He belonged here, with her, she thought, reaching for him, wrapping her arms around his neck. And slowly he entered her, in a long smooth thrust that felt like warm silk sliding on warmer satin. She cried out against his mouth, and his lips caught the sound, held it in him, between them, and being taken like this, filled like this, filled the emptiest part of her mind, never mind what he was doing to her body.

Emotion wrapped around her heart, tight and tighter. Chantal released his shoulders, hands sliding down the back of his thick triceps, to his elbows, then his hips. She felt the powerful muscles in his hips clench, felt his buttocks knot as he buried himself even deeper.

The pressure, the pleasure, it was all so intense and the sensation he created with his body against hers made her want to give him everything, if only for this night.

Because no one had ever loved her this way. No one had ever held her this way. No one had ever kissed her mouth with such tenderness and hunger, passion and need. No one had ever made her feel so feminine and beautiful, and yet intelligent and capable. He was everything she couldn't have and yet right now, he was everything she needed.

Everything she wanted.

I love you, she thought, twin rings of emotion wrapping around her heart. She did love him. She knew now it wasn't lust, wasn't a passing fancy. She also knew that back in La Croix she'd never be able to be with him like this. In La Croix she'd never see him.

Demetrius suddenly shifted his weight, reached around for her ankle. "Wrap your legs around me," he urged, his voice deep, dark, full of passion. "Higher."

She did as he told her, and as she moved beneath him, he kissed her exposed neck and was rewarded with a shiver. She felt his lips curve against her warm skin and he slipped his hands beneath her hips, tilting her even more. "Better?" he asked.

Oh, she was completely his now. "Yes."

"Then hang on," he said with the rough male voice that made her tingle all the way through, "and don't let go."

CHAPTER TEN

CHANTAL woke, and even before she reached out, she knew Demetrius was gone.

And it devastated her. She didn't want him gone. Didn't want to wake up alone. But this is real life, she reminded herself. This is the way its going to be.

She sat up. Her stomach heaved. A violent heave that made her mouth taste funny, all silver metallic tasting.

Slowly she lay down again, placed a hand on her stomach, trying to calm it down. This wasn't a hang over. She didn't even touch her wine last night. Was it food poisoning maybe?

After a few minutes she forced herself up again, dragging herself into a sitting position, giving herself a chance to fight the queasiness, and as she sat there, she felt a whisper of warmth. Demetrius. Demetrius Mantheakis. Darkly handsome. Her sexy, brooding Greek.

Last night had been unreal. By far the most beautiful night of her life. Every moment in his arms was perfect. And yet that kind of emotion, that intensity of feeling, only made everything else pale in comparison.

Don't think about him. Don't think at all. Just get up. Get moving. The night's over. You have to get on with your life.

Pushing off the bed, Chantal did her best to ignore her queasy stomach as she took a bath and dressed before heading downstairs for breakfast.

She stepped out onto the terrace surfaced in buffed limestone. The creamy stones reflected the warm morning sun, and the bright clear sunlight dazzled her, making her head spin.

Where was Demetrius now? What was he doing? She wanted to see him. She was afraid to see him. Yet he was nowhere in sight this morning as she seated herself on the terrace.

The day was already gorgeous, and it had to do with the quality of the light. The air here was luminous—bright, clear, and it glazed the whitewashed walls of the house and garden, shimmered off the green and blue ocean, dappled her table with the bowl of fresh cut fruit.

The breakfast of tea and toast settled her stomach and Chantal was just about to leave the table when Demetrius appeared.

Even though they'd spent the night together, just seeing him this morning sent shock waves through her. God, he was big. Strong. So darkly beautiful.

She swallowed the rush of emotion—love and pain washing through her in fierce waves.

His eyes met hers and for a split-second she imagined she saw the same emotion there in his dark gaze. Her heart ached as she stared up at him. *I love you. I want you. I don't get to keep you, do I?*

A muscle in his jaw pulled, and then his features relaxed, tension disappearing and his expression was impassive...almost bored. "Finished?" he asked, indicating her meal.

No hello, darling. No tender good morning. Nothing to indicate that anything special had passed between them last night.

To hide the intensity of her disappointment she forced a cool smile. "Yes, thank you."

He was wearing denim shorts and a black T-shirt with cutoff sleeves. "Ready?" he asked.

She'd never seen him so casual and her narrowed gaze swept his long muscular legs, the thickly muscled arms, his skin darkly bronzed. "Where are we going?"

"I thought you could use a change of scenery, so we're going to head out. Spend the day on my boat."

It wasn't, she thought later, the best idea, not when her body felt so achy and tired. Her stomach didn't help, either, not with it churning so wildly, but she somehow managed to make it through the afternoon without giving her discomfort away. But in the end, it wasn't her queasy stomach that undid her. It was Demetrius's distance. She'd secretly hoped that on the boat he might be more personal, less aloof. Instead he was the consummate professional. He was near her, but never touched her. He was polite, but not conversational. He was watchful, but detached.

And it was awful. His distance made her feel awful, and instead of enjoying the sail back to the Rock, she seethed inwardly, emotions fierce, wild, nearly impossible to control.

How could he make love to her at night and keep her at arm's length during the day?

Maybe it was the lovemaking from the night before, the day spent on the boat, or the hours in the sun, but whatever it was, on returning to the villa Chantal felt absolutely exhausted.

She couldn't remember when she last felt so tired, and heading upstairs, she closed the wood shutters at the windows, darkening her room. After stripping off her clothes, leaving just her underwear, she climbed into bed between soft cool white sheets.

Dinner that evening was an agony.

It wasn't just Demetrius's company fraying her nerves, it was her body itself. Her body had ceased to cooperate. From the moment she entered the dining room her stomach rebelled.

The very smell of poached fish curdled her stomach, and Chantal took a step back, nearly covering her mouth and nose, fighting the wave of nausea. She hadn't felt all that well today but the fish...no way. She couldn't do it.

Demetrius caught her gaze. His eyebrow lifted.

She returned to her chair, shook her head, forcing a brief smile. Nothing was wrong, she said with her smile. Nothing could ever be wrong.

But sitting down, she felt her stomach do another threatening cramp and fine beads of moisture broke out on her brow and upper lip. She'd been tired and achy all day. She couldn't have the flu again, could she?

Just get through dinner, she told herself, and then go back to your room and back to bed.

But getting through dinner wasn't going to be easy. Her stomach was churning and her body felt so hot and cold she could barely get her water glass to her lips without her hand trembling like mad. Exhausted by the effort to just sit at the table and take the odd sip of soup, she didn't even try to make conversation and Demetrius didn't try to encourage her to speak, either. But he was watching her. Closely. With that unnerving intensity which always made her feel as if she were a science experiment beneath a microscope.

Chantal managed to swallow another tiny mouthful of the spicy fish chowder even though her stomach protested nonstop. She didn't know how much longer she was going to be able to sit here and pretend everything was okay. She didn't feel okay. She felt...sick.

Abruptly Demetrius leaned forward and pressed the back of his hand to her forehead. "What's wrong?"

Her instinctive response was to answer nothing. But her body was overruling her head. She couldn't lie. She was going to throw up—soon. "I need to go to my room."

"What's wrong?" he repeated, rising even as she did.

"I don't know." She wouldn't meet his eyes. She couldn't let him see just how sick she was feeling. Being ill was personal. Private. And worse, throwing up was so undignified. She hated being undignified. "If you'll excuse me—"

"I'm coming with you."

"No."

But he already had a hand wrapped under her upperarm and he was half leading, half dragging her away from the courtyard table back to her bedchamber on the second floor.

Halfway up the staircase her face burned even as the rest of her went cold and clammy. She put a hand out, pushed blindly against him. "Demi—"

He understood, sweeping her into his arms and dashing up the rest of the stairs. She was ill before they reached the bathroom.

Tears burned her eyes, nearly as bitter as the bile in her mouth. In the bathroom he placed her on the edge of the massive bathtub. "I'm sorry," she choked, accepting the damp wash towel he handed her.

"Doesn't matter," he said. "It's nothing." All cold and trembly, she blotted her mouth and forced herself to look at him.

His shoulder was covered.

She closed her eyes, horrified, ashamed. She shouldn't have. Armand would have never forgiven her.

Forcing herself to action, she stood, cleared her throat, even though her stomach was rumbling again. "Let me have your shirt."

"We have staff to do our laundry," he answered, and again he reached out to touch her face, this time her cheek. "When did this first hit you?"

"I haven't felt well much of the day. But I thought it was just fatigue. The walk up and down the hill. The sun." She shrugged. "It's probably just a touch of something," she said, wishing he'd get rid of that shirt, wishing he'd go back to his room, wishing to just escape his hard watchful gaze that suggested both suspicion and danger.

"What?"

"Flu bug," she answered.

His jaw tightened. His eyes narrowed. "Or maybe a touch of food poisoning," she added, uncomfortably.

"We've eaten the same food," he answered.

He trusted no one, she thought, stifling a rather hysterical laugh. Not even her.

"Well, I can assure you I'm not poisoning myself." She placed a hand across her stomach now heaving. She could feel the muscles dance on the insides, tiny pulsating ripples.

Oh, no. Not again. She was going to be sick soon. Too soon.

"You better go," she choked, grateful she was sitting, knowing her legs wouldn't support her now. But even though she sat, she felt so weak she just wanted to slide down, a slow boneless slide to the floor where she could press her hot cheek to the cold white marble surrounding the toilet.

"You're going to be sick again, aren't you?" But he didn't even wait for her to answer. He was already pulling her up, positioning her before the toilet, his arms holding her securely, far too firmly.

Shivering, Chantal felt small and helpless and she hated it. "Please go."

"I'm not leaving you now, Princess."

She didn't miss the grimness in his voice. Why did he insist on calling her princess at the most inappropriate moments? The times she wanted the civility he refused to give it to her, and then when she felt so humble, so ordinary he had to stick her title in her face. "But I don't want you here," she panted, stomach roiling, skin damp, her whole body rebelling. "You're not needed here. This is something I can do on my own."

And before she could utter another word, she was clutching the sides of the porcelain toilet, sick, sicker, and surprisingly grateful when she was finally finished that Demetrius was there to hand her another damp towel and help her strip her dirty blouse off and start the bath.

With the bath quickly filling, he gathered the soiled towels and her blouse and glanced at her where she perched on the closed toilet seat. "I'll go," he said. "But I'm going to be back." He hesitated, inspecting her pale clammy face. "And don't lock the door. I'd hate to break a good door down just to get to you."

"But you would."

"Of course I would."

She gazed up at him through bleary eyes, her hair damp and stringy against her cheek. She felt like hell. Please let this just be a twenty-four hour flu. "Can I just tell you again that you're not a normal bodyguard?"

She was surprised to see a flash of humor in his eyes.

"Good. I've spent my whole life trying to be anything but normal." He nodded. "I'll see you in a few minutes."

Fortunately he gave her ten blissfully undisturbed minutes and by the time he returned she'd already wrapped herself in a plush robe and slipped between her cool cotton bedsheets.

He knocked on her door and entered without waiting for permission, carrying a small woven tray the color of burnt caramel. "Crackers and ginger ale," he said, setting the tray in easy arm's reach on her nightstand. He looked pleased to see her already in bed.

She glanced at the woven tray. Tiny bubbles fizzed in the ginger ale. "Thank you. That's very kind of you."

He gestured impatiently. "It's what any decent human being would do."

"Then thank you for being decent."

The next day, late afternoon, Demetrius walked into her bathroom where she was crouching next to the toilet and dropped a pink and white box on the counter. The writing on the box was in Greek and English.

A home pregnancy test kit.

She swallowed, looked at the box and then up at Demetrius. As usual, his expression was shuttered and impossible to read. But obviously something was on his mind.

"It's not food poisoning," he said, breaking the taut silence. "And it's not the flu."

"You can't be sure."

"Take the test." His deep voice echoed off the polished marble.

"I'm not pregnant." She forced herself up, from the floor of the bathroom to sit on the closed toilet seat. She'd spent more time in the bathroom today then she'd spent in the last six months. "I'd know if I was pregnant—"

"You have morning sickness."

"Afternoon sickness," she corrected, willing herself not to look at the box on the counter, willing him to be wrong even though she knew he was probably right. "I didn't feel this way with Lilly."

"The doctor said every pregnancy is different."

She felt her eyebrows arch even as heat flooded her cheeks. "You consulted the doctor about me?"

"I consulted a physician about my wife's pregnancy." His words were clipped, like splinters of ice. "She had a very difficulty pregnancy. She was sick like this—day and night."

Chantal felt the heat give way to something altogether different. Fingers curling into her palms, she suppressed the wave off emotion rolling through her, working just as hard at resisting the impulse to ask him what happened to this wife and child. Where did she go? Where is your child now?

But even without asking the questions, she saw the answers in his face. His eyes said it all.

The wife was gone. The child was gone. He'd been alone on his own a long time.

Mutely she rose, reached for the pregnancy kit. "How long does it take to get the results?"

"A couple minutes."

She nodded, numb, overwhelmed, resigned. She didn't want to know the truth. She didn't want to see proof when she'd worked so hard to ignore the facts staring herself in the face.

They'd had unprotected sex over two and a half weeks ago. Her breasts were tender. Her emotions were volatile. And she was sick, sick, sick to her stomach. Like the flu, but worse, because this could last for months. Nine months, specifically.

Holding her breath, she opened the box, slid out the foil pouch with the individual test kit. The tester felt so slender, so medicinal. With trembling fingers she opened the pouch. ''I'll let you know.''

''I'll be waiting.''

A minute and a half later the unknown was known. It didn't even take two full minutes. Yes, she was pregnant. Two dark pink lines. Positive.

Opening the bathroom door, she saw Demetrius sitting in a chair by the window. The sunlight poured through the window, illuminating his head and shoulders.

He stood when she opened the door. His eyes met hers. Unable to find her voice, she nodded.

For a heartbeat he did nothing, then he, too nodded. And then he left.

That was it. Nothing had been said, and yet everything had been said. There were moments when words were utterly unnecessary.

Yet just because they didn't speak that afternoon or evening about Chantal's condition, it didn't mean Demetrius was indifferent. It took him hours to fall asleep, and when he did, his dreams were all nightmares, one unending nightmare that clawed at him, holding him transfixed.

Katina in the hands of the enemy, pregnant and terrified. He felt Katina's fear. He saw the terror in her eyes. She didn't understand what was happening, why it was happening, and all she could think about was protecting the baby.

The baby.

In the dream he saw her put a hand up to her swollen belly, the baby's birth just seven weeks away, soothing the baby, reassuring the baby, trying desperately to reassure herself.

In the dream he stretched out an arm to grab her and then the ground opened, swallowed her whole.

In the dream he threw himself at the earth and tried to keep the ground from closing. *Katina!*

Demetrius woke in a cold sweat. He sat up, tossed the covers aside, and headed for the bathroom where he drenched his clammy face with handfuls of cold water.

He hadn't had the dreams in years. He hadn't felt this kind of nameless terror since he bought the Rock. The Rock had given him a sanctuary but Chantal's pregnancy stripped the illusion away.

The pregnancy, he thought, opening the French doors leading to his balcony, changed everything.

His mission had changed. It was no longer a job about protecting a princess, but a job about protecting the mother of his child.

Demetrius's head swam, a dizzying rush of reality and emotion. He couldn't believe it. She was pregnant. This shouldn't have happened but it had.

Leaning against the balcony, he gulped in the cool night air. He'd never thought he'd have another chance. Never thought he'd father another child. He'd been so careful in all his relationships to ensure his lover was protected, that there could be no mistake—that there would be no mistake. His women knew straight off the bat that he wasn't interested in marriage, family, or commitment. He'd had his one family, the only family he'd ever wanted to have, and he'd had no desire to replace what he'd lost. Replacing Katina and the baby seemed cruel. People couldn't be replaced. His wife's tragic death so close to their baby's due date had turned him inside out, taken his mind and shaved it in two. Heartbroken, discipline gone, he'd set out to avenge Katina and their baby daughter's death, and he had.

He had.

He'd done what a good, God-fearing man wouldn't do.

He'd fully expected the Family would answer his vengeance with a retaliation of their own. And he'd been almost disappointed when it didn't come. Truthfully, death would have been easier than life. Truthfully, dying and joining Katina and the baby would have at least given him peace. But peace wasn't forthcoming.

The Family left him alone. The Family let him go.

And that, had been the end of Demetrius Manthakeis, loving father, protective family man.

But now it'd all changed again. Now, somehow, rather miraculously, it seemed, he'd be a father again.

If the princess didn't terminate the pregnancy.

If the stalker didn't terminate the princess.

Exhaling in a slow, hard rush of air, Demetrius stared out at the dark sea, seeing just one small light out on the endless expanse of water. One little boat, he thought, in all that water.

One little life inside Chantal. A life he knew he'd protect with his own.

He joined Chantal as soon as he saw her appear on the terrace for breakfast. "We need to talk."

Her expression wary, she slowly sat down at the table. He was grateful she didn't say anything stupid like *What do we need to talk about?* There was so much unspoken between them, so much heaviness, and silence. He had to know what she was thinking...planning...had to get a sense of what was going on right now inside her head.

"How did you sleep?" he asked, accepting a coffee from the silent housekeeper who appeared and disappeared before anyone could acknowledge her.

Chantal's head tipped, her hair in a glossy brown ponytail. "Not well."

"I didn't, either." The best thing to do was come out and say what was on his mind. "All I did last night was think. Think about you. The baby—"

"Hardly a baby, yet."

His brows furrowed and he was tempted to say something sharp when her head lifted and she met his gaze. Her expression was sober, intense, her blue eyes dark with a night spent soul searching. She was trying to make sense of this just as he was.

"We made a life," he said carefully, still watching her face. He could see she was taking this very seriously. Good. So was he.

She looked away, her eyes narrowing as she studied the horizon. "I'm horrified." She swallowed, her throat bobbing. "Petrified."

He didn't speak. He didn't trust himself to speak, not now, not with so much on the line.

Chantal closed her eyes, breathed deep. Folding her arms over her chest she tried to keep all the wild emotion inside. He had no idea what this meant. He had no idea how much was at stake. Her prenuptial with Armand had been very specific. There were certain duties, obligations, she'd agreed to. No affairs. No illicit conduct. No scandals.

Yes, she was widowed, but pregnant? Unmarried and pregnant? Talk about scandalous behavior. She could lose Lilly. She *would* lose Lilly. "I can't have this baby," she said, pressing her knuckled fists hard against her ribs. "I know it sounds cold, but it's the God's honest truth. The Thibaudets have been looking for a reason to get rid of me. An unplanned pregnancy would give them all the motive they need."

"You don't even like them."

"But my daughter inherits the throne. They could kick me out but keep her."

"That's not permissible by law."

"It is in La Croix. It's an old monarchy, not a democracy. The king and queen still wield incredible power."

"Including holding their own granddaughter hostage?"

Chantal shifted uncomfortably. "They don't see it that way."

His black eyebrows shot up. "You're defending them?"

"Of course not, but I have to be pragmatic."

Demetrius's expression turned brooding. His dark eyes narrowed fractionally, creases at the corners of his full mouth as he studied her taut features. "You're not even considering keeping the baby."

Her jaw ached from grinding her teeth so hard. She'd always wanted more children, she'd love another child, and deep within her she longed to hold one more baby, love one more baby, but she wasn't allowed to have more children.

The price of a pregnancy would be losing Lilly. Permanently.

"No," she answered huskily, breaking away from his piercing gaze. Drawing a shallow breath, she felt the pinch of her bra strap. Her breasts were already fuller. Her body heavier. She couldn't believe how quickly her body was changing, adjusting, growing.

Little baby. Her eyes stung and she bit the inside of her lip. She wanted the baby. She couldn't have the baby. It was horrendous. Heinous. No woman should ever have to be put in her position. To save one child, she couldn't have another.

"So that's it," he said, disgusted. "No discussion, no exploring other options—"

"What other options?" Her eyes blazed. "My daughter is the sole heir to the throne. She's already being groomed as the future queen. There's no way I can leave her in La Croix so I can come play house here!"

"Oh, that's all right, then. All the sacrifice, the loss of freedom, of choice, of love, of life...it's worth it as long as Lilly becomes queen?"

She flinched at his sarcasm. He didn't understand that for a royal there was no choice. For one born a Ducasse or a Thibaudet duty came first.

But Demetrius wasn't finished with her yet. "Are you sure, Princess, this isn't your ambition driving your daughter's future? Are you sure it isn't you that wants to be queen?"

Her head lifted in outrage and her eyes met his. "Being born royal is the last thing I'd wish upon a child, but Lilly is what Lilly is, just as I am what I am."

Her chest burned with bottled emotion. He'd hurt her, deeply. How could he suggest it was her own selfishness that kept Lilly trapped in La Croix? "And you know how much I love Lilly. You know I'd do anything for her, anything to secure her happiness."

"Including abort the child inside you."

CHAPTER ELEVEN

His words lanced deep. Her eyes filled with sudden tears, the shock and pain so deep. My God. How could he?

Staring at him, hurt, appalled, she felt her stomach curdle and heave. "You make me sick," she choked. Literally, she thought, stumbling to her feet. She rushed from her chair, back to her ensuite bathroom where she threw herself over the toilet as her stomach emptied again, and again.

Tears streamed from her eyes as she retched, the sourness in her mouth nothing compared to the fire in her heart. He didn't know. He couldn't know. She'd been through hell. She'd been slapped. Struck. Beaten. She'd endured the worst kind of humiliation to keep her daughter safe. Protected. The shame she'd endured had to be worth it. The bruises and tears couldn't be for nothing.

"I'm sorry." Demetrius's rough voice came from the doorway. "I was too blunt."

Clutching the rim of the toilet, the porcelain cool against her palms, she shook her head, tears still falling, the pain so hot and fresh that she couldn't master her emotions, that control seemed impossible. *Blunt? Was that all? How about harsh? Cruel?*

She stood, rinsed her face, patted it dry and walked out of the bathroom on trembling legs. She'd married Armand, was determined to love him, and he'd hurt her. Not just once. But repeatedly, over and over, and the abuse had lasted for years.

Exhausted, Chantal sat down on the foot of her bed. "I'd die if I lost her," she said hoarsely. The tears had stopped falling and yet she could still feel them on the inside. There was so much sadness there, so much pain buried in her heart, and if he thought she found any of this easy, then he didn't know her at all. Losing her parents, growing up fast to become the big sister Nic and Joelle needed, fighting to preserve the family name and interests...it'd been nothing but a battle for years. "She's all I have left. She's all I live for."

"But you have a new life to think of. And that life needs you, too."

"Oh, God." Chantal's voice broke, a mirror image of her heart, and she looked away, biting her lip so hard she tasted blood. In one hasty night she'd undone all that she'd worked so hard to do.

How could she have been so impulsive? So needy? So *desperate?*

"What's done is done." Demetrius sounded as controlled and as unemotional as she was distraught and broken. "The only thing to do now is move forward."

"I can't. Because I can't lose her. I won't. She's my heart."

He said nothing for a long moment and then she heard him sigh, a hard heavy sigh that seemed to come from deep within his soul.

She looked up, tucked a long strand of hair behind an ear. "I've talked to lawyers. The contract's water-tight."

"Do you have a copy?"

"At the châteaux. In my things."

"I'll request a copy. It wouldn't hurt for me to have a look at it, do some research." He moved into the bathroom, fetched the box of tissues from the marble counter and returned with it.

She took a tissue, wiped her eyes, blew her nose. "Won't do any good." She crumpled tissue in her hands, her chest aching so much it hurt to breathe. She didn't think she'd ever feel the same. To have another child—her cherished dream—but to lose Lilly? What kind of dream was that? "The contract is very specific."

"And it expressly forbids you from taking Lilly from La Croix?"

"The contract prevents me from moving, marrying, or having another child."

His narrowed gaze rested on her face. A small muscle pulled in his jaw. "I won't let them take her from you. We'll find a way to make this work."

"How?" She wiped fresh tears from her eyes and reached for yet another tissue.

"I don't know that yet, but I do know this—there are only two certainties in life—life and death. Everything else is negotiable."

He sounded so hard, so determined. But he didn't know the Thibaudets, didn't know the history. Armand had been there only child, the only son, and his death had changed them. Shut them down. Turned them into bitter, angry controlling people. They weren't going to lose Lilly. They had no one to replace her with. "They can't be bought."

"Maybe not with money."

"How else do you buy people?"

"There are lots of ways."

Her mouth, still so sour, dried. She swallowed convulsively. She needed to wash her face. Brush her teeth. Right now she felt like a mess. "How do you know all this?"

His lips curved but it was a ferocious expression, more snarl than smile. "You can thank my family for my extensive education. Due to their influence I understand what motivates them. People aren't that complicated, *pedhaki mou*. It's just a matter of handling a situation right."

"You're saying you think you could find a way to—" she broke off, searched for the word even as she searched his eyes "—pressure the Thibaudets into returning Lilly to me?"

"Pressure, manipulate, what's the difference?" He shrugged, the thick muscles in his shoulders and chest rippling beneath his loose linen shirt. "I don't really worry about the methods."

"You make it sound as if you were perhaps...not exactly on the right side of the law."

He stared down at her, the shadow of his beard making his jaw look wider, darker. "You understand correctly."

She recoiled and yet she wanted to know more. "How did Malik Nuri find you anyway?"

"We go back a long, long way and when Nuri explained your situation, the danger you're in, and I told him you needed someone good, someone tough, someone heartless. You needed to be protected at all cost.'' His lips curved in a small mocking smile. ''Nuri said that would be me.''

Even inside where the air was warm, Chantal felt chilled. ''You're far from heartless.''

''You don't know me.''

But they'd been together now nearly two weeks, and he'd proven to her that he was strong, focused, serious. He'd proven he wouldn't abandon her—he hadn't on the plane, and he didn't intend to now.

''You don't know me,'' he repeated even more quietly and her heart slowed. Her nerves in state of alert.

''Maybe I don't. But I trust you anyway.''

''You trust too easily then.''

''Why shouldn't I trust you?'' she demanded defiantly.

His dark eyes raked her, taking in her loose hair, her oval-shaped face, the simple dress that clung to her curves, revealing the soft swell of her breast, her smooth throat and bare shoulders, and all of her sweetness and vulnerability. ''Because I'm a man.''

''And?''

His expression turned mocking. ''I'm territorial. Unforgiving. And I protect that which is mine.''

Her veins were dancing now, adrenaline shooting through her. ''I didn't know I'd become yours.''

''You're here.''

''*You* brought me here.''

''Exactly.''

She tensed, growing angry all over again. She didn't understand why he should make her feel this way...so frustrated...so filled with wild and conflicting emotions. There was no reason to feel conflicting emotion. She should want off his island. She should want away from him. She should want nothing to do with him.

''And then there is the baby, which is mine,'' he said, still watching her intently. Possessively. ''It's my duty to protect both of you now.''

''No. It's your *duty* to get me home. Back to Lilly. That was the deal. That was the promise you made me.''

''Before I knew about my child.''

His child. What about *her* child? What about Lilly, her daughter she hadn't seen in three weeks now. "There is no baby yet. I'm barely a week late. My period could still come—"

"It won't."

Her heart pounded. She felt sick all over again. "I haven't spent the last nine years denying myself everything I need, to make a stupid mistake now. And you can't pretend you don't know that I've sacrificed everything—including my pride and dignity—so Lilly can be happy."

"Stop hiding behind your daughter."

"I'm not. I'm protecting her. And if you can't see the difference then I don't know what I ever saw in you!"

"I see the difference. And you know damn well what you saw in me." His gaze locked with hers. "But this isn't the time to fight that one. We've enough to cope with at the moment."

At least he was being calm. Relatively reasonable. She appreciated that someone could keep a level head right now.

"There's no reason to panic," he added. "We've time. You won't show for months. That will buy us a lot of time. And later, if need be, you can dress to hide the pregnancy. Everything seems overwhelming today, but that's part shock, part hormones. Trust me, we can make this work. We can have this baby."

It wasn't until after he left, and she'd begun changing into her swimsuit, that his words hit her forcibly. *We can have this baby.*

Hands going numb, she struggled to slide the slender strap of her black tank style suit over her shoulder. What exactly did he mean?

Brow creasing, she straightened the strap on her and adjusted the suit along her hipbones. When he said 'we', what was he suggesting? Intending?

He knew she couldn't retire from public life and play house. He knew she'd never become Mrs. Demetrius Mantheakis. How did he propose they *have* this baby?

Wrapping the black and white silk sarong around her hips, Chantal tugged a straw hat low on her head and went to the pool. One of the housemaids brought her a light meal and after eating the toasted ham sandwich, she settled into a lounge chair and tried to lose herself in a book.

But she couldn't read, and even the magazines that Demetrius had bought for her were unable to hold her interest. Her thoughts were scattered.

The warm afternoon breeze brushed her skin, and closing her eyes she could picture the baby inside her, could actually feel the baby in her arms now.

She could feel the small weight of warmth against her chest, feel the sweetness, the softness, the tender way babies curved against the breast, their little backs, their little bodies, their hands nestled to their mouths.

The thick emotion inside her grew, swelling, a press against her heart, against her throat. She swallowed, pin pricks of pain against her eyes.

She'd never been able to savor Lilly's pregnancy. From the moment she conceived Lilly, Armand had been angry. Bitter. He hadn't liked Chantal slim, and he hadn't liked her pregnant. Nothing she did was right. Nothing she did was okay. And as she grew, bigger, bigger, Armand's temper flared. After she gave birth, Armand's disgust seemed to know no bound.

He hated her. That was the only conclusion she could come up with. And yet she didn't know what she'd done to provoke such virulent contempt. She'd done everything she was supposed to do. Married him. Slept with him. Conceived his child. What had she denied him? Nothing.

Maybe that's why he hated her.

She'd been his doormat. She was nothing to him but a place for him to wipe his feet as he came and went. Hello, slam. Good-bye, slam.

The lump in her throat threatened to choke her. It hurt to breathe. It hurt to feel, to remember.

Lilly's first year had been a blur of tears and pain. She could remember the slaps, the fists, the punches only because she remembered trying to hold back the tears, stifling the cries, because she didn't want Lilly to hear. She didn't want her shriek to wake the baby.

Don't wake the baby.

Chantal closed her eyes, tightly. It wasn't fair. It had never been fair, but what could she do? Where could she go? With

Lilly's birth she'd effectively given up her freedom, given up her name, her voice, her country. And if she wanted out, she could leave, but leave without Lilly. And God knew, God and all his angels and his eyes and ears knew, there was no way she'd leave Lilly.

Not then. Not now. Not ever.

She reached up, swiped a tear from her lower lashes. Swiped another, chest aching, heartbroken. Wouldn't it be amazing to have a baby, and be free to love the baby? Wouldn't it be incredible to have this baby and just hold the baby, hour after hour, night after night?

She could see herself lying on her side in bed, see her arm wrapped protectively around her swaddled infant and the baby would smell of powder and lotion and love.

"You can't cry." The lounge chair shifted as Demetrius sat down next to her. He tilted her chin up, shook his head. "Crying isn't the answer."

She couldn't whisk the tears away fast enough. "I'm sorry. I can't seem to stop." She scrubbed at her eyes, her throat so raw, her eyes burning like mad. She wanted to pluck them out. Wanted to tear her heart out. She couldn't stand so much emotion. So many memories. So much buried pain. She'd never really dealt with the memories before, the reality of what had happened in her marriage with Armand. She'd thought the best way to recover was to ignore the facts. If she didn't think about it, the truth would fade, the painful details would go away. If she didn't let herself dwell on bad things, the bad things wouldn't hurt her anymore.

But the bad things had hurt her anyway. The bad things had hurt...bad.

"I should be cried out," she said, struggling to get her voice normal, wanting to find calm again. She was exhausted, truly exhausted. She honestly didn't think she could handle much more of this.

"It's the hormones."

"I didn't feel this teary with Lilly—" She broke off, bit her cheek, her eyes lifting, meeting his. That wasn't true, she thought, sick. She might have felt this way with Lilly. She didn't remember. She didn't remember anything about her pregnancy with Lilly except for a pervasive fear. Don't hit me. Don't hit me. It could hurt the baby. Please God, if he hits me, let him hit my face, not my body, never my body.

She placed a cold hand to her face, fingers covering her cheek, her mouth. She was going to be sick again if she wasn't careful.

"I won't have anymore of this." Demetrius voice, hard, tough, unyielding, cut through the fog of her misery. "The crying will only make you sick. It's time for dinner. Go bathe, dress, meet me in half an hour, yes? I won't have you late, and I won't have any more sad faces tonight. Understand?"

She nodded, a wobbily nod, but she got to her feet and drew her sarong snugger around her hips and left the pool for her room. He watched her go and then he, too, headed to his room to shower and dress for dinner.

In the shower, Demetrius turned the water on full force and let the hard spray rain down on him, but the drumming pulse of water did little to ease the tension pounding in his head.

It was easy to protect Chantal here, on the Rock. The families living on the island ensured the safety of the island's perimeter, and the villa itself boasted top of the line security technology—alarmed windows and doors, motion detectors, glass protectors, hidden cameras. He'd know if anyone entered the house. He'd know if anyone left the house. He'd know if anyone called at the house. It was his house. His safe haven. He knew if Chantal remained here, she and the baby would be protected. But she wouldn't be here indefinitely, and he feared what would happen once she returned to her real world.

Toweling off, his whole body still felt hot, hard, his temper simmering just below the surface. Nothing better happen to the princess or the baby. No one better touch them. No man better dare.

He didn't trust himself—didn't trust the outcome—if anyone threatened her now.

He'd always been protective of women, but pregnant women? It was a state of grace, a plane of light and beauty. If he still had faith, his faith was in life, the ability to resurrect in the face of suffering and death.

He, who thought he'd lost everything, had a chance to be a father again, he had a chance to hold his child in his arms, love a child. He saw hope where there had been none.

The key was keeping them here where he and his people could watch over her, ensure that no one would get too close, defend her in the event that security broke down.

But security wouldn't break down, he reminded himself, lathering his face and neck, preparing to shave. Security was his specialty. Security was what he knew. He owned the best equipment. Employed the smartest people. Put his staff through the hardest tests and drills.

His people wouldn't let him down.

Rinsing off his razor with hot water, he reached up for one last stroke on the side of his neck and somehow he caught the skin at an angle and blood spurted through the shaving foam.

Demetrius stared at his reflection in the mirror, stared at the stream of bright blood, and his body went cold. Ice cold.

Katina.

He dropped the razor into the basin and stepped back, grabbed a hand towel and blotted his neck, wiping the remainder of the shaving cream away.

He hadn't protected her.

Tears of rage burned the back of his eyes but the tears didn't come. The tears wouldn't come. He tossed the hand towel onto the counter and stalked from the bathroom to his bedroom and dressed. He'd failed Katina but he wasn't going to fail Chantal. Chantal might not want him, might not love him, but he wouldn't leave her side.

He had a job to do. And he'd damn well do it.

Descending the staircase, Demetrius spotted Chantal wandering outside on the terrace. She was wearing a simple blush colored gown, thin straps, smooth delicate bodice, and a long straight skirt falling to her ankles. She'd drawn her hair back in a loose ponytail low at her nape, leaving her neck and shoulders bare.

On the candle lit terrace she looked fragile. Vulnerable. Nothing like the remote princess photographed in glossy international magazines. Nothing like the sophisticated beauty lauded for her exquisite fashion sense.

Here, with the moon rising overhead and the sea breeze lifting tendrils of her dark hair, he could believe she'd been badly used by her late husband. Without the fashionably cut coats and suits, fitted skirts and slacks, without the Italian leather heels and the chic designer purses, hats, expertly coiffed hair the woman—the real woman—was endearingly simple. Sweet. Touching.

She'd never had a normal life. From birth to her marriage, to her husband's death, she'd been indoctrinated, disciplined, dictated to.

She'd belonged to everyone but herself.

And now he was wanting to do what all the others had done: take control of her life, seize power while he could, wrestle the decision making process from her.

He was no different from the others, was he?

Drawing a heavy breath, he stood there, considering her, considering their options. If he let her go today she'd end up seriously hurt—or worse. If he let her return to La Croix with another bodyguard she might choose to end the pregnancy. If he kept her here, she'd be safe, and she'd give him the child he wanted more than he'd wanted anything since...since...ever.

He swallowed. He was no virtuous man.

Abruptly Chantal turned, spotted him in the doorway. "How long have you been standing there?" she asked.

"Not long."

She didn't know if she should believe him. Didn't know what to believe at all anymore. Funny how just a glimpse of him and she felt lost, drowning beneath waves of contradictory emotion.

Her first reaction when she spotted him had been pleasure—there he was—the man who made her feel like a real woman again. And immediately following that initial response, was a second one—anger. How dare he try to dictate to her? How dare he try to use the pregnancy to control her? She'd had enough of men dominating her, speaking down to her, trying to plan her life for her.

A maid appeared, bobbed her head, murmured something to Demetrius. Chantal watched as he immediately left the terrace, returning to the house. He wasn't gone long, and when he came back five minutes later, he was carrying a sheet of paper.

Wordlessly Demetrius handed it to her.

It was a faxed letter, a letter initially printed on Melio palace stationery. The letter had been written by the palace secretary. *Princess Chantal, we regret to inform you...*

Her hand trembled. She looked up, swallowed, shook her head. Couldn't be. Impossible. She'd had to have read the telegram wrong.

Blinking, Chantal forced away tears, and read the message again.

We regret to inform you of the death of Her Royal Highness...

It was the same.

Ice swallowed her, engulfing her, freezing everything from her heart to her trembling hand. "Demetrius," she whispered his name, her voice failing her. "She's gone."

"I'm sorry."

She swayed a little, stared at the words blurring beneath her vision. *We regret to inform you...we regret...we...we...*

She felt his hand at her waist, felt him guide her to a chair. She allowed herself to be seated, swallowing around the sourness filling her mouth. "Grandmama's gone."

"When are the services?"

"Soon." She clenched her fist, wrinkling the fax. "I can't believe—" She broke off, struggled to take a breath. "I knew it could happen, but...you never do think...you never want to think..."

His hand lightly rubbed her back, calming, soothing. "I'll make arrangements for us to leave first thing in the morning."

She was downstairs early, her things packed by one of the house maids in a leather suitcase, formal dresses zippered into a matching garment bag, make up and hair appliances in another. Somehow she'd arrived on the island with nothing and yet she was leaving now like the princess she was.

Chantal had dressed this morning in a rather severe dark navy suit, the only ornamentation the gold military style buttons on the jacket. She'd twisted her hair up into her traditional chignon, the style she wore most often for public appearances. She couldn't believe this appearance was for her grandmother's funeral. How many funerals had she attended now? Her parents. Her husband's. Now Grandmama's.

Demetrius sat at the back of the plane, left Chantal alone with her own thoughts. They flew into Melio's private airport, the terminal reserved for the royal family and visiting dignitaries. On arriving they discovered the Thibaudets had just flown in from La Croix and Chantal could barely sit still in the back of the limo on the way to the palace.

It was horrible, horrible returning like this, but at least she'd see Lilly.

But on reaching the palace and being ushered into the Thibaudets guest suite, Chantal discovered they hadn't brought Lilly with them after all. Chantal swayed on her feet, stunned. She'd waited so long to see her daughter. She'd counted on having Lilly's company, counted on finally being a family again.

Again Demetrius remained in the background, shadowing Chantal but refraining from speaking. Chantal was aware of his presence but couldn't turn to him, afraid that if she looked at him, or spoke to him, her fragile control would break. She'd wanted Lilly so badly. She'd missed Lilly so much. Three and a half weeks without her daughter. It was a lifetime.

Not even Joelle or Nic could comfort Chantal that afternoon. Nauseous, exhausted, she lay on her bed until the evening reception where the Ducasse royals were to receive visiting dignitaries. She managed to greet guests for two hours until she couldn't smile another gracious smile or speak another grateful word. In the back of her mind she felt only rage and pain.

She'd done everything ever asked of her. How could the Thibaudets keep Lilly from her now?

Finally she left the grand salon and escaped to her room. Demetrius climbed the stairs behind her. She felt him so strongly that her whole body tingled with heat and need.

At her bedroom door she faced him. She knew he'd remain outside her door, ever vigilant. But she didn't want him outside her room. She wanted him in it. And she didn't want him for sex, but for his warmth and strength. "I need you," she whispered.

"I'll be out here—"

"You know that's not what I mean."

His dark eyes met hers. They burned tonight, burned with a silent fire. "I can't do my job here, and the job you want in there."

She flushed at the tone of his voice. *The job in there.* He was reminding her most urgently that he believed all she wanted him for was sex. Her eyes burned, she struggled to smile. "Was it such a job to sleep with me?"

"No. You have a gorgeous body. A very sweet and sexy body, and a lot of men would be happy to give you what you want. But if I have to pick between satisfying your need, Princess, and protecting your life, I'll stay outside the bedroom."

CHAPTER TWELVE

CHANTAL murmured a strangled good night and shut the door, but once inside her room, she crawled into bed fully dressed.

She didn't have Lilly. She didn't have Demetrius. And he was wrong. It wasn't sex she wanted. She wanted him. *Him.* She wanted his arms, and his chest, and his heart beating beneath her ear. But she was afraid of what he'd do—afraid of what he'd do to her life—if he knew how she much she cared for him, how much she wanted the happy ever after ending with him.

Chantal was sick twice before breakfast, and then there was the stiff, silent motorcade ride to the cathedral for the services. Chantal knew her sisters were watching her but she couldn't bring herself to speak. She felt miserable. Absolutely ill-sick to her stomach, sick at heart.

During the memorial service, Chantal had to escape not once, but twice, to throw up in the ladies' restroom.

Hunched over the toilet, she heard footsteps enter the bathroom, a small squeak of the door. They clicked across the floor, the sound definitively female. Chantal spied high heels. ''Princess Chantal?'' the female voice asked, concerned.

''Everything's fine,'' Chantal answered as the door to the stall pushed open. From the corner of her eye she saw a woman peer in and then another wave of nausea hit and Chantal was hugging the toilet hard.

The door squeaked, open, shut. The woman was gone.

A moment later, the door opened again. ''Chantal?'' It was Demetrius's voice this time. ''Who was that?''

''I don't know.'' And then she was getting sick again, and her sour churning stomach fueled fresh panic. What was she going to do? Oh God, how long could she hide this from her family...from the world?

''I'm just outside,'' he said.

''I know.''

143

The rest of the funeral passed in a blur. Between the morning sickness, and the sorrow over her grandmother's passing, Chantal could barely focus on the external events. Dimly she knew that the ceremony itself was beautiful, the music soaring high between the elegant columns, floating up to the cream and gold ceiling. It was a beautiful day, and radiant sunlight poured through the stained-glass windows. It was the kind of day Grandmama would have loved. She'd relished her life on Melio, embracing the sunshine and the long growing season. Grandmama had loved her roses, the rare coral hued and white camellias, the dogwood tree she'd imported and coaxed into blooming a vivid pink every spring.

But the service ended, the last song was sung, the casket removed, and later, after the cathedral emptied, the last condolences were accepted, the last hand shaken.

The graveside internment was private, and this, too, took everything from Chantal. She stood with her grandfather and sisters in the beautiful family cemetery, trying to keep from thinking about the gravestones just behind her, the two beautiful marble stones with her mother and father's names on them.

This wasn't the time to remember. This wasn't the time to think about anything other than Grandfather who looked as if he'd just had the life beat out of him.

Holding back tears, she moved closer to Grandpapa and slipped her hand into his. His hand shook, his skin thin, delicate like crepe. How he'd aged since Grandmama took sick. He'd lost the fire that made him King Remi, fading instead to a shadow of whom he'd once been.

Prayers were said, a murmur of voices around them, and then the casket began its slow descent.

Grandfather's fingers tightened painfully around hers.

She squeezed his fingers back, trying to let him know she was there. But it was a dreadful loss. He and Grandmama had been together nearly sixty-five years. Sixty-five years sharing a room, a bed, a life with someone. How did one say goodbye? How did one ever let go?

Chantal looked up, spotted Demetrius standing on the opposite side of the grave, his narrowed gaze scanning the surrounding grounds. Then he turned his head and looked at her. She had no idea what he was thinking from his expression, there was no tenderness in the hard set of his eyes and jaw. What did he feel about her?

It had been a long twenty-four hours, Demetrius thought, keeping vigil across from Chantal. He couldn't wait until the services ended so he could get Chantal back to the palace, back to a semblance of safety. She was so exposed at the services, both at the cathedral and here, and he felt her vulnerability acutely. It was impossible to get close enough to her today, not with her family taking precedence, but he also couldn't shake the feeling that they were being watched. That *she* was being watched.

Demetrius couldn't explain how he knew, but he just felt the prickle of danger, that uneasy sense that things were not right. Even with additional detectives on the job, and heightened security from Demetrius's Paris and Athens offices, no one had successfully pinpointed the threat yet. Right now anyone from La Croix could be the suspect. Anyone could be targeting her.

It was a quiet ride back to the palace. Demetrius rode in the second limousine with Chantal and her youngest sister, Joelle. He saw the younger princess glance at him, curious, worried. She had Chantal's coloring, but was taller, quite slender, and her blue eyes had more green in them—making them almost turquoise.

Seeing Princess Joelle's wide anxious gaze as she glanced from her sister to him, made him realize how innocent—how *sheltered*—Chantal must have been when she married Armand. She'd known nothing about the world at large. She couldn't have even imagined the abuse she'd suffer at her new husband's hands.

They were silent as they ascended the broad circular palace staircase. A quiet family dinner had been planned for later in the evening and Demetrius would see Chantal to her room, and wait while she changed for the meal. But she'd only been inside her room for a moment when she reappeared, and when she opened the door her face was pale.

''Demetrius,'' she choked out his name, opened her door wider to permit him in.

In her room, a dozen long stemmed roses lay on her exposed

pillowcase, wrapped in gold tissue and tied with a black bow. The roses were dead.

"Have you touched them?" he asked, immediately holding her back.

She shook her head. "No. But there's a card."

"I'm interested in the card, but I want fingerprints first."

Chantal exhaled slowly, rubbed her arms, chilled despite her somber black suit. "This isn't a very nice secret admirer."

"No." He wrapped an arm around her waist and drew her against him. "And the fact that he can access your bedroom, within your family's home, worries me."

All she could think about was going home, seeing Lilly. "Me, too." She drew a shaky breath. "I wish I was in La Croix. Couldn't we go tonight?"

He pulled her closer. "It's too late to fly tonight. I need to arrange security, as well as submit a flight plan, but I promise we'll leave first thing in the morning."

She nodded, shivered. "So where do I sleep?"

"In my hotel suite, with me."

His hotel was luxurious, his suite on the top floor. Chantal noticed the security detail parked out front of the hotel, as well as the men stationed outside Demetrius's suite.

Unlocking the door to his rooms, Demetrius did a quick search, checking closets, bathrooms, beneath the massive king-size bed. "Not taking any chances," he said, catching her eye.

"You never do."

His lips curved, a shadow of a smile. "Not with you." He peeled off his coat, removed the leather holster strap he wore beneath his arm. "Hungry?"

He'd been armed. She shouldn't have been surprised, of course he'd be armed when she was the target of some madman, but glancing at the gun sitting on top of the marble bar counter, she shivered. She hated weapons, had never approved of guns. "I wouldn't mind something light," she said, wanting to get something inside her stomach before the morning sickness returned.

"I'll order," he said, reaching for the phone, "Why don't you relax in the tub?"

The bathtub was enormous, and Chantal poured the rich herbal bath gel provided by the hotel beneath the running tap, filling the steamy bathroom with the heady scent of lavender and citrus.

Eyes closed, and chin deep in warm, fragrant water Chantal heard the knock on the bathroom door, and opened her eyes. "Dinner here?"

"No, not for another five or ten minutes." The door opened and Demetrius leaned against the doorway, eyes hooded, expression pensive. "The detectives have finished dusting for fingerprints at the palace, and they intend to run the fingerprints with local databases, but it could take awhile."

She felt Demetrius's frustration. He didn't like that the investigation was moving so slowly. He was a results man. He backed up his talk with action. "They're doing they're best, right?"

He shook his head wearily. "I wish I had you back on the Rock. I felt better with you there, I could sleep."

She felt a pang. "You're not sleeping?"

"I worry about you being so vulnerable. Being pregnant I—" He broke off, looked away, gaze narrowing. He drew a deep breath, and then another, and yet there was a hint of desperation beneath the surface, an intense emotion that rendered him vulnerable.

He was struggling, truly struggling and Chantal sat up in the bath, her heart wrenched. "Demetrius, I'm pregnant, not sick."

"Yes, but if someone got close to you, someone had access to you—" Again he bit back the words and yet Chantal understood what he was trying to say.

He was afraid she couldn't defend herself properly, afraid that in her condition she'd be even more helpless than before. "Come here," she said softly, extending a hand to him. "Don't stand so far away."

He hesitated before approaching the tub, and dropping to her side.

With him crouched beside the bath, they were eye level and his expression looked tortured. He wasn't the iron man tonight, far from invincible, and Chantal thought she'd never cared so much for him. Gently she reached out to touch his face, his dark jaw bristly. "I don't want you to worry." She tried to smile but her heart felt full and far too tender. "You're doing everything humanly possible to keep me safe and I have full confidence in you, and your security detail."

"Mistakes happen," he said bitterly.

"We can't help that."

"But they shouldn't happen."

She caressed his prominent cheekbone. He was a man that would never shirk his duty. He'd never abandon those weaker, or those in need. "We're human." For the past years she hadn't liked herself, seeing only her weaknesses, feeling only her helplessness, and yet suddenly she felt calm, she felt settled. Demetrius brought balance to her life. Perspective. "And if you honestly believe I only wanted you for sex than you're a bigger fool than—"

He cut her words off with a kiss. Chantal felt the smoldering heat of it all the way through and her lips parted beneath his.

Minutes later when he finally lifted his head, he strummed her soft lips with his thumb. "I'm no fool, Chantal. I know there's a lot more here than sex." At this his dark eyes glimmered with a hidden smile. "But being wanted for my body is kind of a turn on."

He left her to finish her bath but later after room service had delivered dinner and Chantal was sitting in the hotel robe at the dining table with Demetrius, he returned to the subject of the investigation. What the detectives had discovered, and hadn't yet discovered, had been weighing on him all evening. The last thing he wanted to do was upset her on top of such a long, disturbing day, but he needed her help.

"They've had a look at the card left with the flowers in your room at the palace," he said.

Chantal looked up at him, her soup spoon suspended midair. "And?"

He wasn't going to tell her the exact message on the card, it was far too sinister and the peculiar wording had sent chills through him. The stalker had implied he'd be waiting for her in La Croix, that he knew she'd be heading there next and he'd be the first to welcome her home. And the way the word *welcome* had been written in a suspicious reddish ink that wasn't ink at all but dried blood, made Demetrius's skin crawl.

''The card was signed 'S','' Demetrius said evenly, hiding the depth of his concern. Momentum was building. The situation had become extreme. ''Do you know anyone by 'S', first name? Last name? Anyone from La Croix come to mind?''

She leaned forward, propped her elbows on the table, and chewed her thumb. Her forehead furrowed as she seemed to be mentally cataloging names, faces, but after a minute she shook her head. ''Any number of names start with an 'S.' Sabina, Sabrina, Suzette, but no one that I personally know.''

''How about men?''

''I can't think of anyone.''

''Simon? Silvio?''

Again she shook her head. ''I'm sorry. Doesn't ring a bell.''

''That's all right. The detectives are still running tests, trying to match the fingerprint.'' But inwardly he sighed. He was tired. His brain barely functioned these past few days. He knew he needed more sleep than what he was getting but he didn't trust anyone else to watch her, was afraid of what would happen if he fell asleep.

Later when Chantal yawned, he suggested she turn in, get some rest before the flight home. ''You're going to need your energy,'' he gently teased. ''Your daughter is going to be thrilled to see you.''

Chantal immediately brightened. ''I can't wait. It's been forever since I saw her.'' And then she hesitated, her expression uncertain. ''Are you going to sleep in here with me?'' She swallowed, color suffusing her cheeks. ''I'd like you, to. It might be our last—'' She broke off, bit her lip. ''Things will be different in La Croix.''

''I know.'' Very different, he silently added, looking at her for a long, excruciating moment, knowing he had no idea what she'd do once back in La Croix, knowing he had no right to ask her to sacrifice Lilly's happiness for his child's life. But he wanted the baby. He wanted Chantal and the baby desperately.

''I'll come in a little later,'' he said, squashing his emotion, refusing to let her see how much he hated escorting her back into the face of danger. Every instinct in him insisted he take her away from La Croix back to the Rock. His driving need was to protect her and the baby, not deliver her like a sacrificial lamb to the Thibaudet châteaux. "I've some calls to make, and I haven't finished finalizing our security detail for the morning."

He kissed her at the door of the bedroom, kissed her knowing this might very well be the last time he held her like this, and then he clamped control over his emotion and need, and broke away. "Get some sleep."

He turned to leave but her voice stopped. "Demetrius, if Lilly were your daughter, what would you do?"

For a long moment he couldn't answer, then he sighed heavily. There was no way he could lie to her. "I'd do what you're doing. I'd protect Lilly and her future with every bone in my body."

In the bedroom Chantal curled on her side in the big downy bed, staring at the bedroom door which he'd left open a crack. She could see him from the bed. He'd finished his calls, he'd shut down his computer, and now he stood in the semidarkness of the living room, facing the marble fireplace. His shirt was unbuttoned, leaving his chest naked.

He was deep in thought, his hard features severe, and yet she'd never seen him look more beautiful.

He was so troubled. He was agonizing over the baby. She didn't blame him. She was tormented, too.

If there was a way to do this—have the baby, be with Demetrius, keep Lilly—she'd jump at the chance, but at the moment she didn't see a way out. Couldn't see how she'd ever escape the repressive Thibaudets.

Demetrius hoped Chantal was finally asleep. He'd heard her tossing and turning in the bedroom earlier but in the last half hour the room had grown quiet.

He should try to get some sleep, too, but he couldn't go in there, couldn't climb into that bed and be near her and feel her warmth and softness and then climb out in the morning knowing he'd never hold her again, knowing he'd never be so close.

He raised his hands, leaned against the mantle, feeling the muscles in his back harden.

He was in over his head. His stomach knotted. For the first time in his career, he'd lost perspective. He wasn't doing his job anymore. Instead of thinking about the princess's safety, he was obsessing about his own needs.

It shouldn't matter that Chantal didn't want what he wanted. It shouldn't change the way he did his job, and yet he knew he'd lost focus. Knew he was distracted by thoughts of the baby, concerns about the future. A good bodyguard needed a clear cool head. Demetrius had lost his.

He'd been kidding himself when he said he was the best man for the job. It'd been selfish on his part. He hadn't wanted to leave her, hadn't wanted to let go of her. But it was time he faced the truth. His personal interest was jeopardizing her welfare. The fact was, he cared too much for her, and he cared deeply, passionately, about the baby. Unfortunately his needs, his desires, were influencing his thinking.

Earlier tonight he'd put in a call to his office, requested the services of two of his best men. They were both excellent bodyguards, and he trusted them implicitly. It was time they stepped in and did the job he couldn't do anymore.

He gripped the edge of the mantel, muscles in his arms and shoulders tensing all over again.

He'd discovered things that could free Chantal, but it had come at such a price for Lilly that he couldn't tell her. Prince Armand Thibaudet had lived a secret life. Prince Armand wasn't the obedient son his family pretended he'd been.

The Thibaudets had married their son to Chantal to clean up his image. As the eldest of the Ducasse princesses, she was widely loved and admired. Although she was young at the time the engagement was announced, she was also smart, elegant, educated. Chantal was to bring class to a classless son of a bitch, Demetrius concluded bitterly.

She'd been used, and she'd been wronged.

But as Chantal had said, it wasn't about her anymore, it was about Lilly, and if Demetrius revealed what he knew, he'd get what he wanted—Chantal and the baby—but it'd destroy what Chantal wanted for Lilly. It'd destroy Lilly's happiness, her security, her future.

The child had already lost her father. Demetrius didn't believe he had the right to strip her of her title, take her from her home.

He loved Chantal so much that he loved what she loved, and she loved Lilly. Dearly. Deeply. It was one of the things he loved about her most—that she was such a devoted mother, that she'd put her daughter first, time and again.

Exhausted, Demetrius released the mantle. He'd started his business to protect others from suffering. He'd used his own pain to ensure that others wouldn't hurt as he did, and that's what he'd do now. He'd protect Chantal and Lilly. No matter the cost.

CHAPTER THIRTEEN

MORNING arrived, as did breakfast and a stack of international newspapers. Demetrius woke Chantal with a pot of tea and toast. "Plain toast," he said, setting the plate on the nightstand next to her. "We'll leave as soon as you've eaten."

She struggled to sit up, momentarily confused by her whereabouts. Then her grogginess vanished as she realized what he'd just said. They'd be on their way to La Croix soon. She'd be with Lilly before noon.

"I'm also bringing in two new bodyguards," he added tersely. "They're men I've known for years. Alexi will be on the flight. Louis will be at the châteaux. They've been briefed. They know everything I know."

She stared at him for a long moment. His voice was already detached, his body language reserved. "Where are you going?"

"I'll be around. Just not in the foreground."

He was letting her go, she thought, fighting panic, he was already stepping away. "I don't want anyone else."

He struggled to smile, and on him it looked almost frightening. "I'm still traveling with you today. I wouldn't leave you now. I've no intention of leaving you until you're safe."

Her eyes stung. She felt the distance yawning between them. "And when I'm safe?"

He shrugged. "That's for you to decide."

She blinked, but tears were filling her eyes. "I don't want to say goodbye."

"When this is all over, you'll know how to find me. I'll give you my number—"

"Okay. Great." She couldn't do this now, couldn't start the day like this. What did he mean? What about their baby? "I think I'll just get dressed."

The flight was short, from take off to landing, lasting barely forty-five minutes. On board the jet, Chantal was just about to ask Demetrius for one of the newspapers she'd seen him fold and stash in his briefcase, when the plane began to descend.

The plane hit a pocket of turbulence and bounced and she was suddenly vividly reminded of the day they'd met, that terrifying plunge to the earth. Demetrius also seemed to remember, and he looked up, and smiled at her, the first real smile she'd seen in days.

"Frightened?"

Only of being without him, she thought. "No."

They touched ground without a problem, the landing so smooth it felt like they'd touched down on glass. The jet parked in front of the terminal, and Demetrius let the new bodyguard, Alexi, disembark first, then he and Chantal filed off, stepping out into the bright morning light. It was a beautiful day. Clear, sunny, not a cloud in the sky.

They walked swiftly across the tarmac and entered the cool dim terminal. It wouldn't be a long drive to the châteaux. A half hour at most and Demetrius had a car and driver waiting.

Alexi was moving toward the exit. The pilot had promised to carry the luggage to the car. Everything was running smoothly, Demetrius thought. Too smoothly, a little voice mocked inside his head.

He frowned. And yet instinctively he slowed his pace, realizing that Chantal had stopped walking. Glancing down, he saw a ribbon of worry between her fine dark brows. She was looking at something beyond the terminal window, and she was puzzled.

Demetrius tried to see what had caught her attention. The limo. The driver. Alexi at the terminal door.

His narrowed gaze scanned the nearly empty terminal, noted the young attendant at the desk and he shook his head, feeling stupid.

Something was wrong. But what?

His skin fairly crawled as they continued walking toward the door. Every cell in his body was alert as his sixth sense told him to be careful. But careful of what, and more importantly *where?*

Stepping closer to Chantal, he tried to tell himself that nothing was going to happen, that he was here and Alexi was here and they were nearly at the car.

But then the sliding glass doors opened. Demetrius felt a chill. The limousine driver had left the curb outside and entered the building.

Wrong.

A driver never left his car.

Yet right now the driver was heading their way and Demetrius went cold. The driver was nondescript, a middle aged man with fair, thinning hair, but it wasn't his physical appearance which struck Demetrius as wrong. It was the way he was looking at Chantal. His eyes looked hollow, vacant...and he was staring at the princess. And only the princess.

The driver was the danger.

"Do you know him?" Demetrius demanded harshly, drawing closer to her, wishing Alexi was closer, wanting to shield Chantal completely but knowing it was impossible now. She was exposed. He'd left her exposed.

"Yes." Her voice sounded faint. Scared.

Her fear reinforced his worry, and Demetrius felt the muscles in his neck thicken, tighten, tension building through his chest, torso, legs. "Where do you know him from?"

Chantal touched his arm, fingers squeezing his forearm muscle. "Stefano worked for Armand. He was once his driver, and now drives Phillipe and Catherine."

"That's his name?" he managed calmly, grateful to be so cold, so clearheaded. His mouth tasted faintly metallic. *Stefano. S.*

S. The infamous S that had haunted them these past few weeks.

Without taking his eyes off Stefano, Demetrius slid a possessive arm around Chantal's waist. "He's not the driver I requested."

She leaned against him, slipping her body even closer to his, tucking her shoulder beneath his arm. "I should have thought of him before. He's always been a bit odd around me. He doesn't drive me anymore. We had a problem awhile back—"

"We need to get you out of here," He interrupted roughly, not sure where to take her, only knowing that he would not let Chantal be hurt.

He needed Alexi. He needed the backup immediately.

Demetrius called out to Alexi in Greek, alerting him to the danger, and before Alexi could move, Demetrius saw Stefano reach inside his coat.

Stefano moved fast.

Demetrius had just a split-second to register the flash of shiny silver. A gun. Stefano was armed. He'd drawn a gun.

Adrenaline kicked in and everything seemed to happen at once.

Stepping in front of Chantal, he ordered her down even as he pulled his own weapon.

Chantal felt frozen in place. "Get down!" Demetrius's hoarse command echoed in her ears and for a moment she didn't understand, and then it all became crystal clear. Stefano had a gun.

Demetrius had drawn his gun.

She threw herself at the ground as a loud pop reverberated through the terminal. There was another pop and she saw Stefano stagger, and fall.

Demetrius had shot him.

She was up again, on her feet, even as Demetrius rushed to Stefano's side to disarm him. Stefano was on the ground but he was swearing horrendous curses, shouting venomous things at Chantal, hateful names that made her want to throw up, and then Alexi was there, putting his body between her and the others. "You need to go to the car," the young Greek bodyguard said.

She shook her head. "I have to stay with Demetrius."

"He wants you to go."

"No." She pushed against Alexi, but her arms were weak, her body was trembling all over. Hot, cold, terror and shock washed over her in waves.

The wail of sirens pierced the air and moments later a stream of blue and white police cars streaked across the parking lot, drawing up at random angles before the terminal entrance.

The police descended, flooding the building, roughly pulling Demetrius to his feet while Stefano remained on the ground.

Chantal struggled against Alexi as Demetrius was handcuffed. What were they handcuffing him for? "Let me go," she begged, watching the police push Demetrius out the door, toward a waiting police car.

Alexi at least allowed her to the door and standing at the glass, her eyes met Demetrius's as he was shoved into the back of the car. He looked calm, she thought, defiant.

Turning she saw Stefano lifted and strapped onto a gurney before he was wheeled from the building. Then the police car and ambulance streaked off, sirens shrieking.

"That's the end of that," Alexi said, escorting her outside. The limousine was still there but now there was no driver.

Alexi made a phone call. Ten minutes later a black sedan pulled up in front of the terminal. "We'll take you to the château," Alexi said as they entered the car.

"I'd rather go to the police station."

"There's nothing you can do right now."

"I have to go anyway."

Alexi shook his head. He was a younger version of Demetrius. Fierce. Unsmiling. But he acquiesced. "Then we'll go."

The drive to the police station was long, and Chantal stared blindly out the window, her eyes not seeing anything, her brain barely functioning. Demetrius could be in trouble, she thought. La Croix was tough on firearm laws. And Demetrius hadn't just carried a firearm, he'd used it.

She could only pray the police would be lenient.

Arriving at the police station, it didn't take her long to realize the police weren't going to be lenient at all. If anything, they were hostile toward her and refused to let her see Demetrius. "Mr. Mantheakis must be questioned first," the sergeant at the front desk told her.

"His lawyer is coming," she said, trying to stand tall. "You can't question him without his lawyer present."

The sergeant's eyebrows lifted. "Princess Thibaudet, we don't tell you how to run your castle. Please don't try to tell us how to run ours."

There was a derisive note in his voice and she had the peculiar sense that the sergeant was angry with *her*. What had happened? What had she done? "Demetrius Mantheakis works for. He's my bodyguard—"

"But not just your bodyguard," the sergeant interrupted

rudely. Leaning forward on the desk, he pushed an open news-paper toward her with an elbow.

Her gaze fell, dropping to the open paper. Scandalous Affair! The headlines screamed. Princess Chantal Pregnant With Bodyguard's Baby!

Heat burned through her. Her hand trembled as she gazed at the photo beneath the headlines. It was her in the toilet stall at the cathedral, throwing up.

Anger shot through her, anger and shame that her private life meant so much to tabloid photographers and reporters.

It was disgusting. She was disgusted that people could stoop so low.

"It was my grandmother's funeral," she said quietly, looking up into the sergeant's eyes. "Grief's a difficult thing, isn't it?"

The sergeant had the grace to look chagrined. And Chantal used the silence to make her request again. "I'd like to see my bodyguard now. Please."

The sergeant shifted, less confident than he'd been a few moments earlier. "You can't, Your Highness. Your bodyguard resisted arrest. He's being questioned."

"He didn't resist arrest." Chantal's heart tightened, but she wouldn't let herself feel afraid, wouldn't let herself feel anything but fury. "I was at the scene. I was there. Mr. Mantheakis didn't resist arrest. He did exactly as the officer asked. He cooperated completely."

"I'm sorry. You'll have to wait."

She took a seat in the station, ignoring the glances cast her way, ignoring Alexi standing next to her, ignoring everything but the heaviness in her heart. Demetrius was in serious trouble. She felt it in every pore of her body. There was more to this than a simple arrest. This was payback for a commoner forgetting his place and getting close to a member of the royal family.

She waited an hour. Then two. Her stomach began to get that queasy sick feeling but she wasn't going to leave the station without seeing Demetrius.

"You need to eat," Alexi said quietly.

She shook her head. "Not until I see him." But after waiting three hours, and then four, she knew she had to do something.

She didn't want to involve her family. There was no way she'd have Grandfather or her sisters parading into the police station on her behalf, especially not the day after Grandmama's funeral, but Chantal finally used Alexi's phone to call Nicollette, knowing her sister would still be at the palace in Melio.

"I'm at the police station," she said to Nic. "Demetrius—"

"We've heard. It's all over the news. *Everything* is all over the news."

Chantal closed her eyes. She knew what Nic was saying but didn't have the energy to go into that now. What mattered was Demetrius, and getting Demetrius out of jail. "He did nothing wrong, Nic. He took action to protect me. It was purely self-defense, but I'm worried." Chantal was careful to keep her voice down. "Something's not right. I can feel it in my bones."

"Let me put Malik on the phone. He's right here. He wants to talk to you."

"Chantal?" It was Malik's deep voice and he sounded reassuringly calm. "How is it there?"

"Demetrius is in trouble." She couldn't waste time on preliminary greetings. She was too tired, too heartsick.

"Sounds like it. Tell me what's happened so far."

Chantal gave Nicollette's husband a brief rundown of events, exactly as they unfolded, concluding with Demetrius's arrest and her visit to the station. "They say this is about firearms and resisting arrest, but that's not it, Malik. This is about La Croix national pride. They're punishing Demetrius for consorting with a member of the royal family."

"I think you're right."

Shaking, she rubbed her temple. She knew La Croix's culture and politics better than anyone. "He needs a good lawyer."

"I've already sent one. He should be there soon."

"Thank you." She felt a rush of gratitude. "I appreciate it, Malik."

"It's nothing, Chantal. Take care of yourself, and call us as soon as you've more information."

She'd just hung up the phone when a detective appeared at the front. "You have fifteen minutes, Your Royal Highness," he said to Chantal. "Follow me."

Alexi wanted to come but they wouldn't let him. "I'll be fine," she assured the young bodyguard, before following the detective down a gray hallway into an even more gray conference room with a wood table and folding metal chairs. The detective motioned for her to sit. Chantal glanced at the straggle of folding chairs. Paint was peeling off one. The chairs looked so hard and cold.

"Are you going to question me?" she asked, throat dry, sitting down in the chair nearest her.

"No." The detective turned to leave. "There's no need. We have all the information we need."

The door opened again five minutes later and Chantal sat frozen in her chair as Demetrius was escorted into the room, his hands still cuffed behind him.

She stared at him as if she'd never seen him before. Indeed, she'd never seen him like this before.

What had they done to him?

His face was so puffy she could barely distinguish his features, his right eye nearly swollen closed. Blood oozed from an ugly gash on his cheek.

Her heart rose up to her throat. This couldn't be him. He didn't look like anyone she knew at all. "Demetrius." She whispered his name like a prayer, and her eyes, so dry all day, burned hotter, grittier. There were no tears left to cry.

He stared at her as if she were a stranger, no emotion on his face, and the officer leading him into the room gave Demetrius a small push from behind, thrusting him closer to the table and chipped folding chairs.

She saw him stiffen, his jaw thicken as he ground his teeth together in silent protest.

It was Demetrius all right. And yet the knowledge only ate at her, and she sagged in her chair beneath the weight of her shock. Had she done this to him? He'd only been protecting her. He'd put his body between her and Stefano, drawn a gun only after Stefano had drawn his, and yet she couldn't help feeling guilty. If he hadn't tried to save her...

She knew she being illogical, but she also knew the police would have never treated a member of the royal family this way.

They would have never done this to her father. Her cousin. Her late husband. They couldn't have done this to a member of the royal family and gotten away with it.

"Sit down," the officer said roughly. "And Your Highness, you are not allowed to touch him. There is to be no contact between you."

She must have nodded. She felt her head bob but she could think of nothing, look at nothing, but Demetrius. She watched as he slowly sat. His long, powerful legs were braced in front of him and his arms awkwardly cuffed behind him. "What have they done to you?"

He couldn't answer her. He hurt, badly, but it wasn't the physical pain that kept him silent. He'd been hurt worse before, taken a couple beatings before he left the Family, but what he felt now was different. His pain was alive. And it was in his mind...his heart.

He'd succeeded in protecting the princess but at what cost?

"What have they done?" she repeated.

He heard the quaver in her voice and knew she was afraid right now. Afraid for him, afraid for them, and he wanted to smile for her, wanted to show that he was above all this, but his jaw ached and he couldn't move his lips.

"They can't do this," she whispered fiercely.

He smiled on the inside, smiled without any warmth or humor. "They already have," he said through clenched teeth. His jaw throbbed. His face felt huge, prehistoric, like an excavated dinosaur bone.

She scooted forward in her chair, hands on the table. "We'll get you out. We'll make them pay—"

"Chantal." He said her name hard, sharp, to get her attention. "La Croix is very strict about firearms. I'm not going to get out anytime soon."

"I'll help you."

"How?" His dark eyes searched hers. Abruptly he leaned forward, his big chest coming into contact with the table. "Forget about me, Princess. What you need to do now is get on with your life. Enjoy your daughter. Enjoy the time you have with her. You only get one chance at this, *pedhaki mou*. Make it mean something.''

Was he serious? Forget about him? She was carrying his child. She loved him. She'd never forget him and yet time was up, nothing more could be said. The detective escorted her back to the lobby where Alexis waited.

Moments later they were enroute to the Thibaudet châteaux. She'd only been gone a month, Chantal thought as she stepped through the châteaux's doors, but it seemed so much longer. She didn't feel like family anymore, but a stranger as she climbed the staircase to the nursery on the third floor.

Entering the bright yellow room, Lilly flung herself into her mother's arms and Chantal held her daughter tightly. Some of the wretched emotion bottled inside her escaped and tears seeped from beneath her lids.

"Mama," Lilly said, squeezing Chantal even harder.

It'd been such a horrible day. Such a horrible week. But she had Lilly in her arms now and that's all that mattered. "Hello, my darling." She stroked Lilly's soft light brown curls, felt her small straight back, marveled at how much her daughter had grown in the month she'd been gone. And holding her she was again amazed how fast the last four years had passed. It didn't seem very long since Lilly was a newborn.

She was still sitting with Lilly in the nursery, holding her on her lap and catching up on everything that had happened—all the events big and small, including the hurts that had loomed huge in Lilly's mind—when the door opened and Queen Catherine Thibaudet stood in the nursery doorway still wearing her beige wool traveling coat.

"We'd like a word with you, Chantal." Catherine's voice was crisp, no-nonsense. "Phillipe is already waiting in his study."

Dread rushed through Chantal, filling every nerve and pore, weighting her limbs so she trembled a little as she held Lilly. Catherine left and Lilly, sensing Chantal's fear wrapped her arms around her mother's neck. "Don't be afraid, Mama."

"I'm not," Chantal answered, hating that her daughter should already be aware of her fears. It was her responsibility to protect Lilly, not the other way around. Adults were meant to shield children from stress, to ensure they weren't exposed to things they couldn't handle. For God's sake, it was the adult's job to be the adult.

She dropped a kiss on Lilly's head and ruffled her curls, aiming to lighten the mood. "I'll be back soon."

Phillipe and Catherine were waiting for her in Phillipe's study. They were both seated, sharing a late-afternoon tea.

Catherine motioned for Chantal to sit. Chantal gingerly took a seat, knowing that whatever would follow would be miserable.

"Your grandmama's funeral was lovely," Catherine said, breaking the tense silence. "I'm very glad we were able to attend. I knew your grandmother when I was just a little girl. She was already betrothed to your grandfather." The queen struggled to smile, lips pinching. "I admired her very much."

"Thank you." Chantal had heard this a hundred times. This was the way Armand's parents prefaced everything. *Because of the family ties, out of family respect, due to family loyalty...* and of course, whatever followed was bitter and painful. "It's been a very difficult few days."

Phillipe made a hoarse sound as he cleared his throat. "You can imagine our distress on opening the papers this morning. There we were in your family home in Melio, reading a shocking story about—" He broke off, jaw tightening, pale blue eyes narrowing as he focused on a point below Chantal's hips, somewhere between her ankles and knees, "your bodyguard." He swallowed. "Which, I might add, we didn't understand the necessity of you having in the first place."

"I'm certain the Melio palace detectives made you aware of their investigation," Chantal said quietly, refusing to be baited. She knew how Phillipe worked. He'd try to corner her, intimidate her, frustrate her. But it wouldn't work today. "Just as I'm certain you're aware of Tanguy's death earlier this month—"

"Most tragic, yes," Phillipe interrupted, "but these things happen with cars and such."

How could he say that? These things didn't happen. These things were made to happen, and the fact that Phillipe was going to pretend that Tanguy's death was just a random event sickened Chantal.

But she didn't let her outrage show, didn't let any emotion show. She knew too well how Phillipe preyed on weakness. This time, she vowed, she'd show none. "As you've already heard, my bodyguard, Demetrius Mantheakis, saved my life today." She spoke calmly, her voice firm, controlled. "And yet he's in jail facing ludicrous charges." Never mind that he'd been beaten, she thought, trying to suppress the picture of him in her head, his handsome face bruised and swollen. "I want him released immediately."

"That's impossible." Phillipe answered with an equally firm voice. "He committed a crime—"

"Protecting me."

"I'm sorry, my dear. This must be a very trying time for you." Catherine's lightly penciled eyebrows arched. "Now tell us, is there any truth to the story in this morning's paper? You aren't actually pregnant, are you?"

Chantal went cold on the inside. She felt her lips curve but didn't know whether it was a smile or tears.

"Because you know, dear, that's not permitted, not at all permitted." Catherine was trying hard to interject warmth into her voice but her eyes were brittle and her features were rigid and Chantal wondered how it was she'd survived at the chateaux all these years. These weren't warm people, loving people, but ice royals.

"You can't think you'll be able to keep the baby, Chantal, dear. It's just not possible," Catherine added before she and Phillipe exchanged glances. "He's a common man—"

"And a criminal," Phillipe interrupted. "A member of the Greek mafia—"

"No."

"Son of the mob boss himself," the king continued starkly, "It's speculated that he's been part of numerous unsolved crimes."

"I don't believe it."

"Then have a look at this." Anger flared in the king's voice, and drawing a newspaper from the side table he tossed it at her.

Chantal awkwardly caught it, pages slipping half hazardly this way and that. But she didn't need the middle pages. The information Phillipe wanted her to see was right there, on the front page: Greek Mobster Seduces Princess, was the headline and beneath the dark ink was a black and white photo of Demetrius taken years ago. He was dressed in a dark suit, attending a funeral.

"That's your bodyguard." Phillipe's voice came out in ice chips, hard, sharp, frigid. "And that was his wife. Killed by a warring mafia faction. Read all about it and then tell me I'm *wrong*."

CHAPTER FOURTEEN

"I DON'T need to read it. I know the facts."

"*Do you?*" Phillipe leaned forward, stared at her so long and hard that she felt almost ugly, shameful. She didn't understand how he could do that to her. Was it the contempt in his eyes? The ridicule in his voice?

But she was tired of feeling ashamed, tired of the pain and stillness and silence. "I do," she answered quietly, clinging to her dignity. "Maybe you are the one that needs to get your facts straight."

Chantal rose then, but she took the paper with her, carrying it back to her room.

She believed in Demetrius. She believed in him with her whole heart but that didn't stop her from wanting to know more. From wanting to know everything.

Hands shaking, she spread the paper flat on her bed and forced herself to read each agonizing word.

He'd been married, just as he'd told her, and his wife had been pregnant. A rival mob kidnapped Demetrius's wife—

Chantal had to stop reading for a moment, had to draw a breath. Her heart had begun to pound and she felt sick inside, sick and afraid even though the events had happened years ago. Because this wasn't just anyone. This was Demetrius. His world, his wife.

Fighting her revulsion, Chantal struggled to read on, knowing that it was only going to get worse, knowing that what she was going to read would break her heart.

Twenty-three-year-old Katina Mantheakis was held for ransom, and even though Demetrius paid the ransom—paid more than was demanded—the rival mob killed Katina Mantheakis anyway.

Despite the fact that she was pregnant. Despite the fact she just weeks from giving birth to a baby girl.

166

My God.

Chantal squeezed her eyes closed, awash with pain. The story was brief and yet so violent, so horrible that it cut her deeply.

No wonder Demetrius didn't discuss his past. She didn't blame him. Not in the least.

And suddenly, so many things made sense, so much became clear.

The island sanctuary.

The devoted families that lived there.

Demetrius's insistence on protecting her at all costs.

No wonder he didn't trust himself anymore. No wonder he wanted others on the job. She wasn't just a princess, but the mother of his child. His child. And no wonder he needed this child. He wanted to be a father again. Wanted the chance to live again.

And she wanted that for him. She wanted him to have the life, and the family, he'd been denied. But to give him what he needed...what he deserved...meant giving up Lilly.

Could she do it?

Did she have the strength to let one child go to save the other?

Chantal didn't sleep, the hours creeping by, one agonizing minute after another. She left her bed once in the night, went to Lilly's room on the third floor and opened her daughter's door.

A small yellow night-light glowed on the little green painted dresser. In the soft yellow light Lilly's small face glowed. She looked calm. Peaceful.

Chantal's chest squeezed, knotting into a small hard ball. *How do I leave you?* She whispered silently, her eyes burning, too dry now for tears.

And yet her hand moved to her tummy and she placed her palm protectively against her belly. *How do I deny you a chance to live?*

This time her eyes did fill with tears and she pressed her knuckled fist against her face, pressed against her eyes, pressed against the pain.

She had to make a choice. She had to make the right choice. *God, help me do what I must do.*

The long night finally ended and Chantal was in the middle of

dressing when she received a message that the Thibaudets wished
to see her again.

They were requesting her company at the breakfast table. Lilly,
Chantal discovered on arriving in the sunny glass-walled breakfast room, wasn't there.

Taking her place at the formal table, Chantal began to realize
how little she saw of her daughter. How much Phillipe and
Catherine dictated Lilly's life.

But Phillipe and Catherine were smiling at her now, a unified,
almost benevolent smile.

"Good morning, Chantal," Catherine said, starting the conversation as she usually did. "We hope you slept better than we
did." She paused, drew a breath. "As you can imagine, we've
been talking. We've had a great deal to discuss. This doesn't
have to become ugly," she added with her surreal calm and control. "You can put this whole sordid affair behind you right
now."

"That's right. Act now, and this—" the king exchanged sly
glances with his wife "—can all be dealt with. Quickly.
Quietly."

Neatly, Chantal concluded, trying hard to keep her expression
blank. They wanted her to get rid of the baby. Turn her back
into Armand's devoted widow. Pretend nothing had changed, that
nothing would ever change.

"Everyone makes mistakes." The queen was smiling, warmly.
Confidently. Her smile seeming to say, we're both girls. We understand these things, we understand how these things can happen, don't we? "We want to help you, Chantal. Dear. More than
anything we want to make things right for you and Lilly."

The king leaned across the table to cover Chantal's hand with
his. But his hand felt hard, almost punishing and Chantal went
cold inside. He was just like Armand. Too much like Armand.
He'd ruled with a heavy hand, an iron fist throughout his forty
odd years on the throne.

She slid her hand out from beneath her father-in-law's. "And
Demetrius?" she asked. "What about him?"

The queen's smile slipped. The king leaned back a fraction in
his chair. "He'll serve his time, of course."

His time. The way the king said the words made her blood boil. My God, what did 'his time' mean? And who the hell was Phillipe to impose his law onto others? "He was my bodyguard. He was protecting me."

"You know the law. Unless you have a firearm permit from the government, you can't carry a weapon. Concealed or not."

Chantal almost pounded on the table. "He saved my life."

"Dear, do you really believe that?" The queen's expression had hardened, then softened, and now she gazed at Chantal with something between pity and disbelief. "Do you honestly think you were ever in any danger? Or could it be, my dear, that you are simply too sensitive, stressed by the events around you?"

Chantal shook her head, a slow decisive shake. She wasn't going to sit here and listen to this. She'd spent nearly ten years of her life being lectured, controlled, coerced. She'd had enough. She'd had more than enough. "If you'll excuse me," she said, pushing away from the table. "I have things to do."

Chantal met with the lawyer Malik had sent at the lawyer's hotel downtown. "I'm afraid I don't have good news," the lawyer said regretfully. "La Croix laws are rigid, as well as archaic. There isn't much legal ground for us to stand on."

Chantal had been pacing back and forth in front of the brocade sofa. "If Demetrius were royal, this would have never happened. They'd never prosecute a member of the royal family like this."

"But he's not a member of the family. And you're right, there is a bias. But the bias is aimed at you as much as Mr. Mantheakis. As the mother of the future queen of La Croix, you're being held to a different standard. You're to be above reproach."

"And I have been. For nine years I've done everything they've asked of me and how has it benefited anyone? I rarely see my daughter. I'm not allowed to make decisions for her. I'm barely her mother." Chantal's eyes felt hot, scalding and she knew it was the nights of lost sleep, the weeks of fear, the years of loneliness. "But things have changed. *I've* changed. I'm pregnant."

"You don't have to keep the baby." The lawyer slid his glasses back on, picked up a sheath of papers. "No one would know if you terminated the pregnancy. You could call it a miscarriage—"

"No."

"Demetrius thinks you should."

Her body jerked. *"What?"*

"He wants you to do what is best for you. He wants you to do what is best for Lilly."

The prickling behind her eyes made it difficult to see. "I don't believe that for a moment. He wants this baby." The emotion was too strong, her insides churning, the nausea returning. "And I want this baby, too."

"You might want to think on this some more. I've had a look at the contract you signed. There's no way you can have the baby and remain in La Croix. And if you leave, you won't be able to take Lilly with you."

"Maybe that's what I should do." No matter what she did, the Thibaudets would block her, contain her, control her. Even if she ended the pregnancy, they'd still remember, they'd still be ashamed of her. "I'm tired of living like this. I'm done living like this."

She closed her eyes, tried to imagine her future without her daughter, felt the horrible flood of grief and sorrow and nearly recoiled. She couldn't imagine living without Lilly but she couldn't imagine remaining at the châteaux after terminating the pregnancy, knowing Demetrius was paying an unholy price for doing his job.

"They'd still have to let me see her sometimes," Chantal said quietly. "Holidays. Formal occasions."

"It wouldn't be the same as living under the same roof with her."

"No." She stared across the hotel room, trying to see a future without Lilly there every day.

And suddenly she saw it. She knew what she needed to do. Calm swamped Chantal, calm and focus. She knew what she needed to do. "I have an idea," she said. "But I'm going to need your help. King Nuri's, too."

A day passed, night fell, and after another long sleepless night on his cot, morning came. He'd been in the jail three days, two nights. Yesterday had been quiet, no word from the outside, nothing more from the lawyer Malik Nuri had hired. Now it was a new day but nothing felt new.

Footsteps sounded in the corridor, the footsteps ringing extra loud off all the cement walls. The footsteps stopped outside his cell. Demetrius sat up on his cot as the door to his cell squeaked open.

"What's happening?" he asked, shooting the officer a wary look.

"You're wanted in the interrogation room."

"Again?"

The officer shrugged as he cuffed Demetrius. Trailing the man down the corridor, Demetrius tried to rake a hand through his hair, but the handcuffs made even that difficult. It'd been a long night. It'd be an even longer day. He hated not being near Chantal, not knowing how she was, how she was feeling. He just wanted her safe. Happy. She deserved to be happy.

The officer opened the door to the interrogation room, unlocked Demetrius's handcuffs and pushed him into the room. "You've got ten minutes, Mantheakis."

The door closed behind him with a bang. He winced at the loud sound.

"How's the head?" a quiet voice asked behind him.

Demetrius stiffened, turned, faced Chantal. He'd missed her, but he didn't want her here. It'd only make it harder for her. The press would only print more vicious things. "You shouldn't have come."

She didn't look abashed. If anything she looked cool, controlled. "Really?"

"There's nothing you can do to help me now."

"That's not how I see it," she answered calmly. "I think there's quite a bit I can do." She gestured to the gentleman in dark robes seated at the table. "Demetrius, meet Bishop Kazantzakis."

Bishop Kazantzakis? The bishop from the Greek Orthodox Church in Athens? "What are you doing, Chantal?" Demetrius bit out the words, pulse quickening, anger surging through him. He recognized her expression, saw the light of battle in her eyes, but she shouldn't be fighting for him. She should be fighting for her.

"I'm doing what I should have done before." She glanced at her watch. "We don't have much time. So let's get this going. Bishop?"

"Chantal."

She closed the distance between them, moving so close that he felt heat flare through him, heat, desire, possession. She looked beautiful, regal, dressed in a fine crepe suit the softest cream, immaculate pale hose, pale heels, her dark hair coiled at her nape.

"You're not the only one who knows right and wrong," she said, and her blue eyes flashed, bolts of fire in the sapphire. "I know right and wrong, and I can not do what the Thibaudets ask. I know I can not lose this baby, and I can not live without you."

"And I know you. You can't lose Lilly."

Her small firm chin lifted, her full lips pressed giving her classic bone structure the grace and beauty of the ancient Greeks. "I won't lose her. I just won't see her as often. I'm not dying, Demetrius. I'm simply divorcing the Thibaudets."

It felt as if a nail was being driven through his heart. His features tightened, a spasm of pain. He couldn't believe she'd do this for him. He didn't want her to do this for him. Unable to help himself, he reached for her, cupped her pale face, buried his fingers in the coil of hair at her nape. "It'll cost you, *pedhaki mou.*"

Her eyes shone, liquid blue. "And when hasn't it? Being born royal has cost me dearly, every day of my life."

He felt something wild break loose in him, the same thing he'd felt that first night on the beach in Sao Tome. She was breaking his heart. Making him feel an ungodly amount of pain. "I was supposed to protect you," he said hoarsely, his thumb brushing her mouth. "I would have done anything to protect you—"

"You did. You put your life before mine." She struggled to smile but her lips wouldn't work, the tears too close to the surface. "Now it's my turn to put you first. It's what I want to do. It's what I have to do."

"But Lilly—"

"Is loved." She drew a rough breath, the tears clinging to her black lashes. "Her grandparents will always adore her. They'll always be there for her. And so will I. I just won't be there every morning. I just won't be there every night."

"Chantal."

She stood up, pressing close, and covered his mouth with her hand. "Please. This is hard, but it's right. It *is* right. I have a baby inside me, a baby that wants to be born. I have a man I love and he deserves to be a father—" she broke off, bit her lip, fighting for control. "Please, we don't have much time."

Demetrius's eyes burned. His heart burned. He felt as if his body was on fire. "I love you."

She nodded, tears falling. "I know."

He wiped the tears from her face. Her skin was cool, the tears were warm. He couldn't imagine what she'd been going through these past twenty-four hours. He couldn't imagine the soul searching and what it took to come to this decision. "I'd do anything for you," he said, covering her tear-streaked mouth with his own.

Chantal's eyes closed as his tender kiss turned fierce. His desire for her couldn't be contained. It was too strong, too explosive, too much a part of him.

The kiss deepened, and it was like breathing she thought, her arms wrapping around his neck. This was the way it was meant to be. Him, her, them, together. A kiss for a kiss. Air for air. One life for another.

She pressed her hand against his chest, her heart melting, the impossible heat building. "I don't want to be without you," she whispered, turning her lips to brush his beard roughened cheek. "I can't be without you. I can't look at a future without you."

His thumb stroked the side of her face, following the curve of her temple, cheekbone, jawbone. "You're strong. You're stronger than you know."

"I'm stronger than *you* know. I won't let you go. I can survive anything as long as I have you."

He lifted his head, emotion blazing in his eyes. "The Thibaudets will make this miserable for you."

Her lips curved and she felt a welling of intense love. "Maybe. Maybe not. And I'll have the press on my side. They love a good story. We're giving them a story." She saw the flicker in his eyes and her insides were dissolving, love, passion, tenderness. "I'm not afraid of anything anymore. I'm ready to face the world, ready to face the truth. Life is to be lived. I want to live. And I want to live it with you."

"Chantal," he whispered her name deep in his throat and it was strangled, guttural, a sound of pure pain. He was in his own private hell now. "Since Katina died I've wanted nothing for myself. I still want nothing but for you to be happy—"

"Then make me Mrs. Mantheakis," she interrupted. "That would make me happy. I promise."

Bishop Kazantzakis opened his prayer book and in the few minutes they had left, performed the shortest, simplest wedding ceremony ever. There was no time for scripture verses, no time for a homily, there were just the vows, the exchange of rings Chantal had brought with her, and then the blessing. But it was, Chantal thought as the Bishop placed his hand on their joined hands, the most beautiful wedding ever.

"In the power vested to me by God and the Greek Orthodox Church, I now pronounce you man and wife," the Bishop concluded.

Chantal stepped into Demetrius's arms, and kissed him, giving him all her heart, giving him everything she'd ever dreamed, everything she'd ever felt.

The door to the interrogation room opened. The detective had returned. "Time's up."

Chantal stood on tip toe and kissed Demetrius one last time, trying to smile through her tears. "I'll see you soon."

The media were waiting for Chantal outside the La Croix jail. She'd spread the word that something big was going to happen and she used the opportunity as she left the jail to announce that she was no longer Princess Chantal Thibuadet, but Mrs. Demetrius Mantheakis. "As soon as my husband's freed we plan on returning to Greece."

She was done being on the defensive, she thought, sliding into the back of the waiting limousine. From now on she was on the offensive. She was taking control.

But it was one thing to announce her marriage to the eager, story-hungry media; it was another to face the furious Thibaudets.

The chateaux was in an uproar when she arrived, and Chantal was ushered none too gently into a downstairs salon. "What in God's name have you done?" Catherine demanded, voice shaking. "We were going to *help* you. We were going to *fix* this—"

"I didn't want it *fixed*," Chantal interrupted fiercely. She was pregnant. Her beloved grandmother had died. And instead of sympathy, or support, her in-laws were bullying her. Belittling her. Making her life a living hell. "I wanted to do what was right. And I did it."

"Right?" Phillipe repeated, outraged. "Marrying a Greek criminal isn't right. And holding a press conference outside the jail was unthinking...selfish. Have you given a thought in all this to Lilly? Have you even considered *our* feelings?"

"Yes." Chantal straightened, and she realized she was done cowering, done biting her tongue, forever done with running away. "Your feelings are all I ever seem to think about. And I've thought this through, and I know this will impact Lilly, but Lilly can handle this. Lilly's smart, and loving, and she's not going to lose me."

"Wrong." Catherine marched toward her, her slim body shaking. "She did just lose you. Because you're gone. You're out of here now. You'll never see her again."

"You can't keep me from her." Chantal held her ground. "I'm her mother, and I do have rights. No government anywhere would deny me time with her. So maybe she will live here, go to school here, but she'll have weekends and holidays with me."

The salon doors burst open. Demetrius entered the room. He'd showered, shaved, and dressed in a dark suit, and he was accompanied by Nicolette and King Nuri. Nicolette was carrying Lilly, and Lilly looked delighted to be in the arms of her favorite aunt.

"What's this?" Phillipe demanded. "What are you all doing here?"

"Taking Chantal and Lilly home," Demetrius answered, joining Chantal. He shot her a quizzical glance. His way of checking on her.

Chantal would have smiled if she weren't so stunned. "What are you doing here?"

"I think, for once, you have to be thankful to the media. Charges were dropped," he said. "The police chief took pity on me."

"But that doesn't explain what you're doing here," Phillip said, red-faced, agitated. "And it doesn't change Lilly's status. As heir—"

"But she's not heir," King Nuri interrupted evenly. "She's not even your legitimate grandchild."

Chantal couldn't have been more shocked. She rocked back on her heels, absolutely stunned. *"What?"*

Demetrius indicated Phillipe. "He knows," Demetrius said. "He knows your marriage was never legal because Armand's first marriage was never properly annulled."

Armand had a first marriage? There was a first wife somewhere?

"Armand has a son from the first marriage, too. A boy who is almost nine. The boy should be La Croix's heir, not Lilly." Demetrius looked at Chantal, expression strained. "I'm sorry, Chantal."

Philippe's mouth opened, closed. "The first marriage was dissolved. The annulment is nothing but a technicality."

"Just like the prenuptial contract is just a technicality, too?" King Nuri's asked slyly.

There was a moment of strained silence and then Phillipe spoke. "We don't even recognize this other marriage. We never approved of the woman, and have never accepted the son—"

"Too bad. Because he's a really nice kid. A smart, polite kid who could have benefited from loving grandparents."

Catherine pressed her hand to her mouth. Phillipe just looked enraged. "I have a granddaughter and heir. She's right here, right now."

"We love Lilly," Catherine chimed faintly. "We love our baby."

Chantal moved toward Nicollete, whispered in her sister's ear, asking Nic to take Lilly from the room before the scene became even more upsetting for her daughter.

Chantal waited until Nic was gone and the salon doors were closed to answer Catherine. "But she's not your baby," Chantal said. "She's my baby. And you've done everything in your power to take her from me."

Catherine reached out to Chantal. "But we need her—"

"No," Chantal interrupted. "You don't need her. At least not the way you think. She's just a little girl. Why can't she be a little girl?"

"Wait. Stop." Phillipe cleared his throat, obviously struggling to regain control over his emotions. "Can't we discuss this rationally? Let's sit down like reasonable people and talk this out properly."

But there was nothing reasonable or rational left in Chantal. She'd been through hell and back for what? She'd been trapped here for years for what?

"Talk?" Chantal repeated tiredly. "Don't you think, Phillipe, it's a little late to *talk?*"

"Chantal!" Catherine's voice broke. "Please, dear, please."

Chantal held her breath, concentrated on slowing her racing heart. She didn't want to hurt them, and she didn't want to hurt Lilly. "I won't keep her from seeing you. You'll always be her grandparents, but she belongs with me." Chantal shot Demetrius a grateful glance. "She belongs home with us."

They returned that same evening to Demetrius's island in Greece, and back at the large villa with the breathtaking view of the sea, Chantal felt some of the horrendous tension in her shoulders begin to ease.

With Lilly tucked into bed, she and Demetrius faced each other outside on the moon lit terrace. "So much has happened today," she said. "I can't believe we're here. Can't believe we're together—"

"Can't believe we're married?"

She heard the hard note in his voice and grinned a little mischievously. "You imagine I have regrets?"

"You might. It was a rather hasty decision."

Chantal laughed. She couldn't help it. She was feeling so much lighter, the pressure on her chest gone, her breathing easy. "And if I did have regrets, would you let me go?"

"No."

He answered so sharply, so crossly that she laughed again, the sound tinkling like wind chimes. "You're in a bad mood, Mr. Mantheakis."

He glared at her, his jaw still bruised but not quite as swollen. "If you weren't pregnant," he growled, shaking his head.

Her eyes danced. She felt happy, naughty, wicked. "And what would you do?"

"I'd pull you onto my lap and take you here." His dark eyes burned, desire evident in the tightness of his features, in the deepening of his voice. "I'd have you, and make love to you, until you could think of nothing but me."

She leaned toward him, brushed her lips across his cheekbone, near his ear. "So what's stopping you?"

He reached up, captured her face between his hands, fingers twining tight in her long loose hair. "I'm not in a sensitive mood, *pedhaki mou*."

She nipped his earlobe with her teeth. "Good. Neither am I."

"*Chantal.*" His voice deepened yet again, the inflection painfully husky.

Arching against him, she let him feel her breasts, the length of her abdomen, the curve of hips. "Take me. Right here. Right now."

She felt rather than heard the hiss of air as he exhaled, his fingers sliding from her hair, his hands slipping down her shoulders, pressing firmly against her flesh until he'd encircled her waist. "I don't want to hurt you."

"Hurt me?" She lifted her arms, slid them around his neck and kissed him, lightly, playfully, letting her tongue flick his upper lip, feeling the firmness, tasting the wine he'd had at dinner. "You'd never hurt me. Not in a thousand years. I trust you with my life."

His fingers kneaded her hip. "Careful, *pedhaki mou*, you don't want to see a grown man cry."

She pressed even closer to him, and she kissed him more

deeply, offering all of herself to him, offering all of the love in her heart, love that had never been wanted before, love that had never been needed. "Why not?" she whispered, her heart like that of the mythical phoenix, the beautiful bird rising from the ashes. "A few tears never hurt anyone."

"It's not manly," he protested, blinking fiercely.

Her lips curved and gently she reached up, wiped his lashes dry. "There. Strong and manly as ever." And then her own eyes filled with tears. She stared up at him, speechless, heart brimming over, her world so changed she couldn't even take it all in. "You saved me."

"No."

"Yes, Demetrius. You set me free." And she struggled to smile. "I'm free."

He made a rough sound, a little indignant, rather impatient. "I wouldn't call it free. You are married to me."

And Chantal kissed him, the happiness so strong, her lightness so intense, she felt dangerous, wicked all over again. "So prove it to me." She looked into his eyes, daring him, challenging him, wanting to provoke him as much as she could. "Now."

Groaning, swallowing curses, he swept her into his arms, carried her through the house, up the stairs to his bedroom, a room she'd never been in before. It was at the very top of the house, a massive suite with windows on all four walls, windows that captured every view of the island imaginable. Earth, sky, mountain, sea. The moon light bathed the rugged landscape, painting the ground and sea shades of silver and white.

"You're in trouble now," he said, dropping her none too gently on the bed.

"Good."

"Good?" he mocked, his hooded gaze growing hard and hot as he watched her sprawl backward, long brown hair tumbling over her shoulders, skirt hiking high on her thigh. "You might want to rethink that answer."

"Never."

He leaned forward, pushed her skirt up higher until her cream lace panty was revealed, and then slowly, deliberately parted her knees.

She blushed, growing so warm she felt feverish.

He was watching her face, saw her bite her lip. "I think you like living dangerously," he said, hand on her knee, feeling her body tremble with excitement.

"Of course. I've got you around to protect me."

He moved forward, stretching out above her, weight propped on his elbows. "And who, *pedhaki mou,* will protect you from me?"

Her eyes felt so heavy. Her body tingled. Her blood felt sweet and hot. It was like she'd been sipping champagne but she'd had nothing to drink.

It was love.

It was joy.

It was life itself.

She smiled, lips curving with delicious intent, and reaching up, she tugged on his shirt, pulling the tails from his trousers. "So are you just going to talk, Demetrius Mantheakis, or are you actually going to make love to me?"

She helped strip him and then he lowered his weight until the hard planes of his body touched hers. She sighed at the feel of his bare chest, the strength of his corded thighs, the hard press of his erection to her inner thigh. "I had no idea you enjoyed sex this much," he mocked her, dipping his head to kiss her neck, then her collarbone before his lips caressed the swell of her breast and closed over one aching nipple.

She gasped as he kissed her through the thin silk of her blouse. His mouth seared her, his mouth so warm, making her skin burn, her body melt, the core of her damp.

"Now," she choked, dragging her hands through his thick, crisp hair, finger nails raking his scalp. "I want you *now.*"

He made a rough *tsk-tsking.* "You think I'm going to rush this? Sorry, *agaope mou,* I'm not about to hurry anything. You're mine, remember? And what is mine, I cherish and protect."

And that, she thought breathing hard and fast as his hand slid beneath her skirt, beneath her lace panty, was all she could ask for.

By the time he'd peeled the last of her clothes from her warm, flushed body she was trembling all over, her breath trapped in her chest, her imagination stirred. He entered her slowly, so slowly that she needed his kiss to help her remember to breathe. He'd been an incredible lover their first night together, but tonight, their first night as husband and wife he was beyond great, beyond brilliant, he was perfectly wonderfully hers.

Her lover. Her heart. Her future.

Chantal couldn't hold back the tears as he took her to a place she'd never dreamed existed. She didn't understand how it'd happened. One moment she'd been on a silver plane falling from the heavens, and the next moment she was on a shooting star, soaring back across the sky. It was the trip of a lifetime, the most incredible experience.

"Thank you." She pressed her tear-streaked face against his smoothly muscled shoulder, her body still rippling from the aftershocks of their lovemaking. "Thank you from the bottom of my heart."

Demetrius lifted his head, stared down into her wet eyes. "Don't thank me."

"I have to." She tried to hold back the emotion and yet she'd never known such overwhelming happiness. It was like she'd swallowed the sun, and it was glowing full and golden inside of her. "We're here because of you. We have what we have because you treated me like a real person...like an ordinary woman."

"You'll never be ordinary."

"But Demetrius, that's all I want, that's all I've ever wanted to be." She pressed her face to his chest, loving the feel of his damp skin against hers, the steady beating of his heart, the strong powerful arms wrapped around her. "I just never thought I'd have this...never thought I'd feel this way."

It always amazed Chantal how Demetrius made love to her. He could be so hard, so fierce during the day but at night, he was completely hers. With his arms around her she knew she'd found everything she'd ever wanted. She'd always loved being a mother, but she'd never known the pleasure of being a wife...a lover.

But he wasn't just good in bed, he was so good in his heart, and she didn't care where he came from, or what his family had been. She knew him, and she believed in him, and being loved like this, and held like this, was all she needed.

Later, as the moon slipped from one end of the sky to the other, Chantal nestled deeper into Demetrius's arms and let out a contented sigh. "It was a lucky break," she murmured, caressing the sinewy muscles of his upper arm, feeling the hard curve of his bicep, the thick cut of his tricep, "learning about Armand's first marriage. How did Malik find out? Did he just discover the truth today?"

Demetrius dropped a kiss on top of her head. "It wasn't Malik. I found out."

"When?"

"Earlier this week, before we left for La Croix."

She lay very still, her brow furrowing, trying to make sense of what he was telling her. He'd known about Armand's first marriage for days.

He'd known but he'd kept it secret.

"Why didn't you tell me?" she whispered.

"You had enough to think about, enough decisions to make without me forcing your hand."

She shook her head, turned in his arms to face him. The moonlight shadowed his profile, creating stark patterns of light and dark on his proud brow and strong nose. "You could have ended up in jail. You could have ended up..." She swallowed. "But why? I don't understand."

He reached up, tucked a tendril of hair behind one ear. "It's easy. I wanted what you wanted."

Emotion grew hot and thick inside her chest, her heart aching at the idea of Demetrius remaining in jail if she hadn't made the decision she did. "But how could you sacrifice yourself like that? You're so important, Demetrius, you matter so much."

"To you."

"Yes." She hated the prickly sting of the tears burning the back of her eyes. "To me. That's right. You matter so much to me."

"Exactly. Which is why we're here, together—"

"But it could have ended so differently!"

He clasped her face, stared at her long and hard with those

dark impenetrable eyes of his. "No. Not for us. There wasn't a chance in hell we wouldn't be together."

He was impossible. Incredible. So unbelievably arrogant. "How can you say that?"

Pulling her down to him, he let their warm bodies come together and his lips cover hers. "Because I'm Greek. And we're an old civilization full of patience and wisdom."

She laughed against his mouth. "Do be serious!"

"Okay. Because I'm Greek and I love you more than life itself. How is that?"

How could he turn her inside out like that? A shiver raced across her skin. Her heart beat double-hard. "Perfect."

EPILOGUE

Four months later...

THEY'D been out by the pool, enjoying the later summer sunshine when Chantal felt the strangest sensation.

It was like a whisper of sensation, a fluttery feeling in her middle and the hair rose on Chantal's arms. Her eyes opened wide. She lay still, and concentrated. After a moment the delicate ripple returned, a caress inside her, and abruptly Chantal sat up in her lounge chair, hands protectively cupping her tummy.

There. Again. Another little flutter...like a paper boat drifting across the water.

"Demetrius." She said his name before she could stop herself.

He looked up from the edge of the pool where he'd been teaching Lilly to swim, and his black brows pulled, immediate worry in his dark eyes. "What's wrong?"

The baby had moved. She'd felt the baby move. Her eyes watered. "Nothing." And she covered her gently swollen stomach with the palm of her hand.

It was real. The baby was real. Her family here on the Rock was real.

Demetrius set Lilly on the edge of the pool, and stared at Chantal, his dark gaze searching her flushed face. "What's happening?"

She didn't think she could explain. Everything was happening. Everything was turning out just as she'd dreamed. Home. Family. Happiness.

The white plaster house with the blue shutters. The laundry singing on a clothesline. The scent of basil and rosemary in the air.

Tomatoes and cucumbers in the garden.

A husband who meant more to Chantal than anything.

A gorgeous healthy, happy five-year-old and a new baby on the way.

How could it be? How could anything be so wonderful, so incredible? How could she finally feel so much warmth and love?

How could it have really come true for her after all the disappointments, all the pain?

How could the world be so good? Because Lilly was happy here, Lilly had taken to Demetrius and the island and the people and Demetrius smiled frequently—even though fools didn't smile—and they'd settled in together as if they'd always meant to be together.

And maybe they had meant to be together.

"Are you all right?" Demetrius climbed from the pool, and was toweling Lilly off, yet his dark gaze never wavered from her face.

"Yes. I'm fantastic." And it was true. She'd never felt so good. She'd never felt anything this lovely in all her life.

It was like a bubble of laughter caught in the middle of her. The laughter rising a little, sinking a little, a hugely buoyant smile that shimmered on the inside.

Chantal wrapped her arms around her knees, hugged herself, hugged the happiness and vowed she'd never let it go. Never. Ever. She'd waited her whole life to feel this way. She'd paid her dues and she'd sacrificed like crazy.

Now she could be happy. Really happy. Even if the rest of the world went mad, she deserved to keep this little bit of joy inside.

It belonged to her. It felt right inside of her. Her whole body was smiling, her heart grinning, little tears in her eyes.

"Come here," she said to Demetrius, and Lilly, extending an arm. "Please."

Demetrius was at her side, a towel wrapped Lilly in his arms. "What is it?"

She laughed, leaned forward, kissed him on the lips. "Your baby." Her eyes burned with a happiness she never thought she'd know, the kind of happiness she thought was reserved for other people. "Your baby just moved. I thought you'd want to know."

THREE ALONE
VIRGINIA

A surgeon Blake Morley, those old and her new baby on the way...

...incredible. How could she usually feel so much warmth, and let all her appointments slide going?

How could the world be so good? Because Lilly was happy now, Lilly had taken Jenna home, and she stood and she might not...

...

And maybe they had meant to be together.

"Are you all right?" Demetrius climbed from the pool and was dashing Lilly off, yet unheard, gaze never wavered from her face.

"Yes," the fantastic... No, it was true. She'd never felt so good. She'd never felt anything this lovely in all her life.

It was more flashes of incoherence as if the middle of her...

Charlie whispered her arms around her breast, hugged herself, hugged the happiness and vowed she'd never let it go, never lose. She'd lived her whole life in real life, she was sure she'd until her days and she'd mortified late days.

For she could be happy. Really happy. Even if the rest of the world went mad, she determined to keep this little bit of my garden. It belonged to her. It felt right inside of her. Her whole body was smiling, the hour of happiness flute flutes in her eyes.

"Come here," she said to Demetrius, and Lilly expectant, an evil... Please...

Demetrius was, she'd sure, a towel wrapped Lilly in his arms. "What is it?"

She hugged Hamid. He word, kissed him on the lips. "You lady." She just burned with a smile, side never thought she'd know, and a kind of happiness she thought was reserved for other people. "Your baby just named Demetrius you'd want to know."

THE ITALIAN'S
VIRGIN PRINCESS

by

Jane Porter

For Elizabeth Boyle, great author and friend.
Thanks for your faith in me.
Jane.

PROLOGUE

The Ducasse Palace, Porto, Melio

PRINCESS JOELLE DUCASSE studied the sealed letter she'd left on her grandfather's desk. Identical copies of the letter were being couriered to her sisters, Nicolette in Baraka, and Chantal in Greece.

The heavy cream envelope with the gold Palace seal suddenly looked ominous on Grandpapa's desk.

He'd be so hurt, she thought, feeling tears well up. *He wouldn't understand.*

But then, she didn't even understand why she felt so desperate to get away, to escape Melio and the glare of publicity and the camera lenses. She'd never found it comfortable living in the public eye but since Grandmama's death it'd gotten worse. So much worse.

The media wouldn't—couldn't—let her grieve privately. They were there documenting every outing, every appearance, capturing Joelle's weekly visit to her grandmother's grave on film, capturing the sheen of tears in her eyes as she left the royal cemetery, capturing her shell-shocked expression as she climbed into the waiting car.

There was no privacy, no respect, and no time to hide her hurt. Or her confusion.

Grandmama's death had triggered all sorts of pain, pain that must have been buried deep inside of her since her parents' death eighteen years ago. And those tabloid photos, those sensationalized articles, Queen Astrid's Death Rocks The Youngest Princess, only made the confusion worse.

Truthfully, she didn't know what to feel. She didn't even feel. Sometime in the last six months, in the months between Grandmama's funeral and now, she'd lost all feeling, all hope, all courage.

How could she live a public life…a life of public service…if she didn't even know who she was? If she didn't even know *what* she was?

Joelle reached for the envelope on Grandpapa's desk, and her fingers brushed his antique leather blotter, a blotter that had been in the family for over a hundred years, the leather soft and worn, the felt pad replaced numerous times and tears filled her eyes.

She felt so conflicted. So much in knots.

Joelle loved the old leather blotter, loved Grandpapa's handsome paneled study, loved everything about the old limestone palace and she knew intellectually why she needed to marry and remain here—Nic had married the sultan and couldn't return to Melio, and Chantal had married a commoner and the Greek couldn't become king—but she couldn't imagine assuming more duty, more responsibility without recovering her composure first.

She needed a break. Space. Desperately needed privacy. The palace felt so empty without Grandmama, and while she adored Grandpapa, it was Grandmama who'd always counseled her, Grandmama she'd talked to. And now without Grandmama here, she couldn't bear it. Couldn't bear the emptiness, the loneliness, the uncertainty of her future, and yet Joelle knew it was time she started to come to grips with the loss. Even if it meant dealing with the grief her way, without everybody watching, without everybody talking.

Joelle left the letter where it was.

I'm sorry, Grandpapa. Forgive me.

You're only going for a year, she told herself, turning away from the desk and heading for the door. It's not forever. You'll be back in twelve months, you'll marry Prince Luigi Borgarde and life will continue as it should.

But six hours later as she settled into a coach seat on a small European carrier, sunglasses on, a hat pulled down low on her head, she was still trying to shake the guilt and focus on the positives.

She'd have twelve months to find peace, twelve months to come to grips with Grandmama's death, twelve months to grieve without being the focus of cameras and paparazzi.

And yet as the hours passed and Joelle struggled to get com-

fortable in her narrow coach seat, she wished for just one moment that she'd traveled the old way, traveled as a princess usually did—whisked in and out of security, private customs,
private lounges, hidden behind the broad shoulders of bodyguards and airport security. Private protectors. Public defenders.
Plainclothes police and government sharpshooters ever vigilant
on behalf the royal family's safety. Security.

But that was the problem, Joelle thought, tugging her thin
fuzzy blanket higher around her shoulders. There was no way
to be Princess Joelle without the cameras, without the security,
without the palace protocol. And as long as she remained
Princess Joelle Ducasse, everyone would have too much information, would assume they knew everything about her.

But people didn't really know her. They only knew what the
media wrote. They only knew what the palace PR people told
them.

They didn't know her real dreams. Or the depth of her emotion. They didn't know how much she longed for choice. For
independence. For freedom.

Her older sister, Chantal, said personal choice was overrated,
not an essential, and certainly not a guarantee when one's last
name was Ducasse and your lineage dated back to the late thir-
teenth century.

But Joelle didn't want to be a Ducasse. She'd had enough of
the Ducasse lifestyle. All she wanted was to be a regular person.
Private. Independent. Self-sufficient.

For one year she was going to be a regular Jo.

CHAPTER ONE

New Orleans, Eleven months later

"A DRINK, Miss d'Ville?"

The question, asked by a distinctly male voice, a very deep, very quiet voice, sent a ripple of unease through Joelle. Voices like that only came from years of power.

Positions of authority, the kind of authority she'd left behind in Europe. Joelle turned reluctantly, more than reluctantly, knowing by his voice that it was him.

Him.

The one who'd sat in the front row tonight, just left of stage center.

The one who'd distracted her all night with his intense gaze, a gaze that never seemed to leave her.

Twice she'd lost her place in the middle of a song. Twice she'd stood there on stage in the purple and blue gel lights utterly blank—losing all thought, all memory, all words. She'd never forgotten lyrics like that. She'd never stared out at a dark sea of audience and wondered what she was doing with a microphone before.

But it hadn't been an entirely dark sea. She'd seen one face, one man the entire time, and his intense focus had trapped her, called her, just as he did now.

Up close, barely a foot away, he made her feel bare, exposed. She'd never minded dressing sexy on stage but somehow with his dark gaze scrutinizing her, a slow inspection from head to toe, she knew he disapproved.

His censure was nearly as heavy as her guitar case hanging from her shoulder.

"A drink?" she repeated, trying to force her brain to function despite the rather mad thought that if she ever belonged to a man, it wouldn't be to someone like this, someone so over-whelmingly male, so fiercely controlled.

She wanted ease. Charm. She wanted comfortable.

He wasn't comfortable.

"As in a beverage," he answered almost gently, smiling a little and yet the smile remained at his lips, failed to warm his eyes. Instead his dark eyes burned, his dark eyes owned her, possessed her, a hard sexual possession that had nothing to do with civilized behavior and everything to do with bodies. Skin. *Her* skin.

She felt a cool silvery shiver shoot down her spine, and her body reacted—hair at her nape lifting, goose bumps prickling her arms, even her breasts firmed, nipples peaking.

Joelle pressed her guitar case closer to her hip, making it the latest in body armor. "I understand the concept. We have bev-erages in America, too," she said, letting him know she under-stood he was foreign, and yet he couldn't intimidate her.

But she was wary. Not because he posed a physical threat, but because he was different, and she'd always been fascinated by that which was unusual. Intriguing. And he was certainly intriguing.

Tall, darkly handsome and probably very Italian. His accent sounded Italian.

"Then you'll join me," he said, indicating his table.

His stunning confidence dazzled her. "I…I've…plans." Laundry. And packing. She needed to get ready to return home.

"Change them."

There was something…raw…about him, something male and stunningly primitive which didn't go with his superbly tailored suit, the sleek lapel just so, jacket molded, shaping the shoulders and chest, the trousers hanging perfectly, the cuffs hitting the top of his shoe. She'd dated a number of men in the past year and none had been like him. "I can't."

His brow furrowed, his expression hardening. "You must," he said, his tone deceptively soft. "It's important."

Important how? Important to whom?

"Did someone send you?" she asked, looking up into his dark eyes, and once she did, she couldn't look away. He virtually commanded attention, and as she stared at him, she felt the oddest prickle beneath her skin again. More awareness. More unease.

"No."

Her insides tightened. The prickle spread, tingling from her nape to the small of her spine. She didn't know him, did she?

Joelle shook her head, trying to break the strange weave of tension because something *was* happening here and she didn't like it. Her body felt funny. Her chest constricted. She couldn't seem to breathe right. And yet she still couldn't look away.

He knew it, too. His straight black brows were flat, his eyes intently watching hers.

"I'm tired. I've been on stage for over two hours—"

"I know. I was here." He hesitated, as if questioning the wisdom in what he'd say next. "You're very good."

Heat surged through her, a dizzying heat that flooded her limbs, scalded her skin. Somehow it was indecent, this man, his effect on her. "Thank you."

"My table's just here," he said, indicating a table not far from the foot of the stage. "Join me."

"I—" She protested but he was walking away, taking a seat at a small scuffed table bare except for a flickering votive candle.

He flagged down the cocktail waitress and ordered a bottle of champagne, very expensive champagne, before looking up and catching her eye.

He smiled, the smile of one who is used to winning.

Bulldozer, she thought, biting down hard. You can't just come here and take over.

Pulse quickening, she headed toward his table, her leather boots echoing on the hardwood floor. "I'm not joining you," she said, reaching his table.

"Yet you're here."

She hated the sardonic lift of his eyebrow. "I don't want you to waste your money."

"It's just money."

She thought of her kingdom, thought of how close it'd come to financial ruin. Thought of her sisters, how they'd both made marriages of convenience to save Melio. Thought of her past year, and how she'd struggled to get by, how she'd taken two jobs just to pay for the essentials. "It's still wasteful."

"Then you better not let it go undrunk."

Her heart thudded hard, so hard she could feel it pound all the way through her just like the bass guitarist notes had earlier. "What do you want?"

The flickering candlelight played off his face, catching the subtle curve of his lips. There was nothing remotely boyish in his chiseled features. He had a man's face, strong, developed features and she felt something stir inside her, her body betraying her.

Her body liked the way he looked at her.

Her body wanted him to continue looking at her.

He studied her now for a long, level moment, considering her, considering his answer. "I think the question should be, Josie d'Ville, what do you want?"

His answer simply accelerated her racing pulse. Fear, fascination, worry, adrenaline surged through her and her muscles tensed. "This isn't about me."

"But of course it's about you." He gestured to the chair opposite him. "I've come a long way to see you." His inflection firmed. "So sit. *Please*."

What did he mean by that?

Who was he? What exactly did he do?

The dreamer in her hoped he was in the music industry. The dreamer prayed he was someone connected. An agent, maybe. Or even better, a record producer.

Or maybe he was a palace spy. One of those nameless, faceless men who shadowed her this past year, because she was sure her two new brothers-in-law wouldn't allow her to leave home unprotected.

The possibilities filled her, overwhelmed her, and Joelle sat slowly, settling her guitar case at her feet. As she pushed her long hair back from her damp brow she reflected on her performance. Usually she settled into her first set, but tonight nothing had felt right. The energy coming from the audience had felt odd. She'd felt prickly...edgy...not at all her self. More than once she'd had to dig inside herself, finding inner reserves, finding calm to collect her restless thoughts.

She'd tried to tell herself the nerves were due to stress, the fact that she was soon to return home, to return to her duties and the upcoming nuptials to the man she'd never met, let alone seen a photograph of, but duty and marriage had never interfered with a performance before. She'd always loved to sing. Loved being in the moody purple and blue lights, loved the rapt audience, loved the deep bass notes humming through her.

No, it wasn't her imminent return to Melio, which put her teeth on edge. And it wasn't even her impending wedding to a prince she didn't even know. It was this man. He'd skewered her earlier with his eyes, making her feel very naked, and very vulnerable and he was doing it still.

"Why the States?" he asked, breaking the taut silence.

Another current of unease shot through her. *The States,* he'd said, not New Orleans, but the *States.* "What do you mean?"

He leaned back in his chair, arms folded across his chest but he wasn't relaxed. She sensed he was battling to control his temper. "Why do this, here? Why not Nashville? New York? Los Angeles?"

She relaxed a little. Don't be paranoid, she told herself. He's not a palace spy. He doesn't know who you are. "New Orleans is famous for its blues and jazz."

"You've no desire to play in Europe?"

Joelle's nerves danced to life again. Europe. Her world. Home of her kingdom, the two jewel-like islands sparkling in the Mediterranean Sea. "New Orleans is…home."

"You were born here then?"

"My mother was." Or close to here, she silently added, sticking with the persona she'd adopted when she'd first arrived. Eleven months ago she'd gone incognito, darkening her light brown hair, adopting a Southern accent, even wearing funky glasses when she wasn't on stage. Princess Joelle was definitely gone. Josie d'Ville had taken her place.

"Is your mother a d'Ville, too?"

Why all the questions, Joelle wondered? Where was he going with this? "Was," she corrected after a moment. "Before she married." *Before she died.*

Unlike her older sisters, Joelle didn't remember her mother or father. Her parents were just vague memories now, out of her life far longer than they'd ever been in it. Of course she'd wondered about them, endlessly, but it was her mother in particular that mystified Joelle.

Her mother, Star, had been a huge talent. A legendary pop singer. And she'd given it all up to marry a foreign prince.

How ironic that Joelle, a princess, would have given up everything—title, country, prince—to have a chance at being Star.

"So Josie d'Ville is your real name?"

Knots formed in her belly. "More or less."

He laughed softly, mockingly, and the sound pulled her in.

He was magnetic. Compelling. And the intensity in his eyes made her skin sting, her mouth dry. He did this, she thought, fighting panic. But how? Why? And what was he thinking when he looked at her like that? When he stared so long and hard, his expression faintly arrogant, not to mention vaguely amused. Curious. It was almost as if he knew her. Claimed her.

Ridiculous.

He didn't know her. And he couldn't know who she really was. She'd been in New Orleans for over eleven months and no one had even come close to guessing her true identity. And yet there was something in his eyes, something purposeful, masterful, that made her feel small and still. A deer caught in headlights.

The knots inside her grew, the tension filling her until she felt absolutely exhausted from the weight of it.

"More or less," he repeated. "Which really means you're lying—"

"Not lying."

"But not being honest."

She'd never been confronted by anyone with his authority. Power. He exuded power. Overwhelming power. "I'm in the public eye. It's vital I protect my privacy."

"Too little," he said, "too late."

The hair on her nape rose. What was he saying? What did he know?

"You remind me of someone," he blithely continued, "someone in Europe—"

"I have that kind of face. People always think I look like someone they know." Her smile couldn't have been more forced.

"But *you're* not American, are you?"

"My mother—"

"Was American, yes, you've said that." He watched her. Waiting. He knew she was on edge, knew she felt cornered. "How does that explain your French accent then?"

"I don't have a—"

"You do. Beneath the Southern accent there's a very French inflection. It's not always pronounced. I only hear it when you speak quickly. When you're upset."

And he was doing a damn good job of upsetting her, too.

Anxiety rippled through Joelle in waves. "You've a good ear," she answered lightly, even as the panic grew. He didn't know who she was. He couldn't know. He mustn't know. Only a day left, she reminded herself, one day and she'd be on the plane home…

Joelle took a breath, steadied her nerves. There's nothing to fear, she told herself. She knew the bodyguards were out there somewhere, knew she wasn't really alone. "You're right. I did grow up speaking French. My mother's family is from Louisiana. Cajun."

"Cajun?"

"The d'Villes still live just outside Baton Rouge."

"But you weren't raised on the Bayou?"

His words conjured up the wandering Mississippi, the river wide, muddy, the bends ever curving, changing. The great plantations lining the banks, the scattered bayou towns, mostly poor.

It was then Joelle relaxed, the fear easing, turning to something deeper, and far more powerful. He had no idea who she was, what she was. He—like the rest of the world—would never know what she needed, or what she was giving up when she returned home to marry her prince Luigi.

Resentment surged through her. "You're right again." She looked at him hard, fiercely, feeling so much suddenly, feeling the intense pressure and scrutiny she'd been under her entire life. How could he ever know what it'd been like to be little Joelle Ducasse, the orphaned princess? How could he know what it was like to want the world and know you'd only ever get a little island country?

"No, I wasn't raised on the Bayou. But being Cajun isn't about living on the river. It's about having the river in your blood, the river beneath your skin."

"And you have that?"

Her eyes met his, held. "I have so much more than you know." And she wasn't talking about things—possessions—but imagination, hope, and dreams. She'd always had such big dreams.

Silence followed, a long gritty silence that felt like fingernails scraping down a chalkboard and Joelle wished she'd said nothing. Kept her fury and fire to herself. It was none of his business. No one's business. She didn't even know what she was still doing here.

Abruptly she leaned forward, long hair tumbling past her shoulders. "Who are you anyway?"

"Leonardo Marciano Fortino."

She stared at him a long moment, silently repeating the name. He'd spoken his name slowly, carefully, as if imprinting it on her brain, but it meant nothing to her. "Leonardo Marciano Fortino," she repeated. "Quite a mouthful, isn't it?"

Prince Leo Marciano Fortino, of the house of Borgarde, sat back in his chair. She didn't know.

It was worse than he thought, worse than he'd expected…and he'd been prepared for the worst. Not only did his fiancée *not* recognize him, she didn't even know his name.

"Where are you from, Signor Fortino?" Joelle asked, stirring in her seat, fingers flexing ever so slightly.

"Leo," he corrected, biting back a sigh. It was obvious she wasn't ready to settle down, nor was she prepared for the rigors of married life. She was still so young, too young, and he should have listened to his instincts. Her age had troubled him from the start but the palace officials had insisted she was mature for her age. All she needs is a year, they'd said, just give her a year… "Family and friends always call me Leo," he added. "You should, too."

"Yes, but I—"

"Shall call me Leo," he interrupted. "And I've never actually lived in Italy."

"No?"

He saw a flicker of curiosity in her blue-green eyes, and the blue green reminded him of the dazzling Mediterranean waters surrounding her island kingdom. Her eyes hinted at innocence, inexperience, and yet the rest of her exuded sex.

Who was the real Joelle Ducasse?

"Josie." A man approached the table, stopped in front of Joelle. Leo was immediately on guard but Joelle looked completely at ease, and it blew his mind that Joelle lacked proper reserve, lacked any sense of self-preservation.

"You're amazing," the stranger said, standing in front of her, shoving his hands into his pockets. "You're unreal."

"Thank you." Joelle smiled up at the stranger. "That's very kind of you."

"Not kind, honest. I've been here every night you've sung this week, and I've never heard…seen…anyone like you."

Leo felt his gut burn as Joelle's smile dimpled. "What's your name?" she asked.

"Jack."

Leo Borgade remembered the rapt faces in the audience; saw that same combination of lust and longing in Jack's face. Joelle was a bluesy singer, part gospel, part R&B, a little jazz in there, a throaty edge that spoke of big dreams, lots of woes, and the promise of something better coming tomorrow.

Slender, and yet sultry, with long dark hair, lashes so thick and black they made her look both hungry and sleepy at the same time all made her part of the hot steamy New Orleans night. Sexy. Seductive. Mysterious.

No wonder the Jacks of the world wanted her bad.

Leo's lips curved but he wasn't smiling. He was livid. Beyond livid. There was going to be hell to pay.

"Thanks, Jack," Leo said, standing, strategically placing himself between Jack and Joelle. It was a physical gesture. Nothing short of territorial. "It's always nice to hear good things about our Josie. Goodbye. Have a nice night."

Jack nodded dejectedly, and with a wistful look back at Josie, he walked away.

"Our Josie?" Joelle choked.

Leo sat down, shot her a side-glance, and saw she was sputtering mad. Good. Let her wise up. Time she opened her eyes, recognized she was in trouble.

"How could you do that?" she demanded, seething, practically jumping out of her chair, the dim lights overhead casting a sheen on her black leather pants.

"He was drunk."

"He was *nice*."

Leo glanced over his shoulder, caught sight of Jack stumbling out of the bar. "You don't know the meaning of nice, *bambina*."

"It's Josie, not *bambina*, Signor Fortino, and I find your attitude patronizing as well as chauvinistic."

Her Italian accent was flawless. Her temper hot. But she didn't have the right to be angry. She hadn't been deceived. She hadn't been played.

He'd never forget his shock when she strutted onto the stage tonight in her tiny beaded top, low-waisted leather pants, and outrageous stiletto heeled boots. She'd been introduced as Josie—Josie like the name of the kids cartoon Josie and the Pussycats—but this Josie, *his* Joelle, didn't look anything like a kid's cartoon program.

Her face was pale, oval, and luminous in the dark blue gel spotlight. The band members surrounding her were shadowy figures, and in her black beaded cropped top, her tight, black, leather pants and her impossibly high black boots, Josie disappeared in and out of the shadows, with just her pale face and the slim pale patch of midriff reflecting light.

Narrow hips grinding in tight black leather, her breasts pushed up in the tiny top, Princess Joelle Ducasse held the microphone close to her mouth like a long lost lover. And all he could think was, *this is not my fiancée.*

This can't be my fiancée.

Even now it blew his mind. His twenty-two-year-old fiancée was a nightclub singer. She'd spent the last year performing off Bourbon Street in this sleazy little place called Club Bleu.

"I don't want to see you hurt," he said roughly, trying to forget her opening act, trying to forget the way she'd strutted onto the stage.

It wasn't a striptease act but it'd come damn close.

"Why do you even care?" she shot back. "You know nothing about me."

"True."

"And Jack was just being friendly."

"Wild dogs can be friendly."

Her cheeks flamed with color but she eyed him steadily. "You know, you're the one who isn't nice. You're pushy. Domineering. Arrogant—"

"Because I'm honest?" Her directness surprised him. She was far from the sweet, retiring princess he'd been promised.

"Because you're rude. Jack was just paying me a compliment—"

"And you need these compliments?" he asked incredulously, seeing too clearly how at the end of the first set, Joelle had slid to her knees only to slither to the edge of the stage. He'd felt the collective groan of the male dominated audience as she fixed her intense blue-green eyes on the audience, her long dark hair spilling over bare shoulders, her skin gleaming with perspiration.

Every man had wanted her. Every man ached for her.

And he'd understood. She looked sexual. Primal.

"What I need is none of your concern," she snapped, voice husky, breaking.

Wrong, he answered silently, unable to look away from the fire in her blue-green eyes, like late afternoon sun glinting off the Mediterranean. *You are mine, and what you need concerns me in every way possible.*

Tonight, despite his shock, despite his anger at being deceived by King Remi and the Melio palace handlers, he wanted her in the purest, rawest sense of the word. Wanted her to take. To possess. To own. Because she was his.

Physical desire hadn't been part of the equation when he agreed to marry the youngest Ducasse. It'd been business. He was a titled prince without a kingdom, and she was a princess with a kingdom in need of heirs. Together they'd be fruitful and multiply. He'd have his kingdom and children, Melio would have their king and next generation, Joelle would fulfill her destiny.

Or would she?

The cocktail waitress arrived with the champagne bottle and two freshly washed flutes.

Joelle didn't even look at the waitress, her head turned, her gaze averted. He realized she was fighting hard to control her temper.

The waitress popped the cork but still Joelle refused to make eye contact.

He had no patience for theatrics. He was the one that should be angry, not her. Six weeks ago he'd heard the rumors about the Princess Ducasse look-alike in New Orleans. He'd heard rumors that the singer had a voice that could break hearts and a face to match.

More curious than concerned, he'd contacted the Melio palace, and they'd said they'd heard the rumors, too. But it couldn't be true, they told him. Joelle, he was assured, was safe in Europe, immersed in her studies at an exclusive music conservatory, eagerly planning her wedding.

Eagerly planning her wedding.

Indeed. She was the epitome of the blushing bride.

"I was protecting you," he said at last, exasperated by her stubborn silence.

"I don't need your protection," she answered tartly as the waitress filled their flutes, the pale gold champagne bubbling out fast, sending white foam spilling over the delicate glass rims.

He waited for the waitress to leave. "You're naïve."

"You're Italian."

"And that's a problem?"

"Yes."

He sat silent a moment studying her. "Why?"

He looked at her so hard Joelle shivered on the inside. There was something intense in his gaze, something that reached into her and held her still.

She didn't dislike him. She was just terrified of him. Of her response to him. He made her feel painfully self-conscious, far too aware of herself. Far too aware of him.

"And what are your issues with Italian men, *bambina?*"

CHAPTER TWO

HER issues…

Joelle swallowed, shifted. *What were those issues?* Suddenly she couldn't think of anything but how she felt. Because she felt wild, as if there was only chaos on the inside and her skin could barely hold it all in.

She was humming right now, her body literally zinging with nervous energy. It crossed her mind that everything she was afraid of, everything she feared, was everything she'd wanted to know.

Like sex. She wanted to know all about sex. She wanted to live it, feel it, understand it. She wanted to be part of the world before she was locked away in Melio's ivory tower.

"I'm waiting," he said.

But not patiently, she thought, all fire on the inside, an incredible roar of flame and heat. He was doing this to her. He was making her feel hot, irritable, explosive.

He was making her think of all the things she didn't know. Ignition, conflagration, combustion. She felt a tremor course through her. "Italian men are…difficult."

"How so?"

His voice wrapped around her skin, warm, discomfiting. "They're demanding."

"As they should be."

This was madness, she thought, alarm sounding in the back of her brain. You should be home finishing your packing. You should get up and go now. You should be anywhere but sitting here, with him.

But she couldn't move, couldn't look away. Leo Fortino was different from the men she knew, different from anyone she'd ever met. He was thrilling in a heart-stopping kind of way. Thrilling like dancing on the mouth of a volcano. "Possessive."

"A virtue."

20

"Proud."

Leo lifted a flute, held it out to her, the gold liquid shimmering in the votive's flickering light. "Without a doubt."

She hesitated before taking the glass. And once she took the flute, he flashed her a shadow of a smile, looking every bit the predator. Then he lifted his own flute in a toast. "And you're wise to remember that, *bambina*."

Bambina. Baby. Child. But she wasn't a child. And that's exactly what no one in Europe, in Melio, seemed to realize. She might only be twenty-two, but on the inside she was old.

On the inside she was wise. She'd known all along there'd be just this year—one brief year—to pull herself together, to come to grips with Grandmama's death, her Grandpapa's expectations. The past eleven months and odd weeks had been good for her, too. She was stronger. More determined. She'd do what needed to be done. Once she returned. But she hadn't returned yet.

She had one more day of freedom left. One more night of being Josie, not Joelle, of being a woman, not a princess.

"Cheers," he said, lightly clinking his glass against hers.

Glancing across at dark, sexy Leo Fortino, Joelle couldn't help wondering if she still had time to find that romance to last a lifetime, a romance that would carry her through years of cordial marital relations, but relations lacking fire and ice.

And she wanted fire. She wanted sex. Passion.

"Cheers," she whispered, lifting the flute to her lips, knowing Grandmama would be turning over in her grave.

Grandmama had always been so determined to see her granddaughters instilled with the good morals, values and integrity she said the modern young nobles lacked today.

Grandmama said that the new generation didn't understand that to lead, one must sacrifice, and that being able to serve one's country was the greatest of all honors.

I'm sorry, Grandmama, Joelle thought, tipping the flute, *but I need tonight. I need something so hot, so intense I'll remember it forever. I need something that's mine, all mine, something that can't ever be taken from me.*

The champagne tasted cold and fizzed across her tongue and yet when she swallowed it was hot going down.

She could hear Grandmama *cluck-clucking* in the back of her head, preparing to warn her yet again about the dangers of being curious, the dangers of wanting to know everything. *Only foolish women play with fire,* Grandmama used to say, *and don't forget what curiosity did to that poor little cat...*

Carefully she set the glass down, and as she returned the flute to the table, Leo reached out to take her left hand in his.

She shivered at the touch. His gaze lifted, he looked up into her eyes and then back down at her hand. For a long moment he simply inspected her bare fingers.

"No ring?" he asked at last, holding her hand firmly, her palm brushing his, his fingers wrapped around hers.

Heat exploded inside her at the prolonged contact. "I'm not married."

Again he looked up into her eyes. "Surely you're spoken for?"

Joelle hated the sharp nibble of guilt, the bite on her conscience. She knew she'd never be able to sit here, do this, if she could picture Prince Luigi's face, know him as a real person. As it was, Luigi seemed fictional, like a figment of her imagination. Mysterious wealthy prince agrees to marry poor princess...

But why hadn't her prince ever tried to meet her? Why had he cared so little about her? He'd been to Melio. He'd inspected his future kingdom, checked out his future holdings, looked at the ports, the palace, the smaller island of Mejia, but he'd never bothered to even introduce himself to her.

He'd never bothered with her at all.

Hurt, ashamed, Joelle burned hot, then cold. "I'm not much for jewelry."

Leo made a rough sound in the back of his throat, his fingers closing more firmly around hers. "You're not dating, are you?"

Her sense of self-preservation told her to be careful, very careful. She saw the intensity in his expression, the flame in his eyes. He was angry. But why? Joelle swallowed, struggled to speak around the lump filling her throat. "I do go out, yes."

He released her hand and she quickly made a fist, trying to forget how his touch had jolted through her, sharp and hot like the lick of a flame. How could such an impersonal touch, the simple clasping of fingers, make her feel this, or so raw and exposed?

How could the touch of his hand make her want more heat, more sensation, more skin?

Maybe…maybe he could be…

She lifted her head, looked into his face. Their gazes locked and she saw something in his eyes that filled her with fresh heat.

He wanted her.

He claimed her.

But that was crazy. Absurd. She shifted yet again, her tongue sticking to the roof of her mouth. Maybe he was the one. The one who'd take her virginity, give her experience, allowing her to go to her wedding as a woman of the world rather than a sheltered, incompetent, *ignorant* bride.

She'd been waiting for the right man, wanting a sophisticated, intelligent partner, one that would make a satisfying lover. But she'd been picky, too picky, and she was out of time. With the wedding three weeks away, and Grandfather's birthday seven days from today, she needed to act fast. Or accept the fact that she'd marry her Prince Borgarde without knowing what she needed to know. Sex, quite frankly, puzzled her. The mechanics were clear, but the intimacy—the naked body on naked body—unnerved her.

She struggled to find words, to put together a coherent sentence, one that she could actually speak out loud, but her mouth was so dry, her throat felt scratchy and she lifted the flute, took a sip of the tart sweet champagne.

''So what am I doing here?'' she asked faintly, clutching the stem of the flute. ''What am I doing sitting with you?''

His eyes never left her mouth. ''Answering your curiosity, I imagine.''

He had the most piercing gaze, a gaze that made her feel young and inexperienced, a gaze that made her want to find a big comfy sweatshirt and pull it over her head, hiding her hips and breasts…

For a moment she forgot what they were discussing, or where they were. For a moment she couldn't think, too swamped by the sudden heat in her veins and the slow, heavy pounding of her heart.

For a moment there was no one else. No one in the club. No one at the exit. No one at the bar.

And looking at him, she was lost. There was just him, Leo Marciano Fortino, a man with dark eyes that held her fast, that let her know what he wanted, and he wanted her, body and soul.

Then slowly it came back to her, what he'd said, what they'd been discussing. Her curiosity.

He was right. She was curious. She'd always had a problem being so curious, wanting to know so much, wanting to know virtually everything.

When she was growing up Grandmother Astrid was always scolding her about going too far, asking for too much. *Never forget, cherie*, Grandmama would lecture, *curiosity killed the cat. Don't let it kill you.*

But the way things were going curiosity might very well be the end of her. Right now she felt like a dumb moth fascinated by flame. "I do have an insatiable curiosity."

His mouth quirked, a curving that revealed the full sensuality of his lower lip. "And you're curious about me?"

She nodded. She couldn't speak.

His gaze shifted from her face to her tightly closed fist. "Can I offer you one bit of advice, *bambina?*"

Again she nodded.

"You need to be more careful," he said.

Icy heat shivered up and down Joelle's spine. This is dangerous, a little voice whispered inside her. It's one thing to want experience, it's another to get involved. "But I am careful."

She could tell he wasn't convinced.

"There are a lot of men who'd take advantage of your curious nature," he added.

Immediately blood surged through her, flooding her face, melting the bones of her hips and knees. Embarrassed, she looked away, breaking his intense hold.

Leo knocked her off balance, and her brain was no longer in

gear, her body too alive. She was finding it harder and harder to think clearly.

She'd known for years that life was dog-eat-dog. Fierce. Hard. Possibly ugly. Life was Darwinian theory at its best. Survival of the fittest. Only the strong survive.

And that's how she'd tried to live. But she didn't feel strong now. She felt confused. Emotional.

She should have never agreed to an arranged marriage but it was too late to cancel, too late to disappoint Grandfather, the people of Melio, her fiancé and his family. They were counting on a lavish wedding. A properly enthusiastic bride. Somewhere, somehow, she'd have to find the eager expectancy.

Or at the very least, serenity.

Unfortunately the closer it came to the wedding, the less serene she felt. It was bad enough marrying a man she didn't know, a man who didn't care to know her, a man she wouldn't even recognize on the street, but to marry such a man without knowing anything about *sex?*

And that was the real issue. She didn't want to walk down the aisle a virgin. Prince Borgade needed a wife. She didn't have to be inexperienced. The prince was getting her country. He didn't need her virginity.

All her life she'd wanted to be like her sister, Nicolette. Bold. Confident. Brazen. Instead she was more like Chantal. Proud. Shy. Rather reserved.

But shyness didn't excuse ignorance, and she absolutely refused to go to bed with a man—even her husband—without knowing anything. She couldn't bear to think that in three weeks she'd strip off her wedding gown and climb into bed with a husband she'd only just met and lie there naked and wait for God knows what.

The God knows what part really got to her.

There was no way she wanted to feel foolish on her wedding night. There was no way she wanted to be intimidated. Far better to know what to expect. To understand the sequence of events…the sensation…the emotion.

And again the thought hit her— Leo could teach her. She was a fast learner. She really only needed just one night.

Abruptly she reached for her flute, downed the rest of her champagne. The heat and bubbles made her eyes burn. Her stomach lurched a little at the hit of alcohol. ''I should eat something.'' She frowned at her empty glass. ''The bubbles are going straight to my head.''

''You haven't had dinner?''

''I usually don't eat until after the show wraps. Can't eat before. Too much adrenaline.''

There was the briefest hesitation before Leo reached into his wallet, drew out a couple hundred-dollar bills and left them on the table. ''If we leave now we could still make it to Brennan's before they close.''

Brennan's—the famous Brennan's where food was fabulous and the French Quarter atmosphere perfect—was just around the corner and had practically become an institution. ''You're inviting me to dinner?''

His dark eyes met hers. ''You wanted me to.''

True. No point in arguing that.

Joelle swallowed, her throat scratchy dry, rough from the champagne, the smoky club and too much singing. But her scratchy throat was nothing compared to the frantic tempo of her pulse. ''Let me just change.''

Behind the bar, in the small bathroom with the bare lightbulb, Joelle took a paper towel and blotted her face, before taking a Q-tip and makeup remover to lighten some of the stark black eyeliner from around her eyes.

You're sure you want to do this? she asked her reflection, her stomach a ball of nerves. But Joelle already knew the answer to that. Yes. She wanted to do this. Badly.

Leo rose as Joelle emerged from the back of the club. She'd taken some of the heavier eye makeup off and changed into jeans and a long gauzy cream blouse with a lace edged neckline. In her jeans and peasant style blouse she looked even younger than before. And just like that his gut tightened, his body jerking to life, his groin hard, his temper nearly as hot.

Nothing, he thought with a flash of painful insight, would ever be the same for either of them again.

Joelle felt Leo watching her as she approached the table, and slowly, reluctantly she met his speculative gaze.

As his eyes met hers, she felt a funny rush in her middle, the same crazy adrenaline she experienced when on stage, like one of those nights when she wore a micromini skirt paired with thigh high boots.

She felt Leo's narrowed gaze slowly inspect her and she saw herself through his eyes, saw her long loose hair, saw the simple blouse, the tight faded jeans, the open-toed sandals.

''Do you know what you're doing, Josie?'' he said at last.

The air bottled in her lungs and she felt her legs wobble. Then she deliberately exhaled and forced a smile. ''I certainly hope so.''

They left the club, stepping out into the warm humid night of early June and Joelle drew a deep breath, immediately relaxing.

She loved New Orleans, had loved her year in the States. But most of all, she'd loved being real.

Joelle didn't remember when she'd begun to chafe at the royal life, but sometime in the last several years—as both sisters left—she'd grown to hate her life…the structure and routine.

She hated the gowns and gloves, the endless smiling for visiting dignitaries. Hated the formalities, the stiff royal receptions, the lengthy public functions. Chantal was good at shaking hands and kissing babies. Nicolette—smart, witty—was the speechmaker supreme. But Joelle had always found the public attention, the constant demands difficult, but after Grandmama died the burden had become intolerable.

She missed Grandmama so much she couldn't bear to get out of bed, couldn't bear to face people, couldn't bear to smile her tight professional princess smile.

How could she smile when she'd lost the one person who loved her no matter what? How could she smile when she'd lost the person who held her and comforted her all those years after Mother and Father died?

Grandmama was the only one who knew how much Joelle struggled with the pressures of royal life. Grandmama was the only one who knew that Joelle still grieved for her missing parents. Grandmama was the only one who knew that deep down Joelle still hoped, strange and impossible as it was, to someday bump into her mother and her father, to find them strolling down the street, to be reunited with the past she so desperately missed.

The emotion rose up, huge, hot, overpowering.

Grandmama knew Joelle's need to love, and be loved, and she never ridiculed her, never made her feel less, never made her feel anything but good. And generous. And kind.

And now Grandmama was gone and Joelle had to grow up and tomorrow she'd be on the plane home, back to Melio. Back to duty. Back to responsibility.

And she'd do it. She'd do it because Nicolette had shouldered the duties just as Chantal had, and Joelle was determined to do her part now, too. For Grandmama and Grandpapa, if nothing else.

Joelle drew a breath, listened to their footsteps echoing off the pavement as they walked in silence. Brennan's was just ahead, a block away and the quarter-moon gave off dim light.

Tomorrow night she'd be home. A week from now would be Grandpapa's eighty-fifth birthday party. And then in three weeks the wedding. Three weeks and she'd be Her Royal Highness, Princess Ducasse Borgarde.

"That's the second heavy sigh," Leo said, before abruptly shoving his arm out in front of her, stopping her at the curb. A taxi whizzed by, virtually flying through the intersection, bumping over the corner's cobblestones.

Joelle shuddered inwardly as Leo's arm pressed against her chest, the sleeve of his elegant suit rubbing at the thin cotton of her blouse.

"I was thinking," she said, pushing away from the arm, discomfited by the gesture. He'd put his arm out as if she were a impulsive child, just as he'd called her *bambina* earlier.

His arm dropped. He gazed down at her, brows furrowed. "You're reckless."

"I'm not. I know what I'm doing. I walk home every night, and I know this city—"

"You walk home every night?"

"After I finish at Club Bleu."

"Where do you live?"

"Six, seven blocks from here."

"And you walk? Alone?"

Disapproval sharpened his tone, a disapproval so reminiscent of the censure she'd found in Melio when she balked at attending one more luncheon, one more ribbon cutting, that Joelle stopped midstep, anger rifling through her. "Since you disapprove of virtually everything I say or do, why *are* you taking me to dinner?"

The old-fashioned street lamps shone down on them, silhouetting Leo's height, casting dim yellow light on his profile. He looked hard, proud...*Roman.* "I'm trying to understand you."

"What's there to understand? I'm twenty-two, successful, independent. I do what I want, go where I want, make my own decisions."

"Even though it puts you in danger?"

"I'm not in danger."

He shook his head in mute frustration. "How do you know? How do you know *I'm* not dangerous?"

A tremor shot through her. Good question, she thought. She didn't.

Or did she?

She stared up at him, brow creased, studying his hard features. All right. He did scare her. But he didn't strike her as violent. Controlling, yes, but cruel, no. "You wouldn't hurt me," she said at last, burying her hands in her jean pockets. "You're not that kind of a man."

He muttered something in Italian she couldn't completely hear, but she did catch a couple choice swear words along with a very cryptic, "You don't know."

They were walking again and crossed to Royal Street. Brennan's came into view, the exterior painted the softest shade of pink.

Leo held the dark green door open for her and as Joelle moved past him she felt a current of awareness shoot through her, her body prickling from head to toe, her skin painfully sensitive.

She shot him a cautious glance, wondering yet again how he had this effect on her. Yes, he was tall. Yes, he exuded strength.

But it wasn't the physical size of him as much as the energy coming from within.

Leo Fortino would be formidable if crossed.

The hostess seated them almost immediately, upstairs in one of the smaller dining rooms, this one painted a rich dark red, the tall French windows overlooking the lush interior courtyard.

The kitchen would be closing within the hour and after giving the menu a quick perusal, they both ordered.

The soup, Louisiana Crab Bisque, arrived quickly and Joelle, who'd thought she was hungry, could barely get her spoon to her mouth.

It was one thing to find a man heart-stoppingly attractive. It was another to eat sitting across from him.

Leo noticed she'd barely touched her soup. His dark gaze rested on her face. "You don't prefer it?"

Oh, there went the butterflies in her stomach again. When he looked at her like that, so directly, so intently, she felt as if she were lost. Completely. Totally.

"I do. It's delicious," she said, forcing the spoon up to her lips and choking the mouthful down.

But she had his full attention now and the next sip was even harder than the last.

"So what's wrong?"

She pushed back a heavy wave of hair, wishing she'd thought to tie it back but it was too late for that. Just as it was too late to duck out of dinner. Dining at Brennan's with Leo had sounded exciting when she was still at Club Bleu, but now that they were here, seated in a virtually empty dining room, the dark red walls warm and intimate, she was finding the flurry of nerves too much.

"How old are you?" she asked suddenly, setting her spoon down.

"Thirty-two."

Wow. She exhaled slowly, turning into a massive ball of insecurity. He was ten years older than her. Ten years. Imagine the wealth of knowledge he had…especially when it came to women. "When's your birthday?"

"May 4."

A month ago today. She smiled faintly, thinking that his birth date explained a lot "You're a Taurus."

"A Taurus?"

"You know…astrology…the sun signs."

He gestured dismissively. "I don't follow any of that."

The gesture, coupled with his patronizing tone, rankled her. On one hand he was a gorgeous male, but on the other he was hopelessly arrogant. "You don't have to follow anything. It is what it is. It exists even if you don't believe in it."

"But you do?" he persisted, indicating to the waiter that the soup dishes could be cleared.

"It's fun."

Leo's jaw flexed and Joelle felt a tingly shiver run through her. Leo didn't approve.

"It's stupidity."

She blinked, trying to clear the haze of red before her eyes. "How can you do that? How can you be so judgmental?"

"Because you're supposed to be an intelligent woman. You're supposed to think for yourself, not buy into all that New Age stuff. Astrology, sun signs, crystals, palm reading, aura reading—"

"Excuse me, but I never said I was into New Age mysticism. I never brought up crystals or aura readings. I just asked you when your birthday was, and when you told me, I said, you're a Taurus. That was it." What was going on here? Why was she getting such mixed signals?

He'd sought her out earlier. He'd watched her tonight, approached her after the set ended, asked her to join him for a drink. Why?

"You know, Leo, I know you don't approve of me, and I don't know why. Maybe it's because I don't understand what, or who, you think I am. But I'm not a druggie. I don't smoke, inhale, pop pills. I don't drink much. I'm not covered in multiple piercings and body tattoos. I just like to sing." She looked up at him, her gaze meeting his. "And I love to entertain."

As she spoke, her long dark hair fell forward, her right hand fisted on the table, and her voice dropped, deepening with a husky sensuality and fury.

Joelle's gaze held his. "Obviously there are a lot of things you don't like about me. Is there anything you do?"

Is there anything he did?

Leo felt his body respond at the provocative question, and leaning back in his chair he took in her small taunting smile, the cool anger in her blue-green eyes. "Your eyes," he said bluntly. She had beautiful eyes, the lashes so thick and long, even more dramatic now with the extra set of false lashes at the outer corners.

"Your hair." His gaze touched her hair, the incredible length, the rich color. He'd love to tangle his hands in her hair, feel the glossy weight.

"Your mouth," he added, staring at her mouth and watching her bite into her lower lip, chewing on the tender skin. Her lips were full, soft and painted a pale pinky-beige. Her lips were the color of skin, making him think nude, naked, wicked.

He watched her chew on that soft lower lip and felt the silence between them lengthen, felt the tension mount.

She was squirming from the tension. He saw the desire in the darkening of her eyes, the flush in her cheeks, her restlessness at the table.

Would she go to bed with him? Would she sleep with him— a stranger—three weeks before her wedding? "Your body." He felt harsh, cruel, but he needed information. There was so much he didn't know, so much about her he didn't understand.

"And that's all you like about me?" she asked, her voice faint, almost tremulous, in the rich dark red dining room. "Lips, hair, body?"

His chest grew tight, his groin hot and hard. Things were getting complicated. How much did he say? How much did he give away?

He knew his silence hurt her. He saw her smooth throat work, saw her hand tremble as she sorted out her silverware on the linen tablecloth. She was fighting for control, fighting to be calm.

And yet he remained silent, thinking, weighing, deliberating. He sorted through his actions, reactions, examined his motivations.

If he told her who he was, she'd change before his eyes. He

knew she'd hide herself, the true self and become Princess Ducasse. But he didn't want a part. He wanted the real thing.

He wanted to know *her*. Wanted the good, the bad, the ugly.

It was truth he needed now. Truth to cut through the lies and pretense. Truth so he'd know whom he was marrying.

Or if he should even marry her.

But the question of marriage, of suitability of marriage, did nothing to dampen his hunger. He wanted her. His body ached. His trousers cut him.

She was supposed to be innocent.

He was supposed to be the good prince.

Tragically, nothing was as it should be.

"No," he said softly, eyes holding her, eyes taking her, eyes letting her know what he'd do given the opportunity, "I don't just want your body. I want your mind, too."

CHAPTER THREE

JOELLE jerked at the rawness of Leo's answer. He had a hard voice, a decisive voice, and when he said he wanted her—not just her body, but also her mind—she felt as if he'd launched an assault...

Crossbows, battleaxes, and all.

Mouth dry, she stared across at him. And looking into his eyes was yet another mistake in a night of mistakes.

She'd never looked this closely into a man's face before, never let herself look so intimately into someone's eyes, and it wasn't just intimate, it was excruciating.

His eyes were dark, but not brown as she'd thought, but a deep dark green, like the olives of Tuscany, the color of the woods in Melio where sunlight fell in slender streaks between fragrant pine branches.

Cool. Warm. Intelligent. Beautiful.

She felt her lips nearly curve in appreciation, and then small muscles creased at the corner of his eyes and she felt all air leave her body.

The table was too small. They were sitting far too close. Leo was too big.

She shivered all the way through and drew a rough, uncomfortable breath causing the skin on her nape to tingle. The goose bumps returned, this time covering every inch of skin, tightening even her breasts, causing her nipples to peak against the soft contour of her silk bra.

It was a strange response, and such a strong one, too.

Leo shifted and his knee brushed hers beneath the table. Joelle gasped at the sharp heat shooting through her. Beneath the table she pressed her knees together, pressing the muscles of her inner thighs tight, trying to deny the flood of want.

The flood of need.

He'd turned her on from the very first look, and now she was melting on the inside, melting because of him. Just one touch and she tensed, body hot, aching. Damp.

Glancing up, she met Leo's gaze once again. His features were still beautiful but not quite so hard and she didn't know if it was the hidden warmth in his eyes or the fact that his mouth had gentled, accenting his chin, flat across the bottom with a hint of a cleft, but she wanted to kiss him. Felt almost desperate to feel his mouth against hers.

There was so much she didn't know. So much she wanted to understand. Like how a man's lips could stir her imagination and how his breath would feel blowing lightly, tormentingly against her skin...

"You want my mind?" she whispered, thinking, wishing it were so. No one had ever wanted her mind. No one had ever wanted to know her.

"Is that such a bad thing?"

She couldn't help it. She felt her lips curve up, into a wide rueful smile. "They say the best sex starts with the brain."

Leo smiled, but it was different than hers. It wasn't a warm smile, or wry or remotely rueful. No, his smile wasn't one of amusement. Instead he looked as if he were about to declare war.

Joelle went weak in the middle, and the weakness seeped through her limbs. Thank God she was sitting otherwise she would have come crashing down.

Leo's smile faded. "Indeed. The brain is the primary sexual organ. Engage the brain for ultimate pleasure."

She blushed, not just from his words, but the intentness of his gaze. She felt even more aware of him than before. Her heart hammered harder. Her mouth went dry. Muscles clenched deep inside of her.

Joelle felt so hot, so wound up. Eleven months here and she'd never felt anything like this. But the sensations surging through her, the emotions rocking her, weren't gentle, weren't playful, weren't fun.

This was sexual. Brutal.

Fire and ice, she whispered. This is what you thought you wanted...

"You look thirsty," Leo said, his expression lazy, blatantly sexual, leaning forward to fill her wineglass.

But beneath the sexual implication there was a warm, complex sensuality that reached out to her, beckoned her.

She felt fingers of his sensual warmth creep through her.

She *was* thirsty, she thought. But then, she'd been thirsty for years: thirsty for everything she'd never done, thirsty for experience and wisdom, thirsty for knowledge, thirsty for insight, thirsty to be more Joelle.

Her glass filled, Leo sat back. "Drink."

If only it were that easy. Her nose wrinkled as she picked up her glass and set it down again untouched. She honestly didn't think she could eat or drink anything if she tried. "I don't think I can."

"Why not?"

"Too much adrenaline."

Leo thought she'd been beautiful on stage—sexier than hell in the tight flared leather pants, the stiletto heel boots—but nothing was as sexy as listening to her speak, watching her mouth curve, hearing the words "too much adrenaline" in that smoky voice of hers, a voice shaded with dreams and blues.

He understood adrenaline. At one point in his life he'd lived from one adrenaline surge to another, needing huge physical challenges to focus his endless energy, his restlessness haunting him, chasing him around the globe. But there was something about her, and her admission of nerves and adrenaline that touched him.

"What's bothering you?" he asked, filling his glass.

"You."

He looked up in time to see her blue-green eyes flash. "I'm not."

"You are." She inhaled in a rush. More nerves, he thought.

"You're not like most men I know," she added and she touched the tip of her tongue to her upper lip.

Leo's gut felt as hard as his groin. He gritted his teeth, thinking he'd have to peel his skin off in a minute if his body didn't cool down. "And what are those men like?"

"Charming. Easygoing. Harmless."

"That's me."

Joelle laughed. "You're impossible."

"Perhaps." He suddenly reached out, lightly touched her cheek. Her skin was warm, soft and her head jerked up, eyes wide, wary. "You've a beautiful laugh, *bambina.* You should laugh more."

Joelle blushed, looked away, realized dinner was on the way. The waiters presented the plates with a flourish and left them alone to eat. And Joelle realized she wasn't as nervous as she'd been.

Leo's mood seemed lighter as well, his dark gaze warmer, less shuttered, and she continued to relax, enjoying her entrée, giving in to the pleasure of a well-cooked meal.

And sitting there, across from Leo, in Brennan's upstairs dining room, red walls cocooning them, the French cuisine sublime, she thought this was the kind of evening where even the little things took on a larger than life significance.

The flawless white table linens felt silky smooth beneath her fingers. The candle glowed warmly, reflecting brilliantly off the crystal and china. The glimpse of moon outside the windowpane added to the ambiance.

Joelle held her wine goblet by the stem, the glass bowl huge, round, full, the red wine barely filling the basin as she listened to Leo talk about his life abroad, how he didn't live in one place, but many, with homes in London, Santiago, Chile, Zurich. He considered himself a man of the world instead of a man of one country.

She liked the sound of his voice, the strength in his voice and she knew she was smiling as she listened, her eyes resting on his face, her body leaning ever so slightly forward, her legs crossed beneath the table.

It crossed her mind that this is how she imagined America to be—how life to be—the richness, the complexity, the complicated beauty. No easy answers. No right answer. Just life. Just people. Just energy, sound and motion.

"You've traveled extensively," he said, shifting the focus from his own background to hers. "Where have you felt most at home?

"Here." It was easy to answer. She'd never traveled as much as Leo had, but no place had felt like this.

She'd loved the past eleven and a half months. Loved being no one, a nonentity, invisible on New Orleans's streets.

She'd loved walking the French Quarter late at night, guitar slung over her shoulder, heading back to the little apartment she shared with Lacy from Georgia.

She'd loved waking early, grabbing a beignet and coffee across from St. Charles before all the tourists descended.

There'd been so much to embrace here.

Carnival. The sultry heat wrapping the city in summer. The crumbly red bricks of the old buildings. The stately wrought-iron balconies overhanging narrow streets.

Tipping her wine goblet, Joelle watched the wine swirl. "Everything felt right here. *I* felt right here."

"Are you planning on staying in New Orleans then?" Leo's deep voice, rich and cultured, like gold marble shot with veins of black rushed through her, across her taut senses, stirring something deep inside of her.

"No."

"Why not?"

Looking up, she met his eyes, saw that he was trying to figure out where she was, what she was thinking. No one had ever looked at her so long, listened so intently, and she wondered if she'd ever have this again, after she married. Would she ever sit at a table and feel special? Desirable? Would Luigi even want to listen to her?

Resolutely Joelle pushed thoughts of Luigi out of mind, and shrugged in answer to Leo's question. She focused on the candle on their table, trying to keep the tears from burning. "I have to."

"Why the have to? You're an adult. Do what you want to do."

"It's not that simple." She reached out to the candle, put her hand above the flame, felt the lick of heat. "We all have a purpose...something we're supposed to do."

"So it's work that calls you back?"

"Yes. I've a new job waiting."

''What kind of job?''

She laughed without a trace of humor. ''It's awful. Trust me. You don't want to know.''

''That bad?''

She blinked back sudden stinging tears. ''Worse.''

He stared at her long and hard, his black brows furrowed, and then he muttered something intelligible beneath his breath. He stood abruptly, reached for his wallet. ''It's time we go.''

He was angry. Joelle felt a wobble inside her. What had she said? ''Leo?''

But he wasn't looking at her; he was sliding his wallet back into his coat pocket, now heading for the stairs.

Joelle trailed after him on shaky legs. They exited the entrance, reached the street and Leo set off down Royal Street, opposite the way they came. She glanced at him as they walked, tried to read his expression, but it was dark, his profile granite hard, and all she felt coming off of him was waves of anger.

They walked one block, and then another. The French Quarter wasn't all that big and if they continued the direction they were heading, they'd soon hit Canal Street, exiting the French Quarter.

''Leo?'' she asked uncertainly.

''What?''

''Where…'' She swallowed, gathered her courage. It wasn't as if they hadn't just spent three hours together. ''Where are we going?''

He stopped abruptly beneath a street lamp, turned, and faced her. ''Where do you think we're going?''

She shook her head. She didn't understand the look she saw in his eye. At the moment she didn't understand anything.

There was a long moment of silence, a moment where she saw a frustration in his dark eyes, an emotion that held anger as well as passion. Then he backed her into a dark alcove, the large arched doorway a former carriage entrance like so many in the French Quarter.

''We've had drinks,'' he said flatly.

''Yes.''

''We've had dinner.''

She felt his coat fall open, felt the jacket brush against her breasts. "At Brennan's."

He leaned forward, one arm moved above her head, bracing himself against the door. "We've had coffee. Dessert. Now you tell me what happens next."

Joelle locked her knees. Fear mingled with desire. "I don't know."

"Yes, you do."

It was hard to see his face, the shadows hid his expression but she felt the heat radiating from him, felt the warmth of his body without him touching her.

Leo made her feel awash in emotion, and ever since she met him she was swinging like a pendulum from one emotion to another. She was swinging even now and the sense of momentum, the feeling of being in perpetual motion, in perpetual flux, unnerved her more than she could say.

She blinked back tears, knowing they were tears of fatigue, and stress. It'd been a difficult week, packing, saying her good-byes, but the tears were also a release. She'd been so wound up all night…frazzled by a need she couldn't answer.

But he could.

He could quiet the humming in her veins. He could put out the fire.

She felt him move closer, his head bending down. She held her breath, certain he would kiss her. She wanted the kiss. She feared the kiss.

From the corner of her eye she saw his arm move. His thumb strummed her cheek. Her head spun. She needed air but she didn't dare to breathe.

Leo's eyes were dark, his expression intense. "Tell me."

She opened her mouth, stole a breath, and yet her pulse was slowing, desire—anticipation—washing through her in endless waves.

His thumb dropped to her mouth. Lightly he brushed the pad of his thumb across her lips. Pinpricks of light exploded inside her head. Hot sensation rocketed through her and she tensed, hands, arms, legs, everything.

She wanted, wanted, wanted him. She didn't even know

where to begin, what to ask for. The hunger, the need, was alive inside her and she knew nothing could happen here, in this dark alcove, nothing would happen. Leo Fortino didn't strike her as a man who'd taken a woman on a city sidewalk.

She reached up to touch the collar of his shirt, too afraid to touch his skin and yet needing contact, needing to connect. "We go…"

"Yes?" His thumb was drawing circles on her swollen lower lip. The circles were slowly driving her mad.

She closed her eyes, tried to clear her brain. "We go to your—"

"My?"

"Hotel—"

She'd said what he'd wanted to hear. His head dropped. He silenced the rest with a kiss.

His lips were firm, his breath cool and she stiffened with surprise. She'd kissed before, felt rather proficient in terms of kissing but this wasn't a mere kiss, this was like nothing she'd ever experienced before.

His lips moved across hers, deliberately, thoroughly, a sensual exploration intended to stir her, wake every little nerve ending to life and he succeeded. Too well. Her lower lip quivered, tingled and the tingle shot all the way through her, straight to her belly, which felt hot and tight with need.

But that was only the beginning. His mouth drew the heat from hers and the slow exploration flared into something fierce, demanding.

His hard body pressed against hers, his thighs moved between hers and she felt trapped, skewered, the very way he'd trapped her in his gaze earlier, but this time it was with his body.

She felt the hard planes of his chest crush her breasts, the sinewy shape of his thigh between her own and she groaned as he moved against her, his knee up, between her thighs, creating friction, sensation.

Her groan was like tossing gasoline on a fire.

Leo's hands moved from the wall to her head, his palms sliding through her hair, fingers tightening in her long hair, holding her captive.

His desire was raw. His hunger stunned her. He was so not like anything she understood, so beyond anything she could control, and yet she wanted it all—the passion, the fury, the shiver of fraught nerves. All the while her body was melting, her defenses negligent. She'd known from the beginning she couldn't resist him. She'd known from the very first glance that she'd be his.

She felt one of Leo's hands drop from her hair, to her cheek and her jawbone before sliding down the length of her neck. The path his hand took was as tortuous as it was delicious and Joelle arched helplessly up against Leo's body, her hips meeting his, her head tipping, exposing more, more skin.

She felt Leo's fingertips graze her collarbone; stroke the swell of her breast. Shivery pleasure danced through her. Her lips parted, gasped, as his hand moved beneath the thin blouse to find hot bare skin.

It was her soft indrawn take of air that finally penetrated Leo's brain. He was undressing her here, virtually making love to her here, on the street, in a gloomy alcove littered with the day's trash.

What the hell was he thinking?

Drawing back, Leo raked a hand through his hair, trying to quiet the chaos in his body and brain. But it was hard organizing his thoughts, much less organizing himself.

He hadn't lost it like that in years.

"What's wrong?" Joelle asked tentatively, her face dappled by shadows.

She had a smoky voice, a sexy voice, and yet it seemed so incongruous with her wide aquamarine eyes. She seemed so young still, such a girl, and he felt a rise of protective instinct.

Where the hell were her bodyguards? Where was her grandfather? Her older sisters? Where were those who could help her? Guide her?

Princess Joelle knew far too little about the world. Her family ought to be looking out for her. Instead they'd left her alone in a big city like New Orleans, a city designed to seduce the senses, a city that came alive at night with food and sex and soulful sound.

"What are you doing, *bambina?*" he asked, unable to resist stroking the curve of her cheekbone, her skin irresistibly soft, warm.

He heard the catch in her voice at the gentle caress, but shoulders shifted in a careless shrug. "You know the saying, Leo. Girls just want to have fun."

It was true and not true, Joelle thought as he stared down into her eyes. She wanted a man who craved her. A man who wasn't willing to wait years for her, but had to have her, wanted to be with her as much as she wanted to be with him.

"Fun," he echoed softly and his voice had dropped, deep, low, husky and the word hung there between them so sexual, so seductive that it didn't mean anything remotely fun, but had become a challenge.

He stared down into her eyes for so long she couldn't breathe, the air-choked-off panic spread, sweeping through her, confusing her.

She felt her belly clench, tightening hard, tightening so that she felt strangely empty and the emptiness was painful. She wanted anything but emptiness, anything but pain. "Yes."

She saw him swallow, saw the muscle pull at his jaw. "You'd be better off just going home and cooking up a box of mac and cheese."

Joelle had to bite her tongue. *Mac and cheese.* Macaroni and cheese. Kid stuff. For a kid. Her cheeks burned. She looked away, offended. Affronted. "I'm not a child."

"I didn't say you were."

And suddenly his hand tangled in her long dark hair, his palm wrapping her hair around his fist, once, twice, and with her face forced up, his head descended, his lips again covering hers. The touch of his mouth stunned her, the touch, the pressure so different from before.

She twitched, unnerved, her lips parting in surprise and immediately his lips firmed against her parted mouth, his breath warm, the tip of his tongue just barely brushing the inside of her upper lip.

Joelle jerked, muscles tightening, shuddering and she felt like a papier-mâché puppet on strings. It was the strangest response, nerves, muscles popping, but she couldn't help the hot sharp currents surging through her, or the sudden weakness flooding her limbs, her knees, legs, body dissolving, turning to mush.

Her hands rose, pressed against his chest, struggling to balance herself and somewhere in the back of her brain she thought his chest felt unbelievably hard, smooth, thickly muscled. His body felt the way she'd always imagined a man's body to feel and yet the hand in her hair was no nice-guy touch, but the touch of a possessive man, a sexual man, a man that had no problem marking a woman as his.

This is what she wanted but this isn't what she ought to have. She'd told herself she could have a fling, but Leo Fortino didn't strike her as a nice guy, an easygoing guy, the kind of guy to just let a woman walk away from him.

But you're already promised, her conscience frantically reminded her. You can't break off the engagement.

And I won't, she answered her conscience. This is just one night. One time. Once is all, I promise.

Leo must have felt the indecision, the struggle within her. His head lifted, his lips left hers. She blinked, trying to clear her vision, trying to organize her brain. Say something. Do something. Think smart, funny, fun. But for the life of her nothing came to mind.

Leo broke the silence. "How's that for fun?" he asked, his voice deep, grating against her nerves.

She couldn't answer. Her head and senses swam. She'd felt brave during dinner—so brave she'd been numb—but the numbness was gone and all the fears came rushing back, swamping her.

"Change your mind?" Leo asked softly, and she heard the soft taunt in his voice.

She had, or almost had, knowing that a fling ought to be with someone light, someone easy. Leo was far from light. Deep down Leo—and his sexuality—scared her.

She wanted experience, an affair, but she wanted it on her terms. She wanted a relationship she could control, but if she couldn't control conversation with Leo, how could she hope to control what happened in the bedroom?

''The hotel's around the corner,'' he said, stepping away from her, back onto the pavement, putting distance between them. ''I'll put you in a cab there.''

She followed him out, joining him beneath the street lamp. She felt dazed, dizzy, but certainly not ready to be sent home. ''I'm not running scared.''

Leo's eyes glowed down at her in the dark, the elaborate street lamps of the French Quarter reflecting off his hard features. ''I never said you were.''

''So why put me in a cab?'' She lifted her chin, felt her mouth tremble into a smile. ''I haven't seen the inside of your hotel room yet.''

CHAPTER FOUR

So SHE was really going to do this.

Leo allowed the door to his hotel suite to swing closed and watched Joelle enter the suite's living room.

The lights were dim. Housekeeping had visited since he left, tidying the suite, turning down the coverlet on his bed, plumping pillows, but Joelle looked calm, nonchalant even as she wandered around the living room.

He couldn't bear to think she did this sort of thing often. He wanted to believe she wasn't promiscuous, or a party girl, but they'd only just met tonight and yet here she was, alone with him in a hotel room at two in the morning.

Yes, he'd invited her here, deliberately tempted her, and it was a test. He was setting her up, testing her values, her morals, and it might not be right, but it was necessary.

He had to know. The wedding was just three weeks away. Three weeks. How could she behave like this just three weeks before their marriage? Did fidelity…loyalty mean nothing? If she tumbled into bed with him, how many other men was she sleeping with? And if she wasn't faithful before the wedding, why should he believe she'd be faithful after?

The acid taste in his mouth burned all the way to his stomach. He'd known women, royal brides, like Joelle who couldn't, wouldn't, be faithful.

He'd known women, prominent beautiful women—models, socialites, princesses—who needed so much emotionally they couldn't be satisfied with just one man, one relationship. He knew how hurtful these women could be. He knew how their insatiable needs wounded those around them, poisoning relationships, scarring their friends and families.

"Something from the bar?" he asked, setting his room key on the table and sliding his jacket off. "Champagne, wine, a cocktail?"

46

"I'm fine, thank you."

He heard the catch in her voice, heard the nervous edge, and for a moment he felt hope. Relief. Maybe she'd put a stop to this now. He wanted her to put her foot down, be firm, disciplined. He needed her to be a mature woman, one in control of herself, instead of one lost to emotion and whim.

But Joelle turned her back on him, and he saw her examine the suite once again—the subdued elegance of the caramel and bronze interior furnished with pairs of leather club chairs, expensive antiques, and full silk drapes at the window, framing the city nightscape.

"You've a great view of the Mississippi," she said, standing at one of the windows. "I love the river. The action on the river."

He could see the river over her head, spotted the white lights outlining the paddle of a passing steamboat. In the daylight the old paddleboats with their ornate Victorian gingerbread trim looked like miniature wedding cakes.

Wedding cakes. The corner of his mouth curved as cold cynicism ate its way through his heart. Right now there'd be no wedding cake in three weeks. There'd be no wedding at all.

"There's something powerful about water," she added, still studying the river. "I can't imagine not living close to the water, with a view of the water. I think my life has been shaped by tides, storms, boats."

Joelle turned a little, glancing at him over her shoulder. "But you wouldn't have had that where you lived, would you?"

He hesitated a moment, still lost in thought, before forcing himself to answer. "There was the Thames in London, lakes in Switzerland."

Leo shrugged, feeling callous, not wanting to talk about his world anymore. If she wasn't going to be part of his future, she didn't need to know his past.

He crossed to the minibar, opened the small refrigerator and pulled out a bottle of mineral water, popping off the top. He felt as if he were on fire on the inside and he took a long drink, and then another, but the cold mineral water did nothing to cool his temper.

Or his desire.

He wanted her. That was the worst insult of all. He didn't understand how he could feel this kind of anger and betrayal, and yet still be so physically drawn to her.

He shouldn't want her. Shouldn't desire her. She wasn't who she was supposed to be.

It killed him. This wasn't supposed to happen to him. He'd been through this before, had sworn he'd never get trapped by a needy, desperate woman again. And yet here he was, with proof of Joelle's duplicity, and yet unable to act.

He thought he was marrying the innocent Ducasse princess, could remember the discussion with King Remi, Joelle's grandfather, could see the stiff cream folder with gold leaf lying on his desk, the dossier compiled by the Melio palace officials, cross-checked by his own people.

He remembered virtually every word. Every phrase. Every criticism.

Princess Joelle Ducasse, the youngest of Prince Julien's three daughters, has been overshadowed by her older, more ambitious sisters. Although highly educated, and musically accomplished, Princess Joelle is the least extroverted of the sisters and tends to be retiring, even shy in public.

He took a long drink, and then another.

Socially inexperienced, the princess has yet to date, preferring the company of her immediate family over jet-setters her age.

Leo slammed the bottle on the counter.

Joelle jumped, looked at him wide-eyed. "You're very quiet."

"Just thinking." And he was moving toward her, stalking her, anger, desire, frustration coming together in a vortex of emotion.

He saw a flicker of emotion in her blue-green eyes as he approached her. She was afraid, he thought, and his chest tightened. He didn't want her afraid, but he didn't want her behaving stupidly, either. Life was difficult, demanding, even cruel, and trust was even harder to come by.

He'd grown up without knowing what trust was, grew up needing stability…maturity…normalcy—and it'd been denied. His father had been so eager to get rid of his mother that when the divorce came through, his father had gotten rid of Leo, too, and his father was supposed to be the grounded one. The protective parent.

What a joke.

Leo studied Joelle's pale face, the subtle lift of her chin. He didn't understand her, but he did know this—he couldn't marry a woman who lacked stability, or maturity. He could accept youth—but not immaturity.

Placing his hands on her shoulders, Leo fought his own conflicting emotions, torn between throwing her out and tossing her onto the bed.

He wanted to hold her, touch her, and yet he also knew that there was no future for them. That she was the last woman he could marry. He needed a wife he could depend on, a woman he could trust.

He didn't trust her. He'd never trust her.

It burned within him, the deceit, the deception, and he blamed many for this farce of an engagement, including himself. He should have met Joelle earlier, should have investigated her background more thoroughly.

He'd call her grandfather in the morning. He'd call his own father, the various palace officials. They could break the news to the press any way they wanted. He didn't care how the PR folks handled the broken engagement. Leo just knew he wanted it over, and he wanted it over soon.

Everything felt right and yet wrong, Joelle thought, trapped by the weight of Leo's hands on her shoulders. The attraction between them was tangible. She was hopelessly aware of him, and she knew he desired her, it was there in his eyes, in the touch of his hands, but something else was happening, too…

"Those thoughts seem pretty serious," she whispered as he drew her forward, pulling her toward him.

"Yes."

His one-word answer wasn't half as nerve-wracking as his slow, hot glance. He made her feel like dinner. She swallowed hard, heart racing, her panic growing to the point it crossed her mind that she might have been better off going home.

"How far are you planning on taking this, Josie?" he asked,

hands sliding from her shoulders, down her arms to encircle her wrists.

The moment his fingers circled around hers she felt the hottest current shoot through her hand and up her arm.

The sharp sensation electrified her and every nerve in her screamed for her to run. But her body wouldn't move, her muscles were too weak, too warm.

"How far?" he repeated, drawing her closer still.

Her breath trapped in her throat, bottled in her chest. "Tell me something," she said, awed by the differences between them. He was hard. Very hard. The elegant lines of his suit hid the rugged planes of his chest and the steely-strength of his stomach and thighs.

"What?"

He sounded wary, remote even, his smooth brow furrowed, and yet his intense concentration made him more exotic. A gorgeous sleek animal focused. Deliberating.

She knew he must have his pick of women. He was gorgeous, sophisticated, intelligent, wealthy...sexual. She swallowed the butterflies back, her body alive with nervous energy. "You said earlier you wanted my body, and my mind."

He stared at her, said nothing, just waiting.

Her mouth was drying out. She had to swallow again but she couldn't come up with any moisture. "And I was wondering...and forgive me for being blunt, but why would you find me interesting? I'm twenty-two. You're ten years older. What would I have, intellectually, that would appeal to you?"

He didn't answer, but his mouth compressed, his lovely mouth with firm, mobile lips, tightened, and as his silence lengthened, she knew.

He wanted her mind because it was attached to her body, but it wasn't her mind he wanted. It was her body.

"I haven't answered yet, so don't go putting words in my mouth," he said, tipping her chin up. "And yes, your body is beautiful but you've talent—don't forget, I heard you sing tonight—you also play guitar and you probably play other instruments as well."

''The piano and violin,'' she said, swallowing the lump in her throat.

''You're educated, apparently well-traveled, fluent in three languages—''

''Four.''

One eyebrow arched. ''What's the fourth?''

''Spanish.''

''Of course.'' The corner of his mouth tugged. ''And even though you were dressed like a Vegas showgirl earlier, you've beautiful manners.''

''And men like nice manners?''

He grimaced wryly. ''Some of us do.'' His teasing smile faded. ''But what's happening here isn't about love, it's sex. But I think you know that. And I think it's sex you want.''

The word sex sounded so bald, so blunt, and it bounced around her head like a Ping-Pong ball. Sex. Sex with Leo. Sex because she wanted to know more, wanted to have an experience that was hers, and hers alone…sex because it was her choice, her own choice, and probably the last thing that would ever be her choice.

''If you're hoping for more,'' he added, ''you're not—''

''I understand,'' she cut him off.

His lashes had dropped, his expression concealed. ''You don't have to stay.''

''I understand that, too.'' She felt as if he was trying to get rid of her, trying to send her packing and she didn't understand it. He wanted her, but he didn't want her. He was attracted but he fought the attraction. She sensed that beneath all the hardness and cool sophistication, he was very true, maybe even old-fashioned.

It was a shame she wasn't someone else. It was a shame they'd met this way.

For a moment Joelle was filled with indecision, the unknown yawning about her in every direction, and then she did what she knew she needed to do. She touched him. She placed her hands tentatively on his chest, needing to discover him, needing to discover herself, life and sex.

Yet touching him wasn't without pain. With her hands on his

chest, his dress shirt the only thing between her skin and his, she wondered if this was how she was supposed to feel. Conflicted. Wrenched. Overwhelmed.

Touching him made her feel, and her heart felt so tender right now, all her emotions stirred.

His hands moved to her back, and he drew her even closer. "Cold?" he asked, as she shuddered at his touch.

"No." She felt the heat of his body as well as the power of his thighs and hips. He felt hard, aroused, and the ridge in his trousers pushed against her flat belly. "Adrenaline."

"Adrenaline?"

"I think the suspense is killing me." She was scared and yet turned on. Anxious. Excited. "I'm—" She broke off, knowing she couldn't just tell him she was relatively inexperienced, knowing that men were put off by confessions of innocence. She didn't want to risk putting him off. If she only had this one night with him she wanted it to be perfect. "Never mind. It's nothing."

His head dropped, his face close to hers, capturing the warmth of her skin, the flutter of her breath, before his lips touched hers, slowly. It was a light caress and yet there was something fierce behind it, something so hot, so dangerous that she turned her head away, afraid of the flare of heat.

His hand slid up her back, beneath her hair to cup her nape. She tingled every place his hand had touched.

"Your heart's racing," he said as she buried her face against his shirt, drinking in the smell of him, so sensitive to his warmth, his strength, the very texture of his skin.

"You have that effect on me."

He tipped her head back, stared into her eyes. "I bet you say that to all the men."

"No." She tried to smile but failed. Instead she reached up, touched his face. He jerked at her light touch but didn't pull away.

Slowly she trailed her fingertips from his chin—flat across the bottom with just a hint of a cleft—to the strong sweep of jaw. She wanted to know the shape of his face, the lines in his cheekbone and chin, the fragrance that was part skin, part sultry New Orleans tropics. It was like moonlight, musk and jasmine.

"You have a beautiful face," she whispered, awed by the bristles of his beard, the firmness of his skin.

"I don't. It's ordinary."

"There's nothing ordinary about you." She felt him smile and drawing back a little she saw that the corner of his mouth had indeed curved in what she'd come to recognize as his mocking smile. She'd never met any man so young and old. How could he be so jaded at thirty-two?

His smile faded as his eyes met hers, and his dark head dipped, his mouth covering hers again. Oh, how she liked the feel of his mouth against her, liked the smell of him and pressure.

Teasing, she thought, eyes closing, he was teasing her with that warm fleeting touch. It was the perfect seductive kiss—like breathing the aroma of a fine red wine before actually sipping—wakening the senses, stirring the imagination. The tantalizing pressure of his lips seemed to say a kiss wasn't just a kiss, it was pleasure itself.

Then he deepened the kiss, one hand rising to cup her cheek, his thumb stroking near her mouth and hot sensation flooded her limbs, sending rivulets of feeling everywhere. She was melting on the inside even as her breasts ached, her nipples peaking, incredibly sensitive.

Her response stirred him, and heat flared, hot, raw and the kiss changed. No longer tentative, or teasing, Leo's lips were firm, demanding, taking, tasting.

He teased the upper bow of her lip with his tongue and when her lips parted beneath his, he traced the shape of her mouth, the delicate skin inside her lower lip, and then her cheek, the tip of her tongue, saying without words that he would have her and enjoy her but it'd be strictly on his terms.

His hand slid from her cheek, down her neck, over her collarbone to cup her breast. Joelle shuddered at the brush of his fingertips over her nipple. He caressed her again and her belly clenched, tight, hot, aching.

He made her want so much, and the desire made her confident.

This was right, she thought, this was how a first time should be. Powerful. Sensual. Sexual. And his hand slipped beneath her blouse, his palm warm on her bare abdomen, fingers light against her narrow rib cage.

She dragged in another breath, trying to clear her head, trying to shake some of the dizziness away but his touch was too warm, too pleasurable.

When he lifted the edge of the silk of her bra cup, his warm skin against her warmer breast Joelle took a strangled breath and thought for sure she'd melt, dissolving into pure endless need.

No one had ever touched her like this...

No one had ever made her so helpless and hungry at the same time.

She could imagine his hands on her belly, on her hips, between her thighs. It might hurt, she thought, heart pounding, but then it might not, and even if it did hurt, how much better that it happen this way. With him. With someone as sensual and knowledgeable as Leo Fortino.

Suddenly Leo was pushing her backward, setting her firmly down on the edge of the bed.

Dizzily she braced herself, her head spinning, her hands braced on either side of her hips.

Leo stood above her, tall, silent, considering, the electricity between them tangible. She saw the dark flush in his cheekbones, the storm of passion in his green eyes. He was breathing deep, his chest filling, rising, and his lips pressed hard.

Abruptly he leaned forward, wrapped his hand in her hair, lifted her face to his and kissed her hard, a searing kiss, open mouth, a kiss of tongues, a kiss where he took her breath and total possession of her. It was as if he was opening her, rendering her vulnerable, rendering her his.

And as his tongue swept her mouth, probed her mouth, making her want to hold his tongue in her mouth, capturing the fierce rhythmic thrusts that made her belly clench and clench again. The kiss made her think of his hard body on hers, in hers, and heat flooded her womb, sent blood to all the places already far too sensitive.

Fingers still tangled in her hair, he turned his head, ending the kiss. "Take your clothes off," he commanded hoarsely, the bristles of his beard rough against her jaw, his warm breath tickling her skin.

The command, so hard, so direct sent flickers of feeling everywhere. Joelle shivered and clutched at the silk coverlet on the bed.

There were moments she forgot about his power, his authority, but all it took was one demand for her to realize he'd always been in control. That he'd never lose, much less give up, control to her. "Now?" she choked.

He'd straightened and he stood over her, warrior-like, and his dark green gaze stripped her naked. "Yes."

She wanted this, she reminded herself, she wanted to know life.

Wanted to know about power and possession.

Heart thudding, she reached for the strings of her blouse where it was tied in the small of her back. She felt his gaze, felt his intense concentration. Her hands shook as she fiddled with the knot, struggling to undo it.

Seconds crawled. Time slowed. His gaze grew harder. Hotter.

Hands damp, she finally got the knot undone and ties loosened she reached for the hem of her blouse and drew it up over her head and set it on the bed next to her.

He said nothing.

He did nothing.

Joelle blushed, feeling foolish in her faded jeans and push-up bra.

The jeans, she told herself. And standing, nearly bumping into Leo, she unfastened the snap, undid the zipper and breathing shallowly, air hard to come by, she pushed the jeans down over her hips, down her legs until she stepped out of those.

The jeans joined the blouse on the foot of the bed.

She was wearing very simple white silk underwear—white silk panties, the white silk push-up bra. And in her white undergarments she felt even more naked than before.

She glanced up at Leo, saw nothing encouraging in his face, and tears pricked the back of her eyes. Why was she doing this? What was she doing here?

And yet she knew. She was giving her virginity to Leo Fortino to keep from giving it to Luigi Borgarde, Prince of Milano, Count of Venetio, or whatever his official title was.

Although she did think it rather telling that she didn't even know his proper title.

But I'm not marrying for love, she flashed back, tearful, miserable. I've never even met Luigi before. He didn't even try to meet me before the engagement was announced. Instead he just sent some official to the palace, some Borgarde representative to look me up and down, and have me sign the necessary paperwork.

Paperwork. I'm a contract bride. A bargain basement princess. A blue-light special.

Scalding tears burned the back of her eyes and she knew why she never let herself think about Luigi Borgarde. She didn't let herself think about him because she was furious with him, furious that he actually thought it was okay to enter her world, move into her palace, take her parents' old bedroom without ever asking her to her face if she'd like to marry him.

How could a man, a real man, send a representative to handle the engagement?

How could a real man think a woman wanted to be treated like a business deal?

Was it really too much for Prince Luigi to take a day out of his business schedule to meet his future wife? She'd asked Grandpapa to arrange a meeting, asked more than once to allow them time to get to know each other before the engagement was announced to the public, but Grandpapa had said the prince was busy, and that she ought to trust him. *He's a good man,* her grandfather replied, *he's exactly what you, and Melio, need.*

The anger burned hotter, the anger nearly drowning out her passion.

Her grandfather might know what Melio needed, but he didn't know what *she* needed. He didn't know what *she* wanted. No one but Grandmama ever knew her, everyone else assuming she was like Nic and Chantal, assuming duty meant everything.

But duty was the last thing she cared about. Instead she loved music. Passionately, fiercely, with all her heart. When she sang, when she played her guitar, she wasn't a poor princess, or a princess without any position or power. She felt strong. Capable. Beautiful.

The tears continued to burn and gather. Her throat felt raw and the pain she never let herself dwell on threatened to suffocate her. If the Ducasses had been wealthier, if Melio had stronger financial resources—like oil, or exports—she could have married whomever she wished.

Instead she was marrying a stranger because he was wealthy and she was not. Her prince wanted children and she needed heirs. He wanted her kingdom and she—a woman—couldn't rule Melio without a man.

"If you've changed your mind...?" Leo's voice sounded above her head, bringing her back from the life that waited for her in Europe. The life she'd return to tomorrow.

Joelle shook her head, once, twice, fiercely. So many important choices taken from her, so much decided, determined, for her. She'd had this one night. She'd be with Leo, make love because she wanted to make love, to feel something special because it was what she wanted. It was what she *needed*.

"Nothing's changed," she answered, and yet her voice broke.

Pulse racing, Joelle reached behind her back and struggled to unhook her silk bra, peeling the delicate fabric from her shoulders and breasts.

Her hands shook and yet defiantly she lifted her chin, looked up into Leo's eyes. I want to do this, she silently repeated, I want to make love because it's the one thing I can choose for myself, the one thing no one can take from me, the one thing that will mean something to me even when I return home.

Eyes dark, expression shuttered, Leo joined her on the bed. She held her breath as he moved forward, straddling her legs, his knees outside her own. He wasn't even touching her yet, but she felt the warmth of him anyway.

This was it, she thought, the real thing.

And with him so big, so dark above her, she suddenly doubted her ability to see this through.

What did she really know about making love? What did she know about men's bodies?

She closed her eyes as his hands settled on her thighs, the pressure from his hands firm. Compelling. She wasn't going anywhere.

"So," he said, hands sliding ever so slowly up the length of her thighs sending rivers of feeling everywhere. "I take it you're protected?"

Protected? She felt a wall of heat slam through her. She'd forgotten all about that aspect. "Oh, right. Yes." She struggled to sit up but he was above her, still dressed, his body so large, so powerful. "I have um, a—" she looked up, saw the lift of his eyebrows "—a…condom…in my purse."

"You carry your own?"

No, actually, at least, she hadn't until tonight. But tonight she'd grabbed one from the dispenser in the women's bathroom at the club tonight. Just in case.

"I thought I…um, should," she stumbled, but he said nothing, let her flail about, waiting for more. It amazed her how he did that. He got so much information from her by just sitting back, waiting, letting her fill the awkward silences. "You know, take precautions."

"As you should," he answered, leaning forward to grab a leather satchel from the night table. He opened the leather bag, a men's shaving kit with all the gear one would expect before locating a foil pouch. "But I do have my own."

He set the foil pouch on the bed, next to her shoulder, and leaning over he kissed her shoulder. Her nipples peaked, breasts aching. She felt so bare and yet he was in no hurry to touch her.

She drew another quick breath when his lips found the crazy pulse in the small hollow below her ear. She was melting into a molten pool of need.

His lips trailed down her neck, slowly, very slowly until his mouth rested on her collarbone. "Undress me," he said.

His voice vibrated against her skin, sending shock waves through her, shock waves nearly as strong as her jittery response.

"Undress you?" He was so close, so very much on top of her and yet to reach the buttons on his shirt she had to sit higher, leaning toward him.

"Yes."

Joelle felt so exposed, her breasts bare, her hair loose, naked except for her miniscule panties. But she forced herself to ignore her nudity, forced herself to think only of him.

Leaning closer, she breathed in scent of his cologne, the deep woodsy spice, concentrated on the seductive heat of his body. Ignoring the trembling of her hands, she focused her line of sight on the very first button on his shirt. Determined, she undid the button and then moved to the next.

Before she knew it they were both naked and she was lying beneath him. She felt a little foolish, and very inexperienced as he reached out and stroked his hand down her body, from her breast to her hip. Joelle shivered, nipples peaking.

"Nothing's happened yet," he said, stretching out next to her. "Am I that unappealing?"

He made a sound, half laugh, half growl. "You're very appealing."

CHAPTER FIVE

HE DIPPED his head, kissed her, taking his time, slowing the kiss down, slowing Joelle's frantic pulse until she could think of nothing but him and his skin and her desire to be closer to him.

She wanted to feel him on her. In her. She wanted to feel his heat and strength properly.

His hands cupped her breasts, palms grazing across her taut nipples and then down to shape her ribs, her waist, her hips.

He had a great sense of touch, a way of making her feel soft and hot in all the right places. And when his mouth touched the hollow of her neck she gasped, reached for him, let her arms curl around his shoulders. She loved the feel of his body, the hard smooth tension beneath his skin and her fingers gripped the thick muscles of his upper arms as his mouth alternately kissed and bit across her own shoulder and collarbone. She hadn't imagined she could feel anything there, but his teeth and tongue found hundreds of nerve endings that were begging to be stroked and licked and nipped.

With his hands moving across her thighs, between her thighs, and his mouth drawing trails of fire across her breast she felt wild with need.

Helplessly she arched up against him, pressing herself closer, wanting more, wanting the terrible ache inside of her answered.

She sighed as his lips closed around one swollen nipple, sighed again as he parted her thighs with his knee, making room for him. The air felt cool against her skin, she felt so open as he shifted his weight, one leg and then another moving between her knees.

She shuddered as he lifted his head, looked down on her, looked to see her spread out before him. Joelle felt strangely like a sacrificial offering and it crossed her mind—fleetingly—that this is how it would have been on her wedding night if she'd waited, except she wouldn't have been half so attracted, half so turned on. Much better her first time be now, with Leo. Much better she do this her way, have something like this be her choice, within her control.

"I'm losing you," he said, his voice so husky it rasped across her senses, stirring her all over again.

"No. I'm here."

"You're deep in thought."

She reached up to touch his face, marveling at the feel of his beard-roughened jaw. "Just thinking about you."

His black eyebrow arched. He didn't believe it. She smiled. "Do you have so little faith in me?"

His expression hardened, dark green eyes burning hot and fierce. "I don't trust easily."

"Good. Neither do I." And she brought his face down to hers, kissed him slowly, kissed him the same way he'd kissed her earlier, and as the kiss deepened she felt his resistance dissolve.

He shifted, leaned up over her, his hips lowering against her pelvis.

The insistent press of his erection took her breath away, the rigid length between them, hard and hot against her tummy.

"I want you," she said, gathering her courage.

"I'm here."

"Not inside me yet."

And then suddenly he was there, hard against her tender skin, his big body pushing forward. She was warm, slick, but he didn't enter her easily, her body tensing.

Joelle felt his hand move between them, touch her, touch her readiness before he took his shaft in his hand, rubbed the tip across her delicate folds, stroking her once, twice, and she responded instinctively, opening her legs wider, hands moving to Leo's hips.

He stroked his shaft across her once more and as she lifted her hips for him she felt him slide into her, an inch or two and her mouth opened in surprise, stunned by the stretch, the sting of pain.

He pressed harder and again she felt him pull and stretch her. Was this how it felt for everyone? Did it always hurt like this?

Fighting panic, Joelle took a breath, exhaled, tried to relax. And as she said told herself to relax, this was normal, he was just breaking through the hymen, she felt him thrust forward, hard. Harder than she expected. Hard enough her eyes smarted, tears suddenly welling.

She must have made a sound because he stopped moving, lifted his head to look down at her. "Did I hurt you?"

She was panting a little on the inside, trying to get adjusted to his size, trying to accept the feel of him. "You're big."

"Should I stop?"

"No." She pressed her hands to the hollow of his back, her fingers clenched into small, frightened fists. It actually hurt more than she'd expected, and maybe she should have said something to Leo, let him know she didn't have the experience, that she'd never...

Too late anyway, she told herself, trying not to feel so alone, so scared. This was what she wanted to do, this is how she'd wanted it to happen.

"I won't move until it stops hurting," he said, his head dipping to kiss her gently. "Your body just needs to get used to mine."

He sounded very wise and she was grateful for this bit of advice, especially as he was still kissing her, less gently, more passionately, his lips teasing hers, his tongue stroking her tongue, his mouth taking her mind off what was happening in the rest of her body.

This was a kiss, she thought, head spinning, body rippling with delicious sensations and then she shifted beneath Leo and found that the painful sensation had lessened and instead she just felt oddly full, flushed, sensitive.

He started to move, small thrusts of his hips and she felt a ripple of sensation unlike the other sensations, this one a whisper of excitement, a flutter of delicious pleasure. She took a breath, shifted, lifting her hips to see if she could feel it again and he thrust harder, deeper and the pleasure returned, stronger, brighter, like strokes of cobalt-blue against white, color exploding in her mind's eye. And Leo took the lead, thrusting deeply, withdrawing to thrust again and the pleasure of it dazzled her.

He touched her body in so many places and so many ways but it wasn't what she thought sex would feel like. It was a thousand times better.

Her pulse had quickened, her skin felt hot, and as he drove into her she began to tighten on the inside, trying to grip him, hold him, keep him with her but he wouldn't let her hold him, wouldn't let her stop him and the friction built, hot, hotter until her muscles were tightening, tensing on their own, a fierce white-hot heat growing, threatening to explode.

"I can't—"

"Let it go," he answered in her ear, and she shook her head not certain what to do, or how to do it.

"Let it go," he repeated, his hips rocking deep, rocking her keeping her from escaping the delicious torment and just when she didn't think she could hold on, hold back, her body went— a stinging flicker bursting into flame. She shuddered helplessly beneath him, her body gripping his tightly, so tightly, her muscles rippling to life.

She felt his hands bury in her hair, felt his lips brush hers and he groaned her name before arching, tensing, and she felt him go, just as she had.

Later, she wasn't sure when, but she stirred, realized he was still with her, in her, and she felt his gaze, felt him watching her. "What are you doing?" she asked, stretching a little.

"Looking at you."

"Why?"

"You're beautiful."

She smiled shyly and he dropped a kiss on her lips before pulling away. He left the bed momentarily, headed for the bathroom and Joelle reached for the bedcovers and then realized when Leo reappeared from the bathroom that he'd merely discarded the condom.

How silly of her to worry. But how personal it all was. How intimate.

She flushed, embarrassed as she saw him approach the bed, big, muscular, naked. But her embarrassment faded as he climbed into bed, slid between the covers and pulled her back into his arms.

His skin was still warm, a little damp and she nestled closer, feeling incredibly safe. It was so hard to believe they'd just…and it felt like…

"Amazing," she murmured.

"You think?"

She laughed softly, stunned, happy, happy stunned. "Tonight has been…" Her voice drifted off. There were no words. Even if she wanted to explain it to him, share some of the significance of the night, he'd never really know what this—them—meant to her.

With a sigh, Joelle rolled over onto her back, stared up at the ceiling. Her heart was still beating fast. Her skin felt deliciously warm and damp. "I know I'm repeating myself, but I wish I had more time here. I'm not ready to go. There's so much I still want to do. I'd love to play tourist."

"That's the reason you don't want to go home?"

"No. I don't want to go home because I don't want to go to work, but the reason I don't want to leave here is that I love New Orleans." She turned, looked at him, nose wrinkling. "That didn't make any sense, did it?"

"Limited sense."

She laughed a little, savored Leo's gorgeousness. His name suited him. He looked so virile, so primal in bed. All golden muscles. All sexual power. "I've been here nearly a year and there's so much I haven't done yet."

"Such as?"

He reached out, brushed her hair from her breast, letting his palm cover her instead.

She shivered with pleasure as his warm palm cupped her, rubbing lightly, maddeningly across her nipple.

"All of it."

Eyes closed, Joelle pictured the Louisiana she'd yet to see, the colorful brochures pushed on tourists from endless city kiosks. "I'd love to have done the plantation tours, swamp tours, ghost tours, French Quarter walking tours—"

"You're joking." He gently pinched her nipple.

She squirmed against his hand, her body rippling to life all over again, her insides warming, her thighs feeling liquid and hot.

"No." She could hardly speak. She knew now how his body felt on hers, in hers, and she wanted it again. The pleasure. The pressure. The full sensation. But she couldn't be wanton, couldn't demand more, couldn't ask for another go at it. There ought to be some self-control.

She forced herself to think about her tourist wish list instead.

"I'd love a trip to Audobon Park and the zoo," she inhaled, his hand so warm against her breast, the heat intense, making her ache. "A ride on the streetcar, a Mississippi Riverboat cruise, the usual."

"Look at me."

His voice crackled authority, control, and she could only do as he asked. Her lashes lifted and she stared into his eyes, his eyes so dark they looked almost black, like the forest at night, like pine trees with just a hint of moonlight and her heart squeezed.

"You've been here a year, *bella*. Haven't you done any of that?"

She was lost, she thought, lost in him, and she'd done the unthinkable by going to bed with him. She'd given him not just her body, but her heart.

Stupid Jo. Stupid stupid Jo.

"I've been working." She tried to smile, tried to hide the intense emotions filling her. "If it's not one job, it's another."

"Maybe tomorrow," he said.

"Maybe," she answered, knowing tomorrow would be too late.

He didn't say anything and she felt his ambivalence, sympathy maybe. "Don't look at me like that," she said, pulling away from him, pushed on her elbow. "I may look young, but I know everyone has to grow up sometime. Even rebels like me."

He lifted a strand of her hair, twined it around his finger. "I don't worry. I'm the action type. I do what needs to be done."

"Like tonight?" she teased, trying to hide the depth of her emotion. She felt funny on the inside. Tender. Bruised. The sex had been so good, the time with him unreal and yet she knew she was supposed to get up and leave. Walk away. Never look back.

He tugged on the strand of her hair, a sharp painful tug that drew smart tears to her eyes. "This is just the beginning, *bella*."

But it wasn't the beginning, she thought, trying to blink away the tears. It was the end…the end, at least, of what they had here. "So how was I? Good? Bad? Average?" she asked, trying to figure out if he had any idea that she'd been so inexperienced.

"You're asking for a performance assessment?"

She wanted to laugh but couldn't. You didn't just lose your virginity every day. "Yes."

His dark gaze roamed her face. He loosened the tendril of hair wrapped around his finger and smoothed her hair back from her face. "You were good. Very good."

She didn't know why she felt such a strong need to please him. Maybe it was because she wanted him to enjoy the love-making as much as she did. It only seemed right that he felt half the pleasure she'd felt. "You're certain I didn't do anything stupid?"

He rubbed at the worry lines between her brows. "You shouldn't ever worry about such a thing—"

"Women do."

He sighed, shook his head. "Well, you shouldn't. You're gorgeous. You felt unbelievable."

"Good," she answered softly, trying to smile but sadness replaced her anxiety. How odd…this…how bittersweet.

Her first time with Leo.

Her last time with Leo.

Joelle moved closer to him, curving her body against his, not ready to go, not certain she'd ever be really ready. No one had ever held her so close, and yet she knew she'd have to leave soon. Put her clothes on. Head home.

"Stay the night," he said, lightly tracing her spine, his fingertips following the vertebrae until he reached the hollow, the indentation filled with sensitive nerve endings.

"Most men don't like that sort of thing."

"What sort of thing?"

"You know. A woman sleeping over. Commitment."

He laughed. "You know too much about the world, *bambina*. You're only twenty-two."

"I do have older sisters."

"You're close to them?"

"Used to be."

"What happened?"

Her shoulders shifted. "We all grew up."

Leo stirred, and his expression suddenly looked distant. Remote. "I have a conference call scheduled for the morning, but you don't have to leave. I can make the call from the next room."

"Important call?"

Very important, he thought. He'd be calling her grandfather, calling his own father. It wouldn't be a pleasant call.

It wouldn't be a pleasant day at all.

Suddenly Joelle kissed his chest, a little above his nipple, her lips soft and warm against his skin. "Then go to sleep. You'll need your sleep. The last thing you need to do is worry about me."

Joelle woke. It was early, not yet five-thirty in the morning. She dressed quietly in the bathroom, careful not to wake Leo.

She was terrible with goodbyes, had never liked them, but saying goodbye to Leo seemed worse than uncomfortable—it'd be impossible.

After a night in Leo's arms, she felt emotionally spent. She'd known he'd be a one-time only, and while part of her mind was trying to accept it, another part—the part that had yielded to him completely—couldn't let go.

You knew though, there'd be just one night, she lectured herself, hooking her bra. *You knew it was a once-in-a-lifetime fling.* For one night she'd been someone she wasn't supposed to be. She'd been free, warm, passionate. She'd blown caution to the wind, she'd experienced what most women her age were allowed to experience. And that was the beauty of it. For one night she'd been just Joelle and not a princess, and not public property, and not under a microscope.

She'd loved that everything between her and Leo was private. No one would know. No one *needed* to know.

Dressed—except the panties that had gone missing—Joelle dragged her fingers through her hair, pulling the long strands into a loose ponytail. She had a hair elastic in her pocket and she fastened the ponytail at her nape. It was messy, but it worked.

Leaving the bathroom she grabbed her shoes, headed to the living room where she sat down at the elegant writing desk. Using the hotel's pad of paper and pen she tried to scribble Leo a note, but after writing his name, she didn't know what to say.

She stared blankly at the paper. Swallowed. Knew there wasn't much time. *Say something.*

Again she put the pen to paper, hesitated briefly and then just began writing. Soon she'd filled the page. She hoped the words, and thanks, would make sense.

Joelle returned to the bedroom, placed the note on Leo's side of the bed. He was asleep, one muscular arm above his head, his face turned into the crook of his arm. She watched him for a moment, trying to take it all in, wanting to remember the details, the size of him, the shape, the way he seemed to fill not just the bed, but the very room.

She knew she'd never see him again. And yet she also knew he wasn't a man she'd ever forget.

Her veneer of control slipped the moment she walked through the hotel's pretty lobby and exited through the glass front doors.

The sky was still dark except for a slice of steely gray on the horizon and drawing a deep breath, Joelle drew the cool air, heavy with moisture, into her lungs.

She'd thought a night with Leo would answer all her questions, would quell that burning need to know what sex was all about, and yes, the questions had been answered all right. She didn't just like sex. She liked Leo. A lot.

The bell captain assisted her into the back of a waiting taxi and as the cab pulled away from the hotel entrance, Joelle slouched down low on the seat, insides hot, tight, churning.

Don't think about it. Don't think about him. Just don't go there.

Staring blindly out the window, she saw the moment the sun broke through the layers of cloud, turning the sky the faintest shade of pinky gray. And that dusty pink reminded her of Brennan's and the carriage entrance on Royal Street and the feel of Leo's mouth taking hers.

Stop thinking.

Joelle closed her eyes, pressed her thumb to her mouth. Too late for regrets, she told herself. There's nothing you can do about anything now. What's been done has been done. But that didn't help the ache inside her heart.

She'd been prepared for the worst-case scenario. Not the best case. She'd wanted to know what it was like to make love with a real man. To be held in the arms of a man with strength and power, as well as expertise and control.

Well, she'd found out.

Exhaling a little, she pressed her thumb harder against her bottom lip, feeling the softness and soreness, the soreness a memory of a night spent kissing. Making love.

And oh, they'd made love. He'd initiated her into aspects of lovemaking she hadn't known existed, found pleasure in endless varieties of touch. He'd stirred her, tormented her, pleasured her.

Another quick inhale, and Joelle opened her eyes, feeling her chest tighten and burn.

He'd felt so right against her. His skin had felt smooth, sleek, sensuous, warm.

Never had she read anything about the bliss of skin.

Never had anyone spoken to her about the calm even in the eye of the storm.

Never had she suspected such fire, such fierceness, such beauty...and it had been beautiful. It had felt better than anything she'd ever imagined, felt wild, felt strong, felt like a primitive woman. Hungry. Alive. Demanding.

She'd wanted everything from him. She'd wanted to give everything back.

And she knew it wasn't going to be like this with Prince Borgarde. Not even on their best day. And she knew—too late—that no knowledge might actually have been a better thing than some knowledge.

"What's the address again?" the driver asked, breaking the silence.

Joelle saw that they'd reached her neighborhood. "The next block. The brick building on the left side, the one with the black shutters."

Climbing the stairs to her second-floor apartment, Joelle felt the tightness return to her chest, but there wasn't time to do anything but climb into the shower and face the day.

The shower spray pelted warm and hard but it was little relief. She couldn't stop thinking about him. Or the way she felt in his arms. Or the way he'd stretched her out beneath him, his hands on her wrists as he extended her arms high over her head and each time his body dipped into hers she rose with her hips to meet him.

It had been so instinctive. So good. She'd relished the sensation, the pressure, the slow slide of his skin across hers.

The heat of his body…

The strength of his thigh…

The way he kissed her neck just below her jaw…

Reluctantly she turned off the water and stood in the shower, head pressed to the wet tiles, the water dripping off of her.

How had it gone so wrong? Where had she made the mistake? It was going to be easy. She'd thought the whole thing out—analyzed the situation, considered the different scenarios, the various angles it could all play out—and she'd been prepared to suffer a little bruised feelings…a little defeat.

But it hadn't ever crossed her mind that she'd fall for him seriously. She'd thought that good sex or bad sex, she'd at least have experience, but what was happening inside of her had nothing to do with sex at all.

A knock sounded on the outside of the bathroom door. It was Lacey, Joelle's roommate. "Josie, you better hurry. You don't want to miss your flight."

Joelle grabbed a towel. "I'm on my way."

Leo knew Joelle was gone the moment he woke up. He knew before he'd even opened his eyes, and for a few seconds he lay there, arm covering his eyes, seething with frustration.

He wasn't supposed to have slept with her.

He was supposed to have stopped things before they got out of hand.

How the hell had he lost such complete control? He *never* lost control. He was the master of cool, the perfect gentleman as one ex-lover had complained.

Yet he had lost control, and it had been the wrong time, wrong woman, wrong situation altogether.

Livid with himself, Leo threw back the duvet, swung his legs out, and spotting a scrap of white silk—Joelle's panties—between the bisque sheets, he reached down to retrieve them. He froze.

Leo looked up, toward the bedroom door, which stood partway open, and then back down at the bottom sheet. The faint red stain suddenly looked much darker, but that was his imagination. She wasn't a virgin. She couldn't be.

There was no way she was still a virgin, and even if she were, why would she lose her virginity just weeks before her wedding? It didn't make sense. None of it made sense. But his gut felt like he'd swallowed a lead weight.

He'd outlawed the practice of taking virgins years ago, deciding that virgins were for younger men. More sensitive men. Men that still had youth and patience on their side. He had neither. Closing in on thirty-five he'd had women, many women, and he knew what he wanted and what he didn't want.

He'd wanted to prove that Joelle was a fraud…a phony…not the perfect princess the Melio palace had tried to convince him he was getting. So he'd set out to prove them wrong. And he'd seduced her, deliberately seduced her, knowing perfectly well that he was using his expertise with his hands, his body, using his knowledge of a woman's body to bring her to her knees, and yet all the while he'd assumed…

Was so sure…

Exhaling, Leo shook his head, even as little bits of last night returned to him, impressions that had come and gone.

Like her uncertainty at different points, and her body, tight, narrow, tense. It'd been difficult entering her, but he'd put it down to nerves, and yet…

Leo sighed, rubbed his forehead, forced himself to go back, remember.

There'd been resistance, almost a barrier, and he'd wondered briefly, very briefly, if she'd never made love before but she'd said nothing, she'd just reached for him, encouraged him and he—passion blind—had gone.

Had pushed through, pushed into her.

God. The heaviness in his gut seeped through the rest of his body.

Sick on the inside, he climbed from bed and spotted the hotel notepad on the nightstand. A note from Joelle. Cursing, he picked up the notepad, read what she'd written. *Maldezione,* he cursed again.

Leo, I couldn't have asked for a better "first" time, or a more generous lover. Thank you for everything. You were wonderful. Fondly, Josie.

He went cold. Ice cold. His throat worked as he struggled to swallow his shock.

It was a thank-you letter.

She'd left him a thank-you letter. *For taking her virginity.*

Hell.

Hell.

What was she thinking? What was she doing?

The whole thing was too ludicrous for words. He'd never been thanked before for doing this, much less in such a polite manner with the overriding theme being thank you but we're finished. He'd taken her virginity and now she was giving him what amounted to a very polite brush-off.

The ice melted, giving way to poker-hot rage. Dropping the pad on the night table, Leo reached for the phone, then realized he didn't have her home phone number.

Cursing yet again, he slammed the phone back into the cradle, sat down on the edge of the bed, read the note once more.

I couldn't have asked for a better "first" time, or a more generous lover.

Couldn't have asked...

The words went round and round in his brain and his temper grew, threatening to explode. What was she doing? Thinking?

How could she allow herself to be seduced three weeks before her wedding?

It didn't make sense.

She didn't make sense.

He'd thought he'd had her all figured out. Thought she was fast, loose, wanton. She'd been good in bed, but he'd thought it was experience that made her so responsive, not…what? Curiosity? Eagerness? Passion?

The questions screamed at him. Why him, and why last night? Why the seduction three weeks before the wedding? Was she trying to get out of the marriage? And if she wasn't, how could she let a stranger—which is what she thought he was—take what was rightfully her fiancé's?

Rising from the bed, Leo stalked naked to the bathroom. He was angry. Very angry. Last night had been good, and she'd been better than good. She'd been liquid fire in his bed, so hot, so fierce, so everything he'd wanted in a woman, so everything he was sure he'd never find.

But to find it in Joelle, his fiancée, a woman he doubted at every level? How was it possible?

The questions ate at him as he showered, continued to eat him as he shaved and brushed his teeth. He needed answers now. No more games. No more hiding. He only wanted the truth.

Leo felt a savage emotion fill him as he exited the hotel. His driver was waiting outside in the circular brick driveway, the black Mercedes gleaming between lush tropical palm fronds.

''The French Quarter,'' Leo said grimly, climbing in the back seat, giving Joelle's home address.

Traffic was light on Canal Street and they reached her neighborhood in minutes. Leo didn't even wait for the driver to open the door for him. Instead he leapt from the back of the Mercedes sedan.

Leaving him a note. A *note*. A *thank-you* note.

He flashed to the night before, recalled her sweetness in bed, her skin so soft, her taste like honey. She'd felt even better than she'd looked, and when she'd melted into him, against him, her body curved to meet his in all the right ways. She was more erotic than any woman he'd ever known and she was a virgin.

And not just any virgin. His virgin, and what had to be the last of the virgin princesses. And the fact that his princess, his virgin, would give it up to a stranger made him madder than hell.

Leo's gut hurt as he rang her doorbell. So she'd wanted experience? She'd wanted a good ''first time''? Great. He'd show her prowess in bed. He'd show her a lot more than he did last night. He'd teach the little minx everything she'd ever want to know.

And he'd enjoy every goddamn minute of it, too.

He rang the doorbell again. And finally minutes later, the door opened and a young woman peered out, curly hair disheveled, a white bathrobe wrapped about her slender frame. ''Can I help you?'' she asked, hands encircling a ceramic coffee mug.

He glanced up at the house number above the painted door. ''I'm looking for Josie d'Ville.''

''She's gone.''

''To work? The store? Where?'' he demanded roughly, unable to hide his impatience. He had so many questions he had to ask her. So much he needed to understand.

The young woman with the curly red hair smiled apologetically. ''Home.'' The word hung there between them. Lacey's nose wrinkled. ''She left for the airport over an hour ago.''

Four hours later, cabin lights dimmed, Joelle struggled to get comfortable in her narrow uncomfortable seat. She was flying home the way she came—economy class, packed in the back.

It was summer, flights were full and the coach section was crammed with people every direction. Babies wailed. People muttered. The man in front of her had reclined his seat so far it practically rested in her lap.

She tried to plump the flat little pillow, not that the lump of polyester could be called a pillow—and closed her eyes. Goodbye, Leo Fortino, she thought, battling the lump in her throat. Hello, Luigi Borgarde.

CHAPTER SIX

"HE'S arrived, Your Highness." The young uniformed house-maid curtsied just inside Joelle's bedroom door. "I was asked to tell you that Prince Borgarde is waiting with your grandfather now."

"Thank you. I'll be down soon." Joelle tensed as her bedroom door shut, courage flagging.

Why did she wait until the last minute?

Why didn't she tell her grandfather before?

But you wanted to tell him with Prince Borgarde there, she silently argued, you wanted Grandpapa and Luigi to hear it at the same time so there could be no misunderstanding.

There'd be no wedding.

She wasn't going to marry Prince Luigi after all.

Joelle took a deep breath, practiced the words once again. She'd say it flatly, quietly, no emotion in her voice so they'd have no problem hearing her.

There will be no wedding, Grandpapa. I can not marry you, Prince Borgarde.

She'd even prepared for their reaction—steeled herself inwardly for anger, shock. So they'd get upset, they'd talk to her, maybe argue with her, and Grandpapa might even pull her aside, speak to her in that hushed, disappointed tone of his, the tone he'd had when she was small and had broken a rule, but his tone, his disappointment, wouldn't work this time.

She wasn't a child anymore. And she wasn't going to spend the rest of her life trying to make everyone else happy. It had taken that night with Leo to make her understand that no matter how much she wanted to be like Nic and Chantal, she couldn't be them. And maybe they'd accepted arranged marriages, but she couldn't, not if her prospective groom didn't even want to get to know her.

I matter, she whispered, hands growing damp. I'm not just a

princess, I'm a woman. And she couldn't accept marriage to a man who didn't want her for her, who saw her only as means to an end. No, she wanted a man like Leo. A sexy, powerful, passionate man. A man who made her dream.

It's now or never, she thought, catching a glimpse of herself in a mirror above her dressing table—long white crepe dress, a simple gold pendant on a chain around her neck, her hair no longer dark brown but a warm honey shade loosely knotted at her nape. She'd looked just the way Grandpapa liked to see her—pretty, simple, sweet—but she didn't feel simple or sweet. She felt girded for battle.

Joelle exhaled slowly, trying to calm her nerves, and her gaze sought a framed photo on the dressing table. Her mother, the year her first album went platinum. In the color photo her mother, glammed up for a televised award ceremony, was laughing. Young, gorgeous, already hugely successful, she looked like a woman at the top of the world.

Joelle's chest squeezed tight. She envied her mother like mad. *You were lucky, Mum,* she thought, you had everything.

Joelle descended the sweeping staircase, trying not to think, trying not to feel. It was Grandpapa's big party tonight, and everyone near and dear to his heart had been invited, including Luigi Borgarde.

Tonight was their official meet and she found it ironic that he should wait for Grandpapa's party—two weeks before the wedding—to actually meet her. Talk about an eager bridegroom.

She'd known all week she'd see Luigi tonight, had realized with slow but growing conviction that she could never marry Luigi, especially not after what happened in New Orleans.

Perhaps if she hadn't slept with Leo...

But it wasn't even the sex, or losing her virginity that had changed her mind, it was Leo himself. The feelings she harbored.

She'd cared for him. Really, truly cared and since that night nothing had been the same. Nothing within herself felt the same. Leo made love to her so thoroughly, so completely she knew she'd never forget his warmth, or passion.

Entering the Queen's Reception Room, the smallest of the

three palace ballrooms, the white wainscoting and glossy crown molding a crisp contrast to the rich cobalt-blue walls, Joelle searched the room for her grandfather.

And found him. He was standing alone. She felt a tug on her heart.

The five ornate Venetian chandeliers laden with blue and white crystals glittered on King Remi Duccasse in his black evening coat, his thinning hair combed back from his still handsome face.

He was eighty-five and this would be his second birthday without Grandmama.

Joelle swallowed hard, swallowed around the lump swelling in her throat, and as she moved toward Grandpapa, the crowd parted and she realized she'd been mistaken.

He wasn't alone.

Joelle froze, unable to take another step.

Grandpapa was before the massive Titian—Grandmama's favorite masterpiece—and yet his back was to the painting, his attention focused on a guest. She couldn't see the guest's face but the guest was tall—too tall—and his shoulders broad—too broad—and Joelle felt her blood turn to ice.

She knew the guest.

She knew only one man that exuded power. Authority.

Her stomach in a free fall, she could only stand and stare, blood freezing, bones like ice.

For seven days she'd done everything in her power to exonerate Leo Fortino from her memory and yet here he was, standing so casually with her grandfather.

Suddenly the world looked fragile, like one of the delicate blue crystals dangling from the elaborate chandeliers and she realized her curiosity had beaten her this time.

The night she'd spent with Leo in New Orleans wasn't supposed to have left her feeling this way, certainly not so battered. At the time the intimacy felt incredible, but the effort to forget him this past week, the effort it had taken to accept that she couldn't marry Luigi Borgarde, that her feelings for Leo wouldn't allow her to marry another man...a stranger...had drained her.

But part of the detachment, part of the pain, had been accepting that Leo was gone from her life, that Leo would never be part of her life and yet here he was...

Here he stood...

She didn't understand, couldn't grasp how he could suddenly be here, in her world, in her palace, with her grandfather.

But maybe it wasn't really him, she told herself, goose bumps covering her arms, her slim gown feeling sheer, bare. Maybe her need for him was so great that she'd dreamed him up, conjured him like a wizard. He might have the same dark, nearly black hair as the guest, and he might stand the same, but surely there were many Italian, French and Spanish guests, many men with elegance. Sophistication.

Move, she told herself, realizing guests were glancing at her, watching. She forced herself to take a step forward and yet her legs were heavy, her body like lead.

She reached Grandpapa's side, saw her grandfather look up, smile, saw the guest start to turn and shock washed through her in waves.

Leo.

It *was* Leo, and he was looking at her, waiting for her to speak, yet she couldn't make a sound.

What was he doing here? And why did he look so angry with her?

Emotion clawed at her, overwhelming her. She opened her mouth to say his name but no sound came out.

And still he said nothing.

Oh God. This was bad, such a mess. Obviously he now knew who she was, knew about her engagement and from the look on his face, from that hard stony silence, she knew he was livid.

She'd thought of him endlessly this past week, and it had never crossed her mind that she could meet him here, that they'd meet like this. It was too much. Her nerves sparked, hot, sharp, and tears filled her eyes.

''Joelle, love.'' Her grandfather's voice drew her gaze to his.

She could barely see her grandfather through the tears filming her eyes.

She blinked, pressed her nails to her palms, bit down on the inside of her lip to make the tears dry quickly.

She could see Grandpapa now. He was leaning heavily on his cane, but his blue eyes smiled warmly.

She forced a smile to her lips, moved closer to his side. "Happy Birthday, Grandpapa," she whispered, rising on tiptoe to kiss his papery cheek. He smelled of soap and lather and an old-fashioned aftershave, one that smelled of spice, musk and rose.

"Thank you, my darling." King Remi slid an arm briefly around her waist, turning her to face the guest. "And Joelle, love, you must know who this is."

Her breath caught in her throat. Yes, she thought, fighting the wild beating of her heart, she knew who he was. He looked gorgeous, too, dressed in formal evening wear, his white shirt a stunning contrast to the bronze of his skin. She stole a glance up into his face, trying to read something in his expression but he'd closed himself off, leaving just the externals, the dark hair, the hard high cheekbones, the full mouth with the indentation in the lower lip.

And just like that she remembered the feel of his mouth on hers, remembered the way he kissed, he touched and she burned hot, burned feverishly.

This is why you can't marry Luigi, she thought, this is why you can't give yourself to another man. You've already given your heart to Leo.

Not that he seemed very happy to see her.

But Leo couldn't be her first thought. She had to remember what she'd come downstairs to do—to say. She had to deal with Grandpapa and Prince Luigi Borgarde first and then she could think about Leo.

"She's beautiful, isn't she?" Grandpapa said, giving her waist another squeeze.

"She is," Leo agreed, but his voice came out rough, raw, and her head jerked up, their gazes locking.

Joelle couldn't read Leo's expression—his features so hard, so stony they reminded her of a glacier—but that glacier cold sent alarm rushing through her.

Head spinning, she looked away, took a breath, tried to focus. But why was he upset? What reason did he have to be unhappy with her? He was the one who said it was just sex, only sex, and she'd agreed. She hadn't asked for any promises. She'd made no demands…

Her fingers curled instinctively, her heavy engagement ring pinching. Did Grandpapa know about her night with Leo? Was he aware of what had happened?

No, she answered immediately, Grandpapa wasn't. Grandpapa wouldn't be smiling if he knew. Grandpapa was as old-fashioned as his aftershave.

A waiter materialized with silver tray.

"Ah, excellent," her grandfather said, sounding infinitely pleased. "Champagne." He took a flute, handed one to Joelle, another to Leo.

"A toast to celebrate my granddaughter's safe return," he added, lifting his own flute. "I couldn't ask for a better birthday present. It's wonderful to have you home, my darling."

Her throat worked. She struggled to smile. "Thank you, Grandpapa." She clinked glasses with her grandfather, studiously avoiding Leo altogether and yet she felt his attention, felt his intense energy.

Why did she ever go to New Orleans? Why did she ever want passion? What was it about fire and ice that appealed?

She'd had the fire. Now she was getting the ice.

Joelle forced herself to drink, hiding the fact that she felt like a sheet of ice under intense pressure. She was cracking, would soon shatter.

Meeting Leo like this was cruel. Brutally unfair.

She'd wanted to see him again, but not here, not at Grandpapa's party, not when she was still engaged to someone else.

"Ready for the wedding?" Grandpapa asked, grinning, and for a moment he looked exactly like a kid—boyish, excited, eager.

"Grandpapa," she choked, flushing.

He didn't appear to hear. "Just two weeks from now. It'll be here before you know it."

''Please, not now, Grandpapa.'' She wobbled in her shoes, her strappy high heels barely able to hold her.

''No need to be nervous. Prince Borgarde won't rush you. He knows you're young, inexperienced—''

She grabbed his arm, held tight, interrupting him. Her grandfather looked down into her face. ''What's wrong?'' he asked.

She couldn't speak. Fresh ice water sluiced through her veins. She shook her head, removed her numb hand, certain she'd drop her flute any moment.

King Remi patted her shoulder. ''Everything's going to be fine, dear. Every bride feels nervous—''

''We have to talk about the wedding,'' she said quickly, her voice pitched low. ''I wanted to talk to you and Prince Borgarde at the same time, but since he's not here—''

''Not here?'' her grandfather repeated in confusion. ''What are you saying, Joelle?''

''That I can't marry Prince Borgarde.'' Joelle felt so hot and yet she'd begun to shiver in her simple Grecian-style gown. ''And I don't have the feelings—''

''Feelings?'' her grandfather interrupted yet again. ''I don't understand a word you're saying, Joelle. Of course you don't have feelings yet for Leo, you've only just met.''

''You mean Luigi,'' she corrected hoarsely.

Her grandfather tapped his cane impatiently. ''Who is Luigi?''

Joelle knew they were drawing attention and she lowered her voice. ''Prince Borgarde. Luigi Borgarde.''

''There's no Luigi, only Leo,'' her grandfather's voice thundered and Joelle saw guests glance their way.

''What?''

''There's no Luigi,'' her grandfather repeated. ''I don't know where you got this Luigi from.''

She suddenly couldn't breathe, couldn't get air.

''And there will be a wedding,'' her grandfather persisted.

The room swam. The words floated inside Joelle's head. What was Grandpapa saying? He couldn't possibly mean…he wasn't intending…Leo wasn't Luigi…

''I don't feel very well,'' she said vaguely, legs starting to buckle.

Her grandfather didn't hear her; he was lifting his flute, proposing a toast. "To the future," King Remi said, lifting his glass even higher.

She knew Grandpapa's hearing wasn't what it used to be, knew he turned down his hearing aid for noisy functions like this, but his gesture felt unusually cruel considering the circumstances.

"To the future," Leo echoed, raising his own flute, and in the light the silver gleamed, blinding her.

Joelle could see nothing but the tiny beads of moisture glistening on the lower half of the silver flute.

The future...

Her future...

She shook her head, dizzy, disoriented. Nothing made sense. She felt sick all the way through. What she needed was a chair. Someplace to sit, just to get her bearings back.

"I'm feeling—" She broke off, blinked, tried to swallow and a hand touched her elbow.

"Faint?" The hard male voice concluded for her. Leo's voice. Leo's sarcasm.

Yes.

His touch scorched her, his touch so familiar and yet so painful. His touch having turned her inside out a week ago and now he was here, and standing with her grandfather, and making toasts and saying words that confused her.

He couldn't be.

He couldn't be.

He couldn't—

Weakly she looked up, met his gaze, saw the cold fury in his eyes, saw the lines etched at his mouth, saw that she had somehow made a huge mistake.

Fingers numb, she lost her grip, dropped her glass.

The silver flute bounced, a loud noisy clatter, champagne sloshing out, drenching Leo's trouser.

"I'm sorry. I'm so sorry." Torn between relief and shame, Joelle fumbled for a napkin and knelt down. Reaching for the fallen flute, she began mopping up the champagne pooling on the marble floor.

"Leave it, my dear," Grandfather said, his cane moving forward, bumping her hands. "The staff will do that."

She shook her head, body hot, heat scorching through her. "Someone might fall," she choked, her hands trembling like mad as she soaked up more champagne, the linen napkin sopping wet. Oh my God, oh my God…

But Leo wouldn't let her remain on the ground. He wrapped his hand around her upper arm, pulled her none too gently to her feet. "You'll ruin your gown."

Her white gown was the least of her worries but Leo didn't let go, his fingers still wrapped snugly around her arm, close to her elbow.

"I'm sorry," she repeated for lack of anything better to say. "I'm sorry. I made a mess."

"Depends on your definition of a mess," Leo answered, and something in his voice drew her head up.

He was smiling down at her but it wasn't a real smile. She knew him, knew how he smiled. Leo was livid. Beyond livid.

His fury put fresh terror in her heart. "You knew," she choked, her voice dropping, cracking. "You knew in New Orleans."

"Yes."

He sounded so calm, so controlled and she held his gaze a moment longer, sick, so sick at heart.

He'd known and he'd pretended he hadn't.

He'd seduced her knowing she'd be his wife.

He'd played her as if she were nothing. No one. Certainly no one of consequence.

Her hand tightened helplessly around the damp linen napkin, squeezing champagne drops onto the floor. "I trusted you." Her voice, husky with emotion, broke. "I thought…"

Leo arched a brow. "What?"

Grandfather's cane impatiently tapped the marble floor. "What's this? What are you saying, Joelle? Speak up, my dear, you know I don't hear as well as I used to."

"Forgive us, Your Highness." It was Leo who spoke, and although he raised his voice to be heard clearly, his tone was deferential. "But Princess Joelle was expressing her displeasure with me. She claims she didn't know me in New Orleans."

"Not know you?" the king repeated sharply. "What does that mean?"

"It means, Your Highness, she didn't recognize me. Didn't realize I was—" Leo shot Joelle a sharp glance "—her prince."

Joelle's jaw dropped even as spots danced before her eyes. This was madness, utter madness.

But her grandfather's cane was tapping the marble floor with short irritable bursts. "But of course she knew you! She saw you last week in America. You did say you'd had a chance to get to spend time together in New Orleans."

No.

Joelle tried to protest, tried to speak and yet nothing came out. No sound, no breath. Nothing at all.

"You don't remember Leo?" King Remi turned on Joelle, his expression almost fierce, bushy white eyebrows furrowing. "It's only been a week. How can you not remember him?"

"I—" She forced air into her lungs, forced the air out again. "I—remember."

"So what's the problem?"

Hot tears stung the back of her eyes. Her heart felt like glass splintering in a thousand pieces. "There's no problem."

"She's just overwhelmed," Leo said, smiling down at her, the same frightening predatory smile of earlier. "Perhaps the princess and I need some time alone."

A shudder raced through her. Time alone with Leo? Time alone after what he did to her? Time alone after the hurt he'd inflicted? No. Never. *Never.* "I don't think so," she answered stiffly, drawing as far from him as possible. "It's Grandfather's birthday, I don't want to leave him now—"

"Nonsense." Grandfather's cane banged once. "You two obviously need time together. Go out, get some fresh air, but return when dinner is served. You're sitting with me. Prince Borgarde is my guest of honor."

Joelle made a last grab for her grandfather but he was already moving on, leaving her alone with Leo.

There was a moment of heavy silence, the kind that blankets all sound and space.

"Surprised?" Leo murmured at last.

Her heart pounded fiercely. She knew him. She didn't know him. He was a stranger, but he wasn't. How was it possible for so much to have happened between them, and yet in the space of things, it was so little? One night. One brief fling…

But it had never been a fling, not to her. She'd felt something for him, felt something real, and yet she saw now it had been a game to him. He was trapping her, manipulating her…sex was just a test of sorts.

Sick, horrified, she turned away, dragged a shallow breath.

"I hate you," she stammered, aware that he watched her, aware that he was standing close, too close, aware that everything she'd felt was false…a betrayal.

"You didn't hate me when we were in bed."

Bastard. Tears filled her eyes and she took another painful, shallow breath. Her lungs were on fire and yet the fire was nothing compared to the blistering of her heart.

He, Leo, had betrayed her.

Holding back the tears, she looked at him, forced herself to really look at him, a slow inspection from the elegant lapel of his black tuxedo jacket to the crisp white bow tie to the hard square chin. Then she could look no further. It hurt too much. "You knew who I was all along?" she whispered.

"Yes."

She took a step away, cold panic giving way to an even colder anger. "You lied to me."

"No."

She pressed her nails into her palms. "You said you were Leonardo Marciano Fortino—"

"I am."

"What happened to *Luigi?*"

"As your grandfather said, there's no Luigi."

"But you—"

"*Your* mistake."

Her heart pounded, she could barely swallow. This was so

impossible, so incredible. "And the Prince of Borgarde title? Just a convenient omission in New Orleans?"

He shrugged dismissively. "You didn't know my name. I wasn't about to force it down your throat."

"Oh, please!"

"Please what, *bella?* What does your little heart desire now?"

His anger carried a sexual overtone and somehow the anger melted some of the ice in her, reminding her of the heat between them. The passion.

"Surely you desire something?" he persisted, and this time his voice caressed her, tormented her.

He was baiting her, hooking her, trapping her just as he had in New Orleans. But this time it wasn't for a one-night affair. This time it was forever.

And funny how a day ago, even a week ago, she would have been thrilled by the prospect of marriage to Leo, it was different now, now that she knew the truth. He'd deceived her. Betrayed her trust.

Her eyes felt like boiled onions. They burned and burned. "I'm not marrying you."

"Don't be foolish."

"Foolish? I'll tell you what's foolish. This. Us. It's off. The engagement. The wedding." She grabbed at the engagement ring weighing her finger down, struggled to pull the massive marquis diamond surrounded by rubies off her fourth finger. "There's no way I'll go through this now."

His hand covered hers, hard. "Leave it on."

"No." She struggled despite his hand, struggled despite the tears filling her eyes. "You tricked me. You let me think…" She drew a jagged breath. "You let me believe…"

"What?" His fingers squeezed around her own, and holding her, he drew her toward him, closer, so close he could bend his head down and whisper in her ear. "That everything was good and beautiful? That you were sexy and insatiable in my bed?"

"Be quiet." Tears clung to her lashes. She couldn't cry here, couldn't cry in public, especially not in front of one hundred of her grandfather's guests.

"You're the one speaking loudly."

"You're the one being cruel."

People were turning, looking at them, and Leo didn't even bother to smile reassurance.

"As your grandfather said, I think we could use some air." And still holding her hand, Leo tugged her after him, through the crowded blue ballroom, out the tall French doors to the stone terrace outside.

It was a warm night, almost too warm and as soon as she could, Joelle shook Leo off. She hated him. Hated herself. Hated that she felt so much even at a moment like this.

"You can't make me marry you." Her hand grabbed at the balustrade, needing the support. "This might be an arranged marriage, but it was consensual."

"Just like our sex."

Oh, that was low. Her stomach twisted and yet she lifted her chin, trying to cling to what was left of her pride. "What happened that night has nothing to do with us."

"No?"

"It was just…a…one off. Something separate. Something that wasn't—isn't—going to happen again."

"I think you're confused, Joelle…Josie…whoever you are, whoever you want to be. Because it was you and me in New Orleans, you and me at dinner. You and me in the hotel room. You and me in bed."

"No. You were a stranger. You were someone safe—"

"Safe? *Bella,* you obviously don't know me."

His husky inflection made her nerves scream. No wonder she felt so sick inside. Her heart raced madly, her muscles coiled, ready to spring. "Don't threaten me."

The corner of his mouth lifted yet there was no humor in his eyes. "I'm not threatening you." His eyes held hers. "Yet."

God, she was naïve, Leo thought, watching Joelle continue to back away from him, her left hand trailing along the carved limestone balustrade.

She had no idea what he'd been through this past week, no idea how hard it'd been to restrain himself, make himself wait. His first inclination had been to hop on the next plane, confront her immediately, demand an explanation from her. But he knew his temper was too hot. He knew he needed the time, knew she needed the time, too.

So he gave her the week. Allowed her to settle back in. Get adjusted to life in the palace again. But he was done being patient, done waiting.

He wanted answers. Josie had broken every cardinal rule, and he had to understand why. "You slept with me."

"You noticed?"

"Not funny."

"Not trying to be."

"I want a real answer. Why did you sleep with me?"

Her eyes flashed, the blue green darkening in the moonlight. "Because I wanted to."

"Not good enough."

"Too bad. It's all you're getting."

She was hell on wheels. Difficult, temperamental, headstrong. And running scared.

"Wrong," he murmured, knowing he had the upper hand. "I already got more. I got the very thing you never wanted to give me." She blushed, blood suffusing her face from collarbone to hairline. She knew she was cornered.

"That's what upsets you, doesn't it?" he continued. "You thought you were tossing away your virginity, and instead you handed it to me."

"So I made a mistake."

He heard the catch in her voice. "Why then? Why me? You'd never been intimate with a man before."

She took a quick breath, her fingers gripping the railing. "Don't sound so shocked. You saw me at the club. You saw the leather pants, the kohl eyeliner. You saw me perform, and you assumed what you wanted to assume—that I was bad. That I had been around the block before—not just once, but many times." The corner of her mouth lifted in a small, hurt smile. "And you were wrong."

She leaned forward, eyes flashing, revealing the depth of her hurt and anger. "I wasn't wicked and wanton. I was curious, yes. And so I slept with you. Big deal."

He watched her stalk away, across the terrace to stand at the wall overlooking the sea. In the background the lights of Porto shone, the old stone and tile houses hugging the terraced mountain slope.

Joelle braced herself on the balcony railing, the June evening warm, the gentlest of breezes catching at the hem of her long dress, the fabric flowing straight from waist to her feet in the soft folds of a Grecian gown. With her soft honey hair knotted at her nape and the gold pendant hanging low, between her breasts, Leo thought she looked like the mythological goddess Diana outraged she'd been caught bathing by the hunter Actaeon. The goddess had a temper.

"Big deal," he repeated mockingly, feeling momentarily sorry for all the mortal men who angered beautiful Diana.

"Do go away," Joelle shot at him over her shoulder even as voices were heard from below.

Leo glanced over the railing, spotted a couple of the palace secret service patrolling the perimeter of the garden. He raised his hand in silent acknowledgment, then took a seat on the edge of the balustrade. "I'm not going anywhere until we get this resolved."

"Resolve what?" She turned, faced him. "That I was more inexperienced than you thought? That you were the first man to sleep with me? That I didn't want to be a virgin when I married? Well, you figured it out."

Interesting. "Why didn't you want to be a virgin?"

"You're not, are you?"

"Of course not."

"Exactly."

He studied her profile, the small straight nose, dark arch of eyebrow, the full soft mouth. She was beautiful, far more beautiful than he'd thought last week. And the photos the magazines published didn't do her justice, either. Her beauty was too warm, too lush for film.

He found himself responding, just as he had last week in New Orleans.

She did something to him that no one had ever done. She made him feel things, want things, and it felt natural. Comfortable. She'd made him feel amazing, made him hungrier, harder, more giving, more demanding that ever before. And he hadn't been particularly gentle when he took her, either. He'd been burning up, burning for her and if he hadn't seen the sheet, and read her note, he would have never known she was so inexperienced. Especially as everything between them had felt so right.

She'd felt like his. Like she was made for him.

Joelle had been unrestrained, completely without inhibitions, stunningly sexy in her innocence. She'd been curious about everything, interested and open and so damn responsive.

Maybe that's what made him so crazy. She'd been so warm, so passionate and yet she was an ice cube now.

Her haughty aloofness put his teeth on edge. "You don't just sleep with a man, and not tell him this sort of thing."

"Obviously I didn't know I needed to make a big announcement. Thanks, Leo. I'll know better next time."

"You won't be a virgin next time."

CHAPTER SEVEN

JOELLE saw Leo darken, a dark flush spreading beneath the beautiful gold tones of his olive complexion. His high-handed arrogance made her see red. "I can't believe you're making such a big deal about the hymen anyway," she flashed. "It's just a little bit of tissue. Completely irrelevant to the scheme of things."

Leo swore beneath his breath, his hand snaking out, clamping hard on her arm. "I can't believe you actually talk this way. You'd make your poor grandmother faint."

She tried yanking her arm free. "You never met her, you know nothing about her, and even if you did, she's not around anymore, is she?"

"No. But I am." And instead of letting her go, he pulled her against him, drawing her in so hard and fast she felt her breasts crush against his chest, felt the strength of his hips against her tummy, the press of his thighs along hers and she shuddered at the intimate contact, vividly reminded of everything that had happened between them that night.

He threaded his fingers through her knot in her hair, his palm against the back of her head. "Why did you leave before I woke?" He demanded, tilting her face up to his.

"I told you," she answered, trying to desperately hang on to her anger, to not give in to fear, much less desire even though her blood felt thick and slow, so thick and slow that her womb contracted, making her painfully aware that he'd changed everything, made her feel things, want things, she'd never wanted before.

"In a note."

"I could have gone without leaving a note."

"You thanked me for taking your virginity."

Her face felt hot, and with his dark eyes resting on her face her lips felt strange, tingly, very sensitive. "I said I'd appreciated your generosity, and that you were a perfect partner for my first time.''

''And you signed it, Fondly, Josie.'' His fingers tightened, his body pressed against hers. She could feel the steady pounding of his heart through his chest, drumming straight through her.

''Fondly.'' He chewed on the word, furious. *''Fondly.''*

His head suddenly lowered and his mouth covered hers. ''You're going to pay for that, Josie.''

His kiss scorched her, the anger and emotion burning her, and then the anger dissolved, melting into a passion far hotter, far more dangerous than anger could ever be.

It was wrong that she should respond, wrong that her pulse changed, her heartbeat losing speed, and momentum. Already she felt as if she belonged to him, and he knew it, too. He knew he was in control here, merely biding his time, waiting until the moment was right to take her. Possess her.

And fool that she was, she still wanted to be possessed by him. She wanted the hard pressure, the rigid tension, the curve of his lip, the flare of his nostril. He was primal and male—he was hot, hard, everything big and fierce.

But he—and the passion—threatened her.

Joelle pulled away, hard, her heart still racing. She took a breath, and then another. Head turned, she looked to the blue ballroom. ''They've all gone.''

''We should go in.''

We. Like they were a couple. Like they were already meant to be together. Smiling bitterly, she shook her head. ''I'm not going in. Give my apologies to my grandfather, tell him whatever you want…that I was sick, had a headache.''

He laughed. ''I won't tell him anything of the sort. We told him we'd be there, and we will be.''

''I can't do this, Leo. I can't go in—''

''Too bad. Your grandfather expects us.''

The commanding crack of his voice was like a slap in the face. She looked at him, into his eyes, saw the emotion smoldering there, male pride and arrogance, and realized that whatever she'd tried to do in New Orleans, whatever privacy she'd desired, had failed.

Her night with Leo wasn't personal, or private. Her night with Leo had unwittingly made her his property.

"I'm not going to marry you," she said flatly. She'd spent a week trying to battle her emotions, riding a roller coaster of longing and need only to come crashing into this reality. "And if you think I'm going to go inside, play some part, pretend to be your happy little fiancée then you've got another think coming."

"Not even you would be so selfish as to ruin your grandfather's birthday."

"He'll survive," she answered, cringing at her callousness.

"Will he? He's been very ill these past few months—"

"That's not so."

Leo's smile was pure derision. "How would you know, *bella*? You weren't even here."

"Don't you dare lecture me. You're the stranger here. You don't belong here. This is my home, my family—"

"Then if you're such the devoted granddaughter, why didn't you return when your grandfather had pneumonia? Why didn't you jump on a plane the night they thought he wouldn't pull through?"

Joelle's heart stopped. Leo had to be making this up, trying to hurt her. "He was never that sick."

"He nearly died."

The words pierced her, cutting so deeply that tears filled her eyes. "You're exaggerating."

"I wish I was, but I'm telling you the truth. You see, *bambina*, unlike you, I was here. I sat next to his bed in the hospital, held his hand when they didn't think he'd survive the night."

"No one told me. No one called."

"Did *you* ever call?"

"There were conversations."

"How many?"

The breeze felt cold now and it tugged at her hair. With an unsteady hand she tucked a loose tendril behind one ear. It was none of his business, she didn't have to explain to him, didn't have to explain anything. "I was taking a year off..." How insane it sounded now, how impossible to defend but he'd never understand her grief over Grandmama's death, never understand what the loss had done to her. "But of course I would have come, I would have returned if I knew."

Leo's features contorted contemptuously. "He's old. He lost his wife a year ago. And you needed a holiday?"

"It's not like that."

"No?" He looked away, his mouth compressed, expression hard, unforgiving. "You don't know what you have," he said quietly, fighting for control. "You won't know what you have until it's gone."

Maybe, she thought, but he didn't know everything. He didn't know how the grief had beaten her, worn her down, taken everything from her. He didn't know how she couldn't function in the public eye, couldn't make it to church or the cemetery without the press writing things about her, writing about the poor broken little princess.

And he could say what he wanted about her loyalty, about her devotion, but the only reason she'd agreed to the arranged marriage in the first place was because she wanted to see Grandpapa smile again. She'd wanted to make him happy. Even if it killed her. "Why are you doing this? What do you want?"

"What do I want?" He laughed, low, disbelieving. "I want you, *bella,* to do the right thing."

"And what is the right thing?"

"Honoring the commitments you've made."

Dinner was served in the middle ballroom, the ballroom painted the palest shade of coral, the ceiling cream, sconces gilded, chandeliers extravagant, dripping with gold and crystals. Beautiful soft frescoes in aqua and apricot filled the arched spaces above each of the windows, the frescoes romantic depictions of gods and goddesses playing violin, harp, and more.

Joelle was conscious of the attention she and Leo drew as they took their places next to Grandfather at the head table. Chantal and Nic were seated at the same table but they were at opposite ends, too far for conversation.

A butler moved forward to hold Joelle's chair but Leo waved him off, preferring to do the courtesy himself.

Every head seemed to turn, every pair of eyes seemed to fix

on them, and in the warm flickering candlelight Joelle felt herself blush. ''Everyone's staring,'' she whispered, shrinking on the inside from all the attention.

''They're just curious,'' Leo answered, bending low, his mouth brushing her ear even as he scooted her chair forward. ''They're wondering why we're late, imagining what we were doing.''

She looked up, caught the glint in his eyes, felt her belly flip inside out.

Sex, the word whispered inside her. She only had to look at him and think darkness, silence, alone.

Grandfather waited for Leo to sit. ''I like him,'' Grandpapa said to Joelle, covering her hand with his. ''Leo is good. And good for you.''

Joelle bit her tongue. Grandpapa didn't know the half of it. She'd straighten him out—eventually. But Leo was right. It wouldn't be fair to upset him now, tonight, not when he was so glad that his family, his grown-up granddaughters, were all gathered under the same roof again.

Apparently they'd missed the soup course. The salads were now arriving, small colorful plates of beet and goat cheese Neapolitan drizzled with a citron and wasabi vinaigrette.

Joelle glanced at her plate, wished she were anywhere but here. She didn't have the stomach for this, didn't know how she was supposed to sit next to Leo for the next hour or more pretending everything was good, that their marriage was on track.

There'd be no marriage. She'd have to pretend for tonight, but come tomorrow, she'd sit Grandpapa down and set the record straight.

Salad plates cleared, waiters presented lobster and steamed saffron-coconut rice.

''Enjoying your dinner?'' Leo asked politely. His thigh brushed hers beneath the table, once, and again, letting her know the touch hadn't been accidental.

She moved her leg further away. ''Don't touch me,'' she said quietly, smiling through gritted teeth.

''You loved it last week.''

''That was last week.''

''So fickle.''

''No.'' She saw her grandfather look up, saw the furrow between his brows. ''Dear,'' she added, forcing herself to soften her expression, manufacture warmth in her eyes. ''You could have saved us both a lot of trouble if you'd just told me who you were.''

''You wouldn't have slept with me?''

Heat burned in her cheeks. She kept her gaze down. ''No.''

''Why ever not?''

She nudged the lobster with the tip of her fork. ''I didn't want forever, dear. It was just supposed to be a one-night stand.''

For a moment he said nothing. He took a bite. Chewed. Swallowed. Reached for his wine. And when he looked at her, she knew why he'd waited. He was hot. Furious. Features flinty. ''One-night stand?''

Joelle suppressed a sigh. She really didn't want to do this with him, not here, not now, not with one hundred and fifty prominent European friends and royals surrounding them.

That night they'd shared last week had been good. Unbelievably erotic. Everything a first time should be. But partly what had made it so powerful, so sensual was the fact that it was an escape, a night of fantasy. There would be no morning after. No awkward dressing in front of each other. No uncomfortable goodbyes.

She had a fantasy, a fantasy of love, a fantasy of passion, and it was hers, hers alone. ''Don't make me be blunt,'' she said softly, stabbing at the lobster, entreating him to oblige her, remember civility.

His gaze held hers. His jaw tightened. ''Oh, please be blunt.''

His tone, quiet, still managed to cut all the way through her. They were destroying it, she thought. Taking the memory of what it had been, how it'd been, and turning it into something ugly. But she didn't want the ugly. He'd been so generous in bed, he'd taken her as much as he'd given to her and it worked, that raw sensuality, that hunger. She'd loved being wanted like that, loved knowing that sex could not just be intense, but deeply fulfilling. ''Don't ruin what we had.''

''It's already ruined for me.''

She flinched. Her gaze held his. He was furious. Seething. "It was nothing personal, Leo. It was never supposed to be anything more than one night. I never wanted more from you than that."

"Good. That could have been personal."

His taunting tone brought a rush of heat to her cheeks. She stared determinedly at the floral arrangement on their table. "This shouldn't be a big deal. We both got what we wanted. I got experience. You got to test the wares."

"That's not why I slept with you."

She swallowed, and turning her head, she stared hard at him, stared deep into his eyes. "Are you sure?"

She didn't know how they got through the rest of the evening. It was endless, felt endless, felt as if time had stopped and they were simply reliving the same minute over and over.

Dinner dragged on. Then finally they were excused and all moved to the third ballroom, the chandeliers dimmed in the large white and gold room. Ornate gold mirrors hung on the walls, reflecting light and an orchestra played Grandfather's favorite music—Bach and Mozart, with Chopin and even Gershwin sprinkled in.

Thank God Leo didn't ask her to dance. Joelle tried to put as much distance between them, finding refuge in her sisters and their husbands.

"How was it coming home after a year away?" Nic asked, leaning against her Sultan, suppressing a yawn. She was pregnant again, fairly far along and everyone waged odds that it would be another son, but Nic and her sons lived in Baraka, were needed in Baraka. It was odd, but Baraka's future depended on Nic just as Melio's future now depended on Joelle.

"Good," Joelle answered, catching Leo's eye. She averted her head. She didn't want to look at him. Didn't want anything to do with him.

She forced her thoughts elsewhere, forced herself to go back a week, remember her trip home, recalling the moment the jet swooped low over Porto. Porto, the capital city, was one of the most picturesque cities in all the Mediterranean.

She loved Melio and its smaller sister island, Mejia. Several years ago Melio and Mejia were very nearly split. Mejia would have reverted to French rule, and Melio to Spanish rule if the royal Ducasse family couldn't pay their taxes and trade agreements, which is how the first of the arranged marriages came to be.

Nic's marriage to the Sultan of Baraka had saved their country but everyone knew with Chantal in Greece, married to a commoner, it was Joelle's responsibility to provide the necessary heirs. Laws could be rewritten, Chantal's or Nic's children could possibly inherit, but ideally it should be Joelle who would assume the throne, Joelle who'd co-rule with her husband.

And flying home a week ago, Joelle had told herself Melio was worth it. Melio was still such a magical place, the elegant island kingdom had everything—pretty cities, small villages nestled in protective mountains, rocky cliffs, sandy beaches, pastures, crops and fruit groves—she'd felt certain she was making the right sacrifice.

But now...now...

Joelle shook her head, bit her tongue, anger filling her. The way she felt now she'd rather see every Melio law rewritten than marry Leo Fortino, Prince of Borgarde.

"And you, Leo," Chantal said, glancing curiously at Joelle's fiancée. "You've spent a great deal of time here in the past few months. Any doubts about your ability to make Melio home?"

Leo looked at Joelle, smiled coolly. "None."

An hour later he was walking her up the staircase to her room. "This isn't necessary," she said stiffly, conscious of Leo just a step behind her. She felt as if he were her jailor instead of last week's lover. "There's no reason to leave the party—"

"You were tired."

His politeness grated on her. Joelle dragged her teeth together. "I don't need an escort. I've lived here all my life. I know the way to my room."

"But you're my intended. Everyone expects us to need a moment alone, a chance to say good-night properly."

He sounded positively smirky. It was all she could do not to push him down the stairs. "But no one's looking now. You can go."

''And leave a job half-done? Never. I'll see you all the way up, safely to your door.''

''Are you going to lock me in, too?'' she asked sweetly. Having reached the top landing she turned to face him but he didn't smile.

''If I had a key, I'd do it.''

He wasn't kidding. ''You think I'll run away?'' Mockingly she put her hands on her hips, trying to make a joke out of it, trying to laugh, but her voice came out strangled.

''You've run away once—''

''When?''

''Your year in New Orleans.''

''That wasn't running away.''

''No, that was just sneaking out when everyone was still asleep.'' His dark green eyes smoldered. ''Rather like the trick you pulled last week. Leaving before dawn, scribbling a little note.'' He paused, assessed her, his expression critical. ''You're rather good at that, aren't you? Leaving little goodbye notes.''

She ground her teeth together, arms dropping to her sides. ''Twenty years of education,'' she said, thinking that actually, running away wasn't such a bad idea after all. She had no intention of marrying him—not now, not ever. And if he wouldn't accept her refusal to his face, then perhaps he'd have to accept it when she was no longer available.

At her bedroom door, she tried to squeeze into her room without letting him in. But Leo wasn't about to be shut out. ''The problem, *Josie,* is that you have too many.''

He held the door firmly, his strength superior to hers, and simply waited for her to give up trying to lock him out.

It took a few seconds but she finally gave up, abruptly letting go of the doorknob, entering her room with a frustrated sigh. Her shoulders, neck, back tensed as she heard Leo follow behind. Why couldn't he just go away? He'd ruined everything, destroyed even the lovely memory of the night they'd shared.

''What now?'' she demanded, throwing herself down on the pale green velvet chaise at the foot of the bed.

''There's no master plan, *bella.*''

No man had ever been in her bedroom before. Actually few

people outside the immediate family had been here. Her room had always been her haven.

She watched Leo examine her room, first the furniture—including the antique canopy bed hung with green velvet panels the color of tender grass—then the photographs hanging on two of her four walls.

The photos were virtually all of her mother, and they'd once lined her father's study. Years ago the framed photos had come down. Joelle didn't even remember when it'd happened. She'd been away at school at the time. She just remembered coming home and seeing a massive canvas of Greek ruins in the morning mist hanging where the photographs of her mother used to be.

Joelle had rescued what she could, hung them up in her bedroom even though Grandmama didn't approve. Grandmama had claimed that Joelle's bedroom had begun to look like a shrine and it wasn't healthy, but Joelle—who usually acquiesced to Grandmama's wishes—didn't this time.

Leo picked up one of the framed photos from her pretty dressing table. It was a small photo, a candid shot, in black and white. A photographer from a magazine had caught her mother half-dressed, leaning close to the mirror, applying her stage makeup. Star's hair was still pinned up, but the eyebrows were dark, the lips outlined and painted, and yet despite the makeup, the hint of bare breasts, Star looked young. Innocent. Like the girl she must once have been.

"She's beautiful here," Leo said, studying the photo intently.

Joelle nodded, unable to look at Leo. Mother was always beautiful, but she knew what he meant. To become Star, her mother had reinvented herself, losing the small town girl who'd known only hard times and hunger to become special. Mythical. But in that photo, taken at the height of Star's popularity, you could see the small town girl in the mirror, the stigma of being poor and white in the South in her eyes, the memory of the river in the curve of her lips. Her mother had succeeded against all odds.

Her mother had done the unthinkable.

Joelle circled her knees more tightly. "It's my favorite picture.'' Her voice came out scratchy. ''When I look at that picture I almost think I know her.''

Leo looked up at her. ''Chantal said you're obsessed with her, that you've been obsessed with her since you were a teenager.''

A lump formed in her throat and for a moment Joelle didn't trust herself enough to speak. That was unfair of Chantal—if Chantal indeed said such a thing. She grabbed a loose pillow from the chaise. ''When did she say that?''

''The night I stayed at the hospital with your grandfather.''

The night wonderful Leo became part of the family. ''And so she confided in you,'' she said bitterly.

''She was worried about the future.'' His gaze rested intently on her face. ''Worried about you.''

''Then she ought to call me, talk to me.'' Not you. Joelle pressed her fist to the pillow. She hated that her family had taken Leo to their hearts, embraced him as if one of their own. He wasn't one of them. He'd hurt her, deceived her. ''Obviously they knew where I was. You even knew where I was.''

''And that bothers you?''

''Wouldn't you hate it if you were never consulted? If people just assumed they knew what was best for you?'' She turned, shot him a hard look. ''But maybe you never had hurt. Maybe everything's just come easy for you.''

His jaw tightened, thick black lashes lowering to conceal his expression. ''I've known hurt, but I don't live in the past. The past has no hold on me.''

''Lucky you.'' She looked away, swallowed hard, feeling trapped. ''You know, Chantal was twelve when our parents died, Nic was nine. I was almost five.'' She drew a rough breath. ''Nic and Chantal remember Mother. I remember nothing.'' Not even Mother's smile.

Leo returned the photo to the dressing table. ''Is that why you went to Louisiana?'' He walked toward her, hands buried in his trouser pockets, elegant coat hanging open. ''To find your mother?''

''Maybe.'' A needle of emotion pricked her.

Actually, in her grief over losing Grandmama, she hadn't known what she wanted, she'd only known she had to go to

America, had to go to Louisiana. It wasn't a choice. It was a necessity, as if New Orleans was sun or food or oxygen.

It wasn't until she arrived in New Orleans that she began to understand what she was looking for.

Family.

Connection.

History.

Of course she knew her father's family—she and her sisters had all grown up in Melio, and after her parents death King Remi and Queen Astrid raised them in the palace—but it was her mother's family, the mysterious d'Villes, she didn't know. The mysterious d'Villes of Baton Rouge she needed to know.

But once in Louisiana her American relatives didn't exactly open their arms to her, let alone their hearts. They hadn't taken a shotgun to her, but it had come damn close. Visiting their ramshackle house, her uncles and cousins had viewed her with suspicion, first doubting who she said she was, then wondering exactly what she wanted from them.

There'd been no big plan, and she hadn't known what she'd wanted. She didn't know what she'd hoped to find. Love? Hope? Acceptance?

Remembering her visit, remembering the way she'd been coldly rebuffed, Joelle felt a welling of old pain. They made it clear she wasn't one of them, and yet with Grandmama gone she didn't feel like a Ducasse anymore. Sometimes Joelle wondered if she'd ever know who she really was. "Laugh, but I think I thought if I could find Mother, I might find me."

He didn't laugh. "Did you?"

She couldn't meet his eyes. "I don't think so."

He reached out, touched the top of her head. "Can we start again? Try to get this off on the proper footing?"

She didn't answer, she couldn't. He was standing too close, radiating power, authority, charisma. Maybe that was what boggled her mind so. He wasn't just handsome. Wealthy. Royal. He was strong, too. Physically strong. Mentally strong.

She wished he'd say something, wanting him to fill the silence but he wasn't about to speak until he'd heard from her. And so he stood there, waiting, just as he had in New Orleans, forcing her to eventually respond…even when she didn't want to. "I don't know how to start again," she said finally, standing, hoping to escape but his body blocked her in. He didn't move. He wasn't about to let her go again.

"Why not?"

Because I thought you were someone you aren't. Tears pricked her eyes. *Because I thought you wanted me for me.* But she could never say that, never admit how vulnerable she was, how much she'd needed to be loved for herself. "Knowing what I know changes everything," she answered carefully, avoiding his eyes. "I understand your…motives."

"Motives?"

"You were checking up on me, investigating me, weren't you?"

He said nothing and the ache inside her grew, spreading, filling her with utter despair. That night, that incredible night, was quickly becoming so ugly. "You didn't trust me," she continued, the hurt spreading like a dark cold cloud inside her. "And that's why you didn't tell me who you really were, because you wanted to prove to yourself—or Grandpapa or whomever—that I wasn't good, and virtuous, that I wasn't the princess you'd been promised."

She finally looked up at him, her eyes brilliant with unshed tears. "Happy now?"

"No. I didn't want to hurt you. And you're right, I didn't trust you, and I had to know who you were before we married."

"You could have visited me in Melio. You could have given me a chance—"

"I did. I am."

"When?" she sputtered, fury growing, supplanting the hurt. "In New Orleans? Or now?"

"It doesn't matter—"

"It does."

"Why?"

"Because this isn't a one-sided relationship. This isn't just about you, and your needs. I have to trust you, too. And I don't."

He was silent a moment. Then the corners of his eyes creased. "Perhaps it'd help if you'd think of me as Luigi."

He was attempting to tease her, trying to lighten the mood but he didn't understand that she'd fallen for him—really fallen for him—and yet the man she'd fallen for wasn't real.

The man she'd wanted didn't exist.

"You're not a Luigi," she said, voice rough.

"I could be."

He was still trying to tease and she wanted to smile, nearly smiled, but she felt more panic than anything.

Leo was standing far too close. She could see the way his upper lip curved. She felt his power, felt the tension between them. He was merely biding his time, she thought, waiting until the moment was right to claim her, take her, permanently make her his. "No. You're Leo. Definitely a Leo." A lion. A *beast*.

Joelle felt hysteria bubble inside of her. Fire and ice were great for a night of passion but it would never do for real life...the rest of her life...especially if there was nothing real, nothing of substance beneath. Passion only worked if it was based on tenderness...on trust...but she and Leo had no trust, no hope, no chance.

Her gaze searched the planes of his face, the cut of his suit, the hard length of his legs. Beast was right. A hard, hurtful beast at that.

He reached out, pulled one of the shell hairpins from her hair. She sucked in a breath at the intimate touch but couldn't move, helpless, fascinated. His touch did something to her. Made her just want more and more.

He pulled another pin from the chignon, and then a third and finally the loose chignon fell out, her hair tumbling free.

Lifting a long strand, he let the hair slide through his fingers. "Things will get easier. You just have to give us a chance."

"Leo—"

"It will work. Trust me."

Trust him. The words were like poison to her.

Yet as his hands tangled in her hair, and he drew her forward, she closed her eyes, feeling his warm breath brush her forehead, caress her skin.

Taking his time, he tipped her face up to his, and then kissed her, a slow sensual kiss that made her tingle from head to toe. And when he kissed her like that, she felt delicate, beautiful, feminine. He made her feel as if her beauty wasn't just on the skin, but deep, deeper, coming from a hidden part of her.

Her eyes stung, watering, and her lips softened beneath his.

If only he'd never kept the truth from her, if only he'd told her who he was and why he was there…

But he hadn't, and he'd burst her beautiful bubble, the one all women have inside them about chivalrous heroes, handsome princes, white stallions, marzipan castles, and happy-ever-after endings. But as Joelle was learning the hard way, life wasn't sparkling ball gowns and fairy godmothers. Not even for flesh and blood princesses.

After a long moment Leo lifted his head. He strummed a thumb across her tender lips. "Don't forget the photo session tomorrow. Ten o'clock sharp."

Photos?

Her brain felt fuzzy. She couldn't recall anything to do with a photo session. "What session? Where?"

"Our formal engagement portrait. Your grandfather said it's a Ducasse tradition."

"Leo—"

"Remember, at ten. Downstairs." He caressed her mouth again before heading for the door. "Don't be late."

CHAPTER EIGHT

LEAVING Joelle's room, Leo passed Nicollette on the grand staircase. Nicolette, dressed in a smoke-blue beaded gown, her blond hair twisted in an elaborate jewel-studded knot, still looked elegant despite the late hour.

Nic slowed to speak with him. "Enjoy the party?" she asked, smiling warmly.

Yes, if one enjoyed conflict. But he didn't say that, he was rarely rude, self-control something he'd once prided himself on. "Yes, thank you. And you?"

"Very much. I'm just so glad to see Grandfather happy. I haven't seen him this relaxed since before Grandmama died."

Leo really didn't want to hear this. He already felt guilty as hell. "Personally I think he's happy to have his granddaughters home."

"Maybe, but you can see the relief in his eyes. The burden's gone, the worry about Melio's future. Grandpapa has such confidence in you." Nic shifted her weight, protectively touched her pronounced bump, and her expression gentled even more. "We all do."

Nic's words rang in Leo's head even after they'd said goodnight and he'd returned to his suite at the elegant Porto Palace Hotel in the city center.

Standing at the bedroom's window with the panorama view of Porto's bay sparkling with the lights of moored yachts and ships, he tugged off his tie, unbuttoned his dress shirt, and let the shirt hang open over his bare chest.

Nic's voice continued to echo in his head. *Grandpapa has such confidence in you. We all do.*

We all do.

I don't, Leo answered the voice shortly, dropping into a chair in the corner of his luxurious bedroom.

Tilting his head back, he closed his eyes, tried to blot out the whole night, but scenes kept popping up, scenes with Joelle from tonight—scenes where she dropped her champagne flute, the moment she struggled to pull the ring from her finger, and then later at dinner when she looked up at him over her dessert, her blue-green eyes snapping with fury.

Everything had changed, and yet he couldn't articulate the change. He just knew that nothing was as it had been since the night he'd arrived in New Orleans, the night he'd shown up at Club Bleu. That evening the momentum shifted, swung the other way, from the realm of reason and ration to emotion and passion.

He didn't like the shift at all.

He knew what he and Joelle had committed themselves to, knew the marriage was an agreement, a merger of families and power, and yet somehow in the last week they'd shifted from the contract—the business of the marriage—to something far more intimate…far more personal.

This wasn't business anymore. And he felt far from calm.

How could he and Joelle marry like this? How could they enter into marriage with so little in accord? He hated tension, hated conflict, had worked hard to keep control, thereby controlling that which impacted him, but Joelle pushed every button, made him go hot, cold, see red. She turned him inside out and he hated feeling this way.

Marriage should be dignified. Mature. Respectable. And yet Leo felt as if he were losing his grip on dignity and maturity. He felt terribly wound up. Out of control.

Just like the kid he'd been. Just like the childhood he'd know, dragged from one end of the earth to the other with his gorgeous, glamorous mother, Princess Marina, the Princess Marina widely loved by everyone but those who knew her well.

Sick to his stomach, Leo lunged from the chair, headed into the bathroom, turned the shower on. Stripping, he stepped beneath the icy torrent and let the frigid water calm him down.

He wasn't a kid anymore.

He wasn't controlled by anyone.

He was the adult now, he made the decisions, the choices were his.

And as Nicolette said, King Remi was counting on him. King Remi needed him. King Remi was old and needed support.

They'd do this, Leo vowed, lifting his face to the stinging water. He and Joelle would work through their differences, the hurt, the disillusionment, they'd work through this and they'd settle down. Everything would be fine. Everything would work out.

It had to.

But the next morning when Leo returned to the palace, dressed for the formal photo session he discovered that Joelle was not yet down.

He waited fifteen minutes, and then another fifteen minutes and finally he asked that someone go check on Joelle.

The housemaid returned. "Her Royal Highness must be on her way," the maid answered, curtseying. "She's not in her room."

King Remi invited Leo to wait with him in his study, and Leo joined the king, but it was a battle to control his temper.

He was losing patience with the absurdity of the whole thing. He was here, dressed, ready, and yet where was she? How could she be so late? How could she ignore her responsibilities yet again?

Marrying Princess Ducasse had been a business decision. So far it appeared to be the worst business decision he'd ever made. He'd end the whole damn mess now if it weren't for King Remi's age and fragility.

Well, that and the unfortunate fact he'd deflowered his virgin princess bride in New Orleans.

Leo ground his teeth together, clasped his hands behind his back, trying to contain his emotion. He knew who he was and what he was, and while he'd never be a knight in shining armor, even he knew you didn't take a twenty-two-year-old princess's innocence and then throw her back at the family patriarch.

Even hard, cynical royals like himself knew better than that.

"Brandy?" King Remi offered, gesturing to the crystal decanters on the liqueur cart in the corner.

"Too early for me," Leo answered, trying to keep his tone civil, thinking that maybe once he'd wanted to be the storybook prince, the one that'd slay the dragon and rescue the damsel from the dungeon, but that was years ago. Back before he knew who he really was, back before he understood the world he'd been born into, and that his heritage, his very inheritance, would destroy him, if he didn't destroy it first.

His family—the only family he'd known—was as desperate and volatile and dysfunctional as a family could be and yet his parents had actually married out of love.

Love.

If that's what love did to one, he wanted no part of it. And love had never been part of the equation, not when he dated, not when he decided to marry, not when he chose Joelle.

He'd purposely avoided contact until the wedding had drawn close. He'd purposely wanted to keep relations impersonal, polite, civil. Leo could do duty, but not emotion and certainly not passion.

And yet what happened with Joelle in New Orleans had been pure emotion, and even purer passion.

The impersonal, civil marriage had become a nightmare already.

"Maybe I will have that drink," Leo said, changing his mind as the king poured himself a neat brandy.

Remi smiled wryly. "She's driven me to drink, I'm afraid. She's become a stranger to me."

Leo crossed the room, took the glass and stood nearby while the king shifted his grip on his cane and eased himself slowly into a leather wing chair.

"I've sent Chantal after her," Remi said after a moment, trying to sound encouraging. "She'll find her."

Leo didn't think so. He'd suspected Joelle was gone…left the palace gone…left Porto gone. He should have known she'd just leave. She was so good at leaving, so much like his mother, the one who couldn't ever stick around and do what needed to be done.

But then, self-sacrifice hadn't ever been part of Marina's makeup.

"The photographer and his assistant will wait," the king added.

Right, the pictures. The formal engagement portrait.

For a moment Leo had forgotten the photo session, forgotten the reason he was even here this morning.

Pictures.

Posed pictures.

As if he'd even wanted to take the bloody photos in the first place. Growing up he'd had his fill of staged photo sessions…all those tense, forced smiles, everyone's misery tangible, especially the photos from the early days, the ones before his father and mother divorced, the ones where his father and mother looked as if they would spit nails if they had to smile another moment at each other.

But it wasn't just staged photos Leo despised. He hated all photos, including Polaroids.

He'd never smile for another Polaroid camera again. Never let himself be manipulated like that…smiling politely, smiling cheerfully, acting as if nothing disturbed him.

How ironic, Leo thought, running his hand through his hair, that he was trying so hard to be polite now, trying so hard to be kind for Remi's sake while Joelle pulled a Princess Marina trick, running…avoiding…disappearing…

Inevitably without consequence.

"We raised her," Remi said roughly, hands working on the polished wood of his cane, "Astrid and I."

Remi pushed his cane out in front of him, tapped the rubber tip against the carpet, his expression baffled. "Nicolette was always the handful. She gave us fits. But Joelle…" He shot Leo another apologetic glance. "But she'll return, Chantal will find her, Chantal knows all Joelle's favorite hiding places."

But Chantal didn't find her, and it was Nic who discovered the goodbye note in Joelle's room, and it was palace security, which alerted King Remi that Joelle had been spotted boarding a ferry for Mejia.

King Remi called a quick family meeting. His granddaughters and their husbands gathered in Remi's study. Leo was there, too, but he couldn't stand it, couldn't stand how false he felt. He was livid. Humiliated. He didn't believe in hunting women down, much less his own runaway fiancée.

''Since she's obviously going to the island house,'' Chantal said, sitting on the arm of the sofa. ''Leo could take Demetrius's helicopter, meet her, bring her back.''

Nic made a face, nose wrinkling. ''Why bring her back? She obviously doesn't want to be here.''

''But that's because Joelle doesn't like attention. She hates the public scrutiny,'' Chantal answered.

''So stay on the island,'' Malik Nuri, Nic's husband suggested. ''Take advantage of the villa there and try to sort things out.''

''I've my own villa there, too,'' Leo said, fighting his discomfort. He found it embarrassing, discussing his relationship with the others, even if they were Joelle's family. His family had never discussed anything. ''Maybe we'll take a few days—''

''A week.'' Remi interrupted, cane banging. ''Two weeks, whatever it takes.''

''Whatever it takes,'' Leo answered dryly, his mouth curving but it wasn't a smile. He couldn't believe he was doing this, chasing after Joelle yet again.

An hour later, the sun bright as it reflected off the water, Joelle waited patiently for the little ferry to finish docking.

She loved Mejia, had loved the smaller island since she was a girl. The palace at Melio was stuffy, formal, but on Mejia, life was laid back, far more casual.

The ferry's captain held Joelle's elbow as she stepped off the rocking boat. It'd been a slow trip, three hours by boat, but she didn't think she'd been recognized. A large white straw hat covered her upswept hair, big black sunglasses shielded her face, and even if people did know her, they hadn't stared or whispered.

The wonderful thing about Melio and little sister island Mejia is that everyone respected the royal family Ducasse. If the Ducasses were approached it was invariably by strangers.

Now Joelle shouldered her oversize woven bag and headed for the small queue of taxis. The villa wasn't far from the dock, just a ten-minute drive.

''Bella, bella, bella.''

No.

Not him. Not here.

Joelle ducked her head, stared at the ground as if the straw hat could make her disappear. What in God's name was he doing here?

A hand tipped her chin up, forcing her to look up. Broad shoulders. Tall, muscular body. The man had no intention of moving.

Leo plucked the sunglasses from her nose. Sunlight blinded her. She squinted up, seeing the outline of him but not his face. "Leave me alone," she choked, gripping the wood handles of her bag tighter.

"What are we going to do with you, *bella bambina?* Hmmm?"

She felt a rush of cold air dance across her nerve endings. "Forget me."

"And what? Break your grandfather's heart?" He made a disapproving *tch-tching* sound. "I don't think so."

They were standing in the middle of the old wharf, the wooden pier lined with everything from glossy yachts to rusted fishing boats and people pushed past, arms laden with shopping bags, beach toys, fishing gear.

Joelle tried to ignore the interested looks they were drawing, forced a smile. "You don't take a hint very well, do you?"

"You'll soon get to know me." He put his arm around her, drew her close to his side, walked her toward a waiting car. "And happily we've got plenty of time to get properly acquainted."

She resisted moving.

"I'm not going anywhere with you."

He gave her shoulder a little squeeze. "Don't be afraid, *bella.* I'm going to be very patient with you. The wedding is not for two weeks—"

"There's no wedding!"

"Of course there is. Your grandfather's not well enough to be publicly humiliated."

The chauffeur opened the back door as Leo and Joelle approached the elegant sedan. Joelle planted her feet, refusing to take another step. "I'm not going anywhere with you."

"You are."

"No."

With a sigh, Leo scooped her into his arms, tossing her into the back before more gracefully following her.

Inside the car the chauffeur drove as if nothing untoward had happened. But Joelle seethed, her hands fisted at her sides, the big white straw hat resting on her lap. "You've no right. Absolutely no right."

"Maybe not now, but in two weeks—"

"Never!"

He sighed, mildly. "It's going to be a long two weeks."

"You're crazy." They were climbing, leaving the rocky cliffs to the greener hills above. Joelle and her sisters shared a pretty villa on the water with its own private beach but that wasn't the direction they were heading. "Where are we going?"

"Home."

Closing her eyes, Joelle pressed a thumb to her left eyebrow, attempting to ease the massive pain building there. "It's not my home."

He didn't answer. He simply stretched, extending his legs and resting one arm on the back of the leather seat.

She grew hot, her skin prickling from the close proximity of his hand and body. "Do you mind?"

"Josie—"

"Don't call me that."

He turned, put his face in front of hers. "I'm this close, *bella*. This close to pulling you over my knee."

"*What?*"

"Maybe a good swat across your backside would solve some of our problems."

"Just who do you think you're talking to?"

"You."

Before she knew what was happening, he'd lifted her onto his lap, and with her short skirt hiked up he delivered several smart smacks to her backside. Just as quickly he righted her, put her back down.

Mortified, she slid as far from him as physically possible, her skin hot, her backside stinging. "I can't believe you just did that."

"I warned you. It's time you started paying attention. I don't make empty threats." His narrowed gaze raked her. "And forgive me, Princess, but you had that coming."

The car trip did not improve.

Joelle sat pressed to the corner, eyes filling with tears as she silently cursed herself, cursed Leo, cursed her grandfather who liked this arrogant Italian so much.

No one else had ever gotten under her skin this way. No one else had ever made her feel so helpless...so confused...so completely off balance. It only took a couple words from him, one long searing glance, and she fell apart, dissolving into a tearful, jagged mass of emotion.

The fact that he had such power over her scared her. Made her furious. And sitting back on her seat, her behind hot, she felt humiliated all over again. *How dare he?*

How could he?

Mortified that a man, a grown man, would flip her upside down and *spank* made her head spin. "I won't forget this."

"Good."

Twenty minutes later the sedan pulled up to a tall ornate iron gate. The gate swung slowly open and the car drew forward. The gate closed behind the car as they made their way down a long narrow drive, dense green foliage broken every now and then by a tropical palm tree, the walls of green relieved only by arms of purple bougainvillea.

The driver slowed in front of a broad yellow plaster villa, a patch of the turquoise sea visible just on the other side of coral roof tiles.

So they were still on the water, but on the opposite side of the island from the Mejia's quaint port city, opposite side from her family's pretty villa.

The driver turned the engine off and Joelle got a better view of the butter-colored villa, a mix of artisan craft and imagination, with even its own round tower. Part French Provincial, part Spanish colonial, the villa's gently arched windows were framed by soft green shutters, hand carved beams, numerous balconies and fanciful wrought-iron railings.

Leo stepped out, gave Joelle an infuriating smile. "Coming, dear, for the house tour?"

She looked at him and her fingers itched to take her sandals off and throw them at his head. Instead she managed a very regal slide across the seat and an even more regal rise. "But of course. There's nothing I'd like to do more."

Yet as she stood up, and his hand moved to guide her she flashed him a touch-me-and-you-die look. "I'm not yours. Don't think I am."

The house tour was brief and to the point. Leo did a quick walk through the house, opening doors, rattling off names of rooms—salon, dining room, breakfast room, kitchen—and then upstairs to numerous bedrooms and baths, and finally up another set of stairs to a large suite in the tower. "Our room."

Joelle went cold all over. "Whose room?"

"Ours."

She'd gone cold. Now she flushed hot. Suddenly desperate for air, she crossed to a window, struggled with the sash. But the air outside didn't feel any cooler. Joelle leaned on the sill, looked out. The ground was three stories below, and the exterior tower walls were round and smooth, the thick plaster a wash of butter-yellow. "I'd rather have a ground floor room."

Leo dropped into one of the armchairs in the pretty sitting area. He stretched, folded his arms behind his head. He was wearing a white linen shirt and the loose white fabric slid back on his forearms, revealing wide tanned wrists. "I'm sure you would. But I feel better knowing you're safe and sound in here with me."

She turned, sat down on the sill, tried to hide her incredulity. In the white shirt, comfortable chinos and Italian leather sandals he looked like a man on vacation. A man without a care in the world. "Don't you have somewhere you have to be? A job…a princely duty?"

"No."

"Surely you're employed."

"Yes." Sighing, he put his feet up on the matching ottoman. "This feels wonderful. You should come sit here, try this."

Her eyes narrowed to dagger slits. "I'm not sure what you're trying to do, but I don't like it, and I know my grandfather would never approve."

"I've been meaning to talk to you about your grandfather, but that will have to wait for another time. Right now we're just going to have some fun."

Some fun. The words rang ominously in her head. She swallowed, put a hand to her throat.

"Still looking for fun?"

So that's what he was getting at. Her flippant comment in New Orleans. *Girls just want to have fun.* "Is there anything to drink?"

"Lunch should be served soon."

"Good."

"You made a mistake in New Orleans, *bella,*" he added, his expression benign. "There are lots of men who could have given you a good time, but I'm not one of them."

"Obviously I made a mistake."

"*A* mistake? You've made many. You're careless. Reckless. Self-absorbed. You still have no idea what you put your family through—or the palace staff—when you ran off to America last year."

"I've heard this."

"No, you haven't. Your grandfather called an emergency meeting. Asked your sisters to return to Melio. It was the last thing he needed so soon after Astrid's death."

Joelle flushed. No man had ever spoken to her like this. No man—not even her grandfather—had ever tried to shame her, control her. "If you think you're endearing yourself to me, you're wrong."

He hadn't moved, only his mouth quirked, but she felt a sudden rise in tension.

She could almost see a sign over Leo's head.

Dangerous. Do not feed. Keep all hands out of the cages.

Right now he might look calm, but there was nothing calm beneath the warm green-gold gaze, especially when one considered that twice now he'd tracked her down, twice he'd come looking for her. Quite the hunter, wasn't he?

"We're not getting anywhere," he said at length, and stood. A muscle flickered at his jaw, a sign that all wasn't well and for a moment Joelle thought he was going to make a move for her, but then he smiled, a cool hard taunting smile that made her want to scream. "Your lunch will be brought to the room. I'll see you later this evening."

"I—"

But he'd left the room, closed the door and as she stood there, mouth hanging open, she heard the turn of a key.

He locked her in. Her astonishment gave way to fury.

At first she paced, her attention fixed on the beautiful ocean and the gorgeous beach just beyond the villa gardens. She thought of all the things she could be doing. Swimming. Lying on the beach. Reading. But he'd locked her in the room without any diversions—no form of entertainment—no books, not even a radio or TV.

Lunch arrived as Leo promised but the housemaid tried the door, couldn't get it open, and apologizing profusely for being unable to serve the princess, left.

Bastard, Joelle swore silently. Leo would pay she vowed, returning to the window to resume her vigil. The afternoon was picture perfect—just a couple wispy clouds high in a pristine blue sky. The turquoise surf looked so inviting, the water cool, fresh and she itched to reach the water.

Joelle leaned on the windowsill, looked down. Stone pavers below. A couple massive terra cotta pots half-filled with young plants. There was no way she could jump out onto that. And escape via the old tying-the-sheets-together-routine seemed ridiculous at best.

Eventually Joelle gave up pacing, gave up fuming—three hours of anger was hard for even her to sustain—and eventually decided on a bath. There were a dozen different bath products in the blue and white marble bathroom and Joelle determined she'd try them all.

She was still in the bath, reclining deeply in the enormous

tub, when the bathroom door opened, drawing a draft, pulling some of the fragrant steamy air out.

She knew immediately it was Leo just by the sudden rise of tension. Energy literally hummed off of him.

Closing her eyes, Joelle settled back more deeply into the tub, grateful for the mountain of scented bubbles. "Could you please shut the door? You're letting the warm air out."

She heard the door shut, listened intently, and hearing only silence assumed he'd walked out.

But then seconds later her nerves started zinging, again, sending a frisson of intense awareness through her. Her tummy flipped, her skin prickled, even her nipples peaked, tightening.

Joelle opened her eyes.

Leo was standing above her in just loose white linen pants, his skin bare, darkly tan, his powerful body beautifully muscled.

She tried not to stare but he looked lean and hard, his torso cut with muscle and when he slowly sat down next to her on the marble tub surround she knew she was in trouble.

"Have a nice afternoon?" he asked, reaching into the tub, checking the temperature of the water.

She leaned away from him as he dipped his hand into the water. Leo checked his smile. He saw the way she was looking at him, saw her wariness, but also the flicker of curiosity in her beautiful eyes.

And she was beautiful, as well as difficult, and her stubbornness, her *willfulness,* drove him crazy. Almost as crazy as the physical attraction between them.

It had been eight days since he'd had her in his arms, her body beneath his, and he wanted her again. The craving was growing stronger. He didn't know how much longer he'd resist her—or the invitation in her eyes. It was funny how she said one thing, the good and proper thing, but her eyes said something entirely different.

Her lashes flickered up now, her eyes, fiery blue green, met his. "Just because we slept together one time doesn't mean you can join me in the bath."

"I wasn't going to climb in." He cupped a handful of water

and dribbled it onto her throat and collarbone. "But now that you've mentioned it, a bath does sound refreshing."

She threw out a hand, straight-armed him giving him a glimpse of her bare, rosy-tipped breasts. "Don't push me. I've had it today. Had it with you dragging me into your car. Locking me in this room. Spanking me as if I were a child."

She'd thrown an arm in his direction and he took advantage of the defensive gesture, his hand wrapping around her wrist. "That was fun, wasn't it?"

"I'm not laughing." Yet, her cheeks flooded with color, and she tugged at her hand, unable to free herself. "You love this, don't you? Dominating me. Controlling me—"

"You like it, too."

Her lips parted, eyes widening, her irises more green than blue, vivid and intense against her flushed cheeks.

"You love power," he added. "The struggle for power, the use of power, even the abuse of."

"No," she protested, but he wouldn't let her escape.

He momentarily loosened his grip, just long enough to switch hands. "If you didn't love power so much you wouldn't fight me so hard."

She had no immediate answer—he didn't think she would— yet he could see her mind race, her thoughts whirling as she struggled to come back at him with something sassy and flippant.

The king had called his granddaughter demure, timid, sweet. Remi didn't know her.

Joelle was a fighter. And Leo was beginning to comprehend why she needed to go to America, why she'd wanted space from her family. He didn't approve—but that wasn't to say he didn't better understand her motivation. "Give me your other hand," he said.

She shrank away from him, leaning as far back in the bath as she could, yet there was no fear in her eyes, just fire.

"Give me your hand," he repeated. "Save yourself the consequences."

"And what? You plan on tying me up next?"

Heat rushed through him, his body responding, growing hard, painfully hard. "Only if you're naked."

She snapped her mouth closed, but the little pulse at the base of her neck was beating wildly.

And while she processed that vivid detail, he fished beneath the surface of the water for her left hand. She moved to elude him, tried burying her hand beneath her, and yet the moment he caressed her bare hip under water she jolted upright, her left hand suddenly free.

"Thank you." He wrapped his fingers around both her wrists, then slid his palms up, across hers, before linking fingers, locking her to him.

Her eyes flashed up at him. Her long hair was slipping from the knot on the top of her head. Joelle began to shake with anger. "I'm not a second-class citizen. You can't treat me this way."

He lifted her arms, pressed her back against the tub, leaving her breasts exposed, the ripe curves up thrust. "That's right. You're a princess. Princess Josie."

Her eyes flashed at him, daggers of fire. "Let me go."

"And if I don't?"

"I'll…"

"What? Splash me? Call me a name? What's your grand idea?"

Her teeth ground together. Her chest rose and fell. "Why do you enjoy humiliating me?"

He angled his body down, his torso stretching out over hers. He felt her pebbled nipples brush his chest, felt his own body flame in response. "I don't want to humiliate you. But I do want you to understand the commitment you made, the pledge you gave me—"

"Our engagement was by proxy." Her voice wasn't as strong as it'd been. It was rougher, rawer. "You weren't even there for the actual engagement. You let someone else handle the details."

"But so did you."

"Exactly. We'd never even met. We signed a piece of paper. Some commitment."

"I gave you my ring."

"Big deal."

"It is to me." He tipped his head, kissed the side of her neck, and felt her body shudder. "And should be to you. Your word…

your reputation…must mean something.'' He kissed her higher on her neck, just beneath her jawbone. Again she trembled beneath him, and he lowered his weight against her, letting his chest press against her breasts.

He felt her stir restlessly, felt her flat abdomen tense. She pressed up against him, blindly seeking more contact.

"Leo." Her voice broke, husky.

He drew away, looked down at her, his gaze sliding down her, resting deliberately, provocatively on her throat, her bare breasts, the swell of hip, the junction where her thighs met. His gaze was so intimate, so possessive he saw her squirm. "You are mine. Even if you don't know it yet."

CHAPTER NINE

JOELLE could hardly breathe.

She didn't want to feel like this, didn't want to respond like this but whatever it was between them was bigger, fiercer, than anything she'd ever known. He destroyed her reason. Demolished her self-control.

"It was just one night," she insisted, trying to clear her head even as his gaze tormented her, his eyes owning her, claiming her. There seemed no distance between them anymore. The boundaries were gone.

He was dangerous, and yet she still burned for him, her skin flushing, heating, but that warmth was nothing like the core of her, her insides so hot and tight she felt sure she'd melt from desire. Joelle pressed her knees together, pressed her thighs, trying to appease the relentless ache.

"If that's all you wanted, *bella,* you shouldn't have given me your virginity." His head dipped. He kissed her hard, lips parting hers, stealing the air from her lungs, drawing her breath into him.

By the time he broke the kiss off her head was spinning, all thought gone, sense of caution shot.

He released her. She didn't move. She couldn't. She simply lay against the back of the tub, looking up at him with dazed eyes.

He made a rough sound, pressed his thumb to her lower lip, parting her lips wider. "Innocence is valuable."

"I'm not that innocent."

"You know far less than you think." And then he kissed her again, harder, deeper, his tongue teasing hers, before stroking the inside of her mouth.

It was as if he'd lit fireworks beneath her skin and she jerked, body shuddering against his. His tongue stroked her again and one of his hands dipped into the water, covered her breast.

She shook with need, sensation, pleasure. His wet palm rubbed across her breast, torturing her tight nipple.

She whimpered at the touch, her skin so sensitive she wanted to lay down on something soft, escape the scraping of nerves, the bite of hunger. She whimpered yet again as his hand slid down her abdomen, palmed her belly before brushing the wet curls at the V between her thighs, gently parting her thighs.

Oh Lord, she breathed in hard, air strangled, gasped as he stroked the soft folds between her thighs, then parted even those. His fingertips were light, teasing, but he knew exactly what he was doing. She trembled, flexed her hands, shivers of hot-honey feeling racing through her. She knew where she wanted him to touch her, knew how she wanted him to touch her but he didn't touch her there, was in no hurry to do anything but wind her up tighter and tighter.

"Leo."

She felt a flutter of sensation across her clitoris, a flutter and nothing more.

"Yes, Josie?"

She balled her hands. "You're driving me mad."

"Then you know the way I feel." He stroked her tummy, caressed her breast and drew his hand from the water. As he stood up, he reached for a bath towel. "Time to dress, *bambina*. We have dinner plans and can't be late."

Joelle grabbed the towel he held out to her, stepped quickly from the tub, trying to cover herself up as fast as possible. "We're going *out?*"

"Yes?"

"In public?"

"That's the general idea."

The bathroom was steady, the bronze bath fixtures beaded with moisture. She pushed a hand through her hair, knowing it'd be a disaster "But where would we go?"

"We've reservations at Henri's."

Henri's was the island's swankiest French restaurant, sitting high on Mejia's tallest peak, with a treacherous drive up the side of the mountain but with a view so spectacular that no one complained once there.

Visiting film stars and European fashion celebrities loved Henri's. It was said you couldn't dine at Henri's without seeing a half dozen of the most famous faces in the world, and the parking lot certainly had more limos and luxury cars than any other lot on Melio or Mejia.

Her mouth opened, closed, and she stared at him perplexed. She hadn't eaten at Henri's in years, and even then, she'd been with family, and to actually go there tonight with someone like Leo…

And it wasn't Leo's title or wealth that intimidated her, but his sensuality, his frank sexual energy…

She looked up at him, towel pressed tightly to her breast. "Why?"

"You're my fiancée."

He made it sound so normal, as if they were like everyone else, a civilized couple—a cohesive couple—instead of Leo and Joelle locked in a desperate power struggle.

"We're having dinner," he soothed as she said nothing, and he lifted her chin, kissed the corner of her mouth. "You've eaten in public with me before."

"Yes, but I remember how this works. Drinks…dinner…" Her voice trailed off, her eyebrows rose.

"Dessert?"

"Of course."

He kissed the corner of her mouth again, his lips brushing the edge of her upper lip and soft sensitive skin.

She tensed at the coil of pleasure in her middle, felt fresh heat and the shimmer of desire. "I'll dress," she whispered, her grasp on her towel weakening.

"Good idea."

He entered his walk-in closet—they both had their own—and she heard him draw a shirt from a wooden hanger, heard the rustle of clothes and she forced herself to get moving.

In her closet she discovered her wardrobe from the family villa in town—skirts, and dresses, sporty outfits and casual summer wear—a wardrobe usually reserved for the family holidays at the Mejia beach house.

She frowned at the clothes, uncertain what to pick, then

reached for a short red beaded dress tucked between more sedate wear. Nic's Va-va-room dress. Chantal used to give Nic grief whenever Nic wore the dress. Nic claimed the sexy bloodred sequin dress was like a Get Out of Jail free card—whenever she wore it, she got away with anything she wanted.

"You're going to wear that?" Leo's voice came from the closet entrance and she spun around, the dress still pressed against her.

"It's over the top," she agreed, giving the shimmering dress a shake, sequins throwing off little rainbows of light. "And it's actually not mine."

"Wear it."

"You don't like it." But she liked the way he looked. He was wearing black trousers, a thin black turtleneck, expensive shoes and matching leather belt.

"I do."

She looked up at him suddenly, struck again by his intense maleness, his impossibly good looks. Tall, dark, unbearably handsome. What had been a blur became very clear. The dark green eyes. The stubble of a beard on his wide jaw. His thick dark hair, a little long so that it brushed his nape, in equally thick dark waves. "You're conservative."

"Not that conservative."

She heard his tone, felt inflection—wicked—and it was like stoking the fire. Flames shot through her, licking at every nerve, every dangerous thought. Suddenly shy, aware of all she didn't know, Joelle put the red dress back and reached for alternative outfits. She held up the first, a simple cream pantsuit. "I know you'd like this. It's Valentino—"

"No."

She presented the other. "Classic black sheath. Accessorized with pearls—"

"Wear the red. It suits you." He glanced at his watch, turned away. "But hurry. The car is picking us up soon."

She didn't have time to style her hair properly, forced to leave it loose, but she did use mascara and a deep red lipstick that matched the ruby sheen of her dress perfectly.

"Ready?" Leo asked, looking up from the newspaper he'd been reading.

"Yes."

"Good." He rose. "I've something for you," he added, taking a little box from the table next to him. Leo took the lid off, turned the box around.

A bracelet. Rich, heavy shiny silver. Caught off guard, Joelle felt something shift inside of her. "How lovely."

"Isn't it?" He lifted the band, opened the clasp and snapped it around her wrist. He squeezed the band and it mysteriously shrank smaller.

She lifted her wrist, saw her reflection in the polished silver. "When did you get this?"

"This morning."

She felt a pang, imagining how he'd felt when she'd stood him up for the photo shoot. "Thank you."

"My pleasure." His hand circled her wrist and the band briefly, checking the fit. "It was lucky of your brother-in-law to have it with him."

Her brow creased. "Who? Malik or Demetrius?"

"Demetrius, of course. He's the one that specializes in surveillance and security."

Joelle felt a chilly wind blow through her. Her gaze dropped to the bracelet, to Leo's hand still encircling her wrist. "What is this?"

"A wonderfully modern gizmo."

Her niggle of dread roared to life. "What does it do?"

"Keeps track of you."

"A handcuff?"

"It's what white collar criminals might wear for a house arrest."

"A handcuff." Her voice rose. The man was mad. Completely, irrefutably mad. Worse. He was her fiancé. Or so her family thought.

"You know it's not a handcuff," he answered with mock patience. "You're not chained to anybody or anything."

"No, but you'll know where I am at all times."

He looked up, met her gaze, and had the gall to smile. "Yes."

The serenity in his smile made her want to scream, instead, mouthing curses, she tugged at the narrow metal band circling her wrist. "I want it off."

"No."

"Now."

"No."

Frantically she banged the band against the edge of the marble counter in the bath. "You can't do this, Leo."

"I already have."

Her wrist was starting to ache from banging it so hard and hot tears filled her eyes. "Take it off. The band's hurting me."

"It's not. You're hurting yourself. Relax."

"I can't. Not with it pinching like this."

"Nothing's pinching, *bella*. It's just a titanium band." He flashed a smile, evidently quite satisfied with himself. "People will think it is jewelry. You did."

It's true. She did think it was jewelry, and she'd let him put it on her thinking it was a gift, a kind of peace offering.

Peace offering.

My God, how wrong could she be? How hard he must be laughing on the inside.

"How can you do this to me?" She felt like throwing up. Shock and rage washed through her one after the other in waves. "How can you think this will solve anything?"

"You won't run away anymore."

"I never ran away!"

"Josie, *bella,* I found you on a dock in Mejia late this morning. You were supposed to be taking photos with me in Melio."

"They were just photos—"

"And they meant a lot to your grandfather."

"He'll never forgive you when he discovers what you've done to me."

"Your grandfather told me to take advantage of the next two weeks."

Heat rushed through her, her skin so hot she felt certain it would blister. She stared at Leo incredulously. "No."

"Your grandfather is actually relieved you'll be here—safe—with me. He confessed he doesn't know how to manage you anymore. Hoped I might have more success than he.'' Leo stepped back, surveyed her. ''And actually, the band doesn't look so bad.''

''Doesn't look bad?'' Her voice echoed incredulously and she waved her arm back and forth, trying to shake the weight of the snug band, the cool metal slowly warming against her prickling skin. ''It's a metal cuff, Leo. Fastened around my wrist.''

''But no one will know what it's for,'' he answered, lips curving, eyes hard. ''Unless you tell them.'' He shot a glance at his watch, saw the time. ''We better go. I don't want to miss our reservations.''

And that was it? she thought, staring dumbfounded at his broad back, the fine black fabric stretched tight over the muscular planes, revealing every sinewy line and hollow. He was just heading out now. Mission accomplished.

Fury rose up, fury that he could be so high-handed, so arrogant, so insensitive.

''I'm not going,'' she said tightly, deliberately reaching for the zipper in the back of her dress. ''You can go if you want, but I'm not going with you.''

''We're leaving now,'' he said, not even turning at the door.

''Then you're leaving now.'' She unzipped her dress, peeled it from her shoulders, kicked off her shoes, knowing that sooner or later he'd turn, and sooner or later he'd discover her undressed, unprepared, unwilling.

Why couldn't she resist him earlier, she asked herself, why couldn't she be unwilling when he touched her?

Because she loved his damn touch, that's why.

He turned, slowly, very slowly, his hard features even harder. ''I'm not in the mood, *bella*.''

''Neither am I.'' Tears of shame smarted her eyes. How could she be expected to marry a man like Leo? How could she live with someone so arrogant, so chauvinistic that he actually shackled her?

Shackled her.

Joelle shook her wrist, giving the thick silver band an irritated shake. For God's sake the man had put a GPS device on her so he could keep track of her at all times.

"*Bella,* your dress."

She didn't move. Her hands balled at her sides. "Are you going to force me into dressing, too, Leo? Is this how you imagine a relationship to be?"

He looked at her for a long moment. "No," he said at length. "This isn't my idea of a relationship. I thought this was yours. All you've done is fight me—"

"Because you're overriding everything I want, everything I need."

"You need a husband. You wanted me."

"I did need a husband, and I did want you, but that was before I discovered you were my groom-to-be, and the only reason you seduced me in New Orleans was because you doubted my integrity."

His eyes narrowed. "I was concerned about you, yes."

"And so instead of telling me who you were—"

"But I did tell you who I was. I said my name quite clearly. You, *bella,* didn't know me. You, *bella,* weren't at some exclusive music conservatory, and you weren't busy planning the wedding. You, *bella,* were crawling across a dirty stage on your stomach while men drooled all over themselves." He took a rough breath, glanced impatiently at his watch yet again. "Can we go now?"

She didn't have the strength he did, couldn't fight the way he did. Leo seemed to have light-years more experience when it came to conflict. "I'll go," she said stiffly, "but the band comes off as soon as we get home. Is that clear?"

The ride to Henri's in the back of black limousine sedan was very strained, with Joelle sitting as far from Leo as she could manage.

He was worse than awful. He was a beast. A monster. A *devil.*

Balling her hands, she recrossed her legs and felt the sequin dress move with her. She wished now she'd worn something different, something long and loose and black. Instead her snug dress's halter neck bared lots of pale skin, exposing her shoulders, down low between her breasts, and nearly all of her back. Earlier she'd liked how the rich saturated color contrasted with her skin but now she felt vulnerable, a little appetizer to tempt Leo's appetite.

"You're fidgeting," Leo commented, his voice husky in the dark.

"I've a lot on my mind."

"What are you planning now?"

"All the different ways I can kill you."

He laughed. A real laugh, a laugh that came from deep inside of him. "At least you're not boring."

At least.

The fact that he could even say such a thing at a time like this made her see red.

How could she have ever agreed to marry him? But then, how was she to know that he wasn't a regular royal, but a demented prince with medieval ideas of marriage and motherhood? "Is this common practice in Italy? Do men still tether their women?"

She felt Leo's gaze sweep over her. "Only if it gives them pleasure."

And that effectively curtailed all conversation.

Twenty minutes later the driver slowed in front of the restaurant's stone façade. Yellow light glowed from within the restaurant, old wrought-iron chandeliers just barely visible through some of the windows.

Leo climbed from the car and she hesitated a moment in the back seat, trying to gather her courage, as well as her confidence. Dinner with Leo at Henri's wouldn't be easy. She was already on pins and needles.

But inside the restaurant Leo greeted the maître d' warmly, thanking the restaurant host for the warm welcome.

"It's a pleasure to have you here again, Your Highness," the maître d' answered, bowing deeply. "And I don't know if its coincidence or happy circumstance, but your mother is here as well. She's dining in one of the private rooms tonight, but asked me to let you know that she hoped to join you later."

Leo's expression didn't outwardly alter, but Joelle saw all emotion leave his eyes, his easy warmth fading. He was still smiling at the maître d' but Leo looked hard, granite hard, definitely angry.

Even the maître d' sensed that his news had the opposite effect he'd intended, and with another deep bow, he fell into silence and led them to their table in a lovely window bay.

Joelle glanced up at Leo as she was seated. When the maître d' said mother, did he mean Princess Marina or Clarissa, Leo's father's current wife?

Joelle had never cared about society, had never stayed in touch with the other young royals, and certainly didn't read any of the tabloid magazines that would report such things but even she knew that Leo's parents divorce had been the ugliest—most public—royal divorce on record.

The wine steward rushed forward but Leo brushed him aside, asking for time.

Leo was livid, she thought. Livid wasn't quite right. He looked…devastated.

Quietly Joelle waited. She'd never seen him like this. But minutes ticked by and still he hadn't moved, hadn't even looked at her. "Leo?"

He didn't immediately answer and she waited another few seconds before trying again. "Leo?"

He stirred, body shifting uncomfortably. "Yes?"

"We don't have to stay."

His head lifted, his eyes met hers. His eyes searched hers for a long moment before the corner of his mouth lifted. "I'm not going to let her chase us away."

Her…her who? She thought it was his mother, but she couldn't be sure, and she wanted to know. It seemed important to know. "It's not Clarissa, is it?"

"God, no." Leo almost laughed. "Clarissa's a saint. It's Marina, my mother, that's here."

"And that's bad?"

Leo just looked at her.

A few minutes later another waitperson appeared and Leo ordered drinks, a very stiff martini for himself, and a champagne bellini for her.

They didn't speak as they waited for the cocktails to arrive, but then, before the drinks had even reached the table Leo stood abruptly. "I'll be right back."

She knew from his expression where he was going. And again she wondered, just what had happened between him and his mother?

Leo wasn't gone long. He arrived only minutes after their cocktails did. Pale, his features tight, he sat down, took a long drink from his martini before exhaling. "That's settled."

Joelle felt as if she'd swallowed a bucket of nails. Her stomach hurt in the worst way possible. She didn't understand any of this, wished she knew exactly what was happening, why the horrible undercurrents. "What…?"

"She won't be joining us." Leo looked up, dark green eyes blazing, his temper barely controlled. "She understands."

Turning her head, she glanced out the window, saw the lights of the harbor town far below, the reflection of the moon on the water. It was such a beautiful night. "I don't," she whispered, nails pressed to her palm. Her family had fights…conflicts…but nothing like this.

"You don't want to know."

"But what if I did?"

Leo's jaw flexed. "I wouldn't tell you."

Leo heard her inhale, knew he'd hurt her and yet for the life of him he couldn't find any words to fix the hurt with.

His mother *here*. His mother, Princess Marina, "the most beautiful, vivacious, and puzzling royal of her time," as a magazine had once described her. She wasn't here by accident. She must have known Leo was coming.

The magazine forgot a few adjectives, he thought, biting down, trying to control his anger. They could have included voracious, selfish and unstable.

His teeth pressed so hard it became a smile. He should have known better. Should have known he couldn't return to Mejia, should have known to stay on the opposite side of the world.

Lifting his head, he saw Joelle watching him, her face illuminated by candlelight, her reflection caught in the window behind her. She was worried. For him. And the fact that she'd care one way or another stunned him.

He studied her face, her eyes, her mouth, saw what he hadn't wanted to see. Her youth. Her inexperience. "You're beautiful." His voice grated and she shook her head in quick denial, reached for her champagne cocktail and the silver band on her wrist clinked against her water glass.

She stiffened, and he saw the sheen of tears in her eyes.

What in God's name were they doing? What was he doing? He had a responsibility to marry; Joelle had a duty to bear children, but was this the way to go about anything? How could this possibly be the path to happiness?

Or maybe he didn't believe in happiness. Maybe it didn't exist.

He saw silent tears tremble on her lashes and the tears cut him. He didn't want to hurt her, didn't want to hurt anyone, but nothing was easy, and this—them—wasn't about ordinary people making ordinary choices. Neither of them were ordinary, neither of them could afford to ignore their royal responsibilities.

They were privileged. And cursed.

The difference between them was that he'd accepted the curse. She was still fighting it. She was still certain she could have something different…something more.

Something more didn't exist. He of all people knew that.

But she was young, very young, and in the candlelight with her hair loose, her blue-green eyes wide, her lashes damp with tears, she looked like a glorious Rembrandt oil.

Impulsively he leaned forward, cupped the back of her head and kissed her.

Her lips felt soft, inviting, and he deepened the kiss, needing to taste her, feel her. He heard her quick intake, felt her mouth soften and his body hardened instantly. He wished they could skip dinner and just go home, back to the villa. He didn't want to sit and talk, didn't want to sit and feel anything.

"Let's go," he said roughly.

In the car on the ride home Leo sat closer to her, so close she felt the press of his thigh against her own, felt the warmth of his body through his trousers and thin turtleneck.

She remembered how he'd looked at her at Henri's. He'd looked closely, directly, looked so long she hurt on the inside.

People had taken her picture, waited outside restaurants and public buildings to get a glimpse of her, but no one had ever really looked at her, not like Leo, not with his concentration.

She tried not to think during the drive, and he didn't fill the silence, either. But her stillness wasn't that of calm. She felt wild on the inside. Scared.

Leo had always had an edge, but he was positively hazardous tonight.

The car pulled through the villa gates, the driver parked before the house. The lights were out except for one at the door, and another in the hall. It was obvious the staff had all turned in for the night.

Joelle shot a longing glance at the driveway and the car as Leo moved to shut the door. She wanted freedom, wanted to dash outside and just escape. She missed the freedom of New Orleans, missed being independent and unknown.

But, Leo was oblivious to the tension. Either that, or he'd chosen to ignore it.

He carefully locked the front door, flicked off the entry light and turned on a pretty sconce in the stairwell.

''Bed,'' he said bluntly, reaching for her hand.

CHAPTER TEN

HEART pounding she followed him up the staircase to their tower room. Leo held the bedroom door open for her and once she was inside, he shut the door, locked it, pocketed the key.

"Must you lock the door?" she asked, watching him dim the overhead light and close the curtains at the window, the fabric a stunning turquoise silk lined with pale green. She couldn't believe it, couldn't believe they were back to this again.

He was moving toward her, stalking her with single-minded focus. He tugged his turtleneck off, over his head. Undid the belt, pulled the leather from the trouser loops. "Nothing's changed."

Her legs knocked. Her nerves were getting the best of her and she backed up a step, but not very far, and not very fast. He reached for her, his hand on her hip and deliberately he pulled her forward, drawing her to him and her pulse raced, her body hummed.

He was right, she thought, body inflamed, nothing had changed. And her eyes closed as his palm slid up the outside of her thigh, up beneath the hem of her sequin dress. She put her hands on his chest to steady herself as he continued his slow exploration.

He'd found the lace garter holding her thigh high silk hose, and he toyed with the garter, lifting the narrow strap, tugging on it, rubbing the slender strip of lace against her hot skin.

She inhaled, growing dizzy. He was stroking her through the scrap of silk pantie and she leaned against him, her fingers flexing against the warmth of his bare chest. She knew what she wanted, knew how good he felt inside her, but she remembered last time—not the actual lovemaking—but the morning after. Things were already so difficult between them, lovemaking would only confuse everything more.

"We can't," she said unsteadily.

"Okay," he said, even as he pulled the damp silk from her. His head dipped, his lips touching the curve of her cheek as he stroked her beneath the silk again, the tip of his finger stroking back and forth. The sensation was sharp and intense and of course it didn't satisfy. She was ready for him, physically. Her body wanted him but she couldn't bear to feel so conflicted later.

Her hands became fists and she pressed against his chest as hot sensation rushed through her, swamping her, painting stars against her mind's eye. "Can we talk about this?"

"Of course. Talk."

But she couldn't, couldn't find any words, any rational thought. She wanted him, wanted him with her, in her, wanted to be completely his—at least physically—and reaching up, she clasped his face in her hands, pressed a desperate kiss to his mouth. Her breath caught as he slid a finger deep inside her, maddening her senses, making her hot.

He kissed her back, teeth catching her lower lip. She shuddered at the bite of his teeth on her swollen lips and the thrust of his finger inside her.

She leaned against him, legs shaking, threatening to give way. "I can't take much more," she sobbed as his hands took control of her, in her, over her, across her.

He took mercy on her, drew her dress down, covering her lace garter and carried her to the bed.

She felt nerveless, boneless, decadent as he stretched her out on the bed. And as he leaned over her, she reached for his trousers, undid the button and unzipped the zipper.

"I thought you wanted to talk," he said, gazing down at her, his eyes dark with passion.

"We should."

"So?"

"I can't think about the issues now. I can't think of anything but…"

"But?"

"This."

He leaned over her, kissed her and then his hands were slowly moving across her body, down her hips, thighs. She felt his hands slide beneath the hem of her skirt again and deftly he unhooked one stocking from her garter belt, and then the other. Rolling the silk stockings down her legs she felt the air cool her skin, soothe her heated senses.

His head lifted, and he looked at her, expression tense, sober. "If you don't want me, say so now."

He looked strangely young—defiant, troubled, surprisingly vulnerable. Behind his head she saw the sparkle of her dress pattern the ceiling and emotion filled her. She didn't understand any of this. Not him, not herself, not the intense chemistry between them. "But I do want you," she answered, voice husky. "That's the whole problem."

His dense black lashes dropped, concealing his expression, but when he kissed her, it was far more gently, the kiss expressing a tenderness he'd never say with words.

Somehow her dress came off, joining her stockings and heels on the floor. She hadn't been wearing a bra and now she was completely naked before him. He settled her backward, stretched out over her, and then his powerful thighs were parting hers, making room for him between her legs.

She shivered, nerves, expectation and suddenly she felt close to tears again. She didn't know him. She really didn't know anything about him and yet when his skin touched hers, when she felt his warmth, when she pressed her face to his shoulder she knew there was nowhere she'd rather be. How could one feel so close to someone and yet know nothing about the other? How could she want him against her, in her, when he could be so harsh? So unfair?

His hands caressed her rib cage, fingers measuring, counting the ribs and then his palms covered her breasts, her skin heating beneath the delight of his hands. She tensed at the feel of his erection against her. He was very hard, and very big and she suddenly doubted this would work, even though it had worked last time, the first time.

Swallowing her fear, Joelle reached for him blindly, wrapping her arms around his shoulders.

"Don't be afraid," he whispered, his lips brushing her shoulder, her collarbone, the slope of her breast.

It was fine for him to say that, she thought feeling him press against her, feeling her body tighten in response, but it wasn't even her body she was so worried about. Her body was young, resilient, her body could heal. She wasn't so sure about her heart.

But he was moving against her, his weight on his elbows, shifting forward. She felt him push up, push through, entering her slowly. Although hard, he felt warm, sleek, and her body welcomed him, hips lifting to accept him, muscles relaxing, adjusting to the size of him.

The bittersweet emotion earlier was nothing compared to the storm of need, of longing, sweeping her now.

Her whole life she'd felt alone, misunderstood even. Her whole life she'd been the good little princess for everyone, and yet all those years she'd felt so dishonest, she'd felt like a lie. She wasn't a good little princess. She was hungry and wild and fierce and she wanted to be free, and real. She wanted to feel and love.

"Take me," she whispered, emotion drowning her and she was desperate to escape all the feelings she couldn't control. "Take me," she repeated, needing sensation not emotion, pleasure not fear.

His mouth covered hers, his body surged inside her and she forced out all thought but the power of Leo's hard body driving into hers.

Later, bodies satiated, muscles relaxed, they lay close. Joelle was still trying to catch her breath, her body not even close to cooling down but she felt Leo's calm, the release of his tension.

The corner of her mouth lifted. "Maybe you need more sex," she said after a moment, thinking back over the evening. "It'd probably help tame that beast you keep locked up inside of you."

"Beast?"

She tilted her head back, met his eyes. Relaxed, he looked even more gorgeous, his lashes long and thick, his cheekbones high, his lips full, sensual. "Sometimes he's sleeping, which is a good thing, but when he's awake he's ugly."

Leo grimaced. "I'm not that bad."

"No. But the beast is."

His gaze held hers, but he didn't answer, just pulled her back toward him, her breasts pressed to his chest, her tummy against the honed muscle of his abdomen.

He caressed her hip, the curve of her bottom and her breath caught in her throat. They'd only finished making love but he was stirring her again, winding her up, making her want more.

She reached for his hand, attempting to still it, knowing if she didn't stop him now she'd be begging him to take her again. "You've had a lot of practice, I think."

"I've ten years on you, *bambina*."

"And were they all in bed?"

She heard the smile in his voice. "You've a one-track mind."

"Which you've clearly taken advantage of."

"Better me than anyone else."

Her glossy hair fell forward, covering both of them, and Leo picked up a handful of the honey-brown strands, wrapped the length around his hand and tugged. "Most effective," he said, drawing her head back with a tug of his hand, exposing the long line of her throat to his mouth. "I can eat you slowly this way."

Joelle felt heat rush through her. Her cheeks burned hot. "You're not going to eat me."

"Is that a dare or a threat?"

"Neither."

He kissed her chin, and then beneath her jaw. She sighed at the flick of his tongue along her jawbone, and sighed again when he nipped his way down her throat to her ridiculously sensitive collarbone.

"Surely you've had oral sex before?" he asked, his breath warm against her skin.

She shivered as the tip of his tongue drew small slow circles on her collarbone, successfully finding each and every little nerve ending and she was finding it increasingly difficult to think coherently.

"Why surely?" she said, thinking his tongue was awfully clever, seemed to know all kinds of responsive places. "Remember, I was a late bloomer."

"You must have had boyfriends."

"No. I couldn't stomach three-way dates."

Leo lifted his head, looked at her, eyebrows rising. "Three-somes?"

"Me, my guy, and Mr. Secret Service."

Leo laughed softly, a low husky sound that rumbled from his chest straight through her. "I see your point."

"You didn't have security detail on your dates?"

"No."

Leo's tongue flickered across the swell of her breast leaving a damp trail that immediately cooled. Her skin prickled. Her breasts firmed, nipples peaking. His mouth closed over the tip of one breast, and he drew the tight nipple into his mouth.

She reached up, buried her hands in his thick crisp hair, held his head to her breast. "This is getting dangerous," she whispered, her voice husky, and suddenly the tears were there just beneath the surface. The tears felt thick and wet in her eyes. Her heart felt just as wet and heavy, weighted with sadness, weighted with need.

How could she still feel anything for him? How could she imagine she loved him?

Forgetting for a moment whole handcuff security device—forgetting his whole overbearing approach—how could she still be so attracted?

He was tough. Hard-nosed. Stubborn. Proud. Arrogant. Sexual.

And yet, even if he was dominant—aggressive—during the day, he wasn't aggressive in bed. Naked, next to him, he was hard and strong and physical but he didn't hurt her—not ever—not even the first time. His fierceness was tempered by tenderness. His lovemaking had always been intense, passionate, but he'd never marked her, bruised her, intimidated her. Not in bed. In bed he was...generous. Loving.

There, that word again.

But how could a man be loving if he insisted on treating her like a medieval bride, kidnapped, locked up?

How could she think she loved him? How could she want to love him—after everything they'd been through?

It made no sense. And yet what she felt for him, around him, was so much larger than life, so much more powerful than anything she'd felt before. One day she was intrigued by him, the next she was gone. Head over heels.

It wasn't the sex, either, although that was unbelievable. It was something inside her that had shifted, opened, making way for him. She'd found herself in him. Found herself with him. "Did it ever cross your mind, that if we slowed things down, acted like ordinary people, this—us—might work?"

"It works now."

She held her breath, hung on to her temper. "Can we please just talk about this? A little conversation on the topic without threats or talks about throwing me to the lions."

He laughed, softly, but she knew he wasn't amused. "Discussion's moot. We've a contract, made a commitment—"

"Formalities."

"Made love."

She said nothing.

"I didn't wear a condom," he added.

For a moment she didn't understand, didn't see where he was going with this and then it all hit her—like a sledgehammer.

Joelle rolled out of his arms, onto the far side of the bed. No condom. No protection. She hadn't even thought of that. Oh my God. What was wrong with her brain?

Leo rose up on his elbow, looked at her from across the bed. "You could be pregnant."

"I'm not."

"We'll find out soon, won't we?"

Leo's phone rang. He glanced over his shoulder at the armchair where he'd dropped his wireless phone earlier.

The phone rang again and he didn't move. "I'm not going to answer that."

"Fine." She barely heard what he said. She didn't even care what he said, too engrossed in replaying the condom-no condom conversation in her brain. "When did you realize we'd forgotten it?"

He didn't answer immediately. The phone was still ringing.

"Answer it if you care so much," she said, unable to hide her bitterness. They'd just had sex—made *love*—and yet they were back to being strangers again.

"I don't care."

"You do! Just look at you. You're staring at the phone as if it's about to come alive."

"It very well might," he said humorlessly but he did look at her, and his expression wasn't particularly benign. "I knew I wasn't wearing the condom."

She'd rolled onto her stomach to get a better look at him. "At what point did you realize?"

The phone had finally stopped ringing. "I never intended to wear one."

Incredulous she shook her head. She knew he wasn't kidding, knew him well enough to know that he left nothing to chance. If he'd failed to wear a condom it's because he wanted to get her pregnant.

"You need heirs," he said flatly.

Because she was a princess. Because she was the only one who'd remained in Melio, she had to be the one to bring new life and blood to the Ducasse lineage. She had to have children so her children would inherit. She had to have children so Melio would have a future.

A lump filled her throat and her fingers grabbed at the sheets, bunching the fabric in her hands. Again she felt the crushing weight of her position, the weight that had nearly smothered her a year ago when she was grieving the loss of her grandmother, grieving the distance of her sisters. She'd felt so alone then, and she felt just as alone now.

Intellectually she understood that she had to sacrifice personal choice to ensure security for the future, prosperity for her country and people, but emotionally she didn't know if she could do it. Didn't know if she could deny who she was. What she needed.

And she needed a lot.

She needed a strong man, a good man, a man who would love her for herself.

Not for her crown, not for her island, not for her kingdom.

How had her sisters held up? How had they managed to fulfil their duty and yet find happiness? How had they survived the heavy mantle of the Ducasse title—because it was destroying her?

"It's your responsibility," Leo added more gently, as if realizing he'd been too brusque a moment ago.

It didn't help. She didn't need to be reminded of her responsibilities. They were there with her constantly, they were there when she woke, there when she fell asleep, there with every step she took.

The only time she'd felt vaguely free was in New Orleans, dressed in her leather and boots, holding her guitar and pretending she wasn't Joelle but Josette d'Ville—her mother's real name—before Josette became Star.

"We'll get through this," Leo added, reaching for her, trying to draw him to her but Joelle rolled out from beneath his arm and slid off the bed's edge.

"How?" she demanded. "How will we get through this? We know nothing about each other, and what we do know doesn't seem to work." She disappeared into the bathroom, pulled on one of the big plush robes hanging on a brass hook and returned with the robe wrapped snugly around her.

"Look," she continued, and she lifted her wrist, flashing the silver band. "Look at this, Leo. What does this say to you? I know what it says to me—"

"It's just to protect you."

"From whom? From what?" She laughed, a small strangled sound. "Leo, you put it on me to keep me tied to you. You don't trust me. You don't even like me. From the moment you arrived at Club Bleu you've been shocked by me, disgusted by me—"

"Not disgusted. Surprised. Confused."

"Angry." Now that the words had started, she couldn't get them to stop. "You're angry with me, and maybe you have a right to be, maybe the palace PR people did sell you a princess that didn't exist, but at some point you either have to end this— us—or you have to accept me for who I am, because I'm not going to change."

"You don't have to."

"Ridiculous. Of course you expect me to change, otherwise

you wouldn't have done this." And again she flashed her wrist, the band of silver.

He said nothing and his silence galled her.

"You do expect me to change," she repeated, her voice dropping, aching, raw with suppressed emotion. "You expect me to become your vision of a good wife, but I don't know what that vision is...and frankly, I don't want to know, not if it means I can't be me anymore."

"Perhaps we both need to make changes—"

"Perhaps?" she laughed, and jammed her hands into her bathrobe pockets. "But you know, Leo, you won't change, and I won't ever change enough, not enough to satisfy you. And you'll just stay angry with me, and you'll continue to punish me, punish me for being someone...something...I'm not. Punishing me because you can't seem to get past the fact that I'm not—" Damn all, there was a catch in her voice, a rush of emotion. "Not," she tried again, the words still failing.

"Not what?"

"The good princess." Her lips curved but her heart felt like hell. How could he know what it was like growing up in Nic and Chantal's shadows? How could he know that as much as she loved—adored—her sisters, she could never be what they were? And she didn't want to be. She'd just wanted to be herself.

"You're oversimplifying," he said roughly. "I never believed I was getting the good princess, and maybe I have been confused—"

"Angry."

He looked at her for a long, excruciating moment. "Yes, I've been confused, and angry, but I don't believe anyone is all good or all bad...not even you."

He was attempting a joke, and his expression had softened, but she couldn't crack a smile. She hurt too badly on the inside, her chest hot, blazing with emotion she didn't understand.

Earlier wrapped in his arms in that bed she'd come so close to seeing a happy ending, come so close to believing in them, the possibility of them, but there was too much wrong here, too much hurt. Broken.

He left the bed, walked toward her.

She took an immediate, defensive step back. "Stop." But he was still moving and she extended a frantic hand. "Stop, Leo, now."

He finally did, but not before he was just inches from her. And with him standing above her she realized yet again how big he was, how fierce, how overwhelming. Thankfully he kept his hands to himself.

Joelle hugged her robe to her. "You have to see that this—us—isn't working. You have to see that we're not suitable for each other. I can't be who you want me to be and Leo—" she drew a deep breath, heart on fire "—you're not what I need."

He said nothing. He simply stared at her and she balled her hands up, trying to keep the emotion inside her, trying to contain all the chaos and exhaustion. It was over, she thought, and it had never really begun.

She felt tricked. Flattened. Minutes ago they'd been so close, minutes ago she'd felt so much—felt everything—only now to realize it was all a hoax. A game the senses played.

She'd loved being touched, loved the pleasure she'd found in his arms, but what they'd shared had been just about bodies. They'd have fantastic sex, but they'd never made love, and she'd been too naïve, too inexperienced to have known.

"Every relationship is rocky," he said after a moment, no emotion in his voice.

Her eyes burned and she took a deep breath, counted to ten on the inside trying to contain the hurt. "This isn't rocky, Leo. This is abusive." She tried to smile but her lips were frozen and wouldn't move. "You don't trap people. You don't lock them up or chain them to you."

His jaw flexed, dark lashes lowering, concealing his expression. "I wanted to give us time. I didn't want to lose you, and I thought we needed to be together...to get to know each other."

He'd intentionally forgotten the condom. He wanted to get her pregnant. He wanted to trap her. Not out of love, or tenderness, or anything she understood and respected, but out of duty. The very thing she abhorred. "I think we know enough about each other now, don't you?"

She saw him flinch.

"So why did you agree to an arranged marriage?" he asked, voice pitched so low it was hard to hear. "Why put economics before love?"

Her eyes burned. She blinked. "I did it for Grandpapa. He wasn't well last year. He needed something to hope for, something to believe in." She took a breath, exhaled, trying to ignore the ache inside of her. "How can you even think it was economics, Leo? You still have no idea who I am."

The phone rang again.

Leo stiffened, his jaw tightening yet again. Joelle watched him. He didn't move and the phone continued to ring.

"Maybe it's an emergency," she said after the third ring.

"It's not."

"It's almost two."

"Doesn't matter to my mother."

Joelle felt some of her anger deflate. "Your mother?"

Leo gazed down at her, the expression in his eyes tormented. "Princess Marina doesn't have to follow the rules."

Turning away, he headed across the room to retrieve his phone. "Yes?" he answered, and Joelle saw his already forbidding expression darken further, going from angry to positively murderous. He answered in fast, furious Italian, his shoulders twisting, his body tensing with anger.

She caught only bits of the conversation—basically the I've-had-it-with-you, and you-can't-do-this before he slammed the phone shut.

But even with the phone down, Leo drew short, shallow breaths, his temper barely checked. *"Maledionze,"* he swore. "Damn her.

"I can't believe she's doing this again," he added roughly, dragging a hand through his dark hair, oblivious of his nudity.

"What has she done?"

"Same old, same old."

Joelle returned to the bed, sat down. There was something in his answer, in his voice, that wrenched her and she cared that he hurt, cared even though he'd hurt her. "She's been eating at you all night. Tell me why."

He laughed once, a bitter laugh, the kind of laugh that recognized that the joke was on him. "I wish I could—"

"Then do it. Come sit."

"I can't—"

"Fine. Don't talk," she interrupted, icy sheets coating her insides. He was worse than impossible. He was unforgivable. "It's better this way. I'd rather not know you, it'll make it easier to forget you."

"Bella."

The word was dragged from him, an agony of sound but she looked away from him, steeling herself against any more pain. She wouldn't be moved. Wouldn't feel anymore. He'd hurt her at so many different levels—the dishonesty, the manipulation, the domination—and she wouldn't be hurt anymore. Wouldn't let herself slide back into that very bad place she'd been a year ago.

Move on, she told herself. Move on. Let him go.

"We will talk," Leo said, reaching for his trousers and stepping into them. "But I can't now because she's here."

"Here?"

"Downstairs."

CHAPTER ELEVEN

JOELLE felt a pang—didn't know if it was trepidation or remorse. She couldn't imagine what his mother was thinking, showing up now, at nearly two in the morning. "I'll wait up here," she offered, adjusting her robe.

"And what? Miss the fireworks?" Leo mocked, unlocking the door.

Door open, he raked his fingers through his hair, but even with his dark hair combed, he looked wild, just beyond the edge of reason, and then he was gone and Joelle sat on the foot of the bed feeling positively horrible.

Eventually Joelle forced herself to unearth some slacks and a shirt. In the middle of buttoning the white blouse she heard raised voices. A woman's, and Leo's. They were shouting, both of them, back and forth.

Joelle stilled, fingers clutching the last button, ears straining to hear. She'd seen Leo angry but she'd never heard him shout. When he was upset with her he was quiet, contained, seething. But not loud, not unrestrained, not like this.

And what she heard coming from downstairs was nothing short of chaos.

Joelle cinched her hair back in a ponytail, glanced in the bathroom mirror and headed for the stairs.

In the stairwell the voices were even louder, the conversation startlingly clear. Joelle could hear every word being spoken now and she froze, stunned by the bitterness in Princess Marina's voice.

Marina's laugh spiraled, high and brittle. "You'd have more fun, Prince, if you loosened up a little—"

"Not now, Mother."

"No, of course not now. You don't ever have time for me anymore. You're too busy seizing small countries and adding them to your stockpile."

"I've seized nothing."

"But you're marrying profitably, aren't you?"

"Why not? You did."

The hair at Joelle's nape rose and goose bumps covered her arms. She didn't want to hear this, didn't want to hear another word but she couldn't make her legs move. It was as if she'd become cemented to the spot.

"Prince Leo Borgarde, King of Melio and Mejia. Must feel wonderful."

Leo's silence said more than words ever could and yet his silence only provoked Marina.

"Pretty soon you'll own the world," she added flippantly. "You'll just do it one woman at a time."

"That's disgusting."

"But true. You'll have everything. Who could resist you? You're rich, handsome, titled—"

"And it means nothing to me. I'd drop the title if I could. I'd trade it all if I'd had one normal day growing up—"

"I gave you everything!"

"No, Mother. You *took* everything. Even now you need so much, and I can't give anymore, certainly not to you."

"You don't even try!"

Another moment of silence and then Leo laughed, low, harsh. "You're right. I don't try. I'm tired. Done."

Suddenly there came the sound of a slap, a loud sharp ringing crack that carried into the stairwell.

"Selfish! Selfish bastard!" Princess Marina's voice broke. "You're a selfish self-centered bastard just like your father."

Footsteps ran through the hall, the front door opened and the woman—a beautiful tall blonde in a pale blue trouser suit—turned, glanced up the staircase, met Joelle's eyes before rushing out.

The front door slammed shut. Joelle couldn't move, shell-shocked. She'd had fights with her own family, but never anything like that, never such anger, or hatred, never such violent emotion.

Leo appeared in the entry hall. His dark head was bowed,

expression blank and then lifting his head he spotted her on the staircase. "You missed Mother."

Joelle's chest tightened. "Actually I got a glimpse of her."

"She's brilliant with exits, isn't she?"

And entrances, Joelle silently added, overwhelmed. But this stage drama wasn't new to Leo, she thought, seeing the pinched lines at his eyes and mouth. This was very familiar territory. "What just happened here?"

"The usual."

She stared at him a long moment, knowing there was a dozen different emotions going through him and knowing he had no intention of talking about any of them.

"I don't understand you," she said, feeling cold on the inside, but if it was fear, she wasn't about to give in to it. Fear was something she'd been taught to resist, to overcome with action. Decision. The Ducasses couldn't afford to be helpless. As royals, they were leaders. Role models. A Ducasse princess couldn't quit and wasn't allowed to fail.

"And understanding me will accomplish what?"

Anger swept through her. "In the event I am pregnant, and in the event we're forced to marry, I'd like to know something about my baby's father."

A shadow of emotion flickered over his face. Sighing, he switched on the hallway light. "We can talk as we eat."

And he led the way past the stairs, down a narrow hallway to the spacious kitchen at the end.

In the large old-fashioned kitchen with its beamed ceiling and tiled counters and floor, he set to work cracking and whisking eggs, melting butter in a sauté pan, chopping herbs.

He'd directed her to a wicker stool at the edge of the prep counter and she sat there, out of his way, and yet she watched him intently, studying the hardness of his cheekbones, and the press of his full firm lips, anything to keep from looking at the red mark on his cheek from where Princess Marina had slapped him.

But as he reached for the cheese grater his head turned and she saw the mark, the outline of fingers and palm and she felt the cold stunned feeling return, that panic and fear she'd felt when Marina had lashed out at Leo. But it wasn't just Marina's angry words that had sent shock waves through Joelle, it'd been the fact that Marina had hit Leo. Hit him and then walked out.

How could anybody do that? How could any mother treat her own that way?

The lump returned to Joelle's throat. ''Your mother *slapped* you.'' The words came out in a rush, unable to hold them back any longer.

Leo lifted his head, looked at her. His expression was perfectly blank. ''I've been hurt far worse,'' he answered calmly, dumping the grated cheese onto the cooking egg mixture yet she saw the muscle pull at his jawbone, saw the tension return to his face.

He dished the omelet, having cut it in half and he handed her a plate with her half of the omelet and a slice of buttered toast. ''Taste okay?'' he asked, taking a stool across from her.

She nodded, swallowed. It tasted fine, and she'd been hungry, but it was much harder eating than she expected. She felt utterly wretched. She'd wanted to be the good granddaughter for her grandfather, she'd wanted to do her part for Melio, she'd wanted her sisters proud. Joelle wasn't going to marry Leo. Nothing would be as the family hoped.

She and Leo struggled to eat, both picking halfheartedly at their meal. Leo finished first, pushed his plate away, stared at his plate.

Although his black lashes were lowered, she had the feeling he wasn't seeing anything, but thinking. And the thoughts seemed dark, tortured. Joelle shot him a worried glance as she continued to work on what was left of her dinner although after another minute swallowing became impossible.

She set her fork down. ''I'm worried…about you.''

''Don't.'' He grimaced, wearily ran a hand through his hair, messing the dark strands. ''This is nothing.''

But the accusations…the resentment…the anger…how could he say it was nothing? There was obviously so much pain between the two of them and Joelle drew a slow breath trying to find a voice to voice her concerns. ''But your mother hit you… She hit you as if it were nothing.''

"She was frustrated." He smiled but the expression in his eyes grew bleak. "Patience has never been one of her virtues."

His misery was palpable and it washed over Joelle in waves. She realized Leo didn't enjoy conflict at all. He probably never had. "What did she want tonight?"

"I don't know. I never really know… I don't think even she knows. She gets this way sometimes—manic, I suppose you'd call it—and suddenly she wants and needs everything, and doesn't know how to get it."

Tears pricked the back of her eyes. "So she strikes out at you?"

"She strikes out at whoever stands in the way." He looked at her, smiled crookedly. "But I'm probably her favorite target. I'm easy."

Silence hung in the kitchen and then Leo pushed back from the counter, his stool scraping the floor. Quickly he stacked their plates and carried the dishes to the sink where he rinsed them.

Turning around he faced Joelle. "Coffee?"

She sensed he needed a job, something to keep him busy and she nodded. "Please."

It took him a few minutes to make the espresso and when he returned with coffee and biscuits, Leo's hard mask, the stony one, the one without emotion, had slipped back into place.

"I'll tell you a story," he said, sitting down again across from her. He leaned on the counter, elbows braced, shoulders broad. "But you have to promise not to say anything afterward."

She couldn't help the arch of her eyebrows. "I can't say anything?"

"No. I'll tell you this story, but when it's over, it's over, and I don't want any questions or comments, nothing to embarrass me, nothing that will require sympathy from you."

She hesitated, lifted her coffee, blew gently on the steam. "That doesn't sound very fair."

"Life's not fair."

"No, life's dog-eat-dog," she flashed, "But it's just you and me here and you can't offer to tell someone something, and then put stipulations—"

"But it's exactly what I'm doing."

She set her coffee down, stared at him, not understanding him, not understanding anything about him. What motivated him. What emotions mattered. What he wanted out of life.

He was so complicated, too complicated. All along she'd thought his silence and hard edges were arrogance, the arrogance that came from a life of power and affluence, but she was beginning to see there was more here than arrogance. There was a great deal of pain.

Leo intentionally didn't let others in. Leo didn't want anyone close. And Joelle flashed to Chantal, flashed to Chantal's years in La Croix, the terrible mistreatment she'd experienced there with her first husband and in-laws.

"Okay," she said, "tell me your story. I promise I won't say a word when you're through."

"Where to start?" he asked, and then fell silent. It seemed as if he didn't have the words after all. And then he started in, just started talking, quietly, clearly, as if determined to just get the story over with. "My parents separated early. For reasons I won't go into, it was decided I was better off with my mother. I didn't see my father often after that."

"But you're close to him now—"

Leo gave her a long, hard look.

She felt a funny knot in her stomach. "No questions, no comments. Right. Sorry."

"My mother didn't like being on her own. She's not good at being alone. But Mother, being Mother, doesn't behave like other people, nor does she make choices that others might make.

"So we traveled constantly—all over the world. She attempted to make new friendships—liaisons, if you will—and sometimes she was successful and sometimes she wasn't. But the instability of it all wore on her. She's a beautiful woman, knew she was a beautiful woman, and she couldn't be in, be alone on a Saturday night. She'd be almost desperate to be out on a Saturday, desperate to not miss anything."

The corner of his mouth curved in a grim smile of remembrance. "It was even worse if she had to be alone with me," he added after a moment. "I don't think she thought she was cruel. She was just determined."

"We had a little game we played," he continued. "It went like this. We'd both dress up. Put on our best. And we'd set out, like we're on a date. Mother and me. We'd go somewhere nice—ultra-trendy restaurant, luxury hotel, someplace where handsome, wealthy men would go—and we'd go inside, holding hands, and Mother would squeeze my hand, smile down at me. I was her man. Her favorite man."

He looked away, stared across the kitchen, overhead lights gleaming down on limestone tiles and stainless steel. "I loved that part of our nights. I loved it when she held my hand. She'd bend her head, press kisses to my face and her blond hair would envelop me, and she smelled lovely. Sweet. Like gardenias and roses and no one was more beautiful than Mother heading out for a big night."

His lips twisted again, the mockery sharper, the pain deeper. He hated what he was telling her and yet Joelle sensed that now that he'd begun, he wasn't going to stop until he'd told everything.

"Inside the club or restaurant lounge Mother would sort of scope it out. She'd look for the best tables—and that meant tables with optimum visibility—since the whole point of our going out was to see and be seen. And for a little bit, Mother would be content to wait for one of these popular tables to open up, but if nothing seemed to be happening, she'd start working it harder." He laughed roughly. "Holding my hand, she'd take me from table to table, and she'd ask if we could have the table—"

"Have the table?" Joelle couldn't help interrupting. "As in, take it from them?"

His sardonic smile said everything. "Because it was my birthday, you see. And that's when I was pushed to the front, introduced. Her five-year-old. Her six-year-old. Her seven-year-old. And so on. For years we played this game. Sometimes people actually gave up their table to us, other times Mother was asked to move on, but Mother never gave up. I have to hand it to her. She'd find a spot at the bar, leaving me on a seat outside the door, close enough she could see me, but looking far more available than when she had a seven-year-old boy at her elbow."

Joelle was beginning to feel sick. Truly sick. She rather hoped Leo would stop talking, couldn't imagine anyone taking her child to an adult venue and abandoning the child outside.

"Being Saturday nights, they were long nights. We wouldn't arrive until eight or nine. We'd usually stay until midnight—or someone offered to take Mother home. But there were a lot of hours between Mother getting the good table, and Mother finding her mate. And sometimes she'd get so engrossed in a conversation she'd forget I was there."

He tapped his fingers on the counter, tapped to a memory in his head. "I could be outside for hours. Three, four. Inevitably someone took pity on me, inevitably some woman—probably a mother herself, or an older man who'd become a grandfather and couldn't fathom his own grandchildren being neglected— would bring me to their table."

His mouth curved. "That's when Mother would remember me—always in time—just before the restaurant or hotel manager was summoned—and she'd smile gaily, as if everything was just wonderful, and life was a delicious adventure, and she was so grateful someone had taken time to speak to me, especially since it was my birthday."

Joelle's eyes held his, her heart thudding uncomfortably hard. Each of his words seemed to hurt her worse. "You had a lot of birthdays," she said, unable to say nothing despite her promises made.

"Hundreds every year."

Silence fell. Joelle gripped the sides of her stool, the pads of her fingers pressed to the rattan and wood. How could any mother be so callous? So calculating?

Princess Marina was desperate, Joelle silently answered, trying to somehow justify his mother's actions. But the depths of the desperation…the inability to shield one's child, protect and provide boggled her mind.

Her own mother had been so different. Her own mother had fought tooth and nail to provide. Her mother gave up everything—career, identity, culture and country—to provide stability for her children.

"Did you get cakes?" she whispered, trying to hold back the tears, trying to find something positive to latch on to.

"And pastries, tarts, ice cream. Everything arrived with blazing candles, of course. And these nice strangers, these good awkward, uncomfortable people, would sing to me. They clapped when I blew out my candles, and some kindhearted person—I never knew which—would take my picture, my own Polaroid, so I wouldn't forget my special day."

"It's awful."

"What's awful is how these people looked at my mother. I saw how they looked at her. Understood it. At least after the first couple of years. Early on?" His shoulders shifted. "Who knows?"

He fell silent, and after all the talk, the kitchen seemed unnaturally still.

Joelle felt as if someone had let loose a hundred butterflies in her chest, and their wings felt like razor blades, beating at her heart. "Leo."

He shook his head, smiled, and yet there was a sheen in his eyes, a hint of tears he never let himself cry.

"Let me see your hand," he said, and he took her wrist, unlocked the silver band and tossed it across the kitchen into the waste bin. "That's not necessary anymore."

With the removal of the silver band, her wrist felt light, free, and she rubbed her skin. There was no mark on her wrist, no sign that it had ever been there, and yet they both knew. They both understood.

He was letting her go.

He knew it was over now, too.

"I'm sorry," he said roughly. "Forgive me."

Her eyes burned, hot, scalding. She blinked, nodded. "I understand."

"You deserve better. You deserve someone that will love you properly. Kindly." He grimaced. "I'm not a kind man."

Could he mash her heart any harder? Could he notch the pain any higher? "We are what we are," she said, looking away, fighting tears, fighting herself. She was torn between wanting to tell him that maybe they could try again, maybe they could start over, and knowing they both had needs the other couldn't meet.

He didn't trust her, probably wouldn't ever be able to trust her, and she quite frankly, didn't trust him.

And yet knowing that it was over, knowing that she could get up and go, she couldn't leave, at least not yet.

"Let's get some air," Leo said, pushing his stool back. "We could head to the beach."

Joelle wasn't wearing a watch yet knew it had to be close to three in the morning. Although late, a walk sounded infinitely better than tossing and turning in bed.

Leaving the kitchen Leo wondered why he'd been so compelled to tell her everything. He'd certainly never talked about his past before, had never told anyone about life with his mother, and yet he'd told Joelle everything. Each ugly, sordid little detail.

He'd lost control again, he thought, as they walked through the lower garden down toward the beach. He never used to lose control. Until the last couple of weeks he'd been the master of calm.

Even at three-thirty in the morning, the air was warm, almost balmy, and reaching the beach Leo headed straight for the surf. Already barefoot he walked into the water, let the cool tide slap his ankles and cover his feet.

Jesus, he was like a bleeding, gaping wound all of a sudden. Feeling too much. Thinking too much.

He shoved his hands into his pockets, stared out over the water. Clouds had partially obscured the moon. He couldn't see much and yet he felt everything. Amazing, he thought, shoving his hands deeper. You spend fifteen, twenty years suppressing the hurt, and then in just a few days it backfires. The lot of it blows up in your face.

"Children are so goddamn obliging," he said quietly, without looking at Joelle. He was tired, truly tired, and he wondered how it had all gone so wrong. Years ago, after he'd escaped to boarding school, and then university, he'd vowed he'd never be vulnerable again. He'd never let anyone close to him again. And he'd succeeded—brilliantly—until now.

He wasn't supposed to fall in love with Joelle. He'd gone the arranged marriage route precisely because he didn't want to love.

He'd wanted a wife that was strictly business, a steady, intelligent wife who understood the responsibilities of being royal. One that was ready to settle down and start a family. And he'd been assured by King Remi that Joelle was the perfect princess, calling her the "jewel of his heart." According to Remi, the young princess was everything he required—intelligent, stable, a contented homebody.

Leo shot Joelle a wry glance now. Intelligent yes, fairly stable, a homebody, no.

But he was falling in love with her anyway, and Remi had been right about one thing—she was a jewel. Joelle reminded Leo of an exquisite ruby—rich, fiery, passionate, full of light. Her flaws didn't even diminish her beauty. Her flaws made her more rare. He saw the world differently through her eyes, saw things he'd never seen before and somehow he found himself needing…wanting…loving.

The loving broke him, loving her broke him open and he couldn't handle it. Wasn't prepared for such intense emotion. The intensity unhinged Leo. He cared for her, really cared for her, and the caring filled him with fear. And anger.

So he'd done what his mother used to do. He'd tried to trap Joelle to him, chained her to him, used guilt…intimidation…whatever method he could.

"Of all the princesses on the market, why did you pick me?" Joelle turned to look at him and the dim moonlight just barely lit her face.

She'd never looked more beautiful, more honest or natural. And he realized all over again what a mistake he'd made. Joelle had never been like his mother. She wasn't flighty, needy, she was just young. She'd grown up sheltered by her family in the palace, had grown up in her sisters' shadows, and she'd never had time to be her own person. To be her own woman.

He understood now how much he—and even her grandfather—had rushed her, pushed her, forcing their own needs on her.

No wonder Joelle had run away. He would have run away,

too. In fact, he did. He'd run from his family, put as much distance between him and his mother—even his father—trying to keep the pain away.

He groaned inwardly, feeling hard, cruel. "You were a perfect addition to my empire." It seemed surreal now to think he'd wanted her for her title, her bloodline, her country, but that's exactly why he'd wanted her.

"Melio," she said.

"It's an incredible country. I've always felt an affinity for the people…the landscape." Since his family's political exile from Italy, he'd had no country to call home, and having spent summer holidays on Mejia, he'd always been fond of the sister islands, could see himself settled in Melio, see a future there.

"What happens to your empire now?"

"It gets scaled back."

"I'm sorry."

"Don't be. It's better this way."

Is it? Joelle wondered, bending down to touch the water. She'd needed a husband. Melio needed a wedding. In so many ways Leo could have been the right prince, the proper fit.

At twenty-two she didn't know if she'd ever meet anyone like Leo again, a man who made her feel so alive, so aware, a man who made her feel incredibly beautiful in bed. But she couldn't build a future on great sex, nor could she risk building a future on what she and Leo had now. With the wedding only two weeks away she knew there wasn't the necessary time to get to know Leo properly, to have the kind of relationship she wanted to make a happy, healthy marriage possible.

And as impossible as it sounded, as romantic and implausible, she wanted a marriage like her parents, she wanted the same kind of relationship they'd had. Her mother might have been the famous Star, but from everything she'd ever heard, her father had such a good, strong heart. Her father had loved her mother—for who she was, not who he thought she should be.

Joelle longed for that kind of acceptance. "Did you ever meet my parents?" she asked, realizing that Leo might have perhaps crossed paths with them at some point in his life.

"No." He hesitated. "But I attended their funeral."

The admission knocked the air out of her lungs and she took a quick breath, eyes stinging. "I don't remember the funeral."

"You were only four."

She shrugged uncomfortably. "But they were my parents. You'd think I'd have some memory." She didn't remember the real them, just the faces from magazines, the photos, the stories. Her parents, Julien and Star, were like beautiful people in a fairy tale. Girl from poor part of town meets handsome prince and they run off together—no regrets, no doubts—three daughters later and they're still happy ever after.

Joelle drew a breath, ignored the tenderness in her chest. She wished she were Nic or Chantal. They at least had real memories of Mother and Father. They had something to cling to. Joelle just had photos. And the stories others told.

She felt Leo's sympathy, found it excruciating after everything they'd been through tonight. "It was a long time ago." She wrapped her arms around her middle, hem of trousers soaked, body cold, suddenly brutally tired. "Shall we call it a night?"

Returning to the bedroom there was a moment of strained silence where Joelle and Leo just looked at each other, both knowing they'd reached the end and it was a matter of formalities. Civilities. Cleanup, she thought, trying to keep a stiff upper lip.

So do it fast, she told herself. Get it over with. Leo would let her leave. He wouldn't say a thing, in fact, he'd probably be relieved, but he didn't suggest it and as they stood there looking at each other, need and hunger flaring, she wasn't about to offer.

"Can I stay the night?" she asked, knowing dawn would be breaking soon.

"You mean stay until morning?" He moved toward her, took her by the hip, walked her toward him. "You know how men feel about that sort of thing. Smacks of commitment."

"And men are so commitment-phobic."

"Indeed."

She was fighting tears, fighting them tooth and nail. "Will we ever see each other again?"

He clasped her face, thumbs stroking her cheeks and as his

head dipped, whispered, "Maybe," he said softly, before covering her mouth with his.

The kiss was unlike any kiss she'd ever known. It was sweetness and longing, innocence and heartbreak and she felt tears burn beneath her eyelids. They'd come so close to something so beautiful. Perhaps if timing had been different, perhaps if they'd met when they were older...wiser...perhaps if they'd met the way other people did, at a restaurant or club, or introduced by friends...

Joelle wrapped her arms around his neck, held him close, closer, held him trying to remember every second of this last night.

In bed they made love, slowly, leisurely, desperation gone, leaving only pleasure. Leo held himself back for hours, building, extending sensation, both determined to make their time together mean something. It wasn't about sex, Joelle thought, climaxing a second time, burying her face against Leo's warm solid chest. It was about their hearts, about breaking them and trying to patch them together again.

Joelle didn't remember falling asleep. She'd been in his arms, her face damp with tears, lips pressed to his chest, and now she was awake. Alone.

Sitting up, she swung her feet around and tried to stand, her chest feeling as if it'd burst from pain. Something had happened. Something bad. Then she realized what it was. Leo's things were gone.

He'd left while she was sleeping.

It didn't take long to find the note he'd left for her. He'd taken a page from her book, used her favorite means of communication and the tears fell as she read and reread the few, brief words.

Bella, The world is yours. Leo

CHAPTER TWELVE

New Orleans, Louisiana

"HE LEFT a note and that was it?" Lacey repeated incredulously.

"That was it." Joelle leaned back in her chair on the balcony of her and Lacey's French Quarter apartment and stared hard at the beer bottle she was holding, inspecting the label as if it were the most fascinating thing on earth.

She'd been back in New Orleans just a day but planned to stay indefinitely and if she was going to stay, she needed to get through this part, needed to get all the explanations done and out of the way.

"How do you feel?" Lacey persisted.

For a split second Joelle's eyes burned and her throat sealed closed and then she forced herself to breathe. To keep breathing. "Like hell."

Lacey exhaled in a whoosh of air. "I'm sorry."

"It happens."

Lacey shot Joelle a troubled glance and for a moment she chewed on her lip, struggling to find the right words to say. "I think he did love you."

"It was lust, not love," Joelle corrected roughly, and the sudden bitterness in her voice made the lump return to her throat. She felt so hurt...so confused. "I mean, how could it be love? We knew each other for only ten days. You don't fall in love in ten days."

"Those were a pretty intense ten days."

Joelle tried to shrug it off but she couldn't quite hide the hurt. "Everything with Leo was intense," she said at last, lifting her beer bottle and taking a quick drink.

Lacey said nothing and Joelle glanced at her. Lacey was still leaning forward, her blue eyes narrowed, red curly hair even curlier with the humidity.

"Besides, he had no idea what I wanted…needed." Joelle took a quick breath, steadied her voice. She wasn't going to cry, wasn't going to fall apart. She'd loved Leo's body but she wanted more than his body. She wanted his heart. His respect. His faith in her. And without those, the incredible physical attraction, that dizzying chemistry, meant nothing. "I thought I could marry out of duty, obligation, but I was wrong. I thought I could be a contract bride, but I didn't know me. I didn't realize how important it is to me to be loved for me. To have someone want me for me…not my title or my country."

Thunder boomed in the distance and Joelle sighed, the warm moist air as heavy and oppressive as her thoughts. She forced herself to shrug, to mentally move on. "So the wedding's off. The engagement's over. And I'm ready to get back to work. Get on with my life."

"And this time you're here with your grandfather's blessing?"

"Grandpapa agreed that I could use another year or two out on my own."

"Your sisters?"

"They understand, far more than I thought they would. Both Nic and Chantal struggled with the same things I did. I just didn't know. We never talked about it." Joelle took a deep breath, pushed her long hair from her eyes. "It's hot. I'd forgotten how hot it gets here in summer."

"Like a wet oven," Lacey agreed, tilting back in her own chair. She shot Joelle a curious glance. "I have to admit, Jo, I still don't get this whole arranged marriage thing. Would you have really married him if circumstances had been different…if he'd been different?"

Joelle stared out over the street, the dark clouds banking, preparing for the afternoon thunder shower. "I don't know," she said after a moment. "I thought I could do it…marry out of duty, marry because it was what I was supposed to do, but I don't know now. I'm not who I thought I was. I'm—" and she smiled, but it felt tight, painful "—a lot stronger than I thought. Tougher, too. I can't be anyone but me, and as corny as it sounds, only I know what's best for me."

Thunder boomed again and Lacey and Joelle headed back into the apartment just as the clouds overhead burst open. As she closed the doors to the balcony, Joelle suddenly wished she and Lacey hadn't talked, wished Leo's name hadn't come up because she couldn't think about him. Couldn't let herself feel. It was better to forget him—completely.

Joelle had no problem getting her job back at Club Bleu and after a couple weeks she was back in the old routine.

The routine was good for her, too, the singing and performing kept her busy, focused. When she was on stage she forgot about everything, including her own shattered heart.

The hours off stage were the hard ones. Getting through summer was brutal, but then autumn arrived, and the intense heat began to ease, and by winter Joelle felt almost human.

She still had days that hit her from behind, knocking the air out of her, the pain stunning.

Joelle picked up an extra job, waitressing in a nearby restaurant, and the extra money was good, the lack of time even better. She literally ran from one job to the next, and in the meantime she socked away every dollar she could. She was learning to take care of herself, provide for herself, and it felt good paying her own bills…paying her own way. It felt good knowing she was responsible. Capable. It helped, too, living with Lacey. Lacey had such a great perspective on life, such a refreshing sense of humor.

The door to the storage room opened where Joelle sat perched on a wooden crate, a cell phone pressed to her ear. Chet, Club Bleu's manager, held up his hand. "Josie, you're on in five."

She nodded to Chet, indicating she'd heard him and continued listening to the voice mail left earlier by her grandfather. She'd already replayed it twice but she needed to hear it again, missing her grandfather, missing Melio. She'd gone home only once this year and it was for her twenty-third birthday. Maybe it was time for another visit.

"Josie." Chet was back and he shoved his watch beneath her face. "Wake up. You're on. *Now.*"

Joelle saved the call, snapped the phone shut and stood up. "No problem," she answered calmly. On the surface, nothing ruffled her. On the surface, she was New Orleans' hottest nightclub sensation, and it was easy to appear serene. Undisturbed. No one here knew who she really was. No one knew what her heart had been through. "I'm ready."

"You're sure?"

The corner of her mouth curved, silent, wry, catlike. "Baby," she answered, drawling a little, pegging the Southern accent, hiding as always her European roots. "I was born ready."

She took her position on stage and the lights overhead rose, circles of purple and deep blue and as Benny hit the first bass notes, Joelle felt the sultry heat of another summer night.

Opening her eyes, she grabbed the microphone and pulled it close. Club Bleu was packed tonight, every chair filled, filled because they'd all come to see her, filled because she'd become someone in New Orleans—not because of her title or family name—but because she'd earned it by hard work.

Yet Joelle found her success was bittersweet. This is what she'd come to do, and while she'd been offered a generous recording contract, the music hadn't met all her needs. Her taste of success hadn't equaled falling in love.

Don't go there, she told herself, feeling her long dark hair swing against her back, her skin warm, growing damp, don't think about what you can't control. And yet the lump returned to fill her throat and for a moment she nearly lost her composure. She had to fight for the lyrics stuck in the back of her mouth, fight for voice and sound.

She didn't understand what was wrong with her. Nothing felt right tonight. Already she was off, uncomfortable, intense emotion swamping her.

Focus, Jo, she told herself, focus and get through the song. Nothing had changed, nothing was any different, but something inside her keep telling her everything was different.

Everything felt fierce. Intense.

Closing her eyes, Joelle clasped the microphone with both hands, fingers bending protectively, the stainless steel both cool and warm. With microphone pulled forward, tilting it on the stand, Joelle gave it all up to the night, singing about the heartache she'd never talk about in daylight.

Spotlighted by blue and purple gel lights, she admitted what she'd never admit to anyone else.

She still missed Leo. Still dreamed about him nearly every night. She'd gone out with other guys in the past year, kissed her share of men, but none of them had been Leo.

At least you have your music, she reminded herself, no one

can take that away from you. And finally she was able to shut out everything but the bass and the drums and the moodiness of the night, finally she focused and let the scorching emotion pour through her, filling the club, coloring it with powerful sound.

Two hours later, the lights lifted, purple gels fading to white and gold, and the audience erupted in thundering applause. Joelle took another bow with her band but was barely conscious of the whistles. She'd been so immersed in the last song that it was taking her a minute to return to reality.

"Well done," Johnny G, the drummer said, passing her, a towel draped around his neck as he headed off stage.

"You were on tonight, baby girl," Benny added, slipping his bass guitar into his case. "You hit all the notes."

Joelle managed a smile. She'd actually felt funny tonight. Off. Maybe it was the phone call home before she'd gotten on stage, but she felt strangely emotional. Even now tears burned just beneath the surface. "Thanks. See you guys Saturday."

She crouched down to slide her guitar into its case and used the moment to mop her face, wiping away the hint of tears before it smudged her eyeliner. It's just because it's summer again, she told herself. You're just feeling nostalgic.

With guitar strap over her shoulder, Joelle forced herself off stage.

"Josie?"

The deep voice stopped her. Joelle froze, skin prickling.

She'd gone a year without hearing that voice and yet she'd heard it in her sleep, in her dreams, night after night until it made her weep into her pillow.

Slowly she looked up into his face, and he was waiting for her, waiting, and he looked right back, his dark gaze reaching into her, holding her still.

For a moment she forgot time, forgot history, forgot pain. For a moment she stood there, washed in need for him. It had been so long…she'd missed him so much. She stared at him, drinking him in, trying to see everything at once. And his dark eyes let her, his dark eyes held her, his eyes let her know what he wanted, and he wanted her. Body and soul.

Icy heat shivered up her spine and down again. Blood surged through her, flooding her face, melting the bones of her hips and knees. It was all she could do to cling to her guitar case. "Leo."

"You were amazing."

Leo's deep voice wrapped around her heart. She'd forgotten what a distinctive voice he had, so deep, so husky. "Thank you."

Silence followed. Joelle didn't know what to do, what to say. She glanced at him and then away. What was he doing here? It stunned her, him appearing like this. It had been a year without a word, without a single phone call. Why was he here, now?

"How are you?" he asked.

"Fine." She swallowed. "And you?"

"Fine." His lips curved in a wry smile. "You're very polite."

"We're friends, right? Not enemies." But there was a hint of bitterness in her voice and he heard it.

"Friends," he repeated softly, but his green eyes were dark, hard, intense. Everything about him was hard and intense. "Can I take you to dinner?"

Her heart did a funny little beat. "I can't. I've an early morning."

"I see."

His features grew harder. Joelle's heart did another painful stagger and she changed her grip on her guitar case. "I waitress at Brennan's on Sunday mornings. You remember Brennan's?" She saw him nod and she hurried on. "Breakfast at Brennan's is famous. It's quite busy in the mornings. Frantic, really. They run me off my feet."

"I'll have to try it sometime."

Her eyes burned. "I should go."

"You're not walking home, are you?"

"It's just a couple blocks."

His jaw tightened and she saw he was biting back criticism. "I'll walk you home," he said at length. "Give me your guitar."

"Leo—" She broke off when she saw his expression. "Okay."

They walked in silence, the night still sweltering, the clouds banked, the humidity rising. It'd have to rain soon. The air felt saturated with moisture.

On reaching Joelle's apartment building, Leo escorted her up the stairs. There was an awkward moment on her doorstep after Joelle had turned the key. "Do you want to come in?" she asked stiltedly.

He'd heard that, too. "Maybe another time," he answered, turning away. "Good night."

Inside her apartment Joelle shut and locked the door.

He was gone. She should have felt relieved. Instead she felt heartsick.

She shouldn't have let him go.

She should have asked him to stay.

She should have opened a glass of wine and got them talking, really talking. She should have—

No, it was better this way.

Tears filled her eyes. Why was it better this way? What was better?

She drew a breath, tried to calm herself, but she felt lost.

Leo was here. He was *here*. And she let him go.

The pain staggered her, the pain more livid than ever. It's okay, she told herself, it's okay, this is just life, this is just love, this is how it's going to be.

But deep down inside she didn't want it to be true, because when she looked at him tonight, all she felt was want and hope and...

Need.

Need.

The forceful knock on the door made her heart lurch all over again. He'd come back! Relief swept through her and Joelle struggled with the lock. Emotions chaotic she swung the door open but it wasn't Leo on the doorstep, it was Lacey.

"Thank goodness you're home," Lacey said, exhaling with a rush. "I lost my key earlier and was afraid I'd be locked out."

Morning came far too early and Joelle dragged herself from bed, into the shower, out of the shower and into a jean skirt and T-shirt—she always changed into her uniform at work—and grabbed a cup of coffee in the kitchen.

"Hey." Lacey was already up, her curls wild from bed-head hair. "You okay? I haven't seen you look this blue since... well...last June."

Joelle topped her coffee with milk and dumped in a huge spoon of sugar without making eye contact. It had been a long night, a hellish night. "Didn't sleep well."

"Anything happen last night?"

"No. Why?"

"Just wondering."

Joelle downed her coffee and left the apartment, the morning temperature already in the mid-eighties. As she walked the six blocks to Brennan's she wondered why she couldn't tell Lacey about Leo's surprise appearance. Maybe it was because she still hadn't come to grips with his appearance, either. It didn't make sense that he was here, had come to see her, unless...

Unless...

But Joelle couldn't go there, wouldn't let herself go there and once she reached the restaurant was immediately sucked into the frenetic pace of breakfast with a gourmet spin. Brennan's served three-course and five-course breakfasts, as well as famous breakfast libations like Gin Fizzes, Mimosas, Bloody Marys, and the outrageous Mr. Funk of New Orleans.

By the time she'd finished her shift it was nearly two in the afternoon and she was dead on her feet. She'd thought of Leo, but not excessively, and after changing back into her skirt and T-shirt, she stepped out the back door, waved goodbye to the line cooks standing in the brick alley having a quick smoke. It wasn't until she reached the end of the alley that she noticed Leo.

He'd been waiting for her in front of Brennan's, positioned in such a place that he could see her from all the restaurant exits.

She'd half expected to see him, but hadn't expected the fierce jolt of recognition, the electric zing of nerves. He was so familiar and yet so not. So much a part of her and yet so much still hurt when she looked at him, when she thought of him. The emotion had never gentled. The loss had never eased.

"You're not working at Club Bleu tonight," he said, walking toward her, a gorgeous primal grace in just the way he moved.

She'd forgotten that about him, forgotten his grace, his sensuality, his European sophistication. But she couldn't do this, couldn't just hand herself over to him. It had been easy forgiving him, brutal forgetting him, and clearly from the way her body was responding, she hadn't succeeded in distancing herself from him at all.

"I know you're free now," he added, standing over her.

"You're not working again until morning, and Lacey said she was certain you had no plans for this afternoon."

Joelle felt hot, dizzy. Just standing this close to Leo was murder. It didn't help that the afternoon temperature had soared twenty-plus degrees since morning and the dark blanket of clouds overhead pushed the humidity past the point of comfort. Perspiration beaded her skin. Even the air was hard to breathe. "When did you see Lacey?"

"Yesterday when I arrived in town."

"She didn't tell me."

"I asked her not to."

The air seemed to grow thicker, and heavier. Quieter, too. "She's supposed to be my friend."

"She is."

Their eyes locked, another silent battle of wills. Things hadn't changed, Joelle thought, biting her tongue to keep from saying something sharp. He was still trying to dictate everything. Control her.

"Then she should have told me you were here," Joelle repeated, feeling cornered. She hated feeling cornered, especially if it was by him.

"Joelle."

"What?" she flashed, shooting a nervous glance up at the sky. It had become too quiet. It was as if the black clouds overhead had swallowed all sound. It was going to rain soon.

"Never mind. I'm not going to force this, *bella*."

She couldn't look at him, trying to sort through her tangled emotions. In the distance thin white lines ran from the sky, fragments of far away lightning, but so far nothing seemed close.

Except for Leo. He was close, far too close, and with the odd white line illuminating the sky she felt fear.

If he touched her she'd be lost. If he touched her, she'd melt straight into him.

She took a deep breath, tried to be objective. "I don't know how to do this. I've worked so hard to forget you that…" She shook her head, without words. "That it's agony seeing you. It's not something I thought would ever happen."

"You knew I loved you."

"But you left."

"We both know why."

Her throat swelled close and she felt close to tears. The afternoon had gone so dark and quiet she knew the afternoon storm was imminent.

"Want to go inside?" Leo asked, indicating the café on the corner, if one wanted to call it a café.

She knew the café. It was more like a tavern or saloon, the interior dark and cool, fans whirling on the ceiling and music blaring from a jukebox. She'd never liked the café. It served stale soda, flat beer and old popcorn. "Not particularly."

Thunder rumbled across the sky, a slow insistent roll of sound. "It's going to rain."

Joelle glanced a little helplessly out on the street. They'd walked a couple blocks from Brennan's but they were still a couple blocks from her apartment. And he was right. It would rain soon. The street was nearly deserted. Everyone knew the rain was coming, even the tourists. And when it rained in New Orleans, it flooded. They hadn't had a proper rain in days and today promised to be a torrential downpour.

If they were going to make a run for it, they had to do it now. In a minute it could be too late.

"Let's just go to my place," she said, pulling her purse higher on her shoulder.

Then she felt it. The first fat ping.

And then another. And another.

Leo grabbed her elbow, pulled her after him to the café's covered patio as the rain started coming down, hard, and harder.

In less than thirty seconds the shower became a fog, the summer rain so thick and blurry that sheets of steam rose from the street. The water slapped the pavement, bounced from the asphalt.

Like that, the streets were clear. The French Quarter became a ghost town. Cars disappeared. Pedestrians were gone. Shops had all closed their doors.

It was extraordinary. Everyone was gone, leaving just Joelle and Leo alone to watch the pounding rain.

"We might as well get something to drink," Leo said. "It's going to be awhile."

She shot him a frustrated glance. "You're glad we're stuck here."

"Try to think of me as a peace offering," he suggested dryly.

Her hands clenched. "Then why aren't I feeling peaceful?"

He laughed softly, eyes glinting. "That's something only you can answer, *bambina*. Come," he said, holding the door. "Let's find a table before we're drenched."

They ordered bowls of spicy gumbo and glasses of cold white wine at the bar counter and then found seats in a far corner. The café was just as deserted as the street and except for one old man in the corner, they had the place to themselves. "This isn't a sign of good business," Joelle whispered to Leo as they sat down.

"No, but it is dry."

The gumbo wasn't the best Joelle ever had but it filled her up, took the edge off her appetite and at least the wine was chilled. After the bartender cleared away their dishes she went to the door, stared out at the flooded streets. New Orleans had huge drains at every corner but not even the monster drains could handle the slashing rain once it started. From where she stood gutters and downspouts looked like fountains and the lone pedestrian's umbrella had turned inside out.

"Pretty bad out there," she said, sitting down again, trying not to fidget. She felt so hot, unbearably wound up.

"I guess we've got some time to kill."

CHAPTER THIRTEEN

JOELLE felt his enjoyment as his dark green gaze rested on her face, and she could have sworn he was smiling, secretly savoring her misery.

"You planned this," she said, crossing her arms over her chest, trying her best to create distance. Detachment. She hated the way she was feeling...tingly, edgy, all bittersweet emotion. It had been so hard to forget him that she couldn't bear to sit this close now.

Leo's dark gaze gleamed. His teeth flashed white in a pure predatory smile. "I did. I arranged for the thunderstorm when I made my hotel reservations."

She glanced away, fidgeted, unable to return his intense gaze. He was studying her, closely, possessively, and everything in her seemed to unfold, come painfully to life. "We can't just sit here."

"Why not?"

Her teeth ground together and she felt such a welling of need. It wasn't fair that he still looked gorgeous. Wasn't fair that when he focused on her he made her feel like the only woman alive. Wasn't fair that his gaze made her grow hot, tense, hungry. "Because this is miserable."

"I'm comfortable."

She shot him a dark glance. "I'm not. I don't trust you."

"You never have." His teeth flashed yet again and a ripple of unease raced through her

He was bigger than she'd remembered, stronger, more physical. She'd remembered her desire, but not the effect he'd had on her, and somehow, sitting across this tiny bar table, the tavern smelling of beer and stale popcorn she felt incredibly threatened.

He represented everything she wanted. He also represented everything she feared.

He'd change her world. If she let him close enough, he'd

make her his again, and Leo's possession was like nothing she'd ever known. If he should even touch her, she feared for the safety of the walls she'd put up against him, doubted the defenses erected around her heart.

"Did my grandfather send you?" she asked bitterly, balling her hands, arms still pressed tightly against her chest as if she could somehow shut him out, keep her heart safe.

"No."

"Does he know you're here?"

One of Leo's black eyebrows lifted ever so slightly. "No. Did I need to get his permission to visit?"

Her chest squeezed tight, pulled like a rubber band and Joelle briefly closed her eyes, trying to deny the sting of pain. "So what do you want?"

"What do you think, *bella?*"

Her heart twisted yet again, her knuckles pressed tighter to her breasts, her skin soft, her insides hot, livid with emotion…hopes…hurt…dreams. "You can't have me."

"Of course I can. I was meant for you—"

"No."

"Just as you were meant for me."

"Rubbish."

He laughed softly, the husky sound filling her ears, rubbing like the pad of his thumb across her heightened senses. "I let you have time, *bella*. I never let go of you."

Her lashes lifted and she stared at him with disbelief, even as her nails bit into her palms. "It's been a year, Leo, a year. There's no relationship anymore, there's no engagement, no wedding—"

"Not yet."

"Not ever."

"You still want me as much as I want you."

She averted her head, fury making her see red, fury stealing her words, her voice, her breath. How could he do this? How could he come here and sit and make such arrogant statements? How could he even make such assumptions in the first place? "You have no idea what I want."

"No?" He drawled the word so quietly the hair at her nape rose.

Chest on fire she forced herself to lift her chin, meet his mocking gaze. "No," she drawled in reply, matching his tone, matching his taunting edge.

He wasn't going to do it to her again...overwhelm her, steamroll her, use her body against her. This time she was awake. Aware. If he truly wanted her, cared for her, then he'd win her by her heart, not by her senses.

"Let me tell you a story," he said.

She nearly laughed. "I don't think so."

"It's an interesting story."

"I doubt it."

His eyes narrowed, his gaze riveted to her face as fine creases fanned from his eyes, accenting the height of his cheekbones, the hard line of his jaw. "You're giving away your hand, *bambina*. You're revealing too much. If you hope to prove yourself indifferent, then you need less emotion. You need to show indifference."

She flushed and said nothing, seeing where he was going with this and knowing he was right, but knowing he was right didn't help. "So tell me your story," she said, trying to affect nonchalance.

His lower lip curved in the faintest smile of amusement. "You have to promise me that you won't say anything, and you won't interrupt."

Not that again. Joelle could scarcely keep her expression blank. "Fine."

Triumph flared in his eyes. "Once upon a time, not so many years ago, there was a girl named Josette Destinee d'Ville, better known as Star. Star came from a very poor family outside Baton Rouge—"

"I've heard this story."

"But she had an incredible voice and big dreams," he continued as if never interrupted. "No one worked harder than Star and eventually she became America's biggest pop singer. And then at the height of her career, Star met a handsome prince, they fell in love and she moved to Europe with him, giving up her career.''

Joelle's stomach cramped. She felt queasy. ''This isn't my favorite story.''

''It gets better.''

''I don't think so.''

''I do.'' Leo leaned forward, lifted a long tendril of her hair and slipped it behind her ear. She flinched but he kept on talking. ''Since you know this story, you're aware that Star had two little girls, princesses named Chantal and Nicolette, and Star and her prince loved their children very much. But Star didn't feel complete—''

''Because she missed her music.''

Leo smiled. ''No. She wanted one more child, one more Ducasse baby. And Star spent the next six years trying to make this very special baby. She was pregnant three more times and she lost all three babies late in the pregnancy, and after the third miscarriage the doctor told her there could be no more.''

Joelle lifted her chin, lips pressing thin. Leo saw the hurt and pain in her eyes, saw the shimmer of tears of all the years she'd felt alone.

Lightly he touched Joelle's cheek. She didn't flinch this time, didn't pull back.

''But Star couldn't accept that there'd be no third child. She wanted this child, couldn't explain it to Julien, couldn't explain it to anyone. But Star couldn't have another baby so her prince tried to distract her, tried to push her back into music—he built her a studio, drove her to start writing music again—but Star didn't want music. She wanted a baby. There was one more baby for her, one more and she knew it.''

Tears filled Joelle's eyes and her lower lip quivered but she ruthlessly she bit into the lip.

''And against the doctors orders, Star became pregnant again. It was a difficult pregnancy, as difficult as the others but she refused to lose the baby, and she fought for that baby every step of the way. Nine months later Star delivered the most beautiful baby girl of all, and Prince Julien and Star named this miracle baby Joelle. And Star, with all her many accomplishments, and all her staggering successes, finally felt complete.''

Joelle couldn't look at him anymore, couldn't bear any of it. The tears streamed down her cheeks and struggled to wipe them away but there were more tears than hands and she choked on a sob, feeling naked, stricken. She couldn't do this, fall apart like this in front of Leo.

''No wonder you're so driven to be you,'' he said gently. ''You have your mother's heart—and all her dreams and wishes—inside of you.''

She covered her mouth with her hand, knowing she couldn't keep the staggering emotion in, knowing she was about to break, burst, knowing she'd spent too long trying to be strong and independent, trying to be okay on her own. But she'd been lonely. And it'd been hard. And she missed home and she missed her parents and she missed family.

She missed loving and being loved.

She missed romance, missed fire, missed ice.

Missed Leo more than she could ever say.

Suddenly Leo was pulling her into his arms, holding her close against him. ''You deserve better,'' he said, holding her close to his chest. ''You deserved better from me.''

She couldn't answer, couldn't find words to express any of the inarticulate emotion flooding her. It had been such a hard year, a long, lonely year. And while of course part of her hoped she'd see him again, she hadn't honestly thought they'd ever have another chance. She'd started to think their relationship had been just chemistry, a sexy pull that had nothing to do with their hearts, their emotional needs, and yet Leo was here, holding her, his arms wrapped around her, his heartbeat steady beneath her ear.

She buried her wet face against his neck not wanting to think, just feel, and he felt warm, smelled delicious, a heady mix of spicy cologne and endless gorgeous skin. No one had ever held her the way he did. No one had ever made her feel half so alive.

Her hand balled helplessly against his chest. ''I missed you.''

''It was hell to stay away.''

Dragging in a breath, Joelle knew she'd never get tired of his scent, of his strength, of the way he looked at her and made her burn, made her feel so much. "Then why did you?"

She felt his shoulders shift, muscles tightening through his chest, arms like hard bands and he brought her even closer against him. "I had things to work through."

"Like what?" Her voice broke, the hurt and need showing through.

"Like coming to grips with my past. Accepting the fact that I've been very angry with my mother, that I needed to deal with that anger or it'd ruin the future." His hand slid up her nape, wrapped her hair around his hand, held the impromptu ponytail snugly. "That it was already destroying the relationship I wanted with you."

She could hardly breathe, hardly force the air into her lungs, concentrating so hard on the words echoing around inside her head.

"I'm ashamed I put that surveillance band on you, *bella*. I'm ashamed that I hurt you, controlled you. I was just so desperate—so determined—not to lose you. Loving you so much filled me with fear."

Loving you so much…

Loving you…

She closed her eyes against the hot rush of tears. "You love me?"

Fingertips stroked her nape, drawing slow gentle circles so that she tingled from head to toe. "More than I thought I could love anyone." He hesitated. "More than I wanted to love anyone."

Her hands gripped his shirt, squeezing the fabric in fists. He was saying the words she needed, the words she'd craved and yet…and yet…she was afraid, afraid to hope, afraid to believe.

"I've learned a lot this year," he added, "I've worked hard to come to peace with my mother, forgiving her for that which she did, for that which she couldn't give, and I'm ready for a future with you, ready for the life I want to live with you."

"This is about Melio, isn't it?"

He laughed, a low stricken laugh that sounded torn from him. "*Bella*, I'm a disgustingly wealthy man with more chateaus and schlosses and villas than I know what to do with. I don't need Melio or Mejia. I don't need another island—I've one of my own off the coast of Sicily. But I do need you. I love you. I don't want to go to bed anymore without kissing you good night. I don't want to wake up without having you there next to me. I don't want a life alone.''

"I'm sure women are crazy about you," she sniffed, trying to stop the tears welling in her eyes.

"But I want the woman who drove me crazy," he said, lifting up her chin to wipe the tears from her face. "I want the woman who made me grow up, face myself, face my fears. You changed me, made me stronger, kinder, made me real. And there's too much here…too much we feel to let it go without a fight. I'm fighting for us now, Joelle. And I'll keep fighting. Tell me you'll fight, too.''

She searched his eyes, searched his heart and she saw a man unguarded, a man with a strong lovely face, a strong angled jaw, but a man without the hardness, the bitterness, the edges. The anger was gone.

"I'd like to fight for us," she said after a moment, "I want to believe in us…''

"But?"

"You're older than me."

He was trying hard to look serious. "By at least twelve years.''

"And as you said, you're disgustingly wealthy."

"This is true. While most women enjoy a certain lifestyle— clothes, travel, cars and jewelry—I get the sense you don't.''

She nodded. "I find the whole idea of providing a woman with a lifestyle offensive. I don't want to be given a lifestyle. I want a relationship.''

There was a moment of silence.

She licked her lips, mouth drying, heart pounding harder. He was looking at her like a wolf eyeing a little lamb. He'd have her. She knew he'd have her.

"Trust me, *bella*," he said, breaking the tense silence, "you'd get a relationship.''

She heard the possession in his voice and it sent shudders through her.

"Perhaps," he added, "the real issue is that you're not attracted to me."

"Not attracted?"

"Perhaps the physical spark is gone."

The husky, teasing note in his voice sent blood surging, and shivers tingling all the way through her. Not attracted? No physical spark? It would be easy if that were the problem.

"Tell me you're not attracted and I'll leave you alone," he persisted, and yet his dark green eyes heated, a dangerous light flaming there.

Hot. Primal. Sexual.

Her heart slammed into her rib cage. "I'm not attracted."

He smiled. His eyes creased at the corner. "Okay." And then he set out to prove how wrong she was.

He kissed her as the rain poured down, kissed her until she couldn't think, couldn't breathe, couldn't see, kissed her until she was sure he'd stolen all the pain from her, taking it away with his lips and breath, and when he lifted his head, he was smiling faintly, mockingly. "I understand you, *bella,* far better than you think."

Somehow her hands had slid down his chest and rested on his hip bones, holding him steady, holding him, holding him as if she'd never let him go. She put her hands up against his chest to push him away. "What do you know?" she breathed.

"That all you've ever wanted is to be like everyone else. That for once you want to feel like everyone else."

Joelle's heart did a funny twist. The words were familiar, they sounded exactly like her thoughts.

"You want to wear jeans and boots and tennis shoes. Leather coats with lots of fringe."

Those *were* her words, the words she'd written earlier this year and turned into a song. *I want to go to a bar and sit with a beer and get drunk in public if I want…* "You've been listening to my lyrics," she said, frowning at him and then ruining the effect by bursting into laughter. "I can't believe anyone would listen that closely."

"I thought it was about time I paid attention to what you were telling me, thought if we were going to have a chance at succeeding, I needed to get to know you, the real you, the you that's meant to be."

His words made her eyes sting hot all over again and glancing out, past his shoulder she saw the rain was starting to let up, the downpour turning to steamy mist. "You want to know *me*."

"Yes, you, the real you, the you I fell in love with a year ago."

"You didn't like the real me."

He laughed, kissed her. "I loved the real you, even if you were dressed like a sex kitten."

A ray of sun broke through the clouds, a sharp bright streak of yellow white light. "And what's wrong with a sex kitten?"

He muttered something in Italian and then tangling his hand in her hair again, drew her face close, very close to his so that his warm breath caressed her cheeks, her skin, her lips. "Nothing, *bambina*. As long as she's mine."

Suddenly a crease darkened his brow, his eyes narrowing, his jaw jutting. "You are mine, aren't you?"

The ray of sun outside pierced the tavern's gloom, spreading light into every dark corner, the light so bright it nearly blinded Joelle. Wrapping her arms around Leo's neck she put her lips to his ears. "Of course. I've been yours from the moment you first looked at you—yours from the word go."

"The word go?"

Her arms wrapped tighter. She held him closer, held him with all her strength, all her passion, feeling so much. "Make that, hello."

She lifted her head, searched his eyes, saw the brilliant light outside there in his sexy green eyes. "I love you, Leo."

"I know."

EPILOGUE

"WE'RE late," Joelle said for the tenth time in as many minutes. "I can't be late. I don't want to be late."

Nic and Chantal shot her amused but exasperated glances. "If you hadn't started crying, you wouldn't have had to redo your makeup," Chantal said.

"If someone had told me about the veil earlier, I wouldn't have cried."

"You would have still cried," Nic answered, reaching over to straighten the veil. "You look beautiful, Jo. That tiara was made for you."

Joelle reached up to touch the delicate diamond tiara, the tiara in the shape of five brilliant stars supported on a gallery of diamond-studded foliage. Her father, Prince Julien, had commissioned the tiara for his wedding to Star and the tiara had been put away ever since.

Joelle blinked madly, her fingers tracing one sharp star. To think the tiara had been saved for her. All these years. Waiting for her own wedding day and suddenly she didn't think she could keep the tears back another moment longer and using the tip of a gloved finger she dashed away another hot tear. "I'm falling apart!" she choked in protest.

"It's okay, Aunt Joelle." Lilly scooted across the seat, out from beneath her mother's arm to squeeze closer to Joelle. "Brides are supposed to cry."

Joelle laughed, and hugged Lilly back even as she swiped the tears from beneath her lashes. "How do you know so much about life, Lilly?"

Lilly heaved a sigh. "I'm eight now, Aunt Jo. You lost track of time when you and Prince Leo were having all those attitude issues."

Chantal shushed Lilly but Nic laughed and Joelle shot her sisters a wry glance. "Thanks, Lilly. I remember now."

Any other time the drive from the palace to the cathedral would have taken minutes, but with the crowds lining the streets, the driver of their classic cream Rolls-Royce limousine was forced to creep through the old streets of downtown, allowing the crowds on the pavement a chance to see the three Princess Ducasses.

They'd made it, Joelle realized, feeling a lump fill her throat. Somehow, someway they'd survived the leap from girlhood to adulthood and they were happy. Healthy. Safe.

The car drew to a stop in front of the cathedral, the back door opened, the long crimson carpet unfurled, and Joelle leaned forward to impulsively press a kiss to each of her sister's cheeks. "Thank you," she whispered, grateful, touched, incredibly moved to have them with her today. *Her* wedding day. She'd always been the youngest princess, the last of the Ducasse girls, but somehow it felt different…she felt different…she'd changed in the past couple of years. She was ready to belong to Melio again, ready for her future here.

As she stepped from the Rolls-Royce she heard someone cry, "We love you, Princess Jo!"

And the crowds thronging the cathedral picked up the shout, chanting her name as Grandpapa slowly came down the steps, leaning on his cane to take her arm.

"They love you," her grandfather said.

She nodded, her chest burning with emotion. Everyone had been so good to her, so patient, and she was more grateful than anyone would know. "I love them, too," she said, and shifting her bridal bouquet of white lilies, tulips and freesias to her other arm, she lifted a shy hand, acknowledging the cheers.

"They're glad you're home," King Remi added.

She waved to the crows on the other side of the street, smiling as the cheers swelled in volume. "So am I, Grandpapa."

They climbed the front steps of the cathedral, entered the great stone church through dark arched doors, and yet once inside the cathedral the dark stained wood gave way to lavender and white arches supported by gray and white marble columns, the floor a dark rose marble, and the altar a half circle with a dozen stained-glass windows, each window surrounded by the finest white plaster friezes, the detail breathtaking.

Joelle knew the cathedral well. Here her parents and grandparents had been buried, her sisters married, and little Lilly baptized. She knew each of the arches, all the knaves, the choir stalls, the confessionals, but nothing touched her more than the man waiting for her before the altar.

Leo.

He stood waiting for her, flanked by two distinguished groomsmen—Malik Nuri, the Sultan of Baraka, and Demetrius Mantheakis, Greek tycoon who answered to no one, and he was everything she'd ever wanted, everything she'd ever dreamed about.

Prince Leo Fortino Marciano Borgarde. Her heart.

With organ playing and hundreds of candles shimmering, Joelle watched Nic and Chantal and then Lilly precede her down the aisle.

And then it was her turn. At long last. Three years after her engagement to her prince and two years after losing her virginity to him.

She felt wobbly as she walked with her grandfather. Grandpapa needed to walk slowly, and yet he was beaming, infinitely proud. Her own heart pounded with each slow, deliberate step. Life hadn't ever been easy and yet each lesson learned had brought her to this.

She was shaking by the time she and her grandfather finally reached the front of the cathedral, and looking up at her dear grandpapa, a man who'd had to become grandfather and father as well as king, she realized she'd survived the long journey—not just walking the endless white carpeted aisle—but the three years it took to grow up properly, the last year with Leo where they both learned how to love properly, like not to hold grudges, to let an argument die, to gracefully accept an apology.

Her gloved hand squeezed Grandpapa's arm. "Thank you," she whispered, just before he placed her hand in Leo's. "I owe you everything."

"You owe me nothing. Just be happy."

"I am."

Grandpapa kissed her cheek and then he was gone, leaving her in Leo's care and the significance took her breath away, squeezing the air inside her.

The organ died. The bishop began addressing the assembly. "I'm late," she whispered, stealing a glance up at Leo's profile.

"Just a half hour," he whispered back.

She gripped his arm more tightly. "Sorry."

His hand covered hers. He was warm and his warmth relaxed her. "I'm getting good at waiting."

She nearly laughed. She shouldn't laugh. It was her wedding day. She was marrying a prince. Life was getting quite serious now. "You've become a very patient man."

The corner of his mouth lifted. "Why not? We all need some extra time now and then."

The next couple of hours whirled by, music, color, words and sound. And Joelle enjoyed all of it, the ceremony, the reception, the dinner, the dancing but at last it was time for her and Leo to escape. And they escaped to the room at the Palace Hotel that Leo had booked. Tomorrow they'd leave on their two-week Greek cruise, but the rest of the night was theirs and with security at the hotel tight, they were assured a night without any interruptions.

Joelle sat down before the mirror at the dressing table and worked at unpinning the headpiece but it wasn't coming off. "Leo, can you give me a hand? I don't want to tear the veil."

He appeared from the bathroom. She heard water running. He was filling the tub. And in the mirror their eyes met. He was smiling, that dark sexual smile that sent shivers up and down her spine even now.

Silently he crossed the bedroom carpet, his gaze in the mirror never leaving hers. "You're beautiful."

Her heart raced, pulses leaping even as she went liquid on the inside, all hot fire and desire.

He'd moved behind her, one hand brushing her bare shoulders and she sighed, lips parting.

The corner of his mouth lifted and yet he set to work unfastening the headpiece one pin at a time. "It's a beautiful tiara," he said, adroitly freeing the veil and tiara and handing it to her.

Joelle tilted the delicate tiara, the five brilliant stars glittering. "Grandpapa had been saving it for me."

"Your family loves you."

She nodded, bit her lip, overwhelmed by emotion. She felt so lucky, so blessed. Everything good and lovely had come true, all the heartache and heartbreak, none of it seemed real anymore. None of it mattered.

And suddenly she felt a prickle of heat, a rush of energy and glancing up, she discovered Leo looking at her.

Just as he loved her, she thought, feeling his love wash over her, through her, his love so tangible, so visible there in his eyes.

Maybe this is what made life with Leo so intense, so exciting. All he had to do was look at her and she felt him, wanted him, and the desire wasn't diminishing but growing stronger with time.

"You've gone quiet on me," she whispered, her neck feeling bare, her breasts aching, even her lips feeling strangely full, nerves dancing.

His gaze drifted slowly across her face, taking in every bare place of her skin that felt so bereft of his touch, so hungry for his lips.

Her skin warmed, growing pink and flushed even as her tummy knotted again and again, the surge of desire and adrenaline becoming painful.

"I'm just watching you," he said.

True, and the energy between them felt electric. "You really did fight for me."

"I had no choice."

"Why?"

The corner of his mouth tugged. His expression gentled, his green gaze heating. "You already know the answer."

She went to his side, still dressed in her white wedding gown, the silk cool, light against her legs. "I want to hear it again."

He sat down on the edge of the bed, and pulled her down next to him. "I love you."

"Again."

"I love you."

"Again."

"I love you."

And then leaning close, she kissed him, slowly, hungrily, savoring the desire rising through them. "Promise me you'll never stop telling me you love me."

"I promise."

"And promise me you'll still love me even when we're old and gray."

"I promise."

"And promise you'll always remember today."

He laughed, the sound husky. "I promise."

She drew a deep breath, still trying to absorb it all. "You know, we've got the most incredible story to tell our children."

"They won't believe it."

"They'll have to. It's the story of you and me."

"Quite a story," he teased.

"Larger than life."

"Full of stubbornness and one very hothead—"

She kissed him, cutting off his words. "You're describing yourself, of course."

He laughed again, very low and sexy. "Perhaps we need to agree on the story...get the facts right."

"I agree. In fact, maybe while we're on our honeymoon we can start going over the details...agree to agree...agree to disagree as well."

"*Bella,* I think we have time."

"Not that much time." And leaning closer, she pressed her lips to his and whispered, "I'm pregnant. We're expecting a Christmas baby."

Possessed by a passionate sheikh

The Sheikh's Bartered Bride by Lucy Monroe

After a whirlwind courtship, Sheikh Hakim bin
Omar al Kadar proposes marriage to shy
Catherine Benning. After their wedding day,
they travel to his desert kingdom, where
Catherine discovers that Hakim has bought her!

Sheikh's Honour by Alexandra Sellers

Prince and heir Sheikh Jalal was claiming all that
was his: land, title, throne…and a queen. Though
temptress Clio Blake fought against the bandit
prince's wooing like a tigress, Jalal would not be
denied his woman!

Available 19th September 2008

www.millsandboon.co.uk

M&B